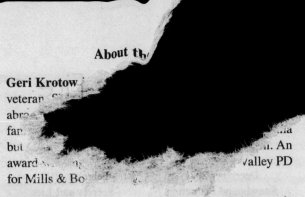

About th...

Geri Krotow

veteran...

abro...

fan...

but... An

award... Valley PD

for Mills & Bo...

Cindy Myers became one of the most popular people in eighth grade when she and her best friend wrote a torrid historical romance and passed the manuscript around among friends. Fame was short-lived, alas; the English teacher confiscated the manuscript. Since then, Cindy has written more than fifty published novels. Her historical and contemporary romances and women's fiction have garnered praise from reviewers and readers alike.

Michele Hauf lives in Minneapolis and has been writing since the 1990s. A variety of genres keep her happily busy at the keyboard, including historical romance, paranormal romance, action/adventure and fantasy. Facebook: MicheleHaufAuthor, Twitter @MicheleHauf, Pinterest at: toastfaery, Instagram: MicheleHauf. visit her website: michelehauf.com, email Michele at: toastfaery@gmail.com

Fire

Love Under Fire: Snowbound Seduction

GERI KROTOW

CINDI MYERS

MICHELE HAUF

MILLS & BOON

First Published in Great Britain 2021
By Mills & Boon, an imprint of HarperCollins*Publishers*, Ltd
1 London Bridge Street, London, SE1 9GF

www.harpercollins.co.uk

HarperCollins*Publishers*
1st Floor, Watermarque Building,
Ringsend Road, Dublin 4, Ireland

LOVE UNDER FIRE: SNOWBOUND SEDUCTION
© 2021 Harlequin Books S.A.

Snowbound with the Secret Agent © 2018 Geri Krotow
Snowblind Justice © 2019 Cynthia Myers
Storm Warning © 2019 Michele Hauf

ISBN: 978-0-263-30298-1

MIX
Paper from
responsible sources
FSC™ C007454

This book is produced from independently certified FSC™ paper
to ensure responsible forest management.

For more information visit: www.harpercollins.co.uk/green

Printed and Bound in Spain using 100% Renewable electricity at
CPI Black Print, Barcelona

SNOWBOUND WITH THE SECRET AGENT

GERI KROTOW

To Michelle Mioff-Haring. Thank you for your
friendship and your tireless support of
Silver Valley.

Chapter 1

Something was wrong in Silver Valley, Pennsylvania, but Portia DiNapoli couldn't put her finger on it. It wasn't the weather, which had been hellacious since Christmas. She couldn't remember such a cold, snowy winter since her childhood. And it wasn't the stress of putting together the town's largest charity event, the gala to raise funds for the library she ran and the homeless shelter where she volunteered many hours. If she thought about it deeply enough, the sense of doom had more to do with the story she'd read in the Harrisburg newspaper that proclaimed the area was under siege from Russian Organized Crime. Silver Valley had been named as the center of ROC's efforts to move everything from illicit drugs to weapons. It struck at her heart, because Silver Valley was where she'd lived her entire life.

Although right now, having to dress in several layers to go anywhere in town, it was hard to believe even ROC could run criminal operations from here. Silver Valley had turned into a frozen tundra from the relentless winter.

She'd arrived three hours before opening to work at the Silver Valley Library. She needed the time to work on the gala, which was now less than a month away. And she loved the quiet of the historical building, the way it always felt like a warm hug, even in the January predawn hours. Pennsylvania remained gripped by the tenacious hand of a polar vortex; arctic air had mercilessly swept the state and frozen everything in its wake. More surface area of the Susquehanna River was frozen than ever previously recorded.

It took her a full two minutes to unwrap from her layers of winter protection. She'd opted to walk the few blocks from her small apartment, even in the cold. Portia loved the four seasons and especially winter, but even she was relieved to be inside the warm building and not on the icy streets.

As she settled into her spot behind the main circulation desk, she tried to let the library's familiarity soothe her, but to no avail. What was different this Monday morning from all the others she'd spent in the facility? Her week had started out great with her usual walk to work, she'd had a great cup of coffee at the local shop in the building next to her apartment and there weren't any pesky emails from the central library staff demanding her attention. But she couldn't shake the sense of danger, the feeling that made her skin crawl and her stomach churn.

This had to stop.

Besides reading about ROC, she'd spent too much time learning about the fight Pennsylvania was waging against the heroin epidemic, finding out that Silver Valley had more than its share of opioid ODs and near-ODs. Since one of her closest friends from high school had become a victim of a lethal dose of heroin laced with fentanyl right before Christmas, Portia had questioned everything about her life and the community she held dear.

She resolved to get lost in the more positive aspects of her job and clicked open the gala files. Reviewing the guest list to date led to perusing the silent auction items, which always buoyed her spirits. The generosity of the average Silver Valley citizen touched her pragmatic heart.

"Portia."

Portia jumped in her seat, startled by the sudden appearance of Brindle, her assistant.

Brindle had joined the staff while still pursuing her undergraduate degree at Penn State, Harrisburg and now was on to postgraduate work.

"What are you doing here so early? And, ah, good morning."

Brindle's mouth twisted into an apologetic grimace. "It's not that early."

Portia looked at the clock. She'd been here for two hours already?

"Sorry to startle you, but I had to get out of my sister's house. Her baby was up all night, and I have two exams this week. I've been at the diner since four, and I was hoping you were in early today. I left my car in their lot and walked over." Brindle knew that Portia came in early many days, especially in January, during the weeks before the gala.

"No problem. As you can see, I came in for the quiet, too." Brindle was taking night and weekend classes to achieve a master's degree in library science, and she also knew from firsthand experience how stressful working full-time and pursuing a degree was.

"I'll use one of the study rooms if you prefer." Brindle seemed truly sorry to intrude upon Portia's space.

"No, that's not necessary. I just boiled water for tea, or rather, I did when I came in. It's in the insulated pitcher. Help yourself."

"Thanks."

They settled into their respective workspaces and Portia's mind wandered yet again. She'd been doing a lot of this lately. Drifting when she should be getting something done, like finalizing the list of items to be auctioned off for the gala. Instead she'd scared herself half to death.

Robert hadn't helped. She'd dated the local politician, helped him organize the personal details of his campaign. She was vehemently opposed to most of his platform, so no way would she help him with the actual campaign events. If she dug deep enough, she had to admit that she'd hoped to change him. Make him at least see her point of view on many issues. But it had never happened. When had trying to change someone else ever worked for her? A snort escaped her and she tried to cover it by sipping her tea. Brindle looked up at her and offered a smile.

"Sorry. Thinking out loud." She raised the ceramic mug as if she hadn't spent another sleepless night tossing and turning, wondering where ROC's next victim would show up.

Robert hadn't supported anything that helped drug addicts, including the fund-raiser she'd done for Silver Valley's homeless shelter, where she volunteered at least one evening or day per week. She was glad she'd dumped his sorry butt. Unfortunately she'd also found out he'd been messing around with one of his supporters, a local lawyer. Her logical side demanded that his cheating ways would make the breakup that much easier, but it hadn't. She'd talked it out with her best friend, Annie, and decided to take a break from men for the time being.

Shoving thoughts of her cheating ex aside, Portia skimmed the morning emails, all the while regularly checking the one monitor dedicated to library security. There were five security cameras in the building, one on each floor and one at each entrance. The back entrance was employees-only and in fact only used as an emergency exit. The screen was divided into quadrants and she'd so far been able to help a senior who'd fallen in the back corner of the cookbook section, break up several different teenaged couples who were clearly aroused by the smell of paper and last fall she'd ushered out a raccoon who'd smelled the tray of cider donuts intended for the toddler Halloween story time.

But she'd never seen a person completely dressed in dark clothing from head to toe, fully hooded, trying to pry open the back door of the building with some kind of instrument. In broad daylight. Well, if not complete daylight, dawn, as the sun was climbing over the Appalachian Mountains.

Portia shot out of her chair and made for the back.

"Do me a favor and keep an eye on the back exit's security screen, Brindle. If it looks like anything serious, call 9-1-1 for me."

Brindle's eyes widened and she got up from the worktable and walked over to the monitor. "Will do." Portia would have laughed at her obvious trepidation but she had to get to the back door and tell the person to knock it off. It wouldn't be the first time she'd had to chase interlopers away from the back door. It was an easy place for teens to hang out, next to the 24/7 diner and two buildings down from the pharmacy.

Even so, she couldn't remember ever having to stop someone from trying to pry the door open before. The images of the headlines about ROC flashed through her mind and she forced herself to take a deep breath. Yes, Silver Valley was under fire from an established crime ring, but what were the odds that ROC had any interest in the town library?

Ludmila Markova couldn't shake the feeling of being watched, but it was nothing she wasn't used to. Whether the police or FBI or one of her superiors, someone was always keeping tabs on her.

So be it. Right now she had to make sure she delivered the goods to the library so that the other worker would know where to find their delivery.

She'd gained many points with Ivanov, ROC's local leader, when she'd come up with the communications plan. Because their cellular phone calls were always in threat of being monitored, and the same with email or SMS, they'd needed a way to pass information back and forth. The transportation manifests were complicated, especially the ones involving shipping heroin.

Exact instructions were needed for each delivery; each pickup and every gram of product had to be accounted for.

Let the American law enforcement groups search her group's technological devices. They'd never find what they were looking for. She was the best, trained by the Federal Security Service, or FSB, in Russia. It had earned her a visa to the US under an assumed identity.

She hoisted her backpack up higher, walking quickly to the library's back entrance. At this hour, with the building still closed for another twenty minutes, she'd get in and out with no fanfare. The only problem was the security camera, which she couldn't risk disabling because she wasn't certain if it was tied to the local police or not.

No matter, this was why she wore a ski mask. The camera would never capture her face, not with enough detail for identification. Someone would have to be in her personal space to see her eyes and her mouth, and even that wasn't always enough. Besides, if anyone got that close, she'd eliminate them. She never left a witness alive. It could spell too much trouble down the road.

She had to keep this job with Ivanov, her current boss. For just one more operation. Anything was better than going back to Russia and having to be at her government's bidding again. A one-nighter with an oligarch led to the slick deal that got her here.

She planned to keep herself out of Russia for the rest of her days. Whether she found a quiet life under an assumed identity in the US or Canada didn't matter to her. She wanted freedom from the constant killing, always having to take orders from above without question. Whether she'd be able to give up the life that she was the best at in the world was a valid question she needed to address, but not now. For now, she had to remain the trained assassin that she was, the best that ROC could ever hope to have on its side.

Only one more mission and she'd disappear, go somewhere where no one would find her. Start the free life she'd always dreamed of. Before her own government had killed her family.

The lock on the door would be an easy pick, but she preferred the much quicker muscle method. She pulled a long knife from her backpack and wedged the thin end into the line that separated the steel door from its frame. Using her body weight as leverage, she began to break into the Silver Valley Public Library. In three more minutes, she'd deposit the laptop where the next operative would find it, where she'd told them to look. It would take them all of thirty seconds to download the information onto a USB stick. If library personnel caught them, they could play dumb and claim they'd forgotten to sign the computer out at the front desk.

Her plan was foolproof, as was everything she did. Two more shoves and the door would open. She was three minutes from completing this part of her mission.

Portia's breathing ramped up as she passed row upon row of books, DVDs and then periodicals, making her way to the stairs, where she sped down to the children's level. The exit door was at the base of the stairs and the stairwell reverberated with the sound of metal on metal. The unknown person was still at it, working on the door.

What the hell?

Portia pushed the long bar handle in, shoved the door open and squinted against the bright motion detector light. The sun had begun its rise behind the building, as well; it was a sharp contrast to the stairwell's dim interior.

"Excuse me, can I help you?"

The person straightened, and the first thing Portia noticed was the cold emotion in the glacial blue eyes under the winter facemask. The second thing was that the person—a woman, judging from the figure under her jacket, the makeup on her eyes and lipstick on her very red mouth—was holding one of the library's dozen laptops. Portia knew it was a Silver Valley Library computer from the identification stickers on its cover.

"Hey, our laptops are for in-house use only. Why are you—"

Before she finished, the woman shoved Portia in the chest, knocking her backward. The assaulter whirled around and ran toward the railroad tracks that divided the library property from the rest of downtown Silver Valley.

Portia scrambled to her feet, and against the voice in her brain that screamed for her to wait for the police, she took off after the laptop thief. Silver Valley Library had mysteriously lost ten laptops in the past six months. It ended with her, today. *Now.* Without hesitating, she took off after the assailant. She hadn't lettered in track and field at Silver Valley High for nothing.

Kyle King swore under his breath, the interior of the beat-up truck he was hunkered down in filling with the crystallized vapor. He couldn't run the engine and heater while he was trying to blend in. He had to make it look like the truck was empty, parked behind the Silver Valley Diner. Right next to the town library, where he'd patiently waited for ROC's thug to show up. He hoped to figure out how the hell they were passing information on illegal drug shipments.

As an undercover agent for the Trail Hikers, a secret government shadow agency, second to none and headquartered in Silver Valley, he knew how critical it was to stop ROC's trafficking of illegal cargo, especially heroin and other drugs, into Pennsylvania. Silver Valley was a short fifteen-minute drive from the state capitol, Harrisburg, and the epicenter of transportation logistics for the entire US Eastern Seaboard.

Typical of ROC's blatant disregard for law enforcement, they'd set up their distribution headquarters in the shadow of a nondescript, medium-sized, everyday American town. Of course ROC had no clue about Trail Hikers, but it was public knowledge that Silver Valley and the surrounding county had succeeded in defeating the most heinous criminals over the last few years. Including an ROC human trafficking ring. Which made the fact that ROC still wanted to stake a claim here stick more deeply in his craw. The latest intel from Trail Hikers and FBI indicated that the criminals were somehow using the local library as a way to pass critical information about their local ops.

Kyle had operated on countless global missions for Trail Hikers over the last several years, after a short stint in the Marine Corps. After two tours to Afghanistan, he knew he wanted to continue serving, but in a different capacity. The offer to become a Trail Hiker agent had been too good to pass up.

That was seven years ago. The ROC op had brought him to Silver Valley three months ago to provide much needed support. He'd welcomed the switch and enjoyed being in an American town for longer than the usual few days his other ops had given him.

Fact was, Kyle was tired of the global travel and wanted to find a place to call home in between Trail Hiker ops. He didn't think it would be Silver Valley, though, as he was born and bred in California and missed the West Coast. He'd purchased land in California while he was still a Marine, needing to know he had someplace to go if he ended up out of the Corps and without a job. But anyplace in the United States was a good place after the rough places he'd been. If he hadn't been so tied up in this op against ROC, he might have enjoyed Silver Valley a bit more.

Kyle wanted to be the agent to smash apart Ivanov's reign of terror so badly that he could taste it. The current gang ROC had sent to Silver Valley was responsible for dozens of heroin ODs in this part of the state, and upwards of thousands nationally. After he solved this case, Kyle was due for time off, a full month. He planned to use it to go back west, see if the property he'd been paying taxes on could become home. The director of Trail Hikers wanted him out there for a bit to set up a West Coast office for the agency, so it all dovetailed neatly. Kyle liked things neat.

It'd be sweet if he could crack open this case sooner than later. Pennsylvania winters were colder than he'd imagined. The last weeks since the polar vortex had dipped down had proved brutal. He'd broken down and bought himself foot and hand warmers for the long hours outside, staking out the library, where he'd confirmed the information drop point was. In classic ROC fashion, they used something that seemed so obvious. Most criminal organizations held meetings or passed information in more clandestine spots, places that were difficult to figure out. Not ROC. By somehow passing information in the library, they'd hidden their methods in plain sight. He just hadn't figured out exactly how yet. The computers were the most likely tools but the Trail Hikers systems forensics expert hadn't found anything unusual on the desktops. Kyle had done a lot of his own recon inside the library, too, hoping to determine a pattern of behavior or repeat patrons who might be up to no good. He'd used different disguises to avoid any kind of recognition. Not just from Markova or her worker bees, but from the library staff.

The librarian in particular. A woman he'd found himself fascinated with. Portia DiNapoli.

But the librarian he'd also happened to monitor the last several weeks wasn't going to make his goal of catching Markova in the act possible. Not today, anyway. As an undercover TH agent, he had to avoid any contact with civilians as much as possible while trailing a target. And Markova was a big one. As he watched, he saw that the librarian was engaging Markova. Portia DiNapoli didn't know Markova was an ROC operative, though.

"Damn it, Portia DiNapoli. Why are you so good at your job?" And why was the town librarian so damn hot? More importantly, why was his dick paying attention at all when he was supposed to be tracking the movements of potential ROC thugs in the library, not Portia's attractiveness?

You're lonely.

Damn it, he wasn't lonely. Okay, he'd appreciate the loving of a good woman right about now, but he was too entrenched in his work to add another concern to it.

Portia DiNapoli was the epitome of distraction. The fact that he was spending mental energy on her when dating her, or anyone else, wasn't in his best interest or the woman's, raised his internal alarm. He needed to get it through his thick skull that he had a job to do that a woman, Portia or whomever, would only complicate. He'd had his share of committed relationships over the years but none had stuck. It always came down to him having to put his career first, and there was the added danger of anyone he was involved with becoming a target of the bad people it was his job to take down. Portia DiNapoli's nearly constant presence in his current surveillance had stirred something in him, though. He probably ought to at least think about dating someone again.

The thing was, he hadn't been tempted by any of the women he'd had the opportunity to flirt with, dance with, talk to at the local bar scene in Harrisburg. And he'd been out so rarely, the case taking up all of his time.

His casual interest, and that was all it was, a fleeting second glance, in Portia, was complicated. It wasn't because she was beautiful, and she was. Big brown eyes with long lashes, a full mouth with lips he'd fantasized doing a lot more than smile at her patrons. She wasn't short, but at least a head shorter than him. The perfect size to pull her in close and lay a kiss on her rosy lips. She always wore rose lipstick, or maybe that was her natural color. Her eyes dazzled behind oversize glasses and her curvy figure was stunning in her sexily delicious pastel cardigans. Portia seemed to have a collection of those, from what he'd noticed. She was all woman, all sexy curves. It might be a record-breaking cold winter, but the sight of Portia each time he'd gone to the library had warmed him up quicker than any wood stove. Today she wore leggings under a body-conscious, curve-hugging dress. The binoculars in his hands were the best technology on the market, but he didn't need them to know the shape of her sweet ass under her clothes. Not that he'd meant to notice it. But when she'd bent over to shelve books the other day, well, he'd happened to catch a glimpse of her sexy rear.

Let it go, man.

She probably had a zillion dudes lining up to take her out. He didn't know, because his physical observation of her began and ended with the library. After he'd found out her apartment was in the one next to his, he'd taken extra care to avoid running into her, using his back entrance almost exclusively. She favored the front, and liked to get a cup of coffee at the shop his apartment was perched over. He knew she wasn't married. And not just from the confidential dossier he'd run on her at Trail Hikers. From her bare left hand to the hours she kept, coming in before the library opened and staying well past closing, Portia DiNapoli was a dedicated career woman. With no commitments outside the Silver Valley Library, except the local homeless shelter. He'd felt no guilt investigating her. He'd had to; when the center of an ROC op was taking place in her library, he'd had to rule her out as a suspect.

Not that his background check on her or anyone was ever considered conclusive. The best bad guys, and girls, were good. Really good. They wouldn't leave any clues that they were doing anything more than visiting a library.

Portia's stance shifted and he recognized the defensive posture—he'd seen her use it last week with a patron who was angry about overdue fines.

But now she wasn't confronting a disgruntled library patron, but an ROC operative, a fully trained, lethal agent. His gut tightened and a distinct discomfort filled his chest. The thought of Portia being hurt by ROC was unthinkable.

Now it looked like the dialogue between Portia and Markova was getting heated. At least, Portia's face was turning red and he'd bet it wasn't from the frigid January temperatures.

"Fuuuudge," he said to himself in the truck, where he'd had his binoculars trained on the library's back entrance since he'd followed Markova here two hours ago. She'd driven from the drab mobile home she kept on the outskirts of town, parked her car behind a restaurant two buildings down and then walked the rest of the way to the library. Kyle figured he was lucky she'd never even looked toward the banged up truck he huddled down in. She never seemed to care about her surroundings but Kyle knew it was all part of her training, to appear as if she were any other civilian—not a trained assassin who didn't miss details others never noticed.

It was freaking freezing and he couldn't risk alerting her to his presence by turning on his engine. Parked behind the 24/7 diner, his vehicle looked like many of the other patrons' wheels: nondescript and dirty from the overdose of salt on the icy roads.

He'd determined that ROC was using the library

somehow to pass information but he didn't know how. And he couldn't directly ask Ludmila Markova, the woman whose file he'd committed to photographic memory months ago. She had to be caught committing a crime before he could tip off SVPD to arrest her.

As he watched, Markova hadn't been successful in getting the back door open, which he found surprising, as well as amusing. The thugs Ivanov employed were top notch and knew their way around locks of all kinds. And they usually were smarter than to attempt to sneak into a public building in broad daylight. But nothing was usual for ROC. They did whatever had to be done to accomplish their jobs, whether that was moving kidnapped underage immigrant women into sex slavery and trafficking illegal drugs, or laundering money made from all of the above.

He watched Portia DiNapoli speak to Markova and a cold sense of dread blanketed him. Emotions weren't allowed during his missions, but he never ignored his intuition. This could go south so very quickly, so very badly. Markova had at least the long knife she'd used to try to pry the door open, and she was adept at using it according to the profile he had on her. Besides her current work for ROC, a number of assassinations were included at the top of the long list of grim accomplishments in her FSB history.

By comparison, Portia DiNapoli's record was as squeaky clean as they came, and reflected an average American who did her job well and contributed to the community with her entire heart. People like Portia were why the Trail Hikers' work was so important. She was not someone who deserved to bleed out in the library parking lot because she'd been in the wrong place at the wrong time with a trained ROC killer.

Kyle eased himself out of the truck's passenger side, using a car parked next to his to shield his movements. His breath steamed in the frozen air and he kept his movements slow and steady. If luck was on his side, Markova would turn and leave without harming Portia.

Kyle never relied on luck. He listened to their conversation, which was taking place no more than ten yards away.

"Excuse me, can I help you?" Portia's voice, normally gravelly and sexy, sounded angry as she shouted at Markova. Making like he was walking toward the diner's back entrance, he hoped to be able to shout and startle the criminal, forcing her to leave the library parking lot.

But the word *laptop* got his radar up.

"Hey, our laptops are for in-house use only. Why are you—" From Portia's tone, there'd be no working it out. He heard it and so did Markova, apparently, who turned and fled. But not before she shoved Portia, who disappeared into the open exit.

Okay, that made it easier, at least. Portia would be safe.

Except that she'd decided the library laptop wasn't going to disappear on her. To his surprise and consternation, Portia was back on her feet and out the door in a blink. He watched her long legs stretch out, her arms pumping, and did what any reputable, competent undercover agent would not do. Kyle ran after Portia.

Portia followed the woman up and onto the railroad tracks, her feet screaming that her simple leather oxfords were no replacement for sneakers or snow boots in the frigid temperatures. Snow crunched under foot and her lungs burned with no scarf to help warm the air.

What was so important on the laptop that the woman would rather risk being criminally charged for taking it than just simply turning it back in and then checking it out again the next day? And why was she running from Portia? Why had she shoved her?

Portia's mind raced with the possibilities, but right now she needed to get the woman, get the library's computer. She was gaining on the woman and gave it ten more strides. As she drew close enough to touch her, she reached for her hoodie and tugged. The woman turned and faced her, still holding the laptop in her arm. Shooting Portia an evil grin that was revealed by the curve of bright red lips in the mouth opening of the knitted mask, she brandished a knife with menacing intent, and the winter sun flashed off the blade.

Portia drew up short, barely stopping herself from falling on the woman—and her knife. She felt the wooden train ties under her thin-soled shoes, her legs trembling, no, *quaking*. But not from the cold. From the shock, the sheer terror of facing down her own mortality. Before Portia could pull back, run from the knife, she saw the woman's eyes glint, narrow, focused on something behind Portia. Her lips curled upward again, as if the laptop thief liked what she saw. Without further threats, the woman jumped off the tracks and ran into the woods on the other side of town. Too late, Portia realized the pounding of her feet on the railroad track wasn't what made the frozen wood ties shake. It was a train. The sound of its whistle blowing was the last thing she remembered before being hit sideways by an overpowering force.

Chapter 2

Kyle chased after Portia as he watched the train bear down on the pair in his peripheral vision. He'd seen it pass through the commercial district several times. A lot of times it slowed to a crawl, and then a complete stop as the tracks were switched to allow the container shipments to go to the other part of town that housed many national distribution centers. But this train didn't slow down, the conductor showing no sign of seeing the women on the tracks as it kept going, way too fast for a local. Kyle figured he had thirty seconds, tops, to prevent Portia from catching up to Markova, or worse, before the train hit them both. Because if Portia caught Markova, the knife blade plunging into her body was the last thing she'd feel.

Kyle couldn't believe that neither Portia nor Markova had noticed the train as he ran toward them. Portia continued her pursuit of the woman she thought was a mere thief, clearly ignorant of how lethal an encounter with her would be. ROC didn't put up with interference of any kind and made it a trademark to never leave a witness alive. No matter how trivial the crime, it left no one living to tell their tales. It was what made them so powerful, enabling their insidious network of crime to reach into the most seemingly solid communities.

He ran in a perpendicular line to the tracks, knowing he risked Markova seeing him, wondering if he was law enforcement, but he didn't care. He had to save Portia. The op would still be there—as far as Markova knew, he was either a Good Samaritan or a friend of Portia's who'd witnessed their altercation. Or even an under-cover cop. Let ROC come after him. He'd be damned if they would add an innocent Silver Valley librarian to their tally of victims.

By the time he was within a few feet of the tracks, the women faced one another, the knife in Markova's hands poised to do maximum harm. He ran toward them and opened his mouth to shout a warning, any-thing to distract the knife-wielding criminal. But it was futile against the roar of the train engine, the wheels of the old cargo car squealing in protest as the engi-neer applied the brakes. Too late, though, to save either woman if they didn't get off the tracks.

He'd practiced so many dangerous scenarios in both his Marine Corps and Trail Hiker training, and expe-rienced countless more in his work as a Marine Scout and then as an undercover operative for the past seven years. There were no surprises as he measured the sit-uation, decided on his course of action and followed through just in the nick of time. Markova jumped the tracks a second ahead of him. As he hit Portia sideways, tackling her off the tracks and holding her as they rolled down the embankment, the roar of the train drowning out all other noise, he had only one surprise.

He hadn't screamed "look out" or "stop" or even "train." The word, the name that had scraped past his throat, dry from the cold air, had been the name of someone he'd never met, not in the conventional way.

Portia.

Portia was aware of a very heavy weight on top of her, her face smooshed against a thick winter coat of some type, the scents of tar, train exhaust, and something else mingling and filling each breath she gasped for. The click of the train-car wheels across the track oddly comforted her, a definite sign that she hadn't been flattened by the engine but in fact had been knocked off the tracks.

"You with me?" A low, rumbling voice filled her ears as much as she felt it through her very center. Her shuddering, shock-affected center.

"Y-y-yes." The chatter couldn't be helped, no matter how hard she clenched her jaw. But it wasn't hypothermic shivers that ran through her; it was so much more.

The weight shifted and she realized someone lay atop her, a very large, lean person, on the ground next to the railroad embankment. An involuntary moan left her lips. Did the man hear it? Did he think she never wanted him to leave her?

"I thought you were a goner back there." He gently rolled them both to their sides, still holding her protectively. Bright eyes filled her vision, a gloved hand cupped her chin.

"Who?" She couldn't manage more than the one syllable; the question *who are you?* really didn't matter, as she was still here, alive, intact. And yet it mattered a whole hell of a lot. Who was this savior?

"Here." Strong arms on either side of her, the weight gone, the sense of being lifted higher, higher, but in reality the man had only shifted her into a seated position on the ground, sitting next to her, his arm still wrapped around her shoulders. "Give yourself a few breaths before you try to stand up. Assess if you're hurting anywhere."

She listened to his voice, acknowledged she could listen to it all day, any day, and never grow bored of it.

"Are you in any pain?" He reiterated his concern as the last few cars passed, revealing a row of Silver Valley PD police cars on the other side of the tracks, back in the parking lot that stretched behind the library, diner and several other Silver Valley businesses.

"No. I'm...I'm okay." She wiggled her toes, her fingers, and mentally moved up her anatomy. Her butt and shoulders were sore on the left side—the large man had somehow cushioned the rest of her from the impact upon stony ground, but since he'd saved her life, she was inclined to agree with him.

"Who are you?" At least her voice sounded stronger. She'd never met him, she was certain, but there was something familiar about him, as if they did know one another. Suspicion stole into her sense of security. Did he know the laptop thief—was he part of some kind of criminal network?

Gray eyes narrowed, thin lines fanning out from their corners. "I'm someone you can trust."

She wiped a shaky hand over her mouth. "That's something after almost being—" She cut off abruptly.

Shudders started to wrack her body and tears spilled onto her cheeks. She'd been that close to dying. To losing it all, forever.

In one moment the importance of her worries and hopes to raise money for the library, to expand its services, her homeless shelter efforts—they all evaporated into what she'd almost become. Oblivion. She looked around her and vowed to never take another day for granted, no matter how cold or how aggravated she was by a laptop thief. It could all be gone as quick as she could say "choo choo."

"Come on." He lifted her to her feet and hugged her to his side. Only when he motioned with his free arm did she notice the pair of police officers who'd walked up to them, followed by EMTs.

"This woman is on the verge of shock." Her rescuer's voice held a note of steel she hadn't noticed as he'd made sure she'd survived their tumble. She turned to thank him but he was gone. Her brain felt like she was thinking in a fog and Portia didn't argue as the EMTs each took an arm and carefully walked her back to the parking area. She wanted to squeeze her eyes shut when they had to briefly traverse the tracks again, but at least it wasn't more than a few paces.

As she received first aid for a couple of cuts and bruises and then was taken to the ER against her desires, as a safeguard, her equilibrium returned. Portia had a lot to do when she got back to the library, but what she wanted to know more than anything was who the man was who'd saved her. And why she could still feel the imprint of his hands, his arms around her as they fell through the air and hit the hard ground, hours later. The matter of the person who'd led her so close to death didn't elude her. Portia wanted to know who she was and wanted the woman to face full criminal charges for all she'd done. But the overarching curiosity that kept her from drowning in the shock and despair of almost dying wasn't over the laptop thief. It was all about her rescuer, the man whose arms made her feel like no one could ever hurt her again.

And his eyes—the color of the Susquehanna in January. But unlike the cold slate of the river that ran through central Pennsylvania, where Silver Valley was nestled, the man's eyes had a warmth in them. And a sadness.

It must have been the shock, as he described it, that made a myriad of emotions assault her as she mentally replayed what had just happened. Because what else explained the instant, white-hot zap of attraction she'd felt for the man, her train-wreck savior?

And who *was* he?

Ludmila Markova wasn't happy. She'd have to circle back, in disguise this time, and drop the laptop off through the front door of the library, to leave it on the circulation desk. The book slot was too small for the computer, no doubt for added security. She'd have to act like a dopey kid who'd accidentally taken the laptop from the library property by accident.

Then she'd kill the librarian. Portia DiNapoli. She'd kept one eye on the bitch each time she'd entered the library, mostly just as herself, since this ignorant American town seemed to have a lot of library patrons. It made it easy for her to blend in.

She swore as she made herself down an entire quart of kefir. The protein was necessary to keep up her strength, and she missed the tang of her mother's home-made drink.

The thought of her mother, gunned down next to her brothers and sisters and Papa, brought tears to her eyes. She viciously swiped at them. No more. After this mission, she'd be free and have the funds to go wherever she wanted. Not back to Russia—never.

Using the tactics ingrained into her by the former KGB official who trained her, she shoved her worthless emotions aside and focused on what the rest of the day would look like. First a stop to the library. Then find the librarian and eliminate the worry of her testimony, no matter how unlikely.

"What do you mean you were almost hit by a train? I thought you were working the ROC distribution network case?"

Silver Valley PD detective Josh Avery looked at Kyle as if his colleague was a new recruit. Kyle's liaison with SVPD was a necessary part of working an op targeting criminal activity in Silver Valley. ROC was a menace to Silver Valley and instead of eradicating the crime ring's reach with the takedown of a human trafficking ring, they'd found themselves looking down the barrel of ROC setting up Silver Valley to be its epicenter of heroin distribution in central Pennsylvania, Maryland and parts of New Jersey. Several of the SVPD detectives and officers were cut into Trail Hiker ops on a need-to-know basis, and often a Trail Hiker agent was paired with a single point of contact at SVPD to minimize leaks and maximize both law enforcement agencies' ability to solve cases. Kyle came into SVPD to debrief Josh, after he was sure Portia was okay and being taken care of by the EMTs. Again, his focus was too heavy on the Portia side for his agent liking.

"I was. I am." Kyle weighed what to say next, even though Josh was his SVPD liaison for this particular Trail Hiker case. But they were working as a team. "I was conducting surveillance, the same kind you do every day, on the library's back entrance. Another agent had the front door covered. When trouble showed up in the way of an intruder—Markova—trying to pry open the locked exit-only door, I paid attention. I never expected the librarian to take off after the assailant, though."

"It's not like we can warn civilians about top-secret ROC details, not if we want to keep our covert ops secret." Josh's face revealed his concern.

"That's the double-edged sword of this work, isn't it? Providing safety for all by tracking the bad guys we can't talk about." Kyle leaned back in the chair across from Josh's desk, in the detective's office. "Who knew a librarian could run that fast?"

"I haven't seen the official report come across yet. Are you sure it was the head librarian, Portia? Or one of her assistants?"

"It was Portia. And we're lucky Markova didn't knife her on the spot at the library." No sense pretending he didn't know who Portia was. "You know Portia?"

"She's my fiancée's best friend." Josh grinned. "Don't get sucked into any librarian stereotypes. Portia doesn't take crap from anyone."

Two strikes against his attempts at staying unseen today. He avoided public venues with any law enforcement agencies, or LEAs, as much as possible while doing his initial surveillance of Markova and ROC. But both Portia and Markova had seen him on the railroad tracks. Portia might believe he was a simple Good Samaritan, as could Markova. But a former FSB agent operated on the belief that there were no coincidences. Chances were that Markova suspected she'd been marked. His days in his undercover guise as a homeless man were numbered now, because Markova was as good as an enemy agent got. She'd put him with his disguise with little trouble. "Hell. Can't one go anywhere in this town without running into another connection."

"It's not that bad. We're bigger than you think, not just because we're over twenty thousand last count. And you could run into the same people in a city of millions, especially in our profession. It happens."

"But it's not supposed to. Not if I'm doing my job right." Kyle's mission was to stay under the radar of a casual observer. He knew that Portia probably hadn't noticed him in the library. He wore various disguises whenever he went there, to keep himself free to be himself during off-hours. He should have worn a disguise this morning, too, but with daylight surveillance, he wasn't as worried—it was easier to pass off someone as inconsequential, normal, during busier working hours.

Josh nodded. He got it—he was an SVPD detective, yes, but also a Trail Hiker Agent as needed, per case. Right now they were using all agencies and means available to eradicate the crime through which ROC had infiltrated Silver Valley.

Kyle happened to have drawn the case of the stolen freight shipments, which amounted to millions of dollars of lost high-end technology goods in the past six months. Televisions, luxury audio systems and scores of top-of-the-line computer systems had been stolen. It'd blossomed into more when he discovered that heroin shipments were part of the ROC clandestine network, too. "I've narrowed down the place where they exchange possible hits and heroin drops to the library. I just haven't spotted them doing it yet."

"You still think it's with the library's computer internal system?"

"I did. But now, I'm not so sure. I've sat surveillance on Markova and the library for almost three weeks with no new leads." The lack of movement on the case had given him too much time to think about Portia.

He wondered if she'd needed stitches, if she was released from the ER yet.

Not your problem.

Josh shook his head. "This is the hardest part. Waiting out the losers to make a wrong move so that we can put all of us out of our misery."

"Yeah." Kyle didn't know Josh that well but knew that he'd recently been involved in a big sting against ROC. "How long did you wait before you saved all those Ukrainian women?" He referred to the human trafficking ROC had conducted in Silver Valley last year. Josh had also been instrumental in helping the wife of a notorious ROC operative get out of a domestic violence situation. He'd told Kyle about it in one of their many liaisons like today's.

"It felt like forever but it came together quickly, once things started falling in place. You know the drill— hurry up and wait. And then be ready to go full throttle."

"Hmph." Kyle tried to review the work he'd done

the past weeks, most of it surveillance, but he couldn't stop the image of Portia's big brown eyes watching him earlier. If he weren't committed to remaining single, putting his career first, always, she'd be…no. He couldn't go there. If he did decide to date someone, as he'd been considering, it couldn't be Portia. Portia was too dangerous, because he barely knew her and couldn't shake her.

"You're still thinking about Portia, aren't you?" Josh's grin rankled Kyle but not as much as his uncanny ability to read him. Few could.

"Why do you ask?"

"I think it's the same expression I had on my face, oh, about six months ago. When I realized Annie was more than a childhood friend."

"Doubtful. I don't know anything about Portia DiNapoli except that she's the town librarian, and also volunteers a lot of time at the Silver Valley homeless shelter. I can only hope she doesn't recognize me the next time I'm there. She's making my job more difficult."

Josh slapped him on the back. "You are so full of crap. You had to have done a quick background check on Portia as part of this case," Josh called him out without hesitation.

Kyle felt his face redden. "Of course I did. But what I mean is that I don't know her personally, at all."

Josh laughed. "You'll figure it out. It's nothing a pro like you can't handle, Kyle."

"Easy for you to say. You don't have to pass as a homeless person a few times a week." Contrary to his words, though, he'd learned more from his undercover work at the shelter than what the case demanded. He'd realized that Portia was a very compassionate, dedicated woman. The kind of woman a man didn't play with romantically.

You're undercover at the shelter for the case, not Portia.

"When are you going back in?" Josh referred to the Silver Valley homeless shelter.

"Tonight. I'll look nothing like this, of course." He motioned to his jeans and flannel shirt. "The other night, I found out that there are three new dealers in town. I need their names. Then I can track down their supplier more quickly with triangulation." And hopefully directly link it to ROC, but he wasn't holding his breath. ROC was notorious for its ability to evade law enforcement. But ROC wasn't used to the state-of-the-art technology and techniques employed by the Trail Hikers. ROC thought they were up against SVPD and the FBI, tough enough adversaries. "I've also got to get into the library to do a thorough search for evidence."

"I've seen your getup. You're right—you don't look anything like the homeless person you use for your cover." Josh paused. "You'll need a search warrant for the library, though."

"Unless we can convince the local librarian to let me in for a look-see." Kyle drummed his fingers on the table, alongside his coffee mug.

"Kyle, you can tell me to mind my own business, but what did you do before TH?" He'd lowered his voice, as the secrecy of the agency meant that the majority of SVPD officers and employees had no idea of its existence. They all thought Kyle was a visiting detective from out of state.

"I was a Marine." He wasn't going to spell it out—Josh wasn't stupid.

Josh's eyes narrowed. "I *knew* it. The US Marine Corps—it explains how cool you are, no matter what."

"And my lack of patience while conducting civilian stakeouts."

"Forget about that. What do you think they're passing in the library?"

"I don't know but from all indications, ROC sends thugs from New York into the library to drop intel for a local operative. Then they split. The local person in charge comes in, gets the information, then passes the information to their local network. It's what TH has put together after collecting information from all available agencies and sources."

"You think there's a tip-off going down soon, for certain?"

"I do. It makes sense, as it's been ten days since the last rash of trailer thefts." Two truckloads of computer equipment and one of wide-screen, high-technology televisions.

"I'm glad they're not doing anything more than knocking out the truck drivers," Josh said, expressing what worried Kyle. It was only a matter of time before ROC left behind their use of chloroform and used weapons that would leave more permanent wounds. Or worse. Escalation was part of ROC's methods. The minute one trucker didn't go down easily with a chloroform-soaked rag, they'd up the ante to let the other truckers in the region know they'd better give up their goods without a fight. His mind flashed back to the image of Portia facing down Markova, and the former FSB agent's knife. He hadn't ever felt that frightened for someone he didn't know. Hell, when was he going to admit to himself that Portia had gotten under his skin?

"You and I both know that they're used to making smaller PD's roll over and get out of their way. They're not afraid to hit at officers as needed. They don't like the press attention, but when it comes down to it, they don't really care. To them, money and power is what matters."

"Not on my watch," Josh said, expressing how Kyle felt.

"I have to admit, Josh, I never know what I'm going to find when I walk into a new PD. Silver Valley PD is solid," Kyle said without thinking and realized he was speaking from his heart. He took a long, hot gulp of coffee. For over a decade, he'd either been a Marine or Trail Hiker, protected the highest officials of government, conducted clandestine ops and never thought much about his dang heart. But since this morning, and coming head-to-head with Portia, he'd—

"Officer Avery? Portia DiNapoli is here to give a statement and she wants to talk to you." The receptionist stood at Josh's desk. "Should I bring her back here or tell her to wait?"

Josh looked at Kyle. "You okay with her seeing you here?"

Kyle wanted to see Portia, know she was okay. It was an unreasonable level of concern for someone he wasn't personally acquainted with. Best stop it before it began.

You're already done for.

"Naw, I'll take off before you talk to her."

"Can you have her wait a few, and I'll come get her?" Josh said to the receptionist.

"Sure thing."

After she was out of earshot, Josh looked at Kyle. "I know you're undercover for TH, but Portia doesn't have to know that. She could think you're a contractor or other LEA, working with SVPD on the ROC case, in general. It's no secret that we've got ROC problems in Silver Valley."

"I know. It's the details that are classified, not the big picture." Kyle's gut clenched. It'd be too easy to let Portia know what he did, that he was someone she could trust, as he'd told her. "But unless she absolutely has to know—"

"I hear you. And I'd do the same." Josh confirmed the conservative approach all undercover agents employed. It was always better to stick to the tightest parameters of operational security possible. Then you could loosen up as needed. But once the cat was out of the bag, i.e., a civilian such as Portia DiNapoli found out you were doing something classified or law enforcement related, you couldn't put it back.

Kyle stood. "I'll check in after my stint at the shelter tonight. Tomorrow morning work for you, unless something important happens?"

"Sure thing. By the way, Kyle? You're doing it again."

"What?"

Josh didn't say anything for a moment while he grinned at him. Kyle braced himself for what he knew was coming, and it wasn't unwarranted.

"One word, Kyle. One woman. P-o-r-t-i-a."

Fuuuuuudge.

* * *

It took most of the morning for Portia to be cleared by the medical staff at Silver Valley Hospital, so she wasn't sure if Josh would be in when she showed up to file a report at SVPD at lunchtime. Annie was engaged to Josh and Portia knew that they enjoyed lunches together during the workweek. She suspected the "lunches" were sexy liaisons, but never pressed her friend on it. Not too much, anyway.

Holding her driver's license up to the security camera, she pushed the button outside the station entrance. She'd had tours of the police department with the library's murder mystery book club and remembered the protocol for civilians.

"Come on in, Ms. DiNapoli." The receptionist's quick acknowledgment didn't surprise her. Portia had been instructed to go straight to the station after she left the hospital, to file her report.

"Hi. Thanks for letting me in so quickly—it's still pretty cold out there." She began to unbutton her coat in the warm entryway. The receptionist nodded.

"You're here to see Detective Avery?"

"Yes."

"Do you know where his office is?" Portia noticed that the entryway had a lot of people coming and going.

"I do."

"Great. Just pass your bag through the scanner and step through the metal detector."

Portia turned to the security guard who led her through the procedure, clearing her to enter the main building.

Portia walked back to Josh's desk once the receptionist cleared her. She didn't have a lot of business at

SVPD, except to ask Josh, a high school classmate, if he'd read to the elementary school students when she'd been working at Silver Valley Elementary. And even then, she called or emailed him, didn't pay the police department a visit. The bustle and sense of many different officers and detectives in constant motion hit her. It matched what she'd read: Silver Valley was in the midst of a crime wave unlike any ever seen before.

A tall man at the end of one of the long corridors made her stomach flip in ridiculous anticipation. Walking away from her, toward the back exit, he could have been anyone. But her body sensed it was the man from the tracks. He was tall, with an angular build that only hinted at his sheer strength—the kind of power that enabled him to knock her out from an oncoming train. Short, military-style hair, a sandy blond. Her gaze travelled down his length. He carried a parka in one arm, the same color as the man who'd saved her wore. Without the extra goose down padding his frame seemed all the more impressive. His butt was all muscle in worn jeans, and his stride in his boots bespoke of stealth. It might not be him, but then he threw her a quick look over his shoulder. His eyes—silver like a wolf she'd seen once, visiting a wildlife preserve. He gave her a curt nod. As if he knew she'd been there all along. Her stomach leaped and she increased her pace, but he disappeared around the corner before she reached him. Clearly, he didn't want to talk to her. She paused right before she got to Josh's office. She'd been through a lot today, and she might be seeing things, seeing *someone* wherever she looked. What were the odds it was the same man who'd saved her from the tracks? The man who'd held her, made her feel safer than she had in a long, long time?

"Hey, Portia. Come on in." Josh Avery's smile was as genuine as his quick, warm hug. He kept a hand on her upper arm after he pulled back and peered into her eyes. "You okay? Really?"

Realization struck her yet again that the morning's events hadn't been a dream, or an almost-nightmare. She'd indeed missed being flattened by a locomotive, with no more than a second or two to spare.

"I'm good." She raked a shaky hand through her curls, not caring what she looked like. "I have some bruises that are going to be pretty ugly, but the man that knocked me off the tracks also protected me from the brunt of the fall, and the hard ground."

Josh motioned for her to sit in one of the seats in front of his desk and sank into his chair. "Did our receptionist get you any coffee or something else to drink?"

Portia waved her hand in dismissal. "No, I'm okay, really. I'm so wired from the adrenaline rush that I'm sure any more caffeine would launch me to the moon."

"Okay." Josh tapped on his keyboard and she watched as his eyes tracked the information on the screen.

"Thanks for making time to take my statement. I know the other police officers are just as able to, but I'd feel better talking to you." And she wouldn't have to explain her hunches—Josh had known her since they were kids and had never patronized her.

"Are you kidding? Annie would have my hide if I didn't take care of this. Besides, it's part of an ongoing investigation I'm working on."

"Really? You mean figuring out who's stealing our library laptops, or something bigger?"

"We'll never figure out who took all of your laptops, Portia. I'm afraid we don't have enough man-hours. But if you can find evidence on your security footage, you know to bring it in."

And she did, but their tapes had been wiped. "Um, speaking of that." Heat rode up her neck, over her face. "The recordings were erased. My staff and I tried to replay the last several weeks' worth, only to discover there was nothing there."

Josh's brows slammed together. "What do you mean 'nothing there'?"

"There's a file on the drive that only I have access to, and I open it up for the staff to watch regularly. We fast-forward through it, pause when we see something suspicious. So far we haven't had any luck figuring out who lifted three computers back in October, and the more recent thefts are even more confusing, as we locked our laptops up overnight. In the mornings, they were gone."

"Yes, I read the reports." Josh kept typing on his computer, taking notes. "Did you say you were able to retrieve the security footage back in the fall?"

Portia nodded. "Yes. But these last two weeks, even after double-checking the camera equipment, doing a trial run on the system, we still lost it all. There's no footage of the library for almost three weeks."

"And yet the video feed is still good? From the cameras to the monitor?"

She nodded. "Yes. Our security specialist monitors the feed all day long. And we have it set for Record, always. Something goes wrong during the archival loop."

Josh frowned. "If anyone understands the information technology around this, you do, Portia. I'm damned sorry this is happening at the local library. Have you noticed anything else unusual?"

She shook her head. "No. Except this morning, when I saw the woman trying to break into the back employee entrance. I should have called SVPD instead of taking her on myself." She inwardly cringed at her transgression. If she'd told Brindle to immediately call 9-1-1, the woman might be in custody.

And you'd never have met the dream man.

She squirmed in her seat. She'd met no one, knew no one.

"Can you give the sketch artist a good sense of the woman—you're sure it was a woman—who took off for the tracks?"

"Only her eyes—they were blue. And her mouth had bright red lipstick."

Josh paused in his note-taking. "I see why you think it's a woman."

"I can't be positive, Josh, but I've seen that woman before. And the fact that she had one of our laptops means she's been in the library at least once before."

Josh paused, as if weighing something crucial. "Look, I don't want to alarm you, but we're working against some bad apples right now."

"You mean ROC? Russian Organized Crime?"

Josh's stern expression broke into a chuckle. "You've been reading the local paper."

"Of course. As well as the police blotter reports on social media. But laptop theft hardly matches the kind of crime ROC participates in, doesn't it? I mean, they'd steal a shipment of computers, I'd imagine. There isn't enough money in a paltry laptop from a local library."

"I'm not going to discuss details of any case other than yours, Portia. What I'm trying to explain is that there are some very unsavory types running about. It's inevitable with the heroin trade and opioid epidemic. And that makes people unpredictable. Paranoid. If the woman you ran after has any suspicion that you might be able to identify her, that might put you at risk. I'm suggesting you be very careful. Don't travel alone anywhere at night."

"You mean the usual way a single woman lives, Josh?" She couldn't help but tease him. "I'm not getting a buddy to walk around Silver Valley—that's ridiculous. But I will be more aware of my surroundings, I promise."

"And you'll call in anything out of the ordinary, no more facing down a criminal on your own?"

"Guilty as charged. For the record, I told my staff to call 9-1-1 if they saw the situation go bad."

"Which they did." Josh's eyes narrowed. "We weren't able to get anything from the security footage, though. The woman knew what she was doing, with a hood and ski mask. I'm not doubting what you say you saw, Portia. But you were under duress, to say the least." Josh paused. "I know you saw a woman, but I can't tell you why I know. Not yet. It's part of the process of taking your report to question what you remember."

Portia nodded. "I get it." She rubbed her upper arms as if to ward off a chill in the well-heated office. "After she shoved me, and I took off after her, yes, but I was calm when we spoke outside the library, at the back exit. I saw red when I saw her on the security camera, trying to open it with a tool of some sort. Now I realize she seemed familiar to me, but of course she had that mask on, so I guess I could be wrong. I'm frustrated that I couldn't get the actual serial number of the laptop. We're missing more than one and it would be helpful to know which one the woman had. Each laptop has different storage capacities and software applications. If we knew which it was, it might help to know why she was trying to sneak into the back with it." The numbers were on the inside of the cases, along with library-specific bar codes. She leaned forward. "You know me, Josh. You've watched me grow up, for Pete's sake. If you're doubting my powers of observation, ask Annie." She had him and didn't feel the least bit bad about it. Portia had been the one to encourage Annie to reconnect with Josh on more than professional matters last summer.

"I'm not faulting your judgment, Portia. I'm questioning what you've just been through, how it may have altered your recollection."

"It hasn't, or else I'd still be in the ER, and you'd be questioning me there."

"True." Josh paused from typing in her account and leveled a look at her. "You're sure you're okay?"

Portia nodded. "Absolutely. The person, the man who…who saved my life, he bore the brunt of the fall." The memory of being in his arms wrapped around her, and it wasn't frightening. The woman who'd have happily left her to be hit by the train, that was scary. But the stranger…he was more.

"By the way, Josh, I was hoping you'd be able to help me out. The man who saved me—he wouldn't give me his name. At the very least, I owe him an apology. Do you know who it was?" She was counting on SVPD's stellar reputation that they'd questioned everyone at the scene, and the man had been the one to hand her over to the EMTs, who arrived after SVPD. But her memory of that was foggy—Josh was right, she'd had a shakeup.

"Aww, Portia, it sounds like a Good Samaritan." Josh's gaze slid from hers, and if the day hadn't already been confrontational enough, she'd call her old school buddy on it. But not now.

It didn't matter. If the man wanted her to know his name, he had plenty of opportunity to tell her. And she wasn't as obtuse as Josh might believe—Annie had told her that there were always cases and law enforcement operations that Josh couldn't talk about. Maybe the man was part of that.

Or maybe she just had a special place in her heart for a hot man, around her age, who had saved her life.

Chapter 3

Portia ignored the ER doctor's suggestion to take it easy for the rest of the day and went back to the library for the rest of the afternoon, after she left SVPD. Sure, the almost-being-killed scene on the railroad tracks had shaken her up for a bit, but there was work to be done at the library, and she had to pull her shift at the homeless shelter tonight. With the record-breaking low temperatures, the fifty-bed facility had been overflowing for two weeks solid. As exhausted as she imagined she was going to feel by later this evening, she knew she had a warm bed to go back to, a roof over her head from any snow flurries. The homeless of Silver Valley and surrounding Harrisburg area had few choices. Silver Valley Homeless Mission was one of them.

The reminder of her empty bed stung in a way it hadn't since she'd broken up with Rob. She had her own bed to sleep in, her own place, but it was always more fulfilling to share it with someone. Rob had been the only man she'd lived with for a short time. The other men she'd dated had, like her, enjoyed their own apartments when they weren't spending time together. Sometimes she wondered if she was destined to be single her entire life. She'd never met a man who'd made her feel she wanted to be with him, live with him, make a lifelong commitment.

Which was another reason why the train track rescue dude intrigued her. How was it that a man she'd never met had left more of an impression on her than guys she'd dated for months at a time?

She grabbed a quick dinner at the local diner, next to the library, before heading to the shelter. It was no more than twenty-five feet to the restaurant and yet she found herself looking over her shoulder, paying extra attention to the patrons entering and leaving the establishment. And she hated the laptop thief for stealing her sense of safety.

Immediately her mind flung back to the stranger, how he'd appeared from nowhere and disappeared as easily.

"Hey, Portia. How are you, honey?" The diner's lead waitress greeted her and grabbed a menu. Molly was a Silver Valley mainstay, the woman who served up hot soup or Belgian waffles when you needed them most. Molly sat her at a single booth, knowing how Portia enjoyed eating in the back corner of the diner, with a table to spread her books out on. "I heard you had a little excitement today."

"I did, and it's over." Portia shrugged out of her parka and hung it on the hook adjacent the bench seat.

"I called my parents right after, so that they wouldn't find out on social media or the online paper." Molly knew her parents, the entire DiNapoli family in fact.

Molly waited for her to sit. "That was smart. I'm surprised your parents aren't here with you now."

Portia smiled, still too worn out to laugh. "Trust me, I had to convince my mother that I'm totally fine. I promised her I was coming here to eat, then spending time at the shelter, where the other volunteers are like my second family."

"It's turned out okay, but honey, you were almost killed. Don't treat it so lightly, give yourself a little time to process. I'm so glad you're okay. That's all that matters."

"I appreciate that." And she did, but she couldn't keep dwelling on the frightening part of the situation or she'd never feel safe in Silver Valley again. "I see the chef made a batch of pepper pot pie." She referred to a local central Pennsylvania dish, which was actually a beef or chicken soup with square noodles, not a pastry-crust pie with filling.

"He did, and it smells divine in the kitchen tonight."

"I'll take that, and my usual."

Molly laughed, shaking her head. "I envy your ability to consume grilled cheese so regularly and not gain an inch."

"I'm on my feet all day." And today she'd earned all the comfort food she could manage to eat. She'd never forget how close she'd come to death, nor the enigmatic man who'd saved her life.

"Do you want hot tea, honey?"

"Yes, please." Molly walked away and Portia counted her blessings. Her parents were still in the area and she saw them fairly regularly, but her two siblings had moved away to Boston and Austin, Texas, respectively. Her brother worked with the FBI and her sister was a medical researcher. Their family times were great when they happened, but they were infrequent. It was nice to come into a diner and be treated like she belonged. Just like it was great to look forward to going to the homeless shelter tonight. Since her high school friend Lani had OD'd, Portia had found herself craving more human connection than what work provided. She wondered if her need to be with others would only intensify after her near-death experience today.

Certainly her obsession over her rescuer indicated she might need more human contact.

As she ate her pepper pot pie and sandwich dripping with Gouda and cheddar, she studied her handheld tablet. In a medium-sized town like Silver Valley, charities often combined events to help individual nonprofits to raise exponentially more cash. Since she'd been the one to suggest marrying the homeless shelter's fundraising efforts to the library gala, Portia knew her professional reputation was at stake. If the gala raised the same amount as last year, that meant less money for the library, as they'd agreed to give the homeless shelter 25 percent of the funds raised. There was less than a month left, and so far they had sold the same number of tickets as last year. She needed to figure out how to sell more by the RSVP deadline, two weeks away. The gala was to be at the end of the month, and would include a Silver Valley ice sculpture festival and contest. She was grateful for five weeks in January this year.

The homeless shelter was a short ten-minute walk from the diner, but it was located at the end of town, where the buildings thinned and the northern wind was a force to lean into. She'd traded her shoes for snow boots and wore her warmest down parka, but nothing seemed enough to stay warm in the sub-zero windchill.

The shelter was a modest craftsman-style home that had been converted to a fifty-bed mission by an anonymous donor three years ago. The porch and entry, usually full with patrons waiting until the last minute to go in for the night, stood empty. It was totally because of the cold, no question.

Still, a shiver raced up her spine and Portia knew a moment of sheer terror as she stared into the dark shadows of the porch. And then made herself look at the windows, aglow with light and promising warmth.

But she couldn't shake the frigid snare of fear that stabbed at her previous sense of safety, of surety about Silver Valley's place in the world. Would she ever regain it?

Kyle hoped tonight's surveillance at the homeless shelter would lead him to whomever might know when and by what means the next heroin shipment was coming in. On a cold night like this, addicts who normally avoided the shelters for fear of getting arrested for carrying illegal substances were sure to come in. He wanted to know who the newest dealers were, and where to find them.

Kyle checked in early to the shelter, well before the time he knew Portia normally showed up. Just in case she did. He'd expect her to go home and take the night off, after what she'd been through today.

Who was he kidding? Portia would no more likely bail on a volunteer shift than he'd quit an undercover op. Wasn't one of the things that he found so attractive about her the dedication she appeared to have to her work, her community? He tried to mentally brace himself to focus on finding someone else to date, to be with. Yet his gut instinct seemed to laugh at him, as if what he felt toward Portia were predestined, beyond his control.

He tried to breathe through his mouth, to not inhale the scent of his unwashed clothes. Part of his successful capture of intelligence regarding ROC's heroin and illegal-goods shipment operation was blending in, no matter the circumstance. As a homeless man, that meant stinking as if he'd been on the streets for several days.

He'd refuse to bathe here, unlike most of the men and women who gratefully accepted a hot shower. He couldn't risk anyone seeing him without the dirty wig or baggy clothes. He promised the intake person that he'd shower before bed. The mission also offered gently used but clean pajamas, to change into and wear so that their dirty clothes could be washed. Kyle found it easiest to play the role of the reluctant shelter-seeker. No one bothered him, save for the social workers who always tried to convince him to let them help him.

He'd found an old, scraggly wig at a used clothing store and wet it thoroughly, doused it with dirt, rubbed it around the attic of the house he rented, until it was sufficiently matted. No one would recognize him as the man who'd knocked Silver Valley's librarian off the local train tracks, in front of an oncoming train, just hours ago.

He scratched his head, hating the wig, and wished he hadn't shaved and had his hair cut. He'd had to, in order to hang around the library and not draw unwarranted attention. He'd needed to blend in, which he did by wearing different types of clothing each day, his wardrobe flexible to accommodate the needs of a farmer, teacher, professional or what he really was. An undercover agent.

After pouring a cup of hot coffee from the urn set up in the dining room area, he settled into a worn sofa and prepared to listen and learn. Observe. It was his job to do so.

A gust of polar air rushed into the room as the front door opened with a bang. His nape tingled and he silently swore to himself. It wasn't a premonition or anything portending danger. It was what he'd labeled his Portia Radar. He'd had to call it something, because as a good undercover agent, he couldn't afford to ignore how he reacted to people.

Before her shiny brunette hair that curled around her face and hung to her shoulders appeared, before the overhead lights reflected off her doe-brown eyes, before her confident, super-feminine laughter bounced off the dining room walls, he knew Portia was here.

A sense of urgency to get the ROC op wrapped up, Ludmila Markova locked up, gripped him. It wasn't so that he'd feel free to pursue Portia, because Kyle didn't do anything long-term, and Portia DiNapoli wasn't the one-night-stand type. Rather, she wasn't *his* one-and-done type. She was the woman that came to mind on the rare occasion he imagined what his "forever" woman would look like, if he were the type to settle down.

Hell. He had to get out of Silver Valley as quickly

as he could. Something about this place had wrapped around him, gotten under his skin.

And they'd never been properly introduced.

"Here you go, Mr. Turner." Portia handed the neatly folded pile of bed linens and towels to the man, still bundled up in his worn puffer down coat that she'd bet was from circa 1995. But it still kept him warm, and that was all that mattered. Still, she was glad he was at the mission tonight.

"Thank you, Portia. You're very kind."

"Just doing my job."

"They give you a raise yet?" He winked at her from behind his thick eyeglasses as he turned to head to his assigned bed. Mr. Turner, as well as most of the clients, she'd assume, knew who the volunteers were. The paid shelter workers included a social worker and counselor, as well as an accountant and grant writer, and were the ones who could get prescriptions filled as needed, medical care when warranted.

As much as Portia remained committed to her time here, she knew her vocation was in library science. Neither social work nor grant writing appealed to her. Her passion lay with seeing patrons find the book that they'd searched for, or a child figuring out that a novel was way better than the film version of their favorite story.

When she walked through the dining room, en route to the library, she couldn't escape the feeling she was being watched. Plain silly, as of course there were several pairs of eyes on her. Several different groups of people gathered around the family-style tables, drinking coffee or tea or hot chocolate. Alcohol and illegal drugs were strictly prohibited at the shelter, but she wouldn't be surprised if some of the hot drinks were spiked.

Portia ignored the urge to sit at one of the tables and find out more about the clients. Her shift was more than half over and she hadn't even started on the library. Before she left the dining area, though, she decided to get a cup of tea. The hot water urn was too tempting to pass up on such a cold night. Even with the house heated, the modern heating units couldn't keep up with the windchill. She pulled a bag of ginger tea from her pocket, ripped open the envelope and dunked the sachet into a thick paper cup. As she watched the boiling water turn golden, the creepy sense of being observed crawled up her back, her neck, and made her scalp tingle. This wasn't her introverted self being aware of the night's clients watching her. It was more.

Portia kept her back to the dining area, where at least twenty people sat around. The hum of their conversations hadn't waned, so it wasn't as if everyone had gone quiet and was staring at her, waiting for her to turn around and face them for an unknown reason. She heard the rush of liquid through the overhead piping, indicating that several overnight visitors were taking advantage of hot running water. Yet she couldn't shake her awareness of being watched in an unfriendly way.

Keeping her movements as casual as possible, she squeezed the tea bag with the paper envelope and threw it out. Hot drink in both hands, she turned carefully toward the door. As she neared the library's entrance, she risked a quick glance about the room. First she swept the dining room at large. No one paid her any attention.

Same with the people chatting in various easy chairs and sofas around the perimeter of the room.

Except for one man, who was sitting in the club chair next to the library entrance. He wasn't looking at her now; in fact, he'd looked away the second her gaze hit him. But not quickly enough. Not before she saw the flash of familiar gray eyes that gave away more than the fact they were watching her.

Her stomach flipped and her body froze. The man who'd rescued her was sitting Right. Here. Right. Now.

Impossible. This man in front of her had shaggy, dirty hair. He appeared filthy, from his worn clothing to the grime under his nails, lying casually atop the chair's upholstered arms.

Yet he had the same cut to his chin, the cleft almost as mesmerizing as his unusual eyes. Portia tried to make her legs move, tried to think and get herself to where she needed to be. But the shelter library's usual lure of a peaceful couple of volunteer hours was nothing compared to figuring out how the hell the man who'd rescued her this afternoon had managed to invade her every thought.

She shook her head and blinked. Forced her gaze elsewhere. Moved one foot in front of the other until she was in the safety of her beloved books. And away from the man who'd rattled her.

She set her tea down and noticed her hands were trembling. So not like her. Maybe she'd hit her head and didn't remember it? But the EMTs, and then the ER staff, would have found a lump during their examination of her, wouldn't they have? Unless she'd had no swelling but in fact had a concussion, or maybe even a hematoma. That was it—she had a hematoma and was about to have a brain bleed.

What else could explain the way her body had reacted to a complete stranger earlier today, a stranger who'd saved her freaking life? And how else to explain her reaction just now, to a homeless man who had nothing to do with what she'd been through? Self-recrimination slammed against her conscience. It was one thing to indulge in harmless fantasy at her own expense. But she'd just mistaken a homeless patron of the shelter, someone who came here out of extreme need, someone with a backstory that had to be pretty ugly to bring them to this point in circumstance, for a man she had an inexplicable draw to. A man she didn't even know.

Portia began to sort and stack the piles of books that were laid out on the few tables scattered around the small room. Maybe keeping her focus on what she knew would bring her sanity back. Otherwise she was going to have to return to the ER. And what would she tell them? That an unexpected attraction to a complete stranger, at the most terrifying moment of her life, was messing with her normally organized, methodical thoughts?

Kyle thought once, twice, three times about giving up and walking into the shelter's makeshift library and telling Portia DiNapoli who he was, what he was doing. Or at least offer a more broad-stroke explanation and tell her he was working with SVPD. ROC's presence in Silver Valley wasn't classified, and in fact only the details of his case were. But he stopped himself. Portia had been through enough. She was an innocent civilian in all of this, and any further contact with her invited trouble. He'd never forgive himself if her involvement with him in any way led to harm, or worse. This was an aspect of the case he'd not counted on: finding out that he cared for a woman he barely knew. And it wasn't just a sexual attraction, though that was front and center. There was something potent between him and Portia, something he'd never experienced with anyone else.

She'd recognized him, he was certain. And worse, by the way she'd halted midstep and locked her attention on to him, he suspected she felt it, too. The most surprising and intense awareness that seemed to connect them in a way he sure couldn't explain.

He grabbed another cup of coffee and headed to the middle of the dining room. He may as well use his time as he always did: listening for any indications of another heroin drop, or notice that another large commercial goods shipment was en route. As he pulled out a chair, he saw a dark shape flit across the frosted windows that lined the back wall of the room. Normally they overlooked a well-kept garden and yard, judging from the photos he'd found online. But in the current winter, it looked like a frozen tundra. The other night, he'd marveled at the way the moon reflected across the crystalline snowpack. But tonight the windows were foggy from the large amount of folks and need for increased heating in the shelter. The motion detector lights had lit up, allowing him to see the quick-moving shadow. His gut raised the alarm, clenching as it always had in Afghanistan, telling him that an attack or explosion was imminent. He'd never questioned his body's third eye of sorts—it was something he'd had as a kid, growing up in a less than desirable neighborhood in San Jose until his father bought an almond farm, and had only grown sharper with his Marine and then Trail Hiker training.

His sensitivity to danger was on full alert. He'd bet his powers of observation that the shadow was Ludmila Markova's, or another thug sent by ROC. The only room accessible from the backyard was the library, which was in fact the former screened-in porch. It'd been built up and insulated to become the library, but the door remained.

An entry point for someone with nefarious intent.

He didn't hesitate. He excused himself before he ever sat down, and headed straight for one of the private restrooms. Once locked inside, he used his phone to alert Josh at SVPD and his boss at TH Headquarters. They'd know to call in backup for him, and to keep it on the down-low until he relayed further information.

He left the restroom and went into the shelter's library, closing the door behind him. Portia jerked up from the pile of books she was bent over, her eyes widened from hearing the door click shut. She opened her mouth, and he saw her chest rise, and he concluded in a split second that she wasn't about to offer a friendly greeting.

Portia was about to scream.

Chapter 4

Ludmila was about to make Portia DiNapoli pay for messing with her, the stupid fool. The librarian actually thought she'd run her off this morning, and she'd had to let her go, find her own cover. She'd come too close to the local police spotting her. As it was they'd seen her running away, but luckily for her, the train provided the divide she'd needed and she'd found cover among Silver Valley's many tiny alleyways and courtyard-style homes. When the law enforcement presence lessened, she'd circled back to her vehicle, a small economy car, just like all the others she rented and traded back in on a regular basis. Using different pseudonyms made her very difficult if not flat-out impossible to trace. The people she worked for provided nothing but the best in the way of forged documents and identification.

She'd had to spend the rest of the day in the mo-

bile home she rented in a rundown trailer park outside town. It was pretty much abandoned and when
she'd researched it, she discovered it had been the site
of a cult that tried to take over the town. Silver Valley
didn't impress her, with its openness and the ridicu-
lously friendly people. Finding out they'd been victims of a cult until it'd been taken out at the very last
minute only increased her derision. What good was
this freedom they spoke about if they allowed outsid-
ers like those people into their communities? Not that
she cared. All Ludmila wanted was her own freedom
from anyone ever telling her what to do, how to live,
ever again. She'd escaped the FSB, virtually impossible for being such a well-trained agent. They didn't let
their assets go, not alive. She'd escape ROC, too. All
she needed was a little more time to pull one over on
Ivanov. It was a shame she wouldn't be around to see
the ROC boss's face when he realized she'd duped him.

Of course, her neighbors' welcoming nature worked
in her favor. No one suspected her of being a lethal
ROC operative. Fools.

The librarian hadn't come back to work today until
much later, and then ate at the diner. She lived near
there. Americans ate a lot of fattening food and very
often—something she at once envied and reviled. As a
top FSB agent, she'd needed to be in top form, and now
working what she hoped was her last time for anyone
but herself, her physicality was one of her best tools.

It was too tempting to drop the laptop today, to get it
out of her hands and ready for the next operator. But it
was too risky. No matter—she had until the end of the
week. Her employer was unforgiving but reasonable
about the length of time she was given to complete her

job. And she'd gotten lucky—the shipment arriving in refrigerator trucks from destinations down south, close to the Mexican border, had been halted halfway across the country due to a blizzard. It bought her time. And her life, some might say, but she wasn't going to let anyone take her life from her. She had to keep going for the sake of her murdered family.

Finally she spied DiNapoli as she left the diner. As soon as feasible, she slipped into the night, following her down the sidewalks of Silver Valley. Dressed as an elderly woman, she was prepared to indicate she lived in a nearby apartment and had only come out to get a meal or a hot beverage at the nearby coffee shop. But she didn't expect anyone to bother her. It was still early enough in the evening for an older person to be out.

She watched DiNapoli turn a corner and cut behind a laundry to pick up her trail more efficiently. The do-gooder was heading for the homeless shelter. Of course she was. It had been part of the job to check out DiNapoli, observe her daily routine so that she'd know when to take advantage of it with the laptop placement. The woman spent a lot of time at the shelter, and from what she'd overheard, also at the library, doing things for others who weren't even her relatives. So as an ROC agent, she scoped the shelter out on a night the librarian wasn't there. Posing as a lost homeless woman had been easy. And had allowed her to commit the entire building to memory, room by room. She'd known immediately the room with all the books and magazines was DiNapoli's doing. It was organized just like the town library, but on a smaller scale. The room opened onto the courtyard—perfect for her plan.

Volunteerism was singularly distasteful to her. If there wasn't a payment, why do it?

DiNapoli paused in front of the shelter and unexpectedly looked around the street. She had to duck into an alcove but was certain the librarian hadn't seen her. The early winter darkness was her ally.

As soon as she confirmed DiNapoli was in the big house that the town used as a homeless shelter, she formulated her plan. She'd break into the shelter wherever the librarian worked and kill her there. Or better yet, she might be able to lure Portia outside, like she'd inadvertently done this morning. Portia DiNapoli was a naive, pampered woman, who wouldn't know the workings of an AK-47 if she were forced to watch an online video about it. She'd never outwit a former FSB agent and current ROC mastermind.

She felt no guilt, not a drop of remorse as she removed her pistol from her parka and prepared to take out Silver Valley's beloved librarian with one shot between her eyes. The woman would die as she lived— with her books.

Portia gasped at the intrusion, the sheer boldness of the intruder who barged into the shelter library and shut off the lights. He'd actually locked the door to the small room behind him. But then she recognized him, his gray eyes, the homeless man who reminded her of the sexy stranger who'd held her close only twelve hours ago. She stopped fighting her intuition that something bad was about to happen. She opened her mouth and prepared to give the loudest scream of her li—

The man moved faster than she blinked, and before she registered his intent, he was next to her, his hand over her mouth. Portia's instincts kicked into hyperdrive as she at once shoved her heel onto the man's instep, attempted to bite his hand and elbowed his ribs.

Her defensive tactics didn't yield a single *ouch*. He was a rock. "Portia DiNapoli, I'm a friend and colleague of Detective Josh Avery's. You know it's me, the man who shoved you off the tracks earlier today. You're in danger and I have to get you out of here ASAP. You have to trust me."

His voice, low and urgent against her ear, made something deep inside her still. It was the same voice; she'd know it anywhere. Or else she had completely lost touch with reality, in which case she was about to be killed by a stalker.

She tugged on his forearm. Slowly, he moved his hand away from her mouth. For as dirty as his hands had looked in the dining room, they were smooth and didn't smell. The scent of coffee clung to his skin, and she caught a whiff of the same scent from this morning. It wasn't a cologne or soap. It was *him*. The musk that she'd been unable to let go of.

"Why do you think I'm in danger?" She remained primed, her back still to his front, ready to lurch for the door and scream bloody hell.

"Like I told you this morning, I'm someone you can trust. But I can't explain it all right now. We don't have time."

She turned on her heel, still in the circle of his arms, and looked up at him. Only the shaft of moonlight revealed his shape, his largeness compared to her. But she knew it was him.

"It is you. But if I can trust you, why am I in danger for the second time in one day?"

The sound of the back door being rattled echoed across the room, and they both stilled, only their breaths between them.

"I want you to stay behind me. Do not come out of here until I come get you. And you can't go back into the dining room or you risk involving everyone else here."

"I'm calling 9-1-1." She was tired of people trying to break into her place of work, places that until now she'd always felt secure in.

"Already done." He put both hands on her shoulders as the door shuddered and she felt the cold air wrap around her legs. "Stay here, behind this shelf."

She didn't see a need to fight him. And what was she going to do, take out the intruder with a book?

He was gone and she hunkered down behind the one long shelf that split the room, the bookshelf between her and the door—and whomever was breaking in. Too late she realized her phone was in her purse—and secured in a volunteer locker. She'd never needed it before, never felt unsafe at the homeless mission. Even if there was an unruly overnight guest, the security guard had always been more than enough to handle it. Always.

Until now.

He knew Markova's tactics. Her weapon would be drawn, ready to take Portia out with one shot. She might make it look like a drug deal gone bad by leaving a packet of heroin with the body, a common ploy by organized crime, but he doubted it. Markova came from a long line of FSB agents, going back to the KGB.

Kyle kept his footsteps soft and swift, mimicking a

female's. He slid into the spot under the low window, next to the door. Markova didn't rely on her primitive tactics from this morning at the library, but instead he heard a succession of clicks, the tumblers freeing the catch. The door swung outward and he waited. It'd be so easy to take her out here, have her arrested and arraigned by a federal court on several counts, including overstaying her original visa, identity fraud and murder. Ludmila Markova was implicated in at least six unsolved ROC-related homicides.

But he didn't know how ROC was passing shipment information yet. He had to scare her off, keep her alive and active until Trail Hikers and SVPD brought the entire op down.

Her silhouette flashed up on the open door, at the precise angle of his line of sight. The handheld pistol was pointed up, but he knew she'd lower it and shoot with zero hesitation.

One boot-clad foot stepped into the room, and he struck. He moved swiftly, using the element of surprise for the split second it lasted. Twisting his hands around her ankle, he ignored her muffled cry of pain and yanked, hard, until she hit her ass on the hard concrete porch. He leaped to his feet and kicked the pistol out of her hand before he dropped onto her, pressing his knees to her chest, holding her arms flat. When she bucked to grab his head with her legs, he was ahead of her, leaning too close to her face, where her soulless eyes glittered under the moon. She'd taken out the motion detector light but couldn't stop Mother Nature. As he peered into her gaze, he noted that she, too, wore a wig and, in fact, was bundled in oversize clothing.

But he'd know her moves, her eyes, anywhere. She was his target.

"Get off me, you stinking pig!" Her voice was low and ugly.

He wanted to shout in victory that she thought he was a homeless person. But it'd be short-lived. In the moment she took him at face value, but later, when she flashed back over the events, she'd figure out he was in the same business she was, except he wanted to save the world and keep people safe. Not watch innocent people die for the sake of the profit made off heroin or whatever the hell ROC had her smuggling for them.

"You're not looking so good yourself. Get the hell out of here. Don't come back."

She spit in his face but he'd already lifted off her, stood between her and the pistol that had slid under the eaves. Markova scrambled to her feet, and without a weapon, took off to the nearest exit from the courtyard. The small wooden gate flapped against the house next door as she shoved it open, never slowing her stride.

Kyle pocketed the weapon carefully, knowing a pro like Markova had worn gloves, but still hoping there might be prints on the pistol.

He'd defeated ROC again, in another battle, just as he had this morning on the train tracks, no matter how convoluted the mission had been. But he hadn't won the war, and now Portia was Markova's prime target.

Portia heard no words exchanged, but she did hear thuds and gasps for air. Each thwack made her jump and it was hard, so hard, waiting and not reacting.

Trust.

The sound of a mewling like an injured cat rent the room, quickly followed by the sounds of fast footsteps.

A quietly spoken but fierce string of swear words, then steady footsteps as he returned.

"You can stand up. All's clear." His face was partially illuminated by his phone, into which he tapped a message. Who was he telling about what had just happened?

"That's it? You let the bad guy get away?" She rubbed the tops of her arms, chilled not only by the back door being open so long and letting the precious heat out, but from the prospect that she'd survived another near miss.

Steel-gray eyes found hers. The colors on the phone screen danced across his face, but his eyes were uncompromising in how he watched her. "I scared them away is more like it. And for the record—you're being targeted by some very bad people. I need to get you out of here."

A knock, then a loud "Portia? You in there?" sounded from the dining room. Gary, one of the other volunteers, was concerned.

Portia turned. "Let me unlock the door at least."

"No!" His hand was on her arm, stopping her. "Not an option. We're leaving out this back door, now."

"But I need my coat, my purse—"

"And I need to keep you alive." His words, exacting and scary in their connotation, seemed at odds with his stance, the expression she could make out in the dim phone light. "Damn it." He quickly tapped on his phone, held it to his ear. They were in the dark again.

More pounding. More people were outside the library room door. "Portia, are you okay? Open up!"

Some of the patrons must have alerted the security guard that she'd been followed into the room by this man. And she didn't know his name.

"Josh, it's Kyle. I have Portia DiNapoli with me and I have to extract us both from the homeless shelter, ASAP. Can you talk to her and tell her I'm good?"

She heard a man's voice answer, but it could be any man. When her rescuer held his phone to her ear, she saw the name across the top—Detective Josh Avery, SVPD.

"Hello?"

"Portia, it's Josh. You must do whatever Kyle tells you. It's a life-or-death situation." Josh's voice conveyed what his words didn't. He was worried for her.

She handed the phone back to the man… Kyle.

"Where are we going, Kyle?"

Chapter 5

Kyle took his keys out of his pocket before he threw his coat over Portia's shoulders and checked out her feet. "I know my jacket stinks, but it'll keep you warm. At least you have boots on tonight. Let's go."

She was a silent, quick partner next to him as they exited the house and ran alongside the walls that were shadowed from the moonlight's reach. He noted that Markova's footprints led to where he'd chased her off—the front of the building, away from the back part of the shelter, where the guests slept. Not that the ROC henchman had wanted anyone but Portia.

Portia stayed with him, thank God.

He'd wanted to take out Markova then and there, but couldn't. He had to have her alive to be able to track her movements, to figure out ROC's next move. But his problem was that Markova had come to wipe out her witness from this morning. The woman who trustingly ran with him, up to the wrought-iron gate that swung out onto the street. The snow around the gate was virgin, so no chance that Markova was lurking at this edge of the property. Yet.

He cleared the area, visually scoured it for any interlopers. Just an empty winter street in downtown Silver Valley, but he knew Markova or another ROC thug could be lying in wait anywhere. Fortunately his vehicle was directly in front of them. He'd planted it hours earlier, during daylight, before he'd assumed his homeless cover.

"Come on. This is my truck." He didn't wait but trusted, this time, that she'd follow without hesitation. He hit his key fob and the lights blinked twice quickly in succession. As he rounded the back, quickly checked under the chassis for explosives and then opened the driver's door, he noted that Portia had already slid into the passenger seat.

He didn't speak until they'd driven away and he'd employed countermeasures to ensure they weren't being followed.

"Thank you."

"For what? Blindly following you to my probable death?"

He laughed, the release of pent-up tension but also from her dry humor in such a dour circumstance.

"I promise you, Portia, you're not in danger from me." He pulled to a stop at a red light and turned to her, held out his hand. "Kyle King."

She looked like she might slap him away, but instead grasped his hand with hers. Her grip was not only firm but surprisingly large, for a woman.

"Portia DiNapoli. But you already knew that." She shook once, then withdrew. Not before she saw his expression at her grip. "Don't look so surprised. I threw shot put in college."

"You look like a runner, and you almost caught your thief this morning."

"I ran in high sch—wait. It *was* you. I'm not crazy." Her bemusement unsettled him. A distraught, scared civilian, he could handle. But Portia's steady thoughtfulness threw him off.

Portia fought to calm herself as Kyle sped through the icy streets. She'd always found the silence of a Silver Valley winter night soothing, but no longer. A lot of things were going to affect her differently after facing down the woman with the knife this morning.

Who was this man who called himself Kyle King? Was that really his name? His profile was exactly as she remembered it, against the morning sky, next to the train tracks as he held her. Rugged but with enough sexiness to make her feel the pulse between her legs wake up and remind her that it'd been too long since she'd been with a man.

But he was about more than the unrelenting sexual attraction she felt for him. This man, this Kyle, was on a mission of some sort. She'd seen that expression on the face of her friends that worked at SVPD, including Josh. And she'd seen it reflected back at her when she was hell-bent on making a community event happen, like the gala.

This mission, or whatever Kyle was about, had nothing to do with warm and fuzzy things like a charity event, though.

Before her nerves blew her anxiety into a full-blown panic attack, she forced herself to take action.

"Can I borrow your phone?" Portia was certain she'd heard Josh's voice on the other end of his cell earlier, but she'd been a little stressed. She prided herself on being a details woman. If she wasn't as safe as Kyle wanted her to believe, she wanted to find out.

"Sure." He pressed the home button with his fore-finger, unlocking the cell phone. Portia wasted no time punching in Annie's number. It was one of the few she still knew by heart, thanks to the ease of a smartphone.

"Hello?" Annie sounded cautious, as Kyle King's number clearly wasn't in her phone.

"Annie, it's Portia. I can't explain a whole lot now, but do you happen to know where Josh is right now?"

"He's next to me. Why? Do you need to talk to him?"

"Yes."

The sound of muffled laughter reached her and heat rushed over her face. Annie and Josh were inseparable since they'd decided to make a go of their relationship and got engaged.

"Portia, Josh here. Everything going okay with Kyle?"

Phew.

"Yes. I had to double-check and make sure it was you I spoke to."

To his credit, Josh didn't laugh at her. "I get it. I'd do the same. Where are you two now?"

She surreptitiously looked at Kyle, whose focus remained on the road, with no hint that he was listening. Not that he could help overhearing, though. "We're heading out of town, toward the catering barn." The town proper fell behind them and they traversed the road that cut like a pale blue ribbon through worn farm fields, blanketed in feet of snow that had fallen over the last month.

"If you're with Kyle, you're safe, Portia. He'll fill you in on what he can."

"Got it. Thanks, Josh."

"No problem. Call anytime, as always. Do you want to speak to Annie again?"

"No, that's okay. I'll catch up with her later in the week. Bye." She disconnected and wished it were already Friday and she was having dinner and a drink with Annie. Their standing girls' night hadn't changed, except for the frequency, since Annie had fallen in love with Josh. Portia slid the phone back across the wide console toward Kyle.

"Feel better?" Kyle's voice was too alive. Too full of sexy vibration.

"Yes. No. How would you feel if a complete stranger first saved you from becoming a human Frisbee earlier in the day, then protected you from some unknown intruder the same night?"

"I'd feel pretty damned lucky, Portia." The lines that bracketed his mouth deepened and she sensed he fought a smile.

"Good for you, Kyle. But I'm a librarian, not a... What are you? Do you work for SVPD?"

"Something like that. I'm a private contractor, law enforcement. I get called in for the cases that require a little more finesse and time than the local LEAs can provide."

"So you're here because of ROC."

He maneuvered the truck around a tight turn before he pulled over to the shoulder and put it in Park. Kyle turned to fully face her, and the sense of comfort she'd started to feel shattered in the face of the sheer power he exuded. From his eyes that missed nothing to his hands that had held her, saved her twice today, to his athletic physique, Kyle King embodied competence and awareness.

"What do you know about ROC, Portia?" Kyle spoke the words with deadly precision, keeping his voice low and purposeful. Gone was the man who'd told her she could trust him. In his place, a predator.

"What's not to know? I read that ROC is fighting a huge battle with local LEAs, all up and down the Eastern Seaboard. Since Silver Valley is in the midst of the logistical hub for the East Coast, it was only a matter of time before ROC's crime affected our town." As she spoke, she noticed that he sat back a bit, his shoulders relaxed.

And he let out a low belly laugh.

"What's so freaking funny, Kyle?" She was almost too tired to get angry at his response. Almost.

He shook his head. "You read about it. The article in the *Silver Valley View*, am I right?"

"What's wrong with that?"

"Nothing. I admire how well-informed you are. And for the record, that article is about 95 percent accurate."

"What's the 5 percent that's wrong?"

"Oh, nothing's wrong. Not at all. But they're missing some crucial facts that are classified. Only SVPD and folks like myself are in on the most critical facts."

That made sense. And frankly, she didn't want to know the other facts the paper hadn't had. Although—

"Don't even bother asking me, Portia."

* * *

"I wasn't going to ask you anything." She bit her lip, angry at herself for showing her thoughts so obviously that he'd read her expression. Heat rushed to her cheeks. "I wanted to tell you that I lost a high school friend to a heroin overdose just before the holidays. It hasn't even been three months yet. I hold ROC responsible for making it so easy for her, and the other victims of this awful scourge, to get the drugs. Not to mention how they cut them with lethal ingredients like fentanyl."

"I'm sorry, Portia."

"Keeping my community the safe place I've always known it to be is what matters to me."

"That's what I'm here for, too." He stared at her and she was immediately aware of being alone with him, on the abandoned road, in the dark. If she wanted to run, she'd never make it back to town before getting hypothermia. They were at least five miles out into the countryside.

"Why are we stopped?"

"I'm not going to hurt you, Portia." Low and seductive, his voice circled her mind, set parts of her on fire that she'd neglected since breaking up with Rob. But even after a good bit of foreplay, Rob had never lit her up the way Kyle did.

"Then why have you parked here?"

"I had to make sure we weren't followed." He hesitated and she knew he was holding something back. Maybe one of those confidential facts he'd mentioned?

"What happened to the person who tried to break into the homeless shelter? Why were they doing that?"

He sighed. It wasn't just an expulsion of air into the

interior. It was as if Kyle wrapped years of longing into his breath, his sigh.

"This morning, when I, ah, shoved you off the tracks—the woman whom you were chasing is a suspected ROC thug. That's more information than I should be telling you, but you asked, and you've done your research." A quick flash of white as he grinned. "My concern then, and now, is that she would come back for you. You identified her, saw her face-on behind the library and then on the tracks."

"That's crazy! I saw her, yes, but she had a ski mask on. I could never in good conscience identify her or have a reliable sketch made of her." Portia's heart began to pound, partially from the fear of being stalked by such a dedicated criminal, and by her growing awareness of being alone with Kyle King. The man was vouched for by Josh, so he was safe, trustworthy. And she'd known that at her gut level, anyhow. If he'd wanted to hurt her, he wouldn't have put himself at risk to save her, twice.

Kyle looked through the windshield as if soaking in the view. When his gaze reclaimed hers, she knew he'd been preparing to give her the news no civilian ever wants to hear.

"Portia, you can't go back to your apartment in town. It's not safe. The fact that you were tracked to the homeless shelter tells me that the ROC thug wants you off their radar."

"Off—as in dead, you mean." She swallowed. "This is unexpected."

His expression changed from the professional whatever-he-was law enforcement person to something far more approachable. Too easy to interpret.

Kyle looked like he cared.

"I know this has to be tough on you. But it'll be a lot more than tough if you wind up dead, another victim of ROC and its attempt to use Silver Valley as its playground."

"So ROC picked Silver Valley as its headquarters in this area?" She'd read the articles thoroughly, and while they stated that ROC's various criminal activities were embedded in central Pennsylvania, she couldn't get her mind wrapped around her hometown being overtaken by organized crime.

"*Headquarters* is too strong of a word. As a main hub, yes. And..." She watched his mouth close, his generous lips thin from the pressure of his thoughts. Disappointment flared deep in her belly. Until she saw the moonlight hit his eyes and illuminate his pupils, dilated against his silver irises. Her regret turned to anticipation as quickly as a flame engulfed dried paper.

Kyle wanted her, too.

Chapter 6

Kyle wasn't a rookie when it came to wanting a woman, and he sure as hell knew when he needed to turn and walk away. But that had been before, with other women. Portia was different. Kyle could fight the erection that strained his battered jeans, he could ignore the heat that ignited each time he set eyes on Portia. And who was he kidding? The warmth that Portia stoked in him lasted all day, hours after he'd been around her.

But breathing the same air as her in the confines of the old truck's front seats made being anything but a human being, aware of every single nuance in her expression, impossible.

Kyle leaned in to kiss her, watched her eyes soak him up, her gaze settle on his lips—

A hard tug on the top of his head halted him mid-motion.

"What the—" He reached up to discover his wig had caught on the rim of the cab's sunroof. *"Fuuuuudge."*

Portia's giggle startled him. It was the first time he'd seen her react without reservation or the guard she kept up around him. And while he knew her defensive stance was important to her well-being, and he in fact would be the first to encourage it, he still reveled in the warmth that rushed over him.

"Who would guess that a wig would save me from a huge mistake?" He spoke his thought aloud: an even bigger mistake. The wariness was back in her eyes and she shrank against the passenger door.

"I'm not used to being referred to as a 'mistake.'" Challenge emanated from her deep brown eyes.

"Portia, it's not you—it's me."

She snorted. "I've heard that one before. Look, spare us both and cut to the chase. Where are we going? I'll need to stop at my place to pack. That's what you're getting at, right? That I can't be seen in town for a few days or I'll be killed by some ROC thug."

His breath escaped in a sharp exhale, as if he'd been gut-kicked. It didn't surprise him, though, that the woman in front of him was incredibly perceptive.

"You're awfully astute and adaptable for a civilian."

"Don't you mean 'for a librarian'?"

"No, I didn't mean that at all." He removed the wig, scratched his head. His hair was close-cropped but it still itched after having a synthetic cap with dirty nylon atop it. "You're remarkable. You went after Mar—that woman without a second thought, all to get the laptop back for the library. It wasn't the smartest move from a safety standpoint, but it took guts." And an excellent level of physical fitness that agents worked hard to maintain. "Are you sure you're not in law enforcement, too?"

She fought it for a second before the grin split her face. "Not at all, but do you think I could be?"

He laughed, more from relief that she was conversing with him, letting go of his stupid comment about the almost-kiss being a mistake. "You're certainly strong and fit enough for it. But working in law enforcement has to be a passion. Like your community work."

"How do you know what my passion is?"

She'd caught him.

"I, er, had to run a background check on you when I began surveillance on the library."

She straightened up, leaned in toward the dash, toward him, watched him closely. "And when, exactly, was that?"

"A month ago."

"Son of a…" She trailed off and he swore he heard the synapses firing in her brain. "That's why your eyes looked so familiar. But I didn't recognize you on the tracks. Or rather, off them."

"A good thing. It's my job to stay under the radar."

"Why wasn't I told there was a case going on right under my nose? I didn't have to know all the details, but maybe I could have helped."

"Which is why we don't tell civilians more than absolutely necessary. You said yourself you read exposes on ROC and how we're fighting it in Silver Valley and all of Harrisburg. It's difficult to know who to trust. And there's no reason to bring innocent civilians into a potentially lethal case. That's what we're trying to avoid."

"Who else besides you has been watching the library?"

He shrugged, tried to appear as nonchalant as possible. And knew he was utterly failing in front of her. What was it with Portia? He'd lied and gotten away with his undercover disguises in front of other people close to him over the years. Yet Portia had immediately pegged him in the homeless shelter, and she didn't take any of his standard lines now. Portia was different.

"SVPD has plainclothes officers circulate through, and there may be other…contract employees like me who keep an eye on things." He wasn't about to reveal anything about Trail Hikers, or any specifics.

"Fair enough. I imagine you'll let me know if you're FBI or another agency when you realize you can trust me." She sniffed and he glanced at the dashboard clock.

"We've got to go." He was certain no one had followed them out here, and he was safe to go back to his apartment. "I have a place for you to stay tonight, but then you'll need something more long-term."

"What? I can't miss work."

"You have no choice. You show up at the library or anywhere in town right now, you risk being killed. ROC doesn't screw around, Portia."

"But what about my purse, my clothes? I need my contacts, my prescriptions—"

"I'll take care of that. I can take care of the shelter and get your purse, phone, whatever." He'd send in an undercover cop or ask a favor from another TH colleague. "You mentioned that Annie is your best friend? We can ask Josh to go with her to your apartment and pack a suitcase. You're looking at two to four weeks of hiding out, Portia."

"This is absolutely ridiculous. In this day and age, with all the technology available, can't SVPD put a security camera or two in my apartment, have a patrol keep an eye on my place? You already said the library's being watched."

"We're keeping surveillance on it. And yet you still were almost killed yesterday, because of your judgment that you could catch a thief." He turned to face the steering wheel and shifted the car into gear. "Trust me, Portia, you're going to thank me for this when it's all said and done."

And he vowed she would thank him. That he wouldn't screw it all up by letting his dick call the shots around her.

Portia took in Kyle's small apartment atop Silver Valley's favorite coffee shop, Cup o' Joe's. "I never knew this apartment existed, and I've lived here my entire life." And he'd been living in the building next to hers.

"So you remember when the coffee shop, this building, was a bank?"

"I do." She watched him, wondered how long he'd been here. How had she overlooked him in the library? The air throbbed with the pure masculinity radiating off him and created a potent sexual aura she found difficult to ignore.

In fact, she'd done anything but ignore it since he'd held her in his arms after saving her life this morning.

"Holy crap," she said to herself as she sipped the weak tea he'd made her. He'd boiled the water in a mug in his microwave and she'd used one of her teabags that she'd stuck in her pocket for the shelter.

"What?"

"It's only been twelve hours since we met. Since that train almost—" She couldn't finish around the huge toad in her throat. Tears ran down her cheeks and she swiped at them. "Sorry. I'm not usually so emotional." She sniffed.

The sofa sagged as he sat next to her and she held her mug out to prevent the warm liquid from spilling.

"Here." He took the mug and placed it on the scarred coffee table. The furniture was all rather ratty and indicative of coming with the place. Kyle King was a man on the move. Did he have a real home, anywhere?

"I'm fine."

"Sure you are." Warm arms came around her and she stiffened but Kyle didn't move as his body heat seeped into her and she accepted defeat. Relaxing into the hug, she leaned her head against his shoulder.

"I'm not the weepy type."

"Of course you're not." Hands smoothed her back, her shoulders, pulled her close. As much as the sexual tension between them was a constant companion, this wasn't a come-on. It was pure comfort and solace. Portia closed her eyes and decided to surrender, to give into the soothing attention. For a few minutes.

"Was today a typical day for you? As far as fighting off the bad guys?"

"No. A typical day for me is boring, actually. Lots of waiting, watching. A good amount of time with my laptop, helping, ah, my colleagues put together information."

"It's okay that you don't tell me everything, you know. I get it. My brother's in a similar job."

"Oh?"

"And you know I won't tell you what he does. I

can't." She heard her voice slur, felt the weight of the hardest day of her life since losing her close friend Lani close in on her.

"No." The vibration of his voice rumbled through her and she could have pulled herself from the undertow of exhaustion. "You don't have to tell me anything you don't want to, Portia."

"Why do I feel that relates to more?"

"Hmm?"

She leaned up and looked at him. "Are you telling me that you won't do anything with or to me that I don't want, too?"

The laughter crinkles at the sides of his eyes smoothed and his hold tightened on her, as if he needed her to know his deepest secrets.

"I've never taken what I haven't asked for first, Portia."

"I know that. And for the record? I trusted you before you got me out of the homeless shelter. Probably from the minute you side-tackled me off the tracks."

He kissed her softly on her forehead, and while she longed to turn the chaste kiss into more, she didn't want to lose this special closeness. This was what she'd been trying to put a finger on when she'd wondered if she'd always be single. *Intimacy.* She wanted to savor it as long as she could.

Kyle couldn't recall the last time a woman had fallen asleep in his arms. He'd planned to put Portia in his bed and take the sofa, but she was out cold, and he didn't want to risk waking her. She'd been through a lot. So much that he was shocked she hadn't had a meltdown of some sort. Most civilians would have. Heck, a lot of agents struggled with compounding events. Anyone would. To have a near miss like what happened on the train tracks was big enough, but then to find out you were being personally targeted by a lethal organized crime group?

He gently laid her down on the sofa, noting how small she looked asleep. As if her personality, at rest, made up for half her size. The soft, worn blanket he used as an afghan on the rare nights when he streamed a show covered her perfectly. But the scratchy throw pillow wouldn't do. He took it and left it on his bed as he brought his pillow back out and tucked it carefully under her head.

Her hair was silky and springy under his fingers and he fought to not run both hands through it. That would be downright creepy, as Portia was sound asleep. He settled for taking a last look at her, noting the way her long lashes contrasted sharply against her high cheekbones, and how full and rosy her lips were.

As he crouched next to her, he smelled not the scent of her floral perfume but something earthier.

Crap. He needed a shower, as he was still in his homeless garb, sans the wig. He stood up and walked back to the bathroom. Had he really been about to kiss Portia while decked out in the filthiest clothing and wig possible?

Humility was a good thing. He switched on the water in the small stall and considered himself lucky to be humbled by the likes of Portia DiNapoli. It reminded him that even he, after years of undercover work and ops against organized crime, wasn't immune to being blindsided by his hormones.

Except, his connection with Portia felt deeper than any potent chemistry he'd ever shared with a woman before. Which made it deadly. Distractions were anathema to any law enforcement agent, especially when working such an explosive case. Neither he nor Portia could afford the chance that their attraction could cost him the case, or worse, her life.

He stripped out of the smelly clothes and shoved them into one of the extra plastic bags he kept under the sink for the wastebasket. He'd toss them. His cover was blown tonight when he'd fought off and scared away Markova. Even if the ROC operative didn't recognize him, she was very good at what she did. Which meant her intuition would alert her, let her know if she encountered him at the mission again.

Damn it. He still had to remain focused on Markova, but it was no longer solely to dismantle the ROC shipment and heroin schedule. It had turned into a way to save Portia's life.

Which meant he'd be seeing more of Portia, something he couldn't afford. He'd call Josh first thing tomorrow morning. SVPD, or someone else at Trail Hikers, needed to take over Portia's safety, because in addition to the case being lethal to her, Portia was also lethal to Kyle's carefully built life. A life that allowed him to move freely from mission to mission, with no emotional ties binding him or his agent work.

And he had California to look forward to. He was only in Silver Valley for the next two or three weeks, enough time to take this ROC op down. There wasn't a future here, on his own or with Portia. He'd best remember that.

The alley was long, dark, with only a huge wall at the end. Portia was trapped, the woman with the evil eyes no more than ten yards behind her. She willed herself to jump, reach for the top of the wall. In an instant she was in the air, flying, until her feet landed on the solid top of the roof.

The sound of metal scraping against the brick wall caught her attention and she hesitated, looked down. Icy blue eyes met her gaze as the woman climbed the wall with the aid of the long-bladed knife. The weapon that could have killed Portia behind the library, and then on the train tracks. The laptop thief smiled and her teeth looked like a rabid animal's. Too late, Portia recognized her mistake. She didn't trust her instinct to keep running, and now the killer was inches away, Portia's fear keeping her from flying off the wall. If she'd listened to Kyle and stayed put, she'd be okay. And now she didn't know where he was.

With a start Portia jerked awake when a shout rang out. She sat up, struggling against the bedclothes. She panicked when faced with the pitch dark, not knowing where she was. In that same instant, she recalled it wasn't her apartment but Kyle's.

"Portia." Strong hands on her shoulders, then smoothing the hair from her sweaty brow. "You're safe. You're with me, Kyle. You've had a nightmare."

Mutely, she nodded. Had that scream been in her mind or had it been her? She swallowed, the rough soreness of it validating that yes, she'd yelled in her sleep.

"Sorry." Her voice was wispy and didn't begin to convey the depth of emotions she'd just plumbed.

He knelt in front of her, but kept a good distance. She got it. As much as she didn't know him, she was a stranger to Kyle, too. She couldn't keep a smile from splitting through her angst.

"That's more like it." Kyle's voice reflected relief, encouragement. And soothed her.

"It's funny that we've gone through so much together in less than twenty-four hours, and yet we don't know one another. But I feel like I've known you my entire life. Is this normal for your kind of work?"

Kyle's breath sucked in, and she waited to hear his exhale. He didn't speak for a good while as she leaned against the sofa back, crossing her legs under her.

"Taking down a criminal ring like ROC is the definition of intense. So yes, it's not uncommon for very strong feelings to surface. It's its own kind of intimacy, I guess you could say." Kyle leaned away from her, shook his head. "But what you and I are feeling isn't usual. It's different."

She peeked at him from under her lashes. "And you're not very happy about that."

"It's not my prerogative to have any feelings about it. I have a job to do, and now we've got the added complication of your life being on the line. It's not like we're at an island resort, where we could have some fun with this, this smoke between us."

"Smoke? Do you mean chemistry?"

"No. I mean smokin' hot heat, babe." The honesty of his bare assessment made all of her most intimate parts tingle, but she saw his quick grin.

"You're joking."

He stood up and stretched. "Actually, no, I'm not. It's nothing to take lightly, but we can't explore whatever kind of connection we're feeling. Feelings are distractions, Portia. In my line of work, they get people killed."

In her life, feelings got her heart crushed. Not anything she wanted to do again, for sure.

"Can't you call Josh and have him guard me, or send over another cop to do the same, while you're chasing down the bad woman?"

"Is that what you dreamed about?" He'd gone still, standing at the end of the coffee table.

She nodded. "Yeah. It was a classic anxiety dream, and more intense than I usually have because of yesterday. I get anxiety dreams all the time. Usually I have to take an exam for a class I didn't attend all year."

"Did you ever skip a class in your entire life?" That flash of white again. His grin could make any woman want to rip her clothes off and encourage him to do the same.

"As a matter of fact, I did."

"I don't believe you."

She shrugged. "You don't have to. I know it's true. Last semester, senior year of college." It'd been her elective class, ballet, that she'd purposefully missed in order to take advantage of a local politician's meet-and-greet. "That's when I started to realize I wanted to be active in my community. Not necessarily in politics, but something that would make a difference."

His grin twisted ruefully. "The last semester of school doesn't count, not really."

"And I suppose you skipped class all the time?"

"Never. My scholarship was at stake, and the cost of the class exorbitant. I would never have risked it."

"So you're the pot calling the kettle—"

"No, I'm the kettle who recognized another kettle."

"Point taken." She tugged the covers back up around

her, not wanting him to think she expected more conversation. "I'm fine, Kyle. You can go back to bed."

"I'm just down the hall if you need me. You can still take my bed and I'll sleep here."

"That's all right, but thank you anyway."

"You're welcome. See you in the a.m." He'd already begun to return to his room. Once she was left alone again, sleep didn't waste time returning. This time it was dreamless.

Chapter 7

Kyle called Josh the next morning, only speaking freely because he was using his TH secure cell phone.

"It's not SVPD's job to provide personal security, Kyle. You know that." Josh sounded annoyed and Kyle knew he'd probably woken up his buddy. The sun had barely breached the horizon when he'd called. Portia was still fast asleep on the ancient sofa. She was going to have a crick in her neck, for certain.

"She needs guarding until Markova is out of the picture."

"Don't you mean until ROC is out of Silver Valley?" Josh took a wider perspective in his Trail Hiker responsibilities, not focused in on one target like Kyle had to be.

"No. I'd bet Markova hasn't told her superiors any-thing about the train track incident, or about the laptops, or her attempted break-in and murder last night. I have no doubt she would have killed Portia on the spot if she had a chance to." He relayed how he'd kept the weapon, and why he believed Portia was in mortal danger. "Markova's doing this on her own, and doesn't want anyone to think she's incompetent."

"Then if we're only worried about one potential murderer, Portia can stay safe with basic countermeasures."

"You mean on her own?" Kyle's insides became as twisted as the web of ROC crime that riddled central Pennsylvania. He knew what the protocol was for protecting innocent civilians. There wasn't much, actually, because the local LEAs were stretched too thin to provide personal security. And TH agents were operatives, not bodyguards. But Portia…

"You're doing it on the phone, man." Josh's voice in his ear yanked him out of the dank mental rabbit hole. "Portia's a big girl. If you want, I have an idea on where she can stay for the next week or two while we ramp up our efforts against ROC."

"Where's that?"

"I have a family friend who invested in a beautiful piece of property that's alongside the Appalachian Trail. Scenic views, privacy, an unexpected place for a town librarian. Anyway, they need someone to housesit while they're on an extended vacation down south. You know, away from this dang winter."

It had been brutally cold, but Kyle hadn't noticed it for the past few days. Not since his case had become so wrapped around Portia DiNapoli. He was in a world of trouble and he knew it. His attraction to her refused to listen to his best mental reasoning.

"The place is available right now?"

"Yes." Josh gave him the address. "Before you go there, bring Portia here so that we can tell her a little more about what she's up against. She can make her own decision about where to stay until we catch Markova and take down the crime ring."

"She'll think she can remain in her apartment." And he hated that she did.

"Not once we fill her in on more than what she read in the paper. The train tracks would be enough to scare away most people, but Portia's always had steel in her spine."

Kyle chuckled. "So I'm not the only one who's noticed it?"

"Hell no. When you meet Annie, ask her. She's known Portia just as long as I have. She'll fill you in."

Only after they'd agreed to talk in a bit and disconnected did Kyle realize he hadn't corrected Josh on his assumption that he'd be doing anything social in Silver Valley. He and Josh had struck up an easy friendship that wasn't just business, as they'd told one another a bit here and there about their personal lives. As a rule, Kyle kept to work and sleep for the entirety of a mission, only allowing himself a social outlet like grabbing a beer once his job was done and he'd left a place. That was fine when his residence had been in New York City and he'd taken shorter Trail Hiker assignments all over the globe as they came up. Trail Hikers paid lucratively and allowed him to enjoy New York when he wasn't on a mission, and kept a nice loft on the Lower East Side. But he'd been in Silver Valley for over a month, with no end in sight to the current op. And now he'd met Portia.

Was she the reason that he felt more at home in Silver Valley than any other place in over a decade? The last few days he'd tried to convince himself that Pennsylvania wasn't for him, but something had changed. The town made sense to him, and he was invested in getting ROC the hell out of it. Not in his usual way—he was an agent and of course wanted to protect innocent civilians wherever the job took him. But he'd inexplicably become more invested in Silver Valley.

You're still going back to California.

He was. His purchase of the small lot adjacent an almond orchard had been his way of promising himself there was more to life than his undercover work, in case he ever tired of it. As the years went by, he also came to the realization that agents couldn't keep up the pace of operations he had much past the age of thirty-five to forty. Sure, there were Trail Hiker and FBI agents twenty, twenty-five years his senior. But they mostly conceded the heavy physical demands of specific ops to the more junior agents. It was life.

And he loved it out west, he really did. Who would willingly accept these freakishly cold winters, the sticky humidity of the summer? Last summer he'd sworn to himself he'd not spend another hot August on the East Coast. Give him the dry air, sunny clime and endless beach of California any day.

Kyle walked out to his kitchen to brew a pot of coffee, but the scent of roasted beans hit him before he left his room. Portia stood in the kitchen, her hands wrapped around one of his mugs, a catlike grin on her face. Her hair tumbled around her scrubbed skin, still damp.

"You took a shower." He hadn't heard or noticed that while talking to Josh. Not very agent-like on his part.

"Good morning to you, too. Yes, I showered. And I'm afraid I used your extra towel—you only have what's in that tiny linen closet, I assume?"

"Yeah." He helped himself to coffee, ignored how she moved far out of his reach. He opened the refrigerator to find the creamer gone. He noticed she'd borrowed his robe, too. And fought the urge to tug at the belt around her waist, open the garment and gain access to her luscious breasts.

"Here you go." Portia held the plastic container out to him. "I wouldn't have pegged you for a chocolate-mint creamer dude."

He couldn't keep the grin off his face. "It was 75 percent off at the grocery. Left over from Christmas."

"You don't have to justify your sweet tooth to me, Agent King. Is that the right title for you?"

"Not at all. It's Kyle. Always." He faced her, allowed his first sip of coffee to be mixed with the delicious sight of Portia in his kitchen. Warmth pulsed through his chest, down his belly and right to his dick. He wanted to brush it away, tell himself that it was just a beautiful woman's effect on him. That it was merely the creamy skin of her cleavage, visible above the V of the robe, the tops of her breasts rounded and highly kissable. As were her mouth, her long throat. But it was *Portia's* energy that wrapped around him, made it feel as if she belonged in his kitchen. With him.

"Okay." She eyed him and he had the startling awareness that he was being studied in a way he knew too well. The same way he watched a criminal target.

He knew Portia wasn't a killer, but why was she looking at him as if she were going to take him out?

Portia had awakened to an ache in her neck from the rickety old sofa, but couldn't deny she'd had the most solid nine hours of sleep since she didn't know when. The blanket she'd tossed back was a clear sign that Kyle had made her comfortable before he left her alone to rest.

As she stared at him, her body so attuned to the sheer strength available in every inch of his frame, she acknowledged that her attraction to this man wasn't going away anytime soon. And that it might be more than a physical connection. Kyle was the first man she'd wanted to know all about, from what kind of kid he'd been to how many women he'd loved, in forever. But he saw her as a job, someone he had to protect.

"How long are you going to have to babysit me?"

His brows shot up. "Ah, that's an interesting question. I just got off the phone with Josh and we're coming up with a solution. You'll have a place to stay for the duration."

"Duration?" *Please don't let it affect the gala.*

"Two, three weeks. Maybe a month, but heaven help us all if it takes that long to drive these losers out of Silver Valley."

"The gala's in two weeks. I can't stop working on it, or miss it. It's taken a year to plan." She'd booked the new venue for this year's bigger, more lucrative fundraiser the week before last year's event.

"You can keep working on it from a distance. How much in-person time does a dance take?"

"It's not a 'dance.' It's the largest charity event in the

Susquehanna region, held right here in Silver Valley. We're expecting almost a thousand guests."

"Great. Among those hundreds of guests, there has to be at least a few people who could take over for you, help you out?"

"No. Not this late." She ran through the list of items yet to finish. It was always tight, this close. Organizing the silent auction items took her an entire weekend last year; this year's contributions were twice as valuable and numbered a third more. "There's a lot of coordination that happens last minute, too. I have to be on-site."

Kyle put his coffee mug down and she mentally smacked her forehead for even noticing the hair on his forearm, the size of his capable hands. Hands that had saved her yesterday, and that she wanted to find out more about. Like for instance, how they'd feel on her breasts, or pressing her buttocks as he brought her pelvis up against his.

She was in deep water with this man, and she'd only known his name since last night.

"Don't worry, Portia, you'll figure it all out. And if we're lucky, it won't be an issue—the case will be finished before you have to be more visible again." The conciliatory softness that played over his hard features made the tight ball of sexual awareness in her belly loosen and spread through her, across her breasts and down to the place between her legs that began to throb for him. Her rational mind didn't even bother trying to fight her want, her need.

When Portia became this mesmerized by a man, she rarely let it go. Not until she explored her desire, found out if it was passing or more substantial. And she'd never felt this strongly this quickly about any other man. Ever.

Mistaking her quiet stare for disagreement, he stepped toward her. "Seriously. It's not anything you can control, the hiding-out part. It's to keep you safe, and the resources we'd need to let you keep up your regular routine can go toward catching the bad guys. It'll work out, Portia."

"I know that. I'm fighting it, but you have to understand I only want what's best for Silver Valley." And she did. If half of what she'd read was true, then Kyle and Josh knew so much more.

The combination of feeling overwhelmed at having to do something she'd never done before, hiding out, and feeling that she somehow had a part in it because she'd stupidly chased the laptop thief instead of leaving it all to the police, wore her out. And made her push past her inhibitions. So what if she barely knew Kyle? They could both die at the hands of ROC, and would she want to die wondering what it would be like to be in this man's arms? To have him in hers?

"Portia..." Kyle spoke her name in a warning tone. His eyes shone bright silver even though the kitchen had light from only the stovetop light and the initial spill of dawn light that crept across the vintage linoleum.

"Don't you ever get tired of being the mysterious man behind the scenes of a case, Kyle?"

"There's nothing mysterious about my work." His breath hitched and she placed her hands on his chest, only his thin, long-sleeved T-shirt between her fingers and his steel-cut chest. His hands came up and wrapped around her wrists, but his touch was gentle, and he didn't try to stop her.

Portia stood on her tiptoes and moved until her face was a whisper from his, noses almost touching, mouths sinfully close. "Let me know you, Kyle. Remove a layer of your mystery for me."

Her excitement ratcheted and she gave him one heartbeat, two, certain he'd snap his agent face back in place and tell her to stop. Tell her that this was a bad idea, a "mistake."

When he didn't, Portia closed the tiny gap between them.

His lips were warm, supple, firm, and Kyle only held back for a nanosecond before he let go of her wrists and buried his hands in her hair, held her face at the perfect angle to allow them to deepen the kiss. She teased the outside of his lips with hers, loving how he let her take the lead while fully responding to every lick and nibble. When his tongue came out to greet hers, she caved and fully opened her mouth, needing him to explore her, too.

Kyle didn't disappoint as he kissed her, tasted her, plunged into every nook of her mouth. It was more than she could have fantasized, the pure, sexual power of their embrace. Portia's hands gripped his T-shirt, but when that wasn't enough, she reached up and clung to his neck, pulling his head down closer.

The kiss lasted minutes but Portia wasn't fooled. This kiss, this intimacy with the man she barely knew, had life-changing abilities. No one had ever kissed her so thoroughly, had turned her on so quickly and intensely that she wouldn't have fought it if Kyle suggested they take it back to his bedroom. Or on the counter.

He lifted his head and she couldn't stop the protest that her voice emitted, a high-pitched cry that left nothing to his imagination, she was certain.

"Portia." His ragged breathing only served to stoke her desire, make her hotter than she'd thought possible. But she remembered his words from inside the truck last night and pulled back, put her hands on his chest again and gently pushed him away.

"Do you still think I'm a mistake, Kyle?"

"You're not a mistake, Portia." He held her, reluctant to let her go, to end this but the only way it would go was problematic for both of them. Her eyes were half lidded, their brown depths willing him back into the warmth of what pulsed between them. Besides his erection. He placed his hands on her shoulders and took a half step back, needing the space to think. "It's what we'll have to face after we take this to the most obvious, and yeah, hot as hell conclusion."

"You're leaving Silver Valley after the ROC mission is over." Her small white teeth peeked out as she gnawed on her lower lip, still swollen from their kissing. "We're both adults, we know where we stand."

"Babe, I want to agree with you. You know I do." He grasped her hand and placed it on his erection, needing her to know he wasn't coming from a place of intellect. He cared about Portia. Too much for someone he'd only just kissed.

"Kyle!" Her breath caught in a sexy growl and she closed her hand around him through his jeans but he pulled away then.

"We've got something that doesn't come along every day, Portia, but we won't have anything if you get killed because of being involved with me. Or if I get taken out, how would you feel? Isn't it better to stop it before we get in too deep?"

She smiled softly and shook her head. "It's funny—just two days ago I would be the one saying this to you. But after coming so close to dying, after seeing what kind of work you do, even just this little glimpse of it, I think I've changed my mind."

"How so?"

"I think that life is short, and sometimes it's the best thing ever to just go for it. To not overthink things so much, to enjoy life one day at a time. Not worry about the future."

Her words were balm to him, and he didn't disagree. But it didn't change the fact that he had to keep her safe and take out Markova. No short order.

"Tell you what, Portia. Let's table this discussion for now. I've got to get you to the safe house and I have a lot of intel data to analyze."

She watched him and his respect deepened for her as she stood her ground, didn't try to convince him to go to bed with her now. As if she, too, knew that sometimes the deepest needs had to wait.

"Then let's get the day going. I want to be a help to this case, not your worry."

He turned to place his laptop and phone in his bag, and heard her feet walk back to the bathroom where he assumed she was getting dressed. This was another first for him. Making the adult decision he loathed, turning away from what he knew would be an explosive union with Portia.

Comfort washed over him and at first he didn't recognize the emotion. Until he heard Portia humming as she dressed behind the closed bathroom door.

Hope. He had hope that somehow, someway, things might take a very good turn with Portia.

Chapter 8

Kyle and Portia didn't waste any more time alone in his apartment. As soon as she was dressed and had her few items in a bag, they left. It wasn't just his desire to be alone with Portia that gave him a sense of urgency, either. He never forgot that Portia had a huge target on her back. As sure as he was they hadn't been followed, and despite the high level of technological security he'd wired the place with, Markova wouldn't give up until she found Portia and divested herself of her witness.

"I don't see what going into SVPD is going to accomplish." Portia argued with him, but she didn't fight getting back into the truck, once he cleared the parking area and surroundings.

"We'll talk to Josh and see where you can stay for the time being."

"Why Josh?"

Kyle gritted his teeth. "He's my point of contact for this case. And without getting into it, you absolutely cannot talk to anyone else about this, Portia." He trusted Josh to reiterate the warning. And yet he also hated that he had to talk in work terms with her at all. This was hard—doing his job with a woman he was more attracted to than anyone else.

"I understand the need for confidentiality. But that doesn't extend to me. I'm the one someone wants to kill!"

He looked over at her after he parked at the police station. While she appeared calm and all together, he knew this was incredibly difficult for her. It would be for anyone, even a tough-as-nails woman like Portia. Her cries during the nightmare had wrenched him awake.

"That's why we're here. You're safe, and I'm going to keep it that way." He waited for her beautiful brown eyes to meet his, to see his sincerity. She managed a smile.

"I know. And I'm sorry, Kyle. I'm being a brat because, well, because I'm sexually frustrated." She let out a self-deprecating laugh. "And that's not something I'd normally admit to anyone!"

He reached over and squeezed her thigh, a friendly reassurance to hopefully break the tension between them. He didn't expect her to cover his hand with hers. The warmth of the skin-on-skin contact stilled him as heat rushed straight to his groin.

When was he going to learn to be extra careful around Portia? The woman wasn't just another civilian witness to protect, nor a casual friend. They had a deeper connection that he couldn't screw around with.

"Kyle." She swallowed, licked her lips. Both signs of nervousness, yet all he paid attention to was how ruby-red her lips were and the fullness of the lower lip. The memory of their kiss seared right through to his dick and he had to make an effort not to groan. In the police station parking lot, no less. Where was his professional bearing?

Right where he'd left it the minute he'd noticed Portia as more than the Silver Valley librarian.

"Kyle." She pressed her other hand under his, gave him an answering squeeze. "Thank you. And if you're anything like me, you're wondering why you're not being totally all about business around me. I'm wondering it, too. I don't usually kiss a guy I hardly know, and I'm not used to such a strong attraction dropping in on me out of the blue." She lifted his hand to her mouth and kissed it. "You're a good man, and I trust your law enforcement instincts. As much as it kills me to say it, if you think I need to disappear from town for a bit, then I do. As long as I can keep working on the gala from a distance. I'll be able to use the internet, I hope."

He stared at her, momentarily stunned into silence. He was darn sure Portia had never been through a clandestine op, had probably never had the occasion to fire a weapon, unless she hunted like many folks in this part of the country did. She was an innocent to the different circles of hell his line of work provided him with on a daily basis. And yet, she'd been the one to step up and call whatever was going on between them what it was. No denial, no hiding it like so many others would.

It made him all the more committed to her. To protecting her, from Markova, yes, but also from himself.

"Portia, you have more balls than a lot of the agents

I work with, and let me tell you, there's no one stronger than an undercover agent most days."

She grinned. "I'm a bit of a control freak, I'll admit. I love the organizational side of library science, and it spills over into my personal life. I've had some…some betrayals and unexpected difficulties with men in the past. I find it preferable to be open right from the get-go, don't you?"

"Whatever you say." He leaned over and kissed her firmly on the lips, a seal of his intent to keep her safe. "Let's get inside."

"I don't need counseling," Portia grumbled at her best friend, who happened to be a police psychologist. Annie Fiero worked for SVPD and also did contract work for other law enforcement agencies.

Annie was at the station when she and Kyle had arrived.

They sat in the nicer waiting area of the police station, reserved for interviewing victims. "And I wasn't a victim." She refused to wear that mantle. Sure, she'd been shoved by the laptop thief, but she'd been on the railroad tracks due to her own decisions. And the almost-attack last night at the homeless shelter was something she didn't want to think about.

"I haven't said a thing." Annie handed her a paper cup from the specialty coffee shop downtown, and Portia bit back the instinct to tell her she'd spent the last night sleeping over it. "I got you a London Fog. The stuff they have here in the station is swill."

"So you knew I was coming back in."

"Of course. I happen to be engaged to one of the men in charge of this portion of the case."

Portia gratefully accepted the drink, her favorite. As Annie knew. "Thanks." She sipped, the warm smoothness of the vanilla flavor mixing with the bergamot and immediately calming her. "This is my go-to comfort drink."

"I know. And before I forget, I brought in a few changes of clothes for you, along with your laptop. It's all in Josh's office."

"Thanks."

"Anytime." Annie smiled, eased back into the easy chair across from the one Portia perched on. "Josh says you came close to getting hit by the train yesterday, and then at the shelter last night you could have been killed. I'm so glad Kyle was there."

"How do you know him?" Was she the last person to meet the sexiest man she'd ever seen walk the streets of Silver Valley? And the most mysterious, at least to her.

Annie's expression faltered, became guarded. "He's a work colleague of Josh's."

"You can quit with the 'it's police business' attitude. It's okay if you can't tell me." She put her cup down so that she could slide back in the chair, just as Annie had. As soon as she did, she realized how tired she felt. It had been a long morning. The time with Kyle this morning had been glorious, if not totally what she wanted. She wanted to have Kyle in every way possible, but not at the expense of his job or this case. When they came together, if they did, she wanted it to be without the weight of worry she saw in his eyes whenever he mentioned the risks to her.

"I'm not pulling the 'it's classified' routine. But some cases are tougher than others, and this one is the mother of all cases Josh has ever worked on, from what I can tell."

"I'm glad you're working at SVPD now. It means a lot to have you here this morning. It's been a rough day or so. How's the yarn shop?" Annie had taken over her grandmother's small business when the woman had suffered a stroke this past summer. Ezzie had returned and ran her shop again but Annie helped her grand-mother in between fulfilling contracts for SVPD as a police psychologist. She'd worked for NYPD for sev-eral years before coming back to Silver Valley when Ezzie had her stroke. While working the yarn shop's register, Annie had encountered a woman she'd sus-pected had been a victim of domestic violence, so she reported it to Detective Josh Avery, now her fiancé.

"Grandma Ezzie is doing fine with the new shop-keepers I hired for her. I'm actually here full-time now, with the recent uptick in investigations."

"The ROC stuff, you mean."

"How much do you know about ROC? We've only talked about it in terms of when Lani OD'd, with the heroin distribution network."

"I read the paper. Everyone knows about it unless they're living with blinders." She couldn't stop the shudder that rolled over her. "What the heck is hap-pening, Annie? Where is the Silver Valley you, Josh and I grew up in?"

"It's still here." Annie leaned forward. "And look, so are we. We're stronger than any group of criminals."

"I don't know. Tell that to Lani's family."

A cloud passed over Annie's expression, the same darkness Portia fought hard to avoid whenever she thought of Lani. They'd lost a few other high school classmates already, to car accidents or premature disease. But to lose one to a heroin epidemic hit her harder. Mostly because she felt it could have been prevented.

"It's tough, as we still don't have answers as to where the fentanyl came from." Annie looked at her. "I don't want to talk about that right now, Portia. I want to know how you're doing, really."

Portia took in a deep breath, held it, forcefully exhaled. "I'm okay. It's probably not totally hit me yet, but I'll get through this."

"You will." Annie looked thoughtful, though, and Portia couldn't help wonder what she knew that she wasn't sharing.

"What's going on, Annie?"

"Nothing more than the usual, since ROC came to town. I want you to know that SVPD will do everything to keep you safe. I'll do whatever it takes to protect you."

"That's quite all right. I've seemed to have made a friend out of someone I've never met before."

"Kyle."

"Yes."

She'd known Annie since they were in second grade, and she knew her friend's moods. Something was on Annie's mind, but she wasn't going to give it up.

And as emotionally spent as she felt, Portia gained tremendous strength from being with her dear friend. And Kyle—Kyle's presence had kept her sane through life threatening circumstances.

"You don't have to say anything, Portia. I see it on your face."

"What's that?"

"You've got a crush on your protector."

"You know me well, but not as much as you think. Yes, there's something there, but it's not a crush, Annie. This is big. I've just been through so much that I don't want to mistake extreme gratitude for…for…" She didn't know what to name it.

"You don't have to do anything but focus on today, Portia. My only suggestion is that you don't let the fact you've known him such a short time prevent you from exploring your feelings. I knew Josh for forever, but when the time was right, our relationship took off and well, you know what happened."

"I do." Annie and Josh were as deeply dedicated to one another as long-married couples, and they'd only been together for the last half year or so.

Could Portia even wish for what her friend had, with a man she'd only just met?

Portia's head swam from all that had transpired but was surprised to find she felt comfortable in Josh's office at SVPD for the second time in twenty-four hours. She couldn't ignore that it no doubt had a lot to do with having Kyle at her side.

"Hello again, Portia." Josh handed her the large laptop bag and purse. "Annie got these for you. She went to your apartment and added more clothes, stuff from your bathroom. I'm sorry you're dealing with more than just a random library-computer theft. Kyle's informed you that it's best that you don't go back to your apartment or the library for a week or two?" Josh looked from her to Kyle as if trying to figure out the extent of what they'd talked about.

"I told her that you and I were coming up with a plan." Kyle looked up from his phone; he'd been texting someone. Portia realized she'd never wondered if he was single, available. She'd let her desire carry her away, because she'd wanted to believe kissing Kyle was a good option. Hadn't she learned from Robert that powerful men rarely had anything less than a bevy of women on their heels? Yet Kyle hadn't struck her as being involved with someone else. He was too focused on her whenever their eyes met. As if she were the only woman he'd ever seen. A delicious feeling, actually.

"Did Kyle mention the house?"

"What house?" She shook herself out of her Kyle daze. "Is it in Silver Valley?"

"On the outskirts. It's a friend of my family's place. They're wintering in Florida, and they've left the keys with me. Annie and I have used it as a getaway from time to time, and I check it out regularly to make sure it's secure. It's up behind its own gated fence, right past the walk-on for the Appalachian Trail."

Portia knew the area and had a friend or two who'd bought land there once they married and decided to start a family. "Sounds beautiful. And very boring."

Kyle's laugh made her jump. "You work in a library. Don't you appreciate a more serene space?"

"Don't mistake quiet for uneventful. The library is anything but peaceful. Recent events notwithstanding, our daily foot traffic is enough to rival any local retail shop. Inquiries about the town and local area are constant, and it's a rare day that I can close up on time." She shifted in the utilitarian SVPD chair. "I could easily rent a house, or own one, for the price I pay for my apartment in town. Silver Valley's not huge like New York City, of course. But I can walk to wherever I need to go, whenever. The part of town Josh is talking about requires a car and I have to plan for an hour round-trip for any errands. It's a full twenty-five minutes just to the grocery store from there."

"Which makes it the perfect place to keep you out of trouble." Kyle looked up from his phone and she allowed the shock of his silver eyes to shoot through her, swirl around in her belly and branch out to every inch of her. "Safety is the priority, Portia."

Josh cleared his throat. "It won't be for long, Portia. Kyle's an expert at what he does and he'll have this case wrapped up in no time."

Kyle remained silent, but she sensed communication between them.

"At the risk of being told I can't know, what exactly is Kyle's job?" She looked at Kyle the entire time.

"Glad you asked. We're going to head over to the conference room about now, and fill you in on some basics. You have a right to know who is protecting you, and for the sake of our operation against ROC, you'll benefit from some background."

Kyle looked up from his texting to respond. "She'll be here in two."

Josh nodded and stood up, indicating that Portia and Kyle should do the same. "Great. Shall we?"

Portia followed the two men out of the small office, down the corridor and into the conference room. She saw a tall, salt-and-pepper-haired man waiting for them at the head of the table. He was in civilian clothes, but with a weapon holstered at his waist.

"Chief," Josh called, and then turned back to usher Portia into the room. "This is Portia DiNapoli, our town librarian."

"Good morning, Portia. Colt Todd." He held his hand out and she shook it.

"Good morning, Chief. We've met several times, at the annual fund-raising gala."

He nodded. "Yes, we have."

Portia waited for him to say more, but he looked past her, toward the door, and his interest was riveted.

"Hello, everybody. Kyle, Josh, Colt." A woman with silver hair in a chic bob strode into the room with a combination of strength and grace that Portia immediately liked. And she was vaguely familiar. Hadn't Portia seen her with SVPD Chief Colt Todd at last year's gala? There'd been hundreds of attendees, so her memory could be faulty. Her laser-focused blue gaze landed on Portia.

"You must be Portia." Everything about this woman screamed total expert, in whatever she did. Confidence and comfort in her own skin radiated from her. "I'm Claudia Michele."

They shook hands, and everyone took seats at the glossy wood table. Portia had been to enough library conferences, book conventions and other business events to know when it was her place to listen and learn.

"We've asked Claudia to come into the station to help explain a different part of the case that you won't read about in the paper," Kyle said quietly. "Claudia's my boss, by the way."

Claudia nodded. "I run a special type of classified law enforcement agency that employs people from all over the world to take on the most difficult cases. We don't take the place of local or even federal law enforcement, but we get in and help where it's challenging, or even impossible, for local LEAs to operate."

"Like CIA and FBI?" Portia didn't want to appear too green in this world she knew nothing about.

Claudia shook her head. "No, not at all. We're more under the radar than either of those agencies, believe it or not." She motioned with her head at Kyle. "Take Kyle. He and I share that we're Marine Corps veterans, and we used what we learned in the military to become fully employed as undercover agents. I don't personally work many cases, as my job is to keep the entire team at my agency running, but I've worked alongside a good number of our agents."

"I'm here to help with ROC's heroin operation in Silver Valley. To infiltrate it and destroy it." Kyle commanded the attention of everyone in the room with his steady, quiet words. "You've gotten caught up in it, unfortunately. Normally we do everything to engage a criminal away from civilians, but it's impossible with the heroin scourge. It's in every city and small town across America."

"It's been all-consuming," Claudia added. "Kyle's worked the ROC crimes that have hit the East Coast especially hard, but when we figured out that ROC was using Silver Valley as its central drug distribution hub, I brought him here."

"I was working out of New York City for the past eight years, ever since I joined." Kyle's expression remained impassive, but in his eyes she saw a flash of concern. Did she imagine it or was Kyle trying to tell her something? "I've been living in Silver Valley, posing as various persons, for the last few months."

"So that's why I didn't immediately recognize you on the train tracks."

His grin broke through. "Off the tracks, and yes."

Heat rushed to her face, not just from his smile. From remembering how close she'd come to losing it all yesterday.

"We're sorry you had to go through that, Portia." Claudia looked at Colt Todd.

"Yes, we're very grateful to Kyle for being there and stepping up. But it's imperative that you understand we don't want you engaging any suspect again until we close this case." Chief Todd's concern was etched in the lines between his brows. "And since I don't have enough officers to spare one for guard duty, we're asking you to lie low for a bit. I'll make sure your paycheck isn't affected, of course."

"Thank you. And I promise I'm not going to give you any trouble—I want to help any way that I can. But I do have to do my work with the gala. Its success this year is more important than ever, with our public funding being slashed every which way. And I'm hoping to earn a nice gift for the homeless mission, too."

"Certainly you can keep working on the gala. We'll provide you with the proper security equipment to scramble your Wi-Fi and internet footprints. I have a special interest in your charity work, as Colt and I enjoyed the gala so much last year." Portia remembered the couple, how attune to one another they'd been. As they were now, but it simmered under their professional demeanors. She wondered at their history, but it wasn't the time to ask.

"Kyle mentioned this could take several more weeks. Can you give me any better idea of the timeline?"

"Annie asks me that all the time about my cases," Josh said. "As with any case, especially undercover, we can't be definitive about how long it'll take. I'm sorry, Portia. One bright spot is that you'll continue to receive your salary. We had the approval signed by a county representative, because you need police protection."

"Rest assured we're working to come up with a solution as quickly as possible." Claudia nodded to Kyle. "Did you bring the nondisclosure forms?"

"Here you go." Kyle slid a folder across the table, toward Portia. "It's up to you, but if you'd like to know a little more about who I'm working for, you need to sign the agreement."

"It's not just for your edification. What we do is need-to-know, but also, Portia, we may ask you for more insight as to how your library works, how you store the laptops, how you maintain your inventory for all your technology."

"Will I get a chance to do any of the surveillance with Kyle?" She felt Kyle's glare and ignored it. Of course he wouldn't want her anywhere near him while he worked. He was a protector, through and through.

Claudia smiled. "No, I can't promise that. Why don't you read over the paperwork and then decide how much you want to know?"

The room grew quiet, but then the three others struck up a low conversation as Portia read over the agreement. It stated she'd never reveal anything she learned from TH, Inc. That had to be the agency Kyle worked for. The one Claudia ran. She signed where appropriate, and the chief witnessed it.

"Okay, so now to put us on the same page, Kyle, Josh, Colt and I all work for Trail Hikers. That's the

TH you see on the document." Claudia went on to explain that the shadow government agency was responsible, behind the scenes, for helping law enforcement agencies at home in the US and abroad. Claudia was a retired Marine Corps General, and she'd taken on the agency right after leaving military service.

"Are all TH agents former military?"

"No, but it's a natural transition, especially for special operatives like SEALs and, of course, intelligence specialists. For every undercover agent working the field, we have at least a dozen personnel working intelligence analysis, communications technology, administrative duties to include travel schedules and logistics, and counterintelligence."

At Portia's blank look, Claudia smiled. "We have a team making sure no one figures out who we are and what we're doing here in Silver Valley. We adopted the name Trail Hikers to fit in with the Appalachian Trail, of course."

"Thank you for the explanation." Portia felt a little bit shaky. She didn't regret signing the papers and finding out more, and she wanted to do whatever she could to help bring ROC down. But it was sobering to realize what was required to keep a country, a state or a town safe. "And thank all of you for doing what you do. I had no idea, beyond what I read online, in papers and in other news sources." She looked them each in the eye, made sure they knew she wasn't speaking platitudes.

"Thank you, Portia. Do you have any questions for us?" Claudia looked ready to go and Portia couldn't imagine how full the woman's schedule was. Unlike running a library, Claudia's job involved life-and-death situations.

"Not a question, but a commitment. I'll stay at the house you've got for me for as long as it takes." She mentally squeezed her eyes shut against the risk to the gala, to her job. The safety of Silver Valley was paramount. "And if you need me to do anything that would help you catch the woman after me, or anyone else, you can count on me."

"Civilians don't participate in law enforcement operations." Kyle's stern admonition sliced across the, until now, cordial ambience. "Stay in the house and you'll be doing your part."

"Thank you for bringing that up, Kyle," Claudia said. "I wanted to point out that it would be most beneficial for you to check in on Portia from time to time. You've got the most expertise with the case, you know how to make sure you're not being trailed and Portia knows you."

Portia's insides immediately froze and flamed hot. What was she getting herself into?

Chapter 9

"I don't like that I won't have my own vehicle to get away in." Portia knew she sounded like a broken record, but it felt good to express her opinion. Not that it was going to change her situation.

"I wouldn't like that, either." Kyle drew to a stop at a traffic light. They were in a nondescript, unmarked police car, to keep Portia's movements under wraps. Kyle had explained that switching up vehicles kept the bad guys guessing. She knew that Kyle must have to keep a low profile, too, but didn't ask him about it. She got it—some of his and Josh's work wasn't any of her business.

Except when it was. "So I'm supposed to hang out with no contact with the outside world until you catch the woman who wants to kill me?"

"Pretty much." They crossed the Interstate 81 overpass and sped into what Portia thought of as the rural part of Silver Valley. Away from the town proper and the main commercial highway that ran around it, they entered the more mountainous, wooded area of the town's outer limits.

"How much longer?" She hadn't paid too much attention when Kyle asked Josh more specific questions about the house. It was hard to imagine she was being plucked from her normally independent life and had to basically hole up like a doomsdayer for the next several days, if not weeks.

"You said you knew the area." Kyle was being very short, deliberate in his words. She didn't like it. She wanted him to bare at least a tiny bit of his soul to her.

"I do, but you have the GPS on it." She took a deep breath as if she were about to plunge into the icy Susquehanna. "Why don't you tell me a little bit about yourself, Kyle?"

Kyle almost swerved the dang car as Portia's request hit him right where he knew she wanted it to. In his soft spot, which was expanding at an alarming rate since he'd met her.

Hell, since he'd first laid eyes on her over a month ago.

"There's not a lot to know."

"Are you going to make me ask it all? Where are you from?" She sounded genuinely interested. When was the last time anyone asked him about himself? Other than for a security clearance?

"I was born and raised in Northern California. My family owned almond farms." Still did, but his dad was getting ready to sell them off, unless he or his brother stepped up to do it. "It was a great way to burn off steam as a kid, helping Dad out during harvest. I knew I wanted to join the Marines from the time I was in high school."

"Your family supported you doing that?"

"Yeah. Not right at first—my mother was freaked out, with the war in full swing after Nine Eleven. But both she and Dad understood my desire to serve. And it provided me with the means to an education, which I got after I left active duty."

"Where did you go to school?"

He looked at her. Yup, big brown eyes soaked up each drop of what he said, as if it mattered to her.

"Boston College."

"Really? I thought you'd go back to the West Coast. To be near your family."

"I got a great deal from the college, scholarship-wise. They matched my GI Bill benefits." The Yellow Ribbon Program had been a godsend, allowing him to go to a top-notch school. By then he'd been tapped by Trail Hikers and knew what his options were after he earned his degree. "What about you, Portia?"

"Nothing nearly as exciting, trust me. I went away to school, but 'away' for me was Penn State, only two hours from here. It was good, though, to have that time out of Silver Valley."

"Did you ever consider living anywhere else?"

"No. This area's in my blood." She gazed out the window and he wanted to watch her expression all day. Except he was driving and didn't think she'd appreciate him running them off the road.

"Have you traveled a lot?"

"Yes. My parents were big on the National Park

scene and took us to many of them each summer, usually for a good week or two. My mother is still a teacher, and has the whole summer off. Dad works for the state, in Harrisburg, so he gets a decent vacation, too."

"We couldn't take off on vacations with the farm to worry about. But we did day trips, especially in winter. Lake Tahoe's only a few hours away from where I grew up, so we went skiing regularly."

"You sound like you miss it."

"I do. As a matter of fact, after this case is solved, I'm taking a month's leave back at home."

"Will you ever move back?"

"That's the plan. Claudia is okay with me moving my home base out west. It'll open me up for assignments not only there but in Asia." It'd be great for his resume, whether he stayed with Trail Hikers for the time being or decided to leave law enforcement.

"So you can retire from the agency, have a pension?" Spoken like a local librarian. Lifelong security would be her primary concern, and he understood it perfectly. He'd had the same questions when he'd joined the Marines.

"Yes. My time in the Marine Corps gets tacked on, too, so I only need sixteen years with Trail Hikers, and I'm at seven now. It's a good option, but part of me would love to start a private investigative firm."

"In California."

"Yes." He didn't want to talk about himself one second more. He'd had a mental safe spot to retreat to these past years, and it'd always been California. He didn't see himself taking over the almond farm, but he'd happily support his brother in doing so. And he'd also enjoy building his own home and office on a portion of his family property. It'd had been his parents' dream when they'd sunk all they owned into the prime real estate, which had exponentially increased in value over the years.

"Here we go." He turned into an asphalt-paved drive, more like a tiny country road. It shot straight back to a copse of evergreens, obscuring anything beyond it from the main road. Only after they'd driven under about a half mile of oak and maple trees did the house come into view.

"Wow." Portia's word hung between them, expressing his reaction, too.

The house looked like a modest A-frame at first glance, albeit huge with an extensive wraparound porch with railings heavily crusted with several inches of icy snow. As his vehicle neared the building, two additional wings emerged, slung low on either side of the main house. He had a twinge of longing in his gut. It reminded him of the mountains surrounding Lake Tahoe, of the ski chalets school friends escaped to during winter break.

He pulled up to the garage door and killed the engine. "I need to do a thorough walk-about. Let's get inside and figure out whatever you need to know to live here."

She laughed. "I think I can manage that on my own, Kyle." The wariness in her eyes didn't match the curve of her lips, though. Had he said something that bothered her, with all his talk of California? The life of a farmer wasn't luxurious, but his family had always thrived. Maybe hers had struggled at times?

"Yes, but you need to learn the first lesson of a good

law enforcement op. Trading information. You know a lot about me now. I still don't even know what you do on a daily basis."

"Oh." Her lips, slightly parted, created a cold-air balloon with her breath.

"Come on, let's get inside. It's freezing out here."

The warm golden hues in exposed wood beams were welcoming and soothing to the eye. Granite and stainless steel stamped the kitchen with a gourmet feel, and the river-stone hearth beckoned for a night of reading while sipping hot chocolate or a hot toddy. Portia appreciated the contemporary sensibilities in the otherwise cozy, traditional home.

But what won her over were the views. Each and every room of the house seemed to have a view of the surrounding hills and rolling mountains that provided the footbed of the Appalachian Trail.

They stopped in the kitchen and she put her purse and laptop on the expansive counter. "I don't think I ever thanked Josh for taking Annie to get this back to me, or for the extra clothes."

"You've had a lot on your mind." He walked up to her and the spacious room morphed to the inches between them. Cool gray eyes appraised her and it was as if this man, a mere stranger only a day ago, read her better than she'd ever done her favorite Dickens stories. "You keep saying you're fine, Portia, but trust me. I've got years of the kind of day you had yesterday behind me, and it was a long day for me. It'd be completely normal for you to think you're losing it a little bit. Or to feel frightened."

She blinked, but didn't break his eye contact. "I

admit I was shaky yesterday, but this…this feels better." She meant the house, the sense of security being away from where the woman had tried to kill her—twice—or knowing that SVPD—no, Kyle—was looking out for her; all of these things made her anxiety melt away. But it'd be a lie. She felt better because Kyle was here. Still.

He's going back to California eventually.

So what? She didn't want anything lasting. Not after the Robert mess. And wasn't it healthy to connect with someone on a sexual level, after such life-threatening events?

"You've got that look again, Portia." The white gleam of his grin told her he was on the same frequency. Which sent thrills from her skin to her deepest, most intimate parts.

"What look?" Her voice sounded breathy and begging for his kiss again, at least to her ears.

He leaned over and stroked her cheek, his finger tracing an electric trail from her cheekbone to her earlobe. Then he moved his hand to her nape. "Like you want to kiss me again."

"I—"

"Do you?"

"Yes."

"You've got to know that I'm a full-partnership kind of guy, Portia. Since you kissed me last time, it's my turn to kiss you."

"Aren't we kissing each other?" she said in a whisper, as she watched his mouth move around his words, saw the flick of his tongue against his teeth. Her knees were wobbly, sure, but it was the insistent hot pulse between her legs that shook her. She'd do anything this man let her, allow him to do whatever he wanted. Portia wanted Kyle as she'd never wanted another man. It didn't make sense; she barely knew him—

His fingers touched her temple. "Stop, Portia. You're thinking too much. If either of us stops to think this out, take it to its logical conclusion, we're going to miss out."

"Yes." Her lips throbbed, too, wanting this kiss to start so that it could never end.

"I'm going to kiss you now, Portia. Is that okay?" His breath warmed her face, and she loved the intimacy of his scent mingling with cinnamon and maybe a linger of the morning's coffee. Other than his hand on her neck, they weren't touching. She swayed and her pelvis moved with her, needing to know if he was as turned on as she.

"Stop talking, Kyle."

His chuckle was the last thing she heard before he hauled her against him, grabbed her ass and held her as he pressed his erection—his wonderfully hard and straining erection—into her heat. Layers of clothes didn't prevent the shock of it from reverberating through her, making her toes clench and unclench in her boots. Her arms went around his neck as his mouth covered hers and sensation assaulted her, blowing away any concerns she had about this being a short-term affair. Any affair with Kyle would be welcome and, in her current state, medically necessary. Because as they kissed, as their tongues stroked, their mouths sucked, their hands explored, Portia felt what she hadn't since before she'd become an ROC target, since before she'd met and been used by Robert.

Portia felt alive. Kyle's touch reminded her that

she loved life, and couldn't wait to see what each day brought.

Today, it handed her Kyle.

Kyle never mixed sex and work. It was a bad combo, not only because of the risk of missing a danger signal but also because emotions ran rampant during a high-stake mission. He'd always preferred to keep his personal commitments completely separate from his duty, which meant he had long-term relationships with women he rarely saw. Since that got old, he'd let go of even trying to form more than a brief sexual bond when opportunity arose.

Portia was different. This wouldn't be just sex and he knew it. He also knew that he'd told her he was leaving after he brought ROC down, going back to California, where he'd pick up the rest of his life.

She'd made it clear she was a Pennsylvania woman, highly educated and well-traveled, at least within North America, but not interested in going anywhere else permanently. Silver Valley was Portia's home, as the tree-nut farms of Northern California were his.

Her kiss was magic, no other word for it. He'd been hard for her all morning, but when she'd turned and looked at him in the kitchen, he'd been unable to maintain his professional demeanor.

"Kyle." She spoke against his mouth as he moved his hand to between her legs, cupped her, intimated with a wiggle of his fingers what he wanted to do once he got her skirt and panties off. Would she even wear panties, or was it a thong, a G-string? He pressed his forehead against hers. He needed oxygen.

"If we keep doing this, Portia, I need all of you. It's been a while, and—"

She silenced him by licking around his lips with her hot, furtive tongue. He wanted to know what it'd feel like on his dick, how she'd take him in her mouth and use it to bring him to full release. When she reached down and stroked him through his jeans, he felt like he was fifteen again and ready to lose it before they even got started. He wrenched his mouth from hers.

"Now, Portia. Here."

"We need a condom." She turned in his arms and grabbed her purse, unzipped it.

He reached into his jacket inside pocket and pulled out the strip of condoms he'd taken from his medicine chest this morning. As much as he'd berated himself for even contemplating involving Portia in his frenetic life, he felt nothing but gratitude.

"Here," they both said at the same time, as she held up a similar strip of protection. Their eyes met and the heat between them evaporated into gales of laughter.

"When did you have time to get condoms?" He hadn't seen her leave his place, but she could have, when he was in the shower. The drugstore was a two-minute walk, tops, from his apartment building.

"After yesterday, at the tracks." Her already flushed face turned a deep crimson. Something warred in her eyes, as if she were on the verge of telling him her deepest secret. "I haven't been held like that, like when you saved my life, in a long time. Maybe forever. It got me thinking that I've been a bit of a…a recluse for too long. It's my way of being prepared, of making an affirmative step toward the life I want."

When her lips formed the word *want*, humor left as

quickly as it'd appeared, and he was a lightning rod full of charged particles—for Portia. All he saw, all he felt, all he wanted was Portia. To be with her, inside her, moving her toward the enjoyment he longed to see her experience.

The insistence of Kyle's lips on hers, the way his fingers dug into her just a bit beyond sexual need, let her know that his desire ran as deep as hers. It wasn't a time for anything but enjoying the present moment with him. They both knew it could end at any second.

The strips of condoms made soft splats as they hit the counter and floor, but not before Kyle had torn off one.

"Do you want to go to a…bedroom?" She didn't know the house, didn't personally care where they came together. All she wanted was him, wherever.

"What do you want?" he asked against her mouth before dragging his to her throat, his hands adeptly circling her waist and lifting her onto the island. "Tell me, Portia."

But she couldn't speak as his hand unzipped her coat and he helped her get her arms out of the sleeves. He shrugged out of his parka, too, and let it drop to the floor. Struck by the urgency of the moment, Portia raised her sweater and shirt over her head, throwing them onto the counter. Clad in only her bra and skirt, she still felt overdressed. She wanted to be skin-on-skin with Kyle.

"You're stunning." His eyes glittered with promise as he looked at her breasts, which spilled over her lacy pink demi-cup bra. He lowered his head and trailed his tongue along the plump skin, the moist heat of him hardening her nipples and making her squirm with desire on the counter. She wanted his tongue everywhere at once—in her mouth, on her breasts, between her legs.

His chuckle vibrated against her and he expertly undid her bra clasp with one hand, while the other gently pinched her nipple. Portia thought she was going to climax on the spot.

"Kyle!" She reached down, trying to get to his belt, but he leaned back, laughed again.

"Patience." As she watched, he unbuckled his belt and shoved out of his pants and underwear in one move. He still wore a button-down shirt and she went to work on unfastening it. Kyle took advantage of her busy fingers to gently blow in her ear, nibble at her lobe.

As soon as his shirtfront was open, he helped by getting out of it and then lifting his undershirt over his head. Portia greedily watched him, saw how his pecs flexed under smooth skin. She leaned over and sucked his nipple into her mouth, but his skin was so taut, he was so chiseled, that it wasn't much more than a nip. But it was enough to make him hiss, and she smiled as he gripped her head and tugged until her mouth was accessible.

This time the kiss wasn't tentative or an invitation. It was full-on passion, with intent to take it as far as they could. When he hauled her up against him, holding her legs, her breasts flattened against his chest, Portia's skin blazed as if he'd touched her everywhere. She linked her feet over his ass and reveled in the erotic sensations that rocked her. Their kiss was a whirl of tongues and gasps and tiny bites and more. It was a promise, a vow that this would be the hottest sex of her life.

Still holding her against him, her arms around his neck, Kyle walked them to the sofa in front of the fireplace and bank of windows that overlooked the rolling Appalachian Mountains. She'd have plenty of time to take in the view in the countless hours and days alone she knew she faced. Right now, she had Kyle and he was all she wanted.

He knelt next to the sofa and set her down. Anticipating their union, she moved to grasp his incredible erection but he stopped her.

"Not yet, Portia. You first."

Before her head had even landed on a throw pillow, he'd spread her legs, held her at the sensitive top of her thighs and covered her sex with his mouth. Never had she been this turned on so quickly. It was as if they'd engaged in leisurely foreplay for hours and now she was primed and ready to come as his tongue did wicked things to her most private folds. Yet they'd only been in the house for what, ten minutes, tops?

He lifted his mouth from her and she looked into his eyes as she moaned her distress at the sudden loss of stimulation.

"Stop thinking. It's you, me and this." He lowered his head, and this time she didn't think about anything but how his mouth felt on her. She reached down, ran her fingers through his short hair and couldn't stop it, wouldn't. The rolling orgasm hit her from her center and exploded out to every nerve ending. Her scream of release echoed around them in the mountain home, as tears streamed down her cheeks. The release was beyond complete.

And they'd only just begun.

* * *

Kyle held on to his erection, refusing to let Portia's cries undo him right then and there, while she pulsed under his mouth. He tasted, smelled, felt nothing but Portia, and it was exquisite. But the best was yet to come. He almost laughed at his mental pun but thought better of it. He wanted this to be perfect for Portia.

Because she was so damned perfect for him.

He leaned up and kissed her forehead, smoothed back her hair. She opened her eyes and, instead of the languorous expression he expected, she grinned.

"You still have that condom?"

He couldn't stop his answering grin if he wanted to. He ripped open the packet and donned protection before he hovered over her, their bodies so close. Portia was freaking beautiful.

"Kyle, stop teasing me. Please. Now."

He'd never paused before, never felt such a need to soak it all in, appreciate every moment. He'd never been with a woman who'd taken him from sexual interest to unstoppable need like this, either.

"You ready, babe?" He gave her one last kiss before he plunged into her, savoring every inch of her sweet hotness as she closed around him. It was as if they'd done this a thousand times and yet, somewhere deep inside of him, he knew that every time with Portia would feel like the first time. Exciting, sexy, special.

Before he went down the feelings rabbit hole, his physical need took over and he pulled out, then thrust in again, harder this time, deeper. Portia's heels lifted to his shoulders and he about died then and there, but managed to channel the turn-on into thrust after thrust, her sighs and moans affirmation that this was so, so good for her, too.

He wanted it to last all morning, all afternoon. He wanted to shove into Portia again and again, never breaking the intimate contact. When she cried out for the second time and pulsed around him, he couldn't fight his release. It wasn't like it had ever been with any other woman before.

With Portia, he'd found his mate. And it was the worst possible time to have found her.

Chapter 10

Kyle and Portia adopted a silent agreement after they'd given into their need for one another a few days ago. She told him that she understood that he needed space to work on the case, and he knew she didn't want to distract him. They slept in separate rooms, he in a guest room and her in the master suite, and avoided being alone together for too long. It worked out, as Kyle was gone for at least fifteen hours a day, keeping track of Markova. He only left when he turned over her surveillance to another Trail Hiker, and arrived at the house each night, well past when Portia had gone to bed. The times they saw one another, usually in the kitchen over breakfast, she'd been quiet, a more reserved version of the woman he knew she was.

Guilt hassled him at every turn. He wanted to draw her out, make her stay here more enjoyable, but if he did, he'd risk getting in too deep with her again. Never a good idea during a case as heavy as ROC.

On the evening that marked the first week since he'd brought Portia to the country house, Kyle knew she needed more than the phone calls with Annie. Brindle was filling in for Portia, with a temporary staffer acting as her librarian assistant, so Portia didn't have any library work to do. He knew she spent hours each day on the gala, but still worried about her. Portia was a woman who thrived on community involvement. She was the epitome of community and she'd been shoved into a strange house, even though it was a beautiful one at that, with no end in sight.

He couldn't shake his sense of culpability over her needing to stay in the strange house, yet keeping her safe remained his priority.

He found her laptop and stacks of papers splayed on the coffee table that separated the huge fireplace from the cozy oversize sofa. But no Portia. A quick glance at the French doors proved they were closed, that she was somewhere in the house. He walked down the hall that led to the bedrooms and saw that the light in hers was on, and heard water running from the master suite. She was taking a shower. Just like she'd done every other evening, after her late-afternoon workout.

Relief was impossible to ignore, and it was exactly the emotion that buoyed his steps back to the kitchen, where he began to set up dinner. The local Greek place was a favorite of hers; she'd told him as much over the deli sandwiches and tomato soup she'd made last night. He told himself he'd stopped and ordered the meal because keeping her fed and her strength up was part of his job.

But he knew it was complete BS. Portia's smile was something he was willing to go to untold ends for, he was finding out.

Soft feet padded on the oak flooring, followed by the scent of her shower soap, or maybe it was her shampoo. Something vanilla but with extra spice added in.

Not that he wanted to pay attention to her that closely. Not touching her this last week had been excruciating, but by a silent agreement they'd both kept things platonic.

"That smells incredible. I didn't know you cook—" She froze in place in front of the island, her mouth agape at the spread of spanakopita, freshly chopped Greek salad with creamy feta dressing, and skewered chicken and lamb.

"You went to Greek Delight!" She regained her composure and reached for the foil packet he'd pulled out of the takeout paper bag. "These toasted pitas are the best."

"You said you liked Greek, so I thought I'd treat."

Her eyes narrowed. "I thought you told me that all of my living expenses were paid for by Trail Hikers. For the duration of your case."

He cleared his throat. "They are. It is."

"But you paid for this out of your pocket?"

"I did." Crap, the way she said it, combined with the quizzical way her brow arched, made it sound like he'd planned a date with her. Or something.

He opened his mouth to allay her misconception but was blindsided by her as she quickly reached up and gave him a sound peck on his cheek. Her lips were smooth and her hair sopping from the shower. The kiss was totally casual, but she may as well have scorched his cheek with a hot brand.

Portia didn't notice that he was dumbstruck as she beamed at him. "Thank you so much. This is very sweet of you."

Now she thought he was sweet. He fought a groan.

"You're experiencing the hardship here, Portia. You've been grabbed from your regular life and forced to live in a strange house with no official deadline. It's the least I can do."

"All you have to do is say 'you're welcome,' Kyle. Don't worry, I'm not misconstruing it for something like a romantic gesture."

"Good. I mean, good that we're on the same page." Hell, how had he gone from a man in charge of a huge secret government stakeout to sounding like a fumbling adolescent? Something about Portia brought out his full range of emotions. Feelings he was more comfortable neatly compartmentalizing and storing far away from the scrutiny of daylight. Or an inquisitive librarian.

"Let's serve it up and enjoy it in front of the fire. It's gotten really cold today—have you noticed it?"

"Heck yeah. I was waiting all day for the woman who's targeted you to show up." At her questioning glance, he continued. "Outside the library."

"Let me guess, you were disguised as a homeless man, without the benefit of your better winter coat?"

"Something like that." He helped himself to several of the lamb skewers and noted that she piled her plate with the salad. They took silverware and napkins and settled on the sofa.

"Here, let me clear my stuff up a bit." Portia balanced her plate in one hand and shoved the papers away from where they sat.

"Don't worry about it." He set his plate in a clear spot and stood back up. "What can I get you to drink?"

"The sparkling water is fine. Thank you."

When he returned with their drinks, he saw that she'd ignored him and cleared her clutter to one side of the cocktail table. She'd also switched on the fireplace, a gas insert. As he sat on the cushion next to hers, he knew that all too easily he could get very used to this.

"Is it always this cold in central Pennsylvania in January?" He dug into his food as he waited for her answer.

"Not this bad, no, but we get our share of bitter cold. This year's been a little worse with the polar vortex deal." She referred to the weather phenomenon that had the local meteorologists all abuzz. The air currents formed in a way that allowed pure arctic air from the North Pole to be channeled south, as far down as the center of North America. That included Pennsylvania, which was currently in a deep freeze.

"It has gotten colder today, by twenty degrees. This salad, by the way, is delicious. You were right."

She eyed his tiny portion of greens, compared to his much larger stack of meat. "You didn't trust my judgment, did you?"

"Hey, don't be so defensive. Salad is known to be chick food. You can't blame me for wondering if you're big on rabbit food like a lot of women are."

She shook her head and grabbed one of his chicken kebabs. "Vegetables are for everyone. And no, I'm not against heavier fare—you saw me polish off that sandwich last night, and I told you I love Buffalo chicken wings."

"You did."

They weren't flirting; they weren't talking about the case, or anything super weighty. And he was happier than he could remember ever being. His mind tried to grab onto what he'd used as his happy place, mentally, these past few years. It'd always been the hope of returning to California, to the year-round sunshine and much more reasonable weather.

But right now, the polar vortex–cursed Silver Valley, Pennsylvania, felt incredible.

Portia savored every last bit of the Greek takeout, almost as much as she did being so close to a man who made her feel things she'd not thought she was capable of. The great sex they'd shared almost a week ago was almost supernatural in its quality, no question. Yet sharing a meal with Kyle proved more intimate to her. As a single woman who spent so much time out of her apartment, working at the library or homeless shelter, she was used to quick meals, most of them alone. Breaking a pita with Kyle proved absolutely the sexiest thing she figured they'd done together.

Not that she'd tell him. By a silent agreement, they'd avoided touching one another since they'd given in to the very strong tension between them. That was still there, but they'd managed to sidestep it.

She was okay with that. Portia didn't want it on her conscience that she'd distracted Kyle in any way from his ROC mission. It was bad enough that he felt he had to protect her by staying here.

"What are you thinking about, Portia?"

She sighed. Should she tell him? "I'm thinking that you're going to ignore what I'll say, but at the risk of repeating myself, you do not have to come back here each night. I know you go out to work at all hours, and driving up here has to be a pain. Your apartment is in the center of town, so much more convenient."

He wiped his mouth with a paper napkin, crumpled it and threw it on his empty plate. Leaning back into the sofa, he stretched his arms across the back of it and let out a long breath. "That is what I call good grub."

She couldn't help but laugh, which only made her more exasperated. "Did you even hear a word I said?"

Silver eyes, so intense, on her. The heat climbed up her throat and face, just like it did every single time he looked at her. He had to know how he affected her. Yet he never took advantage of it, which she gave him kudos for. "I hear every word, Portia. I hear how you take your showers, how you stay in the stall a while as you dry yourself off, then how you open the bathroom door to help let the steam out of the room. Do you want to know anything else that I notice?"

She swallowed. This was going off the rails again, too quickly for her. Their companionable meal was a safer space. Safe from the tantalizing memories of how it felt to have his hands on her...and his tongue.

Stop.

"No, that's enough. I believe you." She forced a smile before she stood up to clear the plates. His arm shot out and his hand gently circled her wrist. "Leave it. And I'm sorry. I'm trying to keep things cool between us."

She sank back into the comfy cushion and faced him. "I appreciate that. It's not easy living in such close proximity after we, ah, had the time we had the first day here."

He watched her, but his arm was back at his side. "No, it's not. I never want you to feel used, Portia."

"I'm an adult. What we shared was mutual. Do you feel used?"

"No, ah, I… Yes, it was mutual." She loved that she'd flustered him. "But I'm leaving Silver Valley after we take down ROC. Especially after I break up the heroin distribution and we capture Markova."

"Markova—that's the woman who wants me dead?" His eyes answered, narrowing and growing angry. "Don't be mad at yourself that you slipped her name, Kyle. I heard nothing."

"It's not something you needed to know, but yes, her name is Markova." He rubbed his temples. "This case has turned into way more than I expected when I first heard of Silver Valley."

"I know that. You've made your reason for being in what I'm sure you consider Podunk, USA." She wouldn't stop her defensiveness over Silver Valley. "I've seen a lot of the US, you know, and I travel overseas every summer for at least ten days, usually two weeks. There are plenty of other places I'd be comfortable living, but nothing compares to Silver Valley. It might just be a place you have to deal with while in the middle of a work gig, but it's a source of great strength for a lot of people."

"Whoa, I didn't mean to get you riled up over this, Portia. I'm going back to California because that's my home. Or it was, until I left for the Marines right out of high school. I get your devotion to this area, really, I do. It's evident in everything you do, you know.

From the library to the homeless shelter, to all the kids I saw you help out who were doing research for high school papers. And you're terrific with the seniors who come in and have a zillion questions about technology." He paused, and she watched in complete shock as he began to chuckle. "Do you know, one day I was hanging around the computers and I watched you help this one older gentleman order a gift for his lady friend at the senior center. He'd found out it'd be less expensive from an online retailer and you patiently led him through all the steps."

"I had no idea you were there." She remembered it as if it were yesterday, because the said gentleman was Mr. Nolan, the retired schoolteacher who'd taught her French classes through high school. He was a community pillar and he'd come in a few weeks before Christmas to order that particular gift. "You've been here since before the holidays? I know you told me that at one point—I just didn't put it together until now."

"Why would you?" His gaze was appreciative and she blushed. It was one thing to know she turned him on, but to realize that he'd seen her in her element, completely unguarded, was a bit overwhelming. "I was just another patron as far as you knew. No one you'd notice."

But Kyle was a man she'd always notice. He had to be very good at his job if he'd escaped her observation until the train track rescue.

He nodded at her work, stacked on the end of the coffee table. "How goes the gala planning? Anything you need me to take care of while I'm out and about?"

"No way. I'd never ask you to do anything but what you're here to do. Save Silver Valley from ROC."

He looked at her like she'd missed something in their conversation. "Ah, you know that I'm just one of many law enforcement types working to make that happen, right?"

Another thing she'd picked up about him, as he'd held her in the shadow of the train that could have killed her: his sincere humility.

"Yes, but you're the one who saved my life and for some reason feel responsible to make sure I'm safe, a week out. Josh has known me my entire life, and while I know he cares, as does Annie, he didn't volunteer to check on me regularly."

"Because he's in uniform, and more visible in the community. He can't send SVPD units out to patrol the area without raising eyebrows. We don't want anything to appear out of the ordinary."

She tore her gaze from him to watch the blue flames in the glass-covered hearth. Her body was too aware of him, but worse, her heart was getting in too deep with Kyle. With a man who was headed for the West Coast the minute the investigation wrapped up.

"Are we going to be able to have the gala?" She voiced her worst fear, as far as her community work went. The other anxiety, over never finding a man like Kyle again, someone who got her right from the get-go, she buried deep.

The cushions moved as he leaned forward on his knees to look at her. "I'm doing everything to ensure you can. But it has to be airtight as far as security is concerned. Why don't we go over the plans together?"

Disbelief made her laugh. "You're kidding." She looked at him and sucked in a deep breath at the light in his eyes. Her heart reacted, too, making her feel as though she'd just run ten kilometers in the bitter cold. "What about a charity ball is interesting to you?" He worked in the most exciting profession she could think of. "There isn't an adrenaline rush involved in planning a silent auction and dance for two to three hundred people, trust me."

The lines around his eyes deepened, but he didn't smile completely. "I'm not an adrenaline junkie, believe it or not. Sure, I've been in tight spots, but that was more likely when I was in the Marine Corps. My job as an agent involves a lot of watching, listening, waiting. And I read a heck of a lot of intelligence reports and criminal profiles. When I'm not actually in the field, I spend eight hours a day at my laptop, wherever I am."

"So while the Trail Hiker headquarters is here, in Silver Valley, the employees don't all work and live here?"

He shook his head. "No, not at all. The staff here exists to keep the agency running, to coordinate the missions."

"And for Claudia to tell her bosses what's going on."

He didn't reply to her comment—she didn't expect him to. "I know that most all of what you do is very classified, and I'm not looking for information I don't have a right to. I suspect you've probably told me a little more than I really need to know, right?"

"Maybe. Claudia wouldn't have told you the basic premise of Trail Hikers, or my role in this particular op, unless she thought it necessary and that you are trustworthy. And don't forget she had you sign the nondisclosure forms."

"You already knew my background when you started surveillance on the library?"

"Yes. Which means, of course, that Claudia had access to the same information."

"Does everyone in your office have access to these files on me?" She was all for supporting law enforcement and helping get rid of the bad guy, or in this case, woman. But having her most personal data out there was disconcerting. As a librarian, she understood the power of information.

"No, quite the contrary. I know you've never been in the military, but as with any government entity, release of classified material is on a need-to-know basis. So other than me, and my supervisor, no one else can read the files. Unless they start to work the same case, or something related to it."

"That makes sense. And yes, I did know that. I regularly read several national newspapers, along with all the local press."

"Yeah, a lot makes it into the papers that shouldn't." He raised a brow. "You probably don't agree, as an information manager."

"Actually I have no problem with the concept of classified information—as long as it's handled that way for the right purpose."

"There's a lot more to you than a lot of people see, Portia." His scrutiny had gone personal again, exactly what she'd hoped to avoid. Unless they were going to make this either a full-fledged fling, or Kyle was going to stay in Silver Valley after ROC was removed, she couldn't let her heart go there.

Chapter 11

Kyle hated to leave Portia again the next morning, but she hadn't seemed fazed. She'd all but shooed him out of the huge house, reassuring him that she'd be safe. It'd taken her no time to master the intricate surveillance system Trail Hikers had installed, but he never forgot who their adversary was. Ludmila Markova knew her way around the most sophisticated technology. His one solace was that he knew Trail Hikers had the best equipment the US government had to offer.

It was his job to protect her, no matter what Trail Hikers or SVPD policy was about providing personal security. Sure, he couldn't stop his mission, but he could damn sure make certain Portia never faced Markova again. To ensure it, he had to get to the bottom of the case ASAP. Markova was the person with the answers as to how the heroin was getting into Silver

Valley, and when. He had two objectives: take out Markova and break up the heroin distribution ring.

His first stop in town was to meet with Claudia at TH headquarters. He made certain he wasn't followed and took precautions with his appearance. Winter and cold weather made it easier, with hats and hoods being commonplace. He entered the building with a card, then passed through three additional security checkpoints that included fingerprint, facial and retina identification. TH hadn't utilized such strident measures during its initial setup, but as their adversaries grew more technologically astute, so had the agency.

"Hi, Kyle." The receptionist tapped on his smart tablet and Kyle knew that Claudia had been informed of his arrival. "Claudia's in a meeting but will be available in five minutes."

"I'll wait." He took a seat in the minimalist but comfortable lounge area. Time with the director of Trail Hikers was precious and he wouldn't be here if he didn't need to.

After the exact time specified, he was escorted to her office and waited for the receptionist to close the several-inches-thick steel door behind him. The entire office building was a fortress, with the agents effectively working in vaults due to the classified nature of the Trail Hiker mission. They would assist international, federal, state and local law enforcement as needed, always maintaining complete anonymity except for the LEA personnel who were also TH. Trail Hiker agents avoided discovery at all costs. What the mission statement didn't reveal was that TH only took on the most difficult and deadly cases, the ones that had to be stopped in their tracks immediately or monitored for the long haul, for the safety of innocent civilians.

"Kyle. Have a seat." Claudia ran a hand through her signature gray hair, and her attractiveness wasn't lost on him, even though she was twenty years his senior. At least. More importantly she was his boss, a fearless leader whom he'd been thrilled to work for when he first learned of the possibility. He'd never worked with Claudia while still a Marine, but her legacy to the Corps was inimitable. To the present day, Marine Corps Intelligence Officers were trained with techniques she'd perfected when she was still a junior officer, before she made General, and long before her retirement as a two-star.

"Yes, ma'am." He never got used to calling her by her first name, no matter that the work environment demanded it. There wasn't the hardline ranking in Trail Hikers like he'd experienced in the military. They were all colleagues, agents all working together for a common cause. Of course there were ranks and definite leaders here, but to minimize the chances of exposure, they didn't refer to one another with anything other than their first names.

"You've got Portia settled at the Olsen house." A statement. Claudia came as close to an omniscient presence as anyone he'd ever met.

"Yes. I'll go back at night to check on her, when I'm not working."

Claudia swiveled in her chair and rapidly typed on her keyboard. He couldn't see her computer display but knew from other times he'd worked a case with her that her monstrous monitor would reflect Claudia's comprehensive assessment of the case.

"It looks pretty tight, security-wise." Cool eyes peered around the monitor at him. "Does she know how to use a weapon?"

"I didn't ask her, but I'd doubt it."

"Why? You're in Pennsylvania. She doesn't have a license to carry in the background check we ran, but she may have hunted before, or gone to a firing range. Find out. I'd like to equip her and you with a few extra firearms, just in case."

"Portia's not a Trail Hiker." He was, and he'd be doing any firing of weapons as needed.

"No, but she knows enough about the case, and of course she's the one Markova's targeting. Have you told Portia anything about her adversary?"

"No. All Portia knows is that ROC is in place in Silver Valley and refusing to leave, and she knows Markova's name. She knows I'm here to help bring the heroin operation down, break up their logistics."

Claudia nodded. "I'm not sure what you pulled up on Portia when you did your background check, but in the profile I have here, it talks about one of her high school friends succumbing to heroin. Annie knew the woman, too."

He hadn't read that part in his file, and he'd been too busy the last week to reread Portia's dossier. He was living with her—that was all he needed. And it made him more aware of Portia as a human being than he had been. Portia had a fire in her belly for charity work. No doubt her high school friend's overdose only further motivated her.

"I do know from her file that she was involved with a local politician. It didn't work out."

Claudia snorted. "Because she ended it, which was a

good move on her part. Robert Donovan is a slickster. He's even accepted donations from out of state donors to include a Mr. D. Ivanov." She met Kyle's gaze again and he registered the same level of disgust.

Dima Ivanov was the head of East Coast ROC, the big kahuna of ROC criminals. He'd alluded capture, even though he'd been in Silver Valley at least a half dozen times in the past eighteen months. Problem was, no one reported him when he was in town. The locals would only see him as a tourist passing through, and frightened anyone who thought they recognized him into keeping quiet. Ivanov knew well enough to keep up a disguise from the local LEAs.

"Is Donovan in with ROC for this operation?" He referred to the heroin distribution chain. It wasn't beyond politicians to convince or at least try to convince LEAs to look the other way when it preserved a solid donor.

"No, not from what we've seen, but nothing would surprise me." Claudia frowned. "You and I have seen so much destruction around the globe caused by greed. I hate that it's come to Silver Valley."

"We're on it, boss."

"We are. So after you find out if Portia can fire a weapon, and train her if she can't, take some extra arms out to the house. Feel free to use our firing range."

"We don't involve civilians in our cases." No way was he training Portia how to fire a weapon. She was a librarian, the town's Mother Theresa of the homeless. Not an undercover agent.

You're getting in too deep.

Maybe he already was.

"Portia's already involved, Kyle." She peered at him from her desk. "Are your emotions becoming involved,

Kyle?" Her astute query was underscored by the blaze of comprehension in her blue eyes.

"No. Maybe. Yeah."

"There's no harm in caring for someone, but it can't affect your mission. It would be rough to reassign you this deep in, but I can make it happen if you'd like."

"No, I'm going to finish this."

"Good." She nodded. "Are you still considering the move to California?"

"As long as the offer to launch the West Coast Trail Hiker office still stands." And even if it didn't, he still wanted to go back to his native state. Didn't he?

He'd thought of it, planned for it for the last year or two. It was as much a part of his everyday awareness as his job. But he hadn't thought about California lately.

Not since he'd held a certain Silver Valley librarian in his arms as he knocked her off the train tracks.

It'd come close for Markova last week at the homeless shelter. So the librarian had a protector—no matter. At some point, the woman would have to go back to work, and then she'd make her move, more exactingly this time. Following her from the library had been foolish, the action of an amateur.

She was not a rookie, as Americans liked to say. FSB training was for only the very best, and when she'd joined them, she'd been young, strong and full of idealistic Russian dreams.

Now she knew they were all lies, but in America with Ivanov, she'd found her place, found a way to use her abilities while still helping her fellow nationals who'd come here looking for a way out. All of them were misfits as far as the Russian government was concerned, all FSB or other government agency throw-aways.

Using her best teenage boy disguise, she'd hung out in the local comic book store since three thirty, the time when high school students liked to relax, she'd noticed. Certain that the man she'd encountered on the train tracks, and again in the homeless shelter, was nowhere in the vicinity, she left the store, entered the library and headed to the classic fiction shelves. There, on the Russian translation shelf, somewhere between *The Brothers Karamazov* and *Anna Karenina*, she surreptitiously placed the USB stick on which she'd copied the most detailed instructions from the site on the dark net. She put the memory device behind the aged volumes, out of sight of a browser. The Russian novels were so obvious a place they would be discounted by SVPD or FBI. They'd had another drop place closer to the front entrance but she'd changed it after the day the librarian chased her onto the train tracks.

Her immediate subordinate in ROC, in charge of the individual dealer logistics for the area, would come and get the stick in the next fifteen minutes.

Not wanting to appear obvious on any security footage that could be analyzed by the local police, and still wanting to drop off the laptop whose hard drive she'd wiped, she went back upstairs and spent the next several minutes browsing the periodicals. She wasn't to know who her handoff was, nor was it her concern. All that mattered was that he or she got the information she'd left.

A group of school-age children, along with a few parents, entered the library, and she used the crowd to her advantage. She pulled the laptop out of the bag and carefully left it on the circulation desk as she exited the library. She couldn't keep the grin off her face. The man who was tracking her would be in for a big surprise, and no doubt infuriated. Ludmila loved aggravating her tails. It was part of her job description as far as she was concerned.

The only thing she hadn't figured out was where Portia DiNapoli was. She hadn't been back in the library, from what Ludmila saw, since the very day she'd almost been flattened by the train.

Outside the library, the air froze the hairs in her nostrils, not unlike Moscow or Saint Petersburg. While she was prepared to work in any climate, anywhere, she had to admit that the cold was her friend, the constant companion of her youth in the block-style apartment building, a holdover from the Soviet era. She'd missed out on it, the glory days of her country. But here in America, she had a chance to see how the system could really work, when ROC's plan to take over the domestic economy came to fruition. At its core was fortifying the influx, distribution and sale of heroin. She was determined to see it work out.

A homeless man sat inside a threshold and she stepped over his feet. And thought about it. She turned back.

"There's a homeless place for you, next block up."

The man shrugged and huddled more deeply into his ragged coat. Ludmila answered with her own shrug and continued walking.

She lit up a cigarette as she walked in the frozen winter twilight of Silver Valley. The smoke fit her disguise perfectly, but also calmed the adrenaline that annoyingly surged through her system. Portia DiNapoli had to go, the sooner the better. Ludmila needed one chance, one straight line of sight, and she'd take the woman out.

Ludmila never left a witness behind, even when what they'd actually seen and could recall for the authorities was questionable. She worked on a zero-risk belief system. It was what had earned her top rankings in the FSB, and ensured her spot as a trusted agent for Ivanov in ROC. And this skill she'd developed so carefully, so thoroughly, was what would allow her to disappear from the face of the earth, take a new identity and leave this life behind for good. All she had left to do was kill Portia DiNapoli.

It was so delicious to think of finally taking out the town librarian she wondered for a fleeting moment if she'd ever be able to stop it—the killing. There was power in taking life, and Ludmila loved having power over people.

Kyle remotely snapped several photos with the miniature camera he'd placed in his ski cap, positioned so that the torn material appeared as any other hole in the fabric and not sporting a lens. The activation button was the crown on the cheap-looking watch he wore.

He'd immediately known it was Markova by the way she tried just a little too hard to appear like an American teen. Markova was good, but not perfect. First, she'd missed him sitting by the front door of the library on her way in. And just now, he was certain she hadn't known it was him. If she had, he'd be fighting for his life or have had to kill her to keep his.

Markova was all about her mission, her survival. He

got it, because he was, too, except his efforts benefited society. Unlike ROC.

He'd called in to another TH agent working the case inside the building to check out the library—everywhere that Markova had walked. All they'd discovered was that the laptop had been left on the circulation desk. It was already on its way to TH headquarters for analysis, but there wouldn't be anything on it. A professional like Markova didn't make those kinds of mistakes, and besides, he knew she'd meant it as a slap.

The question was if she'd left something else somewhere else in the library. He'd change out of his disguise and go in during after-hours to search the place.

As night fell early and snow began to fall, he faced his other conundrum. How was he going to keep his hands off Portia when all he'd wanted, all he craved, since they'd been together, was to be with her again?

Portia didn't go stir-crazy during the first full week of her imposed exile at the mountain home, but by the end of week two, she was beyond antsy. She promised Kyle she'd stay in the house, but surely that had to extend to the immediate property. It was close to nightfall, but she had at least another twenty minutes of sufficient daylight to take a break from the gala planning.

Once outside, her head cleared and the open air immediately soothed her jagged edges. Kyle had checked in on her each day, about midday, then at night, where he'd dutifully slept in a guest room, while she slept in another. He'd not made a move to touch her since their cataclysmic sex the first day she'd been brought here.

And she'd refrained from touching him, too. It was

a silent agreement, as they didn't discuss it. She wondered if his reason was the same as hers, though. Kyle made it clear he was going back to California, which made a relationship with him a nonstarter. Her home was Silver Valley.

Although, in a moment of sheer boredom, she'd looked up open library positions in the northern part of the state, where he'd mentioned he was from. And just as quickly shut the screen down, because in the fantasy of a life with Kyle lay madness.

As she walked off the expansive back deck and onto the concrete patio below, she saw the large cover over a pool, and the surrounding woods appeared frosted with the snow that had begun to fall about an hour ago. According to the weather reports, a flat-out blizzard was headed into the Susquehanna and Cumberland Valley areas. Since Silver Valley was smack-dab in the middle of them, they expected up to three feet, maybe more, in less than twenty-four hours.

She knew it could get ugly outside, but right now it was perfect. The wind hadn't picked up yet and the snowflakes pinged off her parka. Holding out her mittened hands to capture them, she saw that they were tiny ice particles. Standing under the deck, watching nature sprinkle the sparkling snowflakes all about her, it was difficult to imagine she was here because her life was threatened.

Thank God for Annie, who'd talked to her endlessly on the phone these past two weeks. Otherwise being a shut-in would lead to insanity, at the least.

Footsteps sounded on the ground near her and she froze. Kyle always came in through the front door, which was upstairs, on the house's main living area.

He hadn't been on the deck over her head or she would have heard his firm, steady steps.

She shrank back against the house, forcing her breathing to still and her thoughts to focus. Who was here with her?

Chapter 12

Kyle spoke to Josh as he drove up to the house. In a few minutes, he'd be near Portia again. It was at once torture and relief. Relief to see her beautiful smile, know she was safe and unharmed. Torture to be as turned on as a man possibly could be and unable to do a darn thing about it.

"I just talked to Claudia, Kyle. The laptop was wiped, as you expected."

"Yup. It's Markova's way of letting us know she's a step ahead."

"But she's not. You saw her in the library, and the security footage verifies what you described." Josh's laugh sounded throughout the inside of the car, as Kyle used the hands-free phone. "You were spot-on about everything."

Kyle silently thanked Claudia for making sure the library's security feed had been linked to SVPD early in the surveillance operation. It exponentially cut their analysis time down.

"What about the other places she went? Tell me what you saw. I'm going back as soon as I check in on Portia, after the library closes." He couldn't inspect every inch of it as needed with patrons present.

"She walked by the literary fiction section, appeared to linger for a brief moment by the Russian books."

"Aren't you glad I told you where those were?" He poked at Josh, who'd been convinced ROC wasn't so nuanced. But he hadn't had to work against Russian FSB agents before. Kyle had.

"It just seems too obvious."

"And therefore classic. What did you see? Could you see her hands?"

"No, that's the problem. I see her reach up for maybe three seconds, that's it. If she put a piece of paper or a USB of any kind in there, it could be gone by now."

"Go over it again, and go through the next several minutes of footage for me. If you see someone go there, we have our transfer point." And the Silver Valley point of contact for ROC, besides Markova.

"Will do. Also, we just found out that there's definitely a large heroin shipment en route," Josh said with a sigh, which expressed his frustration. "It's the largest sent to the East Coast yet, and it's coming here, to Silver Valley."

They had to stop it. Neither man had to verbalize it.

"We're going to. Keep me posted and I'll check back with you after I get through the library."

"You know about the storm coming in, right?"

"I saw some messages on my phone." He had, but he'd been too busy, first working undercover at the library and then preoccupied with getting back here to check on Portia. He looked at his windshield wiper blades as he turned them off, pulling to a stop in the circular driveway.

"It's not just a storm, Kyle. They're expecting blizzard conditions by midnight, and it won't let up for as much as two days."

"So we need the information Markova left in the library tonight."

"Definitely."

"I'm on it." He disconnected as he killed the engine. It was six o'clock. The library closed in two hours. Enough time to grab a quick meal with Portia and get to the library and back in time for the storm. He did not want her alone at all, but especially during weather that Markova functioned exceptionally well in.

He pulled the couple of bags of groceries he'd brought out of the back and realized that they'd need more provisions to survive a few days, maybe even a week. This wasn't far enough north that they had snowplows standing by to promptly clear rural routes like the one that led to the mountain house. He'd make sure the snowmobile in the garage had enough fuel, and that there was propane for the backup generator.

As he stomped up to the front door, he sent up a thought of gratitude. One nice thing about such a fancy place was that it was set for any kind of weather.

"Hello!"

The greeting had been his usual way of letting Portia know he was here. He knew that he had a habit of stepping softly to avoid detection. A good thing when working undercover, but terrifying for someone like Portia who was alone in this huge house all day.

She didn't answer, and the first niggle of concern tugged at his gut. Portia might be in the shower, or the workout room in the basement. She'd made herself at home, utilizing every space and staying busy beyond her gala planning and the miniscule library work she did long-distance.

He dumped the bags on the island, where he noted she'd left her laptop open, a half-drank mug of tea next to it. He felt the cup—it was cold.

A worm of cold fear began to take root. *Nope, not going there.* She was fine.

But if she wasn't, if Markova had somehow found them, despite his evasion tactics, he couldn't run around shouting for Portia. He had to fight the instinct, not something he was used to. Normally he stayed cool under the toughest situations. But they hadn't involved Portia.

He silently walked to the French doors that led onto the enormous cedar deck, a full twenty feet above ground level. The structure held patio furniture, now covered with weatherproof protection, and a hot tub he vaguely remembered Josh mentioning.

No Portia.

But there were footprints leading to the steps that led to the concrete patio. It was impossible to peer between the slats, as they were laid tightly together. If Portia was down there, being held by Markova, he'd be walking into a trap from which he couldn't save Portia or himself.

Kyle quickly and silently retraced his steps back into the house and locked the French door behind him. He pulled his weapon as he ran back through the house, into the garage and then out the garage's side door. To his relief, there were no prints in the snow that had fallen between the house and the immediate line of trees. His weapon drawn, ready to fire, he pressed forward to the back, northwest corner of the house. Listening for scuffling, any vocalizations, he heard nothing.

He turned the corner with his .45 held in front, ready to fire at the first sign of Markova.

The space under the deck was pitch-dark, the last remaining daylight long gone. He'd not turned on the outside lights, but as he moved to the space farther under the deck, a motion detector light blazed blinding-white in his eyes. He heard a gasp and froze, blinking to regain his vision.

"Kyle!" Portia. Thank God.

"Where are you?" Damn the light.

"Why are you pointing a gun at me? I'm fine." He heard her steps, then she was at his side, away from where he pointed the gun. "Kyle."

Only when he looked into her eyes, allowed himself to accept that she was alone and safe, did he let out his breath. His vision returned and he scoured under the deck for anyone else.

"Kyle, I told you I'm alone. I came out to get a breath of fresh air. I'm so sorry if I worried you." She hugged herself. "Holy cannoli, you scared the heck out of me! I heard your footsteps but you weren't up on the deck, where I'd expect you to be if you came in and saw I was outside. I thought I was done for."

Kyle holstered his weapon and faced her. Snowflakes landed on her soft curls, the white sparkles contrasting with her brunette hair. "You've got a target between your eyes, Portia. Of course I was concerned."

"You seemed a lot more than 'concerned.'" She

made air quotes as her brows rose. "You need to be more careful, Kyle. For a minute there, I thought you cared."

He knew it was her nerves talking. He'd scared her, too, coming up on her like she was his target. "This isn't the time for this." Yet he didn't move. Didn't go anywhere, but instead stayed under the deck with her, where the ambient light from the motion detector allowed him to see her face without totally exposing them to anyone looking at the house.

"There was plenty of time earlier in the week." One side of her lush mouth curved up, and he couldn't take his gaze off the warmth in her eyes. Was it for him? Dare he hope it was?

"I'm not sorry for that, Portia. It was…fantastic. But I'm in the middle of a case. I can't be distracted. And at the end of it—"

"You're moving back to California. You already told me that." She stood her ground. He'd been about to say that he was an undercover law enforcement agent, she was a librarian, they lived in completely different worlds.

"That doesn't bother you?"

"What? That you're moving on? It's not my concern, is it?" She watched him in a way he understood. As if she were waiting until he couldn't take it anymore and admit that there was something deeper brewing between them than the ROC case or lust.

"It'd be your concern if you thought I'd change my mind."

"I'm not looking to change your mind, Kyle. And I know you're not trying to change me, either."

He wasn't, not at all. Because the woman in front

of him was far more than he'd ever dreamed existed. The real deal. The full package—for him.

"Aw, hell." Much against his personal vow to leave her alone, he had to have one more taste. Just a nip. He reached for her at the same instant she touched his face with her mittened hand. The rough texture of the wool scraped against his cheek, but he didn't feel any discomfort the minute his lips touched hers.

Portia's hand overshot Kyle's cheek and she used the momentum to wrap it around his head, to tug him close to her as their lips met. Her fright turned to molten desire as his tongue probed deep, filling her mouth with his taste, his need.

His hands roamed down her back, pulling her in close. The layers of clothing between them were too much. They'd avoided one another all week and it had proved too long. She could blame her emotions, being alternatively scared for her life and then so relieved to have Kyle's hard, reassuring form against her. But it didn't account for the taught tension that strung between them since they'd made love that first time, since she'd become aware of his presence in her life.

She kissed him with all she had. And never felt any less than fully reciprocated as he whispered sexy words against her lips, told her what he intended to do to her. What he wanted her to do to him.

"Kyle." More kissing.

"Mmm?" Another lick.

"There's a hot tub upstairs, on the deck." She fantasized all week about being in it with him, had considered asking him to join her, purely platonically.

But their connection would never be anything but very sexual, incredibly sensual.

"Let's go." He grabbed her hand and tugged her behind as he led them up the stairs. He stopped at the French door. "I have to go in and get a condom, but I locked this door when I saw you were gone." Lines etched around his eyes, the light of the great room spilling a soft yellow glow over them through the door's windows.

"I'm sorry I worried you."

"It seems I did the same to you." He kissed her hard, then smiled. "I can think of no better way to let go of it, can you?"

"No. Here's the key." She handed him the set of house keys that included the one to the back-deck door.

"You carried them with you." He stared at them.

"As you advised. I did listen when you talked to me about safety, you know."

He looked like he had more to say but instead unlocked the door. "I'll be right back. You coming in to warm up first?"

She laughed. "I'm not feeling any of this cold right now. I'll get the hot tub ready."

He disappeared into the house and she took the lid off the spa, watched the steaming water begin to bubble once she found the switches. The snowfall had picked up and was a steady douse of white, piling up on the deck railing and steps where they'd just walked. She quickly unzipped her jacket and walked to the door to strip out of all of her clothes before she made a beeline for the warm water.

Sinking into it was pure bliss. She'd managed to work out each day in the house's high-end gym room, but missed her runs. So she'd pushed it on the tread-mill and elliptical machine, which made her muscles complain a bit. The soothing vibration of the pulsing water was almost as good as—no, it came nowhere near to sex. Not with Kyle, at any rate.

She heard the door click and looked up to see him stride naked across the deck. Kyle's nude body wasn't unfamiliar to her, yet to see his starkly masculine form, underscored by his raging erection, shot a bolt of pure lust through her. If it were any more tangible, the connection she felt to this man would part the water of the hot tub, cause the deck to quake. But she'd settle for making love to him again.

"You didn't waste any time, I see." The flash of his teeth indicated his pleasure as he simultaneously dropped the house keys and a strip of condoms on the deck next to the tub and himself into the water.

Portia couldn't speak. Mesmerized by how his broad shoulders dipped below the water, rivulets running over and down his skin as the steam wove around them, kept her from being able to do anything but stare. Her limbs had no problem reacting, however, as she found herself moving next to him, her fingers running across his skin, cupping his face.

"Where did you come from, Kyle?" She waited for his silver eyes to focus on her, saw the same arousal she enjoyed. And something deeper. Was it the sense of timelessness to their relationship that she felt?

"Snowflakes are sticking to your eyelashes." He held her face, too, as they knelt in the steaming water, keeping it shoulder level to stay warm as the storm intensified around them. When he lowered his head to kiss her, she met him halfway. As under the deck, their need exploded into a desire so fierce that Portia thought she'd never breathe again.

"Oh, Kyle, this is so much." She gasped out the words, unable to focus as his lips landed on her throat and his hands cupped her breasts. He suckled on one nipple, then the other, and as the frozen air hit her skin, it only made her hotter, more desperate to have him inside her.

"Patience, Portia." His mouth came back to hers and she expected he'd reach for the condoms, make short work of foreplay as they both so clearly wanted the ultimate connection. But he instead reached between her legs under the water and stroked her folds with his fingers. Before she got used to the intense sensuality he shoved one, two fingers inside her and caressed the deepest part of her. His caresses bespoke expertise, but so much more. She had no time to figure it out as an orgasm crested and took her out of herself. The only concrete sensation was the feel of Kyle's muscular shoulders under her hands as she held on to him, used him as an anchor in the turbulent onslaught of pleasure. Her cries escaped her throat with no effort from her, and she thought she'd immediately find an apartment to rent that had a hot tub on the deck when this was all over.

"Like that?" Breath from his sexy laugh tickled where he kissed her on her temple. Kyle nudged her cheek with his nose until their lips met again. As she kissed him, she reached for his erection, gripping him firmly and stroking with unquestionable intent.

"Babe." Kyle sat back on the spa's underwater bench and closed his eyes, his head leaned back against the edge as she worked her hands on him, straddled him.

Her body felt weightless, yet she'd never felt more em-powered, been more aware of how her actions affected another human being.

But it wasn't just another human being or man—it was Kyle.

She kissed him as she moved her hand over his shaft and was rewarded with an open, fully exposed kiss that communicated his total need, total trust in her. His erection hardened further, a feat she'd have thought impossible.

His hands were on her shoulders and he gently pushed her away, his eyes heavy with lust. "Careful or it'll be over before we get to the best part, babe."

She laughed softly as he reached for the condoms, tore one off and stood on the spa bench. Only his knees were underwater, and she was transfixed by the water sluicing down his powerful thighs as snow pelted his chest. Kyle had huge, strong hands and even so his erection seemed too big for them. She swallowed, her mouth wanting something that would have to wait for another time.

Once he donned the protection, he sank back down and in one fluid movement pulled her, straddle-style, onto him, pelvis-to-pelvis. Maintaining eye contact, his hands gripped her hips, moved to her buttocks as he guided her over him, onto him, positioned himself at her entrance. The moment she closed her eyes, parted her lips in a sigh of want, he thrust into her, making her already sensitive sex on fire with need.

"Kyle!" She grasped his wrists, which were be-hind her back, and tilted her head to the snow-filled sky as he pumped into her with complete abandon, as she moved over him and pushed back with a ferocity that matched his. They may have been like that for an hour or a minute—it didn't matter, as time never did between them. But their connection, the thing that mattered very much, propelled them to the obvious conclusion as they both reached their releases at the same time, their cries of satisfaction muffled only by the now roaring wind.

Afterward she remained on top of him on the bench as the water bubbled and gently lapped around them. The snowfall had turned into a full-fledged blizzard as the wind drove the flakes into her skin, but she was more attune to Kyle's skin against hers, his breath returning to normal along with hers.

Inexplicably, she'd found her match in the undercover agent she'd known for barely two weeks.

Chapter 13

Kyle left Portia within the hour, as darkness was complete and he was fighting against the snowstorm to get to the library, then return to the country estate before the roads became impassable.

At least this time he didn't have to dress as anyone but an undercover agent with much needed protection from the cold. And he'd accepted Portia's work keys, saving him a trip to Josh's desk at SVPD. Since they coordinated every aspect of the case, they'd agreed to leave most of what they'd need at SVPD. The less Kyle or any agent was seen going in and out of the actual TH headquarters, the better.

Certain he hadn't been followed, he parked his truck in the diner parking lot. There were only half a dozen cars as compared to the usual twenty or so. And the streets and sidewalks were deserted, save for a few intrepid souls scurrying into the local convenience pharmacy, no doubt to get that last loaf of bread or carton of milk. There were plenty of full-size grocery stores on the main pike, but the drugstore, with its few shelves of foodstuffs, was all the people who lived in the downtown area had within walking distance. Kyle knew it well, as he'd subsisted on plenty of its supplies these past weeks.

Maybe that was why he was reacting so intensely to Portia. Not the sex part, which would be out of this world with her no matter what, but the emotional intimacy. The time he was spending with her at that beautiful house, in the perfect natural setting, was the most he'd had to just *be* since he didn't know when. He'd been on this Silver Valley ROC assignment for a couple of months, but it was the culmination of years of following the criminal organization and its key players. He knew he wasn't alone in this, which made it more frustrating that LEA hadn't succeeded in toppling the nefarious empire yet.

As he entered the library through a side entrance, unseen from the front and not in view of the back parking lot, he tried to clear his mind, open his senses to whatever evidence might be available. But Portia's smile, her luminous eyes, the warmth of her, never left him.

He supposed he should get used to it. He imagined she was going to stay with him for a long while, all the way to California and the future he'd counted on for so long.

Whoa. He froze at the bottom of the library stairwell. This was the problem with accepting that he couldn't get a woman out of his soul. His imagination led him to believe she'd always be with him, anywhere he went.

Portia wasn't leaving Silver Valley, and he sure as hell wasn't staying anywhere on the East Coast.

For now, he had a job to do. He made his way to the international fiction section and read the very familiar Russian Literature label at the base of the metal shelf. Replacing his winter gloves with latex, he quickly removed each volume, shaking the books in case a note had been left inside and thumbing through the pages, opening each work to make sure it was a book and did not contain a concealed hiding place. He'd gotten through at least two dozen novels, from Chekhov to Dostoyevsky, when he noticed the small object at the back of the shelf. It had been painted a cream color to blend in with the metal surface and his gut tightened. As he plucked it up with his fingers, he saw immediately that it was a USB. Or at least was meant to look like one. He could do nothing with it until it was back at SVPD, the only "safe" place to take it. When working against the kind of intelligent criminals he did, he had to always assume the worst. Which meant he assumed that the USB port could in actuality be a GPS tracking device, or other technology that could reveal his location.

He placed the device in a plastic evidence bag and pocketed it. Before he left, he continued his methodical search through each book, then replaced them, leaving them as he'd found them. No sense making extra work for the staff, or drawing unneeded attention to the Russian Literature section.

He pulled his phone out to text Josh, so that he could arrive at the library in an SVPD vehicle to retrieve the

USB stick. The face was lit up with weather warnings that urged residents to remain in place at home for the next forty-eight hours.

Two days of storm? It should concern him that the operation would be stymied for that long, or that ROC might still somehow get their heroin shipment delivered under the cover of blinding snow. Instead, he experienced a surge of anticipation. He'd get to be with Portia for two full days.

So much for keeping her at a safe distance.

She watched through the hole she'd rubbed out of the condensation on the diner window as the Silver Valley Police car pulled up and around the diner parking lot, saw it park next to the truck she'd noticed was often in the same spot. One thing none of them expected was that she'd take a job as a waitress, which allowed her to piece together who was who in this simple American town.

The man she'd fought with, thought about killing in the courtyard behind the homeless place, was in the truck. She was certain it was him—he'd come in here for coffee one time when she was on shift. She always took the night shift, as her real job required her to do all ROC duties in full daylight. She was the best at undercover work and they needed her where their other people couldn't operate. So the night, the darkness, was left to the amateurs, as far as she was concerned.

It was an amateur who'd not received the information she'd left in the library, not like he was supposed to. So it sat for another day, until tomorrow, when she'd have to make certain it was picked up. Otherwise Ivanov would have her head on the chopping block. Ivanov didn't like it when anyone screwed up, and this was a costly operation. She'd heard him tell his number two, a new man, since too many others had been either killed or incarcerated, that the sales from the heroin would take ROC to an operating value worth more than many governments.

It didn't matter to her, once this mission was complete. She'd have her new identity, and begin a new life somewhere else, far from this.

As the police officer and other man spoke inside the truck, she couldn't see their lips, couldn't begin to guess what it was about. But she knew the man was at least an undercover cop. Based on his hand-to-hand combat skills, he was former military or FBI, probably both. No matter. All she wanted from him now was to get to the librarian. He had personal interest in the woman or he wouldn't have worked so hard to keep Ludmila from her.

"Melissa, can you take care of table three?" Bob, her clueless night manager, addressed her by the pseudonym she'd carefully generated.

"Sure thing, boss." She prided herself on her faultless American accent, the red wig she wore, the way she walked just like the locals did. Without the constant sense of being followed that most Russians lived with each day. It was something she always lived with, because she knew ROC would cut her from the payroll the minute she was no longer needed. She wouldn't just lose a paycheck, though, but her life. Once an ROC operative, always ROC. There was no such thing as quitting or leaving the group. Which was why she'd planned her disappearance so thoroughly.

* * *

Kyle and Josh sat at the Formica-topped dinette and bantered about the storm as the waitress approached. It was never smart to talk business anywhere but SVPD or TH headquarters, as they didn't know who could be listening.

"Can I get you something to drink?" The redhead's eyes didn't meet his and Kyle figured she wanted to be home for the storm, not taking care of a cop and his buddy in the midst of it.

"I'll have a coffee, black." He'd be up most of the night anyway, sorting through the data he'd downloaded onto his portable laptop in the truck.

"Same." Josh waited for the waitress to be out of earshot. "I'll get the stick to TH tomorrow for analysis. From what you just downloaded, it seems to me it's a normal old USB stick, though." Josh had encouraged Kyle to download whatever was on it.

"I don't think it's anything but a digital storage device, Josh. Which makes me want to put it back on the shelf. We'll catch the handoff."

"True." Josh sat back to give the waitress room to place his coffee cup. He watched her as she walked away. "I don't recognize her. Do you? Not that I know every server in here, but most at least look familiar."

"No. And yes, I'm thinking what you're thinking, but unless she's slapped a bug under the table, she can't hear us."

They both laughed. Kyle knew that as a mission drew to its successful end, tensions made it easy to be paranoid.

"The ROC operatives around here have gotten more

sophisticated, that's for sure. I wouldn't put it past them to have spotters in this diner, the coffeehouse down the road, maybe even the library." Josh's concern echoed Kyle's thoughts.

"They most likely do, but not in the library. There haven't been any new hires there in six months, and they began this particular branch of business only in the last two."

Neither of them spoke for a few minutes, lost in their thoughts.

"How long do you think it'll take you to figure out what's going on with the data?" Josh's voice was quiet, concern in his tone.

"I'll figure it out pretty quickly. Many of the ROC thugs use different idioms, but I've had training in most. Fortunately, they're not usually big on making their directives complicated."

"But they don't usually go to such extremes with their communications, either."

"True." Kyle finished his coffee. "I've got an information technology expert on hand, though. She'll see whatever I miss."

Josh slammed his cup down. "Portia's not law enforcement of any kind, Kyle."

"I hear you. But the information isn't classified on its own, you know. And if she can make it go faster, why not?"

Josh's face brightened. "One thing Portia enjoys is helping out. From what Annie's been telling me, Portia's bored to tears out there."

"She seems to keep herself busy, though. She's still

planning the gala." He noticed the waitress heading back to pour refills. Had she heard him say anything?

They continued their conversation after she walked away.

"Do you think she'll be able to attend it?"

"I'll make sure of it." He hadn't realized it until he'd said it aloud, but he was in fact going to get Portia to that gala if he had to take her himself. He'd worry about it looking too much like a date later.

Portia had never spent so much time without contact with other human beings in her life. And the one person she had access to, Kyle, was the very man she needed to protect herself from.

Sometimes life just wasn't fair. She walked around the house and checked every egress point as Kyle had shown her, making sure the doors and windows were secure. There was no telling when he'd be back, and she needed to get some rest. She had one week until the gala and just as much work to accomplish. It was easier when she was at the library, as she could see at a glance who'd dropped off auction items as they came in. As it was, she had to rely on her staff to email her, and since the gala was a charity event, it didn't trump daily operations. The extra cold winter had a booming effect on library patronage, as reading and watching DVDs were two cold-weather favorites.

As she checked the fasteners on a stair-landing window, she saw headlights approach down the long drive. Fear snuck around her carefully constructed serenity, reminded her that she'd almost died not only on the train tracks but had been targeted by the ROC woman at one of her safest places—the homeless shelter.

Please let it be Kyle. She repeated the mantra, not stopping until she recognized his shape as he got out of the same truck he'd driven her back here in. Relief was short-lived, however, as she watched through the curtain of wind-driven snow and saw him open his back door and pull out several objects. She prayed it was the snow, but the shape of one of them was undeniable.

Why had Kyle brought weapons to the house? She knew he carried a pistol, expected him to always have it on his person. He was law enforcement; it was part of his job. But if what she watched him carry toward the house were indeed a rifle and possibly other firearms, what did he expect to do with them?

She ran down the stairs to the front door and threw it open just as she heard the scratch of his key.

Kyle's face was lit by the foyer light that spilled from behind her. His expression barely registered surprise but she did note something more welcoming—pleasure?

"Here." He didn't greet her except to shove one of the objects at her, which she accepted. Her hands closed around a long barrel, confirming her suspicions.

"What are you doing, bringing these guns out here?" She had to shout over the roar of the wind. How he'd made it back from town safely was beyond her.

"Get in the house." He didn't have to shout—his voice sliced through the high pitch of the wind with little effort. And wrapped around her a little too tightly.

"I don't take orders from you, Kyle." Still, she backed up so that he could come in. He stomped his snow-covered boots on the front porch, and then again after he'd shut the door behind him, locking it with purpose. When he turned to face her, he shoved his hood back and took off his ski cap. His eyes found hers and he waited to make sure he had her attention. As if she'd ever be able to ignore him.

"I meant to tell you about these earlier. We're up against a cold-blooded assassin here. She won't hesitate to kill you. You don't have to like having weapons in the house, but right now we don't have a choice."

Portia's throat constricted against the retort she'd planned to hurl at him, to remind him that she was here willingly but her cooperation stopped short of housing an arsenal of killing machines. Unbidden tears flooded her vision and when she blinked, huge drops fell and ran down her cheeks.

"When you put it like that..." She gulped, steeled her spine. "I've never fired a gun before, but I'm sure you can show me how."

Her stomach sank at the prospect but she was determined to help where she could. If keeping herself safe helped Kyle spend more time on his work, and hastened the capture of ROC's major players, then so be it.

Kyle watched as her conflict played out in her expression. He fought his hands as they itched to drop the weapons and wipe away Portia's tears. To kiss her until she forgot her life was at risk.

But that wasn't what a good protector did. And he was her protector, even if it was a self-assignment.

"Let me get my coat off, and then we'll go through this. I thought you'd be asleep by now."

"I did, too, but the wind is louder than I've ever heard it. And I've lived—"

"Here your entire life. I know." He gave her what he hoped was a reassuring smile. "You've told me, and it's one of your many admirable traits." He hung his parka on the hooks just inside the door.

"Why is that?"

"You could have gone anywhere in the world, still could, but you brought your talents back to Silver Valley after you graduated."

Doubt clouded her eyes. "I keep forgetting that you know everything about me."

"Not everything, just the highlights of your resume. And maybe a little more." Like her birthday, the fact she'd dated a dirtbag politician last year and, much to his great gratitude, dropped the dude when she'd discovered he was a wanderer.

They walked to the kitchen, where he made use of the oversize island and nodded for her to set down the rifle, while he laid down two handguns, his backpack and his personal .45.

"None of these have any ammunition in them yet, that's in my backpack, but I'm going to show you how to check to make sure the chambers are clear and how to use each one. We'll do it in the morning, when you're most alert."

"Fair enough." He loved the steel in her voice. Portia was courageous if nothing else, and she was a lot else. In fact, she could easily become everything to the right man.

It can't be you.

"I'm going to stay up for a while, going through some evidence. I can work in the basement rec area if you need me to."

"Not at all. I don't hear much in my room, unless I walk out onto the balcony, and there won't be any of that tonight."

At the mention of the private deck, his jaw tightened. There weren't any stairs attached, and it was two stories up from the ground that sloped away, as the house was built halfway up a mountain. But still, someone trained in rock climbing or rappelling, or a highly trained burglar, could use it as an entrance point. He mentally saw how he'd do it, with the right equipment. How he'd scale the house wall with the aid of a rope he'd fasten to the deck with one carefully aimed throw. But instead of himself, he saw Ludmila Markova, her profile.

And his insides froze.

"Kyle, what's wrong?"

"Son of a bitch." Quickly he told Portia about the waitress at the diner. "I thought something was unusual about her, but she didn't have an accent and she was in a perfect disguise. But the profile—I know it was her."

"Can I know her name?"

He looked at her, weighed the risks. "Ludmila Markova is the name I have, who she was when she immigrated to the US almost three years ago. She's been working for ROC ever since, under many aliases." So many that he couldn't be certain of all the intelligence TH had on her. Random reports could mean something but could also be throwaway, useless information that was meant to distract American law enforcement.

"Ludmila Markova." Portia leaned her hip on the island. "She sounds like a Russian spy."

"As she was trained to be, most likely. But she's here now, and our problem until we figure out what she's protecting." He pulled his laptop from his backpack. "I have hundreds of pages of spreadsheets loaded on my computer that I'm going to spend the night looking at."

"I'd love to help if you'd like. I don't see myself being able to sleep through this." At that instant a huge gust hit the house and he felt the shudders vibrate through the hardwood floor under his stockinged feet.

Portia's eyes widened. "That had to be a seventy-mile-an-hour gust, at least, to make this big place feel it."

Kyle agreed. The house was the best money could build and he wouldn't have expected it to feel the effects of the storm at all.

As they stood in the kitchen, gazes locked, he felt the heat he'd been fighting return as strongly as the raging snowstorm. Portia felt it, too, and as he wavered between leaning in and kissing her or running down to the basement to keep them both safe from whatever it was that they shared, the lights flickered. Once, twice and then they were plunged into total darkness.

"Kyle?"

"Yeah?"

"Please tell me a house this fancy has a generator somewhere."

Chapter 14

Kyle used the flashlight he kept in his backpack to find and start up the generator, located along one side of the sprawling house. Portia was relieved to know she'd still have access to Wi-Fi and her library system. Although if the rest of Silver Valley lost power, it was a moot point. The library had a generator but it was minimal, existing only to keep the emergency lights on. The computers and server that were the gateway to her work wouldn't be available.

"I have an extra battery charger in my room. I keep it in my bag. It has enough power to restart a dead car battery," she said as she scoured the columns of the spreadsheets on Kyle's laptop. "We don't have to worry about how long this takes."

They sat next to one another at the dining room table, she wrapped in a down throw and he in sweatpants and a long-sleeved thermal shirt, with a flannel shirt as an added layer. The house generator could handle the heating system but not at the constant rate needed to keep up with the plummeting temperatures.

"I'm sure we'll need it. It's going to take days to get through this information." She heard the despair in his voice.

"To summarize, you think that there's a heroin shipment inbound and it's going to be collected here, in Silver Valley?"

"Yes. We know it's inbound but we're not sure when or how. In the past, ROC has used shipping containers, mostly those on long-haul trucks instead of trains. They like to hide the drugs in with random goods being shipped here on a regular basis. Then they take out the truck driver and get the illicit drugs. We've found traces in everything from major appliance to kitty litter shipments."

"Okay. So we need to take a look at these spreadsheets and keep the big picture in mind. Figure out the commonalities, and if we can find a delivery timetable."

"Portia."

She looked up from his laptop. His eyes were on her, his expression soft. "What?"

"I did run it by Claudia to make sure I have the okay for you to see this information. But it isn't your job, babe. I've got it."

"Apparently you don't 'have' it, or you wouldn't look like you're about to pull your hair out." She ran her fingers through his hair and gave him a sound kiss on the lips, surprising herself with how easy it was to partner with this man. "And you have lovely hair, so let's get to it, shall we?"

* * *

"It was insane to think you could ever do this on your own, Kyle. You're looking for a needle in a haystack, you know." Portia spoke as if she were an expert at intelligence analysis, and Kyle's deadpan expression made her giggle.

"Um, yeah. That's why I got permission from Claudia to have you help me with this."

"At least the snowstorm will keep the trains from running, so that buys you some time, right?"

He nodded, his face taut with concentration in the light of the laptop screen.

"Wait—what did you say about a train?" His five o'clock shadow had turned into two-in-the-morning sexy scruff and she longed to touch it. To lick it. Portia blinked, and not just to keep the spreadsheets from blurring. She leaned back from the display, put some inches between her and Kyle.

"You're looking at the products carried on trains that pass through central Pennsylvania, and thus Silver Valley."

"How do you know this, from just looking at these spreadsheets?" His skepticism was punctuated by fatigue.

"You're in luck, Agent King. I happen to have a very good working knowledge of the resources and consumer goods that come in and through Silver Valley, as the graduating senior high school class participated in a nationwide survey on local economies."

"And?"

"These spreadsheets are set up in exactly the same way. Except instead of having every single train, container load and where it's from, this lists what each container will have." She skimmed over the countless processed food, raw grain and other miscellaneous commodities. "We know they're including their heroin shipment in with regular goods, but it won't all be on one train. Which is smart, when you think of it. This way, if they get caught, they won't lose it all."

Kyle's expression morphed to reflect his enthusiasm. "Can you tell which trains will have the drugs in them?"

Portia stared at the data, then smiled. "For sure. If you look at this column, it's the pounds per container of whichever good is being shipped. This column next to it, though, doesn't have a header like the others." She pointed at the container rows, and then the train, time of arrival, gross weight and commercial value columns. "This column header has a summation sign, and look at the numbers—they're all close to the same amount. The rows with summation numbers match certain trains."

"Ten kilos." Kyle's eyes flashed as he scrolled through the long list, pages long, in fact, of the shipments. "If they're adding ten kilos of pure heroin to each of these containers as marked, then it looks like…" He scrolled through the pages of lists. She sat quietly next to him, thinking about whom they could contact at the train depot and the other industry leaders for where the tracks ran. "That's a shipment of just over eleven million, street value."

"And that's just one." She couldn't keep from thinking about Lani and how her OD was just an inconsequential statistic to ROC, meaningless to the drug runners and dealers, except that it meant one less user to give them money. She felt Kyle's gaze on hers and looked at him. "I lost a high school classmate, someone I kept in touch with up until two or so years ago, to an OD. Her heroin dose had been laced with fentanyl."

"I know—Annie knew her, too, right? Claudia told me. I'm sorry, Portia. I have a former Marine buddy from the war who gave in to it, too." Quiet words of compassion that didn't match his tough-guy demeanor. Another reason to fall so damn hard for Kyle.

"I'm sorry for your loss, too." She sighed. "It's all over the news as an epidemic. It shouldn't be a surprise to anyone how deeply entrenched opioid addiction is in our culture. And yet..."

"And yet it still leaves a hole in your gut?" He looked at her with complete comprehension. "Yeah, I get it, believe me."

"Kyle."

"Hmm?" He was scribbling on a notepad with a tiny pencil as he scrolled through the data.

"I will do whatever I can to help you catch these awful people."

"I appreciate that, but you've already done it. It would have taken me hours to figure out this is a train manifest."

"You can thank Silver Valley High and their research assignments." She smiled at the memory of when she'd first learned how to use a spreadsheet.

The power from the generator flickered, indicated by the warning alarm from the refrigerator that the power had gone out.

"Kyle, I think we should back up all of this to the cloud ASAP, while there's still a working generator to keep the Wi-Fi stable."

"I'm on it." The circling symbol in the middle of the

screen confirmed his claim. As they sat there, Portia realized ROC was waiting it out now, too. No trains were moving anywhere from Virginia up through Maine. For all they knew, the drugs could be offloaded in another town or state, far from the madness that was bound to be Silver Valley while the snowstorm raged.

"This is very specific, Kyle. I'd imagine if you are able to compare these with the bills of loading from the matching corporations and the railroad, you'll figure out the dates of the first deliveries."

"I'll pass what we—what you—figured out to Josh as soon as this backup is done." He looked relieved.

"Could it be this simple?"

His eyes widened slightly. "What's that?"

"That you capture the shipment, prevent the bad guys from getting drugs into the hands of users and in turn apprehend Markova?"

A soft smile etched in his handsome face. "It could be." He didn't say anything more and she didn't press it. It made sense that he'd seen so much that she only could imagine, or read about in a spy novel.

"And that's that." He clicked the spreadsheets back open, the digital backup finished. "I'd be happier with a hard copy, but this will do."

"There's a printer in the home office, and if you have the right cable, we can make it happen. The Wi-Fi's out, so we can't do it wirelessly, but the old-fashioned way works."

"Good idea." Within minutes they'd hauled the printer from the office, plugged it into a working outlet and attached his laptop. Page after page printed, making the dark intent of ROC undeniable.

As the last pages printed, she caught Kyle fighting to keep his eyes open.

"Since we seem to have a bit of a reprieve thanks to the storm, I'd suggest we get some rest. The last reports indicate we'll be stuck here for at least the next two days."

"I can't risk missing something." His frown deepened.

She closed the laptop, plunging them into darkness, save for the gas fireplace, which they'd left on to give the living area some heat since the furnace wasn't keeping up with the cold.

"You stand a better chance of overlooking an important detail because you're exhausted." She stood up and carried the laptop to the coffee table, where she had her portable charger. "I'll plug this in so it's ready to roll in the morning."

"I don't know if I can sleep, Portia. The storm could mask an intruder." He'd walked up to the fireplace, where he stood and leaned against the mantel, looking into the flames.

"It could, but did you see the same weather report I did? The gusts are up to seventy-five miles an hour, and look out the window—visibility is what, a foot or less? The governor's declared a state of emergency for the entire state, as has New Jersey and New York. Anyone who ventures outside is subject to arrest. I know I'm not law enforcement but it seems to me that if I were working for ROC, I'd keep a very low profile. Going out now is too risky. No matter how trained they are."

There. That should mollify him. She watched the shadows flick across his face.

"Markova is driven by a need to win. To her, murdering someone in cold blood means nothing if it gets her the prize. Right now her goal is to make sure ROC's plans to distribute heroin through Silver Valley remain intact. She's not going to allow anything to screw it up, including a possible witness. And she won't stop until she knows you're silenced."

Kyle didn't have to tell her how she'd be silenced. By death. Portia knew the woman she was just a little over two weeks ago would have balked at the thought of being targeted by a trained assassin. That woman had changed, though, had faced death twice, survived and also met a once-in-a-lifetime man. A man she couldn't claim, no matter how much she wanted to. They were two different types of people, she and Kyle. He needed to be on the go, constantly in the midst of a mission that somehow involved him saving the world.

All Portia wanted was to make the world more livable. In her library career, she opened worlds to people through books, film, the internet. Her community service work made life a little easier for those who struggled, she hoped.

And she wanted to get back to her life as soon as she could, wanted Kyle and all the involved LEAs to take Markova and any of her pals off the streets. But as she stared at the same flames and Kyle, Portia realized she wasn't afraid. Next to Kyle, she felt invincible, able to tackle anything.

Although the thought of using a gun against any living thing still troubled her, she knew that she'd do what she had to do to stay alive.

"I think it's okay to sleep now. Do another check of the inside perimeter if you want, but I need to get some sleep."

Kyle's gaze sought hers in the dim light and she read weariness, fatigue in the silver depths. "I'll do just that. You haven't considered something else, Portia."

"What now?"

"The house is going to be damned cold once we shut down the fireplace—we can't keep it going all night, if we want the heater to stay decently powered."

She'd seen the thermostat—even with the heater going full blast, the inside temperature of the house was well below a comfortable room setting. "So you want to conserve body heat together? How gallant of you."

He laughed and the warmth that spread through her was all she needed. Nothing delighted her more than to see the serious agent he was 24/7 lighten up.

"It's in my job description."

"Being naked with a civilian?"

He sobered. "No. Not naked. We'll wear our pajamas." His focus on the mission was back full-force.

She scoffed in an effort to help him chill. "Do you even have sleepwear?" She hadn't seen him in anything but his work clothes and naked.

"I have long underwear. It's the only thing that made it bearable to do the long stakeouts I've had to."

Portia felt stupid that she hadn't considered something as simple as long underwear as part of his gear. "I thought you were literally freezing your butt off on the streets, in that awful homeless disguise. By 'awful' I mean it looks really, really authentic."

"Thank you. I appreciate that from you. You'd know right away if someone was a poser in the shelter, I'm sure."

"We've had a few, for sure. One couple dragged their poor kids in with them, said they'd been evicted by an unreasonable landlord."

"And?"

"They'd been evicted, all right, for making meth in the living room. It was a miracle the kids were still healthy enough to walk in with them. The neglect, it—" She broke off, suddenly overcome by tears. "Geez, I'm not usually this emotional."

"You've been under a lot of stress."

"Trust me, there's nothing stressful about this house. And I have all the time I want to work on the gala, so it's been kind of a win-win that way."

"But you're isolated, away from the people and town you thrive on." Kyle rubbed his scruff, shut the fireplace down with one flick of the switch. "Let's do this. We'll use your bed, as it's bigger."

"And has the balcony. So we can escape if we have to. And you can make sure no one climbs onto it. If they do, you'll take care of it then and there. Am I right?"

She couldn't see his face but swore she felt his grin. "You always are." His voice was closer. "Can you follow me back?"

"Yes." She'd follow him anywhere. She'd even looked up the town in California where he'd mentioned he'd grown up. Her job as an information specialist added to her natural curiosity about things in general. Where Kyle was concerned, it could quickly become an obsession. He still hadn't solved the ROC case, Markova remained at large, Portia still had a target on her head, and yet she already felt the pain his departure would leave in its wake.

So much for keeping her defenses up.

* * *

Kyle slid into the bed next to Portia right after he re-checked every single ingress and egress route the large home had to offer. It was a sturdy enough building but even the custom slate roof tiles sounded as though they creaked in the gale-force winds. It was the wind bar-reling through the eaves, and the way it gusseted the large expanses of lumber and river stone that made up the edifice. He'd been through some dicey weather sit-uations during his military and Trail Hiker time, but this was his first full-fledged blizzard.

He knew it wasn't Markova's. The ROC operative had the advantage of growing up in Russia, where to-night's storm wouldn't have been unfamiliar. Kyle took solace in the fact that Markova was on his turf now, and one thing he knew for sure was that the woman wouldn't be able to just take out Portia DiNapoli. Mar-kova would want to ask Portia how much she knew about him, including whom he worked for. Before she killed Portia.

He wanted Markova to know with zero doubt that he was as dedicated as she. He'd pull a trigger when-ever he had to, to stop the threat she brought.

Portia had fallen into a deep slumber—if her light snores were any indication. He watched her sleep for a bit, the soft glow of a night-light his only way to see. True to what he'd promised, he stripped down to his long johns and kept to his side of the bed once in it. Aww, what the hay. He wrapped his arm around her slumbering form and pulled her back up against his front, noting that she, too, was in long-sleeved paja-mas with full-length bottoms.

It was impossible to stop the flood of memories at

the nearness of her, the scent of her hair and skin. He inhaled deeply, then forced his eyes shut. The sooner he could drift off, the better for both of them. He had to keep her safe and she was right—this portion of the storm gave them the most protection. The greatest chance to play house would be another perspective, but he reeled his musings back from the danger zone.

He was Portia's protector, and the agent on the case that had the potential to stop ROC in its tracks. Or at least on the train tracks, with the heroin shipment intact and out of the hands of potential users. And victims.

He closed his eyes again, tried to let the constant howl of the wind and the snow battering the house soothe him.

Because if he couldn't sleep, he wasn't sure he'd be able to resist his body's insatiable need for Portia.

Chapter 15

Portia slept deeply, awaking to a soft sound that didn't match the rhythm of the wind.

Kyle.

He snored softly next to her, his body warm and hard against hers. She'd moved to her back and he lay on his side, his arm across her waist, his face snuggled into her shoulder. She slowly stretched, pointing and flexing her toes, allowing reality to sink back in.

Someone wanted to kill her. It made her think about how comfortable her life had been before, how naive she'd been, in many ways, to go about her business and not even consider what others sacrificed so that she could live in a relatively safe town.

Until ROC showed up. But as she thought about it, Silver Valley had faced its demons these past few years. A cult had almost infiltrated the town, its obsessed leader trying to take several innocent children down with him. Fortunately SVPD had stopped them. With a start, she acknowledged that Trail Hikers must have been a part of that, too.

And now she knew TH was actively fighting ROC, and had no doubt played a big role in the recent apprehension of several criminals involved in a human trafficking scheme. Not wanting to wake him, she inched out of Kyle's hold, reaching for the floor with her bare feet. The contrast of the cold air with the warmth she was leaving made her have to force herself to get out of the bed.

"Where you goin'?" His arm tightened around her waist and she hung in limbo, one toe on the throw rug next to the bed frame as her leg dangled.

"I thought I'd make coffee, get another look at the spreadsheets." Since he was awake, she reached for her phone, still charged. Using her cellular connection, she checked the weather reports. And groaned.

"What?" He was propped on his elbow, watching her. She loved the energy he gave off when he did this, making her feel like she was the only woman in the world, and the most beautiful.

"Four feet have fallen already, with up to another foot expected. The below-zero temperatures are going to make for up to ten-foot drifts. And it's going to last for at least another two days."

Two days stuck in the house she'd been basically exiled to didn't seem so bad, not with Kyle next to her.

"Put your phone away, Portia, and get naked." His huge hand playfully batted at hers. As soon as her phone hit the nightstand, he pulled her ass up against his pelvis.

"Oh." His unclothed erection pressed insistently against her cheeks. "You're fully awake, I'd say." She turned onto her back and looked at him. His silver eyes shone through slits and his nostrils flared. "I thought we were trying to keep our distance. To be professional."

"That was before we survived a night in a blizzard together." He leaned in but remained a breath away from her lips, allowing her to make the choice. It was going to hurt like hell when he left town, but her regret would be even deeper if she didn't make the most of the present. With Kyle.

"It's a good idea to maintain a good working relationship, right? Since we're going to be stuck together for at least another forty-eight hours."

"Kiss me, babe."

She pulled his head down and let his mouth work its magic. In the morning light, which was made paler by the storm's blocking of the sun, she reveled in every touch, every caress as he took his time, kissing her until she was breathless, and then moving his mouth to her throat, her breasts, her stomach, making her quiver with want at each juncture. As he gently sucked on the skin inside her thighs, her need rose and she sat up, pushing him onto his back.

"Let me make you feel just as good, Kyle."

"Babe." He actually looked pained, as if going down on her had been all he'd ever wanted to do. Something deep and lasting tugged inside her but she didn't want to take any time or space away from right here, right now.

She pushed on his shoulders, made him lie back and mirrored what he'd done to her, not stopping when she got to the dip of his belly button in his taut, chiseled abs. Her tongue led the way down the hair that led to his erection, hot and hard. For her.

It was so easy to make love to Kyle. As she took him in her mouth, heard his gasp, inhaled his very essence, she'd never been more complete. This was what a true partnership was about. Not waiting for someone to see that you were just as important as their job, not always wondering if you measured up to their last love.

With Kyle, she knew that, in this moment, she was all that mattered to him, and he was all she thought about, all she wanted.

As her tongue licked and circled, her mouth sucked, and her fingers stroked his shaft, the sensitive area between his legs, he grew harder than she thought possible. When she thought his release was near, she prepared to accept it all, but his hands were on her, lifting her atop him.

"Condom," he said between gasps for breath, and his arousal excited her more than she'd ever experienced. With shaky hands, she placed a condom from the night table on him, the mental effort to focus on the task almost too much. Finally, they allowed their instincts to take over.

Kyle's hands grasped her hips and shoved her down on him with no preamble. None was needed, as she was so hot and wet from their leisurely foreplay.

There was nothing leisurely about how they coupled as he thrust up into her again and again, and she matched his every move not only likewise but also writhed her hips over and around him, clenching and unclenching him as she did so, delighting in every gasp she drew out of him. His hands reached for her as he moved, one between her legs, one on her breast, and when he pressed both her nipple and bud at her center, her climax thundered through her. Kyle's cries sounded almost immediately, and even in the throes of the most sensual, lusty sex of her life, she was aware that he'd waited for her to come first.

Kyle always put her first.

Ludmila Markova knew she was in big trouble with Ivanov. The mark hadn't picked up the USB before the storm hit, and now no one but she had access to the spreadsheets. Ivanov told her that she was personally responsible for making sure the shipment arrived in Silver Valley as planned, and that his dealers received what they expected without a hitch.

But the storm was bigger than this spoiled country was used to. Or the trains. Nothing was moving in the town, or in central Pennsylvania. She knew better than to argue with Ivanov. She'd told his number two that she'd make sure everything worked out. And knew she was lucky that they didn't have anyone else to rely on, or they'd have killed her on the spot. ROC suffered fools almost as infrequently as FSB had. Meaning never.

Her rathole trailer shook with the force of the wind. At least in Moscow the concrete edifices that passed for apartments were strong against the elements. The windows might crack but the building would never shake like this.

She sipped the hot tea with lemon and honey, something she only allowed herself in the trailer. It was too Russian, would make her stick out too much in this average American town that seemed to live on coffee.

As she drank the beverage, she fingered the piece of paper she'd taken from the library information desk. Just in case.

It was what the Americans called a "flyer," a public invitation to attend an annual library fund-raising gala, which she surmised was a dance of some sort. There would be charity activities involved somehow. Most important, it was coordinated by none other than Portia DiNapoli, whose name and email were indicated as the RSVP point. The event coincided perfectly with the first of five drops by their suppliers down south. It made her final actions in Silver Valley more complicated, more risky. Ensure the heroin distribution and kill DiNapoli. But challenge was her specialty. She allowed herself to smile. The shipment via rail had been her idea, and despite the storm, which no one could have predicted, it was perfect for what Ivanov wanted. A crushing hand of control over the heroin trade on the East Coast.

She looked out the small, dirty trailer window as the storm intensified, and she made mental preparations for keeping herself warm. Not only in this hovel, but when she went out to explore a bit. To the place she'd followed the man who didn't leave the librarian's side.

Ivanov and ROC still didn't know that she had a potential witness. Two, actually. The librarian, and the man who'd knocked her off the tracks. The same man who'd been in the diner, and while his gaze had lingered a beat too long on her, she was certain he hadn't immediately recognized her in the wig. When his memory put her with the waitress, it'd be too late. She was going to kill him, along with Portia. If Ivanov knew about her probable witnesses, he'd kill her.

There was always someone else to coordinate his heroin trade.

The man always with Portia DiNapoli was a worthy adversary, as he'd demonstrated at the homeless shelter. She assumed it had been him, keeping her from what she'd hoped to be an easy kill. No matter. His devotion to keeping the librarian safe was his Achilles' heel, and she was at her best when stomping on someone's weakest spot.

Her teacup was empty, the lemon slice withered and cold. Time to begin her plan. First she had a couple to put on edge. Let them know they weren't as safe and sound as they thought.

"Smart thinking on the coffee." He sipped the espresso she'd made with an old-fashioned Italian percolator on the gas-burner stovetop. He'd watched her light a match and then the burner, the electric starters rendered useless by the limited power.

"We're lucky the owners had this pot or I'd have had to make pour-over with the grounds."

"That would be fine, too." Anything with her would be fantastic, in fact. He had a killer to catch, a heroin shipment to interdict and ROC to put a dent into. Normally he'd be wired for sound, unable to do anything but focus on the mission until he successfully ripped all of his targets apart.

But now there was Portia.

"The storm's stalled." Portia scrolled through her phone. "They don't know when it'll move out of here. We could be stuck in this house for days!"

He should care, be concerned about the case, the shipment, Markova, ROC.

All he saw was the beautiful woman standing in front of him.

"Portia."

"Hmm?"

"Put down your phone. Let's go back to bed."

Chapter 16

Sleeping next to a man was a lovely thing. When the man was Kyle King, it was heaven. Portia didn't want to open her eyes, so she snuggled in deeper against him, her body the most relaxed it'd been in months.

She had Kyle's tongue to thank. Unable to remain completely at rest once that thought entered her mind, she carefully rolled onto her back, keeping his arm around her waist. She looked up at his face as he slept. The day's growth of whiskers had been rough against the inside of her thighs, but she'd gladly taken the love injury. And how had he known to use his fingers at the exact right time, to make what his tongue did seem like rookie moves? Desire woke up, deep in her belly, and she smiled, decided to wait as long as it took for him to wake up. She'd watch him until then, get more turned on until he opened his eyes.

A powerful gust of wind rattled the windows, and the French doors that led to the room's balcony shook as if someone was trying to open them.

Portia dragged her gaze from Kyle's gorgeous sleeping face to look through the window. She'd left the blinds up last night, wanting to see the progress of the storm. With the driving snow, there was no chance of anyone seeing inside. Which made it a shock for her to see a person at the window, looking in.

Portia's nails dug into his forearm like a drowning person's death grasp. Kyle opened his eyes, immediately alert, and looked to where her gaze had frozen.

With no preamble, he took them both over the side of the bed furthest from the window, and grabbed one of the pistols he'd positioned on the nightstands—one on each for just such an instance.

Portia scrambled to her knees and crouched as he did behind the bed.

"Did she see us?" Her voice trembled but to her credit she remained at his side, didn't scream or try to run from the room.

"No telling. And we can't be sure it's Markova." Though he'd recognize her shape anywhere. He'd tracked her for months at this point.

You screwed up in the diner. He mentally shoved the accusation away. He couldn't change the past but he could keep Portia safe now.

"Well, since she's out to kill me, I think it's a logical conclusion." Portia's wit was something he loved about her, but right now he recognized it for what it was. Nervous chatter.

"Shh." He leveled his weapon at the door, and saw

the intruder try to peer in. "I agree with you. It's Markova." Who else would venture out in this storm and attempt a break-in, knowing Portia wasn't alone? Because if Markova figured out where Portia was, it had to have been via Kyle's movements. He had to review what he'd done, where he'd been, to figure out how she knew. But not now.

Proof of identity came when the climber removed their black balaclava, probably to see the lock she needed to pick better. Her pale blonde hair fell forward. No red wig this time. Son of a bitch—just as he'd suspected, she'd been the waitress in the diner. She must have followed him out here right afterward. He'd been certain he didn't have a trail, but with the visibility so low, it was conceivable she'd followed him with her lights out, using his to guide her.

And then she'd waited until she'd known they were asleep to make her move.

"It's her, Kyle."

"Yes." He took his phone from the dresser, pressed his finger to it to unlock it and then handed it to her. "Here. Call Josh—he's in my recent calls. Tell him what's going on. And once you hang up, take the rifle from underneath the bed and be prepared to use it."

"You put a rifle under the bed I was sleeping on?"

"Of course."

As she called and spoke to Josh, Kyle watched Markova work the lock. The storm raged and yet to her, a native Muscovite, it was business as usual.

"Josh says he can't get anyone out here right now but he's confident you'll take care of her."

"He's right." He didn't take his focus off Markova. "I want you to take the rifle and get out of this room. Go to the storage room on the top floor like we practiced. Lock yourself in and don't come out until I get you."

"No way! You might need backup."

"I can't do this with you right now, Portia. Get. Out. Of. Here." At his last word, the French doors clicked open, followed by huge double *bams* as the wind blew them against the walls.

Portia escaped just in time, and Kyle was pretty sure Markova hadn't seen her. It didn't matter if she did, because he was taking her down, now.

"Freeze." She did, in the catlike pose she'd assumed on the railroad tracks with Portia. It was a prestrike stance, meant to appear defensive but was, in fact, preparation for a lethal move.

"I will shoot you." He didn't reveal he knew who she was, keeping the power balance of information on his side.

"You would have already put the bullet between my eyes if you meant to." She didn't try to hide her accent, unlike at the diner and the times he'd seen her come and go at the library.

"Put your hands over your head and get to your knees." He didn't have cuffs but he had zip ties in the pockets of his cargo pants, next to the bed. They'd do until SVPD arrived.

"Never." She sprang into action, but instead of attempting to take him out as he'd expected, she ran toward the bedroom door that led to the inside hallway and disappeared. Once around the corner, he heard a weapon fire.

Portia.

He ran into the hall, his weapon drawn. He expected to face down Markova.

But she was ahead of him, opening the sliding doors to the main living room's outside deck. He ran after her and watched as she slipped through the open door, onto the deck, and disappeared over the edge. Kyle ran to the railing, the assault of wind and driving snow fighting his every movement. Looking down, he saw where she'd dropped and rolled. Of course she was trained to scale any height, but the twenty-foot drop was a bit much. Except that it was shorter by at least four or five feet, thanks to the storm. To his eye, it looked like as much as six or eight feet of snow had drifted up against the back of the house, which overlooked the mountains. Her silhouette was quickly swallowed up by the blinding snow.

It didn't mean she was gone, though. Markova was still on the property. He had two options—jump here and risk injury, or go out the front door and cut her off before she reached the main road again. There was no hope for survival in the woods, not in these conditions.

"That was easy." Portia's shout startled him and he stared at her. It was a full second before he noticed the bloodred stain on her pajama top.

"What the hell are you doing outside the storage room?" Didn't she realize that Markova was no match for her? And right now, challenging his every skill. "She shot you."

Portia shot him a wan smile. "Grazed me, is all. I know, it's probably the adrenaline keeping me from hurting or losing it about now. I was hiding behind the kitchen island and had a clear shot of her, but she saw me and fired first. I know I should have listened to you but I thought you'd need backup. She's not going to let you take her down easily. It's me she wants, Kyle."

Portia was shouting over the wind, her thin pajamas flattened against her body in the gale. A sound lower than the wind reached them and they both turned to see Markova speeding away—on a snowmobile.

Kyle hustled Portia back into the house with him and shut the sliding door behind them, cursing that the bedroom French door didn't have an interior deadbolt as this one and all the ground floor doors and windows did. The one fatal security flaw in the huge home and it had to be on the balcony of the room Portia slept in. He'd overlooked it and failed her. Worse, she could have been shot through the heart if Markova hadn't been in such a hurry to avoid capture.

"Let's get your wound checked."

Portia lifted the fabric from her shoulder, stretched to look at the wound. She'd been correct, it was a graze, but it was starting to sting now that they were back inside. It needed to be cleaned and bandaged.

"Does it hurt?"

"More like a sting. Nothing I can't handle. Don't you think we should double-check the house for any other place Markova tried to break in?"

"Yes—let's do a quick check and then I'm bandaging that for you." As they walked, he called Josh and reported what had happened, what direction he'd seen Markova head in. Josh promised to send an SVPD unit out as soon as it was safe, but warned Kyle that it could take a while, depending on the winds and visibility. And since Kyle was the best protection Portia had, if another incident got called in, it might take priority.

Kyle wasn't feeling like he was the best protector for Portia. Not by a long shot. He looked at her face, checked her pupils. She was okay. It was just a graze, and she'd handled herself well, considering she'd blown off his orders.

"I'm going to check the garage to make sure she didn't steal the snowmobile from us."

"I'll stay here." Portia's expression reflected the contrition he knew she'd never verbalize, so he let it go.

"Not this time." He shot the French door an uneasy look. If Markova made it up the side of the house once, she'd do it again. As much as he felt certain he'd scared her away, he couldn't trust his gut, not after letting his physical need for Portia distract him from keeping vigilance on the house.

"Stay with me."

Portia did as Kyle asked, and stayed with him as they searched the bottom floor of the house first. In the garage, they found the snowmobile and doors intact.

"I'm glad she didn't get in here. We may need the snowmobile," Kyle said as they left the garage and began to inspect the main floor for any evidence of a break-in.

"She was crazy to attempt this, in the storm. You're not thinking of going after her, are you?"

"Of course I am. But I won't." The grim line of his mouth was a far cry from the expression on his generous lips that had brought her to climax less than an hour ago.

"Because you're afraid she'll kill me." Portia stopped at the huge picture windows, stared at the snow blowing sideways. Visibility was still at a minimum. Her shoulder was starting to ache and she knew she'd have to draw attention to taking care of it. To her mistake, the error that could have cost Kyle his life, too, and the entire LEA mission. Shudders hit her and while her brain knew it was a delayed reaction, an accumulation of the hell she'd faced ever since the train tracks, she couldn't stop it.

"Hey." He was next to her in a flash, cupped her face in his hands. "Yes, I'm terrified she could have hurt you more seriously. You saved yourself, you know."

"I'm a librarian, Kyle, an information specialist. Fighting bad guys in person, with a weapon, isn't one of my talents."

"It is now." He kissed her forehead and took a step back. "Let's get the inspection finished so that I can tend to your scrape."

She followed him room by room, covering each window and door, but there were no further signs of a break-in. They found a first aid kit and sat in the master bath on the wide edge of a large garden tub as Kyle began to clean and bandage her shoulder.

Portia fought the urge to put her head on his shoulder, to sink into the strength of his embrace. The sting of antiseptic made her wince. To distract herself from the pain, she focused on the case. "How did she know the master bedroom door was the one that wasn't as secure as the rest of the house?"

Kyle met her eyes briefly before resuming his ministrations to her graze. "She didn't. It was an educated bet, at most. She's been out here, watching the house, seeing which rooms light up and when. Then she saw the balcony at the back part of the house, where the big bathroom windows are, and took a chance. With no stairs attached to the small bedroom deck, she knew there was a good chance that the door might not be as secure."

"You've done a lot of the same, haven't you?"

"Yes, but my motives are different."

"Oh, of course! I know that. I wasn't trying to say that you're at all like Markova, or any of these bad guys."

"I know you weren't. And it's undeniable that we employ a lot of the same skill sets."

"Except you're not corrupt. Or working for the bad guys."

His expression grew thoughtful. "No, no, I'm not."

Kyle's phone rang and he answered it, spoke briefly to the caller before disconnecting. He leveled his silver gaze on her, making her feel at once safe and apprehensive.

"What is it, Kyle?"

"That's Josh. He's going to be here with SVPD and a couple of FBI agents within ten minutes, give or take. The gale and low visibility will make it slower."

"I'll get a quick shower." She knew it might be cold, as the water heater had lost its energy source when they'd lost power. The generator could handle only so much of a load.

"Do more than that, Portia. Pack up your things. You're not safe here any longer." He nodded at her shoulder. "I'll resterilize that and patch it up as soon as you're dry."

She was grateful he left the bathroom immediately. It would be the ultimate humiliation for Kyle to see her tears. Hadn't she already caused enough trouble for him? Adding any kind of emotional burden to his plate wasn't fair. She knew it wasn't her fault that Markova was stalking her, trying to kill her. There wasn't blame to speak of, except that she couldn't expect more from Kyle right now than what he was here to do—bring down Markova and the ROC heroin operation.

The sting of the shower spray against her gunshot wound, no matter how minor the graze was, made her grit her teeth. It was still no match for the pain her heart filled with. She'd known it wasn't going to last, her intimacy with Kyle. But to have it ripped away so abruptly, when the damn storm wasn't even over, made big fat tears roll down her cheeks, mixing with the shower water.

After her shower she used the first aid kit to clean the wound again, and put a big bandage on it. Since it was on the front of her shoulder it was easy to reach, and she didn't think she could keep the tears at bay if Kyle touched her bare skin again right now.

When she walked into the kitchen, Josh and other SVPD officers were already there with Kyle.

Josh didn't consider Portia's request to return to her apartment. She'd wanted to go home to her parents, or at least one of her siblings, but that would put them at risk. If Markova was still after her.

"There's no reason to think she'll stop looking for you, Portia." Josh sat at the kitchen island with her and Kyle as the SVPD and FBI officers took evidence from the back bedroom. "You'll be absolutely safe living with me and Annie. We have plenty of room and this way you can go back to work at the library. Annie can escort you there and back each day, and we have a permanent SVPD officer assigned to protect the library until the case is closed."

"What about the library being used as a way to transfer information by ROC? Are you still going to stake it out?" She knew she sounded like the non-LEA civilian she was, but they'd get her drift.

"That's not your concern, Portia. We're on it. If we need to go in after hours, we will. If your staff asks questions about seeing SVPD or me on the security footage, tell them it's extra precautions due to the heroin epidemic. You don't have to mention ROC to anyone, even though it's been in the media. It's better to not confirm or deny anything related to it. For your sake, as well as Silver Valley's."

"Kyle's correct. I know it doesn't come naturally to you, but play ignorant if anyone asks you about it."

"Will do." Josh knew her, knew she'd follow through on the orders. LEA or not, Portia wanted what was best for all.

And that wasn't what she wanted for herself. Kyle leaned over the counter, engaged in the conversation but his mind drifting. Was he counting the minutes until he'd no longer be responsible for her, be free to go after Markova on his own?

"This won't affect the gala, will it?" It sounded shallow to bring up the charity event now, but her mind needed something to hang on to. Something familiar, solid. It couldn't be Kyle—he had a mission to take down the ROC op.

"It shouldn't." Josh ran his hand over his face. The ROC case was taking a toll on everyone she knew in law enforcement. "Kyle explained that you two figured out what's going on with the trains. Once the storm gets through here, it'll take several days to clear the tracks. Then the shipments will arrive, and we'll be ready to get them before any drug dealers do."

"But what about Markova?"

"As long as she thinks her plan is going smoothly, she'll be busy with that. She's tried to take you out two times for certain, a third if we count the train tracks. Although we couldn't have charged her with anything more than stealing a library laptop at that point."

"Josh is about to say that Markova's figured out that you're too hard of a target to catch. And she's going to be more concerned about getting the heroin unloaded and in the correct hands, so that ROC gets paid. Otherwise she'll have bigger problems than us."

Annie showed up two hours later to take Portia to the home she shared with Josh. Kyle couldn't have picked a better place himself. He trusted both of the TH agents and their training. Portia would be safe. Away from him, mostly. He hated to admit it but he and Portia had gotten too close. Not just for the op, either.

He had no business getting involved with a woman he was supposed to be protecting from the very adversary he was assigned to track and eventually apprehend. Yet he had, because Portia wasn't just any woman, wasn't someone he'd hooked up with out of sheer physical need. He had to have Portia on all levels—emotionally, physically, spiritually. And he couldn't. They didn't fit, on paper or elsewhere.

"I'm ready." Portia walked back into the kitchen, where he waited with Josh and Annie. She looked at each of them, her gaze resting the longest on him.

"Let's talk before you go." He looked at Annie and Josh.

"Excuse us."

Portia stilled and he thought she was going to refuse to talk to him. He wouldn't blame her—he hadn't softened any of this. The forensics team was still in the house, and what had been their prison and paradise was gone, another crime scene among the thousands he'd witnessed.

"Sure. Whatever you need." He walked past her and motioned for her to follow him to the back bedroom neither of them had used. It would be too hard to say goodbye in the very room they'd so recently made love in.

If only he'd been able to leave it at sex with her.

Impossible with Portia.

Once in the room, he closed the door behind them. The single large window overlooked the front part of the house and the snowfall continued, although the wind had begun to die down.

Portia's form was in a defensive posture, with her arms crossed over her chest. Meeting her eyes was the hardest mission he'd ever completed.

"What do you want to say, Kyle?" Ah, this was the Portia he knew.

"You never back down from a challenge, do you?" His hands twitched to cup her face, run his thumb along her soft skin.

"By 'challenge,' you mean accepting that there's nothing between us. Don't worry, Kyle. I'm sure you have a string of women behind you. I'm not one of them—I knew what I was getting into when we got together the first time."

As she spoke, it occurred to him that he'd lived a lifetime with her in just a couple of weeks. From the first time he'd seen her, to holding her in his arms after knocking her off the tracks, to their first hot kiss, to the way they'd devoured one another in many parts of this house, including the hot tub.

"Did you, Portia? Because I sure as hell didn't. I had no idea that we'd end up here, having to end something that shouldn't have started in the first place. And I sure as heck didn't know it was going to be this difficult."

She raised her chin and he waited to see a trembling lip, a tear positioned to fall on her lids. But she was tough, his Portia.

"You always have made it clear you're a short-timer here, Kyle. You've made a commitment to move to California. And let's face it, it's for the best, right? If you were going to stay here longer, you wouldn't want a relationship cluttering up your work with Trail Hikers. Silver Valley's not for you, Kyle. It's okay. We got each other through a tough time, with everything going on. Don't worry about me. Josh and Annie are going to keep me safe."

He'd planned to keep this cool, easy. But Portia made everything complicated.

And all he wanted to do was stop all of this, stop time by kissing her.

So he did.

Portia knew she should remain detached, tell Kyle that a kiss wasn't part of a professional send-off. Yet as much as they'd shared by working and solving part of the ROC case together, the bulk of what had passed between them had been incredibly personal.

Like this kiss. When his lips touched hers, Portia grabbed his face and held him there, afraid he'd pull away before she allowed herself this one last long drink of Kyle.

His tongue plunged into her mouth, circled hers, and she sucked on it, wanting to remind him—no, make sure he never forgot—that what they'd shared hadn't been a fling or sexual release. She wasn't the only woman who'd shared his bed. No doubt he'd had women who'd been more worldly and sophisticated than her, for sure. But none had seen into Kyle's soul the way she did. She was positive about this because Kyle had seen the depths of her soul, too. And still cared about her, enough to protect her and make love to her like she was the most beautiful woman on earth.

Had she made him feel the same? She pulled back from the kiss, looked at his closed eyes, heard the ragged intake of breath.

"Kyle. Look at me." Only when his silver gaze focused on her did she continue. "Did you feel it, feel this when we were together? Did you feel like I appreciated you?"

He stared at her and she thought he might let go of her right there and then, refuse to answer. He blinked. One side of his mouth curved up. "Babe, you were the best."

His words cut through the sexual haze he always wove around her and pierced her temporary reprieve from reality. She and Kyle were saying goodbye. He knew it, too, because his smile was gone, his eyes back to the steely hue she'd witnessed so many times over the last weeks.

"I've…I've got to go. To—"

"To Josh's. I know. Listen, I'm not going to be able to text you for the next several days, most likely."

"I understand." She'd never want to distract him in the middle of a life-or-death situation.

He gave her a quick kiss on her forehead, as if she were a platonic friend. "Be safe, listen to whatever they tell you that you need to do. And good luck with your gala."

He turned and opened the door, motioned for her to go first.

Portia left and didn't look back as she returned to the kitchen, grabbed her bags and nodded at Annie. "Let's go."

The advantage of having a best friend like Annie, who'd known her for so long and knew her every expression and mood, was that there were no explanations needed. Annie gave Josh a quick kiss goodbye and left with Portia.

Chapter 17

Portia leaned her head against the passenger headrest in Annie's four-wheel-drive crossover vehicle. Annie expertly drove them to her and Josh's place in the rugged car, the safest bet as the storm still held on for its last gasps. It was supposed to end by nightfall.

They were headed to the home Josh had grown up in and where he had raised his younger sister, Becky, until recently. Becky had mental and emotional disabilities that required constant monitoring, which Josh had done until recently. His sister had moved into an adult community living situation a few months ago, which left a lot of room in the sprawling house.

"How's Becky doing?"

Annie's face lit up. "She's fantastic. Josh couldn't have picked a better place to take her, and she's made so many friends."

"I know you were so worried about her." Portia bit her lip. She wasn't the only one who'd struggled to find the perfect partner. Except unlike Annie, while Portia might have found him, he wasn't going to stay in Silver Valley.

"I was. I'm more concerned about you right now, though. It seems to me that your last few minutes with Kyle weren't great."

They were too great—at least that kiss had been. Nothing she was ready to share with Annie, though. "I'm good. We both knew what we were doing, Annie. It's been an emotional roller coaster, yes. We're also both adults."

Annie opened her mouth to say something, then closed it. They shared several moments of silence, a reprieve Portia was thankful for. She needed space and time between her and Kyle, and some alone time to deal with the burning hole in her heart.

"On another topic, Markova's a wicked person—she has caused a lot of trouble for SVPD and the community, not just you." Annie didn't look at her as she spoke, her attention on the road.

"Besides the library theft and surveillance?"

Annie nodded as she gripped the steering wheel, inching forward slowly to stay within the safety parameters of the visibility. "Hmm. I'm not sure how much Kyle has told you, but I do know you spoke to Claudia."

Portia perked up. "Yes, I have spoken to her. Which of course makes me wonder how you know her."

Annie shot her a sly grin without taking her gaze off the road. "Let's just say that some of my SVPD work spills over into aiding other LEAs with the tougher cases." She didn't have to say that ROC was a harder case than most. Portia knew it, firsthand.

"It's certainly not like the movies. I would have expected Kyle to stop Markova in her tracks once she broke into the house, but he gave her room to be able to take off. I know I'm not cut out for law enforcement because I would have shot first and answered any questions later."

"That's easy, and in this instance, in the master bedroom, fair to say. But it's a perfect example of why someone like Kyle is such an invaluable asset to have on our side. Not just with this case, which affects us locally, but with the bigger, more globally concerning issues. His measure of self-control is unheard of. Trust me, most other agents would have apprehended Markova on the spot, or at least fired their weapon at her. But he kept his head, waited to see what she'd say or do."

"I didn't ask him what she said in the bedroom. I heard her say something." She'd been out of earshot, close enough to know Markova had entered the room but too far to distinguish the individual words.

"We can talk about ROC and Markova for hours on end, Portia. But you're not telling me what I really care about."

Was Annie working another case? "What?"

"You. And Kyle. Josh says you might be more than friendly."

Portia squirmed in the heated leather passenger seat, and it wasn't from the gusts of wind that rocked the vehicle as they left the shelter of the mountain forest and hit the flat road that led into Silver Valley. "We may be. But it doesn't matter. He's leaving as soon as this case is solved. It's been his plan for a lot longer than he's been here."

"You mean, since he's met you."

"Yeah, well, even that is a bit questionable. It turns out he was staking out the library for weeks before I met him. As well as the homeless shelter, can you believe it?" She shot a glance at her friend, who remained intensely focused on the road. "Of course you believe it—you've probably been working this, too, haven't you? Is this why I haven't been able to get you out for our girls' meet-ups quite so often?" She'd thought it had been because Annie and Josh were spending every waking minute together. And sleeping.

The rueful twist of Annie's mouth said it all. "Yes. I wasn't free to tell you why I was working so many hours at SVPD, not when the case was still completely confidential. Of course the details still are, but we couldn't keep the horror of ROC out of the media."

"I'm sure SVPD didn't want to—the citizens who are most at risk from ROC deserve to know what you're fighting. What we're all fighting."

"Yes." Annie's reply was loud in its quietness. "I worked with cops—when I was still on staff at NYPD—who had burned out from trying to crack various ROC factions, stop their crimes before they happened. ROC is merciless, and innocent civilians aren't its only victims. The very people they attract and promise to take care of more often than not also become victims."

"There's nothing good about ROC."

They sat in their very familiar, loving silence. She and Annie had been best friends for so long that they understood one another without question. Annie knew that Portia wasn't blaming the criminals for the ill that befell them from ROC, and she knew that Annie wasn't defending the criminals. They were simply laying out the facts.

She grew so comfortable in the passenger seat that she almost missed the flash of black, followed by two tiny red taillights, in the white haze of the storm. Her eyes fully opened and she gripped the dash.

"Annie, did you—"

"What do you have, Annie?" Josh's voice filled the car. Annie had used her hands-free to phone him.

"Probable Markova sighting, route one-one-four, heading back into town. Dressed in dark clothing, riding a snowmobile going at least sixty. I'm going thirty and she flashed by us."

"Okay, what's your crossroad?"

Portia caught the green sign to her right, through the slanting snowfall. "Hilltop Drive."

"That you, Portia? Thanks." Josh sounded happy to have the information. "I'll turn this around ASAP. You two stay safe and hunker down when you get to our place."

"Will do." Annie answered as she drove.

"Love you." Josh's reply was so casually genuine that Portia blinked at the tears his deep love for Annie prompted.

"Love you, too, babe." Annie disconnected and cast Portia a bemused glance. "He's super affectionate."

"So I hear." They both laughed, and Portia welcomed the release after the constant stress of being on the lookout for Markova. She sobered. "She didn't know we were in this car, did she?"

"Nope. My guess is that she's been taking the back

snowmobile routes down the mountain, and crossed onto the main highway just as we did. If she knew it was us, we'd be fighting her right now."

"You mean if she knew it was me, I'd already be shot."

"Yes."

"She's going to figure out I'm at your place. It's inevitable."

"Not really. I've had some training since I quit NYPD, here with SVPD. Between Josh and me, we'll keep you safe. Just don't go outside the routine we'll establish."

"I'd think routine would be anathema to me staying alive."

"What I mean is our tactical routine. We're going to shake up when you go to the library, your start and stop times, and you'll never be alone. I'll be taking you to and from work, and there will be an SVPD officer with you at all times in the library."

"But cops don't do personal security." Neither did undercover agents, yet Kyle had protected her. The loss of proximity to him was already affecting her and it'd only been thirty minutes. She felt something akin to panic but it wasn't as frightening.

"The entire town is at risk, which includes a public building like the library. Keeping you out of harm's way is an added benefit." Annie gently pressed on the brakes as they came to a four-way stop at the entrance of Josh's subdivision.

Correction, Annie and Josh's neighborhood. A pang of a different kind hit her in the solar plexus and Portia had to sit still and accept that for the first time in her life, she was jealous of her best friend. She wished that she could at least fantasize about having a place of her own with a man like Kyle. Okay, not a man like him, but him. Kyle, the person she'd shared more with in the past week and a half than anyone else in her life.

"We're here." Annie put the car in park and slid out of the driver's seat. Portia saw her friend's slim shape bow against the brunt of the wind, which was still strong, even as the storm was reportedly beginning its departure. She paused before opening her door, and sent up a hope that this would be a new start for her, so quickly after her entire life had changed. But from now on she had to let go of any permanent-type thoughts of Kyle. Their time together had been great while it lasted.

She had a gala to organize.

Kyle had said goodbye to other women he'd dated, accepted a fling for what it was. But as he'd watched Portia shove her things into her backpack, he'd felt like anything but experienced at bidding a woman farewell. Worse, he'd had to fight every fiber of his being that told him not to let her go.

It wasn't ever going to last. There were no guarantees it'd be easy. He'd known it the first time he'd set sight on Portia in the library. She was the woman who'd stay with him years after this. When ROC and Ludmila Markova were distant black-and-white memories, what he'd shared with Portia would be as fresh as the several feet of snow now blanketing Silver Valley.

You could change your mind. Stay here.

He shook off the damning accusation. His involvement with Portia had almost cost her everything. If he'd been more alert instead of sleeping off their most recent

round of lovemaking, he'd have Markova in custody
instead of still out there, targeting Portia.

"You okay, man?" Josh's hand hit his back in a
friendly wake-up. They were alone in the kitchen area
as the SVPD forensic team finished up their work.

"I could have gotten her killed, Josh." The confes-
sion came out unbidden, and didn't do anything to ease
the razor blades of recrimination stabbing his soul.

"Oh, no, you don't. Absolutely do *not* go there. It's
a quick path to insanity. Trust me on this—I was there
last year with Annie, when she got involved in our
human trafficking case."

"You were?" Since Kyle had only been in Silver
Valley for the last couple of months, he'd never known
Josh before he'd been connected to Annie. "I can't pic-
ture you as the overwrought type."

"When it comes to keeping an innocent bystander
safe, we're all vulnerable. The fact that I had feelings
for Annie made it harder to stay detached enough to get
the job done. And I faced what you just did—wondering where I went wrong, seeing only the fact that Annie
could have been hurt or worse, because I'd turned my
head a split second too late or never picked up on a clue
because I was otherwise engaged."

The noose of guilt loosened its hold on him, a tiny
notch. "I had no idea."

"None of us do, until we're in the thick of it." Josh
put his phone down for a minute. "It's never easy, what
we do, but it's a hell of lot simpler when there's not
someone special who's at risk and their life rests in our
hands. And even tougher for me was accepting that I
wanted to come home to Annie every night, which

meant I had to face my fears over leaving her widowed. It's part of our job description."

"Yeah, it is." He wasn't about to divulge all of his thoughts to Josh. Especially when he knew he still had sorting to do. It all had to wait, though, until ROC's heroin shipment was seized, and Markova was behind bars.

"We'll get Markova, Kyle. It might not be here in central Pennsylvania—she's the slippery type. But she'll meet hers. TH is all over the globe, and FBI has had her on their wanted list for a couple of years. Her future's not going to be pretty."

"I know that. I'd like to take down as many of the ROC thugs as we can."

"Me, too, but our priority is to stop the drugs from hitting the street. On that note, you should probably find a different place to stay other than your apartment. You've been made, and Markova knows you're with Portia."

"I'll take one of the TH safe houses." Trail Hikers maintained a half dozen or so apartments that were completely secure, on the outskirts of town. They looked like farmhouses from the road, and unless he was followed directly there, it'd be very difficult to know anyone but a farmer was in residence.

"I was going to suggest that. We can get Portia out to see you, Annie or I. Just let me know."

"That's not on the table." He had to keep Portia alive, and being with him wasn't to her advantage. His stomach rolled into a sickening lead ball and he refused to look at why. If he did, he might hop on the snowmobile in the garage and go after Portia right now.

"Well, if you change your mind." Josh was looking at his phone again, which lit up with a text at the same moment Kyle's vibrated with the same message, from Claudia.

Train's on the move again, from Texas, following back of storm by two days. Expect shipment to arrive SV within the week.

They looked at one another.

"Looks like we're closer than we thought." Josh spoke.

"This is all thanks to Portia's work. She pieced it all together, the shipments and amounts in each."

Josh gathered his laptop and put on his coat. "I'll make the slow drive back to town and see that we have all we need at the station to apprehend whoever Markova brings with her to give the packages to."

Kyle nodded. "I can do the briefing if you'd like." Things were looking up. If they captured this, the largest amount of heroin ever shipped through any East Coast distribution area, they'd send a big message to ROC. Along with arresting their dealers and Markova, it would cripple ROC drug ops for at least a month, maybe six weeks.

And it would keep Portia alive, allow her to return to her regular life sooner than he'd expected. A mental image of her in the library, working with a patron, seared through him as keenly as one of his many sexual memories of her.

But it didn't matter how much, how deeply, Portia DiNapoli was under his skin. As soon as they had Markova, he was headed for California.

Chapter 18

Portia reluctantly set up shop at Josh and Annie's. They'd given her a back bedroom and she had the guest bathroom to herself, so she didn't feel she was in their way. The storm was dwindling and she heard the loud purr of the snowplows on each of the first two nights she slept there, indicating that Silver Valley would soon be back to full operation.

"You're looking forward to going into the library tomorrow, aren't you?" Annie smiled at her over Chinese takeout, a nice treat after the power had been restored to town. Josh was out late, as he'd been the night before.

"Of course." She moved her orange chicken around with her chopsticks. Hunger hadn't been top on her list since she'd left the country house.

"Okay, let's talk." Annie put her napkin down. "You've been moping around since you left Kyle. Have you talked to him?"

"No, of course not. We're not a couple—you know that."

"Except that you've done everything a couple does, Portia. I know it's on an accelerated timeline. Kyle's not a man who has the time to give you the full-blown dating deal. But it doesn't mean he's not more sincere than anyone else you've ever been with."

"I was never with anyone else before. Sure, I thought I was, but Kyle makes all of those men, those relationships, seem adolescent. Even Rob—he looked all adult and fancy in his nice suits and smooth talk. He's a consummate politician. And even if he hadn't been such a dog, I'd still have broken up with him. He didn't hold up the end of a conversation like Kyle does." And no other man's touch aroused her, made her willing to let go and enjoy the moment—no man except Kyle.

"Have you told Kyle this?" Annie asked. Her eyes expressed her concern, her compassion for Portia's pain. It was more than Annie's counseling skills, too. This was what Portia valued about their friendship the most.

"You get me, Annie. I don't know what I'd do if I didn't have you to talk to about all of this."

Annie reached over the island and squeezed her hand. "It goes both ways, sweetie." She pulled back and picked up her chopsticks. "I do think that it'd be worth speaking to Kyle one more time. What do you have to lose, Portia? If he blows you off, then there, you have an answer. But it could work out into something you never expected. Something wonderful."

Portia made a show of rolling her eyes and got the desired laugh out of Annie. "Look, just because you're glowing like the nuclear station at Three Mile Island could have forty years ago, don't think my relationship with Kyle is anything like yours with Josh. First, you knew Josh your entire life until you left Silver Valley. I've only known Kyle for what, two weeks?" She shook her head. "It's not possible to have anything long term between us. Real commitment takes time and that's one thing we don't have. He's going back to California, where he grew up, as soon as the case is over."

"Like I said already, it's not about the timeline, Portia. You know as well as I do that while we have a shared history that cements our friendship, if we met today, we'd still hit it off and be friends. We click, we operate on the same frequency. As, it appears to me, do you and Kyle."

"'Frequency' is a good way to put it." She chewed on her dinner thoughtfully, swallowed and had a swig of the jasmine tea Annie had brewed. "And I do agree— the length of time just isn't a factor. Kyle's the real deal." But it didn't mean they'd make it as a couple.

"Then the next question you need to look at is if you're interested in checking out California."

Portia sputtered. "Wait a minute—that's too far. Kyle hasn't said anything about wanting more than what we've had here so far." And he'd never mentioned nor asked her if she'd want to visit, much less live, there. Would she?

It was too risky to her heart to contemplate anything more with Kyle than what they'd shared here, in Silver Valley. The elation at just the thought of having more time with Kyle scared her in its intensity. Was Annie's question about California reasonable? Sure. And yes, she'd consider going there. But Kyle had never asked her for anything past now. She was pretty certain he'd have already suggested that she at least visit California to see him after he moved back there. Which meant the inevitable ending—the nonending, as far as she could see—was going to be excruciating.

She looked at her friend. Annie was happily in love with the man of her dreams, and that was great. Sure, Annie had left New York City to come back to her hometown, said she was going to, regardless of what happened between her and Josh. But Portia knew her friend. Annie would have been heartbroken, inconsolable, if things with Josh hadn't worked out. She got that, totally.

Of course she did. She was already in the inconsolable phase over Kyle.

Kyle buried himself in the ROC op for the next several days. Without Portia by his side, it was the only remedy for the way his conscience gnawed at him. Finding Markova and tracking her every move had been almost too easy, but he figured it was because the shipment was imminent. Even Markova answered to higher-ups, and if she didn't come through with the coordinated distribution of drugs to preselected dealers, and get the cash from the sales, she'd be out of a job. Except ROC didn't fire people in a conventional way. They killed them.

Claudia had called another meeting, this time at TH headquarters, to go over what they had so far. He sat in the secured office space next to Josh, opposite Claudia and Chief Colt Todd.

"I take it you decided to leave Portia out of this briefing, Kyle?" Claudia never minced words.

"I did. She's done immeasurable good work for us,

helping me figure out what was on the USB stick. My desire is to keep her safe and as far away from Markova as possible."

"The good news is that Markova seems to have switched her focus back to the drug shipment." Colt nodded at Claudia. "We've compared what you've reported from following these last days to the intel we've received from other sources about the shipment and what the East Coast ROC is focused on at the moment." She looked at Josh, indicating he should continue.

Josh cleared his throat. "The train is moving again, after the long wait from the storm. And you already know that Markova is busy making sure every dealer's on the hook for the shipment. We've also gotten reports that this is only the first of as many as six shipments planned this year. We're hoping that by stamping this one out, we'll let ROC know they won't get away with it. But we have to be prepared as a town and community to face repercussions from them."

"Like you haven't already dealt with?" Kyle hadn't been here for it but SVPD and TH had dealt with several different local human trafficking rings, all led by ROC.

"We've only touched the tip of their iceberg." Claudia's proclamation cut through the discussion. "TH is deployed globally, fighting against criminals and despots 24/7. Over the last five years, US LEAs have had to dedicate up to 20 percent more resources in the fight against ROC."

"Why did they pick Silver Valley, Claudia? It doesn't make sense to me. Sure, from logistical and geographical standpoints, but Silver Valley isn't New York or

Miami. While a stranger or new transplant might not stand out as quickly as they would in a small town, Silver Valley isn't big enough for ROC to hide very many of their operatives."

"I don't have the answer to that, Kyle. We're working on it, because there's no such thing as coincidence in the ROC world." Claudia hated admitting she didn't know something, so Kyle knew this had to cut deep.

"The bigger picture isn't what I'm worried about," Colt broke in. "Right now we can make a difference for hundreds, thousands of Silver Valley residents by keeping the drugs from becoming available."

"Not to mention the entire Harrisburg area." Josh added his take on it. "ROC has operated on both sides of the river since they showed up in the area." The Susquehanna River separated the state capitol from many suburbs, including Silver Valley. SVPD was the largest police force on the west shore, though, and often worked closely with the Harrisburg PD.

"Right." Colt looked at Kyle. "We wouldn't have gotten this far without your contribution."

Kyle wished Colt would save the appreciation for after they wrapped up the case. He wouldn't be satisfied until they locked up Markova and every last one of the drug dealers whose hands itched to distribute products that would make them big bucks and keep addicts using, too many becoming OD victims.

He shifted in his seat and focused on what his teammates were saying, but always, always knew he'd be more comfortable if Portia were here. As his partner analyzing ROC data, as his confidante, as his lover.

Good thing he'd learned early in life that you don't always get what you want most.

* * *

On the morning of the gala, Portia made her coffee and grabbed a yogurt from Josh and Annie's refrigerator. The lack of Josh's presence the last couple of days was telling. And it raised her concerns over Kyle, who hadn't contacted her, by mutual agreement, when she'd left the safe house. He had to focus on his job. Still, a text would have been nice.

She heard Annie's footsteps and looked up to see her friend drag herself into the kitchen, circles under her eyes.

"Good morning. I'm guessing your exhaustion isn't from a long night of knitting?" Portia was pretty certain Annie only helped at her grandmother's yarn shop on an as-needed basis, on the weekends or evenings. And she wouldn't be working there while the ROC case was ongoing.

Annie offered a smile. "And you would be correct. I was at the station most of the night, helping Josh and Kyle put together a tactical team."

Portia's concern ratcheted to alarm. Her lungs struggled to grab a breath and her heart felt as though it needed every ounce of energy she had to beat. "Kyle— is he okay? Are they safe, Annie?"

Annie helped herself to a cup of coffee. "They're fine, but the train is due in tonight. Anytime between 7:00 and 9:00 p.m. It made good time after it resumed its trip north, once the storm here cleared."

"Okay, so by the end of tonight, this will all be over?"

Annie slung into a kitchen chair at a large family table. Josh hadn't completely revamped his childhood home, saving sentimental pieces like his parents' kitchen table. He'd lost them both tragically in an auto accident and had singlehandedly raised his sister.

"That's the tough thing, Portia. This case isn't going to be over until the ringleader, the head of the East Coast ROC operations, is caught. And hopefully he'll turn, give us the information we need to eradicate the entire network of criminals."

"Ivanov." She'd read about the man, the swath of crime and murderous devastation he'd cut across the Eastern Seaboard, and now he was digging his claws in deeper, heading toward the Midwest.

"Yes. Did Kyle tell you?"

"Not that much, actually. I've read up on ROC since I saw the news about their connection to the heroin trade. Right after Lani died."

Annie grimaced. Lani had been Annie's classmate, too. "That hit home, didn't it? Have you heard how her family is doing?"

"I spoke with them before the storm, before I met, got involved with, oh, what's the use? Before Kyle."

"And? How were they doing?" Annie wasn't going to put up with Portia's self-pity and she loved her friend all the more for understanding her and not giving her less attractive character traits any time.

"As well as can be expected. As you know from your line of work, better than I, it'll take time. They've thrown themselves into legislative activism, hoping to get the laws changed."

"Just when we think we've handled it from every angle, the opioid epidemic slams us back down." Annie peeled a banana. "There's so much to it. But if LEA does its job, it'll help a lot. Keep the drugs off the streets."

"I've thanked you before, Annie, but I can't tell you

enough how much I appreciate your, and Josh's, service. It has to be stressful on you both when you're working a case like this."

"As the TH and SVPD police psychologist, my job is mostly taking care of the agents and officers, making sure they're getting the practical support they require from their agency. It's a measure of how big this ROC case is that I'm doing as much as I am with the actual tactical operations. I never worked on ops like this when I was with NYPD."

"Was it a hugely hard decision to move back here? I know you loved New York."

"Not at all. I was in the process of figuring out I wanted out of the city, and then Josh came along. Yes, I love New York but I love Josh more. And what's not to like about Silver Valley? We're only fifteen minutes from the Harrisburg Amtrak, three hours from the city. Two from Philly. And two hours to DC, driving. We live in an ideal place."

"We do."

"And that's why we're going to stomp ROC right out of here."

"I'll be at the gala all night, but can you keep me informed?" There were two sets of SVPD patrols assigned to monitor the gala, along with a private security firm, but Portia didn't expect them to be in on all the details of the case.

"Of course I will. I'll be at the gala, too. There won't be anything for me to do during the actual takedown. Claudia and Colt don't allow me near active ops for either TH or SVPD if they can help it. I need to be available afterward, fully functioning to help whomever needs it."

* * *

Kyle stood off from the group of SVPD, FBI and Trail Hiker colleagues who were spread out inconspicuously over a two-mile length of train track that ran straight through the heart of Silver Valley. Their intention was to stop the train at the juncture where the rail curved off and into the part of town where he'd saved Portia from being hit.

"You ready, Kyle?" Claudia's voice reached him on his wireless headset.

"Standing by."

"Train is one mile out." Another TH agent, this one working communications, sounded in his ear. Months of investigation and intelligence analysis, countless frozen nights of surveillance, and more than one hand-to-hand altercation with Markova had led to this. He'd have preferred it was during broad daylight, but the train had been delayed by the storm and they had to work with what was, not wish for a better situation.

As a former Marine and present Trail Hiker, he had every confidence in his ability to complete his mission.

If only he had that with Portia.

He'd stopped trying to fight the visions of her that taunted him day and night. He missed her—not just the sex, and yes, he missed that beyond measure. Portia understood him, accepted him for the man he was. She'd made love to him knowing he couldn't offer her any promise beyond their short time together. And she'd fought alongside him as needed, readily took instruction in weapons and how to avoid getting killed by Markova.

He looked at his watch. Eight fifteen in the evening and it was pitch dark, in the middle of winter. Portia was at the gala she'd so carefully planned. It was the one thing he was grateful for, that she'd be safe and Markova's focus was on the incoming shipment. Still, he hadn't stopped himself from putting on his oversize tuxedo over his body armor, under his plainclothes, also a size too big. He'd used the tux as an undercover agent in various situations, including embassy receptions all over the globe. But tonight, if by some act of God the mission went down more quickly than they'd planned, he'd show up at that gala and…

This is where he was stuck. What would he do? Ask Portia for one last night together before he went out west? Or would he ask for one dance, say goodbye that way?

"Lights." He looked down the track and saw the tiny pinpoint of the engine's headlight. Inhaling the frozen air, he silently practiced his role. The engineer had been replaced by an undercover agent, who would stop the train along this stretch of track to allow for the various LEA officers to board and inspect. Once they found the heroin and any other unknown contraband, they'd replace it with artificial, harmless substances. Then they'd move quickly to be in place where they suspected Markova waited. Where he knew she waited—he'd verified she was in the area just fifteen minutes ago, before he'd driven down here. He wondered if she thought she'd lost him as her tail.

"A quarter mile to go, folks. Stand by."

Kyle waited, wanting the night to be over without incident more than ever before, and knowing in the deepest part of his being that his best course of action was to complete the mission and get out of Silver Valley. Before he risked hurting Portia more than he knew he already had.

* * *

Portia entered the catering barn she'd rented on behalf of the gala committee a year ago and actually had a moment of feeling like a princess. Her sparkling ruby-red halter gown was a far cry from the more practical wardrobe she relied on working in the library, and at the homeless shelter many evenings. She'd splurged on dangling rhinestone earrings and a matching bracelet.

The historical barn had been converted into a remarkable venue, complete with a parquet dance floor, which was large enough for most of the several hundred guests in attendance. It was early yet; the main rush of attendees would begin in forty-five minutes or so.

Satisfaction curled in her belly as she eyed the dozens of round dinner tables, set with the signature Silver Valley colors of forest green, representing the Appalachian Mountains, and a deep agate blue that mirrored the blue shadows of the range from downtown. Gold candles floated in cylindrical vases, imbuing the room with a sense of rich anticipation. Swaths of pale blue muslin reached from the high ceiling and half dozen chandeliers, draping around wrought-iron frames to the floor below.

"What do you think?" Coral Stauffer, the woman who'd bought the barn a few years ago after returning to her hometown after a disastrous divorce from another Silver Valley native she'd happened to meet in California, stood next to her.

"It's spectacular, Coral! I can't thank you enough."

"Aw, honey, you did the hard work. My team put it together like we do for all the other events. Although this is the biggest of the year for us." Coral's bright sapphire-blue eyes reflected deeper emotion than expected for a charity event, but Portia didn't push her school friend. Like Annie, they'd known one another for years and she knew not to push Coral for details on the life she'd had in Southern California before returning to Silver Valley.

"You have been so patient with me."

"You're the expert, Portia. Everyone raves about how nice these evenings are."

"And this will be the biggest and best yet." She held up her hand, fingers crossed.

"No luck needed. Your hard work has paid off." Coral rubbed her bare shoulders. She too was in an evening gown, but one that was much more sedate than Portia's, as it was black and had a simple yet elegant high crew neck. "The storm's gone in time, thank goodness, but I'm going to turn the heat up until the room fills up."

"Do you miss it? The warmer weather in California?" The question came out of her without bidding and she wanted to bite her tongue. And not just from the obvious discomfort she'd brought to Coral, who bit her lower lip. Why was she torturing herself with her obsession over going to California with Kyle? He'd never indicated he wanted her to go with him there.

"I miss some of my friends that I made. I was there for almost ten years, as you know. College and after. But it was the right decision to come back to Silver Valley. Speaking of which, I read in the paper today that you've been through quite a bit lately, with some person stealing laptops from the library, and then you almost got hit on the train tracks? You never mentioned it, even with all the work we've done together."

Portia knew when to play it lightly. "I happened to

be in the wrong place at some of the right times for a criminal to show up. That's all." Her stomach tightened as fierce, protective instincts for the TH and SVPD ops against ROC roared. Who was she kidding, though? It was the only way she could be a part of Kyle's world now. Maintain the confidentiality of the takedown op. Which according to Josh, would have already happened, about an hour ago. She hadn't heard the contrary from Annie and she'd know in about two hours, depending on whether or not they showed up to the gala.

"I have a sneaking suspicion you're playing it far too cool, but we don't have time to talk now. I'm going to turn the heat up and then head for the kitchens. Is there anything you need from me now?"

"No, thanks, Coral. I'll do a quick look-over of the silent auction items." She walked in the opposite direction of Coral, across the dance floor, conscious of her very high strappy silver heels. When was the last time she'd taken such care with her appearance? And why hadn't she ever thought to get made-up for Kyle?

Because they'd been too busy running from a lethal threat or making love.

There, she'd admitted it. It had been making love with Kyle, all of it. She blinked back tears, grateful she'd picked her tube of waterproof mascara. But this was the gala, not a funeral. Lifting her chin and throwing her very chilly shoulders back, she kept going. As she looked at her hands, a huge cocktail ring winked from her right, while her left hand was bare. And would remain so, and that was okay.

It was ridiculous to even think she'd been that close to something big with Kyle. And even after Annie's prompting, she'd decided to be brave and…let Kyle go. She'd pursued Rob and thought she'd successfully landed a good partner, only to be proved wrong, ruefully so. What she'd shared with Kyle had been powerful and she wasn't going to demean it by trying to make it into something it wasn't: permanent.

But as she checked out the tables laden with item after item for the silent auction, in the room off the main dance and dinner area, her heart's whispers haunted her.

Chapter 19

"That was fast, even for TH," said the agent, Benjamin Michaels, who was sitting next to Kyle, whom he was shadowing.

"Don't count on it. The next part is going to be the trickiest. Ready?" Kyle motioned for Ben to follow him and they got to Kyle's vehicle in minutes. Within five more minutes, they were parked in the diner lot, which ran right up to the train tracks. Intel indicated the meeting of the ROC dealers would be in this spot. SVPD would handle the apprehensions, of which they expected at least a dozen. One for every car that they'd found the heroin stashed in.

"Do you think it's all heroin, or is some of it fentanyl?"

"Both the SVPD and FBI substance experts called it half-and-half on the spot."

"Which means it would have for sure been a death sentence. For how many?"

"Too many." Kyle's resolve strengthened. It was good to have a partner to talk to, in the moment. Not that it kept all thoughts of Portia out of his mind, but it did help him keep his A-game going during such a long day and night.

"Look, on the other side of the tracks." As Ben pointed out the five people, all dressed for the weather and with ski masks, Claudia's voice sounded in their headsets.

"We've got affirmative sighting of fifteen possible ROC."

Fifteen? He scanned the other side but the train pulled into view, and even though it moved very slowly, unlike the day he'd had to shove Portia off the track, it wasn't slow enough. Their view of the probable ROC operatives was blocked by the cargo containers.

They waited for the train to stop, as it often did to allow for the track to be switched to allow the cars to continue to the myriad distribution centers on the other side of town.

"We've got to get to other side of the tracks." Kyle was used to a case coming together at the very end, and knew that they were racing against Markova's clock. "Markova won't be here—she'll hang out where more civilians are. It's how she's blended in and disappeared from so many crimes before."

"I'm with you, Kyle." Ben's complete trust in his deduction gave Kyle pause. Another first. Usually he accepted professional respect as another part of the job, just as he gave it to his colleagues. But he'd discovered a new meaning to the word, since meeting Portia.

She'd trusted him to keep her alive.

"Let's go." He drove the vehicle out of the diner lot and headed for the closest cross street behind the train.

"You've done such a lovely job here, Portia." The mayor of Silver Valley shook her hand and she smiled at her.

"Thank you so much! It wouldn't have happened without the support of your office and the Rotary Club." She held her hand out to the woman standing with the mayor, her wife, and thanked her, too. "The community's really come together for this. Did you have a chance to look at all of the silent auction items?"

"Yes, and I'm afraid we may have bid on too many." The mayor cast a mock disparaging look at her spouse. "Why, exactly, did we bid on a fishing trip?"

"It's a perfect gift for your father." The mayor's wife responded with a smile and Portia thanked them for their support. If everyone present had bid as much as these two, they were bound to make a record amount tonight. Good for the library, wonderful for the homeless shelter.

"Enjoy the night. The dancing is about to start." She left the couple and continued to work the room, making sure to thank everyone who'd helped her put the event together. It was really almost everyone in the room.

As she walked from group to group, table to table, couple to couple, she received many compliments for the event, the silent auction items, even her dress. She knew it was pure immaturity that her disappointment was like that of a spoiled child's. But she couldn't help it. She'd hoped Kyle would be here, see her as the woman he'd helped her become. There were transition points in life, clear markers where she'd gone from her comfort zone to who she was meant to be. Kyle had been alongside her for this most recent, most important one. Portia had transitioned from someone content with her status quo, pouring her energy into what her town and its library patrons needed, to a woman who wanted what was best for herself.

Her big problem now was that Kyle didn't think what she wanted was viable. She wanted him.

Kyle looked at his watch for the hundredth time that night. Nine thirty-three. Portia would be announcing the last time allowed for the silent auction bids. He knew because he'd read her paperwork, proofed the program for her, at her request. She'd been all doe-eyed and hopeful when she'd approached him to help her out with the planning. But he knew better. She'd seen that he was bored, once they'd figured out ROC's shipping plans. It had helped the time pass more quickly, as had their lovemaking.

Actions that could have led to her death. He knew he'd never forgive himself for letting Markova get that close to Portia, but he could make a difference now by apprehending Markova the minute she showed up to coordinate the offload.

Kyle and Ben observed from the parking lot of the train station as the train pulled to a stop a full half mile before it was supposed to. It was extremely unusual for a cargo train to pull in at the local, or any, passenger terminal. But not for a shipment that had ROC's backing. Claudia's briefing before they'd prepared to come down here tonight put all the pieces together. ROC had spent almost a million dollars bribing the train conductors along the route from the southern border, where the original shipment of heroin had occurred, to each waypoint where yet another container was loaded with whatever the shipment was, en route to central Pennsylvania.

She reported that Ivanov had been alarmed when the storm hit and shut down all transportation, overreacting a bit by the trains being stuck for so many days. It was record breaking and risky—the shipping companies and receiving customers could have opted to move their goods via other means, like eighteen-wheel trucks. But a storm the size of the one they'd just experienced had shut down all possibilities. A stroke of good fortune for ROC, as far as Ivanov was concerned.

Better luck for SVPD, TH and all the other LEAs working to confiscate the illegal drugs. It meant they'd be able to proceed with the plan of attack they'd practiced for the past several weeks.

"Is that her?" Ben asked and nodded toward a beat-up sedan that had sputtered to a stop in the lot, at the very edge of the plowed pavement, next to a twelve-foot mound of snow.

"Sure looks like it." But before he raised his binoculars to his eyes, gunshots rang through the night air, their pitch higher than the squeal of the train's brakes.

"Go, go, go!" He shot out the order as much to himself as Ben and they exited their vehicle, low on the ground, weapons drawn. Using their doors as shields, they looked around to see the source of the gunfire.

It was two men, from their size, at the engine's door. By the time Kyle ascertained the scenario, one of the shooters was down flat on the ground, and he watched the second drop as the "engineer" dismounted from the engine.

"Two shooters down," a female voice sounded in his headset. So the FBI had used a female agent. And she'd done her job as well as Kyle knew he could have. Probably better tonight, as he was fighting like heck to keep thoughts of Portia from distracting him.

"Copy that. Remove their weapons from the scene and—" Claudia's orders were cut off as more gunfire sounded. The undercover FBI train engineer ducked back, but she needn't have, because the bullets pinged off Kyle and Ben's vehicle.

"Kyle and Ben are under fire, repeat, we are under fire." Kyle issued the report as he stayed low, avoiding the bullets that strafed their car. The initial shots had turned into rapid fire, indicating either a second gunman or weapon. Only an automatic weapon could fire so relentlessly.

"Sounds like AR-15 fire to me," he spoke into his headset but for Ben's benefit. "Trademark Markova. She's happiest with a Kalashnikov, though."

"Stay down and hold your fire. We have the shooter in target range," said Claudia. Her voice revealed nothing but her orders, yet Kyle suspected she wasn't amused by their musings over Markova's weapon of choice.

Another sign that he was tired and had allowed his feelings for Portia to affect him. He was avoiding the reality that he could be killed and never speak to Portia again. It was one thing when he made that choice, decided to go off to California for good. Being killed by his ROC target was a whole other matter, though.

Kyle felt helpless as he and Ben witnessed the takedown of fifteen ROC drug dealers who'd showed up to get their share of the shipment. He wanted to find Markova, be the one to cuff her.

After what seemed like hours, the all-clear came.

"Do we have Markova?" He held his breath, waiting for an affirmative from one of his colleagues.

"Agent Girardi has a female suspect in custody who was driving Markova's vehicle," Claudia informed him, but her statement wasn't good enough.

"Are we sure it's her?"

"You're free to go see for yourself, Kyle."

Kyle didn't spare Ben a glance. "Follow me."

"With you."

They had to walk around several clusters of LEAs, who were taking potential drug dealers into custody. Their statements would be recorded at SVPD, then analyzed to see what new ROC information could be gleaned.

Kyle didn't care about anything but being able to look Markova in the eyes and let her know he'd been on to her all along.

He approached the group of LEAs, three women and two men, who surrounded the petite woman. Anticipation built, but he refused to allow himself the pleasure of thinking about how soon he could see Portia, tell her she was completely safe.

"Excuse me," he said.

The officers parted to let him into the process and he looked for Markova's signature glacial blue gaze. The mark of her sociopathic personality.

Instead he looked into two very wide, very shocked eyes.

"Who the hell are you?"

The woman didn't speak, just trembled as tears rained down her cheeks. He saw the blonde wig on the dirty snow, recognized Markova's clothing on the woman. She spoke in broken English with a good smattering of Russian.

"She says Markova made her do this," one of the FBI agents informed him, while tapping into a tablet. He looked up. "And left you a message." He then read from his notes, "Portia DiNapoli and the man protecting her will enjoy fireworks at the end of the Library Fund-raising Gala. On me."

Among Markova's many criminal skills was a talent for explosives. She'd taken out an entire SWAT team in New York City two years ago. ROC had claimed it but intelligence pointed to Markova as the actual culprit.

Markova was going to blow up the gala venue. With Portia in it.

Kyle leaned past the FBI agent to grab the woman, to find out where Markova had gone, but Ben stopped him. "Easy, Kyle. She's not your target."

He turned toward him, and Ben visibly braced himself. *He thinks I'm going to hit him.* Kyle realized he was tensed as if for the fight of his life.

But it wasn't his life he was concerned about; it was Portia's. And possibly everyone else's at the gala.

He began to run back to his car, with Ben on his heels.

"Where are we going?"

"Gala. At the Weddings and More Barn."

He heard Ben relay the information to Claudia over the wireless headsets but it was in his peripheral awareness. Kyle had no room to focus on anything but getting to Portia.

Before Markova did.

* * *

Markova grinned as she took the best seat in the house at the top of the silo, with a throwaway phone at hand to call in to SVPD when the bomb's timer was at the ten-minute mark. Her rifle was in top shape and ready to go. She'd even splurged on a laser tracer after watching an American war movie. It had inspired her to use their own tactics against them.

She might be working for ROC for another twenty minutes, but she couldn't help her FSB background. It came to the forefront as she faced down what she'd learned was American arrogance. Did Portia DiNapoli and the man she'd seen her with, who she knew had to be an undercover cop or FBI, think they'd survive against the best training Russia offered its agents? Ludmila's training, combined with ROC money and backing, made her invincible.

Almost. What really pushed her abilities into the unstoppable range was her desire to be free of all of this. She had a disguise waiting in the brand-new SUV she'd just stolen and placed fake license plates on. They'd never find her. No one. Not ROC, which would want retribution, nor FSB, which was still sore she'd left after only a couple of tours of duty. And the American law enforcement agencies? Amateurs, all of them.

She looked at her watch, and then called in to the Silver Valley Police Department. It was 9-1-1 that she dialed, but she knew who'd get the message.

"9-1-1. What's your emergency?"

"I don't have an emergency, but your police department does. There's a bomb in place at the Weddings and More Barn on highway two-twenty-two outside Silver Valley. It's going to blow in ten minutes." She loved that she'd perfected her American accent while still in the FSB. It made tasks like this so easy.

"Who are you, ma'am?"

She disconnected and picked up her other cell phone. With a sense of purpose she'd never felt before, because this was not only the end of her duties for ROC, the end of the annoying investigators and agents who'd tried to stymie her efforts, it also was her beginning.

She touched the button and started the bomb timer. A laugh escaped her at her generosity. She'd given the stupid Americans an extra thirty seconds.

Chapter 20

Portia's jaw began to ache from constantly smiling. In truth, it was because as happy as she was that the gala was going well and had raised twice as much as last year, allowing for funding for the homeless shelter, it wasn't completely what she'd envisioned.

Since he'd come into her life, she'd dreamed of Kyle being at the event with her. What good was success if she didn't have someone to share it with?

And she'd shared in Kyle's accomplishment by working on the spreadsheets with him and discovering how ROC was trafficking heroin via rail transport. By now, he'd finished his mission. Markova would be behind bars, and hopefully so would many other ROC operatives.

She couldn't wait to find out that her town was safe again.

"Portia!" Annie appeared from the midst of the

swaying crowd, with at least half of the attendees on
the dance floor following the instructions of the deejay to flap like a chicken. Annie wasn't laughing along
with the dance, though, her face tight with concern.
Portia's stomach flipped. *Kyle.*

"What's going on?"

"I need you to follow me, quickly."

"Can it wait? I've got to announce the silent auction
winners in five minutes."

Annie's expression chilled Portia to the marrow.
She stepped closer and whispered in Portia's ear. "Josh
texted me. They've stopped the shipment, arrested all
the players except one. Markova. Kyle thinks she's on
her way here."

The silent auction items could wait.

"Where do you want me to go?"

"For starters, follow me out to my car. We're getting you out of here."

"I'm right behind you." She followed Annie through
the crowd, danced her way through several overzeal-
ous groups of liquored-up guests. They'd each paid for
their tickets, which included an open bar, and Portia
would have made a mental note about reexamining
that policy for next year's gala. Except she was being
targeted by an assassin.

"Hey, Portia! Come dance with us." Gary, one of
the volunteers at the homeless shelter, circled her waist
with his beefy arm and pulled her off course. In the
center of a dance circle, she lost sight of Annie. Gary
was a friendly guy, and did a lot of the heavy lifting
at the shelter, from repair work to stocking the pantry.
She was no match for his brute strength. What Gary
didn't know, and what she couldn't tell him, was that

his jubilation could very well be what got her killed. Worse, she was putting all of the guests at risk the longer she remained in the barn. She looked around for Annie, knowing her friend would circle back the second she discovered Portia had been waylaid.

But Annie was still making a beeline for the back of the hall, toward the kitchen.

"Annie!" Portia yelled as loudly as she could, but to no avail. Her competition from the partygoers and booming music was too great. She'd have to get out of here on her own.

Forcing a bright smile, she yanked Gary down far enough that she could shout in his ear. "I've got to pee! I'll be right back."

"You'd better!" Gary said, and then guffawed as he made an opening for her, and she wished she'd thought to use the excuse as soon as he'd drawn her in.

Finally she was free, making good headway through the rest of the dancers. Until she slammed into a large man blocking her path. She saw the white tuxedo shirt, the shiny black studs, and looked up to excuse herself as the man's arms encircled her, his hands on her forearms.

"Excu—" She looked up into the only eyes that made her head spin and her heart flip. Silver eyes.

"Portia." Kyle's face was a mask of taut tension and she froze. He was here because of Markova. Of course.

"I know, Kyle. I'm getting out of here, like Annie said to." She looked over his shoulder, searching for her friend. Why hadn't Annie returned to get her?

"Annie's busy taking care of things," he shouted, but then leaned toward her ear, just as Gary had moments before. But instead of sweat and fermenting alcohol, she smelled Kyle's too-familiar musk, mingled with the scent of the bar soap he favored. She fought to stay focused, keep her mind on getting out of the barn, but the assault on her senses threw her. She blinked, and his voice gave her the anchor she needed.

"Listen to me, Portia. Markova's rigged this barn to blow up in six minutes. Five by now. I need you to go to the mic and tell the deejay you have an announcement. Then tell your guests to use the four exits and leave as quietly and as quickly as possible. Stay calm, keep them from panicking. Then you go with them."

She looked into his eyes for a full heartbeat, absorbing all he'd said, knowing from the steady intensity in his gaze that he was telling the truth. They might all die right now.

"Do it, Portia." He gave her a slight shake, a squeeze to her forearms, where he'd gripped her since she'd slammed into him. And then he kissed her, hard, his lips a seal of his promise to keep her safe but more, a show of his confidence in her ability to carry through.

Portia whirled around and made her way to the soundstage, elbowing anyone in her way. Acutely conscious of the ticking clock, which in this case was really a bomb, she got to the deejay.

"Cut the music! We have an emergency!" she shouted in his ear. To his credit he complied, handing her the mic. Before the guests' groans of disappointment turned into a chorus, she held up her hand.

"We have an emergency, folks. Please stay calm. I need you to pick one of the four exit doors around you and leave the building now." She pointed to each door, saw that the guests were paying attention, their heads moving and their bodies following. "We believe there's a minor gas leak in the kitchen but we have to make sure it's nothing serious. Please exit and make your way to the ice sculpture display, in the field directly behind the second barn."

To her great relief, the guests followed her directions. There were whiners, a few people who didn't want to go out into the cold without their coats, but fortunately the more sober and levelheaded attendees prevailed. As she watched the last ones leave, she put the mic down and headed for the nearest exit. Kyle was gone, but this wasn't the time to wish she'd said something to him, told him how she really felt. She had to get out of the building, too.

She stepped onto the exit door threshold, only to notice an odd red line across her arms, which turned into a dot on her chest. Her reaction was automatic as she ducked back behind the doorframe and hit the floor. Shots hit the building on either side of the door and she scrambled to get on the other side of the sound-stage, placing the foot-high structure between her and the open exit.

Kyle and Annie cleared out the few remaining workers in the kitchen area, who might have not been able to hear Portia's announcement. Satisfied that the building was empty, he ignored his mental ticking clock as he worked with Annie to find the explosive. His Marine Corps training had included a rudimentary EOD, Explosive Ordnance Disposal, course but it'd be enough to identify the device and its location for the bomb squad, which was due here imminently.

"What am I looking for, exactly, besides something

with a clock and wires on it?" Annie asked as she searched under cabinets.

"It won't be obvious, out here in plain sight. It's probably close to an energy source." As he spoke, he realized he needed to find where the pipes that brought in the natural gas were. Gas was the primary source of heat and energy in Pennsylvania, second only to electricity. He hadn't seen propane tanks outside, so there had to be a shut-off valve inside the barn, as well as a main switch somewhere on the property.

He stopped to put his hands on Annie's shoulders. "Stop. I need you to get out of here, clear the area surrounding the building."

"You should come with me, Kyle. We don't have more than three minutes left."

"I'm right behind you, Annie. Get out." He didn't look up but heard the sound of her feet hitting the tiles as she reached the ground on the other side of the propped-open door.

The silence that descended made him insane with the need to find the device. It was then that he smelled the telltale scent of natural gas, at the same moment he heard a gunshot. And then several following.

"Kyle, get out behind Annie. Now." Claudia's voice in his ear, he ran to the sound of the shots.

"Gunshots, out by the dance floor."

"It doesn't matter, Kyle. You're down to ninety seconds. *Get out.*"

He ripped the earpiece out and ran into the main room, searching for the source of the shots. He immediately spotted Portia lying up against the soundstage, saw the laser target against the doorjamb as shots continued to hit the building. At least he didn't smell the gas here, or the building would already be gone.

With Portia still in it.

Kyle didn't take time to process or reason things out, or even to figure out the best point of egress. He acted on pure instinct and ran for Portia, not stopping until he slid in next to her.

Portia felt the body slam up against hers and closed her eyes tight. Was this it? Had the building exploded and was she dead, unable to feel any pain?

Familiar hands, arms around her. "Portia. Are you with me?"

She turned and faced Kyle. This had to be heaven. Except he didn't look blissed out but incredibly stressed, an almost animal-like countenance to his expression.

"I'm fine. I'm hiding from the shooter."

"We have to get out of here, now. It's going to blow in less than a minute. Stay behind me, whatever you do." He stood up amid the barrage of more bullets and hauled her up, placing her behind him. They ran for the door, opposite the side where the bullets sprayed plywood from the wall, the doorframe a mess of bullet holes. At the very edge of the exit, hidden from the shooter, he turned and looked at her as if he'd never see her again.

"We are going to run outside, crouched low, zigzagging. We'll make it to the pile of snow and then lie flat." His eyes blazed and Portia wanted to ask him why they were doing this, why they had to leave here right now, in the face of a shooter she'd bet was Markova. Their choices were lethal. And then she smelled it. Natural gas.

"Kyle!" She screamed but he didn't wait, turned with her hand in his and they plunged into the dark night. Into the path of certain death.

Portia thought the air should feel cold against her bared skin, her evening gown no match for the Pennsylvania winter.

Kyle still held her hand, pulling her along, his arm behind his back, blocking her from the shots that rained down on them like errant, lethal snowflakes. The snowbank was so close but Kyle changed direction and she thought she felt a bullet hit him, as he jumped at the moment of impact. Yet he remained on his feet, taking them past the original place he'd set and kept going. Out into the farm field, where a plowed path from the barn parking lot to a silo allowed them traction.

They ran through the night, past the edge of the sculptures, and she had a fleeting thought about the gala guests but they were on the other side of the sculptures, farther from the barn.

"No, no!" she screamed as more bullets hit the snow on either side of them. When Kyle stumbled, her heart seemed to stop. No, no, no—not Kyle.

You should have told him you love him.

Portia opened her mouth to yell at him, to tell him, before they were both blasted into oblivion. But the inevitable explosion happened, rolling across the ground under her feet.

She felt like she was floating, that time was standing still. As she began to fly through the air, all she was conscious of was Kyle's grip on her hand. He'd never let go, never stopped protecting her from the gunfire. His actions resulted in her experiencing every bit of the detonation.

Somewhere in her mind, she registered that the gunfire had stopped.

A sharp flash of light, followed by the loudest sound she'd ever heard, mixed with the hot air that buoyed their flight. A second explosion!

And still they were flying, moving through the air, across the barn's field, as if they were hawks swooping for groundhogs. After they hit the ground, she rolled on the hard packed snow, until coming to a stop atop the frosty white coating.

She looked up to see the barn completely gone, engulfed by flames. Plywood smacked down next to her, narrowly missing her head. And her hands were bloody, but from what? Her hands…

"Kyle!" She screamed but only a croak emerged from her throat. Or was her hearing messed up? Belatedly she discovered that she could hear nothing but a dull roar. She looked around her, saw him lying in the snow no more than a foot from her. Portia tried to move, strained to reach him. His still form shocked her more than any explosion could. He lay on his side, facing her, only a small part of his face visible. Tears and holes in his tuxedo jacket and shirt revealed he'd been hit by bullets. A trickle of blood ran from his nostril to the visible part of his cheek. Shock began to roll through her. Her teeth shattered, her body shook and her heart broke for the love of her life.

Searing pain kept her present, and she looked at its source, the heeled boot painfully crushing her hand.

Raising her gaze up the calf boot to the pants, the jacket, the face of Ludmila Markova.

The woman had a rifle almost as long as her petite torso strapped across her back and a handgun in her grip. But the deadly weapons weren't what frightened Portia. It was the evil smile Markova gave her in the flickering light, the darkness only broken by the burning building behind them. No siren lights, no SVPD units surrounded them.

It was Portia, Markova and an either very injured, or more likely, dead Kyle. Despair that she'd never previously experienced threatened to swallow her as it invited her to a hell she'd only ever imagined.

"Don't look so sad, Portia DiNapoli. They say it's very peaceful after the bullet." Markova kept her pistol pointed at Portia as she kicked Kyle's still body, to no reaction from Kyle. Portia couldn't stop the gagging, the bile that rose as she realized the love of her life was gone, and she was soon going to join him.

This was so not how she'd planned getting back together with Kyle. Her mind flashed to how good she'd felt in his arms, how safe, how protected. How he'd challenged her to face down her choice to settle for her quiet, albeit full, life in Silver Valley. Kyle had invited her to take a chance on having the time of her life with him.

"Your guardian angel has lost his wings, Portia. Time for you to join him."

Portia refused to look at Markova. She kept her gaze on Kyle, knowing that he was the last thing she wanted to see before she died. But the ROC operative denied her that, crouching next to her and placing her face next to Portia's. She must think Portia was injured more than she was.

"You stupid fool. You thought you'd get away from me. Now look at both of you." The cold barrel of the gun felt like ice on Portia's temple and she closed her eyes, acting dead. Before Markova could get a shot off, Portia summoned all the strength she had left and grabbed the hand holding the gun, forcing it away from them. She head-butted Markova, ignoring the smattering of stars across her field of vision. Before Markova regained her wits, Portia rolled her to her back and held the woman's arms over her head, working to get the weapon out of her hand.

But Markova was better trained, more experienced. She flipped Portia off her as if she were no more than a tiny kitten, shoved her heeled boot into Portia's solar plexus. Portia landed hard on her back, the wind out of her sails. She might not have finished the job against Markova but she'd die trying.

Markova loomed over her, furious and prepared to kill her. This time Portia knew she'd reached her limit. She closed her eyes and thought of the one man who'd ever loved her for who she was.

Kyle.

Kyle came to on his right side, in the field, with his face shoved into several inches of snow. He couldn't open his left eye, and from how much it hurt, he figured it was swollen shut. Looking for Portia, his right eye found her, lying just inches from him. She was on her stomach, lifting her head, looking around. Portia had made it.

Thank God.

He focused on trying to assess his injuries, to figure out what he was capable of doing. He could only see Portia, and there was no sign of backup. Not yet.

Markova couldn't be discounted, explosion or not. Years of undercover work and countless situations just like this one had his mind moving automatically into recovery mode. He knew the barn was gone, and that the scene around it would be in chaos until SVPD and TH got everyone taken care of. He sent up another silent prayer that Portia had convinced the guests to leave, that Claudia and he had found out about the explosive soon enough.

His breathing deepened and he winced. His bulletproof vest had done its job; he was alive. But getting hit with automatic weapon ammo still hurt.

He sensed her before he saw her walk into his field of vision. Markova, an AR-47 strapped on her back, a .45 in her hands. She said something to Portia but he wasn't listening. He was watching her actions, preparing to take her out. She turned toward him and he lay still, feigning unconsciousness. The kick wasn't unexpected but still rocked him, and more than anything he had to fight his instinctual reaction to grab Markova's ankle, yank her off balance and hold her down until Josh or someone else arrived.

Her attention was back on Portia and he surreptitiously tested the fingers of his right hand, underneath him. He closed his grip around his weapon, which had landed right in front of his stomach. His left arm had hidden it from Markova.

Before he had a chance to move, Markova's backside was in front of him, and within two seconds, Portia had pulled the woman down—and wait, had Portia just head-butted Markova?

As much as he'd love to see anyone take out Markova, he wasn't risking Portia's life for it. He drew his weapon, took aim and fired.

Markova's form fell, her handgun dropping to the ground, unused. Portia's scream reached his ears, dimly, as the roar of the explosions had made his tinnitus flare. Her scream was enough to tell him all he needed to know. Portia was still alive.

Chapter 21

"You've got several abrasions from flying debris, with your hands being the most severely injured. But they'll heal quickly. Just keep the ointment on them, and replace the bandages after each shower. You're lucky you didn't need any stitches."

Portia paid attention to the ER doctor as much as she could, with her ears still ringing and her head spinning from the night's events. It'd only been twenty minutes since they'd arrived at the ER, an hour tops since the explosion. Since she'd been next to Kyle. But she couldn't stop looking at the door, willing him to walk through it.

"Thank you, Doctor," Annie responded, standing near the exam table. "I'll make sure she waits to sign out."

"Thanks. Best to both of you, and thank you for your service." He nodded at Annie on his way out. She wore her SVPD ID around her neck. While dirty and dusty from all she'd done, Annie looked like a fresh spring daisy next to Portia.

"All I want is my coat and a warm bed." And Kyle.

"I'm afraid your coat, and anything else you had at the gala, is gone."

"Including all the silent auction items."

Annie smiled ruefully. "But you got the pledges. No one will take back their donations, trust me. They're all happy to be alive."

"Mmm." She looked at the door the doctor had just exited. Still no Kyle.

"He's being examined, too. They took him to Harrisburg, in case he needed surgery."

"Surgery?"

"He had several gunshot hits, you know. But his vest caught them all. Josh texted that he's fine and moving around."

But he wasn't here. "Can I go see him?"

Annie looked uncomfortable.

"What, Annie? Tell me."

"Kyle asked that you don't try to find him. He's got a lot of work to do, to wrap up his part of this case, and—"

"No, stop, I don't need to know any more. That's okay." It wasn't okay, though, not really. She ached for him, for the comfort only he brought her. He'd given it so freely, always had her back, kept her alive. She owed him everything, for saving her life twice and more. For showing her what true love really was. Kyle didn't owe her anything, though. And as she'd told him herself, she'd known the deal when she'd been with him. The gaping hole in her heart was something she'd known was inevitable. Kyle was still California-bound, then back to his undercover world, the way he liked it best. With no strings.

"Come on, let's get you home. We'll ask the check-out desk to hurry it up."

"Don't I have to file a report with SVPD?"

"Yes, but your statement will wait until tomorrow. They have their hands full, helping the FBI with Markova's interview."

"So that's it, it's all over?"

Annie shook her head. "Unfortunately, no, as this was just the first wave of several planned shipments. But we made a big dent in their profits, for sure. And Markova, once she recovers from the bullet to her gut, will never see the outside of a prison for the rest of her life, with the charges filed. She singlehandedly orchestrated the shipment of millions of dollars of heroin, including a package of fentanyl that could have killed as many as ten thousand. And she put several hundred lives at risk by blowing up the barn when she knew the gala was there. Not to mention shooting at you and Kyle."

"And breaking into the house." The memories of the days she'd spent snowbound with Kyle overwhelmed her and she let the tears fall. "I'm fine, don't worry. This is probably shock."

Annie's arm was around her shoulders. "More like seeing the person you love take a hit for you."

She sniffed, nodded. No use hiding her feelings from Annie, who saw through her.

"What's this?" Claudia asked as she walked into the room, dressed in casual clothes, her hair messier than its normal smooth bob. It'd been a tough night for the director. "Portia, you have gone above and beyond tonight and this past month. Please accept my thank-you on behalf of my entire agency."

Portia wiped her eyes. "It's been my privilege. Was anyone seriously hurt tonight?"

"Other than ROC's attempt to infiltrate Silver Valley and make it its epicenter of East Coast crime?" Claudia smiled, then shook her head. "No. And a lot of the credit goes to you for staying calm and clearing the barn as quickly as you did."

"Annie helped, in the kitchen, from what she's told me. And I couldn't have done it without Kyle telling me what to do."

"You did it. And you fought Markova—you know, if you ever want to give a job with my group a try, I'd be willing to vouch for you."

Portia managed a weak laugh. "No, thank you. I'll stick to information resources, and the service work I've already signed up for. Finding a new venue for next year's gala is going to be a full-time job!"

Claudia nodded. "Nevertheless, the offer stands. You're adept at intelligence analysis."

"Thank you, Claudia."

"You're getting her home?" Claudia addressed Annie, who nodded. "I'll check in on you next week, Portia. Go home and get some rest."

Claudia left and Annie turned to her. "You're coming home with me, for now. Your apartment is safe, you can go back there, but you shouldn't be alone right now. You've had several major shocks."

Portia didn't argue as she accepted her friend's help. She'd be alone again soon enough.

* * *

Kyle spent the next two weeks wrapping up the case, including several interviews with Markova. True to form, she refused to turn, doing nothing to help any of the law enforcement agencies defeat ROC. After he signed the last reporting document on the case, he loaded his car with his possessions, ended his monthly lease and drove west.

He had to fight from calling Portia, from showing up at her doorstep each minute of every day. But he couldn't go to her until he had his life in order. Until he knew he could be the man Portia deserved.

Chapter 22

One month later

"You'll find a personal hygiene kit, towels and an extra blanket on the end of your bed." Portia gave the newest patron of the homeless shelter a bag of nonperishable food items.

"There's always hot coffee and water, along with fresh muffins, in the dining room. They'll be serving dinner until 10:00 p.m."

"Thanks." The woman met her eyes before she headed for the stairs, which Portia considered a minor victory. It was hard to admit you needed help at any time, but she'd witnessed countless homeless persons struggle the hardest. The cold drove them in from the street, the only place they felt totally independent.

"You're almost done tonight, Portia. Got a hot date?"

Gary joked from the front door, where he added an additional helping hand to the security guard. They'd had a minor altercation earlier in the week with a group of apparent heroin addicts looking for a score. They'd heard a dealer was spending the night in the shelter and wanted to "come in for a quick few minutes." The guard and Gary had chased them off and called SVPD.

"Nope, not tonight, but I'm meeting my best friend for coffee after." She hadn't had any dates or even the dream of one in the last month. How could she, when her heart belonged to a man she'd never have?

Kyle. He'd been in California for a full month, yesterday. Not that she was counting. She'd left Josh and Annie's a few nights after the gala, and without constant contact with Josh, she lost her inside track to Kyle's life. Not that Josh gave away much—he claimed he knew nothing, but Portia knew better. Both men worked with TH and she knew that Kyle was setting up the West Coast TH office. Kyle would have to report back to Claudia on that basis alone, which in turn meant the rest of the agents understandably knew at least a few details of the project.

Portia didn't give a groundhog's butt about the TH project or anything else work-related, including her own job. All she cared was that Kyle was safe and happy.

At least one of them should find joy after what they'd shared.

"You need to go home now, Portia, before the storm hits." Gary treated her like a little sister but she didn't mind. He wasn't patronizing, just caring.

She bundled up in her parka, wrapped the scarf Annie had knit her "just because" and headed into the cold night. Another storm was coming in, accounting for the uptick in shelter patrons. As she walked the few short blocks to her apartment, her cheeks were hit with fat flakes. The last time she'd been snowbound, it'd been in a beautiful home and not her tiny apartment over a coffee shop.

The shop still had its neon OPEN sign lit, and the warm inside light spilled onto the street, where snow quickly accumulated. Annie had sent her a quick text earlier, saying she wasn't sure they'd be able to meet for their girls' night tomorrow, with the storm predicted to bring things to a stop for at least two days. So she'd suggested they meet at the shop next to Portia's apartment.

Portia sighed as she pulled open the heavy door of the former prison, marveling again at how clever the coffee shop owner had been to pick the historical building to begin a new business in Silver Valley. It was a way to preserve the past but infuse it with the promise of tomorrow, and definitely in a more positive way. She preferred it as a café over the local prison it had once been. Scents of coffee and chocolate hit her and she saw a giggling group of teens near the fireplace, their hands holding mugs with the shop's logo. No sign of Annie yet, so she went up to the counter to order a small pot of chamomile tea. She wanted nothing to keep her awake past her usual bedtime. That led to thoughts of Kyle, which led to a sleepless night.

"What can I get you?" The usual college student barista had been replaced since last night. This barista had the same voice as the man she'd dreamed about, been unable to keep her mind and heart off, since she'd met him. Portia's heart swelled, but her fear of having lost her mind tempered her joy.

"Kyle?"

Kyle's silver gaze was lit with a fire she'd only dreamed of, his tall form startling against the backdrop of the espresso machine and pastry case. He didn't speak, as he appeared as hungry as she was, and not for the sweets on the shelf.

"What are you doing here?"

"I'm afraid that's not on our menu, ma'am." His grin was so full of happiness, she wasn't sure if she wanted to jump the counter and kiss him, or turn and run. It was scary, facing her life's dream like this. Her heart's desire.

"I thought you were in California."

His gaze never left hers, but she saw him take her in, really look at her. A worry line appeared on his brow. "You're not eating enough."

"Need some help, Kyle?" The lanky barista she was familiar with appeared next to Kyle, who nodded.

"Thanks, Ryan. I'll be back next week for my shift." Portia watched Kyle as he walked around the counter and put his arms around her. "We're going to be in the front room for a bit, Ryan. A private function," Kyle said to the barista but his eyes never left hers.

"What's this about, Kyle? I'm meeting Annie..." She trailed off as he ushered her into the front room, where she'd often spent long hours reading or going over gala details. Annie had not planned to meet her, after all. It'd been a setup. Portia hoped it meant more than Annie employing her matchmaking tendencies. And what if Kyle only wanted to talk, to have some kind of stupid closure before saying they'd never see one another again?

Although he'd been working behind the counter.

She shrugged away from Kyle, took her coat off and sat in the chair he held out for her. Kyle closed the door, and the room immediately felt smaller, cozier.

Safer.

Kyle sat in the chair opposite her, leaning forward, their knees touching. He reached for her hands and she gave them with no argument. "You'd better have a damned good explanation for disappearing for a month." She'd meant to sound stern but her voice shook and she barely kept from bursting into tears.

"That's for you to decide." He reached up and moved a stray strand of her curly hair behind her ear. The tips of his fingers touched her earlobe and she closed her eyes against the assault of emotions.

"Kyle."

"I need your eyes open for this, babe. When they're closed like that, all I want to do is get to the kissing and I've got some talking to do first."

She opened her eyes, ready to listen. "Shoot."

Kyle's eyes glistened. No way. Was her secret undercover agent tearing up?

"I had to go back to California to take care of some business. The least important was what you know, to set up the office Claudia wants out there. But the other part…" He squeezed her hands and she squeezed back. It was automatic to support him in whatever he had to say.

"Go on."

"I bought a piece of land years ago, to give myself an anchor. A place I'd have to go back to, whether between missions, on leave or for a permanent residence. I went back there—it's next to an almond farm—and I took time for myself. The last several years have been one op after another. That worked for me for a long time, but no longer." He looked away as if gathering his thoughts. When he met her gaze again, she swore she saw down to his soul. And knew he saw the same in her eyes.

"The thing is, Portia, none of it's the same anymore. Since I first laid eyes on you, I knew you were special. I'm not one for woo-woo stuff, but I swear my soul recognized you. And then when we were together— there's no one else for me, Portia."

"Kyle, I feel the same."

"I was hoping you'd say that, but here's the deal. I'm not going to push you on this. You take as long as you want. But I'm putting my roots down here, in Silver Valley. I'll still work for TH, of course, and I'll work in this coffee shop. Maybe pick up some other part-time jobs, too. They're all good cover for when I'm not out on an op."

She couldn't keep the grin from stretching across her face if she wanted to. Portia took her hands from his and cupped his face, leaning in close. "I never thought of you as a barista, but I kind of like it. Imagine what we could do with frothed milk."

He sucked in a breath and his pupils dilated in the brightly lit room. She'd missed turning him on so much.

"Hold on, babe." His hands were on her waist, his fingers digging in just enough to make her go hot all over. He'd better say whatever else he wanted to quickly, because she was about to jump him.

"I'm not doing this to see how it works out, or worse, if it'll work out. We're going to do whatever it takes to make this work, Portia, because what we have is big time. The kind of thing that lasts a lifetime."

"'Kind of thing,' Kyle?" She wanted to hear him say it.

"Love, Portia. I love you and I will until my last dying breath."

"I love you, too." She leaned in then but he was already there, kissing her with as much love and abandon as she had.

"Um, I think we'd better get upstairs to my apartment." She didn't want to have her first time with Kyle since he'd returned be on top of the coffee shop table. Although...

"Well, since you've mentioned it, there's a storm coming. And I happen to have the keys to a place with a hot tub. We could get stuck there for several days..."

She kissed him. "Quick then, let's go. Let's hurry up and start the rest of our lives together."

"Oh, we've already begun that, babe. The day I first laid eyes on you."

* * * * *

SNOWBLIND JUSTICE

CINDI MYERS

For Gay and Reed.

Chapter One

Snow sifted down over the town like a downy blanket, turning trash piles into pristine drifts, transforming mine ruins into nostalgic works of art, hiding ugliness and danger beneath a dusting of wedding-cake white.

The murderer lurked behind a veil of snow, fresh flakes hiding his tracks, muffling the sound of his approach, covering up the evidence of his crimes. Deep cold and furious blizzards kept others indoors, but the killer reveled in his mastery over the landscape. His pursuers thought he was soft, like them. They couldn't find him because they assumed conditions were too harsh for him to survive in the wilderness.

And all the while he was waiting, striking when the right opportunity presented itself, his intellect as much of a weapon as his muscles. The woman who lay before him now was a prime example. She hadn't hesitated to stop when he had flagged her down on the highway. He was merely a stranded motorist who needed help. He was good-looking and charming—what woman wouldn't want to help him?

By the time she realized his purpose, it was too late. Like the officials who tracked him, she had underestimated him. The lawmen doubted his ability to instill trust in his victims, and were awed by his talent for killing quickly and efficiently while leaving no trace.

He lifted the woman's inert body into the car, arranging it into an artful tableau across the seat. There was very little blood—none in the vehicle—and no fingerprints or other evidence for the sheriff and his deputies to trace. They would search and examine and photograph and question—and they would find nothing.

He shut the door to the car and trudged away as the snow began to fall harder, a sifting of sugar over the bloodstains on the side of the road, and over his footprints, and over the signs of a struggle in the older snow beside the highway. The killer ducked behind a wall of ice, and disappeared out of sight of the empty road. Wind blew the snow sideways, the flakes sticking to the knit mask he had pulled up over his face, but he scarcely felt the cold, too absorbed in the details of his latest killing, reveling in his skill at pulling it off—again.

There were no witnesses to his crime, and none to his getaway. The lawmen thought they were closing in on him because they had linked his name to his crimes. But they didn't realize he was the one drawing nearer and nearer to his goal. Soon he would claim his final victim—the woman who had brought him to Eagle Mountain in the first place. After he had taken her, he would disappear, leaving his pursuers to wonder at his daring. They would hate him more than ever, but some part of them would have to admire his genius.

"I FEEL LIKE I should apologize for seventeen-year-old Emily's poor taste in prom dresses." Emily Walker looked down at the dress she had unearthed from the back of her closet that morning—too short in the front, too long in the back, entirely too many ruffles and a very bright shade of pink.

"It will be fine as soon as we straighten out the hem and maybe take off a few ruffles." Lacy Milligan looked up from her position kneeling on the floor beside the chair Emily stood on, and tucked a lock of her sleek brown hair behind one ear. "You'll look great."

"Everyone is supposed to be looking at you when you walk down the aisle in that gorgeous bridal gown—not at the clashing train wreck of attendants at the front of the room," Emily said. Watching Lacy wouldn't be a hardship—she was gorgeous, and so was her dress. The same couldn't be said for the bridesmaids' makeshift ensembles. "Let's hope the highway reopens and the dresses you chose for your wedding can be delivered."

"Not just the dresses," Lacy said. "The wedding

favors and some of the decorations are waiting to be delivered, as well. Not to mention some of the guests." She returned to pinning the dress. "With less than a week to go, I can't risk waiting much longer to figure out how to use what we have here—including this dress." She inserted a pin in the hem of the skirt and sat back on her heels to study the results. "As it is, I may be going through the wedding shy one bridesmaid if the highway doesn't open soon."

"The road is going to open soon," Emily said. "The weather reports look favorable." Since the New Year, the southwest corner of Colorado had been hammered by a wave of snowstorms that had dumped more than six feet of snow in the mountains. The snow, and the avalanches that inevitably followed, had blocked the only road leading in and out of the small town of Eagle Mountain for most of the past month.

"Travis tried to talk me into delaying the wedding." Lacy sighed. "Not just because of the weather, but because of this serial killer business."

A serial murderer who had been dubbed the Ice Cold Killer had murdered six women in the area in the past few weeks. Lacy's fiancé—Emily's brother Sheriff Travis Walker—had been working practically 'round the clock to try to stop the elusive serial killer. Emily thought postponing the wedding until the killer was caught and the weather improved wasn't such a bad idea, but she wasn't a bride who had spent the past six months planning the ceremony and reception. "What did you tell him?" Emily asked.

"I told him I'm willing to postpone my honeymoon. I understand that being a sheriff's wife means putting my needs behind those of the town. And I've been patient—I really have. I haven't seen him in two days and I haven't complained at all. But Sunday is my wedding day. All I ask is that he be here for a few hours. The case will wait that long."

"It's not just Travis," Emily said. "Half the wedding party is law enforcement. There's Gage." Emily and Travis's brother was a sheriff's deputy. "Cody Rankin—he's technically on leave from the US Marshals office, but he's still working on the case. And Nate Harris—he's supposed to be off work from his job with the Department of Wildlife to recover from his ankle injury, but he's as busy as ever, from what I can tell. Oh, and Ryder Stewart—he's had plenty of time to help Travis, since most of his highway patrol territory is closed due to snow."

"Then they can be here for a few hours, too," Lacy said. "That may sound terribly selfish of me, but I put so much of my life on hold for the three years I was in prison. I don't want to wait any longer." Lacy had been wrongfully convicted of murdering her boss. She and Travis had fallen in love after he had worked to clear her name.

"Then you deserve the wedding you want, when you want it," Emily said. "I hope my brother was understanding."

"He was, after I whined and moaned a little bit." Lacy stood and walked around the chair to take in the dress from all sides. "I didn't tell him this, but another reason I want to go ahead with the wedding is that I'm beginning to be afraid the killer won't be caught. Travis and every other lawman in the area has been hunting this guy for weeks. It's like he's a ghost. Travis and Gage and the rest of them work so hard and the murderer just thumbs his nose at them."

"It's crazy." Emily climbed down off the chair and began helping Lacy gather up the sewing supplies. "At first I was terrified. Well, I guess I'm still terrified, but honestly, I'm also angry." She patted Lacy's shoulder. "Anyway, I'm not going to let the killer or the weather get me down. The weather is going to hold, the road will open and you'll have a beautiful wedding, without my fashion faux pas spoiling the day."

"I hope you're right and everyone I invited can be here," Lacy said.

"Who in the wedding party is still missing?" Emily asked.

"Paige Riddell. She recently moved to Denver with her boyfriend, Rob Allerton."

"Of course." Paige had run a bed-and-breakfast in town prior to moving away. "I never knew her well, but she seemed really nice."

"She is nice. And I really want her here for my wedding. But you can't fight nature, I guess, so we're going to make do no matter what." She turned to

Emily. "Thank you so much for everything you've done to help," she said. "Not just with the wedding preparations, but all the work you've put into entertaining the wedding guests who are already here. I forget that the weather has forced you to put your own life on hold, too."

Like everyone else who had been in town when the first blizzard struck, Emily had been stuck in Eagle Mountain for most of the past month. "The first few weeks I was on my winter break," she said. She was working on her master's at Colorado State University and was employed by the university as a teaching assistant and researcher. "It's just the last ten days that I've missed. Fortunately, the university has been very understanding, letting me complete some of my coursework and research online, delaying some other work and arranging for another researcher to teach my undergrad class until I get back."

"I'm glad," Lacy said. "Can you imagine having to delay your master's degree because of snow?"

"Snow has its upsides, too," Emily said. "That sleigh ride last week was a blast, and I'm looking forward to the bonfire Wednesday."

"Every party you've thrown has been a big success," Lacy said. "I'm sure most brides don't entertain their guests so lavishly."

"Well, everything has gone well except the scavenger hunt," Emily said. "I wouldn't call that a success."

"It's not your fault Fiona was murdered during

the party." Lacy hugged herself and shuddered. "I thought for sure Travis would catch the killer after that—he was so close, right here on the ranch."

Just like that, the conversation turned back to the Ice Cold Killer as the two friends remembered each of his victims—some of them locals they had known, a few tourists or newcomers they had never had a chance to meet. But every person who had fallen victim to the killer had been young and female, like Emily and Lacy. They didn't have to say it, but they were both keenly aware that they might have been one of the killer's victims—or they still might be.

Emily was relieved when the door to the sunroom, where they were working, opened and Bette Fuller, one of Lacy's best friends and the caterer for the wedding, breezed in. Blonde and curvy, Bette always lit up the room, and today she was all smiles. "Rainey just got back from town and she says the highway is open." Bette hugged Lacy. "I know this is what you've been waiting for."

"Is Rainey sure?" Lacy asked.

"Rainey isn't one for spreading rumors or telling lies," Emily said. The ranch cook was even more stone-faced and tight-lipped than Travis. Emily looked down at the dress she was wearing, now bristling with pins and marks made with tailor's chalk. "Maybe I won't have to wear this old thing after all."

"Rainey said there was a line of delivery trucks coming into town," Bette said. "Which is a good thing, since the stores are low on everything."

"I'm going to call Paige and tell her and Rob to drop everything and drive over right now—before another avalanche closes the road," Lacy said. "And I need to check with the florist and look at the tracking for the bridesmaids' dresses and the wedding favors and the guest book I ordered, too."

"I can help you with some of that," Bette said.

"You two go on," Emily said. "I'll finish cleaning up in here." The prom dress—pins and all—could go back in the closet. If she was lucky, she'd never have to put it on again.

As she gathered up the clutter from around the room, she thought of all the work that went into weddings. This was only her second time serving as a bridesmaid, and she was looking forward to the ceremony, though she was a little nervous, too. Mostly, she hoped she wouldn't get too emotional. Weddings were supposed to be hopeful occasions, but they always made her a little melancholy, wondering what her own wedding would have been like—and how different her life might have turned out if she had accepted the one proposal she had had.

Who was she kidding? If she had agreed to marry that man, it would have been a disaster. She had been far too young for marriage, and he certainly hadn't been ready to settle down, no matter what he said. At least she had had sense enough to see that.

She was stowing the last of the sewing supplies and looking forward to changing back into jeans and a sweater when the door to the sunroom opened again and a man entered, obscured from the waist up by a tower of brown boxes. "I met the UPS driver on the way in and he asked me to drop these off," said a deep, velvety voice that sent a hot tremor up Emily's spine and made her wonder if she was hallucinating. "Whoever answered the door told me to bring them back here."

"Thanks." Emily hurried to relieve the man of his burdens, then almost dropped the boxes as she came face-to-face with Brodie Langtry.

The man who had once proposed to her. She felt unsteady on her feet, seeing him here in this house again after so long. And if she was upset, her family was going to be furious.

"Hello, Emily." He grinned, his full lips curving over even, white teeth, eyes sparking with a blatant sex appeal that sent a bolt of remembered heat straight through her. "You're looking well." A single furrow creased his brow. "Though I have to ask— what is that you're wearing?"

She looked down at the prom dress, the hem lopped off and bristling with pins, one ruffle hanging loose where Lacy had started to detach it. She looked back up at Brodie, feeling a little like she had been hit on the head and was still reeling from the blow. "What are you doing here?" she asked.

"As it happens, the Colorado Bureau of Investigation sent me here to help your brother with a case," he said. "I hear you've got a serial murderer problem."

"Does Travis know you're coming?" Her brother

hadn't said anything to her. Then again, he was probably trying to spare her feelings.

"He requested assistance from the CBI, though he doesn't know it's me. Is that going to be a problem?"

She bit her lower lip. "I don't know."

"It's been five years, Emily," he said.

Right. But it might have been five minutes for all the pain that was twisting her stomach. She hadn't expected to react like this. She was supposed to be over Brodie. "You never answered my letter," she said.

The crease across his brow deepened. "You sent me a letter?"

"You mean you don't even remember?" The words came out louder than she had intended, and she forced herself to lower her voice. "I tried calling, but your number had been changed. Travis found out you'd been transferred to Pueblo, so I wrote to you there."

He shook his head. "I never received your letter. Why did you write?"

Did he really not know? She pressed her hand to her stomach, hoping she wasn't going to be sick. This was too awful. "It doesn't matter now." She turned away and tried to make her voice light. "Like you said, it was five years ago. I'm sure Travis will appreciate your help with the case." Her brother was nothing if not a professional.

Brodie was silent, though she could feel his eyes boring into her. She began looking through the stack of packages. "I'll ask again," he said after a moment. "What is that you're wearing?"

"It's a prom dress," she managed.

"Isn't it the wrong time of year for prom? And aren't you in graduate school?"

Her eyes widened and she froze in the act of reaching for a package. "How did you know I'm in graduate school?"

"I might have checked up on you a time or two. They don't have proms in graduate school, do they?"

He'd *checked up* on her. Should she be flattered, or creeped out? "It's the new thing. Haven't you heard?" She continued scanning the labels on the boxes. She picked up the one that surely held her bridesmaid's dress. Maybe instead of stuffing the prom dress back into her closet, she'd burn it at Wednesday night's bonfire. That would be appropriate, wouldn't it?

"What is all this?" Brodie swept his hand to indicate the piles of boxes, bits of tulle, sewing supplies, silk flowers and other flotsam piled around the room. "Are you getting ready for a big party?"

"Travis is getting married on Sunday," Emily said. "I guess you didn't know." Then again, why would he? He and Travis had stopped being friends five years ago.

"No, I didn't know. Good for him. Who's the lucky woman?"

"Her name is Lacy Milligan. I'm sure you don't know her."

"No, but I know of her. Now it's coming back

to me." He grinned. "Lacy is the woman Travis arrested for murder—then after new evidence came to light, he worked to clear her name. I remember the story now, though I didn't know a wedding was in the offing."

It hadn't taken long for the media to latch onto the story of a wrongly accused woman falling in love with the law enforcement officer who had sent her to prison in the first place, then worked to clear her name. Most of the state was probably familiar with the story by now, but Emily didn't want to discuss it with Brodie. "Travis is at his office in town," she said, deciding it was past time to send Brodie on his way. "It's on Main. You can't miss it."

Before he could answer, her cell phone buzzed and she grabbed it off a nearby table. "Hello?"

"Hey." Travis's greeting was casual, but his voice carried the tension that never left him these days. "I was trying to get hold of Lacy, but I can't get through on her phone."

"I think she's talking to Paige, letting her know the highway is open."

"She's terrible about checking her messages, so do me a favor and tell her I'm not going to be able to take her to dinner today. I'm sorry, but we've had a break in the case."

Emily's heart leaped. "Have you made an arrest?"

"Not exactly, but we know who the killers are. One of them is dead, but the other is still on the loose."

"A second murderer?" Travis had long suspected

the Ice Cold Killer might be more than one man. If he had caught one of the killers, surely that meant he was closing in on the second. Maybe the case would be solved before the wedding after all. "Lacy will be glad to hear it," Emily said.

"Maybe not so glad when you tell her I have to miss dinner. I need to focus on tracking down the second man."

Which meant he probably wouldn't be home to sleep, either. "Travis, you can't keep working around the clock like this."

"We're going to get some help. The Colorado Bureau of Investigation has agreed to loan us one of their investigators. Now that the road is open, he— or she—should be showing up anytime."

She glanced over her shoulder at Brodie, who was looking out the window. The past five years had been kind to him, filling out his shoulders, adding a few fine lines around his eyes. He wore his hair a little longer than when she'd last seen him, and sunlight through the window picked out the gold streaks in the brown. Add in chiseled cheekbones, a dimpled chin and a straight nose and it was no wonder he could be mistaken for a model or a movie star.

As if sensing her staring at him, he turned and met her gaze, then cocked one eyebrow, lips half-curved in a mocking smile.

"Emily? Are you still there?" Travis asked.

"Um, your help from the CBI is here," she said. "It's Brodie Langtry." Not waiting to hear Travis's reaction, she thrust the phone at Brodie. *It's Travis*, she mouthed.

Brodie took the phone. "Travis! It's been a long time. I'm looking forward to working with you on this case…Yes, I volunteered for the job. To tell you the truth, I thought it was past time we mended fences. I know we didn't part under the best of circumstances five years ago and I'd like to clear the air. I've been catching up with Emily."

She cringed at the words. She and Brodie didn't need to "catch up." They had had a fun time together once, and if it had ended badly, she took most of the blame for that. She'd been young and naive and had expected things from him that he had never promised to give. She wouldn't make that mistake again.

While he and Travis continued to talk about the case, she turned away and began opening the boxes, enjoying the way the scissors ripped through the tape, letting the sound drown out their conversation. As an investigator with the Colorado Bureau of Investigation, Brodie would no doubt bring a welcome extra pair of eyes to the hunt for the Ice Cold Killer. She needed to remember that he was here to help Travis and probably didn't have the least interest in her. So there was no need for her to feel awkward around him.

Brodie tapped her on the shoulder and held out her phone. "Travis didn't sound very happy to hear from me. Why is that, do you think?"

"You'll have to ask him." But she would make

sure Travis didn't tell Brodie anything he didn't need to know. Best to leave the past in the past.

"I'm going to meet him in town and get caught up on this case," he said. "But I'm hoping to see more of you later."

Before she could think of an answer to this, he leaned forward and kissed her cheek. "It's great to see you again, Emily," he murmured, and she cursed the way her knees wobbled in response.

Then he strode from the room, the door shutting firmly behind him.

Emily groaned and snatched a pillow off the sofa. She hurled it at the door, half wishing Brodie was still standing there and she was aiming at his head. Brodie Langtry was the last person in the world she wanted to see right now. This next week with him was going to be her own version of hell.

Chapter Two

Brodie drove through a world so blindingly white it hurt even with sunglasses shading his eyes. Only the scarred trunks of aspen and the bottle-brush silhouettes of pine trees broke the expanse of glittering porcelain. If not for the walls of plowed snow on either side of the road, it would be difficult in places to distinguish the road from the surrounding fields. After five hours of similar landscape between here and Denver, Emily, in her crazy ruffled pink dress, had stood out like a bird of paradise, a welcome shock to the senses.

Shocking also was how much Travis's little sister had matured. She'd been pretty before—or maybe *cute* was the better word—vivacious and sweet and attractive in a lithe, youthful way. She had filled out since then, her curves more pronounced, her features sharpened into real beauty.

She seemed more serious, but then so was he. Life—and especially a life spent working in law enforcement—did that to people. He'd seen a dark side to people he couldn't forget. It was the kind of thing that left a mark. He couldn't say what had marked Emily, but he saw a new depth and gravity in her expression that hadn't been there before.

He had been such a rascal when they were together five years ago. He had thought Emily was just another fling. He had felt a little guilty about seducing one of his best friend's sisters, but she had been more than willing. And then he had fallen for her—hard. He hadn't been able to imagine a future without her, so he had laid his heart on the line and asked her to spend the rest of her life with him. And she had stomped his heart flat. The memory still hurt. He had offered her everything he had, but that hadn't been enough.

So yeah, that was in the past. He wasn't here to rehash any of it, though he hoped he was man enough to treat her with the respect and kindness she deserved. He owed that to her because she was Travis's sister, and because she had given him some good memories, even if things hadn't worked out.

And now there was this case—a serial killer in Eagle Mountain, of all places. Remote tourist towns weren't the usual hunting grounds for serial killers. They tended to favor big cities, where it was easy to hide and they had a wide choice of prey, or else they moved around a lot, making it tougher for law enforcement to find them. Yet this guy—this Ice Cold Killer—had targeted women in a limited population, during a time when the weather kept him trapped in a small geographic area.

Then again, maybe the killer had taken advantage of the road reopening today and was even now headed out of town.

Brodie steered his Toyota Tundra around an S-curve in the road and had to hit the brakes to avoid rear-ending a vehicle that was half-buried in the plowed snowbank on the right-hand side of the county road. Skid marks on the snow-packed surface of the road told the tale of the driver losing control while rounding the curve and sliding into the drift.

Brodie set his emergency brake, turned on his flashers and hurried out of his vehicle. The car in the snow was a white Jeep Wrangler with Colorado plates. Brodie couldn't see a driver from this angle. Maybe whoever this was had already flagged down another driver and was on the way into town. Boots crunching in the snow, Brodie climbed over a churned-up pile of ice and peered down into the driver's seat.

The woman didn't look like a woman anymore, sprawled across the seat, arms pinned beneath her, blood from the wound at her throat staining the front of her white fur coat. Brodie was reminded of going trapping with an uncle when he was a teenager. They'd come upon a trapped weasel in the snow, its winter-white coat splashed with crimson. Brodie hadn't had the stomach for trapping after that, and he hadn't thought of that moment in twenty years.

Taking a deep, steadying breath, he stepped away from the vehicle and marshaled his composure, then called Travis. "I'm on County Road Seven," he said. "On the way from the ranch into town. I pulled over to check on a car in a ditch. The driver is a woman, her throat's cut. I think we've got another victim."

BRODIE KNEW BETTER than to tell Travis that he looked ten years older since the two had last seen each other. Working a long case would do that to a man, and Travis was the kind who took things to heart more than most. Brodie was here to lift some of that burden. Not everyone liked the CBI interfering with local cases, but Travis had a small department and needed all the help he could get. "It's good to see you again," Brodie said, offering his hand.

Travis ignored the hand and focused on the vehicle in the ditch, avoiding Brodie's gaze. A chill settled somewhere in the pit of Brodie's stomach. So this really was going to be tougher than he had imagined. His old friend resented the way things had ended five years ago. They'd have to clear that up sooner or later, but for now, he'd take his cue from the sheriff and focus on the case.

"I called in the plate number," Brodie said as Travis approached the stranded Jeep. "It's registered to a Jonathan Radford."

Travis nodded. "I know the vehicle. It was stolen two days ago. It was driven by the killers."

"Killers? As in more than one?"

"We've learned the Ice Cold Killer isn't one man, but two. One of them, Tim Dawson, died last night, after kidnapping one of my deputies and her sister. The other—most likely Alex Woodruff—is still at large."

"And still killing." Brodie glanced toward the Jeep. "Most of that blood is still bright red. I think she wasn't killed that long ago."

Travis walked around the Jeep, studying it closely. "Before, Alex and Tim—the killers—always left the victims in their own vehicles."

"Except Fiona Winslow, who was killed at the scavenger hunt on your family's ranch." Brodie had familiarized himself with all the information Travis had sent to the CBI.

"They broke their pattern with Fiona because they were sending a message," Travis said. "Taunting me. I think Alex is doing the same thing with this Jeep. He knows that we know it's the vehicle he was driving until recently."

"Do you think he's driving this woman's car now?" Brodie asked.

Travis shook his head. "That seems too obvious to me, but maybe, if he hasn't found another vehicle. He thinks he's smarter than we are, always one step ahead, but we know who he is now. It won't be as easy to hide. And it will be harder for him to kill alone, too. He's going to make mistakes. I can see it with this woman."

"What do you see?" Reading the case files Travis had emailed was no substitute for eyewitness experience.

"The woman's feet aren't bound. The others were. Maybe that's because he didn't have time, or without Tim's help he couldn't manage it." He moved closer to look into the car once more. "The collar of her fur coat is torn. I think she struggled and tried to fight him off. Maybe she marked him."

"The others didn't have time to put up a fight," Brodie said, recalling the case notes.

Travis opened the door and leaned into the car, being careful not to touch anything. With gloved hands, he felt gingerly around the edge of the seat and along the dash. When he withdrew and straightened, he held a small rectangle of card stock in his hand, the words *ICE COLD* printed across the front. "He's following his pattern of leaving the card," Brodie said.

"He doesn't want there to be any doubt about who's responsible," Travis said. He pulled out an evidence envelope and sealed the card inside. "It's another way to thumb his nose at us."

They turned at the sound of an approaching vehicle, or rather, a caravan of two sheriff's department SUVs and a black Jeep, traveling slowly up the snow-packed road. The vehicles parked on the opposite side of the road and two deputies and an older man bundled in a heavy coat got out.

"Hello, Gage," Brodie greeted one of the deputies, Travis's brother, Gage Walker.

"You're about the last person I expected to see here," Gage said. He seemed puzzled, but not unfriendly, and, unlike his brother, was willing to shake Brodie's hand. "Typical of CBI to show up when we have the case half-solved."

"Dwight Prentice." The second deputy, a tall, rangy blond, offered his hand and Brodie shook it.

"And this is Butch Collins, the county medical examiner." Travis introduced the older man, who nodded and moved on to the car. His face paled when he looked into the vehicle.

"Something wrong?" Travis asked, hurrying to the older man's side.

Collins shook his head. "I know her, that's all." He cleared his throat. "Lynn Wallace. She sings in the choir at my church."

"Do you know what kind of car she drives?" Brodie asked, joining them.

Collins stared at him, then back at the Jeep. "This isn't her car?"

"It was stolen from a local vacation home two days ago," Travis said. "We think the killer might have been driving it."

"I don't know what kind of car Lynn drove," Collins said. "Only that she was a lovely woman with a beautiful soprano voice. She didn't deserve this. But then, none of them did." He straightened his shoulders. "Are you ready for me to look at her?"

"Give us a few seconds to process the outside of the car, then you can have a look." Travis motioned to Gage and Dwight, who moved forward.

Travis indicated Brodie should follow him. "I need you to get to work on identifying Lynn Wallace's vehicle," he said. "I think Alex will ditch it as soon as he can, but he might not have had a chance yet. You can use my office."

"Tell me what you know about Alex," Brodie said.

"Alex Woodruff. A college student at the Colorado State University—or he was until recently. He doesn't have any priors, at least under that name, and that's the only name I've found for him."

"Emily goes to the Colorado State University, doesn't she?" Brodie asked. Knowing he was coming to Eagle Mountain, he'd checked her Facebook page. "Do they know each other?"

The lines around Travis's mouth tightened. "She says he participated in a research study she and her colleagues conducted, but they weren't friends, just acquaintances."

"What brought him to Eagle Mountain?"

"He and Tim supposedly came here to ice climb over their winter break and got stuck here when blizzards closed the highway. They were staying at an aunt's vacation cabin until recently."

"I'll get right on the search for the car," Brodie said. As he walked to his SUV, he considered the connection between Alex Woodruff and Emily Walker. His work investigating crimes had taught him to be skeptical of coincidence, but until he had further proof, he wasn't going to add to Travis's concerns by voicing the worry that now filled his mind. What if the thing that had brought Alex and Tim to Eagle Mountain wasn't ice climbing—but Emily?

Chapter Three

"Thank you, Professor. That would be so helpful. I'll review everything and be ready to discuss it when I see you next week after the wedding." Emily hung up the phone and mentally checked off one more item on her Tuesday to-do list. All her professors had agreed to excuse her for another week so that she could help with the preparations for Travis and Lacy's wedding. Though she could have made the six-hour drive back to Fort Collins to attend a few classes and try to catch up on all she had missed while stranded by the snow, the last thing she wanted was for the road to close again, forcing her to miss the wedding.

Instead, someone in her department had volunteered to make the drive out here to deliver files for Emily to review. She had protested that it was ridiculous to make such a long drive, but apparently more than one person had been eager for the excuse to get off campus for a while. The risk of getting stranded in Eagle Mountain if another storm system rolled in had only heightened the appeal.

She moved on to the next item on her list. She needed to check on her horse, Witchy. The mare had developed inflammation in one leg shortly after the first of the year and veterinarian Darcy Marsh had prescribed a course of treatment that appeared to be working, but Emily was supposed to exercise her lightly each day and check that there was no new swelling. Slipping on her barn coat—the same one she had worn as a teenager—she headed out the door and down the drive to the horse barn. Sunlight shimmered on the snow that covered everything like a starched white sheet. Every breath stung her nose, reminding her that temperatures hovered in the twenties. She still marveled that it could be so cold when the sun shone so brightly overhead, giving the air a clean, lemony light.

The barn's interior presented a sharp contrast to the outside world, its atmosphere warm from the breath of animals and smelling of a not-unpleasant mixture of molasses, hay and manure. A plaintive *meow!* greeted Emily, and a gray-striped cat trotted toward her, the cat's belly swollen with kittens soon to be born. "Aww, Tawny." Emily bent and gently stroked the cat, who started up a rumbling purr and leaned against Emily's legs. "It won't be long now, will it?" Emily crooned, feeling the kittens shift beneath her hand. She'd have to make sure Tawny had a warm, comfortable place to give birth.

She straightened and several of the family's horses poked their heads over the tops of their stalls. Witchy, in an end stall on the left-hand side, whinnied softly and stamped against the concrete floor of her stall.

Emily slipped into the stall and greeted Witchy, patting her neck, then bent to examine the bandaged front pastern. It no longer felt hot or swollen, though Darcy had recommended wrapping it for a few weeks longer to provide extra support. Emily breathed a sigh of relief. For a brief period during her childhood, she had considered studying to be a veterinarian, but had quickly ruled out any job that required dealing with animals' suffering.

"Are you contemplating climbing down out of your ivory tower and hiring on as the newest ranch hand?"

Emily froze as Brodie's oh-so-familiar teasing tone and velvety voice flowed around her like salted caramel—both sweet and biting. She was aware of her position, bent over with her backside facing the stall door, where she sensed him standing. She turned her head, and sure enough, Brodie had leaned over the top half of the stall door, grinning, the cat cradled in his arms.

With as much dignity as she could muster, she released her hold on the horse's leg and straightened. "Brodie, what are you doing here?" she asked.

He stroked the cat under the chin. Tawny closed her eyes and purred even louder. Emily had an uncomfortable memory of Brodie stroking *her*— eliciting a response not unlike that of the cat. "I was looking for you," he said. "Someone told me you're in charge of a bonfire and barbecue here Wednesday."

"Yes." She took a lead rope from a peg just outside the stall door and clipped it onto Witchy's halter. The mare regarded her with big gold-brown eyes like warm honey. "What about it?"

"I was hoping to wrangle an invite, since I'm staying on the ranch. It would be awkward if I felt the need to lock myself in my cabin for the evening."

She slid back the latch on the door and pushed it open, forcing Brodie to stand aside, then led the mare out. "I have to exercise Witchy," she said.

He gave the cat a last pat, then set her gently aside and fell into step beside Emily, matching his long strides to her own shorter ones. "I didn't realize you were staying at the ranch," she said. He hadn't been at dinner last night, but then, neither had Travis. The two men had been working on the case. Frankly, she was shocked her parents had invited Brodie to stay. They certainly had no love lost for him, after what had happened between him and Emily.

"When the CBI agreed to send an investigator to help with the Ice Cold Killer case, Travis asked your parents if they could provide a place for the officer to stay. They were kind enough to offer up one of their guest cabins."

"Wouldn't it be more convenient for you in town?" she asked.

"There aren't any rooms in town," Brodie said. "They're all full of people stranded here by the road closure. I imagine that will change now that the avalanches have been cleared and it's safe to travel again, but in the meantime, your folks were gracious enough to let me stay." He fell silent, but she could feel his eyes on her, heating her neck and sending prickles of awareness along her arms. "Does it bother you, having me here?" he asked.

"Of course not."

She led Witchy out of the barn, along a fenced passage to a covered arena. Brodie moved forward to open the gate for her. "Are you going to ride her?" he asked.

Emily shook her head. "She's still recovering from an injury. But I need to walk her around the arena for a few laps."

"I'll walk with you." He didn't bother asking permission—men like Brodie didn't ask. He wasn't cruel or demanding or even particularly arrogant. He just accepted what people—women—had always given him—attention, time, sex. All he had to do was smile and flash those sea-blue eyes and most women would give him anything he wanted.

She had been like that, too, so she understood the magnetism of the man. But she wasn't that adoring girl anymore, and she knew to be wary. "Of course you can come to the bonfire," she said. "It's really no big deal."

She began leading the mare around the arena, watching the horse for any sign of pain or weakness, but very aware of the man beside her. "Tell me about Alex Woodruff," he said.

The question startled her, so much that she stumbled. She caught herself and continued on as if nothing had happened. "Why are you asking me about Alex?"

"I've been reviewing all the case notes. He was here, at the scavenger hunt the day Fiona Winslow was killed."

"Yes. He and his friend Tim were here. I invited them."

"Why did you do that?"

"I knew the road closure had stranded them here and I felt sorry for them, stuck in a small town where they didn't know many people. I figured the party would be something fun for them to do, and a way to meet some local people near their age." She cut her gaze over to him. "Why are you asking me about Alex?"

He did that annoying thing Travis sometimes did, answering a question with a question. "You knew Alex and Tim from the university?"

"I didn't really know them." She stopped and bent to run her hand down Witchy's leg, feeling for any warmth or swelling or sign of inflammation. "They both signed up as volunteers for research we were doing. Lots of students do. Most of the studies only pay five to ten dollars, but the work isn't hard and cash is cash to a broke student."

"What kind of research?" Brodie asked.

She straightened and looked him in the eye. She loved her work and could talk about it with almost anyone. If she talked long enough, maybe he'd get bored and leave. "I'm studying behavioral economics. It's sort of a melding of traditional psychology and economics. We look at how people make the buying decisions they make and why. Almost every choice has a price attached to it, and it can be interesting what motivates people to act one way versus another."

"How did Alex and Tim hear about your experiments?"

"We have flyers all over campus, and on social media." She shrugged. "They were both psychology majors, so I think the research appealed to them. I ran into Alex in a coffee shop on campus two days later and he had a lot of intelligent questions about what we were doing."

"Maybe he had studied so he'd have questions prepared so he could keep you talking," Brodie said. "Maybe he was flirting with you."

"Oh, please." She didn't hide her scorn for this idea. "He was not flirting. If anything, he was showing off."

One eyebrow rose a scant quarter inch—enough to make him look even cockier than usual. "Showing off is some men's idea of flirting."

"You would know about that, wouldn't you?"

His wicked grin sent a current of heat through her. "When you're good, it's not showing off," he said.

She wished she was the kind of woman who had a snappy comeback for a line like that, but it was taking all her concentration to avoid letting him see he was getting to her. So instead of continuing to flirt, she started forward with the horse once more and changed the subject. "Are you going to be able to help Travis catch the Ice Cold Killer?" she asked.

Brodie's expression sobered. Yes, nothing like a serial murderer to dampen the libido. "I'm going to do my best," he said. "We know who we're looking for now—we just have to find him."

She managed not to stumble this time, but she did turn to look at him. "You know who the killer is?"

He frowned. "Travis didn't tell you?"

"I haven't seen Travis in several days. He's either working or spending time with Lacy. He told me on the phone that one of the men he thought was involved is dead, but that there was another one he was after."

Brodie said nothing.

She stopped and faced him. "Tell me who it is," she said. "You know I won't go talking to the press."

"The man who died was Tim Dawson," Brodie said.

All the breath went out of her as this news registered. "Then the other man is Alex Woodruff." She grabbed his arm. "That's why you were asking me about him. But he and Tim left town when the road opened briefly a couple of weeks ago. Travis said so."

"They moved out of the cabin where they were

staying, but now Travis believes they stayed in the area. If you have any idea where Alex might be hiding, or what he's likely to do next, you need to tell me." She released her hold on him and stepped back, the mare's warm bulk reassuring. If her suddenly weak legs gave out, she'd have the animal to grab on to. "I hardly know him," she said. "But a serial killer? Why would a smart, good-looking guy from a well-off family want to murder a bunch of women he doesn't even know?" And how could she have spent time with Alex and Tim and not seen that kind of evil in them?

"You're more likely to have an answer for that than I do," Brodie said. "You're conducting a lot of research on human behavior and motivation. Didn't you do one study on what motivates people to break rules or to cheat?"

"What did you do—run a background check on me? That's creepy."

"All I did was look at your public Facebook page," he said. "And there's nothing creepy about it. I knew I was coming here and I wanted to see how you were doing—as a friend. I guess you never did the same for me."

She couldn't keep color from flooding her cheeks. She had, in fact, perused Brodie's Facebook page more than once, as well as Googling his name for tidbits of information. Not because she still felt anything for him, simply because she was curious. "All right," she said. "As long as you're not being a creep."

"Such technical language from a psychologist."

"Behavioral economics is different," she said. "There's psychology involved, of course, but nothing that would give me insight into the mind of a serial killer."

"I think you're wrong," he said. "I think you probably can tell us things we don't know about Alex Woodruff. You've always been smart about people."

I wasn't smart about you. She bit her lip to hold back the words. "I'm sure the CBI has profilers who specialize in this kind of thing," she said.

"Yes, but they don't know Alex, and they don't know Eagle Mountain. You do."

She searched his face, trying to read his expression. He was focused on her in that intense way he had—a way that made her feel like she was the only person in the world he wanted to be with right this second. "What do you want from me?" she asked.

"I want you to think about Alex, and about this area, and see if you can come up with any ideas that might help us."

She shook her head. "I think you're grasping at straws. You need to consult a professional."

"We will. You're just another avenue for us to explore. You never know in a case like this what might be the key to a solution."

"Does Travis know you're asking me to help?"

"No, but I can't see why he'd object. I'm not asking you to do anything dangerous."

She nodded. "All right. I don't think it will do

any good, but I'll think about it and see what I can come up with."

He clapped her on the shoulder. "Thanks. I knew I could count on you."

How had he known he could count on her? But she couldn't ask the question. He was already striding out of the arena, his boots making neat prints in the raked dirt.

Brodie had to know she would do anything to help her brother. If Travis had asked her for help with the case, she wouldn't have hesitated. That she was less willing to cooperate with Brodie probably said more about her feelings for him than she cared to admit.

Never mind. She would try to come up with some ideas about Alex and—with her help or not—Travis and Brodie would catch him and put him in jail for a long time.

Then she could go back to her normal life, with no serial killers—and no former lovers—to unsettle her.

"YOUR SISTER HAS agreed to serve as a consultant on the case."

Travis was so even-keeled and unemotional that Brodie considered it a personal challenge to attempt to get a reaction from him. He'd scored a hit with this announcement.

Travis looked up from the file he'd been studying, eyes sparking with annoyance. "What could Emily possibly contribute to the case?" he asked.

Brodie moved out of the doorway where he'd been

standing and dropped into one of the two chairs in front of Travis's desk. The small office was spartan in appearance, with only a laptop and an inch-high stack of papers on Travis's desk, and a few family photographs and citations on the walls. Brodie's own desk at CBI headquarters in Denver was crammed with so many books, files and photographs his co-workers had hinted that it might be a fire hazard. But hey, the clutter worked for him. "Emily knows Alex Woodruff and she's studied psychology," he said. "She can give us insights into his character and what he's likely to do next."

"She's an economics major—not a profiler."

"We'll still consult the CBI profiler," Brodie said. "But I think Emily will come to this with fresh eyes. Besides, she knows this county almost as well as you do. She might be able to give us some new ideas about places to look for him."

Travis shook his head. "He's probably left the county by now. The highway is open, and he has to know we're on his trail. A smart man would be half-way to Mexico by now."

"You and I both know criminals rarely behave the way most people would. Alex may be smart, but he's arrogant, too. He's been taunting you, leaving those business cards, killing a woman on your family ranch, going after one of your deputies. He still thinks he can beat you."

"Maybe." Travis fixed Brodie with a stare that had probably caused more than one felon to shake in his shoes. "This isn't some scheme you've come up with in order for you to spend more time with Emily, is it?" he asked. "Because I'm not going to stand by and let that happen again."

"Let what happen?" Brodie had a strong sense of déjà vu. He recalled another conversation with Travis that had begun like this, five years ago, when his friend—only a deputy then—had accused him of trying to seduce Emily.

"Emily really hurt when the two of you broke things off," Travis said. "It took a long time for her to get over you. I don't want her to have to go through that again."

Brodie bristled. "She's the one who ended it, not me."

"You must have had something to do with it."

Brodie ground his teeth together. He did not want to argue about this with Travis. "I didn't come here to get back together with your sister," he said. "I came to help with this case. I asked Emily to consult because I think she's another resource we can draw on."

Travis uncrossed his arms, and the tension around his mouth eased. "Fair enough. I won't rule out anything that might help us catch Alex Woodruff. Speaking of that, have you had any luck tracking down Lynn Wallace's car?"

"Not yet. She drove a white Volvo." Brodie opened his phone and read the license plate number from his notes. "Nothing flashy. Fairly common. Easy to hide."

"Right. I'll put my deputies on the lookout." He turned to a map pinned to the wall of his office. Pins showed the locations where each of the Ice Cold Killer's seven victims had been found. "Alex and Tim working together concentrated the murders in three areas," he said. "Christy O'Brien and Anita Allbritton were killed within Eagle Mountain town limits. Kelly Farrow and Michaela Underwood were both murdered in the area around Dixon Pass and the national forest service land near there. Fiona Winslow, Lauren Grenado and Lynn Wallace were all killed within a couple of miles of the Walking W ranch." Travis indicated a third grouping of pins on the map.

"Does that tell us anything about where Alex might be hiding now?" Brodie asked.

Travis pointed to a red pin on County Road Five. "We know Tim and Alex were staying at Tim's aunt's cabin, here, when the first three murders took place. They spent some time in a vacation home here." He indicated another pin. "And they may have been at this summer cabin in the national forest, here, for the other murders. Now—who knows?"

A tapping on the door frame interrupted them. Both men turned to see office manager Adelaide Kinkaid, a sixtysomething woman who wore what looked like red monkeys dangling from her earlobes, and a flowing red-and-purple tunic over black slacks. "We just got word that a fresh slide on Dixon Pass sent one vehicle over the edge and buried two others," she said. "Fortunately, they were able to dig everyone out pretty quickly, but the road is closed until they can clear up the mess."

Brodie groaned. "How many delivery trucks do you suppose got caught on the wrong side of this one?" he asked.

"Probably about as many as were able to leave town when the road opened," Adelaide said. "Everyone is just trading places."

"I'll take your word for it," Brodie said. "You do seem to know everything." He leaned toward her. "Are those monkey earrings?"

"Yes." She tapped one earring with a red-painted fingernail. "Do you like them?"

"Only you could pull off a look like that, Adelaide," Brodie said, grinning.

She swatted his shoulder. "You're the kind of man I always warned my daughters about."

"What kind is that?"

"Too smart and good-looking for your own good. The kind of man who's oblivious to the broken hearts he leaves behind."

"Adelaide, Brodie is here as a fellow law enforcement officer," Travis said. "He deserves our respect."

"I'm sure he's a sterling officer," Adelaide said. "And a fine man all around. Just not marriage material—which is probably okay with him." She grinned, then turned to Travis. "And speaking of marriages, don't you have a tux fitting to see to?"

Color rose in the sheriff's cheeks. "I don't need

you to keep track of my schedule, Addie," he said. "Right now I have a case to work on."

"You always have a case to work on," Adelaide said. "You only have one wedding." She whirled and stalked away.

Brodie settled back in his chair once more. "Do you have a tux fitting?" he asked.

"I canceled it."

"Unless you're going to get married in your uniform, are you sure that's a good idea?"

Travis scowled at Brodie. "They have my measurements. They don't need me." His phone rang and he answered it. "Hello?"

He listened for a moment, then said, "I've got Brodie in the office. I'm going to put you on speaker." He punched the keypad. "All right. Say that again."

"I've got what looks like another victim of the Ice Cold Killer," Deputy Dwight Prentice said. "Taped up, throat cut, left in her car near the top of Dixon Pass. Only, she's still alive. The ambulance is on its way."

Travis was already standing. "So are we," he said.

Chapter Four

The woman—a once-pretty brunette, her skin bleached of color and her hair matted with blood—stared up at them, glassy-eyed, her lips moving, but no sound coming out. "You're safe now," Brodie said, leaning over her. "We're going to take care of you." He stepped back as the EMTs moved in to transfer the woman to a waiting gurney.

"We've already called for a helicopter," the older of the two paramedics said. "I think this is more than the clinic in Eagle Mountain can handle. They've agreed to meet us at the ball fields, where it's open enough for them to land."

Brodie's gaze shifted to the woman again. She had closed her eyes and her breath came in ragged gasps. He wanted to grab her hand and encourage her to hang on, but he needed to move out of the way and let the paramedics do their job.

Travis, who had been talking to Dwight and highway patrolman Ryder Stewart, motioned for Brodie to join them. "Her name is Denise Switcher," Ryder said. "We found her driver's license in the purse on the passenger floorboard, and the registration on the car matches. Her address is in Fort Collins."

"Did she say anything about what happened?" Brodie asked.

"I don't think she can talk," Dwight said. "One of the EMTs said the vocal chords may be damaged."

Brodie winced. "How is it she's still alive?"

"I don't know," Travis said. "But I hope she stays that way." He nodded to Dwight. "You must have come along right after it happened. Did you see anything or anyone who might have been Alex?"

"No." Dwight hooked his thumbs over his utility belt and stared toward the EMTs bent over the woman. "A trucker who was pulled over taking off his tire chains flagged me down and said he spotted a car on the side of the road near the top of the pass. He didn't see anyone in it, but thought maybe I'd want to check." Dwight pulled a notebook from inside his leather coat. "Gary Ellicott. He was delivering groceries to Eagle Mountain and somehow missed that the road had been closed again. When he got to the barricades, he had to back down a ways before he could turn around. He thinks about fifteen minutes had passed between the time he spotted the car and when he talked to me."

"I don't think she was lying there very long," Brodie said. "A wound like that bleeds fast." If much more time had passed, she would have bled to death.

"The road closed seventy-five minutes ago,"

Ryder said. "There was a lot of traffic up here and it took maybe half an hour to clear out. If the killer was cutting her throat then, someone would have seen."

"So this most likely happened between thirty and forty-five minutes ago," Brodie said.

"But he would have had to have stopped the car before the road closed," Travis said. "The car is on the southbound side of the road, headed toward town. That seems to indicate she was arriving, not leaving."

"We'll need to find out if she was staying in town," Brodie said. "Maybe she has family in Eagle Mountain, was leaving and, like the truck driver, had to turn around because of the barricade."

"If this is Alex's work and not a copycat, that means he didn't leave town," Travis said.

The paramedics shut the door of the ambulance and hurried to the cab. Siren wailing, they pulled away, headed back toward town. "Let's take a look," Travis said, and led the way to the car, a gray Nissan sedan with Colorado plates. It was parked up against a six-foot berm of plowed snow, so close it was impossible to open the passenger side door. The snow around the vehicle had been churned by the footsteps of the paramedics and cops, to the point that no one shoe impression was discernable. "I took photographs of the scene before I approached," Dwight said. "But I can tell you there weren't any footprints. If I had to guess, I'd say the killer used a rake or shovel to literally cover his tracks."

Brodie continued to study the roadside. "I don't see any other tire impressions," he said.

"He could have parked on the pavement," Ryder said.

"Or he could have been on foot," Travis said.

"It's four miles from town up a half-dozen switchbacks," Ryder said. "That's a long way to walk. Someone would have noticed."

"Not if he stayed behind the snow." Travis kicked steps into the snowbank and scrambled to the top and looked down. "There's a kind of path stomped out over here."

Brodie climbed up beside him and stared down at the narrow trail. "It might be an animal trail."

"It might be. Or it could be how Alex made his way up to this point without being seen. Then he stepped out in the road and flagged down Denise and pretended to be a stranded motorist."

"How did he know the driver was a woman by herself?" Brodie asked.

"He could have studied approaching traffic with binoculars."

The two men descended once more to the others beside the car. "Why would any woman stop for him, knowing there's a killer on the loose?" Dwight asked.

"She was from Fort Collins," Travis said. "I don't know how much press these murders have been getting over there. It wouldn't be front-page news or the top story on a newscast."

"He's right," Brodie said. "I've seen a few articles in the Denver papers, but not much. It would be easy to miss."

"Alex is a good-looking young man," Travis said. "Clean-cut, well dressed. If he presented himself as a stranded motorist, stuck in the cold far from town, most people would be sympathetic."

"Maybe he dressed as a woman, the way Tim did when they were working together," Dwight said. "People would be even more likely to stop for a woman."

"Alex and Tim were both amateur actors, right?" Brodie asked, trying to recall information from the reports he had read.

"Yeah," Ryder said. "And we know that, at least a few times, Tim dressed as a woman who was trying to escape an abusive boyfriend or husband. He flagged down another woman and asked for help, then Alex moved in to attack. One woman was able to escape and described the scenario for us."

Travis pulled on a pair of gloves, then opened the driver's-side door. He leaned in and came out with a woman's purse—black leather with a gold clasp. He pulled out the wallet and scanned the ID, then flipped through the credit cards until he came to a slim white card with an embossed photograph of a smiling brunette—Denise Switcher. "Looks like she worked at Colorado State University," he said.

The hair rose on the back of Brodie's neck. "Emily's school," he said. He didn't like another connection to Emily in this case.

"Alex's school." Travis slid the card back into the wallet. "I wonder if he chose her because he recognized her."

"That might have made her more likely to stop to help him out," Dwight said.

Travis returned the wallet to the purse and rifled through the rest of the contents. Expression grim, he pulled out a white business card, the words *ICE COLD* in black ink printed on one side.

The card taunted them—a reminder that, yes, they knew who attacked Denise Switcher, but they weren't any closer to catching him than they had ever been.

They were still silently contemplating the card when Travis's phone rang. He listened for a moment, then ended the call. "That was one of the paramedics," he said. "Denise Switcher coded before Flight for Life arrived. She's dead."

Brodie silently cursed the waste of a young woman's life, as well as their best chance to learn more about Alex's methods and motives. He turned to walk back toward the sheriff's department vehicle, but drew up short as a red Jeep skidded to a stop inches in front of him. The driver's door flew open and Emily stumbled out. "Is it true? Did the killer really get Denise?" she demanded, looking wildly around.

Brodie hurried to her. She wore only leggings and a thin sweater and tennis shoes, and was already shivering in the biting cold. He shrugged out of his jacket. "What are you doing here?" he asked.

She waved off his attempts to put his jacket around her. "You have to tell me. That ambulance I passed—was it Denise? Does that mean she's still alive?"

Travis joined them. "Emily, you shouldn't be here," he said.

"I was in the Cake Walk Café, waiting. Then Tammy Patterson came in and said she heard from a source at the sheriff's department that the Ice Cold Killer had attacked another woman. I had the most awful feeling it was Denise." She bit her bottom lip, her eyes fixed on Travis, her expression pleading.

He put a hand on her shoulder. "It was Denise Switcher," he said. "But how did you know?"

"Tammy said the woman was from Fort Collins. I was hoping that was just a coincidence, but…" She buried her face against Travis's shoulder.

"Emily?" Brodie approached, his voice gentle. "What was Denise doing in Eagle Mountain?"

She raised her head and wiped away tears. "I'm sorry. I thought I said. She was coming to see me."

BRODIE WORE WHAT Emily thought of as his cop face—grim determination and what felt like censure, as if he suspected her of withholding important information. She refused to give in to the temptation to cower against Travis, so she straightened and wiped the tears from her eyes.

Brodie, still scowling, thrust his jacket at her once more. "Put this on. You're freezing."

She would have liked nothing better than to refuse the offer, but the truth was, she was so cold she couldn't stop shaking. She'd been so upset she had left her own coat behind at the café. She mutely accepted his jacket and slipped into it, his warmth enveloping her, along with the scent of him, clean and masculine.

"Why was Denise coming to see you?" Travis asked.

"The lead on the research project I'm involved in had some files he wanted me to review," she said. "Denise volunteered to deliver them to me."

"She drove six hours to deliver files?" Brodie asked. "Why didn't they transmit them electronically? Or ask you to make the trip?"

"These are paper surveys students filled out," she said. "And the professor had already agreed I should stay here in Eagle Mountain until after the wedding." She hugged the coat more tightly around her. "Honestly, I don't think he would have bothered, except Denise wanted to come. She said it was a great excuse to get out of the office and spend at least one night in the mountains."

"The two of you were friends?" Travis asked.

She nodded, and bit the inside of her cheek to stave off the fresh wave of tears that threatened with that one change of verb tense—*were*. "She's the administrative assistant in the economics department and she and I really hit it off. I'd told her so much about Eagle Mountain and the ranch that she was anxious to see it." She swallowed hard. If Denise had stayed in Fort Collins, she'd be alive now.

"When did you talk to her last?" Travis asked.

"She called me when she stopped for gas in Gunnison, and we agreed to meet at the Cake Walk for lunch."

"What time was that?" Brodie asked.

"About ten thirty."

"Did Alex Woodruff know her?" Brodie asked.

Had Denise known her killer? Emily shuddered at the thought, then forced herself to focus on the question. "Maybe," she said. "Students can register online to participate in various research studies, but they can also come into the office and fill out the paperwork there. If Alex did that, he would have met Denise. And a couple of times she's helped check people in for studies."

"So there's a good chance he did know her," Brodie said.

"Yes." She glanced toward the gray Nissan. "What happened to her? I mean, I know she was killed, but why up here?"

"It's possible Alex posed as a stranded motorist in need of a ride," Travis said. "If your friend recognized him from school, do you think she would have stopped?"

Emily nodded. "Yes. Denise was always pitching in to help with fund-raisers or any extra work that needed to be done. She would have stopped to help someone, especially someone she knew." Again, she struggled for composure. "I'm sure she has family in Denver. Someone will have to tell them."

"I'll take care of that," Travis said.

She wanted to hug her brother. He had had to break the awful news to too many parents and spouses and siblings since the killings had begun. "Why is Alex doing this?" she asked.

"We're hoping you can give us some insight into that," Brodie said. "You might talk to some of the professors who knew him. We could call them, but they might be more inclined to open up to you. You're one of them."

"What is that supposed to mean?" she asked.

"You're an academic," he said. "You speak their language. I'm just a dumb cop."

Under other circumstances, she might have laughed. Brodie was anything but dumb. But there was nothing funny about what had happened here today. "I'll see what I can find out," she said. "But I'm not promising I can help you."

"We'd appreciate it if you'd try." Travis patted her shoulder. "I'm sorry about your friend, but I think you'd better go home now. There's nothing you can do here."

She nodded, and slipped off the jacket and held it out to Brodie. "You keep it," he said. "I can get it tonight."

"Don't be silly," she said. "I'm getting back in my warm car, so I don't need it." And she didn't want to give him an excuse for looking her up again later.

He took the jacket, then turned toward her Jeep, frowning. "You drove up here by yourself?" he said.

"Yes."

"You shouldn't be out driving by yourself," he said. "Alex Woodruff targets women who are in their cars alone."

"I'm not going to stop if he tries to flag me down," she said. "I'm not stupid."

"He knows that," Brodie said. "He would use some subterfuge. He's done it before."

"Brodie's right," Travis said. "From now on, when you have to come to town, take someone else with you. And don't pull over for anyone—no matter what."

She stared at them, fear tightening her throat and making it hard to breathe. Of course she knew there was a killer preying on women. But it was hard to believe she was really in danger. That was probably what those other women had thought, too. She nodded. "All right," she said. "I won't go out alone, and I'll be careful."

Brodie followed her to the Jeep and waited while she climbed in. "I know you think Travis and I are overreacting," he said. "But until this man is caught, you're not going to be truly safe."

"I know." She didn't like knowing it, but there was no use denying facts. For whatever reason, Alex Woodruff was targeting women who were alone— women in her age group. "I do take this very seriously," she said. Having a brother who was sheriff and another brother who was a deputy didn't make her immune from the danger.

Chapter Five

Emily couldn't shake a sense of guilt over Denise's death. She could have refused her friend's offer to bring the student surveys to her. She could have at least warned Denise to be careful, and made sure she knew about the serial killer who had been targeting women in the area. But she couldn't change the past, and guilt wouldn't bring Denise back to her. All Emily could do was to try to help Travis and his officers find Alex and stop him before he killed again.

With this in mind, she called the professor who had taught several of the undergrad psychology courses she had taken at the university. "It's always wonderful to hear from a former student," Professor Brandt said, after Emily had introduced herself. "Even if you did forsake psychology for economics."

"I still have one foot in the psychology camp," she said. "And I use things you taught me almost every day."

Professor Brandt laughed. "You must want a big

favor indeed if you're ladling out flattery like that," he said. "What can I do for you?"

"I'm calling about an undergrad, a psychology major who participated in some research I'm conducting," she said. "I need to get in touch with him, but I'm not having any luck. I'm wondering if you know how to reach him. His name is Alex Woodruff."

"Yes, I have had Alex in several classes," the professor said. "He was enrolled in my experimental psychology course this semester, but my understanding is that he never reported for classes."

"Do you know why?" she asked. "Has he been in touch with you?"

"No. There are always a number of students who drop out each semester for various reasons."

"Do you have any idea where he might be? Did he mention moving or anything like that?"

"No. But then, I doubt he would have confided in me. He wasn't the type to seek out faculty for conversation."

"What type was he?" Emily asked. "What were your impressions of him?"

"He was intelligent, good-looking. A bit arrogant. The type of student who doesn't have to work very hard or put forth much effort to get good grades. If I had to describe him in one word, I'd say he was superficial."

"Superficial?" she repeated. "What do you mean?"

"He was chameleonlike, adjusting himself to his

circumstances. He could play the part of the studious scholar or the popular jock, but I always had the impression they were all just roles for him. Watching him was like watching an actor in a play. I never had a sense that he ever really revealed anything about himself."

"Yes, I saw that, too," Emily said, a chill shuddering up her spine. When she had met Alex, he had played the role of the eager research participant, an average student earning a little pocket change, no different from the majority of other students who filled out her questionnaires. But chances were his fantasies of murdering women had been well formed by then. The literature she had read about serial killers pointed to their compulsions building from a young age.

"I do remember one time the subject of future professions came up in class, and Alex said he wanted to go into law enforcement. He specifically mentioned becoming a profiler."

Another shudder went through her. "Did that strike you as odd?" she asked.

"Not really. Television has made the profession glamorous. I always point out to students that they'll need experience in some other branch of psychology before they can make the leap to criminal profiling."

"Did Alex have any particular friends at the university?" she asked. "A girlfriend?"

"I don't know," the professor said. "Why your interest in Alex? If you're unable to follow up with him, you can always discard his responses from your research."

"It seems odd to me that such a promising student would suddenly drop out of school," she said, grappling for some plausible explanation for her interest. "I know it's none of my business, but someone must know something. I guess I hate leaving a mystery unsolved."

"Now you've got me curious," he said. "I tell you what—I'll ask around a little and see what I can find out. Is this a good number for you?"

"Yes. I'm staying with my parents for my brother's wedding this weekend. I appreciate anything you can find out."

"I'll talk to you soon, then."

She ended the call and stared out the window at the snow-covered landscape. What role was Alex playing today? Was he safe and warm in the home of an unsuspecting friend, or hunkered down in a cave or a remote cabin, preparing to kill again? Why hadn't she—or the other people who knew him— seen in him the capacity to murder? Was it because he hid that side of himself so well—or because as humans they shied away from admitting the possibility that such evil lay in someone who was, after all, so very much like themselves?

BRODIE HAD NEVER thought of Emily as a serious person. He had a fixed image of her as young, fun and carefree. But maybe that was only because they had been like that when they had been a couple five years before. Time and the job had made him more somber, and he could see that in her also. He stood in the doorway of the sunroom that evening, studying her as she sat on a love seat across the room: legs curled under her, head bent over a thick textbook, dark hair in a knot on top of her head, brows drawn together in concentration. Travis's words to him earlier still stung—had she really been so hurt by their breakup? It had been what she wanted, wasn't it—to be rid of a man she couldn't see herself with permanently?

She looked up from the book and noticed him. "How long have you been standing there?" she asked.

"Not long." He moved into the room and held out the stack of file folders he had tucked under his arm. "I retrieved these from Denise Switcher's car. I think they're the files you said she was bringing to you." The box the files had been packed in had been spattered with blood, so he had removed them. No need to remind Emily of the violent way her friend had died.

She hesitated, then reached up to take the folders. "Thank you."

When he didn't leave, but stood in front of her, hands tucked in the pockets of his jeans, she motioned to the love seat across from her. "Do you want to sit down?"

He sat. "Are you okay?" he asked.

"Why wouldn't I be okay?" She pulled a pencil from the back of her head and her hair tumbled down around her shoulders. He'd always wondered how women did that—styled their hair with a pencil or a chopstick or whatever was handy.

"It's hard, losing a friend to murder," he said.

She nodded. "It's worse knowing someone you knew killed her." She shifted, planting her feet on the floor. "Did you have something to eat? I think Rainey kept back some dinner for you and Travis."

"I'll get it in a minute."

He let the silence stretch. It was a good technique for getting people to open up. He used it in interrogating suspects—though he wasn't interrogating Emily, and he didn't suspect her of anything more than being uncomfortable around him. He'd like to change that.

"I talked to one of Alex's professors," she said after a moment. She glanced at him through a veil of dark lashes—a look that might have been coy but wasn't. "I wasn't sure if I should let on that he's a murder suspect, so I pretended I was doing follow-up for the research he participated in for our department. I told the professor I hadn't been able to get hold of him—which isn't a lie. He confirmed that Alex didn't return to classes this semester."

"We already knew that. Did you find out anything else?"

"I'm getting to that."

"Sorry. Go on."

She sat up straighter, prepared to give a report. He imagined her in the classroom, making a presentation. She was probably a good teacher—well-spoken and direct. Pleasant to listen to, which probably wasn't a requirement, but he was sure it helped. He liked listening to her, and he liked sitting across from her like this, breathing in the faint floral scent of her soap and enjoying the way the light of the lamp beside her illuminated her skin. "Alex is studying psychology," she said. "So I asked the professor what kind of person he thought Alex was. He said he was superficial."

Brodie considered the word. An unusual choice. "What do you think he meant?"

"He said Alex struck him as someone playing a part. He knew how to act like a serious student or a popular friend, but the professor always had the sense that beneath the surface, there wasn't much there. Or maybe, that there was something darker there that Alex didn't want to show to anyone else."

"Did you ask the professor if he thought Alex was a sociopath?"

"No. And I don't think he'd make that kind of diagnosis on the basis of their relationship. It wouldn't be professional."

"I'm no psychologist, but I'd say a man who kills eight women in cold blood doesn't have normal emotions or reactions."

"I wouldn't disagree." She met his gaze and he felt the zing of attraction. However else they had both changed in the past five years, they hadn't lost this sense of physical connection. He had always believed

the physical side of a relationship was the most superficial, based on hormones and basic drives. With
Emily, even this felt different.

"Did the professor say anything else?" he asked,
determined to keep things loose and professional. He
had meant what he said to Travis about coming here
to do a job, not to resume a relationship with Emily.
After all, she had made it clear when she had refused
his proposal that she didn't see him as the kind of
man she wanted to spend her life with.

"Only that Alex was very intelligent, made good
grades when he applied himself and had expressed
an interest in going into law enforcement work," she
said. "Specifically, he mentioned he wanted to be a
criminal profiler."

Another surprise. "That's interesting. And a little
unnerving. I hate to think law enforcement would
be attractive to someone like that."

"I don't know—if you wanted to commit crimes,
doing it as a cop, where you would be privy to all
the information about the investigation, would allow
you to stay one step ahead of the people looking for
you. You might even be able to guide them to look
in the wrong direction."

"Now I'm a little unnerved that you've put so
much thought into this." He tried for a teasing tone,
letting her know he wasn't serious.

"You asked me to get inside Alex's head." She
shifted position on the sofa. "Though I have to admit,
it's not the most comfortable place to be."

"Do you have any ideas where he might be hiding out, or what his next move might be?" Brodie asked.

"I'm a researcher, not a clairvoyant," she said. "But I am working on it. The case feels really personal now, with Denise's death. I mean, I knew a lot of the women he's killed, but this hits a little close to home."

He nodded, but said nothing, debating whether he should mention his concerns about a connection to her.

She must have sensed his hesitation. She leaned toward him, her gaze searching. "What aren't you telling me?" she asked.

"I don't want to alarm you."

"I'm already alarmed."

He blew out a breath. Maybe if he shared his theories, she'd help blow them out of the water. "I'm wondering if you might be on Alex's radar as a possible target," he said. "If, in fact, you're what brought him to Eagle Mountain to begin with."

"Why would you think that?"

"Maybe he fixated on you."

"He's killed eight other women and hasn't even threatened me."

"Maybe he's biding his time, waiting for the right opportunity."

She didn't look frightened—only skeptical. "And the other women were what—practice?"

"The first one might have been. Then he discovered he liked killing. Or maybe he's done this before, someplace else."

"I'm sure Travis has already thought of that," she said. "I don't think he found any like crimes."

"You're right. And Alex is young. His first murder may very well have been Kelly Farrow."

"I think it's just a coincidence that he ended up here," she said. "He came here to ice climb with his friend, they got stranded by the snow and he killed Kelly—maybe he'd always had a sick fantasy about killing a woman and he thought doing so in this out-of-the-way place, with a small sheriff's department, would be easier."

Brodie nodded. "And once he started, he felt compelled to continue."

"From what I've read, that's how it works with many serial killers—they're fulfilling an elaborate, engrossing fantasy."

Brodie hoped she wasn't part of that fantasy, but decided not to share that with her. He didn't want to frighten her—only make her more aware of possible danger. "I told Travis I'd asked you to help with the case," he said.

"What did he say about that?"

"He reluctantly agreed to let you help, but I don't think he was too happy about getting his little sister involved." Or about any possible involvement between Brodie and Emily.

"He and Gage both tend to be overprotective. I've learned to humor them and do what I want, anyway."

"They have a right to be concerned. I hope you took what we said this afternoon—about not going anywhere alone—seriously."

"I did."

"It applies to all the women here at the ranch, and all the women you know."

"We do talk about this, you know? I don't know any woman who goes anywhere by herself without being alert to her surroundings."

"When you live in a peaceful place like Eagle Mountain, I can see how it would be easy to get complacent."

"But I don't live in Eagle Mountain," she said. "I live in Fort Collins. And I have two brothers who are cops. I know more than I want to about how dangerous it can be out there."

"Point taken," he said. And maybe it was time to shift the conversation to something more mundane and less stressful. "How do you like living in the big city? It's a lot different from life here on the ranch."

"I love it," she said. "I really enjoy my work, and I like all the opportunities and conveniences of a bigger city."

Footsteps approached and they both turned toward the door as Travis entered. He stopped short. "Brodie, what are you doing here?"

"I dropped off the files from Denise Switcher's car," Brodie said. "The ones she was bringing to Emily."

"I could have brought them," Travis said. He was

studying Brodie as if he was a perp he suspected of a crime.

"I'm sure Brodie didn't want to bother you with such a little errand," Emily said. She turned to Brodie. "Thanks again for bringing them to me."

"It's been a long day," Travis said. "I'm sure Brodie wants to get to his cabin."

Brodie resisted the urge to needle Travis by protesting that he wasn't tired in the least and had been enjoying his visit with Emily. But the sheriff looked in no mood for teasing. For whatever reason, Travis still harbored hard feelings about Brodie and Emily's breakup. At times, the sheriff seemed more upset with Brodie than Emily did. Brodie stood. "Travis is right," he said. "And I've kept you long enough."

"I enjoyed your visit," Emily said. Brodie wondered if she was saying so to goad her overprotective brother, but she sounded as if she meant it.

"Yeah, we'll have to do it again sometime." He didn't miss the dark look Travis sent him, but sauntered past the sheriff, head up. Brodie hadn't come here intending to renew his relationship with Emily. But if that did end up happening, maybe it wouldn't be such a bad thing.

As long as the sheriff didn't decide to run him out of town first.

Chapter Six

Reviewing the student surveys would have to wait until after Wednesday's barbecue and bonfire, the latest in a series of events at the ranch that Emily was hosting in an attempt to entertain friends and family trapped in town by the weather. Wednesday morning found Emily in the kitchen with Bette and Rainey, reviewing the menu for the evening. "Good plain food to help warm folks up in the cold," Rainey declared after describing the chili she would make and the kabobs Bette would assemble. "The kind of food I've been making all my life."

The ranch cook was an angular woman in her late forties or early fifties, who had reigned over the Walker kitchen for the past decade. Though she shooed Emily and her friends out of the kitchen whenever they invaded that sacred territory, she had also been known to spoil the youngest Walker sibling with homemade cookies and grilled pimento cheese sandwiches at every opportunity. Rainey's son's recent incarceration had subdued the cook a little, but she had also confided to Emily's mother that she felt less stressed, since at least now she knew her son was somewhere safe, and not causing trouble for anyone else.

"Everything will be delicious," Emily said, and handed the menu back to Bette. "And I definitely want to keep this simple. This close to the wedding, I don't want to burden either one of you."

"She's got this, and the wedding, taken care of," Rainey said.

"Rainey has been a big help with the reception preparations," Bette said, quick to praise the woman who, on her initial arrival at the ranch, had been her biggest foe.

Emily's cell phone rang. She fished it from the back pocket of her jeans and her heart sped up when she saw Professor Brandt's number. "I have to take this," she said, and hurried from the room.

Alone in the sunroom, she answered the call. "Hello, Professor."

"Hello, Emily. I asked around about Alex Woodruff and I found out a few things, though I don't know if they'll help you much."

Emily grabbed a notebook and pen from the table and sat on the sofa. "I'm all ears."

"This is an odd situation," he said. "And I'll admit, I'm curious now, too. Alex doesn't have any close friends that I could find, though he spent more time with Tim Dawson than anyone else. Do you know him?"

"Yes."

"Oddly enough, Tim failed to return to school also," the professor said. "I wasn't able to learn anything about him. When I contacted his family, they didn't want to talk to me about him. His father hung up on me."

Maybe the Dawsons didn't want to reveal that their son had been killed while committing a crime, or that he was a suspect in a series of murders. Emily was pretty sure Travis had talked to Tim's parents, but she had no idea what had come of that conversation. "What about Alex's family?" she asked.

"He's apparently estranged from them, though he has a trust fund that pays for his schooling and living expenses, and from what I gather, anything else he wants."

"Oh." That explained how he was able to spend a month in Eagle Mountain with no worries about money.

"I have a name for you, of a young woman he apparently dated for a while. Grace Anders. She's a student here. You understand I can't give you her contact information."

"I understand." If she couldn't figure out how to get hold of Grace on her own, Brodie or Travis could help her.

"When you return to school, you shouldn't have much trouble finding her here on campus, if you want to talk to her."

"Okay, thank you. Anything else?"

"No, that's all. But do me a favor and let me know what you find out. Like I said, I'm curious now."

"I'll do that." Though if things went well, Professor Brandt would be able to read about Alex and his arrest for murder in the Denver papers.

She hung up the phone and stared at the name she had written on her pad. Grace Anders. She could give the name to Travis and have him or Gage or one of his officers contact the young woman. They were trained to elicit information from witnesses. But would Grace really confide in them? Wouldn't she be more likely to open up to another woman at the university, someone close to her own age?

She picked up her phone again and punched in the number for the sheriff's department. Adelaide answered, all crisp professionalism. "The sheriff is out at the moment," she said, after Emily identified herself.

"It's really you I want to talk to," Emily said. "I'm doing a little job for Travis and I need help finding a phone number for a friend of Alex Woodruff. Grace Anders, in Fort Collins."

"Travis did mention something about you helping with the case," Adelaide said. "He wasn't too happy about the idea, if I recall."

"I'm staying safe, just making a few phone calls for him," she said. "Can you find Grace Anders's number for me?"

"Hold on a minute."

Emily doodled in her notebook while she waited

for Adelaide. She was coloring in circles around the word *trust fund* when the older woman came back on the line and rattled off a phone number. "Thanks, Adelaide," Emily said, and hung up before the office manager could question her further.

Before she could lose courage, Emily dialed the number Adelaide had given her. On the third ring a young woman answered. "If you're trying to sell something, I'm not interested," she said.

"I'm not selling anything, I promise," Emily said. "I'm calling about Alex Woodruff."

The silence on the other end of the line was so complete, Emily feared Grace had hung up. "What about him?" she asked after a minute.

"My name is Emily Walker. I'm a grad student at the university. Is this Grace Anders?"

"Why are you calling me? What has Alex done?"

Emily thought it was interesting that Grace assumed Alex had done something. Something wrong? "I understand you dated him at one time."

"Not for months. I haven't had anything to do with him for months and I'd just as soon keep it that way."

No love lost in her tone, Emily decided. "I'm trying to help a friend who had a rather unpleasant encounter with Alex," she said. That wasn't a complete lie—Denise was her friend, and Alex had killed her. Emily was trying to help find him and see that he was punished for the crime.

"Sorry about your friend," Grace said. "Alex is a creep."

"But you went out with him."

"Because I didn't know he was a creep at first," Grace said. "He was good-looking and he could be charming. We had a good time, at first."

"But something happened to change that?" Emily prompted.

"What did he do to your friend? I mean, did he steal money from her or something?"

"Did he steal money from you?"

"No. He had plenty of money of his own. I just wondered."

"He didn't steal from my friend." How much should Emily say? She wanted Grace to feel comfortable confiding in her, but she couldn't say anything that might jeopardize Travis's case against Alex.

"Did he assault her?" Grace blurted. "I mean, rape her or something?"

"Or something."

Grace swore. "I knew it. I should have said something before, but what would I have said?"

"Did Alex rape you?" Emily asked, as gently as possible.

"No! Nothing like that. It was just… I got really bad vibes from him."

"What kind of vibes?" Emily asked. "I know that's a really personal question, but it could really help."

Grace sighed dramatically. "We had sex a couple of times and it was fine, and then he wanted to do things different." She paused, then continued, "It feels so icky even talking about it, but he wanted to choke me."

Emily gasped. "Choke you?"

"Yeah, you know that autoerotic thing some people do where they choke themselves while they're getting off. It's supposed to give you some super orgasm or something, but it's crazy. People have died like that."

"But he didn't want to choke himself—he wanted to choke you."

"You get how creepy that is, right? I told him no way. I was really freaked out."

"How did he react when you refused him?"

"He got all huffy. He really pressured me, and that made me freak out even more."

"Because you had a really bad vibe."

"Yeah. I guess. It just seemed to me that it wasn't the sex he was so into, but the choking. I was worried he might like it so much he wouldn't stop. Is that what happened to your friend?"

"Something like that. You've been really helpful. If the police were to contact you about this, would you be willing to talk to them?"

"I guess. I'm sorry about your friend."

"Do you know of any other women he dated?" she asked.

"No. Like I said, I've stayed as far away from him as I could. Somebody told me he didn't come back to school this semester. I was relieved to hear it."

"Did Alex ever threaten you?" Emily asked.

"No. I just never felt comfortable around him after the choking thing came up."

"You were smart to turn him down. You have good instincts."

"Maybe I've had too much practice dating creeps. I just want to meet a good guy, you know?"

They said goodbye and Emily reviewed the conversation, organizing her thoughts to present to Travis. Maybe Alex had merely been interested in experimenting sexually, but her instincts told her Grace had read him correctly—he wasn't so much interested in the sexual experience as he was in choking a woman and knowing what that felt like.

He hadn't choked his victims, but maybe he had ruled out that method after being turned down by Grace. Or maybe he had intended her to be his first victim. He could murder her, and if anyone found out, he could claim she had died accidentally while they were experimenting. He might even have been able to get away with it.

Maybe he *had* gotten away with it. Maybe somewhere in Denver was a young woman who had died at Alex's hands, though he hadn't yet been charged with the crime.

With trembling hands, Emily punched in Travis's number. "Are you calling to tell me you've decided to cancel the bonfire tonight?" he asked.

"No! Why would I do that?"

"I told Lacy I thought you should. I'm concerned

Alex will try to repeat his performance at the scavenger hunt."

"Alex is not invited to this party."

"That might not stop him."

"It's too late to cancel the bonfire," she said, trying to quell her annoyance and not succeeding. "All the invitations have already gone out, and the ranch hands have been accumulating a mountain of scrap wood and brush that needs to be burned. Not to mention Rainey and Bette have been cooking party food for days. I'm certainly not going to tell them their extra work will be wasted."

"Which is pretty much what Lacy said. But she agreed that I could station a deputy and one of the ranch hands at the gate to check the ID of every person who enters against your guest list. So I'll need a copy of the list, first chance you get."

"All right." Part of her thought this was overkill, but the rest of her was grateful for this extra measure of safety.

"If you didn't call about the party, why did you call?" Travis asked.

"I talked to a woman Alex used to date," she said. "She said they broke up when he tried to talk her into letting him strangle her while they had sex."

"That's interesting. Does she have any idea where he is right now?"

"No. She hasn't had anything to do with him for a couple of months. But do you think this is how he started? What if some other woman agreed to his proposal and she died and everyone thought it was an accident, when really it was murder?"

"I haven't found anything like that in my research, but I can add it to his file."

"You could call someone in Fort Collins and Denver and try to find out."

"I could. But that won't help us discover where Alex is right now, and that's what I need to know if I'm going to stop him."

"No one in Fort Collins knows where he is," she said. "His professor told me he didn't have any friends but Tim, and he's estranged from his parents. Oh, and he has a big trust fund that pays for everything."

"Yes, we knew that."

"Then why did you even ask me to try to find out about him?"

"You've learned useful information," Travis said. "I don't want you to think I don't appreciate your help. But we really need to focus on where Alex might be hiding right now. Did he know anyone in Eagle Mountain before he arrived here? Does he have any relatives who live here? Did he ever complete an outdoor survival course or express an interest in winter camping?"

If Travis wanted her to ask questions like that, why hadn't he given her a list? "I don't think any of the people I talked to know those things," she said.

"Maybe no one does," Travis said. "But it's important to try everything we can think of. Is there anything else you need to tell me?"

"No."

"Then I have to go."

He ended the call and Emily frowned at her phone, fighting frustration. She felt like she had learned something important about Alex, but Travis was right—it wasn't going to help them find him and stop him. The longer it took to locate him, the more time he had to attack and kill another woman.

She studied her notebook, hoping for inspiration that didn't come. "Emily?"

She turned toward the door, where Lacy stood. "The ranch hands brought up that load of hay bales you asked for," she said. "They want to know what to do with them."

"Sure thing." She jumped up, pushing aside thoughts of Alex for now. Time to distract everyone else—and herself—from the danger lurking just outside their doors.

For the rest of the day, Emily focused on making sure the party was a success, and counted it a good sign that, though the highway was still closed due to multiple avalanches, no new snow had fallen in a couple of days, and clouds had receded to reveal a star-spangled night sky and an almost-full moon like a shining silver button overhead.

As an added bonus, though the wedding favors and guest book hadn't been delivered before the road closed again, Paige Riddell and her significant other, DEA agent Rob Allerton, had arrived and moved into the last empty guest cabin. Lacy was thrilled her friend had made it and had thanked Emily half a dozen times today for arranging the bonfire.

All the guests seemed happy to be here, gathering in a semicircle as Travis, Gage and Emily's father lit the bonfire, then cheering as it caught and blazed to life. Even before the blaze gave off much warmth, the sight of it made everyone more animated. The flames popped and crackled as they climbed the tower of old pallets, scrap wood and brush the ranch hands had spent days assembling; the sparks rose like glitter floating up into the black sky, the scent of wood smoke mingling with the aroma of barbecue and mulled cider.

From the fire, guests gravitated to a buffet set up under tents. Rainey and Bette had prepared big vats of chili, pans of corn bread and half a dozen different salads. They had also arranged skewers of kabobs and sausages guests could toast over the fire. Guests could opt for cookies for dessert, or create their own s'mores.

Seating was provided by hay bales draped in blankets and buffalo robes, shaped into surprisingly comfortable couches—some long enough for half a dozen people, others just the right size for cuddling for two. Two of the ranch hands played guitar and sang for the appreciative crowd. Alcoholic and nonalcoholic beverages added to the festivities.

"Travis tells me you're the genius behind all this." Brodie's voice, low and velvety, pulled Emily's attention from the music. She hoped the dim lighting hid the warm flush that seemed to engulf her body at his approach. He indicated the crowd around the bonfire. "It's a great party."

"Travis wanted to cancel the whole thing, but I had Lacy in my corner," she said.

"He doesn't look too upset right now." Brodie nodded toward the sheriff, who was slow dancing with Lacy on the edge of the firelight, her head on his shoulder, both dancers' eyes half-closed.

Emily couldn't help but smile at the lovebirds. "They're so good together," she said. "It's great to see Travis so happy."

"Gage has found his match, too," Brodie said.

Emily shifted her attention from Travis to her other brother, who sat on a hay bale with his wife, Maya. The two were feeding each other toasted marshmallows and laughing, eyes shining as they gazed at one another. Emily sighed. "I never would have guessed my two brothers could be such romantics," she said.

"Are you kidding? When it comes to love, most men are completely at a woman's mercy. We may not always show our romantic side, but it's definitely there."

"I'm not talking about buying a woman flowers and delivering a convincing line to get her to go out with you—or to go to bed with you," Emily said.

"Neither am I. I think most people want to be in relationships, to love and be loved. Maybe one of the reasons a lot of men—and maybe women, too—have a hard time expressing that desire is that they know it's so important. They're really afraid of messing things up and getting it wrong."

Brodie was the last person in the world she had ever expected she'd have a philosophical conversation about love with. "Excuse me?" she asked. "Are you sure you're really Brodie Langtry? Mr. Heartbreaker?" He certainly hadn't hinted that he was so keen on that kind of deep relationship when the two of them had been together. And she still wasn't sure she believed he had never received the letter she had sent to him after their breakup. Pretending he'd never seen it made him look much better than if he had read the letter and decided to blow her off—which was what she had always believed.

"I grew up," he said, her own image shining back at her in the reflection of the firelight in his eyes. "We all do. Besides, I was never as shallow as you thought I was. When someone is important to me, I will do anything to protect them and support them."

Now he was getting really hard for her to believe. "Have you ever had a serious relationship with a woman in your life?" she asked.

"Once."

A sharp pain pinched her chest. Who was this woman who had captured his heart? And why did it hurt to hear about her? Emily wet her lips. "When was that?"

"A long time ago."

She thought she heard real regret in his voice, but why was she feeling sorry for him? "I don't believe you," she said. "You can have any woman you want. If you commit to one, you have to give up all the others, so why should you?"

"What about you?" he asked. "Are you serious about someone? Or have you ever been?"

He was the only man she'd made the mistake of falling for. "I'm getting my degree and focusing on my career. I don't have time for a relationship."

He moved closer, blocking the firelight, the sheepskin collar of his heavy leather coat brushing against the nylon of her down-filled parka. Layers of fabric separated them, yet she felt the contact, like current flowing through an electrical cord once it was plugged in. She couldn't make out his features in the darkness, but was sure he was watching her. "Now who's avoiding commitment?" he asked.

She told herself she should move away, but couldn't make her feet obey the command. "I'm not avoiding anything," she said.

"Except me. You don't have to run from me, Emily. I would never hurt you."

Hurt wasn't always a matter of intent—maturity had taught her that, at least. This knowledge made it easier for her to forgive him, but she wasn't going to forget anytime soon how easily he had wounded her. She would have told anyone that she had gotten over him long ago, then he showed up here at the ranch and all the old feelings came surging back like the tide rushing in. No good would come of revisiting all that.

"I have to go check on the food," she said, finally forcing herself to take a step back, and then another.

He didn't come after her, just stood and watched her run away. Maybe he didn't pursue her because he didn't really want her, she told herself as she hurried toward the buffet table.

Or maybe he didn't chase her because he was so sure that if he bided his time, he could have her, anyway. That, on some level, she had never really stopped being his.

BRODIE LET EMILY walk away. Maybe what they both needed right now was space. He had never expected to be so drawn to her. He had thought he was over her years ago. He'd been angry and hurt when she turned down his marriage proposal, and had spent more than a few months nursing his hurt feelings and wounded pride.

And now that he was back in town, Emily's family acted as if he was the villain in the whole bad scene. Had Emily made up some story about him dumping her, instead of admitting that she'd turned him down? She didn't strike him as the type to lie about something like that, but as he had told her, they had both done a lot of growing up in the past five years.

He helped himself to a kabob from the buffet table and tried his hand grilling it over the fire. Gage, a skewered sausage in hand, joined him. Of the two brothers, Gage had been the friendliest since Brodie's return to Eagle Mountain. "How's it going?" Gage asked.

"Okay." Brodie glanced around to make sure no one could overhear. "I'm trying to figure out why your family is giving me the cold shoulder. I mean, they're all polite, but not exactly welcoming."

Gage slanted a look at him. "You dated Emily for a while, right?"

"Yes. Five years ago. And then we broke up. It happens. That doesn't make me the bad guy."

Gage rotated the sausage and moved it closer to the flames. "I was away at school when that all went down, so I don't know much about it," he said. "I do know when I asked about it when I came home for the holidays, everybody clammed up about it. I got the impression you dumped Emily and broke her heart. You were one of Travis's best friends, so I guess he saw it as some kind of betrayal."

"I asked your sister to marry me and she turned me down," Brodie said. "That's not exactly dumping her."

"Does Travis know that?"

"I'm sure he does. Emily didn't have any reason to lie about it."

Gage shook his head. "Then maybe you'd better

ask Travis what's on his mind. You know him—he keeps his feelings to himself, most of the time."

"Maybe I will." But not tonight. Brodie looked across the fire to where Travis sat with Lacy in the golden glow of the fire, their heads together, whispering. The sheriff looked happier and more relaxed than he had since Brodie had arrived. Amazing what love could do for a person.

Someone shouting made him tense, and he turned to see Dwight helping Rob Allerton into the circle of firelight. Rob dropped onto a hay bale and pushed Dwight away, as Paige rushed to him. "What happened?" she asked, gingerly touching a darkening bruise on his forehead.

"I left my phone back in our cabin and decided to go get it so I could show someone some pictures I have on it," Rob said. "As I neared the ranch house, I noticed someone moving around by the cars. At first I thought it was someone leaving the party early, but as I drew nearer, the guy bolted and ran straight at me. He had a tire iron or a club or something like that in his hand." Rob touched the bruise and winced. "I guess I'm lucky he only struck me a glancing blow, but I fell, and by the time I got to my feet and went looking for him, he had vanished." He looked up and found Travis in the crowd gathered around him. "I think he did something to your sheriff's department SUV."

Brodie followed Travis, Gage and most of the rest of the guests over to the parking area in front of the house. Travis's SUV was parked in the shadows at the far end of a line of cars and trucks. The sheriff played the beam of a flashlight over the vehicle, coming to rest on the driver's-side door. Someone had spray-painted a message in foot-high, bright red letters: *ICE COLD.*

Chapter Seven

Emily dragged herself into the sheriff's department the next morning, the two cups of coffee she had forced down with breakfast having done little to put her in a better mood. She hadn't slept much after the party broke up last night—something she probably shared in common with everyone else in attendance at this meeting the sheriff had called. Most of the law enforcement personnel who gathered in the conference room had searched the ranch and surrounding area for Alex Woodruff late into the previous night. Once again, after leaving his blood-red taunt on Travis's SUV, he had disappeared into the darkness.

She took her place to Travis's left at the conference table, nodding in greeting at the others around the table and avoiding lingering too long when her gaze fell on Brodie. She had missed him at breakfast this morning. Her mother had mentioned that he'd left early with Travis. Though the two men hadn't been friendly since Brodie's arrival at the ranch, they did seem to work together well.

Her feelings for Brodie seemed to fluctuate between regret and relief. Regret that they couldn't pick up the easy exchange they had enjoyed Tuesday evening in the sunroom. Relief that she didn't have to revisit the tension between them beside the bonfire last night. Other people got through situations like this and were able to put the past behind them. She and Brodie would learn to do that, too.

Travis stood and everyone fell silent. "I think you all know my sister, Emily," he said. "She is acquainted with Alex Woodruff and is completing her master's degree in behavioral economics. I've asked her to sit in on some meetings, to help us try to get into Alex's mind in hopes of anticipating his next move."

"I pity you, being in that guy's mind," someone—she thought it might be Ryder Stewart—said from the other end of the table.

Travis ignored the comment and projected a map of Rayford County onto a wall screen. "As I believe all of you know, someone—we're operating on the assumption that it was Alex—vandalized my department SUV last night at my family's ranch during a party."

"How did he get by the security you had set up?" wildlife officer Nate Harris asked.

"He parked around a curve, out of sight of the guards," Travis said. "He approached the ranch house on foot, and circled around through the trees. We were able to trace his movements that far at first light."

"He must have run track." Rob Allerton had joined them this morning, the bruise on his forehead an angry purple, matching the half-moons under his eyes. "He raced out of there like a gazelle."

Travis projected a color photo of his SUV onto the wall screen. The large red letters stood out against the Rayford County Sheriff's logo. "He's always enjoyed taunting us. This seems to represent an acceleration of that."

"He knows we know who he is and he doesn't care," Ryder Stewart declared.

"He thinks he's better than all of us," Brodie said.

"We're looking for anywhere Alex might be hiding," Travis said. "We've ruled out the two sets of forest service summer cabins where we know he and Tim Dawson spent time before." He circled these sites in red on the image. "We know Alex and Tim used an unoccupied vacation home as a hideout previously, so we're working our way through unoccupied homes but we haven't hit anything there, either. We've also published Alex's picture in the paper, on posters around town and on all the social media outlets. We've alerted people to let us know if they spot him."

"If he's using someone's vacation home, the neighbors are bound to see him," Dwight said.

"Maybe he's using a disguise," Deputy Jamie Douglas said.

"Alex was in the drama club at the university," Emily said. "But I don't think he would hide in a place with a lot of people—not now when he knows you've identified him. He takes risks, but they're calculated risks." She had lain awake for a long time last night thinking about this, and searched for the right words to share her conclusions. "He knows you're looking for him, and he wants to be free to come and go as he pleases. That freedom is important to him—he has to be in charge, not allowing you to dictate his movements. Showing up at the ranch last night and vandalizing your vehicle is another way of asserting that freedom."

"He could have moved into an abandoned mine," Nate said from his seat beside Jamie. "There are plenty of those around."

Travis nodded. "We'll check those out."

"He could be in a cave," Dwight said.

"He could be," Travis said. "But remember—wherever he is has to be accessible by a road."

Emily leaned forward, trying to get a better look at the map. "What's that symbol on the map, near Dixon Pass?" she asked.

Travis studied the image, then rested the pointer on a stick figure facing downhill. "Do you mean this? I think it's the symbol for an old ski area."

"Dixon Downhill," Gage said. "I think it's been closed since the eighties. When they widened the highway in the nineties, they covered over the old access road into the place."

"I think part of the old ski lift is still there,"

Dwight said. "But I'm pretty sure they bulldozed all the buildings."

"Gage, you and Dwight check it out," Travis said. "See if there are any habitable buildings there where Alex might be holed up."

"I'd like to go with them," Brodie said.

"All right," Travis agreed. "Dwight, you and Nate can work on the mines." He gave out assignments to the others on the team.

"What would you like me to do?" Emily asked, as the others gathered up their paperwork and prepared to depart.

"You can go home and write up your thoughts on Alex," Travis said.

A report he would dutifully read, file away and consider his obligation to her met. Her brother might have agreed to let Brodie ask for her help, but that didn't mean he was going to let her get very involved. "I'd like to talk to Jamie," she said. "She spent time with Alex's partner, Tim, when the two kidnapped her and her sister."

"Her statement is in the file I gave you," Travis said.

"I want to talk to her," she said, with more force behind the words.

Travis gave her a hard look, but she looked him in the eye and didn't back down. "All right," he said. "Set it up with her."

"I'll see if she can meet me for lunch." She started to leave, but he stopped her.

"Emily?"

She turned toward him again. "Yes?"

"Alex Woodruff is very dangerous. Don't get any ideas about trying to get close to him on your own."

A shudder went through her. "Why would I want to get close to a man who's murdered eight women? Travis, do you really think I'm that stupid?"

"You're not stupid," he said. "But you tend to always think the best of people."

She wondered if he was talking about more than Alex now. Was he also warning her away from Brodie?

"I'll be careful," she said. "And I won't do anything foolish." Not when it came to either man.

To REACH WHAT was left of the Dixon Downhill ski area, Brodie and Gage had to park at the barricades closing off the highway, strap on snowshoes and walk up the snow-covered pavement to a break in a concrete berm on the side of the road, where an old emergency access road lay buried under snow. Reflectors on trees defined the route. The two men followed the reflectors to a bench that was the remains of the road that had once led to the resort.

The resort itself had been situated in a valley below the pass, with lift-accessed skiing on both sides. "You can still see the cuts for the old ski runs from here." Gage pointed out the wide path cut through stands of tall spruce and fir.

"Is that the lift line there?" Brodie indicated a

cable running through the trees to their right. A couple of rusting metal chairs dangled crookedly from the braided line.

"I think so. There's the lift shack, at the top."

The small building that housed the engine that ran the old rope-tow lift really was a shack, cobbled together from rough lumber and tin, a rusting pipe jutting from the roof that was probably the engine exhaust. Brodie took out a pair of binoculars and glassed the area. From this angle, at least, it didn't look as if anyone had been down there in a long time.

"They used old car motors to power some of these things," Gage said. "I'd like to get a look at this one."

"Does the lift still run?" Brodie asked.

"I don't think so," Gage said. "Though if a mechanic messed with it, he might be able to get it going again. Those old motors weren't that sophisticated, and it's been out of the weather."

Gage led the way as they descended into the valley. With no traffic on the closed highway above, and thick snow muffling their steps, the only sounds were the occasional click of the ski poles they were using against a chunk of ice, and their labored breathing on the ascent.

Brodie tried not to think of the mountain of snow on either side of them. "Did you check with the avalanche center before we came down here?" he asked.

"No," Gage said. "We probably should have, but I was too eager to get down here and see what we could see." He stopped and glanced up toward the highway. "We'll be all right as long as he doesn't try to climb up and disturb the snowpack up there."

Brodie hoped Gage was right. After ten minutes of walking, they were forced to stop, the old road completely blocked by a snowslide, the wall of snow rising ten feet over their heads. "I think it's safe to say no one has been down here in a while," Gage said. "This didn't just happen." Dirt and debris dusted the top of the slide, and the ends of tree branches jutting out of the snow were dry and brown.

"At least now we know no one has been here," Gage said.

"Is this road the only way in?" Brodie asked.

"In summer, it might be possible to climb down the rock face from the highway," Gage said. "Though I wouldn't want to try it." He shook his head. "Even if Alex could get here, there's no place for him to stay. That lift shack isn't going to offer much shelter. At this elevation nighttime temperatures would be brutal. And the only way in and out is to go up this road—which is blocked—or scramble straight up."

"Wherever he is, it's somewhere he can go with ease," Brodie said. "This isn't it."

Gage clapped him on the back. "Come on. Let's go back."

The trip up was slower going, in deep snow up a steep grade. "We should have thought to bring a snowmobile," Gage said when they paused halfway up to rest.

Brodie took a bottle of water from his pack and

drank deeply. "And then if Alex had been down there, he would have heard us coming miles away."

"He's not down there." Gage looked around at the world of white. "I wish I knew where he is."

Brodie started to replace the water bottle in his pack when a loud report made him freeze. "What was that?" he asked.

"It sounded like a gunshot." Gage put a hand on his weapon.

"Not close," Brodie said. "Maybe someone target shooting?"

"It sounded like it's up on the highway," Gage said. "Maybe a blowout on one of the road machines?"

"Let's get out of here," Brodie said. They started walking again, but had gone only a few steps when an ominous rumble sent his heart into his throat. He took off running, even as a wave of snow and debris flowed down the slope toward them.

Chapter Eight

Emily arranged to meet Deputy Jamie Douglas for lunch at a new taco place on the south end of town. The former gas station had half a dozen tables inside, and a busy drive-up window. Jamie, her dark hair in a neat twist at the nape of her neck, waved to Emily from one of the tables. "Thanks for agreeing to talk to me," Emily said, joining the deputy at the table.

"Sure. What can I do for you?"

"Let's order lunch and I'll fill you in."

They ordered at a window at the back of the room, then collected their food and returned to the table. "Travis asked me to put together a kind of profile of Alex Woodruff," Emily said when they were situated. "Not as an official profiler, but because I knew him slightly from the university and he hoped I'd have some insights. You probably spent more time with his partner, Tim, than anyone else, so I thought you might have some thoughts I could add to my assessment."

Jamie spooned salsa over her tacos. "I never even met Alex," she said.

"I know. But I think more information about Tim would help me clarify some things about their relationship."

"Sure. I'll try. What do you need to know?"

"I read your report, so I know the facts about what happened when Tim and Alex kidnapped you, but I'm more interested in other behavioral things."

"Like what?"

"When you came to, you and your sister were alone in the cabin with Tim?"

"Yes."

"And he told you he was waiting for Alex to return?"

"That's right. Well, he never named him, but we knew his partner was Alex."

"Did you get the impression that Alex was the leader—that Tim was looking to him to make the decisions?"

"Yes. Tim got a phone call from his partner— from Alex—who apparently told him he had to kill us by himself. Tim didn't like this, so then they agreed that Tim would bring us to wherever Alex was waiting, and they would kill us together."

"Do you think the idea of the killings started with Alex, or was it Tim's idea?"

"Definitely Alex. Tim said the first killing freaked him out, but then he started to like it. Or, at least, he liked getting away with the crimes."

"Alex must have recognized a similar personality to his own," Emily said.

Jamie nodded. "I guess it's like they say—birds of a feather flock together."

"My understanding is that Tim acted as the decoy, dressed as a woman, while Alex came up out of the woods and attacked women?" Emily asked.

"Yes. And Tammy Patterson's description of her ordeal confirms that." Tammy was a reporter for the *Eagle Mountain Examiner* who had managed to get away from Alex and Tim after they waylaid her one snowy afternoon.

"I don't think the two were equal partners," Emily said. "Alex was dominant. He's the man who chose the targets, and probably the one who did the actual killing. Tim was his helper. I wonder if Tim would have eventually killed on his own, without Alex around to goad him into doing it."

"I don't know," Jamie said. "But I believe Tim was prepared to kill me and Donna on his own. At least, that's what he told Alex."

"How is your sister doing after this ordeal?" Emily asked. Donna was a pleasant young woman with developmental disabilities who worked at Eagle Mountain Grocery.

"She's doing good." Jamie's smile at the mention of her sister was gentle. "She had some nightmares, but Nate has moved in with us and that's helped. She gets along really great with him, and she says having him in the house at night makes her feel safer." She blushed. "He makes me feel safer, too."

Emily hadn't missed that Jamie had been sitting next to Nate Harris at the meeting this morning. "It's great that the two of you got together," she said.

Jamie rotated the small diamond solitaire on the third finger of her left hand. "We're going to be married in the spring and Donna is almost more excited than I am."

"Congratulations." Emily couldn't quite hide her surprise. The last she had heard, Jamie and Nate had only recently started dating. "You obviously don't believe in long engagements."

"We were high school sweethearts, you know," Jamie said. "We broke up when he went away to college. I thought it was because he was eager to be free of me and date other people. He thought he was doing me a favor, not leaving me tied down to a man who wasn't around. Anyway, I guess we needed that time apart to really appreciate each other."

Emily nodded. So Jamie and Nate weren't strangers who just got together. They had dated and split up before—like her and Brodie. Except the situation with Brodie was entirely different. The circumstances of their split, and everything that had happened afterward, made things so much more awkward between them now.

Jamie's radio crackled with words that were, to Emily, unintelligible, but Jamie set down the glass of tea she had been sipping and jumped to her feet, her face pale. "I have to go," she said.

"What is it?" Emily asked, as the alarm from the fire station down the street filled the air. "What's happened?"

"An avalanche on Dixon Pass," Jamie said, already moving toward the door. "Gage and Brodie may be caught in it!"

As THE WAVE of white moved down the hill toward him, Brodie tried to think what he was supposed to do. He had taken a backcountry rescue course once, and he struggled to recall what the instructor had said.

Then the avalanche of snow was on him, hitting him with the force of a truck, sending him sprawling, struggling for breath. Instinct took over and he began swimming in the snow, fighting to reach the surface before it hardened around him like concrete. He fought hard for each stroke, his thoughts a jumble of images—of Gage's startled face just before the snow hit, of his mother the last time he had seen her and finally of Emily.

Emily, the hardness gone out of her eyes when she looked at him, head tilted to look up at him, lips slightly parted in a silent invitation for a kiss...

Then he popped to the surface of the snowslide, like a surfer thrust forward by the momentum of a wave, gasping in the achingly cold air. A tree branch glanced off his shoulder with a painful blow, then a rock bounced off his head, making him cry out.

Wrenching his head around, he saw that he was on the very edge of the slide, which had probably saved him. He struggled his way out of the snow's grip, like a man floundering out of quicksand. "Gage!" he screamed, then louder, "Gage!"

Relief surged through him as a faint cry greeted him. He fought his way toward it, clawing at the snow with numbed and aching hands, repeatedly calling, then waiting for the response to guide him in the right direction. "Gage! Gage!"

At last he located the source of the cries, and dug into the snow, first with his hands, then with a tree branch. He uncovered Gage's leg, the familiar khaki uniform twisted around his calf, then he dug his way up to Gage's head. When he had cleared away enough snow, he helped Gage sit up. They slumped together in the snow, gasping for air. A thin line of blood trickled from a cut on Gage's forehead, eventually clotting in the cold.

"We need to get out of here," Gage said after many minutes.

"We need help," Brodie countered, and shifted to reach his cell phone. The signal wasn't good, but it might be enough. He dialed 911 and said the words most likely to rush help their way without long explanations. "Officer needs assistance, top of Dixon Pass."

The phone slipped from his numb grasp and he

watched with an air of detachment as it skidded down the slope. Gage struggled to extract his own phone, then stared at the shattered screen. "They'll find us," he said, and lay back on the snow and closed his eyes.

Brodie wanted to join his friend in lying down for a nap. Fatigue dragged at him like a concrete blanket. He couldn't remember when he'd been so exhausted. But the danger of freezing out here in the snow was real. "Wake up, Gage," he said, trying to put some force behind the words. "You don't want to survive an avalanche only to die of hypothermia."

"There are worse ways to go," Gage said. But he sat up and looked up the slope, to the scarred area that showed the path of the avalanche.

"What do you think set it off?" Brodie asked.

"I don't know. Maybe that sound we heard earlier. That engine backfiring."

"Or the gunshot." The more Brodie thought about that report, the more it sounded to him like a gunshot.

"Somebody target shooting in the national forest?" Gage suggested. "Sound carries funny in the canyons."

"Maybe," Brodie said. "But what if someone set off the snowslide deliberately?"

"Why would they do that?"

"Because they didn't like us taking a look at the old ski resort?"

"I don't know who would object. And you saw

yourself—no one has been down there in weeks. Since before that older snowslide."

"Can we find out when that snowslide happened?" Brodie asked.

"Probably," Gage said. "Maybe. I don't really know." He tilted his head. "Does that sound like a siren to you?"

It did, and half an hour later a search-and-rescue team had descended and was helping them back up the slope. The SAR director had wanted to strap Brodie and Gage into Stokes baskets and winch them up the slope, but the two victims had persuaded him they were capable of standing and walking out under their own power, with only a little help from the SAR volunteers.

An hour after that, Brodie was in his guest cabin on the Walker ranch, fortified with a sandwich and coffee, fresh from a hot shower and contemplating a nap.

A knock on the door interrupted those plans, however. He glanced through the peephole, then jerked open the door. "Emily, what are you doing here?" he asked.

She moved past him into the room, her face pale against her dark hair. "I wanted to make sure you were all right," she said.

"I'm fine." He rolled his shoulders, testing the statement. "A little bruised and tired, but okay."

She touched his arm, and the purpling bruise where he had collided with a tree branch or boulder in his frantic effort to escape the snowslide. That light, silken touch against his bare skin sent a current of heat through him.

He moved toward her, drawn by the scent of her mingling in the lingering steam from his shower. Her eyes widened, as if she was only just now seeing him—all of him, naked except for a pair of jeans, his skin still damp, droplets lingering in the hair on his chest.

She jerked her gaze back to his bruised arm. "You should put something on this," she said, her voice husky.

"Would you do it for me?"

"All right."

He retreated to the bathroom and fetched the ointment from his first-aid kit. Did he imagine her hand trembled when he handed it to her? Her touch was steady enough as she smoothed the ointment on, so careful and caring, and so incredibly sensuous, as if she was caressing not only his wound, but the invisible hurts inside of him.

She capped the tube of ointment and raised her eyes to meet his. Time stopped in that moment, and he had the sensation of being in a dream as he slid his arm around her waist and she leaned into him, reaching up to rest her fingers against the side of his neck, rising on her toes to press her lips to his.

He had a memory of kissing her when she had been a girl, but she kissed like a woman now, sure and wanting, telling him what she desired without the need for words. When she pressed her body to his, he pulled her more tightly against him, and when she parted her lips, he met the thrust of her tongue with his own. He willingly drowned in that kiss, losing himself until he had to break free, gasping, his heart pounding.

She opened her eyes and stared up at him with a dreamy, dazed expression. Then her vision cleared, eyes opening wider. She let out a gasp and pulled away. "I can't do this," she said, and fled, out of his arms and out the door before he had time to react.

He wanted to go after her but didn't. He lay back on the bed and stared up at the ceiling, marveling at the twisted turn his life had taken, bringing him back here, to this woman, after so long.

And wondering where it all might lead.

Chapter Nine

Emily read through the first of the surveys her professor had sent for her to review—then read through it again, nothing having registered on the first pass. Her head was too full of Brodie—of the pressure of his lips on hers, the strength of his arms around her, the taste of his kisses. For all she had been enthralled by him five years ago, she had never felt such passion back then. The Brodie she had faced in his cabin yesterday had been more serious, with a depth she hadn't recognized before. He was stronger—and far more dangerous to her peace.

At this point in her life, she thought she could have handled a merely physical fling with a fun, hot guy. But she could never think of Brodie as merely a fling. And she didn't know if she would ever be able to completely trust him with her feelings. Even five years before, as crazy as she was about him, she had never been able to fully believe that his feelings for her were more than superficial. She was another conquest, another victim of his charm. He hadn't acted particularly torn up when she had turned down his marriage proposal, and he hadn't made any effort to persuade her to change her mind.

Even if he hadn't received the letter she had sent to him later, if he had really loved her, wouldn't he have kept in touch? He could have used his friendship with Travis as an excuse to at least check on her. But he had simply vanished from her life. That knowledge didn't leave a good feeling behind, and it made getting involved with him again far too risky.

But she wasn't going to think about him now. She had work to do. Determined to focus, she started reading through the survey once more. She had just finished her read-through and was starting to make notes when her cell phone buzzed, startling her.

Half afraid it might be Brodie, she swiped open the screen, then sagged with relief when she read her brother's name. "Hi, Travis," she answered.

"There's someone here at the station I think you should talk to," he said.

"Who is it?"

"Ruth Schultz. She says she knows you."

Emily searched her memory for the name, but came up blank. "I don't think—"

"Hang on a minute… She says you knew her as Ruth Parmenter."

"Ruthie!" Emily smiled. They had been classmates in high school. "Why does she want to see me?"

"It has to do with the case. Could you come down and talk to her?"

Puzzled, but intrigued, Emily glanced at the folder full of surveys. Not exactly scintillating reading. And not all that pressing, either, not with a murderer on the loose. "Sure. Tell her I'll be there in half an hour."

Twenty-five minutes later, Adelaide looked up from her desk when Emily entered the sheriff's department. "Mrs. Schultz is in interview room one." Adelaide pointed down the hall. "She said she can stay until twelve thirty. That's when her youngest gets out of half-day kindergarten."

"All right." Emily headed past the desk, intending to stop by Travis's office first to ask what exactly she was supposed to be talking about with Ruthie, but before she could reach the sheriff's door, Brodie stepped out and intercepted her. "Travis had to leave, so he asked me to sit in with you and Mrs. Schultz," he said.

Running into him this way, when she hadn't had time to prepare, unsettled her. She took a deep, steadying breath, but that was a mistake, since all it did was fill her head with the masculine scent of him—leather and starch and the herbal soap that had surrounded them last night. She stared over his left shoulder and managed to keep her voice steady. "What is this all about?"

"She says her younger sister, Renee, is missing."

Emily had a vague memory of a girl who had been three years behind her in school—a pretty, sandy-haired flirt who had been popular with the older boys, and thus, unpopular with the older girls. "How long has she been missing?"

"Four days. At first Mrs. Schultz thought she had left town when the road opened and got caught when the road closed again. But she hasn't answered any calls or texts and that's not like her."

"Maybe her phone lost its charge or broke," Emily said. "Or maybe she's somewhere she doesn't want her sister to know about."

Brodie frowned. "Maybe. But Mrs. Schultz is worried because she said Renee knew Alex. She went out with him at least once."

Emily sucked in her breath. "That is a frightening thought. But why does she want to talk to me?"

"Because you knew Renee, and you know Alex. Travis explained you were helping us put together a profile of Alex and he thought the information she had might help. But most of all, I think she's looking for some reassurance from you that her sister is all right."

"I don't think I can give her that," Emily said.

"Probably not. But maybe telling her story to a friendly face—someone who isn't a cop—may help her."

"Then of course I'll talk to her."

Emily remembered Ruthie Parmenter as an elfin figure with a mop of curly brown hair and freckles, a star on the school track team, president of the debate club and senior class president. She had talked about going to college on the East Coast, then taking off for Europe with a camera, maybe becoming a war correspondent or a travel journalist or something equally exciting and adventurous.

The woman who looked up when Emily and Brodie entered the interview room was still lithe and freckle-faced, though her hair had been straightened and pulled back from her face by a silver clip. She wore a tailored blouse and jeans, and an anxious expression. "Emily, it's so good to see you," she said, standing and leaning over the table to give Emily a hug. "You still look just the same. I'd have recognized you anywhere."

Emily wasn't so sure she would have recognized Ruthie. Her former classmate looked older and more careworn, though maybe that was only from worrying about her sister. She indicated Brodie. "This is Agent Brodie Langtry, with the Colorado Bureau of Investigation."

"Yes, Brodie and I have met." The smile she gave him held an extra warmth, and Emily inwardly recoiled at a sudden pinch of jealousy. Seriously? Was she going to turn into that kind of cliché?

"Why don't we have a seat?" she said, pulling out a chair.

They sat, Brodie at the end of the table and the two women facing each other. "Brodie said you haven't been able to get in touch with your sister," Emily began.

"Yes. Not since Monday afternoon, when the road opened again for what was it—less than a day? I wasn't worried at first. I assumed she'd gone to Junction to shop and maybe take in a movie. But when I called the next day and she didn't answer, I was a little concerned. And when she didn't come to dinner last night, I knew something was wrong. It was my son's birthday—he just turned six. Renee would never have missed Ian's birthday."

"Was your sister dating anyone in particular?"

"No." She waved her hand, as if brushing aside the suggestion. "You know Renee—she always liked men, but she was never ready to settle down with anyone. She hasn't changed in that respect."

"But she had dated Alex Woodruff?" Emily asked.

"Yes." The faint lines on either side of her mouth deepened. "When I saw his picture in the paper and read that he was a person of interest in the Ice Cold Killer murders, my legs gave out and I had to sit down. And I knew I had to contact the sheriff. In case…" She paused and swallowed, then forced out the next words. "In case he's the reason Renee is missing."

Emily reached across and took Ruthie's hand and squeezed it. She could only imagine how worried Ruthie must be, but she wasn't going to offer hollow words of comfort. "When did Renee last go out with Alex?" she asked.

"I'm not positive, but I think they only had the one date. I think she would have told me if there was more than one—that was back on New Year's Eve.

She went with him to the Elks' New Year's dance. My husband and I met them there."

"Was that their first date?" Emily asked.

"Yeah. She told me she met him at Mo's Pub a couple of nights before. He and a friend were there, playing pool, and she thought he was cute, so she asked him to the dance."

"She asked him?" Brodie asked. "He didn't approach her?"

"Not the way she told it." Ruthie shrugged. "That was Renee—she liked calling the shots in a relationship and wasn't afraid to make the first move."

"What did you think of him?" Emily asked.

Ruthie made a face. "I didn't like him. He struck me as too full of himself, and a phony. I told Renee that, too, and she said they had a lot of fun, but she didn't think she'd go out with him again—he wasn't her type. To tell you the truth, it surprised me she went out with him that one time. She generally likes older men who are a little rougher around the edges, you know? Outdoorsmen and daredevils. Alex was close to her age, and far too smooth."

"Did Renee mention anything that might have happened later that night, maybe when Alex took her home—anything that seemed off or upsetting?" Emily asked.

"No. Nothing like that. She just said he wasn't her type. My husband didn't like Alex, either. In fact, he and I left the dance early. I was afraid if Bob had one too many drinks he might end up punching Alex.

Alex kept popping off like he was an authority on everything and I could tell it was getting to Bob."

"You married Bob Schultz?" Emily asked, picturing the rancher's son who had never really been part of their group.

Ruthie smiled, her expression softening. "Yeah. I came home for Christmas after my first semester at Brown and he and I met up at a skating party my church had organized for the youth. We just really hit it off. I ended up transferring to Junction to finish my degree and we got married my sophomore year. We have two kids—Ian is six and Sophia is five."

"Wow," Emily said, trying—and failing—to hide her surprise.

Ruthie laughed. "I know! I was going to save the world and have all these adventures. But marriage and motherhood and running our ranch is adventure enough for me."

"You sound really happy."

"That's because I am." Her expression sobered once more. "Except, of course, I'm worried about Renee."

"Now that we know she's missing, we'll be looking for her," Brodie said. "You gave Travis a description of her vehicle, right?"

Ruthie nodded. "She drives a silver RAV4. Travis said he would put out a bulletin to let law enforcement all over the state know to be on the lookout for her. Maybe they will find her in Junction with some new guy she met." She smiled, but the expression didn't reach her eyes. "That would be just like Renee."

Brodie rose, and the women stood also. "Thank you for talking to me," Emily said.

Ruthie reached out and gripped Emily's wrist. "Be honest with me. Do you think this guy went after Renee?"

"I don't know," Emily said. "He hasn't had a previous relationship with any of the other women he's killed—at least not as far as we know. And all of them have been found very shortly after they were killed—within minutes, even." She gently extricated herself from Ruthie's grasp. "But people aren't always predictable. All I can tell you is that this doesn't follow his pattern so far."

Ruthie nodded. "I know you can't make any promises, but I'm holding out hope that it's just a sick coincidence that she knew this man." She shuddered. "I can't believe we spent a whole evening with him. I thought he was a bit of a jerk, but I never in a million years would have pegged him as a killer."

"If we could do that, we could prevent crimes before they happened," Brodie said. "But we can't."

They walked with Ruthie to the front door, where she offered Emily another hug. "We'll have to get together after this is all over," Ruthie said. "I'd like you to meet my family."

"I'd like that, too," Emily said.

Brodie waited until Ruthie was gone before he spoke. "What do you think?" he asked.

Emily worried her lower lip between her teeth. "Alex went out with Michaela Underwood, too," she said. "So we know he has used asking women out as a way to get to them."

"But he killed Michaela on that first date. Renee Parmenter went out with him at least once and lived to tell the tale."

"That was about a week before he and Tim killed Kelly Farrow and Christy O'Brien," Emily said. "Maybe Alex was still working on his plan, or maybe killing women was still a fantasy for him then."

"She didn't tell her sister about anything unusual happening on the date, but that doesn't mean nothing did," Brodie said. "She might not have wanted to worry her sister."

"If Renee was wary of Alex, she probably wouldn't have gone out with him again," Emily said.

"So you don't think he used a second date as a way to get to her so he could kill her?" Brodie asked.

"I don't know," Emily said. "Maybe he charmed her. Or she was physically attracted to him in spite of her misgivings. Attraction can make people do things they know they shouldn't."

Her eyes met his, hoping he'd get the message that what had happened between them in his cabin yesterday was not going to be repeated. Brodie wasn't a bad person—far from it. But she didn't like the way he made her feel so out of control and not in charge of her decisions.

His gaze slid away from hers. "I hope Alex didn't

murder Renee Parmenter. But I can't say I've got a good feeling about this."

"No, I don't, either," she admitted.

"Have you come up with any ideas about where he might be hiding—or what he intends to do next?"

"No, I haven't."

He clapped her on the back. "Then you'd better get to work. I still think you can give us something useful if you put your mind to it."

"Because of course you're always right."

"I've got good instincts. And so do you, if you'd pay attention to them."

He strode away, leaving her to wonder at his words—and at the look that accompanied them. She and Brodie seemed to specialize in nonverbal communication and mixed messages. It was probably time they cleared the air between them, but coming right out and saying what she felt wasn't something she had had much practice at. Like most people, she liked to protect her feelings. She had allowed herself to be vulnerable to a man exactly once, and the ending made her unwilling to do so again.

BRODIE HAD CLAIMED a desk in the corner of the sheriff's department conference room that had been turned into a situation room. The faces of the victims of the Ice Cold Killer surrounded him as he worked, and the scant evidence collected in the case crowded a row of folding tables against one wall. He hunched over his laptop, scanning databases, trying to trace Renee Parmenter's movements since her disappearance.

Travis had asked Ruth to run a notice in the paper, asking anyone who had any knowledge of Renee's whereabouts to contact the sheriff's department, but that wouldn't appear until tomorrow. As it was, Renee had been missing four days. Brodie feared they might already be too late.

The door to the room opened and Travis entered. He scanned the room, his gaze lingering a moment on the faces of the dead before he shifted his attention to Brodie. "Are you coming up with anything?"

Brodie pushed his chair back from the table that served as his desk. "The report from the CBI profiler came in a few minutes ago," he said.

"And?" Travis asked.

Brodie turned back to the computer, found the file and opened it. "I forwarded the whole thing to you, but the gist of it is, she thinks now that Alex is working alone, and he knows we know his identity, that's increasing the pressure on him. He's likely to kill more often and perhaps take more risks. He's trying to relieve the pressure and attempting to prove to us and to himself that we can't stop him."

"We have to find him in order to stop him," Travis said. "Does the profiler have any idea where he's likely to be hiding?"

"She doesn't mention that," Brodie said. "I'm still hoping Emily will come up with some ideas."

Travis shook his head. "I don't think my sister can

help us with this one. We're going to have to keep looking and hope we catch a break."

"I've been working on trying to track Renee Parmenter," Brodie said. "It looks like she bought gas here in town, charging it to her credit card, the afternoon she disappeared. After that, there's nothing."

"Maybe she ran into Alex at the gas station, or he flagged down her car on the side of the road and she stopped because she recognized him," Travis said. "He asked her to give him a lift and he killed her."

"And then what?" Brodie asked. "Did he hide her car with the body? He's never done that before."

Travis rubbed his chin. "Hiding her doesn't fit with what we know about him, either," he said. "Alex wants us to know he's killed these women—that he got away with another murder. He wants to rub it in our faces that we aren't even slowing him down."

"He and Tim kidnapped Jamie and her sister and planned to kill them later," Brodie said. "Maybe that's a new MO for him."

"They kidnapped Jamie's sister in order to lure Jamie to them," Travis said. "Tim told her they wanted to kill a deputy as a way of getting to me. Fortunately, she was able to fight off Tim until we got to her."

"If Alex did kidnap Renee, he'd have to keep her somewhere," Brodie said. "We should consider that when we're focusing on places he might be hiding."

The phone on Brodie's desk beeped. He picked it up and Adelaide said, "Is the sheriff in there with you?"

"Yes."

"I've got a caller on the line who wants to talk to him. They were pretty insistent that I had to put them through to Travis. They won't give a name and I can't tell if it's a man or a woman."

"You record the incoming calls, right?" Brodie asked.

"Of course."

"Travis is right here." Brodie hit the button to put the call on speaker and handed the handset to Travis.

"Hello? This is Sheriff Walker."

After a second's pause, a wavery voice came on the line. "I saw that girl you're looking for. She was hitchhiking on Dixon Pass. That's a dangerous thing to do, hitchhiking."

Travis's eyes met Brodie's. He could tell the sheriff was thinking the same thing he was—how did the caller know about Renee when the story hadn't even come out yet in the paper? "Who is calling?" Travis asked. "When did you see this hitchhiker?"

"Oh, it was a couple of days ago." The man… woman…sounded frail and uncertain. "I just wanted you to know."

"Could you describe her for me, please?" Travis asked. "And tell me exactly where you saw her."

But the call had already ended. Brodie took the

handset and replaced it. "I'll contact the phone company and see if they can tell us anything about who made the call," he said.

Travis nodded. "I'd bet my next paycheck they don't find anything," he said. "I don't think that was a random Good Samaritan."

"Me, either," Brodie agreed. "Alex Woodruff is used to acting. It might not be too difficult for him to disguise his voice."

"Yes. Maybe he's annoyed that we haven't found Renee's body yet and decided to give us a hint."

"Or maybe he's set a trap."

"Come on," Travis said. "Let's go up to Dixon Pass and find out."

Chapter Ten

On the way up to the pass, Travis called Gage and let him know where they were headed and why. "I don't want the whole department up there in case this is a false alarm," Travis told his brother. "And I also don't put it past Alex to do something like this to draw us away from town. Just be alert if you don't hear from us in twenty minutes or so."

"Will do," Gage said. "But if that was Alex calling to give you a clue as to where to find Renee's body, it was a pretty vague one. Where are you going to look?"

"I have some ideas."

They parked Travis's sheriff's department SUV, which still bore faint traces of Alex's graffiti on the driver's side, at the barricades two-thirds of the way up the pass. They walked the rest of the way, past two dump trucks waiting to carry away loads of snow and an idling front-end loader. Travis stopped at the post that indicated the turnoff to the former ski area, most of the old road now buried under the avalanche that had almost killed Brodie and Gage. "The highway crews were able to clear this section of road pretty quickly," he said. "Apparently, most of the snow that came down was below this point."

"I still wonder what set off the slide," Brodie said. "Gage and I thought we heard a gunshot right before it came down."

"The road crew swears they had nothing to do with it," Travis said. "They were on a break when the avalanche happened. They don't remember seeing anyone around the road who wasn't supposed to be here, either."

Brodie continued to stare down at the river of snow. Sometimes things happened for no discernable reason, but the investigator in him didn't easily accept that.

"Gage said you didn't see anything suspicious down there before the slide," Travis said.

"No. It didn't look like anyone had been around for a while. I didn't see anywhere Alex might have been hiding—though we weren't able to get down there to take a closer look at the buildings. But if we couldn't get down there, neither could Alex, so I'd rule him out."

"Let's find someone to talk to about Renee Parmenter." They set out walking again. When they rounded the next curve, they could see a wall of blinding white, easily fifteen feet high, obliterating the roadway. A massive rotary snowblower was slowly chewing its way through the wall, sending a great plume of snow into the canyon below.

A man in a hard hat, blaze-orange vest over his parka, approached. "What can I do for you officers?" he asked.

"We're looking for a missing woman," Travis said.

The man scratched his head under the hard hat. "We haven't seen any women around here."

"What about cars?" Brodie asked. "Do you ever come across cars buried under these avalanches?"

"Sometimes. But we usually know they're there going in because someone reports it. If there was a driver or passenger in the vehicle, emergency services would have already worked to dig them out, and they usually flag the car for us so we can work around it. Hitting one could wreck a plow, but our guys watch out. There are all kinds of hazards that come down with the slides—rocks, trees. Once we found a dead elk."

"You might want to keep an eye out for a car up here," Travis said.

"What makes you think your missing woman is up here?" the man asked.

"We got a call," Travis said. "She's been missing since Monday—before the slide."

The man nodded. "Okay. We'll keep our eyes open."

He walked away and Travis and Brodie stood for a few minutes longer, watching the steady progress of the blower, until Brodie's ears rang with the sounds of the machinery. "Let's get out of here!" he shouted to be heard above the din. The noise, the endless snow and the eeriness of a highway with no traffic were beginning to get to him. Or maybe he was just twitchy after almost being buried alive in an avalanche.

Back in Travis's SUV, the sheriff didn't immediately start the vehicle. "If Alex killed Renee Parmenter, I have to believe he chose her because she knew him and was inclined to trust him," he said. "He took advantage of their previous relationship."

"Same with Denise Switcher," Brodie said. "She knew him from the university, so was more likely to stop when he flagged her down. He doesn't have Tim to help him lure and subdue his victims, so he's searching for easier prey—women who are more inclined to trust him."

Travis turned to Brodie. "Who else does he know who might trust him?" he asked. "Answer that question and we might be able to figure out who his next victim will be."

"We could start by interviewing single women in town, find out who else he—or Tim—might have dated in the weeks they've been here," Brodie said.

"Emily mentioned a woman he dated in Fort Collins," Travis said. "She dropped him because he wanted to strangle her while they were having sex."

Brodie scowled. "Maybe he planned to keep on choking her until she was dead." The more he learned about Alex, the greater his urgency to stop him.

"I'll ask to dig a little deeper. Maybe he had another girlfriend who came here for a visit and we haven't heard about her yet." He started the SUV and pulled out to turn around. But before he could make the turn, the man in the hard hat and orange vest ran toward them, waving his arms. Travis stopped and rolled down his window. "What is it?" he asked.

The man stopped beside the SUV, hands on his knees, panting. "We...found something," he gasped. "A car. And there's a woman inside."

"Poor Ruth." Emily's first thought on hearing of Renee Parmenter's death was of her sister. Yes, Renee had suffered at the hands of a murderer, but Ruth had to live with the knowledge that the person she loved had been taken so brutally. "I guess there's no doubt Renee was murdered?"

"No," Travis said. "She was killed just like the others."

"Alex even left his Ice Cold calling card," Brodie said. He and Travis flanked Emily on the living room sofa. A fire crackled in the woodstove across from them and a pile of wedding gifts that had been delivered when the road reopened waited on a table against the wall. Everything looked so ordinary and peaceful, which made the news of Renee's murder all the more disorienting.

"Have you told Ruth yet?" Emily asked.

"No," Travis said. "I was on my way there after I talked to you."

"I want to go with you," she said. "Maybe it will make it a little easier on her if she has a friend there."

"I was hoping you'd say that," Travis said. He stood. "Let's go see Ruth. If we wait too long, she might hear about this from someone else, and we don't want that."

By the time Ruth answered Travis's knock, Emily could see she had prepared herself for the worst. Her gaze slid past Emily and fixed on Travis. "Have you found her?" she asked, her voice tight, as if she had to force the words out.

"May we come in?" he asked.

She stepped back to let them pass. The house was an older one, with nineties-era blond wood and brass fixtures, the room cluttered with toys and shoes and a pile of laundry on one end of the sofa. A large window looked out onto pastures and hayfields, now covered with snow. "The kids are in school and my husband is out checking fences," Ruth said as she led the way to the sofa. She moved a child's book off the sofa and picked up a pillow from the floor, then sat, holding the pillow in her lap. "Tell me what you've found. It can't be anything worse than I've already imagined."

Travis removed his hat and sat across from Ruth while Emily settled in next to her. "We found your sister's body at the top of Dixon Pass, in her car," Travis said. "She was murdered—probably by Alex Woodruff."

Ruth made a short, sharp sound and covered her

mouth with her hand. Emily took her other hand and squeezed it. Ruth held on tightly and uncovered her mouth. "When?" she asked.

"The car was buried by the avalanche that closed the road on Tuesday morning," Travis said. "She was killed before then."

Ruth closed her eyes, visibly pulling herself together. "Is there someone you'd like me to call?" Emily asked. "Your husband, or a friend?"

"Bob will be in soon." She opened her eyes, which shone with unshed tears. "If you know who did this, why don't you arrest him and stop him?" she asked.

"When we find Alex, we'll arrest him," Travis said. "Do you have any idea where he might be hiding? That night you and your husband met him, did he say anything at all that might give us a clue?"

She shook her head. "I'm sorry. We talked about school and the dance and the weather—just ordinary small talk among people who didn't know each other well."

"And you're sure Renee never mentioned seeing or talking to him after that night?" Travis asked.

"No. I really don't think she heard from him or saw him after that one date," Ruth said.

"You said you didn't like him," Travis said. "Maybe knowing that, she decided not to talk about him."

"Renee wasn't like that," Ruth said. "If she liked someone and I didn't, she would have made a point of mentioning him, just to give me a hard time." She shook her head. "She was really definite about not wanting to see him again. If he had called and asked her out again, she would have been on the phone to me as soon as she hung up with him." Her breath caught, and she swallowed, then added, her voice fainter, "That's how we were. We talked about everything."

"I'm very sorry for your loss," Travis said. He stood, hat in hand. "Once the medical examiner has completed his autopsy, we'll release the body to the funeral home of your choice. Call my office if you have any questions."

Ruth stood and walked with them to the door. "Are you sure you don't want me to stay until your husband gets here?" Emily asked.

"I'll be okay." She took a shuddering breath. "I do better with this kind of stuff on my own—but thank you."

Emily squeezed her arm. "Call me if you need anything. Or if you just want to talk."

Ruth nodded, then looked at Travis again. "You'll find him and stop him, won't you?" she asked, the words more plea than query.

"Yes," he said.

He and Emily didn't say anything until they were almost back to the sheriff's department. "Denise was killed the same day," Emily said. "Right before the avalanche. And her car was found at the top of the pass."

"The first two murders—Kelly Farrow and Christy O'Brien—happened within hours of each other," Travis said.

"I think he gets a charge out of getting away with not one, but two killings," Emily said.

"The profiler from the Colorado Bureau of Investigation said he's feeling more pressure from us now that we know his identity," Travis said. "She believes he'll continue to kill, as a way to relieve the pressure."

Emily nodded. "Yes, that sounds right. And he wants to prove that he can still get away with the crimes—that you'll never catch him."

"He's by himself," Travis said. "Wherever he's hiding can't be that comfortable. We're doing everything we can to alert other people that he's dangerous, so he can't move safely around town, or rely on others for help. He's going to run out of victims he can fool also. We're going to run him to ground."

"I've been thinking," Emily said. "Maybe I can help you find him."

"Have you thought of someplace he might be hiding?"

"No. But he knows me. Maybe I could lure him out of hiding by agreeing to meet him."

"No." Travis didn't look at her, but the muscles along his jaw tightened.

"I'm serious," she said. Her brother wasn't the only stubborn member of this family. "I've lost too many friends to this man. I'll do whatever I can to stop him." Alex was a killer, but she knew him. Maybe she could get to him when no one else could.

Chapter Eleven

"Over my dead body."

So what if it was a cliché? Brodie thought, as soon as he had uttered those words. Travis's announcement that Emily wanted to try to lure Alex to her had prompted a visceral reaction that went beyond coherent speech. The thought of her anywhere near that monster made his blood freeze.

"I already told her the idea was out of the question," Travis said.

"It's a stupid idea." Brodie dropped into the chair across from Travis's desk at the sheriff's department, not sure if his legs were steady enough yet for him to remain standing. "What makes her think he'd come anywhere near her?"

"She fits the profile of the other women he's murdered," Travis said. "Alex knows her. And she's my sister. He's made it clear he enjoys getting back at me and my department—it's why he went after Jamie."

"How can you even look at this logically?" Brodie groused. "She's your sister."

"I made it clear it wasn't going to happen," he said.

"We don't even know where he is," Brodie said. "What was she going to do—put an ad in the paper asking him to meet her? He'd see that as a trap right away."

"Maybe. Or maybe he'd be too tempted by the chance to get at her."

Brodie glared at the sheriff. "You've actually considered this, haven't you? You've run all the possibilities through your head."

Travis shifted in his chair. "It's not going to happen," he said again. "But if anyone is to blame for her coming up with the idea, it's you."

"Me?"

"You're the one who asked her to help with the case. You gave her the idea that she knows Alex better than anyone, and that her insight could help."

"Insight. Her thoughts. I never meant for her to put her life on the line—or anything close to it."

"I know. And I know she really wants to help. But this isn't the way to do it."

Brodie slid down farther in his chair. "I think this case is getting to us all."

Deputy Dwight Prentice stopped in the doorway to the office. "Abel Crutchfield just called in with a tip we ought to check out," he said.

"Who is Abel Crutchfield?" Brodie asked.

"He's a retired guy, spends a lot of time ice fishing in the area," Travis said. "He was the first one to report a blonde woman hanging around near where

Michaela Underwood was murdered. That woman turned out to be Tim Dawson in disguise."

Brodie nodded and sat up straighter. "What's the tip?"

"He says he saw smoke coming from some caves over by Eagle Creek," Dwight said. "Like someone was camping up there. He figured we might want to check it out."

"Take Brodie over there with you and have a look," Travis said. "But call for backup if it looks like anyone is up there."

"Right." Brodie rose. "Much as I'd like to get hold of this guy, better not try to do it by ourselves."

"We should be able to get a good look from across the way," Dwight said. "Enough to see if it's worth going in. Maybe Abel just saw snow blowing off trees and mistook it for smoke."

The drive to Eagle Creek took twenty minutes, most of it on narrow, snow-packed forest service roads. "It doesn't look as if anyone lives out here," Brodie said, staring out at the landscape of snowy woodland.

"They don't," Dwight said. "This is all forest service land. A few snowmobilers or cross-country skiers use the road, and ice fishermen like Abel."

"Sounds like a good place for someone to hide out if he didn't want to be seen," Brodie said.

The caves themselves sat above the river in a limestone formation, centuries of dripping water having hollowed out the rock to form the openings. "Most of these caves are pretty shallow," Dwight said as he led the way through the snow along the riverbank. "There are only a couple that are deep enough to provide any real shelter."

"Deep enough to live in?" Brodie asked.

"Maybe. It wouldn't be very comfortable. You'd have to have a fire to keep from freezing to death, and there would be a lot of smoke and dampness. Not to mention bats, bugs and wild animals."

"It doesn't sound like Alex Woodruff's kind of place," Brodie said. "He struck me as someone who likes his creature comforts."

"Yeah, but he's desperate now. He can't be as choosy."

They halted on a bench of land across the river from the largest opening. Dwight dug out a pair of binoculars and trained them on the cave. "The snow around the opening is churned up," he said. "Someone—or something—has been going in and out of there." He shifted the binoculars. "And there's a definite path leading up there."

Brodie sniffed the air. "I can smell smoke—like a campfire."

Dwight handed him the binoculars. "There's no smoke coming from there right now."

Brodie focused the glasses on the cave opening. It was impossible to see into the dark space, but there was definitely no movement at the entrance. He returned the binoculars to Dwight. "What do you think we should do now?"

"I'd like to get a little closer before we call in the cavalry," Dwight said. "We can approach from below and anyone inside wouldn't be able to see us until we were almost on him."

"Sounds good to me."

It took twenty minutes to retrace their steps along the river, negotiating over icy rock and snow-covered deadfall. They had to walk farther downstream to find a place to cross—a bridge of felled trees that required stepping carefully and balancing like a tight-rope walker. But when they reached the other side, they found the worn path through the snow that they had glimpsed from the other side.

Weapons drawn, they moved cautiously up the path. The rushing water tumbling over rocks and downed trees drowned out all other sound. Dwight took the lead, while Brodie covered him, staying several yards behind. They reached a series of rock steps that led up to the cave and halted. "Let me go up first, while you stay down here," Dwight whispered. "I should be able to get right up on the entrance without being seen. You come up after me and we'll flank the entrance and demand whoever is in there to come out. If we don't get an answer, we'll shine a light in, maybe try to draw his fire."

Brodie agreed and Dwight started up, keeping close to the cliff side, placing each step carefully, the rush of the water below drowning out his approach. When he was safely up the steps and stationed on the left side of the cave entrance, he motioned for Brodie to follow.

Brodie moved up more quickly and took up a position on the opposite side of the cave entrance. "Is anyone in there?" Dwight called.

The words bounced off the canyon walls and echoed back at them, but no sound came from the cave.

"This is the Rayford County Sheriff's Department!" Dwight called. "You need to come out with your hands up!"

No answer or movement. Dwight unsnapped his flashlight from his utility belt and trained the powerful beam into the cave entrance. A rock fire ring sat about two feet inside, full of dark ash and a couple of pieces of charred wood. Brodie stooped, picked up a rock and tossed it inside the cave. It bounced off the stone floor and rolled toward the back, then all was silent again.

Dwight's eyes met Brodie's. He jerked his head toward the cave and indicated he was going in. Brodie nodded. Instincts could be wrong, but it didn't feel to him as if anyone was in there. Dwight swung the flashlight in ahead of him, then entered the cave, staying close to the wall. He had to duck to enter. Weapon ready, Brodie watched him disappear from sight.

"Come on in!" Dwight called a few seconds later. "There's no one in here."

Brodie unhooked his own flashlight and followed

Dwight into the cave. He swept the light over the mostly empty space, coming to rest on a pile of garbage in the corner—tin cans, beer bottles and food wrappers. He moved closer to the fire. "Someone was here for a while," he said. "And not that long ago."

"The ashes in the firepit are still warm." Dwight crouched beside the rock ring and held his hand over the charred wood.

Brodie holstered his gun and played the flashlight over the scuffed dirt on the floor of the cave. The space was maybe ten feet deep and eight feet wide, tall enough to stand up in, but barely, with a ceiling of smoke-blackened rock and a dirt floor. It smelled of smoke, stale food and animal droppings. "Not exactly the Ritz," he said.

"No one would be camping here in the middle of winter unless he had to," Dwight said. "It has to be Alex."

Brodie trained his light on the garbage pile again. "He's buying food somewhere." He nudged a beer bottle with his toe. "Lots of craft beer, chips and canned pasta."

"That sounds like a college guy's diet," Dwight said.

"If he's shopping, someone in Eagle Mountain must have seen him," Brodie said. "Why haven't they reported him to the sheriff's department?"

"He could be breaking into summer cabins,"

Dwight said. "Or shopping at the grocery store wearing a disguise."

"If he was here this morning, it doesn't look as if he intends to return," Brodie said. "There's no sleeping bag, no stash of food—not even any firewood."

"We'll watch the place for a couple of days, see if he comes back," Dwight said. "But I agree—it looks like he's cleared out. Maybe he saw Abel looking up this way and decided to leave."

"There's not much here, but we'd better look through it, see if we can find anything significant," Brodie said. He smoothed on a pair of gloves and began sifting through the garbage, while Dwight examined the firepit. He combed through half a dozen beer bottles, two empty ravioli cans, several candy bar wrappers and two chip bags, but found nothing that told them where Alex might be now. They took photographs and bagged everything as evidence. They might be able to get DNA off the beer bottles that would prove Alex was the person who had hidden in this cave, but Brodie didn't see how that would be useful in their case against him.

"I may have found something," Dwight said. He used a pen to lift something from the ashes and held it aloft. Brodie recognized the coiled binding of a pocket-size notebook. "The cover is gone, and the edge of the pages are charred, but most of it's intact," Dwight said. He spread the notebook on the ground and Brodie joined him in leaning over it. Dwight flipped through the pages, which appeared to contain everything from grocery lists—*chips, lunch meat, cookies, soda, razor*—to cryptic numbers and calculations. Most of the pages were blank.

"We'll have to go through this at the office and see if there's anything significant," Dwight said. He reached into his coat and pulled out a plastic evidence bag.

Brodie continued to flip through the pages. He found what looked like phone numbers, notes on what might have been climbing routes, then stopped on a page that was simply a column of letters—*KF, CO, FW, LG, AA, MU, TP, DD, JD, LW, RP, DS, EW*.

"What have you got there?" Dwight asked. "Are they some kind of abbreviations? For what?"

Brodie repeated the letters under his breath, then stopped in mid-syllable as the realization of what they represented hit him. "They're initials," he said. "Of all the women he's killed."

"Kelly Farrow, Christy O'Brien, Fiona Winslow, Lauren Grenado, Anita Allbritton, Michaela Underwood, Lynn Wallace, Renee Parmenter and Denise Switcher," Dwight said. "There's a line through *TP*—Tammy Patterson. She got away from him. Another line through *DD* and *JD*—Donna and Jamie Douglas. They escaped, too."

"They're in order of the attacks," Brodie said. "He must have killed Renee before Denise." He frowned at the last letters on the page. "Who is *EW*?"

"Is there a victim we haven't found yet?" Dwight asked. "Or someone he's gone after today?"

Brodie stood, his stomach heaving and a chill sweeping through him. "*EW* could be Emily Walker." He clapped Dwight on the shoulder and shoved the notebook toward him. "Bag that and let's get out of here. We have to make sure Emily is all right."

Chapter Twelve

"I'm fine, and I think you're both overreacting." Emily had been up to her eyeballs in surveys to review when Brodie and Travis had burst in on her late Friday afternoon, demanding to know what she was doing and if she had talked to or seen Alex Woodruff. "Alex hasn't been anywhere near here, and as for what I'm doing, I'm working. And I don't need you interrupting."

"You could be in danger," Brodie said. "Promise me you won't go anywhere without me or Travis or Gage with you."

"What are you talking about?" She turned to Travis. "Why are you both here this time of day? What's happened?"

Travis pulled a plastic evidence envelope from his coat and held it out to her. "Brodie and Dwight found this in a cave over by Eagle Creek," he said. "We think it belongs to Alex."

She studied the half-charred notebook, and the

list of letters inscribed on the page in front of her. "What does this have to do with me?"

"The letters on that page are the initials of the women Alex killed," he said. His face was pale and drawn, like a man in pain. "The crossed-out letters are the three women who got away."

She read through the list again and nodded. "All right. I can see that."

"The last letters are *EW*," Brodie said. He put a hand on her shoulder. "Emily Walker."

This announcement elicited an astonished laugh from her. "*EW* could stand for anything," she said. "Ellen White. Elaine Wilson—there are a lot of women with those initials."

"What were those names again?" Brodie had pulled out a notebook and pen and was poised to write. "We'll need to check on those women, as well."

She shifted in her seat. "I don't actually know any women with those names," Emily said. "I was just giving you examples of women's names with those initials."

"We'll research tax rolls and any other records we can find for women with the initials *EW*," Travis said. "But we wanted to be sure you're all right."

"I'm fine." Some of her annoyance receded, replaced by a cold undercurrent of fear. She thought Brodie and Travis were overreacting—but what if they weren't? "I'm smart enough to stay far away from Alex Woodruff," she said.

"Last I heard, you were volunteering to lure him to you," Brodie said.

"I did. But Travis persuaded me that was a bad idea." She shrugged. "It wouldn't work without the sheriff's department's cooperation. I mean, I'm not misguided enough to try to do something like that without a whole bunch of law enforcement watching my back."

Some of the tension went out of his shoulders. "I'm relieved you're all right," he said.

His real concern for her touched her, so that she had to look away. She focused on Travis. "I'm fine. It was sweet of you to worry, but don't."

"What are you doing the rest of the day?" Brodie asked.

She really wanted to tell him that was none of his business, but that would only lead to another argument. The man never took no for an answer. "Since the favors for the wedding didn't get here while the highway was open, a bunch of us are getting together with Lacy in a little while to make everything she needs. We're going to do crafts, drink wine, eat a lot of good things and stay right here on the ranch."

"Good." Travis tucked the evidence bag back into his pocket. "Don't say anything about this to anyone."

She shook her head. "Of course not."

"Come on, Brodie. Let's see about those other women."

They turned to leave, but she stopped them. "Did you say you found that in a cave?" she asked.

Travis nodded. "It looked like Alex had spent at least a couple of nights there, though he isn't there now. We've got a reserve deputy watching the place, in case he returns."

She wrinkled her nose. "That doesn't sound very comfortable—not like Alex."

"We agree," Brodie said. "It shows how desperate he's getting. The pressure on him is increasing."

"Then he's liable to become even more violent and unpredictable," she said.

"He's more likely to make mistakes," Travis said. "We're going to take advantage of that."

"Be careful," she said, but the two men were already turning away again.

She tried to put their visit, and the disturbing news about the list of initials, out of her mind and return her focus to the student surveys. But that proved impossible. She kept repeating the names of the murdered women, and picturing that *EW* at the bottom of the list. Surely that didn't stand for Emily Walker, but the idea that it *might* definitely shook her.

Travis and Brodie and Gage and her family and friends and everyone else she knew would protect her. They formed a living barricade between her body and anyone who might try to harm her. But could they really keep Alex away? He had proved so sly and elusive, slipping in and out of crime scenes unseen, leaving scarcely a trace of evidence. Every law enforcement officer in the county had been tracking him for weeks, yet they hadn't even touched him. Could he somehow get past all her defenses and take her down when she least expected it?

She shuddered and pushed the thought away. Alex wasn't a mythical boogeyman who could walk through walls. He was flesh and blood and as vulnerable as anyone. And she was safe. She was smart and wary and protected by all those who loved her.

She didn't believe Brodie loved her—not in the way she had once wanted him to. But she believed he would protect her. He might be glibly charming and socially superficial at times, but he took his duty as an officer of the law seriously. She tried to take comfort from that.

She was grateful when Lacy came to her and asked for help setting up for their get-together with the other women in the wedding party. "This is so nice of everyone to help," Lacy said as she and Emily and Bette set out craft supplies and readied the refreshments.

"You deserve every bit of help we can give," Bette said, arranging paintbrushes at each place setting down the long dining room table, which had been spread with brown paper to protect its polished wood surface. "Besides, this is going to be fun."

At six o'clock, the other women began arriving: Lacy's mother and all the bridesmaids—Brenda Prentice, Gage's wife, Maya Renfro, and Paige Riddell—as well as wedding guests veterinarian Darcy Marsh, Deputy Jamie Douglas and her sister, Donna. Along with Emily, Travis's mom and Bette, they made a lively party. "We're going to be decorating fancy sugar cookies," Bette explained, passing a plate of cookies shaped liked butterflies and birds. "We're using colored frosting that's the consistency of paint. Use your paintbrushes to decorate the cookies however you wish. When the cookies are dry, we'll package them up with fancy wrappings."

"I'm not very artistic," Jamie said, looking doubtful. "What if my cookies turn out ugly?"

"Then we can eat them," Donna said, sending a ripple of laughter around the table.

"I don't know," Maya said. "That might be an incentive to mess up."

"They'll turn out great," Bette said. "And when we're done, we have more cookies and plenty of other yummy party food."

Emily dipped her paintbrush in a small pot of yellow icing and began to decorate a butterfly. Though she had never considered herself an artist, the results of her efforts pleased her. "Everyone is going to love these," she said.

"Probably more than the drink cozies and pens I ordered," Lacy said. She held up a purple hummingbird. "I kind of like the reminder of spring amid all this snow."

"The weather is breaking all kinds of records this year," Darcy said. "Ryder says no one he works with can remember the highway closing so often and for so long due to avalanches and the sheer volume of snow."

"The science classes have been measuring snow amounts and tracking the weather data," Maya, a high school teacher, said. "Word is forecasts look promising for a shift in the weather to a drier pattern. That will give the snow time to settle and the highway department to get the roads in good shape to stay open."

"That's good news." Emily turned to Lacy. "You shouldn't have any trouble getting away for your honeymoon."

"Travis has to catch the Ice Cold Killer first," Lacy said. "He'll never leave town with the case still open. I'll be lucky to drag him to the altar for a few hours."

"We're getting close," Jamie said. "Now that we have a good idea who the killer is, we have everyone in the county looking for him. Someone is going to see Alex and tip us off in time to arrest him."

"I just pray they find him before he kills someone else," Bette said. The others murmured agreement.

"Do any of you know a woman in town with the initials *EW*?" Emily asked. She had promised not to tell anyone about the notebook with Alex's supposed list—but that didn't mean she couldn't do a little digging of her own.

"You mean besides you?" Lacy asked. "Why?"

She shrugged. "No reason. Just wondering."

"That's not the kind of question a person asks for no reason," Brenda said. "What's going on? Does this have something to do with Alex?"

Emily grappled for some plausible story. "I, um, saw the initials in graffiti on the bathroom stall at Mo's Pub," she said. "I was just curious." She hoped the others didn't think the story was as lame as it sounded to her.

"There's Ellie Watkins," Maya said. "But she's only six—a classmate of my niece, Casey. So I don't think anyone would be writing about her on bathroom walls."

"Elaine Wulf is one of the museum volunteers," said Brenda, who managed the local history museum. "But she's at least eighty and I can't think she'd have been up to anything that would warrant writing about it on a bathroom wall."

The others laughed and Emily forced a weak smile. "It was probably only a tourist, then. Never mind."

"What did the message say?" Lacy asked. "It must have been pretty juicy if you're asking about it now."

"Oh, it was nothing." She held up her finished butterfly. "What do you think?"

They all complimented her and began showing off their own work, but Emily was aware of Lacy eyeing her closely.

When the women took a break to eat, Lacy pulled Emily aside. "What is going on?" she asked. "What was all that about a woman with the initials *EW*? And don't give me that lame story about graffiti in the restroom at Mo's Pub. There is no graffiti there. Mo wouldn't allow it."

Emily chewed her lip. "You have to promise not to let Travis know I told you this," she said.

"I can keep a secret—within reason."

"Dwight and Brodie checked out a cave where Alex might have been camping. They found a half-burned notebook in the fire ring. In it was a list of initials that matched the initials of all the women he's killed—or attempted to kill. The last set of initials on the list was *EW*."

Lacy's face paled. "Emily Walker—you!"

"It's not me!" Emily protested. "I mean, I'm not dead, and Alex hasn't tried to get to me, so it must be someone else. I was trying to figure out who it might be."

"I'm sure Travis is looking for her, too."

"Of course he is. I just thought with a room full of women here, someone might know a woman with those initials that Travis could check on—just to make sure she's all right."

Lacy rubbed her hands up and down her arms. "I hate to think the killer is out there stalking another woman."

"And I hate that I've upset you." Emily put her arm around her friend. "Come on. Let's go back to the others and do our best not to think about this anymore. Think about your wedding and how wonderful it's going to be when you and Travis are married."

For the rest of the evening, Emily did her best to put Alex out of her mind. She ate and drank, and listened as the married women in the group told stories of their own weddings—Travis's father had apparently been late to the altar because he got lost on the way to the church, and Lacy's father had proposed by hiding an engagement ring in a piece of cheesecake... and her mother had almost swallowed it.

After they ate, Bette led them in making wedding-themed wreaths to hang on all the outside doors of the ranch house, as well as the doors of the four guest cabins. They wrapped grapevine wreaths in white tulle and silver ribbon and added glittered snowflakes and feathers. The end result was surprisingly delicate and beautiful.

They wrapped the cookies and placed them in baskets, to be handed out at the wedding in two days. "They look like little works of art," Maya said.

"Definitely too pretty to eat," Brenda said.

"You have to eat them," Bette said. "They're delicious."

"They were!" Donna said. She, like everyone else, had eaten her share of "mistakes."

After everyone had left, Emily volunteered to help Bette hang the wreaths. "I'll get the cabins, if you'll do the doors in the house," she said, draping four of the wreaths over one arm.

The four guest cabins sat between the house and the barn, along a stone path through the snow. The porch lights of each cabin cast golden pools across the drifted snow, islands in the darkness that she headed for, the chill night air stinging her cheeks and turning her breath into frosty clouds around her head. Emily hung a wreath on each door, smiling at how festive each one looked. The last cabin in the row—the one farthest from the house—was where Brodie was staying. Emily approached it quietly, not anxious to disturb him. He'd been hovering over her even more than her brothers and all the attention made her uncomfortable. The sooner the case was solved and the wedding was over, the better for all of them. Brodie could go back to Denver, she'd return to Fort Collins and everyone could go about life as it had been before.

She hooked the wreath on the nail in the cabin's door and stepped back to make sure it wasn't crooked. Satisfied, she started to turn away, but the door opened and Brodie reached out and took hold of her arm. "Come inside," he said. "We need to talk."

She could have argued that she didn't want to talk to him, but arguing with Brodie never went well. He was too stubborn and determined to be right. If he had something he wanted to say to her, she might as well hear him out now. And then she'd make him listen to a few things she needed to say, too.

Once inside, he released his hold on her and she sat in the room's single chair, while he settled on the side of the bed. He didn't say anything right away, merely looked at her—or rather, looked through her, as if he was searching for some unspoken message in her face. "What did you want to talk about?" she asked, forcing herself to sit still and not fidget.

"Why did you turn down my proposal?" he asked.

She frowned. "Your proposal?"

"I asked you to marry me and you said no."

She couldn't have been more stunned if he had slapped her. "Brodie, that was five years ago."

"Yes, and it's been eating at me ever since. I figured it was past time we cleared the air between us."

Maybe he thought that was a good idea, but did she? Was she ready to share with Brodie all she'd been through—and maybe find out he'd known about her troubles all along? That he had received the letter she had sent to him, and chosen not to get involved? She pressed her lips together, searching for the right words. "I turned you down because I wasn't ready to get married yet—and neither were you."

"You said you loved me."

"I did! But marriage takes more than love. I was only nineteen—I had so many other things I needed to do first."

"What other things?"

Maybe he should have asked these questions five years ago, but he was asking them now, and maybe answering them would help her put herself back in that time and her mind-set then. "I was only a sophomore in college. I knew I needed to finish my education and get established in my career before I married."

"Why? Lots of people get married while they're still in school. I wouldn't have held you back."

"You would have, even if you didn't intend to." She shifted in her chair, trying to find the words to make him see. "You know my family places a lot of value on education and being successful in whatever you choose to do," she said.

"I think most families are like that," he said.

"Yes, but mine especially so. My mother has a PhD, did you know that? In entomology. And my father has built the Walking W into one of the largest and most successful ranches in the state. Travis is the youngest sheriff our county has ever had, and Gage is a decorated officer with a wall full of commendations."

"I wouldn't have held you back," he said again.

"You were established in a job that could require you to move across the state at any time," she said. "In fact, you did move, right after we broke up."

"The department takes spouse's jobs into consideration," he said, for all the world as if he was making an argument all over again for her to marry him.

"You weren't ready to settle down," she said. "Not really."

"How do you know?" he asked.

She straightened. Why not come out and say what she had been thinking? "If you really loved me so much, you would have tried harder to persuade me to accept your proposal. Instead, after I said no, you simply walked away."

He stood and began to pace, his boot heels striking hard on the wood floor. "Did you really expect me to browbeat you into changing your decision—or worse, to beg?" He raked a hand through his hair and whirled to face her. "Did you ever think that I didn't walk away because I didn't love you, but because I respected you enough to know your own mind?"

His words—and the emotion behind them—hit her like a blow, knocking the breath from her. "I...I still don't think we were ready to marry," she managed to stammer. "So many other things could have happened to tear us apart."

"Like what?" His gaze burned into her, daring her to look away. "What would be so bad our love wouldn't have been enough to overcome it?"

She wet her lips and pushed on. "What if I'd gotten pregnant?"

"We'd have been careful, taken precautions."

"We didn't always do that before, did we?"

He stared at her, and she saw doubt crowd out defiance. He studied her, eyes full of questions. "Emily, is there something you're not telling me?" he asked, his voice so low she had to lean forward to catch all his words.

She was not going to cry. If she started, she might never stop. "I told you I wrote to you after you moved," she said, speaking slowly and carefully.

"And I told you, I never received your letter." He sank onto the edge of the bed once more, as if his legs would no longer support him. "Did you really think I would ignore you?"

"I didn't know. I didn't know what to think."

"What did the letter say?"

She sighed. Did this really matter now? It did to

her—but would it to him? "After you left, I found out I was pregnant," she said.

"Emily." Just her name, said so softly, with such tenderness and sorrow the sound almost broke her. She blinked furiously, but couldn't hold back the tears. "My parents, of course, were very upset. Travis was furious. He's the one who insisted I contact you, though at first I refused."

"Why didn't you want me to know?" he asked. "I would have done the right thing. I already wanted to marry you."

"That's exactly why I didn't want you to know," she said. "I was going to have a baby, but I still didn't want to be married. And I didn't want you to marry me because you had to. It felt like I was trapping you into something I couldn't believe was right for either one of us."

He leaned forward and took her hand, his fingers warm and gentle as he wrapped them around her palm. "What happened to the baby?" He swallowed. "To our baby?"

"I'm getting to that." She took a deep breath, steadying herself, but not pulling away from him. "My father finally persuaded me that you had a right to know you were going to be a father. So I tried to call and your number had changed. I wrote and the first letter came back, so Travis got your information from the CBI. The second letter didn't come back. I thought that meant you'd received it and decided to ignore it."

"I never would have ignored it." He moved from the bed to his knees in front of her. "I wouldn't ignore you."

"I was going to try to contact you again, but then…" She swallowed again. "Then I lost the baby."

He said nothing, only squeezed her hand and put his other hand on her knee.

She closed her eyes, the sadness and confusion and, yes, relief of those days rising up in her once more like water filling a well. "The doctor said it wasn't anything I'd done—that these things just happen sometimes. I was sad, but relieved, too. I went back to school and went on with my life. We…we never talked about what had happened again."

"Did Gage know this?" he asked, thinking of his conversation with Gage at the bonfire.

She shook her head. "No. He was away at school and then summer school. He knew that something had happened with us, but he never knew about the baby. Just my parents and Travis. I— It felt easier, the fewer people who knew."

"I would have wanted to know." He stroked her arm. "I would have wanted to be there for you."

She nodded, crying quietly now, more comforted by his sympathy than she could have imagined.

"No wonder Travis insists on keeping everything strictly business between us. He thinks I deserted you and our baby when you needed me most." He looked her in the eye, his gaze searching. "I wouldn't have done that, Emily. Never in a million years. I'm sick, hearing about this now."

She put her hand on his shoulder. "I believe that now," she said. Now that she had seen the real pain in his eyes. "I'm glad you know the truth. But we can't go back and change the past. Both of us are different people now."

"Different," he said. "Yet the same." His eyes locked to hers and she felt a surge of emotion, like a wave crashing over her. Brodie still attracted her as no other man ever had. But she was no longer the naive, trusting girl she had been five years ago. She didn't believe in fairy tales, or that either she or Brodie were perfect for each other.

But she did believe in perfect moments, and seizing them. She leaned toward him, and he welcomed her into his arms. She closed her eyes and pressed her lips to his, losing herself in sensation—the scent of him, herbal soap and warm male; the reassuring strength of him, holding her so securely; the taste of him, faintly salty, as she broke the kiss to trace her tongue along his throat.

"I don't want to let you go just yet," he said.

"I'm not going anywhere." She kissed him again, arching her body to his.

"Stay with me tonight," he murmured, his lips caressing her ear.

"Yes." She began to unbutton his shirt, kissing each inch of skin as it was exposed, peeling back the fabric to expose muscular shoulders and a perfectly sculpted chest. She pressed her lips over one taut nipple and he groaned, then dragged her away and began tugging at her clothes.

She laughed as he fumbled with her bra strap. "I never could get the hang of these things," he muttered as she pushed his hands away and removed the garment herself.

Together, they finished undressing and moved to the bed, where they lay facing each other, hands and eyes exploring. "You're even more beautiful than I remember," he said as he traced the curve of her hip.

"Mmm." She kissed her way along his shoulder, smiling to herself as she thought that he was exactly as she remembered him—strong and male and exciting. He slid his hands up her thighs, calluses dragging on her smooth skin. The heat of his fingers pressed into her soft flesh, and into the wetness between her legs.

He leaned into her, the hard ridge of his erection against her stomach making her gasp. He caught the sound in his mouth, his lips closing hungrily over hers, his fingers moving higher, parting her hot folds.

She squirmed and moaned, the sound muffled by the liquid heat of his tongue tangling with her own. He dipped his head to kiss her breasts—butterfly touches of his lips over and around the swelling flesh—then latched onto her sensitive, distended nipple, sucking hard, the pulling sensation reaching all the way to her groin, where she tightened around his plunging finger.

He slid his finger out of her and gripped her

thighs, spreading her wide, cool air rushing across her hot, wet flesh, sending a fresh wave of arousal through her. "What do you want?" he whispered, his voice rough, as if he was fighting for control.

"I want you."

He leaned across her and jerked open the drawer of the bedside table. When he returned, he had a condom packet in his hand. He ripped it open with his teeth and smoothed on the sheath, then pushed her gently onto her back. "Are you ready?"

She nodded. More than ready.

He drove hard, but held her so gently, his fingers stroking, caressing, even as his hips pumped. The sensation of him filling her, stretching her, moving inside her, made her dizzy. "Don't stop," she gasped. "Please don't stop."

"I won't stop. I promise I won't stop." She slid her hands around to cup his bottom, marveling at the feel of his muscles contracting and relaxing with each powerful thrust.

He slipped his hand between them and began to fondle her, each deft move sending the tension within her coiling tighter. He kissed the soft flesh at the base of her throat. "I want to make it good for you," he murmured. "So good."

She sensed him holding back, waiting for her. When her climax overtook her, he swallowed her cries, then mingled them with his own as his release shuddered through them both.

"I'm glad you stopped fighting this," he said.

"I wasn't fighting," she said.

"You kept pushing me away."

Only because he had such power over her—power to make her forget herself. She didn't trust his motives—or her own.

Chapter Thirteen

Emily woke the next morning with the sun in her eyes and a smile on her face. Last night with Brodie had been better than her best fantasies—and better than she remembered from their younger alliance. There was something to be said for a little maturity when it came to sex.

She had remembered to text Lacy before she went to sleep last night, letting her know she was tucked in safely for the night, in case her friend worried. But she hadn't mentioned she was spending the night with Brodie. For now, she wanted to keep that information to herself. But she supposed she should get back to her own cabin soon, in case someone came looking for her.

She rolled over to face Brodie, who lay asleep on his back, dark stubble emphasizing the strong line of his jaw, his sensuous lips slightly parted. She was just about to lean over and give him a big kiss when pounding on the door shook the cabin. "Brodie, wake up!" a man shouted.

Brodie sat up, instantly alert. "Who is it?" he called.

"It's Travis," Emily whispered, even as her brother identified himself.

"Quick, go in the bathroom." Brodie urged her toward the one interior door in the cabin, then swung his feet to the floor and reached for the jeans he'd discarded last night.

Emily gathered the sheet around her and shuffled to the bathroom, only partially closing the door and positioning herself so that she could see out. Brodie opened the door and Travis—scarily pressed and polished as always—said, "They've found Lynn Wallace's car."

"Where?" Brodie held the door partially closed and stepped back. Emily realized he was attempting to kick the clothing she had left on the floor under the bed.

Travis frowned and tried to move into the cabin, but Brodie blocked the move. "Never mind. You can give me all the details on the way there. Just give me a minute to get dressed."

Brodie tried to shut the door, but Travis pushed past him. "What are you trying to hide?" he asked.

"Nothing, I—" Brodie protested, but Emily had heard enough. She moved out of the bathroom, still clutching the sheet around her.

"Brodie is trying to be a gentleman and hide me," she said. "But there's no need for that. We're all adults here."

Travis's face turned white, then red. "Emily, what do you think you're doing?" he finally snapped out.

As gracefully as she could, she bent and retrieved her clothes from the floor. "I'm going to get dressed so that I can come with you to look at Lynn's car."

"You are not coming with us," Travis said.

"I'm part of the investigative team," she said. "I want to see where the car was left and what kind of condition it's in. That may help me reach some more conclusions about Alex." Plus, she knew how annoyed Travis would be at having her push her way in like this. Her brother was a good man, but he was far too uptight, and she saw it as her duty to force him to loosen up a little.

"We don't need a civilian at a potential crime scene," Travis said.

"You can ride with me, but you have to stay in the vehicle until I clear you to get out," Brodie said.

Travis glared at him, no doubt perturbed at having Brodie overrule him. But Brodie didn't work for Travis, so Emily supposed he could make his own decisions.

"Okay." Clothes in hand, she turned back toward the bathroom.

"It is not okay," Travis said.

"Just give me a minute to get dressed," Brodie said. "I'm sure we can work this out."

Smiling to herself, Emily shut the bathroom door behind her. Later, she was sure she'd have to endure a lecture from her brother about how she was making a big mistake getting back together with Brodie. And maybe he was right. But at least this time she was going into the relationship with her eyes wide open. She would have a good time with Brodie now, and avoid thinking about forever.

TRAVIS INSISTED THE three of them travel together in his sheriff's department SUV. Brodie reluctantly agreed. He firmly believed in picking his battles, and arguing over how they were going to get to a crime scene wasn't on his list for today. Not with the promise of a bigger fight looming, judging by the icy stare Travis kept giving him. Fine. The two of them could clear the air later, preferably when Emily wasn't around.

As for the woman in question, Travis's little sister looked smug and satisfied, which should have felt more gratifying than it did. Brodie wasn't certain if she was so pleased with herself because of the fantastic sex they had enjoyed the night before—or because she'd managed to upset her usually unemotional brother.

Dwight met them at the barricade that blocked the still-closed road. He shifted the orange-and-white pylons to one side to allow Travis's vehicle to pass, then walked up to meet them after Travis had parked behind Dwight's cruiser.

Lynn Wallace's white Volvo sat crookedly across the northbound lane, both front doors open. "The crew working to clear the road found it like this when

they reported for work this morning," Dwight said.
"They left at about five o'clock yesterday, so someone drove it up here after that."

"Were the doors open like that, or did they open
them?" Travis asked.

"They said they were open," Dwight said. "I think
whoever dumped it here wanted to make sure it was
noticed, and that people saw what was inside."

"What was inside?" Emily asked. She was pale
and looked a little frightened, but stood her ground.

"Not another body, thank goodness," Dwight said.
"Come take a look."

"Emily, you stay back here," Travis said.

"I won't compromise your crime scene," she said.
"I know better than that." Not waiting for an answer,
she started toward the car, so that Travis had to hurry
to catch up with and pass her.

Brodie followed more slowly, so that by the
time he arrived at the car, the others were gathered
around, bent over and peering into the open doors.
Emily took a step back and motioned for him to move
in ahead of her.

The white upholstery of the Volvo, both front and
back seats, had been slashed, long diagonal cuts leaving leather hanging in strips, stuffing pulled out and
spilling onto the floor. Dull red liquid lay in pools
on the seats and dripped onto the floor. "It's paint,
not blood," Dwight said. "Regular latex. Most of it
is still wet, probably from the cold. I took photos
when I arrived, but the snow around the vehicle was

pretty churned up. I think all the construction guys probably had a look."

The car's windshield had been smashed, the glass a spiderweb of cracks, green glass pebbles that had broken off from the cracks glittering on the dash.

Brodie rejoined Emily a short distance from the car. She stood with her arms folded across her stomach, staring at the pavement. "Are you okay?" he asked softly.

She nodded, but didn't speak until Travis joined them. "Alex is really angry," she said, looking at her brother. "Enraged. And he's coming apart."

"You think Alex did this?" Travis asked.

"Yes. I'm not an expert, but I think doing this, leaving the car up here like this, where it was sure to be found, he's sending you a message."

"What kind of message?" Brodie asked.

She glanced at him, then back at her brother. "The next woman he goes after, I think it's going to be more violent."

"And he's going to blame law enforcement for the violence," Brodie said. "We're making him do this because we won't leave him alone."

"Yes," Emily said. "I think you're right."

Travis looked back toward the Volvo, the silence stretching between them. Dwight shifted from one foot to the other. The rumble of the road machinery sounded very far away, muffled by distance and the walls of snow.

"Dwight, take Emily back to the ranch, please,"

Travis said. "Brodie and I will wait for the wrecker to tow the car to our garage for processing."

Emily stiffened, and Brodie expected her to argue with her brother, but she apparently saw the sense in not standing out here in the cold with nothing to do. She headed toward Dwight's cruiser, leaving the deputy to follow.

Brodie waited until Dwight had driven away and he and Travis were alone before he spoke. "If you have something to say to me, say it," he said.

Travis took a step toward Brodie, the brim of his hat shading his face, hiding his expression. Brodie braced himself for a dressing-down. Travis would tell him he had no business sleeping with Emily, that he was here to do a job and not to seduce his sister, that he had used their friendship to take advantage of Emily—nothing Brodie hadn't already told himself or heard before, five years ago, when he and Travis had also argued about Brodie's relationship with Emily. He would let Travis get out all his words and not try to defend himself. Once Travis had exhausted his anger, maybe they could have a civil discussion about Emily and Brodie's feelings for her.

But Travis didn't say anything. He reared back and belted Brodie in the chin, sending him staggering.

Brodie let out a yelp of surprise and managed to stay upright. He rubbed his aching jaw and stared at the sheriff, who was flushed and breathing hard, hands at his sides, still balled into fists. "I reckon you think I deserve that," Brodie said.

"You don't think you do?"

"I had a long talk with your sister last night—before we went to bed together. She told me about the baby." He paused, gathering his emotions. The reality that Emily had been pregnant with his baby—that he could have been a father—was only just beginning to sink in. "I never knew, I swear. She said she wrote to me, but I never got the letter. If I had, you wouldn't have been able to keep me away from her."

Travis glared at him, wary.

"You know I asked her to marry me, right?" Brodie said.

Travis nodded.

"And she turned me down. I didn't dump her—she dumped me. But I would have come back to help her with the baby—in whatever way she wanted me to help."

He could tell the minute the fight went out of Travis. The sheriff's shoulders sagged and he bowed his head. "I'm sorry I let my temper get the best of me," he said.

Brodie rubbed his jaw again. "Maybe it was good for both of us." He offered his hand.

Travis stared at Brodie's hand. "Maybe it's none of my business, but what happens with you and Emily now?" he asked.

"I don't know. A lot of that is up to her. But it's

not going to be a repeat of last time, I promise. Is that good enough for you?"

Travis grasped his hand, then pulled him close and thumped him on the back. "You and Emily are adults, so what you do is your business," he said. He pulled away and his eyes met Brodie's—hard eyes full of meaning. "But if you hurt her again, I promise, I will hunt you down."

Brodie had no doubt of the truth behind those words. "You don't have to worry," he said. "Now come on. The killer is the only man you need to worry about hunting down right now."

"YOUR FIANCÉ ATE my prosciutto."

Saturday afternoon, Emily and Lacy looked up from the place cards they were hand-lettering for that night's wedding rehearsal dinner. The caterer, Bette, stood before them, hands on her hips and a stormy expression in her eyes. "How do you know Travis ate it?" Lacy asked.

"Because I caught him finishing off the last of it before he headed out the door this morning."

Lacy set aside the stack of place cards. "The poor man has been working so much, eating at odd hours. I hope you didn't fuss at him too much."

"I didn't. But I need that prosciutto for the dinner tonight."

"If you think the grocery in Eagle Mountain will have it, I can run and get it for you," Emily said. "I need to go to the office supply store, anyway."

"They don't have it," Bette said. "But Iris at the Cake Walk said she had some she would sell me. If you could fetch it for me, that would be a big help. I have too much to do to get ready for tonight to leave."

"Of course I'll get it." Emily looked at the place cards spread out in front of her. "Lacy and I are almost finished here."

"Don't go to town by yourself," Lacy said. "Find one of the ranch hands to go with you."

"All right." Emily wanted to protest that she would be fine on her own, but the other women Alex had killed would have probably said the same thing. And the possibility that the *EW* on Alex's list might mean her made her even more cautious.

She and Lacy finished the place cards, each handlettered, with a tiny silk rose glued to the corner. "They turned out really nice," Emily said as she passed the last of the cards over to Lacy.

"They did." Lacy sighed. For a bride on the eve of her wedding day, she didn't look very happy.

"What's wrong?" Emily asked.

Lacy looked up, her eyes shiny with tears. "I'm being silly. I mean, women have died, and here I am, worrying about my wedding. It's ridiculous." She pressed her fingers to her eyes, blotting the tears.

"You're not being silly." Emily squeezed Lacy's hand. "The wedding is going to be beautiful. By tomorrow afternoon, you'll be married and it will be beautiful."

"I'm so worried something is going to happen to

mess things up," she said. "Not just the wedding, but Travis—this killer hates him." She sniffed. "I know he has a dangerous job, and I told myself I could handle that, but when I think about something happening to him…" She pressed her lips together and looked away.

"Travis is smart and careful, and he loves you so much," Emily said. "Nothing is going to happen to him." She said a silent prayer that this would be true.

Lacy nodded and stood. "You're right. And my worrying won't accomplish anything." She gathered the place cards into a neat pile. "Thanks for your help with these. I think I'll go see if Bette needs me to do anything in the kitchen."

Emily wished she had had more to offer her friend than words. If only she could figure out where Alex was hiding. Finding and arresting him would allow Travis and Lacy to start their marriage off right, with a honeymoon away from all this stress and no lingering worries about local women dying.

She gathered her purse, slipped on her coat and went in search of someone to accompany her to town. She searched the barns and outbuildings, and stopped to check on Witchy, who was contentedly munching hay, her leg showing no signs of further inflammation. No one was at the bunkhouse or in the machine shed. Maybe the men had decided to make themselves scarce while the last frantic preparations for tomorrow's wedding were being completed.

On her way back from the barn she walked past

the row of guest cabins. The door to Brodie's cabin opened and he stepped out onto the porch. Odd that he'd be here this time of day. "Brodie!" she called.

He turned to face her and she winced. The left side of his jaw was red and swollen. "What happened to you?" she asked, hurrying up the steps to him.

He gingerly touched his jaw. "I put ice on it, hoping to get the swelling down."

"What happened?" When she had left him and Travis on Dixon Pass, they had been waiting for the wrecker to arrive.

"It's no big deal." He took her arm and urged her down the steps alongside him. "By tomorrow you won't even know it happened."

"You're not answering my question." She studied the injury more closely. She was no expert, but she was pretty sure someone had punched him. "Who hit you?"

"You don't want to know."

Had he tried to arrest someone and they fought back? No, he wouldn't bother hiding that information from her. In fact, she could think of only one person he might try to shield. "Did *Travis* punch you?" The last word came out as a squeak—she couldn't quite hold back her shock at the idea. Travis was so even-tempered. So aggravatingly calm almost all of the time.

But he definitely hadn't been pleased to find her and Brodie together this morning.

"It's no big deal," Brodie said again.

"Did you hit him back?" She clutched at his arm. "Lacy is going to be furious if you broke Travis's nose or something on the eve of the wedding."

"No, I didn't hit him back." He stopped walking and turned to face her. "I figured he needed the one punch to let off some of the pressure that's been building up with this case."

"Then he should go split wood or something— not punch you."

"Don't worry about it," he said. "We cleared the air, and everything is okay now."

"What did you tell him?"

He caressed her shoulders and spoke more softly. "I told him I never got your letter about the baby— that if I had, I never would have left you to deal with that alone. I still hate that you had to go through that by yourself."

The pain in his voice brought a lump to her throat. She moved in closer and his arms went around her. They couldn't do anything to change the past, but at least now she knew he really hadn't deserted her when she needed him most. She wondered what would have happened if he had received her letter and come back to her. Would they have married, anyway? She knew she'd been right to turn down his proposal, but would knowing a child was on the way have changed her mind? She closed her eyes and pushed the thought away. The answer to that question didn't matter now.

Brodie patted her back. "What are you thinking?" he asked.

"Travis still shouldn't have hit you," she mumbled against his chest.

"It's okay," he said. "It was something we both needed, I think."

She raised her head to look at him. "Men are weird."

He laughed. "Now that that's settled, what are you up to?"

"I promised Bette I'd run to town and pick up some prosciutto for her. I was looking for someone to go with me. Want to volunteer?"

"Absolutely. What is Bette doing with prosciutto?"

"Something wonderful, I'm sure. It's for the rehearsal dinner tonight."

"I'd almost forgotten there's a wedding tomorrow."

"How could you forget? There's a big silver-and-white wreath on every door in the house—and the door of your cabin. Not to mention the wedding gifts in the hall and everyone running around like crazy people trying to get ready."

"I said almost. Besides, I've been focused on other things."

Right. Everything always came back to the killer. Alex would probably be thrilled to know how much he was directing all their lives. She couldn't even go to the store by herself because of him. "Come on," she said. "Let's go. I have a million things to do before the dinner tonight."

On the way into town they didn't discuss Alex, or the wedding, or even the weather—all topics Emily felt had been exhausted in recent weeks. Instead, they talked about their lives on the other side of Colorado—she in Fort Collins and he in Denver. "In the spring there's a great farmers market every weekend," she told him. "I go sometimes just to hang out and people watch."

"Do you ever go hiking out around Horsetooth Falls?" he asked.

"It's been a while, but it's a great area."

"We should hike it together sometime," he said.

Her heart gave a funny little flutter. "Yeah. Yeah, we should."

He parked at the curb in front of the Cake Walk Café and followed Emily inside. The lunch crowd had dissipated, but people sat at a couple of tables, nursing cups of coffee or polishing off the last of a meal. The café's owner, Iris Desmet, waved from behind a counter at the back of the room. She disappeared into the kitchen and emerged a moment later with a paper-wrapped parcel. "I warned Bette that I've had this in my freezer for a while," she said as she punched keys on the cash register. "But she said she was desperate, so I told her she could have it for a discount."

"I'm sure it will be fine," Emily said. "Will we see you at the wedding tomorrow?"

"Of course. There's nothing like a wedding to cheer people up, and we could certainly use a little of that—though I hear the road may open tomorrow, and the weather forecast doesn't show any more snow for a couple of weeks. Maybe the rest of the winter won't be as hard."

"I hope that's true." Emily handed over her credit card and waited while Iris swiped it, then she signed the receipt and tucked the package of prosciutto into her purse.

On the sidewalk, Dwight hailed them from across the street. "I thought you'd want to know what we found in the car once we started going through it," he said.

"Let me guess," Brodie said. "One of the Ice Cold calling cards."

Dwight nodded. "Better than that—we found some good prints in the paint. They match ones on file for Alex Woodruff."

"I don't think we had any doubt who was responsible, but it's nice to have more evidence," Brodie said.

"When you get a chance, we've got a couple of questions for the CBI profiler."

Emily put a hand on Brodie's back to get his attention. "You two talk shop. I'm going to the office supply store to pick up a few things."

Brodie frowned. "I'll only be a minute."

"And the store is only two doors down." She

pointed to the building with the oversize gold paperclip over the door. "You can see it from here."

He nodded, then turned back to Dwight. Smiling to herself, she hurried toward the office supply. She couldn't say why she was so happy—there was still a killer on the loose, the highway leading out of town was still closed and everyone around her was keyed up over the wedding tomorrow. And it wasn't as if she and Brodie had resolved anything. She felt closer to him now, and they'd had a night of great sex. Maybe after this was all over, they'd get together again to hike or, who knows, maybe even go out on a real date. That was still no reason for the almost giddy lightness that made her want to skip down the sidewalk and had her fighting back a goofy smile.

The bells on the door of the Paperclip jangled as she entered. The owner, Eleanor Davis, who had taught Emily when she was in third grade, waved from in front of a display of earbuds and went back to assisting an older gentleman. Emily wandered down the aisles of office supplies, admiring a beautiful pen here or an attractive notebook there. She could have spent hours in here, running her hands over the displays and breathing in the scents of ink and paper, but settled for choosing a package of colorful note cards, a sturdy wire-bound journal and a purple gel ink pen. What could she say—some women experienced euphoria when buying new shoes, while office supplies did it for her.

Outside on the sidewalk, she almost collided with

an elderly man. "So sorry, miss," he said, holding out his hands defensively. He stared out at her from behind thick glasses, his expression confused and his eyes bloodshot. His gray hair hung lank to his shoulders and a wisp of a gray beard stood out against sallow skin and sagging jowls. "Clumsy of me, I…" He looked around, blinking. "I think I need some help."

The poor dear looked really out of it. Emily glanced across the street, hoping to see Dwight and Brodie and wave them over, but they must have gone back into the café—probably to get out of the biting wind. She shifted her purchases to one hand. "What can I do to help you?" she asked.

"It's my car. There's something wrong with it."

"Let me call someone for you." She fumbled in her purse for her phone.

"No." He put out a hand to stop her. "Don't go to so much trouble. I know what's wrong. I just need to find the auto parts store."

"There's one out on the highway," she said. "Near the motel. But it's a little far to walk in this weather."

"You could give me a ride," he said. "I know it's a lot to ask, but it would help me so much."

She glanced toward the café again. "I'm with someone," she said. "But I'm sure he wouldn't mind giving you a ride—"

"No!" The man's hand clamped around her wrist—hard. Startled, she stared at him. The confused look had vanished from his eyes, and he no longer looked so old. Something sharp pricked her side—a knife. "Come with me now, and don't make a scene," he said.

Chapter Fourteen

Emily opened her mouth to scream, but no sound emerged. The old man put his arm around her, pulling her close. The odors of wood smoke and sweat stung her nose, and the knife dug into her side, so that it hurt to even breathe deeply. She dropped her purse, the contents spilling out onto the sidewalk, the package of ham coming to rest in a snowbank. "That's right, come along nice and easy," the man—she was sure it was Alex—crooned.

He still looked like an innocent old man, but nothing about him was harmless. He had a grip like iron—she imagined him breaking her wrist if she tried to jerk away. And then he would slash her open with the knife before she had time to run.

"Hey!" The shout boomed out, making her jump. Alex turned, dragging her around with him, and she stared as Brodie raced toward them. She had the sensation of being somewhere outside herself, watching a slow-motion movie—Alex opening his mouth to say something, Brodie reaching into his coat and pulling out a gun—the knife pressing harder against her side.

Then everything sped up. Someone screamed, Brodie shouted, then Alex shoved her away, so hard that she fell, slamming her knees into the concrete of the walkway. Brodie's boots thundered past her, then a woman knelt beside her, trying to help her to her feet.

But Emily didn't get up until Brodie returned. He bent over her, chest heaving, the gun out of sight now. For a long moment, neither of them said a thing, their eyes locked, his expression reflecting all the terror she felt. "Are you…all right?" he managed to gasp at last.

She nodded, though she still couldn't seem to speak. By now a crowd had gathered, everyone wanting to know what had happened, and if they could help. Brodie grasped Emily's hand and pulled her to her feet. She caught her breath at the sudden sharp pain in her side, and clamped her hand over the spot. "He had a knife," she said.

Brodie pushed her hand away, then yanked down the zipper of her coat and shoved it aside. She stared at the quarter-sized blossom of red against the white of her sweater. "We need to get you to the clinic," he said, then, without waiting for a reply, scooped her into his arms and started across the street.

"Brodie, put me down. Please!" She beat her fists against his chest, but his expression never changed. People called after them, a car braked to a halt as he stepped in front of it and horns honked, but Brodie appeared to hear none of it. He burst into the Eagle Mountain medical clinic and everyone in the small waiting room stared at them.

"She's hurt," he said. "She needs to see the doctor now."

She wanted to demand once more that he put her down, but doubted he would even hear her. When the door leading to the examination rooms opened, he carried her through it and into the closest empty room. A woman with a stethoscope followed them inside. "What is the meaning—"

But she got no further. Brodie took out his badge and shoved it at her, then pulled back Emily's coat to show the spot of blood. "She's been stabbed."

The woman's eyes widened, but she recovered quickly and took charge. She pushed Brodie out of the way, then eased the coat off Emily and pulled up the sweater.

In the end, Emily needed four stitches, a tetanus shot and some antibiotics to ward off infection. Brodie sat in a chair, scowling and silent, while the nurse practitioner on duty stitched up Emily. No one talked about what had happened, and Emily didn't know if she was relieved about that or not.

The nurse had just finished administering the tetanus vaccine when someone knocked on the door. "It's the sheriff," Travis said. "May I come in?"

"You might as well," the nurse practitioner said, and shifted so that Travis could squeeze in behind her.

"I'm fine," Emily said, sliding off the exam table, wincing a little at the pain in her side. "It was just a little cut."

Travis's answer was to pull her close and squeeze her so tight she couldn't breathe. Her brother wasn't much for words, but the concern in that hug made her tear up, and she had to force herself to smile and push him away. "I'm okay," she said. "Really."

Brodie stood and Travis turned to him. "I've got everyone available out looking for this guy, but I'm afraid he's done another disappearing act."

"Let's talk about this outside," Brodie said. He picked up Emily's coat and helped her back into it. Then, one hand on her back, he followed her into the waiting room, where, once again, everyone stared at them.

"Someone brought these for you," the receptionist said, and handed over Emily's purse, the package of office supplies and the paper-wrapped parcel of prosciutto. Emily stared at the ham, teary again. It felt like hours since she had set out to run a simple errand for Bette, yet the prosciutto was still cold.

"Let's go to my office," Travis said, and escorted them out of the clinic. The three of them piled into his cruiser, Brodie in the back seat with her. She lay her head on his shoulder, closed her eyes and tried not to think about what had happened, although she knew she would have to give a statement to Travis. All she wanted was a few more minutes to pretend she hadn't just come within seconds of death.

At the station, Adelaide clucked over her and brought her a cup of tea. "Drink that," she ordered. "And don't let these two bully you into anything." She scowled at Brodie and Travis as if she blamed them for the attack, then left, closing the door to Travis's office behind her with a solid *Click!*

"I'm not going to bully you," Travis said. "But we need to know what happened. We got a description of the man who attacked you from a few people, but about all they said was that it was an old guy with a patchy beard, and none of them remembered seeing him before."

She took a long sip of the sweet, hot tea, then set the cup on the edge of the desk and took a deep breath. She could do this. She was alive and safe and what she had to say might help Travis and Brodie stop this man. "It was Alex," she said. "I didn't recognize him because he was wearing a disguise. A good one. But I'm sure it was him."

"Start with a description," Travis said. "We'll go from there."

She described the old man who had approached her—his glasses and long hair and saggy jowls. "He looked confused and harmless," she said. "Stooped over and a little shaky. I felt sorry for him. He wanted me to feel sorry for him, to not see him as a threat. I'm sure that's what he did with the other women, too."

"He didn't run like an old man," Brodie said. "He

took off like a track star. He ducked down an alley and I lost him within seconds."

"He said he was having car trouble and asked me for a ride to the auto parts store," Emily said. "When I told him I was with someone, and started toward the café, he grabbed my wrist and stuck the knife in my side. His whole demeanor changed. That's when I knew it was Alex." She swallowed hard, remembered terror making her light-headed.

"I came out of the café with Dwight and saw Emily cozied up with this old guy," Brodie said. "Even though her back was to me, something about the situation didn't look right. When I called to them, the guy swung her around toward me. He looked angry—enraged—and I could see that Emily was terrified. I drew my weapon and ordered him to stop. At first I thought he would resist, or try to use Emily as a shield. Instead, he released her and took off running." He raked a hand through his hair. "I should have insisted you stay with me. And I never should have gone into the café with Dwight."

"I was in a public place with other people all around," Emily said. "What was Alex thinking?"

"He thinks he's invincible," Travis said. "That law enforcement is stupid and we'll never catch him. But we will."

A knock on the door interrupted them. "Come in," Travis called.

Dwight entered, a bundle of cloth in his hand.

"We found these in the trash bins behind Mo's Pub," he said, and laid the bundle on the desk.

Emily stared at the drab shirt, thick glasses with scratched lenses, and thin gray beard and long hair. "That was his disguise," she said.

"I figure he ditched the clothes and either put on another disguise or walked away as himself," Dwight said.

"He's good at blending in," Emily said. "He can be noticed when he wants to be, but when he doesn't, he fades into the crowd."

"I interviewed some of his professors over the phone," Travis said. "Most of them didn't even re-member him."

"He's decided to go after you now," Brodie said.

"But why? Because I knew him at school?"

"Maybe," Brodie said. "Or because you're Travis's sister. He wants to prove he's better than any cop."

She welcomed the anger that surged through her at the thought. It made her feel stronger. She stood. "I'm not going to sit quietly and play victim for his sick fantasies."

"No, you're not," Brodie agreed. "And he's not going to get close enough to hurt you again." He stood also, and took her hand in his. "Because from now on, I'm not letting you out of my sight."

THAT EVENING, BRODIE sat in the Walkers' living room as Emily descended the stairs to the strains of Pa-chelbel's Canon. Something tugged hard at his chest as she paused at the bottom of the stairs and met his gaze, then she ducked her head and turned away to take her place in front of the fire, where the officiant, a plump woman with auburn hair, waited for the run-through of the wedding ceremony.

The other bridesmaids followed—Gage's wife, Maya, Paige Riddell and Brenda Prentice. The music switched to the traditional bridal entrance tune and Lacy, in a blue lace dress, carrying an imaginary bouquet, appeared at the top of the stairs. Even though this was only a rehearsal, Brodie and the other observers rose as Lacy descended the stairs.

Rather than watch the bride, Brodie kept his eyes on Travis, who stood with Gage, Ryder Stewart, Nate Harris and Cody Rankin in the archway between the living and dining room. The sheriff's stance was casual: hip cocked, face impassive. But as Lacy neared, Travis straightened, then reached out his hand to her. In that moment, Brodie was sure Travis wasn't thinking about a killer or the women who had died, or about anything but this woman and their future together.

Love had the power to do that—to push aside every worry and distraction, to focus attention on what mattered most, on life and hope, even in the midst of tragedy.

Brodie shifted his gaze to Emily. She was watching her brother and Lacy, eyes shiny with unshed tears, joy radiating from her smile. Brodie's heart hammered and he had trouble catching his breath, the knowledge of how much he loved her a sucker punch to the gut.

If only she would look at him, and let him see that she felt the same—that she loved him. But her eyes remained fixed on the bride and groom as the officiant explained what would happen next.

"You may practice kissing the bride if you like," the officiant said. Everyone laughed as Travis moved in to kiss Lacy and the spell was broken.

"Now that that's over, we can eat," Gage said, ignoring the scolding look from Maya.

Brodie stood and went to Emily. Though he was not a member of the wedding party, and had not even received an invitation to the wedding, Travis had embraced the idea of Brodie as Emily's bodyguard. He had also apparently persuaded his mother and father that Brodie was not the scoundrel they had assumed and now they, too, seemed happy to have him protecting their daughter.

As for Emily, he wasn't certain what she felt about him becoming, by default, her "plus-one" for the wedding. She smiled as he held her chair for her, next to his at the table, then quickly turned her attention to the other guests. Most of the wedding party was made up of other law enforcement officers and their spouses or significant others.

Travis and the bride-to-be sat side by side in the middle of the long table, Lacy smiling and beautiful, Travis stoic and tense, his smiles doled out sparingly for his beloved. He was putting on a good show, but

Brodie knew his mind was back on Alex. Like Brodie, he was probably wondering if, while they ate and drank and toasted the happy couple, the Ice Cold Killer was claiming another victim.

The officiant, Reverend Winger, sat across the table. As Bette and the ranch cook, Rainey, set salads in front of the guests, she leaned across and asked, "Are you in law enforcement, too?"

"Yes, ma'am. I'm a detective with the Colorado Bureau of Investigation."

"This must be the safest place to be in the whole county right now," Reverend Winger said.

"Reverend Winger, I understand you vacationed in Italy last year." Lacy leaned across to address the pastor. "What was your favorite thing about that trip?"

As the reverend launched into a description of her visit to Tuscany, Brodie silently applauded Lacy. Before the rehearsal began, she had laid down the law—absolutely no discussion of the case tonight. *We're going to focus on the wedding and be happy*, she had insisted.

"The prosciutto doesn't look any worse for wear," Emily leaned over and whispered to Brodie as a plate of prosciutto-wrapped asparagus and petite sirloin steaks was set before each of them.

"No one will ever know," he said, and popped a bite of the asparagus into his mouth. No one would know what Emily had been through earlier that day, either. If he detected a little more tension around her eyes, that was only because he was so focused on her.

"You know, it's hard to eat when you're staring at me like that," she said.

"Sorry." He was tempted to say something about her being so beautiful he couldn't keep his eyes off her, but he was sure such a cheesy line would only make her groan. He focused on his own food. "This is delicious," he said. "Bette did a great job."

"She really did," Emily agreed. "Though in addition to the stress of my prosciutto problem, she had to deal with a no-show by the florist." She gestured toward the center of the table, where an arrangement of greens and pine cones, tied with silver ribbon, filled a silver vase. "This was a last-minute substitution."

"What did the florist have to say about the failed delivery?" he asked.

"By the time Bette had a chance to call, they were already closed. But she left a stern message—and she's going to double-check with them in the morning to make sure the wedding flowers get here in time."

"I'll be sure and tell her everything looks—and tastes—great."

"Speech! Speech!" Nate Harris, at one end of the table, tapped his spoon against his water glass.

Travis's father shoved back his chair and stood as the guests fell quiet. "Thank you, everyone, for coming here this evening," he said. "I especially want to thank Bette and Rainey for putting on such a lovely dinner."

Cries of "hear, hear" and light applause followed this remark.

Mr. Walker turned to Travis and Lacy. "Your mother and I have looked forward to tomorrow for a long time," he said. "We're so happy to welcome Lacy into the family and we wish you only the best." He raised his glass in a toast and everyone followed suit.

"Is this where everyone else in the wedding party feels compelled to also give a toast?" Emily whispered to Brodie. "If it is, I'm going to need more wine."

But instead of toasts, Bette arrived with dessert—a baked Alaska that Brodie, at least, would have awarded first place in any bake-off.

Half an hour later, stuffed and happy, the guests who weren't staying on the ranch made their way to the door. Brodie stood with Emily, saying goodbye. When everyone was gone, Brodie led Emily aside, where they could talk without being overheard. "About the arrangements for tonight," he said. "I meant what I said before about not letting you out of my sight."

"So you're saying we have to sleep together?" He couldn't decide if the look in her eye was teasing or not.

"I'm saying I'm going to spend the night in the same room as you—sex is optional."

"Alex isn't going to come into this house and up to my bedroom," she said. "He wouldn't dare!"

"I wouldn't put anything past him at this point." After all, Alex had tried to crash the barbecue Wednesday night. Brodie took her arm and pulled her closer. "I'm not going to give him any opportunity to get to you again." The memory of her crumpled on the sidewalk, bleeding from Alex's knife, still made it hard to breathe.

"All right." Her smile made the tight band around his chest ease. "I was planning on sneaking out to your cabin later, anyway." She snuggled against him.

"Oh, you were?" He lowered his head to kiss her, but an uproar at the front door made them pull apart and turn toward the clamor. Lacy's parents, who had been among the first to leave, stood with Travis and Lacy—Mrs. Milligan in tears, her husband white-faced. "That poor woman," Mrs. Milligan moaned.

Brodie moved toward them, Emily close behind, as Dwight shoved through the crowd. "The florist van is blocking the end of the driveway," he said. "The delivery driver is inside, dead."

Chapter Fifteen

Emily urged Brodie to go with Travis and the others to investigate the crime scene, but he insisted on staying by her side as she helped her mother and Lacy soothe the Milligans. She volunteered to let Lacy's parents stay in her room that evening. Her own parents didn't ask where she planned to spend the night, though she was aware of her mother watching her and Brodie more closely as the evening progressed.

Several hours passed before the other guests could leave. While they waited for the crime scene investigators and coroner to finish their work, for the ambulance to remove the body and for the wrecker to arrive to tow the van to the sheriff's garage, Emily poured coffee and served snacks that no one ate, and tried to make small talk about anything but the murders.

It was after midnight before she was able to retrieve her clothes and toiletries, along with a change of clothes for the next day, from her room and go with Brodie to his cabin. She should have been exhausted by the strain of the day, but instead felt hyperalert and on edge. Halfway down the path to the cabins, she put her arm out to stop Brodie. "Stop just a minute," she said. "This feels like the first time things have been quiet all day and I want to take it in."

She closed her eyes and breathed in deeply of the cold, clear air, then tilted her head back and stared up at the night sky, thousands of stars glittering against the velvet blackness.

"It's beautiful," Brodie said, standing behind her and wrapping his arms around her.

"It's surreal to think of violence in the midst of such peace," she said. "Especially while we were celebrating such a happy occasion."

He kissed the top of her head—such a sweet, gentle gesture. "Come on," he said. "You're shivering. It's warm in the cabin."

The cabin was warm and neat, the bed made and clutter put away. Was this because Brodie had been expecting her to stay with him tonight, or because he was a neat and organized guy? She suspected a little of both. "I want to change out of this dress and these heels," she said, staring down at her fashionable, but definitely chilly, attire.

"Go right ahead," Brodie said.

She retreated to the bathroom, where she changed into yoga pants and a T-shirt. She studied her reflection in the mirror over the sink, hesitating, then turned on the water and washed off her makeup, then brushed out her hair. It wasn't as if Brodie hadn't seen her like this before.

"How is your side doing?" he asked when she emerged from the bathroom. He had removed his shoes and untucked his shirt, and his gun lay on the table beside the bed.

She made a face. "It hurts some," she said. She had been mostly successful at distracting herself from the pain. "It's more annoying than anything."

"Do you mind if I have a look?" he asked.

"All right."

He crossed the room to her and carefully lifted up the T. When she had changed for dinner earlier, she had removed the dressing, so that the stitches were exposed, the skin slightly puffy around the neat row of dark thread. Brodie studied the wound for a moment, then bent and gently kissed the skin above the stitches.

She threaded her fingers through his hair and held him to her for a moment, before dragging his face up to hers and kissing him. She molded her body to his, enjoying the feel of him so close, the anticipation of spending another night getting to know him even better like a pleasant hum through her.

"I don't want to hurt you," he murmured, his mouth against her hair.

"You won't." Not physically, at least. She wouldn't think about what might happen if he left her again.

They kissed again, heat building, and were moving toward the bed when someone knocked on the door. Brodie turned toward the sound. "It's Travis. Can I come in?"

Brodie opened the door and Travis entered. He looked cold and exhausted, Emily thought. He needed a hot drink and a good night's sleep, but she doubted he would get either. He glanced at Emily, then turned to Brodie. "I wanted to update you on what we found," he said.

"Emily will have to stay and hear." Brodie sat on the side of the bed and Emily settled next to him.

"All right." Travis took the chair and sat with his elbows on his knees, head down. "The woman is Sarah Geraldi, a part-time delivery person for the florist," he said. "She was killed like the others, hands and feet bound, the Ice Cold calling card tucked into her bra." He glanced at Emily again. "You were right. There was more violence this time. He cut her up pretty badly, and there was more blood."

"He would probably have blood on him," Brodie said. "He's not being as careful."

"He knows you know who he is," Emily said. "He's not trying to hide his identity anymore. In fact, I think he likes knowing you know that he's the one who's getting the better of you. At least, I think that's how he sees it."

Travis nodded. "The medical examiner thinks she was killed much earlier today, hidden in the van, then driven here a short time ago. The delivery van's engine was still warm."

"He killed her someplace else and brought her here to taunt you," Brodie said.

Travis nodded. "It looks that way."

"If Alex drove the van here with the body in it, how did he get away?" Brodie asked. "Has he recruited another accomplice? Stashed another vehicle somewhere? It's still seven miles to town."

"Maybe he didn't leave." Travis raised his head, his gaze steady, his expression grim. "Maybe he's still here, hiding somewhere."

TRAVIS'S ANNOUNCEMENT DID nothing to help Emily or Brodie sleep. They made love tenderly, but with an air of desperation, eager to suppress, at least for a little while, thoughts of the horror that might lurk outside the door. They both woke early and dressed without saying much, then made their way up the path to the house. Brodie walked with one arm around Emily, the other hand on his gun, constantly scanning around them for any sign of an intruder.

"I'm jumpy enough without you acting as if Alex is going to leap out of the bushes and grab me," she said. "You heard Travis—he had every extra man searching around here last night. Alex isn't here."

"I don't believe in taking chances when the stakes are so high," Brodie said.

The look he gave her had a lot of heat behind it, and she had to look away. She really needed to keep her emotions in check so that she could support Lacy today. She couldn't afford to let her confusing responses to Brodie reduce her to a sodden puddle of feelings.

The wedding was scheduled to take place at five o'clock. Before then, there was still a lot to do to prepare for the ceremony. Bette appeared in the doorway to the dining room as Emily and Brodie were finishing up breakfast. "I need you two to help with the decorations," she said.

"Sure." Emily handed her dirty dishes to Brodie, who had volunteered to carry them into the kitchen. "What can we do?"

"Give me those." Bette took the dishes, then dumped them in a bus tub on the end of the sideboard. "Needless to say, things are as chaotic at the florist's this morning as they are here, and we may not be getting all the flowers we ordered, so we're making some last-minute adjustments. Come with me."

She led them through the living room, where she had assembled a pile of evergreens, silver ribbon and a mass of white silk flowers. "I raided the attic and the rest of the house for every flower arrangement on the premises," Bette explained. "Now we're going to use them to transform this room into a woodland winter wonderland."

Under Bette's direction, Emily and Brodie began cutting and wiring the greenery to make garland. Bette came along behind them and attached ribbons and flowers. "I guess the florist was pretty upset when she got the news about her employee," Emily said as she snipped a section of pine branches.

"It's even worse than you think," Bette said. "The woman who was murdered was the shop owner's daughter."

"Oh, no!" Emily's chest tightened in sympathy for the poor woman.

"Believe me, I'd gladly throttle Alex Woodruff with my bare hands if I could find him." Bette yanked hard on the end of a silver bow. "Not only am I sick over all the women he's killed, but I hate that this has cast such a pall over the wedding. Lacy, of all people, deserves to be happy on this day."

"Of course she does," Emily murmured in sympathy. Travis deserved to be happy, too—and he wouldn't be until Alex was arrested and locked behind bars, where he couldn't hurt anyone else.

"Oh, Bette, it's going to look wonderful."

The three of them turned to see Lacy, dressed in black yoga pants and a too-large sweatshirt that had *Rayford County Sheriff's Dept.* emblazoned across the front, her hair rolled up in large foam rollers, her face pale from both lack of makeup and lack of sleep, and her eyes dull with a frazzled, distracted expression. She moved into the room and fingered a white silk rose, and a single tear rolled down her cheek.

"Oh, honey, it's going to be all right." Bette enfolded her friend in a hug.

Lacy gave in and sobbed on Bette's shoulder. "This is supposed to be the happiest day of my life," she said between tears. "And I'm so worried and scared and angry. What if something happens to Travis? What if someone else gets hurt? It's just so awful." And a fresh wave of weeping engulfed her.

Bette patted her back and looked over her shoulder at Emily and Brodie. "You two can finish up here, can't you?" she asked. "The garland is mostly done—you just need to add a few more bows and then put it around the archway." She indicated the arch between the living and dining room, where Lacy and Travis would stand to recite their vows.

"Of course we can," Emily said.

Bette nodded. "Come on, Lacy, let's go fix you a cup of tea and get something to take the puffiness out of your eyes," she said, leading the distraught bride away. "Everything is going to be fine."

Emily and Brodie finished the garland. Emily didn't think her bows looked as professional as Bette's, but she told herself everyone was going to be focused on the happy couple, and not the decorations. "You'll have to start attaching this over the archway," she said, handing Brodie a length of garland. "I'm not tall enough to do it without a ladder."

"What do I attach it with?" he asked.

She searched the table and spotted a staple gun. "Use this." She handed it to him. "If Mom complains later, I'll take the blame."

He positioned the garland, pressed the staple gun against it and…*click!* He frowned. "I think it's out of staples."

"I know where they are," she said, and raced to retrieve the box. Her mother kept all her household tools in an old pie safe at one end of the front porch. She hurried to the cabinet and found the box, half full of staples, and let out a sigh of relief. One less thing to worry about.

She was halfway back to the front door when a plaintive cry stopped her. She held her breath, listening, and it came again. "Tawny?" she called, and the cat answered, sounding even more distressed than before. She must have decided to have her kittens near the house, but where?

Emily moved to the end of the porch. "Tawny?"

The cry came again. Was the cat under one of the cars? Was she hurt? Heart hammering, Emily hurried toward the sounds of distress. "Tawny!" she called again, and bent to look underneath Brodie's SUV.

Strong arms grabbed her from behind, and a hand slapped over her mouth so that she couldn't cry out, and she couldn't move. She stared up into Alex's face. "Isn't this going to be a nice surprise for the sheriff on his wedding day?" he asked.

Chapter Sixteen

Brodie was about to go after Emily when Bette called to him from the other room. "Brodie, can you come in here a minute, please?"

He looked after Emily, who was closing the front door behind her.

"Lacy wants to speak to you," Bette said.

Telling himself Emily would be fine, he followed the sound of Bette's voice to the sunporch, where she and Lacy sat with teacups in hand. Lacy beckoned him. "I have a favor to ask," she said, and patted the love seat beside her.

"Of course." He perched on the edge of the seat, anxious to get this over with so he could check on Emily.

"Promise me you'll see that Travis gets to the altar for the wedding," she said. "There are plenty of other law enforcement officers here today who can handle things for a while. All I need are a couple of hours of Travis's undivided attention so that we can get married."

He nodded. "Of course." Though the sheriff was in charge of the case, there was no reason he couldn't take a break for a few hours.

"I'm going to find Gage and make him promise the same thing," Lacy said. "And any of the other officers who are here today." She set her teacup aside and stood. "And now I'd better get upstairs and take my bath. Paige is coming by soon to do my nails."

"I've got plenty to do, too," Bette said, standing also. "Brodie, did you and Emily finish the decorations?"

"Emily went to get more staples. I'll go find her." She had been gone much too long, he thought, quickening his pace through the house.

He grabbed his jacket from the hooks by the door and pulled it on as he stepped out onto the porch. The door to a cabinet at the end of the porch stood open. The cabinet contained a hammer and other small tools, paintbrushes, some flowerpots and other items that might be useful for minor repairs or outdoor decorating. Was this where Emily had retrieved the staples? But where was she?

A gray tabby cat came around the side of the house, heavily pregnant belly swaying from side to side. She jumped up onto the porch and rubbed herself against his legs. Brodie ignored her and stepped off the porch, studying the snow. Footprints overlaid each other in the snow on the edges of the shoveled path, but none stood out as particularly fresh, and he couldn't tell if any of them were Emily's.

A sheriff's department SUV pulled up in front of the house and Travis climbed out. "Are you hiding out here from the wedding chaos?" Travis asked.

Brodie opened his mouth to share his concern about Emily, then closed it again, remembering his promise to Lacy. Travis needed to focus on the wedding today. If Brodie needed help, there were plenty of other people around here who were qualified to give it. "What are you doing in uniform today?" he asked.

"I had to get a haircut and I stopped in the office to check on a few things," Travis said. "The wedding is hours away and there's not much for the groom to do but show up and say his lines when the time comes."

"I think Lacy is upstairs getting her nails done or something," Brodie said.

"That's okay. I really came by to take another look at the crime scene." Travis scanned the area around the house. "The searchers never found any sign of Alex last night, but I can't shake the feeling that he's hiding somewhere close by."

"We're all keeping an eye out for him," Brodie said.

Travis nodded. "I think I'll go in and check in with Lacy," he said. "She's a little stressed about all of this. I think she's worried I'm going to leave her at the altar or something."

"You wouldn't do that," Brodie said.

"Of course not." Travis moved past him. "Not permanently, anyway."

Brodie headed to his cabin, telling himself Emily might have gone there in search of something she had left behind the night before, maybe. But the place was empty, though the scent of her perfume lingered in the rumpled sheets on the bed, recalling their night together and how much she had come to mean to him.

He turned on his heel and headed to the barn. Maybe she had gone to check on her horse. But Witchy was contentedly munching hay in her stall. The mare swiveled her head to look at Brodie when he leaned over the stall door. She shook her head and whinnied, as if impatient that he was invading her home. "Next time, I'll bring you a carrot," he said, and headed back to the house.

After checking that no one was lurking around to ask him what he was up to, he made his way up the stairs to Emily's bedroom. Five years ago, he had done much the same thing, sneaking past Emily's parents to rendezvous in her room, embracing the role of the dangerous bad boy up to no good with his best friend's sister.

He was cautious this time, not because he thought he had to hide what he was doing, but because he didn't want to upset and alarm the family if there was no need. He knocked softly on the door and relief surged through him as footsteps approached from the other side.

Mrs. Milligan blinked at him, her hair in curlers and some kind of greenish cream on her face. Brodie took a step back. "Have you, um, seen Emily?" he asked.

"No, I haven't."

"Thanks." He backed away, then turned and hurried down the stairs, heart pounding. Something had happened to Emily. She was gone. Now it was time to panic.

"WHERE ARE YOU taking me?"

Alex hadn't bothered to gag Emily, though he had bound her hands and feet with tape, holding her in an iron grip that had left bruises on her upper arms. He had dragged her through the woods to a dirty white van and belted her into the back seat, her head at an uncomfortable angle, every jolt of the vehicle on the uneven ground sending pain through her bound arms.

"You'll see." Alex, his head almost completely covered by a knit cap pulled low and a scarf wound over his mouth, nearly vibrated with suppressed elation. "The sheriff and his deputies were so sure they could stop me this time," he said. "They don't realize who they're dealing with. I'm an expert who's making them look like a bunch of amateurs."

"Why would you want to be an expert at murder?" Emily asked. "You're smart enough you could have excelled at almost anything." She figured it couldn't hurt to flatter him—and as long as they were talking, she could remain alive. Brodie would have missed her by now. He and the others would be looking for her. All she had to do was stay alive until they found her.

"Murder is the ultimate crime," Alex said. "The one that captures everyone's attention and focuses all the effort and money on the killer." He pounded the steering wheel with the heel of his hand. "Talk about a rush."

"Why come to Eagle Mountain?" Emily asked. "Couldn't you have gotten away with a lot more in Denver?"

Alex laughed—a maniacal chuckle that made the hair on the back of her neck stand on end. "You don't get it, do you?" he asked. "You're as clueless as the rest of them. Honestly, I expected better of you."

"Get what?"

"I came to this 'middle of nowhere' excuse for a town because of you!"

You came here to kill me. But she couldn't say the words.

"When we first met, I was intrigued," he said. "You were pretty and smart, and you had a certain *fragile* quality I appreciated. I thought about asking you out, but as I observed you, I noticed that you didn't appear to date anyone—male or female. If I asked you out, chances were you would turn me down. And sex wasn't what I was really after. No, I wanted a much deeper connection. Do you know what that is?"

"No." She had to force the single syllable out. Alex's words terrified her even more than his actions. He had seemed so normal on the outside, yet talking with him now, she understood clearly how unhinged he had become.

"Before I kill someone, I look into her eyes and she realizes her life—her very existence—is in my hands. It is the most profound connection I could ever have with another human being. The feeling I have at that moment, the power and, yes, the love, is incredible. I wanted to experience that with you."

She said nothing, no longer wanting to encourage him.

But he didn't need her encouragement. "I decided I needed to work my way up to you," he said. "I had to experiment and perfect my methods."

"What about Tim?" she asked, hoping to change the subject.

More stomach-turning laughter. "I asked him to come with me because I thought he could be my first victim. But he turned out to be useful."

"He helped you murder the first few women."

"He did. Turns out, he had a taste for killing and I was able to exploit that. Of course, he was nowhere near my level of genius. Which is why he was caught in the end." He giggled. That was the only way Emily could think to describe the sound he made, like a little child chuckling over a silly cartoon. "Things kept getting better and better for me after I came here. The local sheriff's department was as tiny as the town, and they had tiny brains, too. And then I found out your older brother was the sheriff. Such delicious synchronicity. As if this was all meant to be."

He had turned onto the highway up Dixon Pass. Emily craned her head to see out the window. "Is the pass open now?" she asked.

"It doesn't matter if it is," Alex said. "We're not going all the way to the top."

Emily strained forward, staring down the empty road. They passed a sign warning of the road closure, then the orange barricades loomed in sight. But before they reached the barricades, Alex jerked the steering wheel to the right and the van lurched to the side. Unable to brace herself with her bound hands and feet, she jerked painfully forward against the seat belt and her head bounced against the window. Tears stung her eyes from the pain.

The van jolted to a stop, the vehicle's nose buried in a snowbank. Alex shut off the engine, then came around and slid open the side door. He leaned in to unbuckle Emily and she wondered if she could find a way to fight him off. But then he was pulling her from the vehicle. He dumped her into the snow like an old suitcase and slammed the door shut behind her.

"Come on," he said, then grabbed her by the ankles and began dragging her through the snow.

She screamed, hoping to attract the attention of one of the highway workers who were clearing the pass. "Shut up," Alex said, no heat in the words. He climbed over a snowbank and came down in a narrow alley cut through the snow. The passage was just wide enough for one person to walk. He strode down it, dragging Emily by her heels after him. The packed snow scraped her body and sent stabbing pains through her arms. The cold bit into her until her teeth were chattering, and tears streamed down her face from the pain as her head repeatedly pounded against the ground. She wanted to protest, to beg him to stop hurting her, but what difference would it make? He was going to kill her, unless Brodie and Travis and the others got here in time.

Then, as suddenly as he had started, Alex stopped. Emily lay in the snow, staring up at the blue, blue sky, wondering if this would be the last sight she would ever see. Alex came and bent over her, the scarf no longer hiding his face. "Wait for me at the bottom," he said, then gave her a hard shove.

She flew down a steep slope, over the packed snow, sliding on her back, and then she was falling, tumbling. She pressed her arms tightly to her body and tried to curl into a fetal position, sure she was going to break something. Her body turned and bounced and slid some more, until at last she came to rest in a drift of snow, so cold she could no longer shake, numb with fear and the certainty of impending death.

Then Alex was standing beside her. "Was that fun?" he asked. "It looked like it might be." He hauled her upright and tossed her over his shoulder, as if she weighed no more than a sack of flour. "One more trip and we'll be home."

She heard the sound of a motor coming to life, and the creak of turning gears. She craned her head to look and saw an old ski lift with chairs wide enough for two people. Alex shoved Emily into one of the chairs, then sat beside her, and they started up at a rapid clip. She thought of jumping from the lift, but the fall would probably hurt, and with her hands and feet still taped, she wouldn't be able to get away. "Is this where you've been living?" she asked.

"Pretty cool, huh?" he asked. "I got the old ski lift going, and I fixed up the lift shack at the top as a cozy little hideaway."

"Did you set off the avalanche the day Brodie and Gage came here?" she asked.

"They were stupid enough to come here when the avalanche danger was so high. I figure I did a public service, reminding them."

"Are you going to kill me up there?" Emily asked. Maybe it was a stupid question, but she wanted to know. If he answered yes, maybe she would risk jumping off the lift, and find a way to take him with her. With luck, he'd be the one to break a bone or hit his head when they landed.

"I'm going to kill you eventually," he said. "That's the point, isn't it? But not right away. First, we're going to wait."

"Wait for what?"

"For your brother and his men to come after you. I have a big surprise in store for them."

Chapter Seventeen

Brodie descended the stairs two at a time. He met Bette crossing the living room. "Have you seen Gage or Cody?" he asked.

"They and the other groomsmen went into town to pick up their tuxes. And I think they were all going to have lunch together. Why?"

He shook his head and went past her, back onto the porch. He could call Gage and break up the lunch—and probably end up disrupting the whole wedding. Or he could try to locate Emily and Alex on his own, and summon help then. He surveyed the empty porch again, then moved into the yard and parking area. He was staring at the ground, trying to find what might be Emily's footprints, when he spotted something he hadn't noticed before.

He picked up the box of staples, a cold piercing him that had nothing to do with the outside temperature. Something protruded from the corner of the box. He lifted the lid and shuddered as a small white card fluttered to the ground. He could read the words printed on it without bending over: *ICE COLD*.

Alex had Emily, and he wanted Brodie and the others to know he had her. Maybe he even wanted them to come after him.

Brodie picked up the card and tucked it back into the box of staples, then slipped them into his pocket. He surveyed the snow near where the card had fallen, the surface smooth and undisturbed. But a short distance away, he spotted an area of churned-up ice, with drag marks leading away from it.

He followed the marks for several hundred yards, to a wooded area on the edge of the Walker property. Someone had parked a vehicle here, the impressions from the tire tread making a distinctive pattern in the snow, dripping oil forming dark Rorschach blots between the treads. The tracks circled back to the road that led away from the ranch. When Brodie reached the road, he turned and jogged back toward the house to retrieve his truck. Travis's SUV was still parked in front of the house, but the sheriff must still be inside.

Good. Brodie would follow Alex, and once he found him, he'd call for help. And heaven help the man if he hurt one hair on Emily's head.

The oil drip made Alex's tracks relatively easy to follow. Brodie wondered once again if Alex had planned it that way. The man didn't seem to do anything by accident. Had he set up an ambush to take down any law enforcement who followed him? Did he really think he could defeat a whole phalanx of lawmen? Maybe he thought Emily would be enough of a shield to protect him.

The idea made Brodie's stomach churn, but he told himself if Alex intended to use Emily as a shield, he would keep her alive as long as she was useful to him. And no matter what the murderer thought, he wasn't going to be able to outwit and outrun them much longer.

The oil drips turned onto the highway leading up to Dixon Pass. Brodie followed them, keeping his speed down, watching the roadsides for any sign of Alex or Emily, or anything that looked like a trap. Alex might be in disguise, or he might use other people to help him, as he had done before. But Brodie saw no other traffic or pedestrians as the road climbed toward the pass. He sped by the sign warning of the road closure, and was almost to the barricades when he spotted an old van, nose first in the snowbank that marked the site of the avalanche he and Gage had been caught in.

He pulled the truck in behind the van, blocking it, then sat for a long moment, staring at the empty vehicle, noting the puddle of oil beneath the rear axle and the opened passenger-side sliding door. The van had no license plate, and was scratched and battered, the bumper wired in place and a deep scratch running the length of the driver's side. Minutes passed, with no sign of life from the vehicle, and no sound but the ticking of the truck's cooling engine.

Weapon drawn, Brodie eased open the door and

exited the truck, then approached the van. The vehicle was empty, the keys dangling in the ignition. A glance inside showed a roll of duct tape on the back floorboard, and a single long, dark hair caught in a tear in the upholstery on the back seat. Brodie stared at the hair, struggling to rein in his emotions. Emily had been in this van. So where was she now?

The deep snow made it easy to follow a set of footprints and drag marks from the van, up over a berm of snow to a perfectly carved channel, just wide enough for one man to pass through.

Brodie crept down this channel, the cold closing in around him, as if he were passing through a freezer. He kept his weapon drawn, alert for any activity over and above him. But the only sound was the heavy inhale and exhale of his own breath.

He emerged at the top of a rise and stared down at the old Dixon Downhill ski resort. As before, all was silent. A single chair dangled from the old lift and no life stirred below him.

Except... He sniffed the air. Yes, that was smoke, rising in a thin ribbon from a stovepipe on the other side of the canyon, where the old ski lift shack huddled at the top of the lift line. Brodie stared at the smoke, a vise clamped around his heart. Then he turned and walked back to his truck, where, fingers shaking so hard he could hardly make them work, he punched in Gage's number. After three rings, Gage answered. "What's up?" he asked, the sounds of laughter behind him.

"I've found Alex," Brodie said. "He's got Emily. We've got to stop him before it's too late."

ALEX FED MORE wood into the cast-iron stove that crouched at one end of the lift shack, until the flames leaped and popped, the heat almost overpowering, even though Emily was sprawled on the bench seat from an old pickup truck that had been placed in the opposite corner of the little wooden building. Alex—or someone else—had also brought in a rusting metal table, two wooden stools and a cot draped in blankets, presumably where Alex slept. "They should be able to see the smoke from the highway," he said, closing the door of the stove and standing. "I did everything I could to draw them here, but they're so dim, I need to practically lead them by the hand."

"There'll be more of them than there are you," she said. "You can't kill them all."

He turned to face her, firelight reflecting in his eyes, making him look as insane as he probably was. "But I can." He swept a hand toward the slope opposite them. "I've got explosives planted everywhere on that slope. I stole the dynamite and fuses from the highway crew. They use them to set off avalanches when the road is closed. There's enough gunpowder out there to take out half the mountain."

"If you do that, you'll be killed, too," she said.

"I'll be gone before it blows. Of course, you'll still be here." He tilted his head, studying her. "Do you think I should kill you before I go—or let you die with your brothers in the explosions?"

She closed her eyes, unwilling to look at his face any longer. The mania in his eyes frightened her. Had the insanity been there all along and she had simply failed to see it, believing he was just another undergrad, not someone she really noticed?

"They're here." She opened her eyes at his words, in time to see him pick up a rifle and carry it to the sliding window that filled half of one side of the shack. Originally, the window had allowed the lift operator a view of the lift line and the skiers unloading at the top of the lift. Now it gave Alex a view back toward the opposite slope, beyond which the van was parked. "They're really going to make this too easy for me," he said, sliding the window open a few inches.

She tried to rise up and look past him out the window, but the pain in her arms and legs made movement difficult. The best she could manage was a view of the sky and the back of his head.

Without warning, a blast echoed through the shack. Emily screamed. Alex steadied the rifle against his shoulder and fired again. The smell of gunpowder filled the air, and cold from the open window settled over her like an icy blanket. Alex straightened and laughed. "You should see them out there, running around like frightened rabbits," he said. "I can't believe they thought they were just going to walk up here and take me."

Emily closed her eyes again and said a silent prayer that no one had been hurt.

A melody full of Celtic pipes and drums filled the small shack. Alex whirled to face Emily once more. "What is that?"

"I...I think it's my phone." How was that even possible? She'd been carrying the phone in her back pocket when she stepped out onto the porch, but she would have thought it would have either fallen out or been damaged as she was dragged, and then pushed, down the snowy road.

The music continued to play. Still clutching the rifle, Alex stalked over, shoved Emily onto her side and extracted the phone from the back pocket of her jeans. He studied the screen, then swiped to answer. "Emily can't take your call," he said. "She's a bit tied up at the moment." He laughed, and her stomach churned.

Alex moved back to the window, his back to her. "Who do you think this is? This is the Ice Cold Killer. Who is this? Wait. I'm going to put you on speaker."

"What have you done to Emily?" Brodie's voice boomed over the phone. She choked back a sob, though whether of relief or panic, she couldn't say.

"I haven't done anything to her...yet." Alex held the phone out toward her. "Say hello to Agent Langtry," he said.

"Brodie, it's a trap," she said. "He's—" But before she could finish her warning, Alex hit her, hard, almost knocking her off the seat. She tasted blood from her split lip.

"Let her go now." Brodie's voice was louder, more urgent. "Release her and we can negotiate with you."

"You don't expect me to believe that, do you?" Alex said. "After all, you think I murdered ten women. Besides, I need her. The sheriff and his deputies won't dare hurt me if it means hurting his dear baby sister, too."

"Let her go and take me," Brodie said. "They won't hurt you with a fellow cop as a shield."

Emily held her breath, not sure she had heard correctly. Why would Brodie offer to take her place with a killer?

"Oh, you do tempt me," Alex said. "But I'm not interested in you. I came here originally to kill Emily and I believe in carrying through with my plans."

"What do you want from us?" Brodie asked.

"I want you to play a game with me. You won't win, but I'll try to make it challenging."

"What is the game?"

"Where is the sheriff?" Alex asked. "I want to talk to the sheriff."

"He isn't here."

"Why not? Does he think his wedding is more important than me? More important than his sister?"

"Tell me what you want," Brodie said.

"No. I'm done talking with you now. And I'm destroying this phone. Don't bother calling back." He hit the button to end the call, then jerked open the door to the stove and tossed the phone inside. The smell of burning plastic filled the air.

"Isn't that noble of him, wanting to take your place?" Alex said.

Emily didn't have words to explain how Brodie's offer made her feel. Was he only doing his job as an officer of the law, or did she really mean that much to him?

BRODIE, GAGE, DWIGHT, Jamie, Nate, Ryder and Marshal Cody Rankin gathered at the top of the rise looking down onto the ski lift, just out of range of Alex's rifle. Brodie punched Emily's number again and listened to it ring and ring. "He probably really did destroy the phone," Ryder, who was standing next to Brodie, said. "He doesn't strike me as one to bluff."

"Maybe we should get Travis out here to talk to him," Dwight said.

"Not yet," Gage said. "Rob is with him. His job is to keep him occupied and in the dark." DEA agent Rob Allerton was Paige Riddell's boyfriend and had the least involvement of any of them in this case.

"Alex might make a deal with Travis," Dwight said.

"He's more likely to kill him," Gage said. "I promised Lacy I'd do my best to see that she wasn't a widow before she was a wife."

"How are we going to get closer to him?" Nate asked.

"The snow down in the valley must be six feet

deep," Jamie said. "You'd never get through there without a snow machine. Even if you could somehow manage on snowshoes, you'd have to climb down there first, and Alex would have plenty of time to see you and pick you off."

"How did he get up to the lift shack?" Brodie asked, studying the steep, rocky incline from the bottom of the lift to the top. "And how did he get Emily up there with him?"

"I think they rode the lift," Dwight said.

"The lift's broken," Gage said. "It hasn't worked in years."

"Maybe he figured out how to get it running," Brodie said. "Didn't you say it's powered by an old car motor?"

"That doesn't help us," Nate said. "If we try to start the lift, he'll just shoot us. He can let us get almost to him and pick us off."

"Maybe we could lure him out of the shack and pick him off with sniper fire," Ryder said.

"He'd never come out of that lift shack," Gage said. "Not without Emily as a shield. He's too smart for that."

"I still say we need to get Travis here to talk to him," Dwight said.

Brodie studied the scene below him while those around him debated the best approach. "What if instead of climbing up to him, we climb down?" he asked after a moment.

"Climb down from where?" Jamie asked.

"From above the lift shack." He indicated the cliff that rose behind the shack, part of a long ridge that formed the east side of the pass. "That may be how Alex got down there in the first place. He's a rock climber, right?"

"How would you even get there?" Gage asked, squinting at the mountain that rose above the lift shack.

"There's an old mining road that runs along there, just above the ski area," Nate said. "See that narrow ledge." He pointed, and Brodie thought he could make out the relatively horizontal path along the cliff face. "Climbers use it in the summer. You can take a Jeep up there then, but you'd have to snowshoe in now."

"And if Alex did turn around and see someone up there, he could pick them off with that rifle." Gage shook his head. "It's too risky."

"He hasn't got a view of the slope behind him from the lift shack," Brodie said. "He'd have to step outside to see anyone up there, and we've already established he's unlikely to do that. The thing we need to do is keep him distracted."

"How?" Jamie asked.

"We could take turns approaching behind cover and taking potshots at him," Dwight said. "Or launch flares at him."

"Have to be careful with that," Nate said. "You don't want to set off another avalanche."

"Okay, so we could probably distract him,"

Dwight said. "But who are we going to get to make the climb? It looks pretty technical."

"I've done some climbing," Brodie said. All of it in a gym, but they didn't have to know that. He knew how to use the equipment, and he was desperate to get Emily out of there before she suffered even more than she already had.

"It's too risky." Gage shook his head.

"It's our best chance of getting to him," Brodie said. "He won't be expecting it because he sees himself as the expert and we're all the amateurs. He's probably made the climb, but he believes we'd never attempt it."

"He's right. You shouldn't attempt it," Dwight said.

"If it was Brenda trapped there, would you do it?" Brodie asked.

Dwight compressed his lips together. "I don't know," he said after a moment. "I'm just glad my wife isn't in there with him."

Emily wasn't Brodie's wife, but if things had worked out differently, she might have been. He wasn't going to let her die if he could do something—even a crazy, reckless stunt like rappelling down an icy cliff—to save her.

He turned to Gage. "Where can I get climbing gear?"

Nate clapped Brodie on the shoulder. "I've got a friend who can fix you up."

"Then let's go. We don't have any time to waste."

Chapter Eighteen

Alex paced back and forth across the floor of the lift shack, alternately cursing to himself and stopping to stare out the window. "Why aren't they doing anything?" he asked. "Nobody up there has moved for the past half an hour." He turned back to Emily. "Maybe they've decided to just let you die. What do you think about that?"

She swallowed and held her head up, though every movement sent pain shooting through her. Alex had let the fire go out and the cold made the pain worse. She couldn't stop shivering, but Alex, dressed in a fleece top and jeans, didn't seem to notice. "Maybe they went to get Travis," she said. "You burned my phone, so they don't have any way of letting you know."

"They better not be planning any tricks. They'll find out soon enough they can't trick me. Do you know why I chose this place for this standoff?" He put his face very close to hers, so that she could smell his stale body odor. It must have been a while since he had showered. How long had he been living up here in this primitive shack? "Do you know?" he demanded.

"No."

"It's because that road up there—" he gestured with the rifle he still held "—that road is the only way in here." He laughed. "Unless they decided to try to land a helicopter down here. Not easy, and if they do, I'll just set off the explosives as soon as it touches down." He returned to watching out the window. "They can't get at me any other way."

"If they can't get in, how are you going to get out?" she asked.

He grinned, the expression in his eyes telling her he was long past any concrete grip on reality. "I'm going to climb out." He gestured behind them. "That cliff is a 5.9, maybe a 5.10 route. Expert only. But I've done it half a dozen times. I could do it with my eyes closed. By the time I make it to the top, they'll be trapped down here under tons of rock. I'll be far away from here, with a new identity, before anyone even starts to look for me."

"It sounds like you've thought of everything." She was back to flattery—anything to keep him talking and get on his good side.

"Of course I have. It's how I've been so successful so far. These country rubes aren't used to dealing with genius."

"You told them on the phone that you had a game for them to play," she said.

"For the sheriff. Of course, it's a game he can't win. I'm not stupid enough to design it any other way."

She wet her dry, cracking lips. "What is the game?"

"He has to guess the way I've planned for him to die."

"Why would he want to play a game like that?"

"If he guesses right, I'll slit your throat and you'll die quickly. If he guesses wrong..." He let the words trail away, leaving her to imagine the dozens of ways he might choose to make her suffer. She pushed the thoughts away. She wasn't dead yet. She wasn't going to give up hope. A person could live a long time on hope, or so she had read.

Hurry, she sent the thought to whatever rescuers might be mustering to help her. *Hurry, because I don't know how much longer I can hang on.*

"I'VE DONE THIS climb before, but not with the snow and ice." Nate's friend, a wiry thirtysomething who went by the single name Truman, handed Brodie a climbing helmet. "You're certifiable if you want to do it now."

"I don't have any choice." Brodie tugged the helmet on and fastened the chin strap, then reached for a pair of climbing gloves.

"We could try to bring in a helicopter," Nate said. "I bet he'd come outside when he heard that. We could probably get a good shot at him from inside the chopper."

"Or he could decide to kill Emily then and there." Brodie pulled a down jacket over his wool sweater. A Kevlar vest and thermal underwear added extra protection from the cold and gunfire, though he had doubts the vest would stop a bullet from a high-powered rifle—or prevent him from breaking every bone in his body if he fell from the cliff.

"The safety harness should protect you from a fall." Truman demonstrated hooking into the safety line. "It won't help if you bash into the rocks while you're swinging there, but if you lose contact with the cliff, we'll do our best to haul you up."

"I feel so much better now," Brodie said.

Truman made a face and ran through a checklist of the gear. None of the terms were new to Brodie, and he was beginning to feel more confident. "Come on," he said. "We need to get to the site where I'll start the downclimb." Every minute that passed was another minute that might cause Alex to lose patience and take his frustration out on Emily.

They drove as far as they could in Truman's Jeep, then strapped on snowshoes for the rest of the journey. They had to snowshoe almost two miles until they reached a point directly above the lift shack. Brodie peered down at the little tin-roofed building. "There's no smoke coming out of the stovepipe now," he said.

Nate was on the phone with Gage and relayed Brodie's observation. "Gage says Alex and Emily are still in there. He can see them through his binoculars."

"What are they doing?" Brodie asked.

"Just sitting there, he says. Waiting."

"Somebody's been climbing this route recently." Truman pulled back a tarp underneath a spindly fir to reveal a pair of snowshoes.

"Alex," Brodie said. "I figured he had to be getting to and from the shack this way, at least part of the time."

"Then you might be in luck," Truman said. "He may have set anchors in the rock that you can hook on to. Watch for areas cleared of snow—that might mark his hand- and footholds."

Brodie nodded and focused on checking and double-checking his safety harness.

"Why can't he just rappel down?" Nate asked. "It seems like that would be a lot faster."

"It would, if the cliff was straight down," Truman said. "But it's not. There are a lot of rocks and trees and stuff that stick out. Try to rappel that and you'll just smash into stuff. No, our man is going to have to downclimb." He grinned at Brodie. "Sucks to be you, dude."

Brodie grunted and moved to the edge of the cliff. "You two just hang on if I slip."

Truman moved up beside him. "The route is hard to see from this angle," he said. "We're sort of jutting out over most of the area you'll be descending. But there's a ledge about fifteen feet down that will be a good place to stop and rest."

"If we can't see him, how are we going to know what to do to help him?" Nate asked.

"You can get a good idea of what's happening by the feel of the ropes." Truman clapped Brodie on the back. "Ready?"

Brodie nodded. His brain was telling him he was crazy to risk his life this way, but he was ignoring his brain. His heart was saying he didn't have a choice, and he was choosing to go with his heart. "Tell the others it's time to start whatever they've come up with to distract Alex."

"I've told them," Nate said. "Good luck."

The first step off the cliff, blindly groping for a foothold in the slick rock, was the worst. Relief surged through him as his foot found purchase and he was able to steady himself, but he couldn't stop to enjoy the sensation. He had to keep going. Glancing down, he could see the shallow rock ledge Truman had mentioned, and he focused on getting to it. One foot here, one hand there. Test the next foothold to see if it would support his weight. Reject another foothold as too weak or too slick. He wedged his foot into a niche in the rock. It felt secure, so he lowered himself down, searching for the next foothold.

Then the rock gave way. He flailed around, seeking purchase and finding none, swinging free against the rock face, like a pendulum in a crazy clock. Truman, very pale and very far away, looked over from the top. They had agreed that they couldn't shout to one another for fear of attracting Alex's attention.

Nate also leaned out and gave him a thumbs-up. Truman pointed to the ledge and pantomimed lowering the rope. Brodie nodded. They were going to lower him to the ledge. Good idea.

Once safely on the ledge, he rested a moment, his body plastered to the rock, the cold seeping into him despite the layers of clothing. In contrast, the sun at his back burned. When he was breathing more or less regularly again, he tugged on the rope, a signal that he was ready to start down once more.

He fell three more times on the way down, each time the safety harness catching him, the rope stretching and bouncing him slightly. He learned to relax until the swaying slowed, then to find purchase in the rock once more. As Truman had guessed, Alex had hammered pitons into the rock face, allowing Brodie to clip into these as he moved down the cliff, untethering from Truman and Nate above.

About three-quarters of the way down he realized he was no longer afraid. He was actually doing this. The adrenaline rush was exhilarating, and if what awaited him at the end of the climb wasn't so important, he might have lingered to enjoy himself.

But he had no time to indulge himself. He moved as quickly as possible. When he touched ground only a dozen feet behind the lift shack, his hand shook as he unhooked from the safety rope and climbed out of the harness. He took the time to roll up everything and stash it underneath a tree, not wanting to provide an escape route if Alex managed to make it out of the lift shack before Brodie got to him.

He straightened, drew his weapon and started toward the shack. His plan was to go in, surprise Alex and make an arrest with no one getting hurt. It was a good plan, but he had no idea if it would really work.

EMILY HAD FALLEN into a kind of stupor on the old car seat, while Alex slumped on a stool in front of the window, the rifle propped against the wall beside him. Earlier, she had spent some time groping around the seat, hoping to find a popped spring or a protruding bit of metal to cut the tape at her wrists or ankles, but no such luck. All she could do was wait and pray. She tried asking Alex questions about himself, but after a while he had stopped answering her.

Suddenly, he shoved back the stool and stood. "It's about time," he said.

Emily pushed herself up straighter. "What's happening?" she asked.

Alex gestured toward the window. "They've found a way to communicate."

By arching her back and craning her neck, Emily was able to make out someone holding what looked like a poster with writing on it. But it was too far away to read. "What does it say?" she asked.

Alex pulled out a pair of binoculars and studied the sign. "*THE SHERIFF IS READY TO TALK.*"

"Travis is there?" Emily's heart pounded. Travis shouldn't be here! He should be with Lacy, getting married.

Alex scowled. "There's someone there in a sheriff's department uniform, with a big hat and a star on his chest, but I can't tell if it's your brother." He set down the binoculars and looked around the lift shack. "I need something to write on. I need to tell him to move in closer—and to take off the stupid hat."

"You should have thought of that before you burned up my phone." Emily braced herself for another blow, but Alex only scowled at her and began digging through the debris against the walls of the shack. Amazingly, he came up with a small whiteboard, roughly two-foot square. Emily recalled seeing similar boards at lift shacks at other resorts, used to convey messages such as "Mr. Reynolds, contact child care" or "New snow overnight 4 inches!"

In a drawer, Alex found a set of dry-erase markers. He scrawled his message, *COME CLOSER AND TAKE OFF THE HAT.*

"They're not going to be able to see that from in here," Emily said. "You'll have to go outside."

"And give them a clear shot at me?" Alex shook his head. "No, you'll go out." He pulled the knife from his belt and she shrank back in fear. But he bent and cut the tape from her ankles, then did the same for her wrists.

She cried out as she brought her hands in front of her again, the stabbing pain doubling her over.

Alex chafed her ankles between his hands. "You'll be fine in a minute." He straightened and thrust the sign and the marker at her. "Go out there and hold this up. And don't try anything. If you run, I'll shoot you in the back." He held up the rifle.

She gripped the board with numb, aching fingers and he tucked the marker into the pocket of her jeans and hauled her to her feet. She could barely walk, much less run. Alex took her arm and dragged her toward the door of the lift shack. "Get out there!" he called, and thrust her out the door.

She landed sprawling in the snow, the sign face-down beside her. "Get up!" Alex shouted, and she looked back to see the rifle pointed at her.

Clenching her teeth, she shoved to her knees, then slowly stood, bringing the sign with her. Holding on to the lift shack for support, she made her way around to the side facing the road, moving through snow that came past her knees. Finally she stopped and held up the sign. Seconds later, an answer appeared: *YOU OKAY?* in letters large enough to be seen clearly even at that distance.

She nodded, hoping someone was watching through binoculars. Then she scrawled *YES* beneath Alex's message. A cold wind buffeted her, and she was shaking so badly she had trouble holding on to the sign. "Get back in here!" Alex shouted.

She wanted to ignore the command, to run as fast and as far as she could. But that wouldn't be very far. The snow here was several feet deep and she could scarcely move. She would be dead before she took more than a few steps.

"Get in!" Alex shouted again.

Instead, she moved up against the lift shack once more, the thick logs providing a barrier to the wind and, she hoped, bullets from the man inside. She sank into the snow and sat, arms wrapped around her knees. Alex couldn't see her from here, and he wouldn't be able to shoot her without coming outside—something he apparently was loath to do. She would sit here until her strength returned and some of the pain in her limbs subsided. By then, maybe someone below would have come up here to her, or found a way to get to her. Having her out of the way might even help them.

Alex was screaming now, a stream of profanities aimed at her. She closed her eyes and shut him out, focusing instead on the whistle of the wind around the corner of the lift shack, and the creak of the chair on the overhead cable.

And the sound of footsteps moving through the snow.

Her eyes snapped open, fear choking her. Alex's rage at her must have overcome his fear of leaving the shack. But instead of Alex, she was amazed to see Brodie standing at the corner of the shack, one finger to his lips. "How?" She had scarcely uttered the single syllable before he shook his head. He motioned for her to stay where she was, and indicated he intended to go inside the shack.

She shook her head. If Brodie went in there, Alex

would kill him. He had the rifle, and a knife, and then there were the explosives everywhere on the mountain. How could she warn Brodie without Alex overhearing? She picked up the sign and rubbed out the message there with the sleeve of her sweater, then wrote, *HE HAS EXPLOSIVES ALL OVER THE MOUNTAIN. WILL DETONATE.*

Brodie read the message and nodded. Then his eyes met hers, and the determination and, yes, love in that single glance made her almost giddy. Then he was gone, around the back of the shack once more.

Emily shoved to her feet. She couldn't sit here, not knowing what was happening with Brodie and Alex. She followed Brodie around the back of the shack, floundering through the thick snow, which covered the sound of her approach. At the door of the shack he stopped, weapon raised, then burst inside.

She braced herself for the blast of gunfire or the sounds of a struggle, but only ringing silence followed. Cautiously, she moved forward, until she was just outside the open door. "What's happening?" she called.

"He isn't here," Brodie called. He stood over the table, examining the items scattered across it. "He must have slipped out while I was with you."

"A very good deduction," Alex said as he grabbed Emily from behind and put a knife to her throat.

This can't be happening, Emily thought, as Alex crushed her against him. The knife bit into her throat, but she scarcely felt it, as if her body was becoming immune to pain.

"Let her go," Brodie said, his gun leveled at Alex.

"Drop the gun or she dies now." Alex pulled her more tightly against him, so that she could hardly breathe, her body angled so that she was between his legs, one hand almost resting on his groin.

Brodie tossed the gun aside. It sank out of sight in the snow. "What now?" he asked.

"That's right," Alex said. "I'm calling the shots."

Emily gripped the dry-erase marker in her hand. As weapons went, it was pathetic. But it was all she had. Several years before, when she was an under-grad, she had attended a presentation on self-defense. All she could remember was the instructor's advice to use whatever was at hand as a weapon. Most of the feeling had returned to her fingers. She made a fist around the marker, then drove it as hard as she could into Alex's groin.

The knife slid across her throat, but she was able to shove out of Alex's grasp as he doubled over. Brodie jumped on him and the two grappled in the snow. Emily knelt by the shack, watching in horror as blood stippled the pristine surface of the snow with red.

The two men rolled over and over in the snow, first Brodie on top, then Alex. With a cry of rage, Alex heaved Brodie off him and jumped to his feet. Then he was running, headed for the cliff. He began to climb, clambering up the steep slope without aid of harness or ropes or even gloves.

Brodie knelt beside Emily. "It's bleeding a lot, but I don't think the cuts are too deep," he said. He stripped out of his jacket, peeled off his sweater and wrapped it around her neck.

"There's a rifle in the shack," she said through chattering teeth. "You need to get it and go after him."

"It's okay," he said, one arm wrapped around her. "Nate and another man are waiting at the top of the cliff. He won't get away from them."

They stared as Alex scaled the cliff, swarming up the rock face. Emily gasped as he slipped, then regained his foothold. "He's going too fast," Brodie said. "He's being reckless."

He was almost to the top, where the rock jutted out and he had to pull himself over it. He had almost made it when something at the top caught his attention. "It's Nate," Brodie said. "He's got him covered."

A rope dropped over the edge of the cliff and dangled beside Alex. "Nate will pull him up and arrest him," Brodie said.

But Alex didn't take the rope. Instead, he looked back over his shoulder. He took one hand from the rock and balanced for a second, before releasing the other hand and falling backward.

Emily buried her face in Brodie's shoulder. Alex's cries echoed around them, then all fell silent. "Is he dead?" she asked.

"If he isn't, he's badly hurt." He stood. "Gage is

sending a couple of snowmobiles down to get us. Let's go meet them."

"Can we sit here a little bit, until they get here?" she asked.

"Are you too weak to walk?" His voice rose in alarm. "Do you want me to carry you?"

"No, I don't want you to carry me." The idea made her want to laugh.

"What's so funny?"

"I'm wondering if there's a statute of limitations on proposals."

He hesitated, then said. "What do you mean?"

She pressed her palms to his chest, over his heart, and looked into his eyes. "I mean, I don't want you to carry me. But I might want you to marry me."

"Because I scaled a cliff and faced death to save you?"

"Because you did those things. And because I love you. More than I was willing to admit before."

"Why weren't you willing to admit it?"

"Are you always so full of questions?"

"I want to be sure you're not out of your mind from loss of blood."

"I turned down your proposal before because I was afraid of what I would have to give up if we married," she said. "Now I'm old enough to see that marriage isn't about giving things up—it's about gaining a partner who can help you get even more out of life."

He gently brushed her hair back from her face

and looked into her eyes. "Emily Walker, will you marry me?" he asked.

Tears—of relief, and such joy she could hardly contain it—flooded her eyes and she pressed her lips to his.

The roar of an approaching snowmobile interrupted their kiss. Two more snowmobiles followed. They stopped nearby and Gage pulled off his helmet. "Are you okay?" he asked.

"Emily's wounded," Brodie said. "I'm fine." He looked toward the cliff. "Alex is either dead or wounded."

The man on the second snowmobile collected a medical kit from the back of the machine and started through the snow toward the cliff. The driver of the third snowmobile, a woman, approached Emily. "Let's take a look," she said, and began to unwind Brodie's sweater. She surveyed the wound. "It's mostly stopped bleeding. You might need a few stitches and you might be more comfortable wearing scarves for a while, but in a year or two I'll bet the scar hardly shows."

"I'll take a scar over the alternative," she said.

"I'll just get you cleaned up a bit," the woman said, and opened her medical kit.

The other paramedic returned, shaking his head. "That one doesn't need me anymore," he said.

Emily tried to feel some sympathy or sorrow for the man Alex might have been—handsome, smart, with every advantage. But she felt only emptiness.

She didn't have it in her to hate someone so twisted, but she could admit she was relieved he would never terrorize anyone else again.

The paramedic helped her to the snowmobile and assisted her in climbing on. Brodie rode behind Gage. They were at the top again before Emily remembered one of the most important questions of the day. She looked at Gage. "Where is Travis?"

Gage checked his watch. "I hope he's getting married about now."

"But you're the best man," she said. "And I'm one of the bridesmaids."

"I think they can finish the ceremony without us," Gage said.

"He's going to be furious when he finds out what happened," Emily said.

"He is. But he'll get over it."

"Get over what?"

They turned to see Travis, a leather duster pulled on over his tux, striding toward them. Lacy, a down parka over her wedding dress, and the rest of the wedding party trailed behind. "What are you doing here?" Gage demanded.

"I came to see this case to the finish." He turned to Emily. "Are you okay?"

She nodded. "I'll be fine." At least, she would be, given time to rest and heal.

Travis nodded and turned back to Gage. "Alex?"

"He's dead."

"He jumped off the cliff, rather than face arrest," Brodie said.

"It's over," Emily said, the impact just beginning to hit her. "It's really over."

"It is." Gage put one arm around his brother. "You can leave the mop-up to us. Now you can get on with the honeymoon."

"We have to get married first," Lacy said.

"You're not married yet?" Emily asked.

"We couldn't get married with most of the wedding party—and some of the guests—up here on the pass," she said.

"You all weren't coming to the wedding, so we decided to bring the wedding to you," Bette said. She indicated everyone around them. "We're all here, but it's a little chilly, so let's get going, why don't we?"

Emily put a hand to her throat. "But I'm not dressed for a wedding."

"No one is looking at you." Bette handed her a bouquet. "Now hold this, stand over there. Lacy, you stand here."

Bette arranged everyone, and within five minutes Emily was blinking back tears as her eldest brother and her dear friend promised to love, honor and cherish each other for the rest of their lives. The officiant pronounced them husband and wife and they kissed as a tinny rendition of the Wedding March—courtesy of someone's phone—serenaded them.

"Now everyone come back to the reception," Bette said. Gage started to object, but she held up a hand. "I know what you're going to say. You have a crime scene to process. I'll send refreshments back to you."

"If it's all right with you, I'll stay with Emily," Brodie said.

"You do that," Travis said. "I think I can trust you to take good care of her this time."

"This time, and for every time to come," he said.

The others piled into their vehicles and drove away, Travis and Lacy in a white pickup truck with tin cans tied to the back and *Just Married* scrawled across the back window. Then Brodie walked Emily to the ambulance and climbed in after her. "I don't think you ever gave me an answer to my proposal," he said, taking her hand.

"Yes," she said. "Yes, I'll marry you."

He held her gaze, steady and sure. "I never want to hold you back from your dreams," he said. "I only want to be part of them."

"You are." She kissed him, a sweet meeting of their lips full of promise and hope and all things she was determined to never give up again.

* * * * *

STORM WARNING

MICHELE HAUF

Chapter One

Jason Cash squeezed the throttle on the snowmobile he handled as if a professional racer. The five-hundred-pound sled took to the air for six bliss-filled seconds. Snow sprays kissed Jason's cheeks. Sun glinted in the airborne crystals. The machine landed on the ground, skis gliding smoothly onto the trail. With an irrepressible grin on his face, he raced down an incline toward the outer limits of Frost Falls, the small Minnesota town where he served as chief of police.

Thanks to his helmet's audio feed, a country tune twanged in his ears. His morning ride through the pristine birch forest that cupped the town on the north side had been interrupted by a call from his secretary/dispatcher through that same feed. He couldn't complain about the missed winter thrills when a much-needed mystery waited ahead.

Maneuvering the snowmobile through a choppy field with shifts of his weight, he steered toward a roadside ditch, above which were parked the city patrol car and a white SUV he recognized as a county vehicle. Sighting a thick undisturbed wedge of snow that had drifted from the gravel road to form an inviting ridge, Jason aimed for the sparkling payload, accelerated and pierced the ridge. An exhilarated shout spilled free.

Gunning the engine, he traveled the last fifty feet, then braked and spun out the back of the machine in a spectacular snow cloud that swirled about him. He parked and turned off the machine.

Flipping up the visor and peeling off his helmet, he glanced to the woman and young man who stood twenty yards away staring at him. At least one jaw dropped open in awe.

A cocky wink was necessary. Jason would never miss a chance to stir up the powder. And every day was a good day when it involved gripping it and ripping it.

Setting his helmet emblazoned with neon-green fire on the snowmobile seat, he tugged down the thermal face mask from his nose and mouth to hook under his chin. The thermostat read a nippy ten degrees. Already ice crystals formed on the sweat that had collected near his eyebrows. He did love the brisk, clean air.

It wasn't so brutally cold today as it had been last week when temps had dipped below zero. But the warm-up forecast a blizzard within forty-eight hours. He looked forward to snowmobiling through the initial onset, but once the storm hit full force, he'd hole up and wait for the pristine powder that would blanket the perimeter of the Boundary Waters Canoe Area Wilderness, where he liked to blaze his own trails.

Clapping his gloved hands together, he strode over to his crack team of homicide investigators. Well, today they earned that title. It was rare Frost Falls got such interesting work. Rare? The correct term was *nonexistent*. Jason was pleased to have something more challenging on his docket than arresting Ole Svendson after a good drunk had compelled him to strip to his birthday suit and wander down Main Street. A man shouldn't have to see such things. And so frequently.

He almost hated to share the case with the Bureau of Criminal Apprehension, but Marjorie had already put in a call to them. Someone from the BCA would arrive soon. Standard procedure when a homicide occurred within city limits.

"Cash." Alex Larson, who had just graduated from the police academy and headed north from the Twin Cities to find work, with hopes of eventually getting placed on search and rescue, nodded as Jason walked nearer. The tall, gangly man was twenty-four and had an eye for safety and a curiosity for all things female. Unfortunately, most of the women in Frost Falls were over forty. Not many of the younger ones stuck around after high school. Smart move in a dying town. The Red Band iron mine had closed four years ago. That closure had sent the migrant workers—and far too many locals—packing in search of a reliable paycheck.

Alex was the only officer Jason needed in the little town of Frost Falls, population 627.

Though, from the looks of things, the population was now 626.

A middle-aged woman, wearing a black goose-down coat that fell to her knees and bright red cap, scarf and mittens, stood beside Alex. Elaine Hester was a forensic pathologist with the St. Louis County medical examiner's office. She traveled the seven-hundred-square-mile area so often she joked about selling her property in Duluth and getting herself an RV. She gestured toward the snowy ditch that yet sported the dried brown heads of fall's bushy cattails. The forthcoming blizzard would clip that punky crop down to nothing.

"What have you got, Elaine?" Jason asked, even though his dispatcher, Marjorie, had already told him about the body.

Jason led the team toward the ditch and saw the sprawled female body dressed in jeans and a sweater—no coat, gloves or hat—long black hair, lying facedown. The snow might have initially melted due to her body heat, so she was sunk in to her ears, and as death had forfeited her natural heat, the warmed slush had iced up around her and now crusted in the fibers of her red sweater.

"Female, mid- to late-twenties. Time of death could be last evening," Elaine reported in her usual detached manner. She held a camera and had likely already snapped a few shots. "Didn't want to move the body for closer inspection until you arrived, Cash. You call in the BCA?"

"On their way. We can continue processing the crime scene. The BCA will help, if necessary. Last night, eh?"

"I suspect she was dumped here around midnight-ish."

Jason met Alex's gaze, above which the officer's brow quirked. They both tended to share a silent snicker at Elaine's frequent use of *ish* tacked to the end of words when she couldn't be exact.

"How do you know she was—" Jason drew his gaze from the body and up the slight ditch incline to the gravel road. The marks from a body sliding over the snow were obvious. "Right. Dumped."

Jason studied the ground, noting the footprints, which were obviously from Elaine's and Alex's boots, as they'd remained only on this side of the body. They hadn't contaminated the crime scene. That was Elaine's forte: meticulous forensics.

Jason walked a wide circle around the victim's head and up the ditch to the road. As he did so, Elaine snapped away, documenting every detail of the scene with photographs. Though they were still within city limits, this was not a main road. Rather, it was one of four that left the town and either dead-ended or led deeper north into the Boundary Waters Canoe Area Wilderness, a million-plus-acre natural reserve within the Superior National Forest that hugged the Canadian border. The only people who used this road were two families who both lived about ten miles out of Frost Falls. The gravel road showed no deep tracks in the mix of snow, ice and pebble, like if a vehicle were to take off quickly after disposing of evidence. But there were boot prints where the gravel segued into dead grass long packed down by snow.

Jason bent and decided they were a woman's boot prints for the narrowness.

"Marjorie said a woman called in the sighting?" Jason asked Alex.

"Yes, sir," Alex offered. "Call came from Susan Olson, who works at The Moose in the, er—ahem—back." If Alex hadn't been wearing a face mask, Jason felt sure he'd see him blush. The back of The Moose offered a low-class strip show on Saturday nights—basically, Susan and a few corny Halloween costumes that had fit her better back in high school. "Miss Olson was driving out to her aunt's place to check in on her when she saw something glint in the ditch."

Jason shuffled down into the ditch, avoiding Elaine as she stepped around the woman's head. "Evidence?" he asked Alex.

"Just the body and the clothing on it. No phone or glasses or personal items that may have fallen out from a pocket. I'll bag the hands and head soon as Elaine gives me the go-ahead. Any tracks up there?"

"They're from the caller, I'm sure. But take pictures of the tracks, will you, Elaine? We'll have to see if Susan's fashion lends to size-eight Sorels, if my guess is correct."

"Of course. Nice thing about snow—it holds a good impression of boot tracks. I hope it's Ryan Bay with the BCA."

Jason cast her a look that didn't disguise his dislike for the guy for reasons he couldn't quite place. He'd only met him twice, but there was something about him.

Elaine noticed his crimped smirk and shrugged. "Guy's a looker. And he's easygoing. I can do what I need to do without him wanting to take charge."

"A looker, eh?"

There it was. She'd nailed his dislike in a word. A looker. What the hell did that mean? Wasn't as if handsome held any weight in this small town. Least not when a man was in the market to hook up. Again, no eligible women as far as a man's eye could see.

"You're still the sexiest police chief in St. Louis County, Cash." Elaine adjusted the lens on her camera. "But if you won't let me fix you up with my niece…"

The niece. She mentioned her every time they had

occasion to work together. Blind dates gave Jason the creeps. His brother Joe had once gone on one. That woman had literally stalked him for weeks following. Yikes.

"Didn't you mention she was shortish?" Jason asked with a wink to Alex.

"Short girls need love, too, Jason." The five-foot-two-inch woman laughed. "Don't worry. I know she's not your type."

Jason squatted before the body, thinking that if Elaine actually did know his type— What was he thinking? Of course, she did. Along with everyone else in the county. The gossip in these parts spread as if it had its own high-speed internet service.

Focusing on the body, with a gloved hand he lifted the long black hair that had been covering the woman's face. Her skin was pale and blue. Her lips purple. Closed eyelids harbored frost on the lashes. No visible signs of struggle or blood. She was young. Pretty. He'd not seen her in Frost Falls before. And he had a good mental collection of all the faces in town. A visitor? She could have been murdered anywhere. The assailant may have driven from another town to place her here.

In the distance, the flash of headlights alerted all three at the same time.

"BCA," Elaine said. "We'll review the evidence with them and then bag the body."

"You'll transport the body to Duluth?" Jason asked.

"Yes," she said. "You going to follow me in for the autopsy?"

"You going to process it this morning?" Duluth was about an hour's drive to the east.

Elaine shook her head. "Probably not. But I will get to it after lunch. If you can meet me around oneish, that would work."

"Will do."

The white SUV bearing the BCA logo on the side door pulled up twenty feet from Alex's patrol car and idled. Looked like the driver was talking on the phone. Jason squinted. Couldn't make out who the driver was. A looker, eh? Why did that weird comment bother him?

It didn't. Really. He had a lot on his plate now. And he wasn't the type for jealously or even envy.

He glanced over the body of the unfamiliar woman. Pretty. And so young. It was a shame. "Any ID on her?"

"No, but she's probably Canadian," Elaine said.

Jason raised a brow at that surprising assessment.

Elaine bent and pushed aside the woman's hair with the tip of her penlight to reveal a tiny red tattoo of a maple leaf at the base of the victim's ear.

"Right." Jason frowned. "Are those ligature marks on her neck?"

"Yes." Elaine snapped a few close-up shots of the bruising now revealed on the woman's neck. "There's your signs of struggle right there. Poor thing." She replaced the victim's hair in the exact manner it had been lying and stood. "Looks like you just might have a murder case on your hands."

He'd suspected as much. Even though the weather could be treacherous and oftentimes deadly in the winter, the evidence screamed foul play.

"We'll get the BCA up to speed here, then I'm heading in to talk to Susan Olson," Jason said.

Jason had seen a lot, and he wasn't going to allow

some psychopath to think he could get away with murder. As well, this was his first big case since his humiliating demotion from the CIA. The timing was either laughable or fortuitous, depending on how he looked at it. Because he'd just received notice that the police station had been marked for budget cuts. In all likelihood, it would close in March and Frost Falls would send all their dispatch calls through the county. The tiny town couldn't afford to pay Jason's meager salary anymore. But the notice had also mentioned it wasn't necessary to employ someone who was merely a town babysitter and not involved in real criminal procedures.

That one had cut deep. He was not a babysitter. Sure, he'd taken this job out of desperation. Getting ousted from the CIA was not a man's finest moment. Yet he had made this job his own. And he did have a lot on his plate, what with the domestic abuse calls, the poaching and—the public nudity.

Time to prove he wasn't incompetent to all those who were watching and taking notes. And with any luck? He might earn back his pride and a second chance.

Chapter Two

Nine a.m. on a lazy Sunday. Most of the Frost Falls inhabitants were at church in the neighboring town or sat at The Moose noshing on waffles and bacon. Most, but not all.

Susan Olson yawned and scrubbed a hand over her long, tangled red hair. Her eyes were smeared with dark eye makeup, and one streak veered up toward her temple. She wore a Black Veil Brides T-shirt and bright pink sweatpants. They might have graduated the same year, but Jason had been born and raised in Crooked Creek, a town sixty miles west from here. Susan had lived in Frost Falls all her life.

Another yawn preceded "Really? Do you know what time it is, Chief Cash?"

"I do," Jason reported. He turned his head to block the wind that whipped at the front of the house. "Heard you found something interesting this morning."

"I knew you'd be stopping by. Just thought it would be at a decent hour. Come in."

Jason stepped inside the tiny rambler that might have been built in the '40s. It boasted green shag carpeting in the front living area; the walls were painted pink and—

did they have glitter on them? He stayed on the rug before the door. His boot soles were packed with snow.

"Just have a few questions, then you can head back to bed," he said. "I know Saturdays are your busy night. Hate to bother you, but a woman has been murdered."

"She was murdered?" Susan's eyes opened wider. She clutched her gut and searched the floor. "I thought maybe she just died from, like, frostbite or something. Oh my God. I remember her. I mean, I didn't touch the body, but I did see her face this morning. I always run to check on my aunt Sunday mornings, even though I'm so raging tired after my shift."

"You..." Jason leaned forward, making sure he'd heard correctly. He tugged out the little notebook he always carried from inside his coat. Pen at the ready, he asked, "Remember her? The woman in the ditch?"

"Her and three others. It was Lisa Powell's clique. Must have been someone's birthday. They were loaded and loose last night. But the woman in the ditch didn't look familiar to me. I mean, I don't think she was from around here. It's not difficult to know all the locals."

Jason nodded and wrote down the information.

"She tipped me a ten," Susan said with a curl of a smile. "Doesn't happen often, let me tell you. The people in this town are so stingy."

"She was with Lisa Powell, and—do you know the names of the other two?"

"Hannah Lindsey and, oh, some older woman. Might have been one of their mothers. They are all older than me, don't ya know." She tilted out a hip and fluffed back her hair with a sweep of hand. "Must be in their late thirties, for heaven's sake."

Jason placed Susan at around thirty, same as him.

"Not an issue right now," Jason said. "How long were the women in The Moose? Did they all leave together? Who else was watching your performance?"

Susan yawned. "That's a lot of questions, Cash."

"I know. You got coffee?"

"I do, but I really don't want to wake up that much. I usually sleep until four on Sundays. Do we have to do this now?"

"We do. You'll remember much more detail now as opposed to later. And I have an appointment in Duluth in a few hours I can't miss."

Susan sighed and dropped her shoulders. "Fine. I got one of those fancy coffee machines for Christmas from my boyfriend. I'll make you a cup. Kick off your wet boots before you walk on my carpet, will you, Cash?"

"Will do."

Jason toed off his boots, then followed Susan into the kitchen, where a strange menagerie of pigs wearing sunglasses decorated every surface—all the dishware and even the light fixtures.

Yvette LaSalle wandered down the tight aisles in the small grocery store set smack-dab in the center of Main Street in Frost Falls. The ice on her black hair that had sneaked out from under her knit cap melted and trickled down her neck. If she didn't zip up and wrap her scarf tight when she went outside, that trickle would freeze and— *Dieu.*

Why Minnesota? Of all the places in the world. And to make life less pleasant, it was January. The temperature had not been out of the teens since she had arrived. Sure, they got snow and cold in France. But not so utterly brutal. This place was not meant for human survival. Seriously.

But survive she would. If this was a test, she intended to ace it, as she did with any challenge.

This little store, called Olson's Oasis, sold basic food items, some toiletries, fishing bait and tackle (because crazy people drilled holes on the lake ice and actually fished in this weather), and plenty of cheap beer. A Laundromat was set off behind the freezer section. It boasted two washers and one semiworking dryer. The store was also the hub for deliveries, since the UPS service apparently didn't venture beyond Main Street.

Frost Falls was a virtual no-man's land. The last vestige of civilization before the massive Superior National Forest that capped the state and embraced the land with flora, fauna and so many lakes. This tiny town reminded Yvette of the village where her grandparents had lived in the South of France. Except Frost Falls had more snow. So. Much. Snow.

"Survival," she muttered with determination, but then rolled her eyes. She never would have dreamed a vacation from her job in gorgeous Lyon would require more stamina than that actual job. Mental stamina, that was.

But this wasn't a vacation.

Something called lutefisk sat wrapped in plastic behind the freezer-case glass. Vacillating on whether to try the curious fish, she shook her head. The curing process had something to do with soaking the fish in lye, if she recalled correctly from a conversation with the store's proprietor last week. It was a traditional Nordic dish that the locals apparently devoured slathered in melted butter.

Not for her.

Fresh veggies and fruits were not to be had this time of year, so Yvette subsisted on frozen dinners and pre-packaged salads from the refrigerator case.

Her boss at Interpol, Jacques Patron, would call any day now. *Time to come home, Amelie. The coast is clear.* Every day she hoped for that call.

Unless he'd already tried her. She had gotten a strange hang-up call right before entering the store. The number had been blocked, but when she'd answered, the male voice had asked, "Yvette?" She'd automatically answered, "Yes," and then the connection had clicked off.

Wrong numbers generally didn't know the names of those they were misdialing. And an assumed name, at that. Had it been Jacques? Hadn't sounded like him. But he'd only said her name. Hard to determine identity from one word. Impossible to call back with the unknown number. And would her boss have used her cover name or her real name?

The call was not something to take lightly. But she couldn't simply call up Interpol and ask them for a trace. She was supposed to be dark. She and her boss were the only people aware of her location right now. She'd try her boss's number when she returned to the cabin.

Tossing a bag of frozen peas into her plastic basket, she turned down the aisle and inspected the bread selections. Not a crispy, crusty baguette to be found. But something called Tasty White seemed to be the bestseller. She dropped a limp loaf in her basket. She might be able to disguise the processed taste with the rhubarb jam that she'd found in a welcome gift basket when she'd arrived at the rental cabin.

When the bell above the store's entrance clanged, she peered over the low shelves. A couple of teenage boys dressed in outdoor gear and helmets joked about the rabbit they'd chased with their snowmobiles on the ride into town.

Town? More like a destitute village with a grocery/post office/fish and tackle shop/Laundromat, and a bar/diner/strip joint—yes, The Moose diner offered "pleasure chats" and "sensual dancing" in the far back corner after 10:00 p.m. on Saturday nights. The diner did dish up a hearty meal, though, and Yvette's stomach was growling.

Her gaze averted from the boys and focused beyond the front door and out the frost-glazed window. Had that black SUV been parked before The Moose when she'd arrived? It looked too clean. Not a beat-up rust bucket like most of the locals drove. And it wasn't dusted with a grayish coating of deicing salt that they seemed to sprinkle on their roads more than their meals around here. She couldn't see the license plates to determine if it was a rental.

Yvette was alert for something she felt was imminent but was unable to say exactly what that could be. It reminded her of when she'd worked in the field. A field operative had to stay on her toes and be constantly aware of her surroundings, both physical and auditory. A wise state to embrace, especially in a town not her own.

She'd take a closer look at the SUV after she'd purchased her groceries.

The teenagers paid for energy drinks and left the store in a spill of laughter. Making her way to the checkout, Yvette set her basket on the counter.

"Bonjour, Yvette." Colette, the shop owner, a Canadian expatriate Yvette had bonded with because she spoke fluent French, fussed with the frilled pink polka-dot apron she wore over a slim-fitting black turtleneck and slacks. "Twenty dollars will do it."

Surely the bill was thirty or more.

Yvette nodded, unaccustomed to kindnesses, yet receiving such generosity felt like a warm summer breeze brushing her icy neck. Very much needed lately.

She handed over the money. Colette packed up her provisions and helped Yvette fit it all into the backpack she brought along for such trips. She looked forward to riding the snowmobile into town for twice-weekly grocery trips. And today, despite the single-digit temperature, boasted bright white sunshine. A girl could not ignore fresh air and the beautiful landscape. She always brought along her camera and stopped often to snapshots. It was a good cover for an agent, but photography had also always been a hobby she'd wanted to take to the next level.

"Those wool leggings look *très chic* on you," Colette commented, with a slide of her gaze down Yvette's legs. "But you really do need to wear snow pants if you're snowmobiling in this weather."

"I've got on layers." Yvette waggled a leg. The heavy boots she wore were edged with fake fur, and the leggings were spotted with white snowflakes on a blue background. Beneath, she wore thermal long johns, an item of clothing she hadn't been aware existed until she'd arrived here in the tundra. A quilted down coat topped it all.

Fitting the backpack over her shoulders, she paused at the door while Colette walked around the counter and met her with a zip up of her waterproof coat and a tug at her scarf (which happened to match her leggings—score one for fashion).

"You don't have a helmet to keep your ears warm?" Colette asked. She eyed Yvette's knit cap with the bobble of red pom-pom on the top. "You foreigners. I'm surprised your ears don't drop off with frostbite. It's colder than a polar bear's toenails out there. And with the wind chill? *Uff da*." The woman shuddered.

"Don't you mean *mon Dieu*?" Yvette countered.

Colette laughed. "Minnesota has gotten into my blood, *chère*. It's *uff da* here. Want me to order a helmet for you?" She tapped the pom-pom. "We order directly from the Arctic Cat supplier in Duluth. Takes only a day or two. And some are even electronic so you can turn on the heat and listen to music."

"Sounds perfect. The helmet provided by the cabin is too big for me and tends to twist and block my vision. Thanks, Colette."

"You heading across the street for a bite to eat? I see the chief's snowmobile just pulled up. That is one fancy machine. And I'm not talking about the snowmobile."

"The chief?" Yvette glanced across the way. "You mean a police chief? What's up?"

"Nothing of concern, I'm sure. It's just, have you met Chief Jason Cash?"

"Should I?"

Colette winked. "*Uff da*, girl, he's the hottest catch

this side of the Canadian border. Young, handsome and cocky as hell. But none of the local girls can seem to turn his eye."

"I am hungry," Yvette said with a wistful glance across the street. For so many things she'd not had in almost two months. Sunshine. A buttery croissant. Conversation. Sex.

"Good girl. Tell the chief I said hello." Colette pushed the shop door open and virtually shoved Yvette out.

Bracing for the blast of cold, Yvette cursed how easily she had succumbed to the suggestion she hide out overseas until the heat on her blew over. Her boss had chosen this location and given her a cover identity. He hadn't told her exactly what it was that could implicate her, but she knew it had to do with her photographic memory. Thing was, she never really knew what some of the stuff that she worked on meant, as it was generally out of context and merely a list or scramble of information to her brain.

Boots crunching on the packed snow, she crossed the wide double-lane Main Street. A couple of pickup trucks with snow chains hugging the tires were parked before The Moose, as was one of the fanciest, most powerful snowmobiles she had seen. Walking by it, she forgot about the mysterious SUV she'd noticed earlier and instead took in the sleek black snowmobile dashed with neon-green embellishments. The body was like a blade, streamlined for speed.

The owner was handsome, eh? And single?

She wasn't looking for romance, that was for sure. But a woman could not survive on staticky rerun episodes of *Sex and the City* and her vibrator alone. Might as well *give the man a gander*, as she'd heard people say in these parts.

But for the official record, she was just here for the food.

Chapter Three

Jason took in the woman who sat before the diner counter. Two stools separated them. After setting a backpack on the floor, she'd pulled off a knit cap to let loose a spill of long black hair. Unzipping her coat halfway revealed a blue-and-white wool sweater that featured snowflakes and reindeer. Looked like one of Marjorie's knitted projects. Jason had one of those ugly sweaters—it featured a moose and possibly moose tracks (because he could never be sure it wasn't moose scat)—but he wore it proudly because someone had made it especially for him.

The woman at the counter was not a resident of Frost Falls. And today, of all days, he was particularly alert to strangers. This morning had brought a dead stranger onto his radar. Lunch had found him standing over an autopsy of the same woman. When driving back to Main Street, he'd sighted a shiny SUV that did not belong to a local. He'd run a plate check. Belonged to a Duluth resident. No police record or accidents reported. Worked for Perkins. Probably in town visiting friends.

And now Miss America was sitting ever so close.

She ordered mint tea and the club sandwich with

extra bacon. The waitress winked and commented that she was glad to finally use up the tea she'd had stashed under the counter for years.

Jason noted the woman's cringe when she heard the date of the tea, and he chuckled.

"Not many tea drinkers in these parts," he said. "I haven't seen you in The Moose. You passing through Frost Falls?"

"In a means, yes," she said with an accent that sounded familiar to Jason.

She was an exotic beauty. Her skin tone was olive, and her features were narrow. Bright blue eyes twinkled beneath delicate curved black brows. She didn't fit the standard profile of the Scandinavians who populated a good portion of Minnesota's frozen tundra. Gorgeous, too, far prettier than most. And she didn't appear to be wearing a lick of makeup. Something about natural red lips...

Jason shook off a bittersweet memory of red lips and sly winks. Weird that he hadn't heard about this beautiful woman from the town's gossip mill. He turned on the stool to face her. "Name's Jason Cash," he offered. "I'm the town's chief of police."

For another few months, at least. If and when he lost this job, what would he have to show for his years of service to both his country and this small town?

Not a hell of a lot.

"Nice to meet you, Chief Cash. I'm Yvette LaSalle. I'm not exactly passing through this cozy town. I've been here a few weeks. For a, um, vacation. Decided to stop in the diner today because I was across the street making a grocery run."

"LaSalle." Must be French Canadian. Nix the Miss America idea, and replace it with…hmm… Her tone didn't seem to possess the rugged edge the Canadian accent offered. Interesting. And come to think of it, he had heard Marjorie mention something about a newcomer sitting in The Moose last week. Why had Marjorie failed to point out how drop-dead beautiful the woman was? Her gossip was usually much more on point. "I'm glad our paths crossed today."

The waitress set Yvette's plate and tea before her.

"Mind if I slide over?" Jason asked. "Then we don't have to yell across the room at one another."

"Go ahead." She pulled a strip of bacon out of the sandwich and munched the crispy slice. "Mmm, meat, how I have missed you."

"You go off meat for some crazy reason?"

"I am a vegetarian," she said, prodding another bacon strip, then eyeing it disdainfully. "Or rather, was." She took a big bite of the sandwich. "*Mon Dieu*, that is so good!"

Miss France, he decided. He'd only been assigned a single two-day Parisian job while serving in the CIA. He knew a handful of French words, but beyond that, his capacity for learning foreign languages was nil.

"You must not order the tea very often, eh?"

She rolled her eyes. "I had a misguided craving. I think this'll be the last time I get tea here."

"Stick with the root beer," Jason said. "Root beer never lets a man down."

"Sounds like a personal issue to me, but to each his own. I like your snowmobile," she said. "The one parked out front, yes? It looks like a racing machine."

"Oh, it is." Jason's back straightened, and he hitched a proud smile in the direction of the powerful machine parked outside. "Could have been a professional racer. I love burning up the track. But I don't have the time. This job keeps me on call 24/7."

"I suppose there is a lot of crime in this sleepy little town." She tried to hide a smirk, but Jason caught it. A fall of dark hair hid half her eye. Oh, so sexy. And every part of him that should react warmed in appreciation.

The last time he'd felt all the right things about a woman had been two years ago in Italy.

And that had ended disastrously.

"Someone has to keep the Peanut Gang in line," he offered.

"The Peanut Gang?"

"Bunch of old farts who think poaching wolves isn't harming the ecosystem. Idiots."

"I'm not afraid of wolves. I think they are beautiful animals."

Jason nodded. "They are. But I'll leave it to my brother, the wolf whisperer, to kneel on the ground and pet them. It's always best to be cautious around wild animals."

Yvette nodded, but then said, "I got a great shot of a moose last week. On film, that is."

"Is that so?"

"I've learned to snowshoe out in the forest behind the cabin. Always take my camera along."

"You should be careful. Those beasts look gawky, but a moose can run fast."

"Tell me about it. I was photographing the snow-laced birch trees and out of nowhere a moose charged through the deep snow. It was beautiful. But I'm cautious to check for big critters now when I venture out."

"You should stick to the trails. Safer."

"Safe is good, hmm?"

Jason almost responded with an immediate *yes*, but he sensed by her tone that she was angling for bigger fish. Were those thick lashes as soft as they looked? And did she prefer not so safe? Now that was his kind of woman.

"Depends," he said. "There's safe and then there's, hmm…wild?"

"*Wild* is not a word I'd ever place to anything in this town."

If that wasn't some wanting, repressed sexual desire in her sigh, Jason couldn't guess otherwise. She had been in Frost Falls a few weeks. Why had he never noticed her before? And could he hope Alex hadn't already hooked up with her?

"You, uh, like wild?" he asked.

"I do." She finished off one triangle of the sandwich, but from his side view Jason noticed her smile did not fade.

Oh, he liked the wild, too. In so many ways.

The waitress set his bill down before him. He did not put it on the station's expense account. He couldn't see asking the town to pay for his meals. And now with the closure notice hanging over his head, he wanted to be as frugal as possible with the city budget. Much as he didn't like sharing the investigation with the BCA—yes, Ryan Bay, the looker, had arrived in town—it was a good thing, considering they had the resources and the finances to serve the investigation properly. As soon as the final autopsy report arrived, Jason intended to meet with Bay at the station house and go over the evidence.

Reaching for her backpack, Yvette shuffled it on over her arms. Ready to head out so quickly? She still had half a sandwich on the plate. He couldn't let her leave. Not until he'd learned more, like where she was staying, and did she have a significant other? And did her hair actually gleam when it spilled across her shoulders?

Briefly, Jason frowned as memories of his early morning stop resurfaced. The deceased had long black hair and a beautiful face.

At that moment, his cell phone buzzed with a text. Elaine had ID'd the victim as Yvette Pearson.

"Yvette," he muttered and wrinkled a brow. That was a weird coincidence.

"Yes?"

He looked up and was met with a wondering blue gaze. He'd once fallen for a pair of blue eyes and a foreign accent—and life had changed drastically for him because of that distraction.

"You said my name?" she prompted.

"Huh? Oh. No. I mean, yes. Not you. It's a text." He quickly typed, Thanks for the info. Forward the final report to me and Ryan Bay. He tucked away the phone and said to the very much alive Yvette, "It's a case. Not you. Sorry. Police business."

She nodded. "Yvette is a common French name."

"You betcha. Lot of French Canadians living up in these parts."

"These parts." With a sigh, she glanced out the front window.

Jason noticed she eyed the black SUV parked across the street. The one that hailed from Duluth.

"Friend of yours?" he asked, with a nod out the window.

"You mean the owner of that SUV?" She shook her

head. "Despite my sparkling personality, and a desperate desire for good conversation, I don't have any friends in this town. Other than Colette at the market. She's the only French-speaking person I've run into."

"You speak French? I was wondering about your accent."

"I'm from Lyon."

Lyon, eh? That was a major city in France.

"So, what is there to do in this town that is more interesting than Friday night at the Laundromat slash grocery store?" Yvette asked.

"Let's see…" Jason rubbed his jaw. "A guy could nosh on some of the amazing desserts they have here at The Moose. I have to admit, I'm a big fan of their pie. You want a slice before you rush off?"

"Much as I would love to, I'll have to pass. Wasn't as hungry as I thought I was." She pushed the plate forward to indicate she was finished. "But I won't rule out pie in my future," she said with a teasing tone. "What else you got?"

"Well, there is Netflix and chill," Jason suggested slyly.

"I don't understand."

"It means…uh…" A blush heated Jason's cheeks. Since when had his flirtation skills become so damned rusty? And awkward. Mercy, he was out of practice.

"More coffee, Jason?" the waitress asked.

Saved by the steamy brew. "No, thanks, I should get going. Marjorie is waiting for me back at the office to sign off on some…paperwork."

The last thing he wanted to do was let the cat out of the bag that a body had been found so close to town.

On the other hand, he expected when Susan Olson next went on shift at the back of the diner, it wouldn't take long for word to spread.

He pulled out a twenty and laid it on the counter. "That should cover both our bills."

Yvette zipped up her jacket. "Thank you, Chief Cash. I'm going to look up Netflix and chill when I get home."

"You do that," he said. And when she learned it meant watching Netflix together, then making out? "I'm down the street at the redbrick building if you ever need me. Used to be a bustling station house, but now it's just me and dispatch."

"Keeping an eye on the Peanut Gang."

"You betcha."

He walked her to the restaurant door, and she pointed across the street where a snowmobile was parked before Olson's Oasis. It was an older model, similar to the one he'd once torn through ditches on when he was a teenager.

"That's me," she said.

"How far out do you live?" he asked.

"I'm renting. Here for a short stay. It's a cabin about five miles east. Lots of birch trees. Very secluded."

"Everything around here is secluded. You step out of town, you're in no-man's land. That's what I love about this place. And lots of powder."

"Powder?"

"Snow. When I'm not working, I spend my time on the cat, zooming through the powder. Er, *cat* is what some locals call the snowmobile. At least, those of us with an inclination to Arctic Cat sleds and racing."

"Ah, a thrill seeker?"

"You nailed it. You must be staying at the Birch Bower cabin?"

"Yes, that's the one."

Jason nodded. The owners rented the place out in the winter months while they vacationed in their Athens home. Nice place, Greece. Beautiful blue waters. Fascinating local culture. Ouzo in abundance. He'd nearly taken a bullet to the stomach there a few years ago. Good times.

"Thanks again," Yvette called as she walked away.

Feeling as though he wanted to give Yvette his phone number, Jason also suspected that would not be cool. Not yet. They'd only chatted ten minutes. So instead he watched her turn on her snowmobile and head off with a smile and a wave.

Besides, he knew where to find her now if he wanted to.

A glance to the SUV found it was still parked. Exhaust fumes indicated the engine was running. Hmm…

Jason strode across Main Street toward the SUV, boots crunching the snowpack. The vehicle shifted into gear and drove past him. It slowed at the stop sign at the east edge of town. And sat there. Yvette had crossed to the town's edge and taken a packed trail hugged by tall birch trees.

The thunder of Jason's heartbeats would not allow him to dismiss the SUV. It was almost as if the driver had been parked there, watching… Yvette?

He looked at his cell phone. Elaine's message read, Yvette Pearson.

As the very much alive Yvette LaSalle had said, it was a common French name. But two Yvettes in one small town? Both, apparently, visiting. And one of them dead?

Unable to shake the itchy feeling riding his spine, Jason returned to his snowmobile and pulled on his helmet. By the time he'd fired up the engine and headed down Main Street, the SUV had slowly moved toward the birch-lined road heading east. Yvette's direction.

Jason pulled up alongside the SUV, switched on the police flasher lights and signaled the driver to pull over. He did so and rolled down his window. The thirtysomething male wearing a tight gray skullcap and sunglasses tugged up a black turtleneck as the brisk air swept into the truck cab.

"Chief Jason Cash," Jason said as he approached the vehicle. A nine-millimeter Glock hugged his hip, but he didn't sense a need for it. Nor did he ever draw for a routine traffic stop. Not that this was a traffic stop.

"Hello, Officer," the man said with an obvious accent. Texan? A Southern drawl twanged his voice. "Is there a problem?"

"No problem. I've not seen you in Frost Falls before, and it is a small town. Like to introduce myself." He tugged off a glove and offered his hand to the man. The driver twisted and leaned out the window to shake his hand. A calm movement. Warm hand. But Jason couldn't see his eyes behind the mirrored lenses. "Your name?"

"Smith," he said easily. Which was the name Jason had gotten from the plate check. "I'm visiting the Boundary Waters tourist area. Just out for a drive. Beautiful day with the sunshine, yes?"

"You betcha."

Definitely a Texan accent. Fresh out of high school, Jason had served three years in the marines alongside a trio of Texans who had extolled their love for hot sauce whenever they were bored.

"You got some ID and vehicle registration, Smith?"

The man reached down beside him. Jason's hackles tightened. He placed a hand over his gun handle. Smith produced a driver's license and, opening the glove compartment, shuffled around for a paper. He handed both over.

Hiding his relief that he hadn't had to draw against a dangerous suspect, Jason took the items and looked them over. It was a Minnesota license, not Texas, but people moved all the time. The name and address matched the vehicle registration. It also matched the info he'd gotten earlier. Thirty-seven years old. Brown hair. Brown eyes. Donor. A Duluth address. Hair was longer in the photo, but the man looked like he'd recently had a clipper cut.

"You a recent move to Minnesota?"

"Why do you ask?"

"There's not a lot of *uff da* in your accent."

The man chuckled. "Born and raised in Dallas. But I do enjoy the winters here."

"I gotta agree with you there. You must enjoy outdoor sports."

"Mostly taking in the sights."

"Uh-huh. You got the day off from work?" Jason asked.

"You bet."

"Duluth, eh?" Jason handed back the license. "Where do you work?"

"Perkins. Just off Highway 35 west."

Jason had eaten at that location before. So that checked out, too. In town to take in the scenery?

"Thank you, Mr. Smith. You should turn around here before the road gets too narrow," he said. "It's not for tourism. And it's also not a through road."

"I had no idea, Officer."

"That's part of my job. Making sure everyone stays on the straight and narrow."

The man furrowed his brows. And the fact he'd misnamed the Boundary Waters Canoe Area Wilderness gave Jason another prickle down his spine. A strange mistake for someone who should be familiar with the area.

"The Moose serves up some tasty meat loaf with buttered carrots," Jason offered. "Stop in before you head out of town."

"Thank you, Officer. I will. Is there anything else?"

"No. You can go ahead and turn around here. Road's still wide enough. But watch the ditch. The snowpack is loose. You'll catch a tire and have a hell of a time getting out. Tow service is kind of sketchy in these parts."

"Sure thing."

The window rolled up, and Jason walked back over to his snowmobile. The SUV sat for a bit, not making any motion to turn around. Clouds of exhaust formed at the muffler.

Jason sat on his cat and swung the driver a friendly wave. If he had been following Yvette, there was no way Jason was going to leave his post. And if the driver had known her, he would have mentioned he was following a friend. Maybe?

When the vehicle finally began to pull ahead, turn,

back up, turn some more, then make the arc around to head back the way it had come, Jason again waved.

"Something up with Smith," he muttered.

He could generally spot a fake ID at a glance. The license had been legit. Everything checked out in the police database. But still, his Spidey senses tingled. Sure, Frost Falls got sightseers. The town's namesake, the falls, froze solid in the winter months. It attracted thrill seekers. And idiots.

But the man hadn't mentioned the falls specifically. And if that had been his destination, he should have headed out of town in the opposite direction.

Jason had met three strangers today. And one of them had been lying dead in a ditch. He wasn't going to let this one sit.

Firing up the cat, he headed back into town to keep an eye on Smith.

Chapter Four

Jason breezed into the station but didn't unzip his coat or stomp his boots. Marjorie had gotten used to his tromping in ice and snow and had laid down a rubber runner mat a year ago. She still complained about the mess, but when he'd given her a budget for a monthly rug cleaning, she'd settled.

That would all change soon enough. He wasn't sure how to tell her the station might be closed in March. He had to tell her. Maybe if he waited, it would never happen?

"There's a message," Marjorie started as he walked by.

"From the BCA?" Jason asked.

"No, Bay's in your office—"

He strode into his office and closed the door behind him. "Bay."

The agent was seated in the extra chair against the wall beneath a sixteen-point deer rack with a laptop open and his focus pinned to the screen. "Cash. Give me a minute."

"Minute's all you get. I'm investigating a murder. Have to get out there. Talk to people. Gather information."

Walking across the room, Jason pushed aside the shades to give him a view of Main Street. He'd seen Smith's SUV heading east toward Highway 35. The man had taken the hint.

On the other hand… He glanced down the street toward the gas station that sat at town's edge.

"They still renting snowcats from the gas station?" Jason called out to Marjorie.

"You betcha. Jason, do you want some krumkake?"

That invite turned his head. He strode back into the next room and eyed the plate of sweet treats Marjorie pointed to on the corner of her desk. Half a dozen delicate rolled sweets sat on a Corelle plate decorated around the circumference with green leaves (just like his mother's set). Krumkake were like crunchy crepes, but so light and delicious.

"You make those?" he asked.

"Of course. I use my grandmother's krumkake iron. They don't make those things anymore, don't ya know."

He grabbed one of the treats and bit into it, catching the inevitable crumbs with his other hand. Two more bites and it was gone. He grabbed another, then tugged out his notebook and tore out a few pages to hand to Marjorie. "Can you type up these notes I took while talking to Susan Olson?"

"Of course. I've already got a case file started. Elaine Hester forwarded the autopsy report for the woman in the ditch. I left a copy on your desk, and Bay's got a copy as well."

"Yeah, she texted me the name Yvette Pearson." Jason wandered back into his office and closed the door behind him.

Ryan Bay stood and set the laptop on Jason's desk. "I've got family info on the victim."

"Lives in a Minneapolis suburb," Jason said. Susan had been sure the women at the club the other night were from the Twin Cities, because one had worn a jacket with a high school logo embroidered on the sleeve. "Blaine?"

"Yes, Blaine. I've already contacted their police department so they can get in touch with the family."

"I've got a list of the deceased's friends I intend to question as soon as I step out of the station. But first, I'm going to head east and check on—"

"That pretty young woman you talked to in The Moose?" Marjorie asked as she entered with the plate of treats in hand.

Marjorie took his silence as the hint she needed it to be and, after handing him the plate, she left the office with a promise to get right to his notes.

Jason closed the office door again and nodded to Bay, who turned his laptop toward him. "Classic homicide. Ligature marks. Struggle bruises on forearms and DNA under fingernails."

"Yep, I was there for the autopsy. It was all very clean. Generally there's much more bruising on the body as the killer struggles to complete the unfamiliar—or unintended—task. Anger and aggression."

Bay shook his head and exhaled heavily. "You said you talked to the woman who found the body?"

"Yes, she gave me the names of the women the victim was last seen with. That's where I'm going next—"

"I thought there was a pretty young woman?" Bay said with a smirk.

"A…" Jason closed his eyes and shook his head. Marjorie really needed to stay out of his personal life. But the worst part of it was that she knew about his personal life before it tended to get personal. "Never mind," he said. "You don't want to question the victim's friends, do you?"

Bay tilted his head, a casual thought process taking place inside his perfectly coiffed head. He wore a suit, for some damn reason, and it looked like his fingernails had been manicured for the glossy shine. Was that what women found attractive? Yikes.

"Go for it," Bay said. "The locals are more likely to be comfortable talking to someone they know. When I consult on a case, I like to guide and keep track, but ultimately, this is your case, Cash. I'm not going to trample on your turf. And I'm starving. I haven't eaten yet today."

"Then The Moose is your next stop." Jason picked up the documents Marjorie had left for him on his desk. "You staying in town?"

"There's no motel. Snow Lake has a halfway decent Best Western and free coffee."

"Not a problem. My office is yours. I'll let you know what I learn." Jason strode out and through the reception area, pleased that Bay was easygoing. Which would give him all the rope he required to control this investigation. He really needed this one. It was an opportunity to show the powers that be that he had what it took to manage real police work, and that the Frost Falls police force, as small as it was, was a necessity.

Instead of the snowmobile, he'd drive the Ford. He could use some warmth. Turning up the car heater to blast, Jason rolled down Main Street, the car tires crunching as if across Styrofoam as they moved over the packed snow. He loved that sound. It was hard to describe to anyone who didn't live on snow six months out of the year. To him it meant home.

From here he could see the small parking lot in front of the gas station. No business name on the broken red-and-white sign above the station. It had been called just "gas station" forever, according to an elder member of the town.

And yet, when Jason cruised closer to the gas station, he saw the black SUV parked around the back side of the white cinder-block building. It was the one licensed to James Smith.

"What the hell?"

He pulled into the station lot. Hopping out of the truck and blowing out a breath that condensed to a fog, Jason quickened his pace into the station.

"Afternoon, Cash," the owner said from his easy chair placed on a dais behind the cash register. Easier to see out the window and watch the town's goings-on from that height.

"You rent out any cats this afternoon, Rusty?"

"I just did, not ten minutes ago. Local fellow."

"Local?"

"Well, you know, he mentioned he was from Duluth. That's local."

It was. The port city that sat on Lake Superior was an hour's drive east and within the St. Louis County lines.

"Gave him directions to the falls and told him to stick to the trails," Rusty said, "but I think he went east. Idiot. Your brother still with the State Patrol?"

"Justin? Yep. He's stationed near the Canadian border right now. Big drug-surveillance op going on."

"Those marijuana farms." Rusty shook his head.

"You betcha. What was the name of the renter?"

Rusty tapped a crinkled piece of paper hanging from a clipboard to the right of the register. "Smith. Sounded foreign. And not Canadian foreign. He was a mite different. Like those duck hunters they got on that television show."

"Thanks, Rusty. Gotta go."

Jason made haste to the truck, and before the door was even closed he pulled out onto the main road and turned to hit the eastbound road that led to the Birch Bower cabin. It was only five miles out, but with each mile the forest thickened and hugged closer on both sides of the narrowing road. It was as desolate as a place could get so close to a small town.

As he drove down the gravel road that the plow only tackled every Monday morning, he noted the snowmobile tracks lain down on the road shoulder. A couple of them. Freshly impressed into the crusted snowpack. One set must belong to Yvette. The other?

"Smith."

In his next thought, Jason wondered if he were getting worked up over nothing. No. She'd said she didn't know anyone in town. And yet she had looked at the SUV for a while.

Didn't feel right to Jason. And if he'd learned anything over the years, it was to trust his intuition.

ONE OF THE reasons Yvette hadn't minded leaving home for a while was that she'd been questioning her job choice for some time now. She'd never been fooled that being a field operative for an international security agency was glamourous or even 24/7 action-adventure. The job could be tedious at times. Mildly adrenalizing, at best. Most people associated spies with glamour and blockbuster movies. In truth, the average agent spent more time doing boring surveillance than the few minutes of contact with a suspect that might provide that thrill of action.

Yet beyond the intrigue and danger, a surprising moral struggle had presented itself to her when she was faced with pulling the trigger on a human target. She was not a woman prone to crying fits. And yet, the tears had threatened when she'd been standing in the field, gun aimed at a person and—she'd been unable to pull the trigger. Human life meant something to her. Even if the human she had been charged to fire at was a criminal who had committed vile crimes. She'd not expected to only realize such moral leanings until the heat of the moment, but that pause had changed her life irreversibly.

She asked for a change of pace and had, thankfully, been allowed to continue her work in data tech. A job that didn't fulfill her in any tangible manner. It had become an endless stream of data on the computer screen.

Now seclusion in a snow-covered cabin offered an excellent time to consider her future. Did she really want to continue on this career path? Days ago, she'd started a list of pros and cons regarding her current employer.

Yvette tapped the pen beside her temple as she delved deep for another pro. She felt it necessary to write down the good as well as the bad reasons to stay or leave. Solid and tangible. Easy to review. Difficult to deny once inked on paper. Because she'd followed in her parents' footsteps, career-wise. Had thought she was cut out for the gritty hard-core work it required.

Yet to her surprise, the desk job had, strangely, become more dangerous than fieldwork. She had seen something on the computer screen that she was not supposed to see. She just didn't know what that something was, because it had been a list, and perhaps even coded.

Setting aside the pros and cons list and getting up to stretch, she exhaled. She'd been working on the list for an hour while listening to the wind whip against the exterior timber walls. A blizzard was forecast.

"Joy," she muttered mirthlessly and wandered into the kitchen.

No thought cells could operate without a healthy dose of chocolate. Plucking a mug out of the cupboard, she then filled the teapot with water and set that on the stove burner.

She shook the packet of hot chocolate mix into the mug. Right now, she needed a heat injection. Her toes were freezing, even though she wore two layers of socks. And her fingers felt like ice. She'd turned up the heater upon returning from the grocery run, but it didn't want to go any higher than seventy-four degrees.

With the wind scraping across the windows, she felt as if she sat in a wooden icebox. A glance to the fireplace made her sigh. A woodpile sat neatly stacked outside and behind the house. The owners had suggested she carry some in before too much snow fell, but she'd not done that. After she'd fortified her chilled bones with hot chocolate, she'd have to bundle up and bring out the ax to chip the frozen logs apart. The night demanded a toasty fire in the hearth.

The teapot whistled, and she poured the steaming water into the mug. Oh, how she missed the thick, dark chocolate drink served exclusively by the French tea shop Angelina. Unfortunately, the shop hadn't come to Lyon, but she visited Paris often enough and stocked up when there.

Tilting back the oversweet chocolate drink, she sighed and took a moment to savor the heat filling her belly. Who would have thought she could enjoy a moment of warmth so thoroughly? It was a different kind of warmth from the one she'd felt sitting in the diner talking to the chief of police. Colette had been spot on regarding her assessment of the man. He was a handsome one. He'd seemed about her age, too.

A knock on the front door startled her. That was—not weird. The postman knocked every day with her mail in hand. Not that she got personal mail. It was always ads and flyers for retirement homes. But she did appreciate his smile and some chat. He often asked if she was comfy and did she like fruitcake? His wife had extra. Yvette always declined with the knowledge that fruitcake was not a culinary treat.

Yet something stopped her from approaching the door. She still couldn't erase the police chief's question about the mysterious SUV. It had seemed out of place in the small town. And she was no woman to ignore the suspicious.

Grasping a pen from the kitchen counter, Yvette fit the heavy steel object into her curled fingers, then walked cautiously over to the door. She stood there a moment, staring at the unfinished pine wood that formed the solid barrier. There was no peephole.

"Who is it?" she called.

"Delivery," answered back. "Is your name…Yvette?"

"Yes, but…" Yvette frowned. It was her cover name. She hadn't ordered anything. And she'd only this morning asked Colette to order the helmet.

"It's from The Moose," the man said. "You didn't order anything?"

"No," she called back. "It's food? Who sent it?"

A pause, and then, "Note says it's from a new friend."

A new friend? And The Moose? But she'd just—had the police chief sent her a gift? Of food? They had discussed pie. How nice of him. And if it was a flirtatious move, she was all in.

Yvette opened the door.

The man standing on the snow-dusted front stoop was tall and dressed all in black, including the black face mask he wore that concealed all but his eyes. He growled and lunged for her. He fit his bare hands about her throat, and Yvette stumbled backward.

Chapter Five

Jason ran in through the open doorway and encountered a struggle. In front of the floor-to-ceiling windows that overlooked a snow-frosted copse of maples, he witnessed a man shove a woman—Yvette LaSalle—against the wall. Her painful grunt fired anger in Jason's veins. He dashed over a fallen chair and toward the struggling duo.

Suddenly, Yvette swept her hand forcefully backward, her elbow colliding with the attacker's neck. She twisted and plunged a fist against his head. The man—Smith—yelped and gripped his bleeding scalp.

Jason charged across the room. With a swift right hook, he connected under Smith's jaw and knocked him out cold. The man dropped to his side, sprawling on the floor.

He spun around to find Yvette behind him, clutching a tactical pen in one hand. A fierce, huffing demeanor held her at the ready before him. Her stance declared she was prepared for more fight.

"It's okay," Jason reassured. "He's out."

She nodded, but her defensive pose remained. Impressive. She'd been terrorized. The adrenaline must be coursing through her like a snowmobile around a racetrack.

"That was— You were—incredible." Jason finally found the right words. "You are certainly no damsel."

"No, I'm not." She winced, but lifted her chin. "He was strong. Stronger than…"

Jason sensed the adrenaline was beginning to rapidly drop from the high that had served her the strength to defend herself. Yvette's body began to shake. He rushed over and took her in his arms.

"It's okay." He hugged her firmly, pressing his face against the crown of her head. She smelled like salt and summer. A sweep of soft hair tickled his nose. His thundering heartbeats thudded loudly. But was it from the moment of attack, or from the surprising feeling of holding a trembling woman in his arms? Mercy. She had reacted unexpectedly bravely. And her sudden surge of strength may have saved her life.

"You did good, Yvette. Guy's out like a light." For now. "I need to cuff him. Can I let you go?"

She nodded against his chest, though her fingers clung to his biceps, unwilling to relent. Jason stepped back but bowed to check her gaze. When she offered him a wincing smile, he slowly extracted himself from her grip. She wasn't going to faint. Not this brave woman.

Digging out the cuffs from his jacket, he bent to secure the suspect's hands behind his back.

"You know this guy?" he asked over his shoulder.

"No. Do you?"

"He's the guy from the black SUV."

"I told you I didn't know him when you asked in the diner."

"I know, but he put up my hackles. I pinned him for something more than a guy taking in the scenery. He was following you."

"He was? How did you— Why didn't you stop him before he got here?"

"I thought I had." Jason stood and grabbed the back of a fallen chair and righted it. He lifted a boot, realizing the papers scattered on the floor were wet and torn. No saving them. "I didn't expect him to rent a snowmobile and go after you. Why was he after you?"

"We've been over this, Chief Cash. I've never met him."

"How did he get inside the cabin?"

"I, uh…" She clutched her throat. Her fingers visibly shook. "Opened the door."

Jason stopped an admonishing retort and instead asked carefully, "You always let strangers inside?"

"He said he had a delivery from The Moose. Why did you talk to him in town? What made you wonder about him?"

"He looked suspicious. We've got an active investigation going on and—"

"Investigation? Like what? A man attacking women?"

She was close. Jason never gave out details of an ongoing investigation. Was the man on the floor the one who had murdered the woman he'd found in the ditch this morning? He had been attempting to strangle Yvette. The one in the ditch had died by strangulation. And Jason never subscribed to coincidence.

Yet would a stalker, or even some sort of serial strangler, have allowed a woman to get the upper hand with a weapon so simple as a tactical pen?

As well, how many seemingly innocent women vacationing in a secluded cabin carried a tactical pen on them? It was a self-defense weapon that most did not know about or bother to keep close enough to use.

"That's a handy thing, isn't it?" He gestured to the rugged black steel pen she still held.

She clutched it against her chest and lifted her chin. "I never go anywhere without it. It's something I was trained—"

"You've taken self-defense training?"

When she looked up quickly, as if he'd discovered a secret, a moment of clarity softened her features, then she shrugged. "Like you said, I'm not a damsel."

"I guess not. But didn't the training class teach you never to open the door to a stranger?"

Another shrug. She avoided his gaze, as well. Hmm…

"Are you going to get him out of here?" she asked with a gesture to the fallen attacker.

"I'll give Officer Larson a call." Jason wasn't ready to leave without asking more questions. And he couldn't do that and watch the perp at the same time. "You sure you're okay?"

"Of course I am," she said a little too quickly. Then a sweep of her hand through her hair preceded a hefty sigh. "But if you'll excuse me, I'm going to step into the, uh…little girls' room for a bit."

"Go ahead. I won't leave until this guy is out of your hair." He tugged out his phone and dialed up dispatch. He and Alex alternated shifts, but both were on call 24/7. And he'd rather have him come and assist than the lackadaisical Ryan Bay.

Yvette closed the bathroom door behind her and exhaled. Her shoulders hit the door. She caught her head in a palm. Her entire body shook, but she didn't cry. She sank, bending her knees, until she sat on the tiled floor.

That man could have killed her.

She was thankful that the police chief was here and had rescued her in the nick of time. But a retreat to the bathroom had been necessary. She hadn't wanted him to see her break down. And what was this shaking about? She was better than this—trained for such encounters, and well able to defend herself against some of the strongest attackers.

Yet she hadn't panicked when he'd come at her. She had done her best to protect herself from what could have been a terrible outcome. Because the man had had his hands about her neck and his thumbs pressed against her larynx. She'd gasped and had felt her lungs tighten.

It had been over a year since she'd worked as a field agent and had exercised her defense skills. Had she gotten so out of shape and ineffective in such a short time?

"Get it together, Amelie," she whispered. "Why did this happen?"

Because Amelie Desauliniers had been sent out of the country to hide under an assumed identity. But hide from whom or what hadn't been made clear to her. Surely this hadn't been a random attack. And yet she was undercover. Dark. Who had found her?

A quiet knock on the door preceded "Yvette? You okay in there?"

She closed her eyes.

"Yvette?"

"Oh." Despite embracing the name, it just didn't click sometimes. As well, she'd have to form words to reassure the police chief. Inhaling a quiet sniffle, she said, "Sorry. Yes, give me a few minutes. I'm a little shaken."

"Thought you might be. I'll be out in the living room. Another officer is on the way to pick up the perp."

She waited until his boots echoed away down the hall. Amelie stood and walked to the sink. Twisting on the water spigot, she splashed her face but let out a gasp. She would never get used to the fact the water took a good three or four minutes to reach room temperature. But the frigid water did work to shock away her tears.

Pressing a towel over her face to dry it, she then nodded at her reflection. The agent she had once been must be tugged out of retirement. For survival purposes. "I can do this."

But she couldn't ask the sexy police chief for help. Her stay here in Minnesota was classified. And not knowing what she knew had suddenly become a detriment. She had to speak with her boss. And soon.

Returning to the living room, she walked around the prone body on the floor. The attacker was coming to, groaning. Another knock on the door sounded. Amelie jumped. A pair of gentle, warm hands settled onto her shoulder.

"It's Alex, my assistant," Chief Cash reassured her in a deep voice that hinted at the strength she desperately required. "Why don't you sit on the couch." He touched her upper arm, and she winced. "Looks like you got hurt. Your sweater is torn. I'll take a look after I get the perp out of here."

He opened the door, and the waiting police officer nodded and introduced himself to her as Amelie settled onto the couch. He was tall and attractive. Not handsome sexy, more like boy-band cute. The thought summoned her out of the heavy tension that had made her clutch the tactical pen. She set the pen on the coffee table and inspected her sweater.

She'd been hurt? She hadn't noticed while shivering in the bathroom. Yet now that Jason had pointed it out, she felt the sting of pain in her biceps. Her sweater was torn and bloody. And…yes, the pointed tip of the pen was bloodied, so she'd caused her attacker some damage.

The two men picked up the suspect by his upper arms. He growled and struggled against the handcuffs. Both officers had to move him out of the cabin, kicking and gyrating across the threshold. As they exited, the attacker called, "I will be back for you!"

Amelie swore and turned to clasp her arms about her legs, pulling them tight against her chest. Her heart thudded up to her throat.

She knew something dangerous. It was locked away in her brain, and only she possessed the key to dredge out the information.

Chapter Six

Standing on the front stoop, Jason watched Alex back the patrol car out of the double-wide drive. Alex gave him a thumbs-up as he headed toward town. He'd secure the perp behind bars, and Ryan Bay could help book him and start an interrogation.

He leaned back inside the cabin and called, "I'm going to take a look around the cabin and surrounding area. Look for clues. You okay alone for a bit?"

"Of course."

The answer was the right one, but it sounded shaky. To be expected.

"Give me half an hour. I'll stay close. If you need me, just shout out the door."

Wind and snow crystals scoured Jason's face as he rounded the side of the cabin, following the faint traces of boot prints that were neither his nor did they belong to a female. Another hour of wind and the tracks would be gone.

An outjut of stacked pine logs formed a two-sided protection from the wind and elements for the generator. He lifted the blue tarp cover and looked over the machine. Some snow had drifted up about the base, but it all looked in working order. He might turn it on to check it out, but it was windy, and he wanted to beat the storm before it erased all evidence Smith had left behind.

Picking up his pace through a foot of fluffy, dry snow, Jason passed the detached double garage behind the cabin. He sighted sunken boot prints. They did not reveal sole design because the snow and wind had already filled them, but he could see they walked toward the cabin. Scanning ahead, he noticed the line of tracks and veered toward the line of white-paper birches that edged a forest fifty yards ahead. The footprints disappeared for ten feet, but then he could pick up the sunken smooth imprint when he flashed the flashlight beam over it. But he didn't need the tracks when he spied the snowmobile in the woods.

Hastening his steps, he entered the woods, which blocked the wind. Thankful for that reprieve, he huffed out a breath. The cold was something he was accustomed to, but when the wind beat directly at his face, it took a man's breath away.

Tromping over fallen branches and loose snow made footing difficult. The snowmobile still had the keys in the ignition. A rental sticker on the hood told him it had come from the gas station. Smith had likely intended to do the deed and head back to the snowmobile for a quick getaway.

Jason sat on the snow-dusted vinyl seat cushion and flashed the light beam about the sled. The gas station kept its rental machines in tip-top condition, even if they were decades old. This one was fully gassed up. The seat was comfy and not torn. The outer fiberglass hood was not scuffed, save for a small crack where the windshield connected.

The footprints, which now he could plainly see were from cowboy boots, took off from the sled and walked straight on toward the cabin—no pacing about the vehicle, deciding to get up his courage. The man had been focused, set on his task. He'd wanted to get at this second Yvette.

Had it been the same man coming after yet another Yvette? The implications pointed toward some type of serial stalker. A man obsessed with Yvettes?

He tipped open the cover of the small supply box on the back of the seat cushion. Nothing inside. If the man had intended to use a weapon against Yvette, he would have brought it along with him into the cabin. Jason hadn't removed any weapons from him when cuffing him and patting him down.

Jason flipped the box cover shut. He would check on Yvette, and—hell, she had been bleeding.

BACK INSIDE THE cabin, Jason kicked off his boots. When he wandered into the living room and sat next to Yvette on the couch, he sensed her shivers before seeing them. She was still frightened. The tactical pen lay on the pine coffee table. He would secure that as evidence.

"You were very brave," he said in his reassuring officer's tone. Something a guy cultivated with experience. "Can I look at your arm?"

She nodded but didn't speak as he carefully pulled away the torn knitted threads from her arm. There was a good amount of blood, but it looked like it might be road rash. Nothing deep. She must have rubbed against something rough when struggling with the perp. All the furniture in this cabin was fashioned from heavy, bare pine logs, so it was feasible she could have fallen against a chair leg or arm.

"I found the snowcat the perp drove out here in the woods. I'll have a tow come get it after the storm threat passes. I think you should come to town with me and have Marjorie, my dispatcher, look at that. Just to be safe. And I do need you to give me an official statement."

"I'm okay."

"Marjorie used to be a nurse," he encouraged.

"It's just a bruise. And I know you have questions—standard police procedure, and all that—"

"I really do need to talk to you while the incident is fresh in your mind. It's just odd. The guy was following you. He sat outside on Main Street, watched you walk across from the grocery store, stayed there while you had a bite to eat and then…" He sighed heavily.

"I've never seen that man before, Chief Cash."

"Then why did you let him inside the cabin?"

"I called out and he said he had a delivery and asked if my name was Yvette."

"A delivery?"

"Said it was from a new friend. I assumed it was from you. We *had* talked about pie."

"You thought I sent you pie?"

"It sounded reasonable at the time. I opened the door, and then he lunged. You arrived a minute or two later. *Merci Dieu*."

"So he called you by name?"

She nodded.

"Your full name?"

Yvette thought about it a moment. "No, just my first. I did have the clarity to grab the tactical pen before answering the door."

"So you were suspicious."

"I was until he said the—er, my name. Then I believed he was a deliveryman."

"Right. So, he started to choke you immediately? Or did you have a conversation first?"

"No, he immediately went at me. I was able to struggle and move the two of us across the room toward the table, where you see the mess."

"Those papers on the floor…" Jason looked over her shoulder. "Important?"

"Uh, no. Just some journaling stuff. Why? You think he was after something of mine?"

"I don't know. You have to tell me."

"He didn't speak after I'd let him inside. Didn't ask for anything, like where my valuables were. I don't believe he was here to rob me. He wanted to hurt me. Possibly even…"

Jason nodded and tugged out his notebook to make a few notations.

"How many people know you're staying here?" he asked.

"One," she said, then offered him a shrug as if to apologize for that low number.

"No friends? Family?"

She shook her head, keeping her lips tight.

"Sounds kind of odd," he remarked. "Single woman off alone in a country foreign to her, and only one person knows about it? Boyfriend?"

She shook her head again, choosing silence. A silence that niggled at Jason's trust. Why not provide the person's name without his prompting?

"Who knows you're here, Miss LaSalle?"

"Just my boss. This was a retreat," she added quickly. "A photography excursion. A last-minute decision sort of thing, so I didn't announce it to everyone I know. Just…got the time off I needed, and…here I am."

"Here you are. You work as a photographer?"

She nodded.

He wasn't buying it. Wouldn't a photographer have equipment? He hadn't noticed any cameras in the open-layout cabin. "Your boss is a photographer as well?"

She shrugged. "It's a hobby. I'm trying to expand my portfolio."

Jason closed his notebook and stuffed it inside his coat. "Anything else you want to tell me about what happened?"

"No."

"So he was only in the cabin a few minutes before I arrived?"

"Yes. Or it felt that long. I can't be sure, but I'd guess that's about as long as I'd last against someone so strong."

"Fine. I have to head in and help process the suspect." And he'd been on his way to talk with the victim's friends before the detour out here to the cabin.

"I'm going to call you in an hour," he said. "To check in with you. You should be safe now."

She nodded. "Thank you." She glanced to the papers strewn on the floor.

"Will you also promise not to open the door for anyone except the mailman?"

"That's a deal. Write down your number on one of those papers before you leave."

He stood and picked up a paper from the floor. It was a lined notebook page. He read the header. "Pros and cons?"

"Just doing some journaling."

Wanting to read more, but respecting her privacy, he tugged the pen out of his coat and scribbled down his number on the back of the paper.

When he handed her the page, Jason felt her shiver again. "What is it, Yvette? There's something else. I can feel it."

She exhaled heavily. "Did you hear what he said when the other officer took him away?"

Smith had called out that he'd be back for her. The audacity.

Her serious blue eyes searched his. Seeking a comforting reassurance that Jason gave her without asking. It was easy, because he couldn't imagine being alone in this country, with no friends, and having been attacked.

"This town is small, but I take protecting the residents seriously," he said. "Do you want me to stay awhile?"

"No, I'll be fine. And you do need to take care of that man. Lock him up, will you?"

"That's my job. Just call me, okay?"

He headed to the door and pulled on his gloves. As he shoved his feet into his snow boots, he turned to look at her. She still sat on the couch, back to him, gaze focused out the tall windows that overlooked a snow-frosted birch forest not far behind the detached garage.

Was he doing the right thing? Leaving her here alone? The perp had been secured. But he couldn't know whether or not Smith had been acting alone. He'd make a point of checking in with her soon.

Jason couldn't shake the fact that there was a stranger staying in Frost Falls, and for some reason she had attracted danger to the small town. He believed that she didn't know Smith.

But what wasn't she telling him? What woman left for another country and only told her employer? Felt wrong. But he could attribute her nervousness to having just gone through a traumatic event. He'd give her some space.

"An hour," he said as he opened the door. "I want to hear from you!"

PULLING THE TRUCK along the side of the police station, Jason dialed up the radio volume just as the meteorologist announced everyone should head out for groceries. The blizzard was on its way and would be full force by tomorrow afternoon, possibly even the morning. He turned off the engine and got out with a jump. An inhale sucked in icy air. It was too cold for a storm, but the weather was always crazy in the wintertime.

Making a quick stop inside the station's ground level, Jason grabbed another krumkake from the plate on Marjorie's desk, then stepped right back outside. He swung around the building corner and opened the heavy steel back door. Down a short hall and then to the right, he clattered down the stairway that led to the basement cells. He hated this setup, especially when he had a drunk or violent perp to contain. More than a few times, he'd almost tumbled to the bottom with the prisoner in hand. Not the most well-designed police station, that was for sure.

The heater kept the cinder block–walled basement at a passable sixty-eight degrees and each of the three cells even held one of Marjorie's homemade quilts, along with a fluffy pillow. Jason had spent a night in one of the cells a few months earlier after a long night of reading over boring expense reports.

"We have a new guest in the Hotel Frosty?" he asked Alex and Ryan as he joined them before the middle cell.

"Just got him locked up. He's a fighter," Alex said. "Bay had to help me fingerprint him."

Jason noticed the black ink smear on Alex's jaw. "I see that. You get anything out of him, Bay?"

The man's focus was on his laptop again, set on a small table beneath a landline phone that hung on the wall opposite the cells.

"Not yet."

"All he's said," Alex added, "was a whole lot of words that were not favorable toward my mother."

"Is that so?"

Jason stepped up to the cell bars. Inside, the perp leaned against the back wall, one leg bent with his sole flat against the wall. Cowboy boots, not snow boots with traction on the soles. Idiot. The man lifted his chin. A position of challenge that didn't give Jason any more worry than if he'd spat at him.

"You are under arrest for assault," Jason stated. "James Smith, eh? I ran a trace on your plates earlier.

You live in Duluth and work at Perkins. What's a line chef doing in Frost Falls strangling women?"

The man mumbled something and ended with two very clear swear words.

"He doesn't like your mother much, either," Alex said.

Jason smirked. "My mother would arm wrestle this skinny guy under the table if she heard him talking like that."

The Cash family—all three of the boys and both mother and father—was an athletically inclined bunch. Their father had been a marine before purchasing the Crooked Creek land and settling into dairy farming and to raise his family. And their mom, well, she was always trying new martial arts classes and once had flipped the eldest son, Justin, onto his back in an impressive move that had left their brother red-faced and Joe and Jason laughing like hyenas. Jason was never ashamed to admit it had been his mother who taught him some keen defense moves, including the more relaxed tai chi she practiced religiously.

The prisoner lifted his chin haughtily and then flipped them the bird.

"This is going to be a fun afternoon." Jason nodded to Ryan. "Why don't you get the paperwork started and bring down the DNA kit. You get mug shots?"

Alex blew out a breath and offered an unsure shrug. "Bay was taking the shots. Not sure."

"My camera was out of focus," Bay provided on a mumble. "I'm going through the shots right now. Might be one usable image."

"I get it," Jason said. "We'll mark this one down as

uncooperative. Wait for fingerprints, then we'll check the CJRS." The Criminal Justice Reporting System was the US database for tracking and identifying criminals and those with police records.

"Will do, boss." Alex started up the stairs.

"And next time you come down, bring some of those krumkakes, will you?"

"If there's any left when I get through with them." Alex's chuckle was muffled by the closing of the upper door.

Jason turned, crossed his arms over his chest and couldn't help a smile. The man giving him the wonky eye might very well be a murderer.

"You interview the dead woman's friends?" Ryan asked as he joined Jason at his side.

"Haven't gotten that far yet."

"Storm's moving in. I hate Minnesota. I put in for a position in an Arizona county office."

"I'm sure they'll be happy to have you," Jason said. Bay was distracted, or probably didn't care much about the situation. Burnout? Maybe. Or it could be the weather. Damn cold was enough to make any man lose focus on what was most important.

And right now, Jason had added a beautiful French-woman to that list.

"I should head out before it gets nasty outside," he said. "Ask this guy about girlfriends named Yvette. Or maybe it's his mom he's trying to strangle? Check the family stats on him."

"Will do," Bay said as Jason left him and headed out.

Chapter Seven

Amelie dialed the international number, and it went straight to her boss's voice mail. It was nearing midnight in France. Jacques needed to know about the attack on her, but, when fleeing France, she'd been instructed to keep any voice messages she left general and vague. He'd warned her not to communicate with him unless the situation were dire.

One man's definition of dire could very well be another man's idea of a challenge. It wasn't dire. She'd survived. Had the attacker intended to kill her? Rubbing her neck where his hands had clasped without mercy, she nodded. He would not have released pressure until she'd ceased breathing. But the police chief had arrived—the American expression was, in the nick of time.

So, not quite dire, but getting there.

Forgoing a message, she almost set down the phone, but then she remembered she'd told Jason she'd check in with him.

She dialed the number the police chief had written down for her. This call also went straight to message. She quickly relayed that she was fine and thanked him for his worry. Then without thinking, she added, "I owe you dinner at The Moose for your timely arrival to fight the bad guy. See you soon."

Dinner? Where had that come from?

She told herself that it made sense to befriend the chief of police—after all, she was alone here. It couldn't hurt to have an extra set of eyes watching out on her behalf, even if those eyes belonged to the most handsome man she'd seen in years.

"I'm just being practical," she said to the empty room.

Hanging up and tossing the phone onto the couch, she added, "Netflix and chill, indeed."

Wandering into the living room, she picked up a stray paper she'd not noticed earlier when cleaning up the mess from the struggle. It had slid partially under the couch. It was the beginning of her pros and cons list. One con read: *no love life*. Because working for an international police organization did tend to put a damper on relationships. Certainly, it was much easier when working in the tech department as opposed to having to go out in the field and never knowing where the job might take her. But still, it wasn't a job she could talk about with civilians. And that made getting close in a relationship difficult.

She set the paper on the desk, and as she did, the lights flickered but did not go out. She suspected the electrical wiring for this old cabin was doing the best it could, given the harsh weather conditions. The rental owners had left instructions on how to use the generator, which sat outside hugging the east wall. As well, candles were in abundance, tucked in drawers, on windowsills, and placed in a box on the fireplace mantel.

Taking the lighter from the hearth, she lit the three fat candles fit into a birch log on the rustic wood coffee table. The ambience was nice, but the flickering flames didn't erase her lingering unease.

She rubbed her palms up and down her arms. She wasn't afraid. Not a damsel. But the question was: Was she safe here? Had someone found her because of what was in her head? What *was* in her head? She'd read a document on the computer. It had only showed up on the screen for ten minutes, and then it had disappeared. She had it all stored in her brain. And someone—her boss—had suspected what she'd seen could be dangerous.

The attack hadn't been random—someone seeking an easy victim in a desolate cabin far from town. He'd known her name. And in further proof, as the officers were dragging him out to the waiting vehicle, the attacker had said something about coming back for her.

An impossible task if he was in jail. But had he acted alone?

It wasn't uncommon for Interpol agents to go dark, especially when they were deep undercover. She wasn't exactly deep undercover, but Jacques had been adamant about keeping her off the grid. She may not have been out on assignment, but the extensive information lodged in her head made her dangerous, whether she liked it or not. She'd always trusted Jacques before. She'd continue to trust him now.

"Another week," she muttered. "That's all I'll give him before I reassess and change tactics."

"YOU LISTEN TO your messages?" Marjorie asked as she popped her head into Jason's office to say goodbye for the evening.

Jason had left Ryan Bay below to interrogate the prisoner, while he was still on his way out to question the other women who had been with Yvette Pearson on Saturday night at The Moose. He hadn't even glanced to his phone yet.

"Will do," he absently replied to Marjorie, his focus on the computer screen. James Smith did not have any known relatives listed.

"Uh-huh." Not convinced at all. "How's the prisoner?"

"Think he's from Texas. But we can't have a decent conversation with him that isn't three-quarters expletives."

"How's Ryan doing with him?"

"Guy's lackadaisical. He feels like one of those mosquitoes that a guy always has to brush away, but the bug never gets too close to bite."

"Annoying?" Marjorie asked.

"That's the word."

"You taking the night shift to keep an eye on him?"

"No, Alex has the night shift. I'll come in early to relieve him. Unless the storm arrives. Then I might have to go for a ride."

"I know you're excited for the fresh snow." Marjorie chuckled. "You need to start racing, Cash."

"I would love to, but can't afford to take time off now. This is a big case."

"That it is. And I trust you'll handle it well."

"You've never seen what I can do with homicide. How can you be so sure, Marjorie?"

"Because you're smart and not about to take crap from anyone. Especially a man behind bars who may have murdered an innocent woman."

"Thanks for the vote of confidence."

"Yes, well, I see how you sometimes doubt yourself, Chief Cash."

He raised an eyebrow at that statement.

"You put yourself out there like the got-it-all-together, cocky police chief. And that's well and fine. You do have it all together. More than most of us do. But I know you were hurt by something right before you came here."

He'd never told Marjorie everything about his reason for taking the job at the station, only that he had come fresh from the CIA.

"You're doing a good job, Cash," she said. "Don't ever forget that."

He nodded, finding it hard to summon a response. He tried his best with what he'd been given. And now he'd been handed a homicide investigation. How he handled this would prove to all watching him that he was capable and trustworthy.

He winked at her. "See you tomorrow, Marjorie," Jason said. "Tell Hank hey from me."

She waved and closed his office door.

Jason returned his attention to the police database. Along with the fingerprints, he entered a description, possible alias of James Smith, nationality and crime. Smith was not his real name. Well, it could be, but a search for "James Smith" brought up far too many hits, none remotely similar in looks to the man sitting below. And none matched the Duluth address from the license, which meant the owner of the license might never have committed a crime and had reason to be booked and have his fingerprints on record.

And that meant that whoever sat in the cell below had stolen the license and the vehicle.

Jason sat back in his chair and flicked the plastic driver's license Alex had taken from the man's wallet. It was easy enough to fake a license, but to take the time to coordinate that match with vehicle registration? Had to be stolen. By force?

Tugging open his top drawer, he pulled out a magnifying glass and studied the microprint on the license. The virtual image of the state bird—the loon—appeared to float and then sink on the card's surface as he viewed it from different angles. A rub over the surface felt like all the other licenses he'd held over the years. The card was not flimsy, either. The photo showed a nondescript man in his midthirties with brown hair and eyes who wore a green collared polo shirt. He looked like the man in the cell below, but—well, hell, anything was possible.

The SUV hadn't been listed as stolen when he'd run the check earlier. But if the original owner had been harmed in some way—or even murdered—the car may not yet have been reported stolen.

He picked up the phone and then called out to Marjorie, "You still here?"

"What do you need?"

Jason smiled. It always took her a bit to gather her things, and shut down the computer, and do a bit of dusting before she felt able to leave the office. "Will you patch me in to the Duluth desk?"

When the call was transferred, he gave the officer the VIN and the license info. There were no reports of theft.

"Will you drive out and check on James Smith?" Jason asked the officer. "I've got a perp here with his license and his vehicle, but I don't think he is who he wants us to believe."

"Will do. Give me an hour."

"Thanks." Jason hung up.

Time to head for Lisa Powell's place. He'd wanted to go sooner, but one of the drawbacks of being on a police force of two was that he had to do almost all of the work himself, from questioning to data search to writing reports. And Bay wasn't as helpful as he needed him to be. Fortunately, Powell lived down the block from him with her husband and a couple of kids. She had to know that Yvette Pearson was dead, but just in case, he'd proceed carefully. Being a Sunday, the whole family would be home. This was not going to be easy, but he did enjoy the interrogative procedure and modulating it for a nonaggressive subject.

Pulling out his phone, he spied the voice mail waiting for him. From Yvette. He hadn't forgotten about asking her to check in with him. She reported she was fine and…

"Dinner?" Jason nodded appreciatively. "Perfect opportunity to figure out who the hell Yvette LaSalle is."

Because in a short time, there had been a murder and then an attack on another woman. Coincidence? He didn't think so.

Chapter Eight

Both Lisa Powell and Hannah Lindsey had been upset
to hear about Yvette Pearson's death. Both had known
her from Blaine High School, where they'd graduated
three years earlier. They, along with Hannah's mother,
had been celebrating Lisa's birthday and had far too
much to drink. Lisa had been inconsolable, so Jason
had left her to her husband. Hannah had been in tears
as well, but she'd said that Yvette had left The Moose
to head back to the Snow Lake motel where she was
staying. When he'd asked why they'd let their drunk
friend drive, Hannah had broken out in a bawling fit.

Neither had mentioned a strange man watching
them while they'd been partying in the back of The
Moose. But would they even remember if they'd been
that wasted? Yvette Pearson had gotten a ride to The
Moose from Lisa, and yet no one in the Powell family
had noticed the maroon Monte Carlo—Yvette's car—
still parked out behind their garage in the alleyway
until Jason had arrived. Yvette hadn't made the short
four-block walk from The Moose to her car. Smith—if
he were indeed the murderer—had to have offered her

a ride. Very possibly, he'd ended her life somewhere in town.

That would have been an aggressive move on Smith's part. Not taking her to a private place to do the deed. It indicated he'd simply wanted her dead, and quickly. And he hadn't driven far to dispose of the body. Another indication of a rushed job.

Had he known Yvette Pearson? Had anger over something pushed him to take her life? Had she known him from Blaine? Did they work together? They might have known one another and he followed her here and waited until she was alone so he could strike. A crime of passion.

Except that those sorts of crimes were messier, more involved, and didn't involve the perpetrator going after yet another woman with the same name.

Unless, of course, an Yvette had hurt him in some way and he was taking out his anger on any random Yvette he stumbled upon?

Very possible. And the two women did bear a resemblance, both young and beautiful with long dark hair.

Now that Jason had spoken to the friends, he could go back to the office and, along with Bay, figure out a new interrogation strategy. Pearson's family would need to be interviewed, as well as those she worked with.

But really? If Elaine's final report showed Smith's DNA taken from under Pearson's fingernails, then the interrogation wasn't necessary. And the suspect had yet to ask for a lawyer. A good time stall on Jason's part.

He'd had the Monte Carlo towed to the station so Alex could give it a thorough once-over. And Marjorie would type up his audio notes from the interviews with the women in the morning.

Before it got too late, now was a good time to check in on Yvette. And maybe delve deeper into what the hell was happening in Frost Falls.

"WHY DO I suspect ulterior motives?" Yvette asked as he stepped inside the cabin.

"Just a routine check to ensure you're safe." Jason had handed her a heat-safe sack of food from The Moose. She *had* suggested dinner. "The meat loaf might need warming," he offered. "It's my favorite."

"I'm not sure I've had loaf of meat before," Yvette teased.

After he'd peeled away all his outer gear layers, Jason settled before the table as Yvette dished up warm meat loaf, mashed potatoes and the soft, buttered dinner rolls The Moose's owner made from scratch. Now this would hit the spot. She bustled about the kitchen while he attacked the meat loaf.

She'd seemed distant since the attack, and instinctively, he wanted to allow her space. But professionally? He could dig for a few relevant clues while engaging in casual conversation.

"I'm surprised a woman who seems prickly about our winter chose to vacation in Minnesota."

Yvette sat across the table from him and tore her bread roll in half. "The trip was a gift," she said. But he knew, from her inability to meet his gaze, that she wasn't being truthful. Not completely. "A friend of a friend knew the owner of this cabin. I thought I'd give it a try. And with the photography opportunities…like I've said."

"Fair enough." Using a quarter of the roll, Jason sopped up the butter melted in the concave top of his mashed potatoes. "I thought you said you trust me, Yvette?"

"I do."

"Then why are you lying to me?"

She pressed her fingers to her chest and gaped at him. Those blue eyes were hard to accuse, so he tried not to look into them for too long. But, man, what about those lush lashes? A guy could get caught in them and never wish to escape.

"You would never in a million years choose to vacation here," he said. "Or maybe it started out as a spur-of-the-moment trip, but I sense things have changed for you. You know why that man was after you, don't you?"

"I honestly don't. Swear to you that I don't. You can even give me a lie detector test if you need to." She bowed her head and poked at the mashed potatoes.

That was an odd defense. Bringing up the lie detector suggestion was something only those who were deeply worried being caught out with their lies would suggest. Was she shaking? Sure, there was a draft sitting here by the window, but he sensed she was not comfortable. And it wasn't because this could be misconstrued as a first date. It wasn't. But he sensed a little of that "get to know you but I'm nervous" vibe about her.

"Can you give me the name of the friend of a friend who suggested you vacation here?" he asked.

Now she looked at him straight on. And he didn't

sense any shyness in that gaze. "You're investigating me now?"

"No, just trying to gather as many useful details as I can. You're a stranger to our town, and you've been targeted. I need to put together possible connections."

"I don't have the friend's name. I took the offer as a means to fill out my photography portfolio. I've always wanted to turn nature photography into a career. And I've never taken snowy shots. It was an opportunity, so I grabbed it."

Jason sat back. "Fine. But if I look you up in the international database, what will I learn?"

She shrugged. "That I live in Lyon, France. I have a job, rent an apartment, drive a Mini Cooper and—what else do those things reveal?—I've no police record. I've been hired for a few nature photography assignments for small publications over the last year."

"Kind of vague."

"Chief Cash, I'm not the criminal here. And I'm a bit offended that you're treating me like one."

"I'm offended that you don't want to help my investigation. Anyone with nothing to hide should be happy to help. The man could have killed you, Yvette."

"I know that." She took a sip of water and closed her eyes, looking aside.

Had he pushed too hard? Admittedly, Jason had never ranked high on the compassion stuff. Comforting victims after a crime was always a challenge for him.

Jason placed a hand over hers, and she flinched but then settled and allowed him to keep his hand there. "I've not had a case like this in…" She didn't need to know he was desperate to prove himself. "I've never had a homicide. Small town, you know? I just want to do things right. But if I've offended you, I'm sorry. It's hard for me to keep business separate from other things in this situation."

"Other things?" She lifted a brow.

Hell, he'd gone and said something he probably shouldn't have. And yet, if he couldn't be honest with her, then she had no reason to reciprocate. "I like you, Yvette. I feel protective toward you, and not just because it's my job to keep you safe."

Her nervous smile was too brief. "I like you, too, Jason Cash. I wish we could have met under different circumstances."

"Doesn't mean things can't go how we want them to."

"No, it doesn't." Now the smile returned, more confident.

"But I promise you," he said, making a point of meeting her gaze, "if I ever want you to have pie, it will be delivered in person, and shared."

"Makes sense. Now. It was a stupid thing to open that door. I should have been more suspicious."

Jason lifted his chin. "You have a reason to be suspicious?"

She shrugged. "Shouldn't any woman staying alone in a cabin in the middle of nowhere be cautious?"

He nodded, but again, his Spidey senses tingled. There was something she wasn't telling him.

The phone in Jason's pocket jangled. He reluctantly pulled his hand from Yvette's and checked the message. It was from Ryan Bay. He'd gotten a fingerprint hit on their prisoner. It was not a match to James Smith, line chef at the Duluth Perkins.

"I need to head in to the station," he said to Yvette.

"The investigation?"

"Yes. Sorry." He stood. "I hate to eat and run. And to leave things…well…"

She took his hand and squeezed it. "You know where to find me. Go. Do your job. Text me later if you can."

"That I will."

He almost leaned forward, but then Jason realized it would be for a kiss and—it didn't feel quite right. She'd been angry with him for the way he'd gone about asking her questions—a bit too angry for someone with nothing to hide. And he wasn't even sure what he wanted right now. To interrogate her or to romance her? Best to dial down the need for tasting her lips that he got every time he looked at those lush ruby reds. He had a job to do. He didn't need distractions.

Damn. Why did those blue eyes have to be so stunning? They possessed powers. He could feel them weakening his resolve as well as his legs. If he didn't move now, he'd sit and stay for a while.

Jason moved to the door and got dressed, backing out the front door with a silly wave as he did so. When he stood out on the snowy stoop and the chill clenched in his lungs, only then did he blow out a breath and shake his head.

"What's she doing to your head, man?"

RYAN FLAGGED DOWN Jason as he was driving toward his house. He pulled over and rolled down the truck window. Ryan leaned out the window of his white SUV. "I'm headed to Marjorie's house for supper. Wasn't sure when you'd be back, but I left the perp's outstanding arrests report on your desk."

"You got a digital file?" Jason asked.

"Sure. I can text it to you now." The man punched a few buttons on his phone, and a minute later Jason's phone rang with a message. "Perp's got some deep stats. Connects him to the Minnesota mafia."

Jason lifted a brow. The Minnesota mafia wasn't an official term; it was what those in the know used because it was easier to say than "the group of half a dozen families who joined with the infamous Duluth gang, the MG12, and were involved all over the state in everything from theft to money laundering, gun running and human trafficking."

And Jason had one of their ilk in his jail?

"I'm going to read up on them after I eat. Apparently Marjorie's husband, Hank, makes a mean roast beef and dumplings," Bay offered, as he was already starting to roll up his window. "It's cold out here! Stay warm, Cash!"

And with that, the man headed south toward the dispatcher's house. Hank did have a talent—Jason never passed up an invite for dumplings.

Now he could only sit there in the idling truck, window still down and cold air gushing in, as he scrolled through the report.

"I'll be," he muttered after he'd read it all. "Mafia. Really?"

The report named their James Smith as one Herve Charley, a Texas native who had no current known residence. Last three reports connected him to the Minnesota mafia. As a hit man. He specialized in close elimination, meaning he preferred to use his hands and not a weapon.

Jason swore. Yvette had managed to avoid harm from a hit man? Possibly the very same hit man who had taken out Yvette Pearson, a woman who bore a striking resemblance to Yvette LaSalle. What the hell was going on?

The last time he'd been in such proximity to a woman capable of handling her own against a dangerous predator had been in Italy, two years earlier…

Jason lay on the rooftop, peering through the sight of the .338 Lapua sniper rifle. He could hit a target a mile away with ease. Today the target was closer, less than a third of a mile in range. He'd tracked the suspect's movements from the Accademia hotel down the street.

He made a minute adjustment to the rear sight. In forty seconds he would be in position for a kill shot.

It was a windless day, and fluffy off-white clouds dampened the sun. A bird chirped from a nearby tin flue that capped an air vent jutting up from the roof tiles. Perfect conditions to make the shot.

Behind him on the roof he heard Charleze click off on a phone call and say something to him. He ignored her. He was in the zone. No interruptions. She should know better. Thirty-five seconds…

"Jason?"

She had to know he could not chat with her now.

"It's off," she said.

He heard that. He didn't want to hear it. But he processed those two words and grimaced. Twenty-eight seconds…

"Jason Cash, did you hear me? Interpol wants the suspect alive."

Not according to his orders from the CIA. And he didn't answer to anyone but the Central Intelligence Agency. Charleze may have been his liaison here in Verona, Italy, helping him to navigate the ins and outs of this foreign land, but she was not his boss. And she didn't call the shots. Unless they were in bed. And... that had happened, too.

Sixteen seconds. He wouldn't increase pressure on the trigger until the eight-second mark. And he always shot on empty lungs. He began the exhale. The increase in oxygen to his eyes would help his visual acuity.

"Jason." Her hand slapped over his trigger hand.

The suspect wobbled out of sight. Jason lost the mark. He reacted, gripping Charleze by the shirt and pulling her down, nose to nose with him. "Do you know what you've done?"

"We want him alive," she repeated succinctly.

He squeezed the shirt fabric and shook his head. "We? Who we? The target wasn't yours to have. My orders were to take him out. And now you've spoiled that."

He rolled to his back, knowing he could set up and take another shot, but not without causing a commotion on the ground. He'd chosen the perfect kill shot, a place where the suspect would fall next to a brick building, out of the public's view.

Had she known that all along? Had she been stringing him along? Using him to get to the target?

He hated her for that. Wanted to grip her by the shoulders and force the truth out of her. But he couldn't do that until he got the full story from both his boss and hers.

"You're a sore loser," Charleze suddenly said. She stood straight, looming over his prone position on the rooftop. The floaty white pants she wore listed against his forearm. The touch was mutinously soft. "He's one of our own, Cash. The FSB wants him alive to prosecute for crimes in our own country."

"Your own? The FSB is Russian federal security. You're with Interpol."

"Most of the time." Had red lips ever smiled with such evil relish? "I do enjoy this vacation in Italy. A breath of fresh air, if you ask me. Not to mention the sex with an American agent."

A double agent? Jason blew out a heavy breath. She was a honeypot. "You cost me the hit. He's killed dozens in the US. The CIA had jurisdiction on this case."

"If that's how you want to play it. I've done my job of babysitting you. Ciao!"

She turned on her sexy red heels and strutted across the rooftop to the door, walking inside and closing it behind her.

Babysitting him?

Jason turned to his side and swore.

He'd been played. She'd used him to track the target. She'd probably been relaying his position to her team while he'd been lining up the shot. *Idiot!* How had he allowed this to happen?

Because he'd slept with her and had let some long blond hair and pouty red lips sway his better judgment.

His boss would have his ass for screwing up this one.

Rightfully so. The target had been on a most-wanted list. His death had been imperative.

Now Jason pounded a fist on the steering wheel as he still sat idling on Main Street. He'd never run after Charleze. He'd lain there on the rooftop, stunned, his blood draining from his extremities as he'd processed the shock of it all. He should have gone after her. Should have...

Would have...

Could have...

There hadn't been a thing he could have done to change the outcome after he'd missed the shot. He'd known that then; he knew that now. And he had been punished for that screwup. But he'd always tried not to look at his employment in Frost Falls as punishment but rather, a new opportunity. And it had grown into a job he could be proud of. He loved the people who lived here. Sure, he wished for more real police work. Procedural stuff like the homicide he currently had on his docket. But what else to expect in a small town?

And now they would take that away from him, too.

Chapter Nine

The next morning, Jason hopped out of his truck behind the station house and closed the door. The patrol car, which Alex drove, was parked next to his.

The wind whipped at his face, and he smiled. Despite the ghosts of CIA past that had threatened to haunt him, he'd woken bright and shiny this morning, singing in the shower, and after rereading the report on Charley, happier than a clam that he had him behind bars. He'd nabbed a mafia hit man. That should prove to those who had the inclination to keep an eye on him that he was worthy of a second chance. He seriously wanted to maintain his position as chief of police here in Frost Falls. It was small potatoes, sure, but it was a job he'd made his own.

He'd dressed quickly and headed for the station. The storm had arrived early. He looked forward to it, because in its wake the forecasted two to three feet of snow would invite him to plow through it going well over one hundred on the snowmobile. If he had a clear, open road to race along, he'd push the machine beyond 150 miles per hour. Grippin' it and rippin' it!

His phone jingled with the second reminder tone that

played ten minutes after an initial message. Must have missed the first one. Pulling it out from inside his coat, he read the one-word text: Hurry! It was from Alex.

Jason crossed the lot in a race and pulled open the basement door. He called down to the cells, "Alex?"

He descended the stairs quickly. Half a bloody footprint stamped the bottom step. And there before an open cell door lay Alex, sprawled on the floor. His face bled, and he was out cold. His fingers were still wrapped about his cell phone. No sign of the prisoner.

Jason lunged to the floor and shook the officer.

The man roused and groaned, touching what Jason figured was likely a broken nose. It was then Jason noticed the bruise marks about his neck.

Alex coughed and gripped his throat. "Sorry, Cash. I had to open the cell to push in the food. The Moose packaged it up in a box and bag, and I didn't have a plate to slide through the meal slot, so…"

"It's all right, Alex. He tried to choke you?"

Alex nodded. "He was strong. Think I saw my life flash before my eyes. I can't believe I let him get the better of me."

"That's a pattern," Jason said.

"What?"

Jason tapped Alex's throat where the skin was already turning deep purple. "The girl in the ditch. Yvette LaSalle was almost strangled. And now you. They're all connected. Have to be."

"Last night…I asked him how long he'd been in town." Alex gasped and winced, touching his nose tenderly. "You know, trying to tease out more information from him."

"And?"

Alex clutched Jason's sleeve. "He said…since Saturday morning."

"Really?"

"Yes, and then I asked if he'd visited The Moose that night, and he grinned like the Joker. I could feel his evil slide over my skin like some kind of nasty weeds at the bottom of a lake. Creepy."

"He was there," Jason guessed. "I bet he was watching Yvette Pearson, then he followed her."

Wincing and easing his fingers over his neck, Alex asked, "How long have I been out?"

"The text rang through ten minutes ago. I only just noticed it. I gotta get out there now. Pick up his trail. I'll call Marjorie and have her come over to fix you up!"

Dialing Yvette's number while he stomped up the stairs, out around the side of the building and into the station, Jason swore when his call went to messages. He left a quick one: Lock your doors. Don't answer any knocks unless it's me.

He shoved the phone in his pocket, realizing that had been cryptic and would freak out a person. He'd not take more than a few minutes here before heading out to pick up the suspect's trail. He dialed Marjorie and told her he'd found Alex in bad shape. She could be over in less than five minutes, because she was pulling out her laundry at Olson's Oasis.

A few minutes later, Marjorie stomped into the station house and set a laundry basket aside on the floor.

"Marjorie, I need you to put out an APB on the suspect Herve Charley. Using the false name James Smith. Put it out across the Boundary Waters, St. Louis County and the rest of the state. The BCA hasn't reported in yet this morning. Give Bay a call and ring Robert Lane to come in and give us backup."

The county frequently spread their law enforcement employees from town to town when help was needed. Small towns like Frost Falls generally never required more than two at any given time. But Jason had a potential murderer on the loose, and with Alex injured, he couldn't do this himself. Nor would he want to risk screwing up the case because he was too proud to ask for help.

"Check your messages!" Marjorie said as he paced his office.

"Will do. I'm heading out to take a quick run through town, but—" He knew the suspect could only be moving in one direction. "On second thought, I'm headed for the Birch Bower cabin to check on Yvette."

"The dead woman?"

"No, Miss LaSalle. The French chick renting the Birch Bower cabin."

"Oh, right. He attacked her yesterday."

"And he might be going back for a second attempt."

"Take the four-by-four with the snow chains on the wheels," Marjorie offered.

"Nope. The cat will get me there faster, and if the snow drifts, I'll have to dig the truck out. Won't have to do that with the snowmobile."

Marjorie sighed. "Fine. But take one minute to listen to your messages before you leave. There's a weird one on there from Interpol asking about Emily."

"Emily?"

"Something like that. Just listen to it."

Jason eyed the blinking red light on the desk phone, indicating he had a message. She had told him to listen to his messages yesterday, but he'd gotten distracted. A weird one?

He pushed the button on the phone and listened to the male voice, which had a French accent similar to Yvette's.

"I am Jacques Patron, assistant director with Interpol in Lyon, France. This is urgent. My employee Amelie Desauliniers is staying in your town. I've been unable to reach her. She is in danger. You must—"

A crash sounded in the background on the phone line. Jason gripped the edge of the desk.

"Protect her!" shouted over the phone.

The next sound was too familiar to Jason. A gun fired. And then an abrupt shuffle was followed by static.

Had the caller just been shot? Not *just*. This message had been on his phone for over a day. Jason winced. What the hell?

Jason called out, "Marjorie, when you're finished nursing Alex, I need you to trace the call that was on my messages. I think it's recorded another murder."

"*Uff da*, are you serious? I thought it sounded odd. And who is Emily?"

"Amelie. And I don't know."

Jason rubbed his jaw. This new development only added to the mystery. He needed to call Interpol, verify that the caller was indeed who he said he was and then find out if he were dead or alive. He'd asked about Amelie? An employee of his.

He had a foreign spy hiding out in Frost Falls?

And there was a strange Frenchwoman staying out

at the Birch Bower cabin who seemed oddly capable of defending herself and yet protective of personal details.

Could Yvette LaSalle be undercover? Using a different name? Or was there another Frenchwoman hiding out in the town?

"I have to get out there." Jason checked the Glock holstered at his hip with a clasp over the solid shape, then zipped up his coat. "Sorry you had to come in when you should be home with Hank preparing to ride out the storm. Call me when you've got a trace on that call. And…have Bay call Interpol and verify a Jacques Patron is assistant director."

"Sure thing, boss." She bent to scribble that information on a piece of paper. "You check in with me once you're out at the Birch Bower place. I don't want to learn you've gotten stuck in a snowbank."

"You know I'm smarter than that!" Jason pulled the door shut behind him. The wind blasted him so fiercely, he took a step back to counter his sudden loss of balance.

Straddling the snowmobile, he fired it up. Pulling on the helmet stopped the pricks of icy snow crystals from lashing at his eyes and face. The storm had picked up. Soon enough, the winds would be vertical. The music blasted inside his helmet, and he turned it off. He wanted to hear when he got a call from dispatch.

Or if he got a plea-for-help call from Yvette.

Pulling up to the gas station, Jason ran out and into the store. He'd had the SUV towed after Alex had given it a once-over, finding no evidence. It was in a Duluth impound lot by now. And of course, it was stolen, belonging to a man he'd yet to learn was safe or even alive.

"Any new rentals this morning, Rusty?"

The old man shook his head. He had a coat on and keys in hand. He stood up straighter at the sight of Jason's urgency. "What's up, Cash?"

"Just following a lead."

"Did that foreigner take off with my rental?"

"If you consider Texas foreign, I suppose so. I found it out near the Birch Bower cabin. It's been impounded as evidence."

"Ah, shoot."

"Don't worry. You'll have it back in a month. You haven't seen that man in the last half hour, have you? Looking for another rental? Walking the streets?"

"Nope, and I pay close attention to what's going on in this little town. You know all I have to do during the day is sit and stare out at everything."

"I do know that. But you're headed home now?"

"No one needs gasoline during a storm."

"And if they do, they can help themselves," Jason said of the station owner's generosity at allowing customers to pay him the next day if they ever needed a fill-up at odd hours. "Give me a ring if you see him on your way home. Deal?"

Rusty nodded. "Sounds like you've got something exciting going on."

"Nothing I can't handle. Talk to you later, Rusty."

Jason got back on his snowmobile and turned on the ignition. Smith, aka Herve Charley, could have fled town. But without killing his target? Didn't sound like a reliable hit man. He must be lying low. That's what Jason would do if he were in the man's shoes.

That message from Jacques Patron bugged the hell

out of him. It almost felt…staged. But he'd heard the gunshot. Or had he?

Jason tugged out his cell phone. Bay would have contacts in the FBI. They might be able to get more from Interpol, and quicker, than a simple small-town police chief.

THE WIND WHIPPED blinding snow through the open cabin door as Amelie welcomed Jason Cash inside. He stomped his boots and slapped his gloved hands together. That was followed by a short jump, which successfully released most of the snow from his head, shoulders and boots to the door mat.

Closing the door behind him, he offered her a rosy-cheeked smile, but concern flickered in his green eyes. "You okay?"

"Yes. Two visits in as many days. A girl could only get so lucky." And maybe she'd been wrong earlier to think he was suspicious of her. "Why did you brave the storm to come out here?"

"Didn't you get my message?"

"No, my phone is dead. Was just going to charge it when you knocked on the door. The electricity keeps flickering on and off. I suspect it'll be a cold, dark day." She noticed his tense jaw. "What's going on, Jason? Now you're frightening me."

"Sorry, didn't mean to. You're safe. That's what matters." He glanced out the window, where only a sheet of white could be seen. "Visibility on the main roads is already less than zero, but if a guy knows where he's headed, he can make it a few miles out here. As for the electricity, you're probably right to suspect it could cut out on you. You should start a fire in the hearth."

"I'd love to, but the wood out back is frozen. I was going to head out with an ax, but it's not that difficult for a girl to talk herself out of hard labor."

He seemed like he had something else to say, but he only clenched his jaw. "I'll bring in some wood," he said after a moment. "Safety precautions first." He slapped his palms together. "I'll head around back and—where's the back door?"

She pointed across the living room.

"I'll bring the wood to that door. Uh…you might want to gather some candles and check if there's a radio as well. With predicted snowfall of twenty-four inches, you're going to get snowed in for sure," he said as he stomped across the living room to the back exit.

He left, slamming the door shut, which whisked in a mist of icy crystals that shivered across Amelie's face. The wind howled and whipped wickedly outside. She could barely make out the man's silhouette as he walked by the back window. His black snow gear was obliterated by the whisks of wind and snow. Kind of him to bring in some wood. And much appreciated.

He had been worried about her? That went beyond nice. That was plain sweet. But also, a policeman doing his job. She'd been attacked. She appreciated having a hearty, handsome man show up when she felt most vulnerable.

Back in the kitchen, Amelie plugged her cell phone in to recharge. With hope, there could be a message on it from Jacques Patron.

Chapter Ten

Amelie met Jason at the back door after he'd made four trips and had deposited some surprisingly dry logs in the iron fire dogs designed to hold half a cord of wood. It was already growing dark outside, and with the visibility so low, the sky was fuggy and gray.

Now he pulled off his outer gear and she hung his hat, gloves and scarf on a hook by the front door. He'd brought in a palpable chill, but it was tinged with his cologne, which was a mix of pine and spice. Maybe it was his natural scent? She could breathe him in all day.

"I've water on the stove for hot chocolate, then I'll start the fire," she said.

"You take care of the treats. I got the fire situation under control. Looks like there's some of those handy fire starters on the mantel." He crossed the room and placed a few logs in the hearth.

Checking that the water wasn't yet boiling, Amelie glanced at her phone, charging on the little stand next to the toaster. "You said you'd left me a message?"

"No need to check it," he called from before the fireplace. He knelt, clicking the lighter until the starter he held took to flame. He nestled it within the logs, holding it there until the wood started to smolder. When satisfied he'd gotten a flame going, he stood. "I called because…"

She wandered over, gesturing he take a seat on the couch while they waited for their respective projects to heat up.

Jason settled onto the old yellow-and-green-checked couch and sighed. "The prisoner escaped. Tried to strangle Alex when he was serving him breakfast and took off. That's why I headed out here. To make sure you were safe. After cruising around town and not finding any trace of him, I suspect the guy has holed up somewhere. That's a good thing. Maybe. He could be inactive until the storm passes."

"He tried to strangle an officer?" Amelie clamped her fingers about her neck. She had faint bruises from the attack, which was why she'd put on a turtleneck this morning. "You think I'm in danger? Again?"

"The man's on the loose, Yvette. You were lucky that I arrived in time yesterday."

She nodded and glanced to the desk where she'd been writing out her pros and cons. Another con? Being pursued by a relentless killer.

A log in the fireplace snapped and took to a glowing yellow blaze. The heat wasn't yet palpable, and the cozy scene didn't settle her nerves. Amelie pulled a blanket folded over the back of the couch about her shoulders.

"If he was intent on harming you, or ending your life, I have to believe he won't leave until the job is done." Jason glanced to her. "Sorry. Shouldn't have said it like that. But I won't lie to you."

"Of course not. I need to know the truth." She tugged the blanket tighter around her shoulders.

"And then there's the phone call from Interpol," Jason said.

She sat upright. She hadn't told him she worked for Interpol. Unless Jason had talked to Jacques Patron? Had the assistant director filled him in? Could she come clean to Jason?

The police chief tilted his head and eyed her fiercely. Amelie felt as though he were trying to read her, to look inside and divine her truth. Truths she had been trained to protect at all costs. He knew something. He must.

"Jacques Patron," he said. "From Interpol." He rubbed his hands together, blew into them, then shot her another delving look. It felt like a blade stabbing at her throat. "Are you a spy?"

"No!" And then she said more quietly, "Yes. I'm not sure. Maybe?"

Did the man have a thing about spies? He wasn't making a point of being open-minded, at least not with his actions. Spies weren't all evil and double-crossing.

"Why would you guess at something like that?" she asked.

"Maybe? Seriously?" He rubbed his jaw with both palms. A sigh had never sounded more exasperated. "How can you not know if you're a spy? It's time you let me ask you some questions."

"What did Jacques tell you, exactly?"

He compressed his lips and nodded. "I get it. Not going to spill the details. Just like a spy."

"I'm not a spy, Jason. I mean…"

"Listen, Yvette—or is it Amelie?—this is serious.

And I need your help. Before I met you in The Moose, I'd just come from a crime scene. Dead body of a young woman found in the ditch. Homicide. Ligature marks around her neck. She had long dark hair, and I'd place her at about your age. And…we got an ID on her. Her first name was Yvette."

"That's…"

"Not a crazy coincidence. We have more French Canadians up in our parts than in the lower region of Minnesota. If you're in the business, you know this is all tied together. Or you have to suspect as much."

"But that would mean—" Amelie swallowed. "The man who attacked me killed an innocent woman because he thought…she was me? What about her family? Oh my goodness."

"I don't normally divulge details of an ongoing investigation to citizens, but it seems like you are involved in some way. And the call from Interpol really threw me for a loop. What is going on? Is your name Yvette or Amelie?"

"I…" Jacques had used her real name. That was the only way the police chief could know such a thing. Unless he'd had her checked out—no. Yvette LaSalle, aspiring photographer, was a hastily created cover that only she and Jacques knew about.

"He specifically asked for Amelie?" she asked carefully.

"Yes. Amelie Des—something or other. He was speaking quickly. Listen, I know something is up with you. You haven't felt right to me since I met you in The Moose. If you're on some kind of a mission—"

"I'm not. I promise."

"Then why do I have a dead body sitting in the Duluth morgue? And an escaped strangler who may or may not be pursuing any woman named Yvette?"

Why, indeed. If someone had truly discovered she had been hiding out here in Minnesota, would they have actually gone after the wrong Yvette? That would make for a very inept hit man.

And yet, someone was after her. She couldn't ignore that fact.

An innocent woman had been murdered. And the killer was now on the loose. She could tell Jason some of her truth. She had to. "I'm no longer a field operative."

He lifted a brow.

"I was a field agent for Interpol for six months."

Jason nodded and clasped his hands before his nose. Thinking. Deciding whether he could trust her? He could. The question was, could she trust him?

"Why didn't Jacques call me?" she asked. "I've been waiting to hear from him."

"The message said he wasn't able to get in touch with you. Amelie. Is that your real name?"

She nodded. "That's strange. The burner phone Jacques gave me—" She stopped before it was too late.

But it already was.

"There's only one reason a person has need for a burner phone, Yvette. Amelie."

"Actually, there are many reasons for any person to want to keep a phone not connected to a network."

He gave her another look of exasperation.

"You're with law enforcement, Jason. You know I can't tell you things."

"If you were on an active case, I might accept that excuse. *Are* you on a case?"

She shook her head.

"But you're not telling me something because…? Do you know why that attacker was after you? Why he wanted you dead? And why would your boss call and beg me to protect you, the call ending in the sound of a gun firing?"

"A gun? What happened? Is Jacques all right? What's going on?"

"You tell me. All I know is the man pleaded with me to protect Amelie, who he said was an employee of his, and then I heard a gunshot and a struggle before the connection went staticky. Marjorie is tracing the call, but I'm going to guess you can give me a direct number."

"He's assistant director at the Lyon office of Interpol. Of course you can get that number. I tried to call Jacques on his personal line earlier, and it went to message. Again."

She caught her forehead against her palm and exhaled. Her world had just tilted. Again. And this time she wasn't sure how to right things herself. She had to tell Jason her story. It was the right thing to do. Especially if she wanted help from law enforcement.

"I am supposed to be dark," she said. "No contact. Wait for Jacques to call me. The last time I spoke to him was on the evening that I hopped a flight to the US. And now such a strange call to you." She stroked her throat and swallowed roughly. "I am in danger, Jason. For something I know."

"Yeah?" He lifted his chin. His gaze was not soft or

reassuring. He wasn't willing to give her the benefit of the doubt. She didn't blame him for his caution. Certainly, she would be cautious in this situation. "And what is it you know, Yvette?"

"That's the problem. I have the information in my head, but I don't know what it means."

She exhaled, her shoulders dropping. In the two weeks she had been hiding out here in the States, she'd gone through a list of those people she trusted, who might help her, if she needed to reach out. That list had included only Jacques Patron. She had no close family. And her few friends were all clueless as to her real job.

If she was going to survive, she needed to give Jason as much information as she was able. And then hope that she could trust him.

"It's why I'm here. My boss sent me into hiding after I told him about a strange list I read. I work in information systems and technology. Data tech, for short. We receive coded documents and dossiers all the time. The information is sorted and filed. But the last email I took in was something I'd not seen before. I thought Jacques should know about it. I didn't print it out—there wasn't time to—but I had skimmed it as I was wondering what it was about. I went to his office to tell him."

"And?"

"He asked me to write it out for him, which I did. After he glanced at it, he expressed worry that what I had seen would attract danger to me. He immediately sent me home. Then, in the middle of the night, I got a call from him telling me to be at the airport in two hours. I grabbed my bugout kit, was given a fake passport for

Yvette LaSalle and hopped in a cab, headed to Lyon-Saint Exupéry airport, and…here I am. Still waiting."

Jason swiped a hand over his chin. "You know something but you don't know what it is?"

"Exactly."

"But you just said he asked you to write it out for him. You remembered the whole list you'd read on the computer screen? I don't get it."

"I have a photographic memory for certain instances, like when reading. I never forget a single sentence in any book I read. And documents and lists that I've read? I can recall them perfectly. Coded lists? I may not know what they mean, but I retain all the data like a computer. Even uncoded items may baffle me if I don't know the original context."

Amelie pressed her palms together before her lips and closed her eyes. Her worst nightmare was coming true. "Jason, I've got a list in my head, and someone wants to kill me for it."

Chapter Eleven

Amelie rushed into the kitchen to remove the boiling kettle from the stove. She busied herself with pouring water into mugs to make hot chocolate. But more so, she simply didn't want to face Jason's questions. Because he would have a lot. His gaping expression after she'd confessed what was going on had spoken volumes.

But she couldn't avoid those questions. No smart agent would withhold information that could help to solve a case.

Placing the mugs on a tray, she turned to find Jason standing right behind her. She hadn't heard him approach and was so startled she sucked in a breath. He steadied her hold on the tray as she felt it slip. His warm palm slipped over the back of her hand, and all her focus went to that touch.

"Sorry," he offered. "Didn't mean to pull a sneak on you."

Were his green eyes freckled with brown? Mercy. Why did he have to be such an attractive man?

"So what do I call you now? Amelie or Yvette?"

Just when she was getting used to the cover name…

"Amelie is my name. But I wonder if keeping the cover name might be easier when we're around others."

He shook his head. "Woman, you are full of surprises today. Let me get this for you, Yvette." He pronounced it purposefully. "Smells great. I love hot chocolate." He carried the tray over to the couch.

While she pressed a palm over her thundering heart. Chocolate. Handsome man. Sneak charm attacks? A tantalizing touch? Nothing about this day was going to be easy.

Over on the couch, Jason patted the seat beside him. Mug in hand, he put up his feet, clothed in striped wool socks, on the coffee table and sipped.

"I don't know if I can do this with you being Mr. Casual," she blurted out.

He sat upright. "Sorry, thought I was making you comfortable. Making it easier to talk and tell me your deepest, darkest secrets."

"That's a covert tactic."

"You know that from experience?" His tone was still calm, but that question had been edged with a sharp interrogative skill.

"I'm not a spy, Chief Cash. Not anymore."

Amelie sat a few feet away from him on the couch and grabbed the other mug from the tray. It was too sweet, but it was warm, and she needed that right now. The heat from the fireplace didn't quite reach the couch, for the logs were still kindling to flame.

"Please, call me Jason. And I'll stick with Yvette, since I agree that would be wisest. For now."

"I'm good with that."

"And, uh…with the snow blowing like a banshee,

I think I'm stuck here for a while, so I hope you don't mind me getting comfy. And asking you the hard questions."

Amelie nodded. "Snowed in with…" She thought, *a sexy cop*, but said "…the local law enforcement. I'm feeling very safe, indeed. As for the hard questions?"

Time to come clean. With hope, she'd gain an ally and not be put on his suspects list.

After a sip to fortify her courage, she started, "Like I said, I'm a data technician. For Interpol. I sit in an office and type reports and do field research. Of course, my field is bits and bytes. It's something I excelled at in college but had set aside for the excitement and adventure of being a field operative. Until that position no longer fit me. Anyway, I was learning to program and hack all sorts of electronic and digital devices from a distance."

"You a code breaker?"

"Not as accomplished at that skill as I'd like. But with more training, it could happen."

And was that what she wanted to happen? Her pros and cons list was weighted to one side. And no matter how many ways she found to list "using my intellect" and "keeping up with technology" as pros, the heaviest side remained the cons.

Jason cast her a quirk of brow and a gaze that said she wasn't going to get away with any lies. "And does what's up have to do with something related to an Interpol case? You said something about having information but not knowing what that was."

"Exactly. But I don't know if it's an active investigation. Is it covert? Need to know? What's going on in my absence? I haven't been informed beyond 'keep your head down and we'll call you.' I thought the document I viewed was random business details. It looked like an invoice. My boss didn't clarify anything about it."

"So less than twelve hours after you brought it to his attention, he asked you to assume a new identity, leave the country and…you just did?"

"I trust him."

"Why is that?"

Amelie narrowed her gaze on the man. Was he intimating something deeper existed between her and Jacques? There wasn't anything between them. Not that she hadn't had the occasional fantasy. The man wasn't married, but she knew he had a model girlfriend who liked to be treated as if a queen.

"Jacques Patron had been on the same training team as my father decades ago. My dad always had good things to say about Jacques. That he was kind and had the other guy's back. I've known Director Patron over the years, but only from answering phone calls to my parents, and once I met him at a holiday party. After my hire at Interpol, I immediately trusted him, simply knowing how much my father trusted him.

"Jacques was the one I went to when I realized I couldn't cut it in the field. He didn't judge. Instead, he helped to reassign me. And when he learned about my memory, he started using me for special assignments."

"Such as?"

"I can't tell you about them."

"Right. Need to know and all that secure state secrets stuff."

"Exactly. But I can explain how my brain works. My

current position sees me sitting before the computer, sometimes mindlessly typing in lists or code, or whatever comes across my desk. I don't process it in the moment, but trust me, it all gets retained here." She tapped her skull. "My ability sounds weird to others, but I've known nothing else since childhood."

"Like a kid who has colorblindness?" Jason asked. "He never knows he sees the world differently until someone points it out to him?"

"Exactly. I retain it all. And yet, not all. It's termed eidetic memory, or photographic memory. The eidetic term refers more to recalling memories like a photograph, and the photographic memory is more related to lists, text and detailed information. What is weird is that sometimes I'll get to the grocery store and realize I've forgotten what I'd gone there for. I don't remember short lists, appointments or even conversations. It's only long lists and random coded data that seem to lodge in my brain. Book text, as well. But if I could ever remember what day my yoga class was scheduled, my instructor would stop giving me the side eye when I wander in on the wrong day."

Jason smirked. "Yoga and covert operations. You're a very interesting woman."

She'd take the compliment, but only because she needed it right now. Anything to make her feel safe and accepted by the one man who could very well make her life miserable. Because if he wanted to, he could turn the tables and investigate her, insist she tell him the things she didn't dare reveal. Or force her.

Jason took another sip of the hot chocolate, then asked, "You've been in Minnesota how long?"

"Two weeks."

"Witness protection?"

"We call it going dark."

"So still working for Interpol, but for all intents you're on an extended vacation."

"Exactly. Let me explain from the beginning. I originally trained as a field operative."

"A spy." He hung his head, and his grimace was obvious.

"Yes, you can call me a spy." Because she did like the term. Something strangely romantic about it. "Former spy, that is. My parents both worked for their respective governments. My father was Interpol and my mother, well…"

Telling him that sad tale wouldn't be easy, and it wasn't necessary to this case. If she were to keep the tears to a minimum, all information about her mother had to stay in the past. Where it belonged.

"The desire to serve my country is in my blood," Amelie continued. "And I've told you about Jacques Patron, and how I grew up trusting him. But after a few months of fieldwork, it grew apparent to me that I would never be able to take another person's life if it became necessary. I couldn't do what I'd been trained to do. Sure, I can use martial arts to defend myself and fend off an attacker. Though I was a bit rusty yesterday. Anyway, I can track and follow, surveil, assess a dangerous situation, but…" Amelie bowed her head and exhaled. "I couldn't bring myself to pull the trigger at a moment when it was necessary to stop a suspect. I choked. Aiming at a human body is a lot different than shooting at targets and ballistic dummies."

"That it is," Jason agreed. "You didn't think, during training, that your job might lead you to life-or-death situations?"

"Of course. But training and real-life experience are vastly different. It's hard to explain. And I'd been surrounded by other recruits eager to prove themselves. I fell into the tough-girl mien. But that has never been me. Or at least, I thought it *could* be me. You know, grow up and take after your parents. Show them you've got the same grit in your blood." She sighed heavily. "I learned differently."

"You handled the attack from Smith like a pro. Make that Herve Charley."

"That's the perp's real name? Where is he from? Did you get a rap sheet on him? Who is he?"

"I'm asking the questions here, remember? What I just told you is what I know so far. And you were telling me how a spy came to sit behind a desk typing in coded lists."

"Sorry, it's natural to want to know everything I can about the guy who tried to kill me."

"I'll grant you that. Go on."

"Fine. After I realized I couldn't pull the trigger, I went to Jacques Patron. They'd spent a lot of money training me. I was disappointed in myself. In an effort to maintain some dignity and save face, I blurted out that I had a photographic memory."

"That didn't come up in training?"

"It really is something innate to me. I don't bring it up because…" She shrugged. "It's my normal. And the skill may have helped with maps and topography and following long, detailed instructions in training, but for the real world, action, think-on-your-feet stuff, it doesn't make much of a difference. But Patron was intrigued at my, as he termed it, 'superpower,' so he put away the dismissal form and assigned me to the tech department. He tested me with a few assignments. I'd receive a classified document that I was to memorize and then later repeat when it was needed. I call it parlor tricks. But Patron was impressed."

"Sounds a little underhanded to me, but go on."

She'd never call it underhanded, but there had been times Amelie had wondered if Jacques was using her for reasons that no one else in Interpol was aware. Sort of his secret data weapon. And she'd not questioned him. In fact, it had made her feel more useful, like a part of the team again.

"One day an unconfirmed email arrived in my box. All incoming documents go through a secure server and are verified with a four-point internal security check. No one can hack into the system. And hacking *out* is even harder. I initially thought it was a regular invoice that got misdirected. I see them once in a while. Agent reports. Expense summaries. Purchase orders. I forward them to Accounts. It didn't give me pause. Until I started reading the data. Dates, dollar amounts, locations. And that mysterious fourth column. I'd never gotten something like that delivered by email. I was going to transfer it to Accounts when I noticed the sender's email was untraceable. That put up an alert. And…for some reason, I read it. Just sat there and read each line. It only took ten minutes."

"You went against protocol?"

"Yes, and no. It hadn't specifically been assigned

to me, but Jacques was aware I retain all the information I see. Because it was an odd thing, I knew I had to tell him about it. I called him, and when I was going to transfer the email to him, it blew up."

"Blew up?"

"It was on a timer. It had been set to destruct so many minutes after an open reference was received, and then it did the cyber version of self-destructing. The weird thing was, after I'd written out the list at his request, Jacques merely glanced at it and seemed to know what it was for. I mean, he didn't state that specifically—it was a feeling I got at the time. He suggested I resume work, not worry about it. But he called me twenty minutes later and told me to go home for the day."

"You didn't think that was strange?"

"A little, but he didn't sound upset. And, as I've said, I trust him. I knew whatever I had seen was out of the ordinary."

"The guy must have known it was sensitive information."

"He did, but he didn't tell me what it was. He burned the list I'd written for him."

"So he just burned it? Never to be seen again?"

"He knew that the information could be accessed anytime because it's always in my head, no matter if I write it out or not."

"You must have a crowd in your brain."

She smiled. "I sometimes wonder about that, and then I realize the reason I can't remember to pick up milk along with cereal at the grocery is because my brain is crammed with too much other stuff. Ninety percent of which means nothing to me."

"You sure you don't have some international secrets locked away up there?"

"Well." Amelie set down the mug and tucked her palms between her legs. She faced Jason on the couch. "It is always a possibility."

His lift of brow told her he was intrigued.

"That night," she continued, "Jacques called me at home. It was after midnight. He'd booked a flight for me that left in two hours. He'd also given me a new passport and a new identity. He said the data I had in my head was so sensitive he feared for my safety and that I needed to go into hiding for a few weeks."

Jason whistled. "You gotta love the international spy game. But you've been trained to bug out?"

"Of course. I had a bugout bag packed for such an occasion. It was scary, but at the same time, I've been trained to handle situations like that. I took a cab to the airport. Nine hours later I arrived in Minneapolis, then a car drove me four hours to…this strange land that reminds me half of the tundra and half of a bizarre movie I've seen where the bad guy gets stuffed in a wood chipper."

"I love that movie." Jason cleared his throat. "Ahem. You said you've been here two weeks."

Amelie sighed and nodded. "I'm waiting for the all's clear from my boss."

"The same boss who called me and…" He winced.

She had forgotten about that strange message he'd received. Ending with the sound of a gunshot? Was Jacques okay?

"It baffles me," Jason said, "if a professional was sent

after you, that he could make such a stupid mistake. To kill the wrong person?"

"He had to have asked her name." Amelie worked it out. "Might have looked her up. Followed her."

"But then he would have had her last name and should have known she wasn't the right target. And she's from a suburb north of Minneapolis. Was visiting friends here in town. Was in The Moose Saturday night, partying."

"He tracked her from Minneapolis?"

"I don't think so. I'm guessing he knew to look for his target in Frost Falls and, well—he found the wrong Yvette. That woman was in the right place at the wrong time."

Amelie started to work it out. The only person who knew she'd been staying here as Yvette LaSalle was her boss, and now Jason. So if she had been targeted because of her assumed name...

"Is your boss the only one who knows you're here?" he asked.

She met his pointed gaze with a gape. "But Jacques would never..." No, she trusted him. He'd given her a second chance when he didn't have to. "On the other hand, someone purchased my plane ticket. Made arrangements for the car when I arrived here. Jacques can't be the only one aware of my location, or that I'm hiding under an assumed name. And you know the spy trade. If someone wants to find another, they will."

"True. But there's something I'm missing. If you can help me to understand what it is you know that someone would kill for, that would help."

"That's the thing. The only way I can learn what I

have in my head is to write it out. It's how the memory process works. I can't jump into the middle of a list of data. I need to write it from beginning to end."

"You didn't think to write it out when you got here?"

She shrugged. "I've been settling in, adjusting to this cold place, and what good would it have done? I've looked at it before. I didn't know what it was then—why would I know now?"

"I'd like to take a look at it. I'll keep the fire stoked if you will put your pen to paper. Are you willing to give it a go?"

She nodded.

"Sounds like a plan. I'll check in with Marjorie. See if she's gotten a trace on the call from your boss. I'm going to run out and park the snowmobile in your garage. With the way the wind is blowing, if I leave it out, the snow might drift over the top of it."

"Thank you, Chief—er, Jason. I know this is the last thing you want to do on a stormy day."

"Actually, this is what I most want to do. You're in danger? I want to protect you. It's my job. But also…" He winked. "I'd hate to see the prettiest woman in Frost Falls get harassed by a hired killer."

"Harassed?" Amelie laughed at that, only because it was so assuredly not what had happened to her. The man had meant business. She was lucky to be alive.

"I know." He stood. "But I'm trying to not be so direct."

"Please. Be direct. I'm a big girl. I can handle the truth. You want to protect me from someone who has me on his hit list? I'm glad to have you here. I'll even make you soup for supper."

"My night gets better and better."

"Don't get too excited. It's from a can. I just have to heat it up."

"If it's hot, I get excited." He winked and then got up to stoke the fire.

And Amelie felt that fire transfer to her chest, where her heartbeats fluttered. She'd opened herself to him, and he hadn't accused her. She could trust him. And she could drop her brave front and allow a bit of the damsel to emerge. Because, truthfully, it was getting harder to keep up the courageous facade. She was being hunted by a killer.

But now her protector was close.

Chapter Twelve

Jason loved a good blizzard. Snow slashing at his cheeks, eyelids and nose. Veins chilled to the bone. Visibility reduced to zero. Good times. But only when he was out having some fun on the snowmobile. When it arrived while he was in the thick of a homicide investigation, he preferred calmer weather.

He secured his snowmobile in the garage out behind the cabin beside the older Arctic Cat model the owners provided for their guests. With a tug of his scarf to tighten it about his neck, he stepped outside. The wind nearly pushed him over. Or it might have been the ice patch in front of the garage door. Steadying himself, he leaped up two feet onto the snow berm that had formed behind the house. There was already a solid foot of powder on the ground, but wind would lick it up in dunes that could get as high as his hip if the storm lasted through the night.

Boots crunching over the snow, he wandered around behind the log cabin. The snow glittered like diamonds. The smooth surface hadn't had a chance to take on rabbit tracks. Those critters were too smart to be out on a night like this.

And with hope, so would a killer.

On the other hand, if someone did have it in mind to return and finish the botched hit job, Jason wanted it to happen when he was here. Yvette needed protection. And that was something he could do. Even as his better judgment warned him—another beautiful female spy in his life? The last one had changed his life forever, leaving him humiliated and scrambling to prove himself.

This new woman appealed to him both physically and by prodding his innate need to protect. But could he trust her? Her name wasn't even Yvette. And did she know more than she was letting on? How could she *not* know what she had in her head? He wanted to trust her, but it was never that easy. She had been trained in evasive tactics. A man should never let down his guard.

His cell phone rang, and he stepped around to the side of the cabin where the generator was protected from the wind.

"This is Robert Lane. Your dispatcher wanted me to check in with you."

"Hey, Robert, good to have you in town." Robert had helped out last fall when Alex had been sick for a week. The man preferred to move around St. Louis County, filling in, rather than settling in one station. He was good folk. "I'm currently at the Birch Bower cabin east of town," Jason said. "The renter was the escaped perp's target. I want to stay close. Did Marjorie get a trace on the call?"

"Not yet, but I've been looking over your escaped perp's stats," Randy said. "You've got an interesting one, Cash. Looks like a pro hit man. You say you managed to intercept his attack on a woman?"

"Yes. Actually, the victim held her own until I arrived. Surprises me if his stats are so deep," Jason said. "A hit man right here in Frost Falls. Something's not right with this situation. You talk to Ryan Bay?"

"Yes, and he was in contact with Interpol."

"Did they provide information on Jacques Patron?"

"Gave Bay the runaround. Said the assistant director would contact him soon."

"Seriously?" Jason toed the snowy base of the generator. "So he's alive?"

"Interpol wouldn't say anything more than they'd get back to him. Bay was swearing about it."

"Strange. Well. Okay. I'll, uh…" Think on that one when he was inside and warm.

"I'll hold the fort here in town," Robert offered. "Most of the county roads are closed. I don't think anyone will be cruising around tonight, not even on a snowmobile. I might catch a few z's later in the basement. You still got those cozy blankets down there?"

"You betcha. Thanks, Robert. Call me at any hour."

"Will do."

Jason hung up and leaned against the cabin wall. The flurry of snow whipping about darkened the air.

"A hit man," he muttered.

Yvette's boss had sent her out of the country until the heat blew over. Jacques Patron had then called the local police to warn them that his employee was in danger—and, in the process, he'd been silenced.

Or had he? Interpol said Patron would call them soon. Why hadn't they patched him through to Bay when he'd called?

That weird instinctual creep at the back of his neck

wouldn't allow Jason to dismiss the boss as dead. Did Interpol really know where he was? Could the call to the station have been staged? To make it seem as though Patron was out of the picture? Because…he was involved and wanted to erase his tracks?

"I need to know what Yvette knows."

But she didn't know what she knew.

"This is crazy."

As THE WIND pummeled the windows in a fierce symphony, Amelie was happy to be spooning up hearty beef-and-vegetable soup with the sexy police chief. Inside, protected from the bitter chill. She hadn't had company since moving here. And despite the reason for his presence, she found herself enjoying simple conversation about snowshoeing on bright winter days.

"The cabin does keep a good stock of outdoor gear," she said when Jason asked if she had problems getting a good fit on the snowshoes. "The mudroom is filled with things like snowshoes, boots and helmets, fishing poles, and a strange long drill that I can't figure out."

"Sounds like an ice auger. There's a lake eight miles south from here. Great ice fishing. I believe the cabin even puts up an ice house for its renters to use."

"There might have been something about that in the information packet, but I'm sure I breezed over that detail. I'm not much for fishing for my supper. I'll take a breaded, prepackaged hunk of cod any day. As long as it's not been soaked in lye."

"Oh, lutefisk. I love that stuff."

Amelie gaped at him.

Jason chuckled and nabbed another roll from the plate and dunked it in his soup. "It's an acquired taste."

Dark stubble shadowed his jaw and emphasized the dimples in his cheeks that poked in and out as he chewed. And those green eyes. They were as freckled as the spots dotting the bridge of his nose. They appealed to her on a visceral level. Due to lacking sexual satisfaction of late—well, she was thinking about a few things she'd like to do with those freckles. Starting with touching each one. With her tongue.

"I challenge you to come out on the ice with me someday," he said. "I bet I can make you a fan of ice fishing."

"I do love a good challenge."

"A woman fashioned from the same mettle as myself." He winked at her.

Could she get swept off her feet by a mere wink? Most definitely.

His phone buzzed, and he tugged it out of a pocket to look at it. "Got a dossier from Marjorie earlier. It's on the perp. I want to finish reading it and…we heard from Interpol."

"Yes?" She leaned forward. If Interpol were actively involved now, she need no longer worry about remaining undercover and could very likely return home.

"Ryan Bay spoke to them. Sounded like they were unaware there were any issues with Jacques Patron. Said he'd contact us in a few days."

Amelie let out an exhale. "He's still alive?"

"Well." Jason pushed his empty bowl forward on the table and clasped both hands before him. "You say you can't make contact with him?"

"No."

"But you've left messages?"

She nodded.

"Sounds like he's avoiding you. If he is alive. And why make such a strange call to the station, and make it sound as though he'd been shot? And yet Interpol also thinks he's alive. Something does not add up, Yvette. Amelie."

"Just stick with Yvette."

He winced.

Because it was easier for her to have him use her alias. Less personal. On the other hand, she could really use a confidant. Someone to trust.

"Maybe it's time I checked in with Interpol," she offered. "That should clear things up. But I know Jacques was keeping this situation dark. If he didn't tell anyone…"

"And why wouldn't he?" Jason leaned forward. "Unless the man is hiding something he doesn't want anyone in Interpol to know about?"

Amelie gaped. A niggle of that idea had occurred to her, but she'd pushed it back, unwilling to believe that Jacques could be dirty. He'd worked so closely with her father. They had been good friends. Jacques Patron would never do a thing to harm her or her family.

"I'll let you think about that one." Jason stood. "Thanks for the meal." He wandered into the living area and plopped down on the couch before the crackling fire.

Amelie caught her chin in hand. She didn't want to think about it. But he was right. Something didn't add up.

Gathering the dishes, she set them in the sink and rinsed them. A glance to her cell phone saw it was fully charged. To pick up the phone and try Jacques one more time?

He wouldn't answer. She instinctively knew that. Which meant she had already fallen to the side of distrust for her boss.

It felt wrong. She had always been loyal to him and Interpol.

"You going to write up that list?" Jason called to her.

The list was the one thing that might hold a clue to Jacques Patron's actions. She'd write it out and let Jason take a look at it. If that didn't spark any clues, then she'd go over Patron's head and call the director.

Amelie settled into the easy chair before the fire with a notebook and pen, but it was difficult not to notice the man sitting so close. He smelled like the wild outdoors. And he sent out crazy, distracting vibrations that she felt sure hummed in her very bones.

Jason looked up from his phone and asked, "You know the name Herve Charley?"

Startled out of her straying thoughts, she shook her head. "No. You said that is the name of the man who attacked me?"

"Yes. He showed me a license that identified him as James Smith. The real James Smith—let's see… Marjorie dug up details on him—has been located in the Duluth hospital. He was attacked, nearly strangled. Has been in a coma for days." Jason whistled. "I'll have to call the investigator for that case ASAP. He'll need to know what's going on here. Anyway, our suspect identifies as a known hit man," he read as he scrolled. "No known address in the past five years. But most recent activity has been noted right here in northern Minnesota. I suspect he might be tied to the Minnesota mafia. You ever hear of them?"

"No. Should I have?"

He shrugged. "Interpol knows things."

"Not everything," she replied with a touch of annoyance. He'd grown distant in demeanor since supper. Of course, the man had a lot on his mind. And police work was first and foremost. And yet, she needed to become an active part of this investigation. And the answers could lie in her placing the list onto the paper in her hands.

"Bunch of families in Minnesota all connected," Jason continued as he scanned his phone. "Involved with a gang out of Duluth. We've got a family living nearby at the edge of the Boundary Waters that's into all kinds of criminal endeavors. Poaching is their favorite."

"Is that even a felony here in the States?"

"Misdemeanor. But they're into a lot of stuff, including assault and transporting stolen goods. Charley has a list of crimes half a mile long, but all minor infractions. Never able to pin the big stuff on him. That's how those guys work. Their lawyers are paid the big bucks."

"So he's a legitimate hit man?" Amelie leaned forward on the chair. "But that's so—"

"Big? Serious? You bet it is. The Minnesota mafia is involved with some European big shots. They handle guns, ammunition, sometimes stolen art. That's common for mafia families."

Unable to focus on what Jason was currently musing over, Amelie raked her fingers through her hair.

Because to think about it, why would someone send a hit man after her? For an *invoice*.

She tapped the pen on the blank notebook page. The list she had absently read was so much more. Did she want to know what it really was?

Yes.

Jason scrolled up on his phone. "The Minnesota mafia has strongholds in Marseille, Berlin and Amsterdam. There's your French connection." The man whistled and shook his head. Then he looked at her point-blank. "You sure you know everything that's going on with this forced vacation of yours?"

"Apparently, I know very little. Jacques has all the answers."

"Right. Jacques Patron, assistant director of Interpol, Lyon, France. Marjorie also sent a report on him." He scrolled for a few seconds then swore. "Wi-Fi just gave out. Surprised it lasted that long. Can you put in a call to Interpol for me?"

"I intend to. But if the Wi-Fi is out…"

"Should still get cell service."

He leaned over and placed a hand on her knee. "I need you to be smart and help me as much as you can." His intense gaze pulled her up from a swirl of emotion, and she focused on those mesmerizing freckled green eyes. "You are strong and brave, Yvette. I saw that when I arrived to find you fending off the attacker. But now you need to stay strong and keep a clear head. Can you do that?"

She nodded. Gripping his wrists, she gently pulled his palms away from her face and yet didn't let go of him. He was warm, and despite the crackling fire, she had begun to shiver.

"I can do that," she said. "I just… Interpol's lack of concern could mean many things. One, they know exactly what happened to Jacques Patron, but they are unwilling to divulge that information. Or they were not aware of a problem until your dispatch contacted him and they are looking into it."

"I'm going with number one. Because they sure as hell would have noticed if their assistant director went missing a few days ago."

She nodded, knowing that was the likeliest of the two. But that still didn't answer another question: Was Jacques dead or alive? If he was dead, wouldn't Interpol call her back in? Had Patron kept her leave a secret to the organization? If so, then that added another suspicious notch to his tally. "I don't understand any of this, Jason. I'll contact Interpol. We need to sort out the facts."

"Thank you." He waggled his phone. "But calls might not be possible right now. I just lost cell service. Until it comes back, if we can figure out what you know, that might help."

"I've got the list right here." She tapped her temple. "I'm sure I can get it out and onto paper."

"Great. I'll stoke the fire and you do what you need to do. Once you get that list written, I'm going to need you to talk to me about your work and anything you can think of that led up to you being sent to a remote cabin in the Minnesota Boundary Waters to hide. Deal?"

She clasped the hand he held out, wanting to not let

go, to use it as an anchor as she felt the world slip beneath her. But instead Amelie sucked in a breath and gave him another affirmative nod. "Deal."

Chapter Thirteen

Jason wandered down the hallway into the bathroom and splashed his face with water. He needed a shower, but he'd survive until morning. Heading out here during the storm, he'd known the options would be few regarding sleeping arrangements. He probably wouldn't sleep much. If anyone who wanted to harm Yvette managed to brave the storm, then he dared them to. He'd like to stand against someone with such moxie.

Smirking, he tossed the towel into a hamper and shook his head. Had he been craving some action so desperately that he'd mentally invited a hit man to come at him?

A smart man would wish for a quiet night and a clear morning. With Bay holed up in a motel until the storm passed, Jason needed to get out there and search for the escapee. He didn't like the unknown. He preferred to know every player's position on the board. He was the knight protecting the queen. And somewhere out there the rook could still be lurking. He had to be. His mission to take out Yvette had failed. What sort of hit man walked away from an assignment after failure?

Jason had never walked away from failure.

Until he'd been forced to walk away or risk endangering so many more. It sucked that he'd left the CIA under such circumstances. And now being around Yvette, despite the fact she wasn't an active field agent, stirred his blood for just such fieldwork. He had loved the job—working undercover, researching, tracking and surveilling, and finally apprehending and making an arrest. On more than a few occasions, his objective had been to eliminate a target. His sharpshooting skills had not been exercised lately, but he was confident with his aim. Always.

Despite the mark against him, he'd served the CIA well. As he currently did as Frost Falls' chief of police. Yet losing the perp could be counted as a failure. He should have been the one to take Herve Charley in for booking, and then stand guard.

Maybe he wasn't cut out for this sort of police work?

He shook his head. Stupid thinking. He was just distracted, that was it. And the distraction—another beautiful spy—was his key either to solving this case or, once again, to ruining his career.

"It's finished," Amelie said. "The list." She nodded over a shoulder while wandering into the kitchen to meet Jason at the fridge. She'd left her pen and notebook sitting on the rug beside the easy chair. "You'll have to look at it."

"I will. You got anything to drink in here?"

"Beer and orange juice."

"Beer will work." He opened the fridge. "Now that you've written it out, do you have any idea what the list is for?"

"Like I said, I initially thought it was an invoice. But who kills for an invoice?"

"Not many, I figure." Jason popped open a beer can and leaned against the counter. "You don't know what it means?"

She shrugged. "It can be any number of things. Invoices would normally go directly to Accounts. So I have to believe it was either sent to the wrong email address or, if it was sent to me purposely—"

"It wasn't sent to a wrong address. It freaked the hell out of your boss enough that he sent you out of the country. Someone sent that to you on purpose. Maybe because they knew your connection to Patron and that you would go to him with it."

She rubbed her arms and gave it some consideration. Why would someone want to get to him and do it through her? "Then why not send it directly to Jacques?"

"When involving someone else can twist the screws a little tighter?" he prompted.

The suspicion in his voice troubled her. She hadn't initially thought to suspect Jacques of any wrongdoing. Yet now, all clues pointed to that very real possibility.

"Can I ask what led you to working for Interpol?" Jason asked. "You said something about your parents working for the agency?"

"My dad was with Interpol. That's how he met my mother."

"She worked for them too?"

"No, she was a spy for the Russian FSB. I know, cliché. Not because she chose to, but because she was desperate to protect her family. Her father had been indebted to the Russian government, and he had some black marks against him that the government used to twist the screws. When he grew ill, my mother stepped in and did what she had to do. Which was whatever the FSB told her to do."

"That's tough. But sounds like it ended well? If they met and—she must have gotten away from the Russian government's control?"

"My father helped make that happen. I wish I could tell you my parents lived happily ever after..." Amelie closed her eyes. Memories of that morning flooded back. Her father had been away on assignment. She had been nine.

"What happened to them? If you can tell me. You don't have to tell me," Jason rushed out.

She didn't want to tell him.

She *did* want to tell him. Anyone. Just to release it from her memory. Amelie had thought she was over the grieving—and she was—but it still hurt to think of her mother. And sometimes blurting it out, whether to a stray cat or a cabdriver who didn't speak her language, seemed to alleviate some of the pain.

"My mother was executed," she spilled out.

Instantly, Jason's hand covered hers. His warm fingers curled about hers, and she reactively curled hers around his. "I'm sorry," he said quietly.

"I was nine," she said. "There was a knock at the door. My mother grabbed me and said I should hide. I started to beg for a reason. What was wrong? She said she had done something bad to help good people. I'll never forget that." She met Jason's gentle gaze. "She did something bad to help good people."

He nodded and bowed his head. He understood. It was a spy's lot in life. But a spy's safety was never ensured, even from those he or she worked for.

"I heard a man enter the house," she said quietly. "They exchanged few words." The accent had been French. But her fright and the strain to try to hear the short conversation had kept Amelie from hearing anything more than syllables and sounds instead of actual words.

"My mother cried out. The front door slammed. I knew whoever had come inside the house had left. I waited for my mother to call out again. I waited so long. Then finally I crept out and found her in a pool of blood. It's all a blur after that. I didn't see my father until two days later. He was on a covert mission, and it took that long for Interpol to contact him. I realize now they could have contacted him at any time. They simply wanted him to complete his mission before giving him the terrible news."

Amelie sighed and pulled her hand from Jason's. She wrapped both arms across her chest. No tears. It was what had happened and it couldn't be changed. There had been a formal investigation, but no suspect had ever been found.

"My father died when I was twenty. It was…alcohol poisoning. He drank himself to death. He couldn't handle my mother leaving his life. I almost wished it had been him in her place that day. He was never the same. Doesn't matter now. They are both gone. And I have accepted that."

Jason hugged her, which startled her, but she melted into the warmth of his embrace and managed a smile.

She'd never gotten a reassuring hug following either of her parents' deaths. This was a long time coming. She closed her eyes and just let it happen. To feel his heartbeat against hers. To accept that he cared about her. To allow herself to sniff back a tear.

When after a bit he pulled back to look at her, he asked, "You still wanted to work for the government even after all that?"

"I know how things work in the security agencies. Everything is a big secret. Don't tell. Need to know. I signed on for that at a time…let's say I was still reeling from my father's death. But I walked in, knowing what to expect. And that's why I'm here now."

"Gone dark."

"Exactly."

"I'll keep you safe." He squeezed her hand, and his eyes met hers. "Do you trust me?"

"I do. Thank you for listening to my sorry little story."

"It's not sorry. It's tragic. I wish things could have been better for you, Yvette. Amelie." He kissed the crown of her head. He smelled so good. Warm and just so…there.

"I had a great childhood," she offered. "My parents were the best. And you know, they were always honest with me. Telling me they worked for an organization that saved others, sometimes, as my mom put it, forcing them to do something bad. I always had a sort of knowing that something could happen to them. Didn't make it any easier to accept. But it was almost not a surprise, if that makes any sense."

Jason blew out a breath. "My parents are both still

alive. Simple, humble dairy farmers. Well, my dad used to be a marine until he had to muster out with a bad back. They are both retired now. And happy. I'm thankful for that."

"I bet having a son working law enforcement makes them both proud and nervous."

"I know my mom was pleased when I, uh…left the CIA."

"You were in the CIA?"

"Not anymore. And that makes my mother a very happy woman, because I could never tell her what I was doing, and the not knowing part is hardest. Now that I'm watching over Frost Falls, she's decided that at least the one son isn't in as much danger. My other two brothers. Well."

"What do they do?"

"Joe works for the DNR. Department of Natural Resources. He's a nature boy, but I wouldn't mind having his daily patrol out on a lake or tromping through a beautiful forest."

"That does sound like a perk. What about the other?"

"Former State Patrol. Uh, Justin got hurt last year. Crazy woman shot him during a routine traffic stop. Left him with some neurological issues. He's doing good though. But that one certainly tried my mother's heart, let me tell you. Mostly, we don't tell Mom about the serious stuff." He cast her a wink. "How you holding up?"

"Honestly? Since I've been staying here at the cabin, I've had a lot of time to think about my life and the choices I've made. Even made up a list of pros and cons regarding returning to my job."

"Which won? Pros or cons?"

"I'm not finished. No matter what I ultimately choose to do, I don't want to die in this terrible, cold no-man's land."

He smiled at that. "It is terrible in the wintertime, but it's my home. For now, I'm focused on protecting you and solving this case. If there's a killer loose, we'll round him up and bring him in."

Amelie believed him. Even though she knew that if whoever was pulling strings behind whatever was going on wanted her dead, they could make that happen. And she knew Jason knew that, too.

"So you're CIA? Jason, why didn't you tell me that?"

He shrugged. "Haven't known you that long. I'm not much for laying it all out there."

"I can believe that. If I ask nicely, would you tell me about it?"

"Everything you do is nice, Amelie. I like that name. Well, I like them both. But Amelie fits you." He turned and propped his elbows on the counter.

Everything about his physicality fit her just fine. He was so…there. All man, and smelling so good. The sadness over telling him about her parents had slipped away. Hard to stay sad when talking to such a sexy man. Their closeness niggled at her. The idea of tracing his freckles returned, but Amelie pushed it back. He'd revealed he used to work for the CIA. She wanted to know more.

She leaned in beside him. "Tell me what you're willing to divulge."

"That isn't much. You know the drill. I was in the

CIA for four years. Circumstances forced me out. That's all I want to say. For now."

He eyed her then, making sure she got his point. She did. Intelligence agencies guarded their secrets. A good agent did the same. Unless she was alone and confused, in a country not her own.

Nodding, she said, "Got it. I didn't tell you my secrets right away. You've a right to yours."

"Thanks for respecting that. You know," Jason said, "all this snow really is a lot of fun. You just haven't done the right things in it yet."

He had dismissed the CIA conversation quickly. She would give him that. For now.

Amelie leaned against the counter, which put her toe to toe with him. "Is that so? Well, according to the instructions left by the owners, I've shoveled, deiced the truck windows and broken icicles from the roof so water doesn't leak in. And I've learned I do like to snowshoe."

"See? That's a lot of fun. You said you take photographs? Or is that just your cover story?"

"Yes and yes. It's my cover, but it's also a hobby I'd like to turn into a career. I'll show you the picture of the moose I told you about." She grabbed her cell phone and tapped into the photographs app. Finding the picture, she turned it toward Jason.

"Wow. That is beautiful. The snow spraying about the moose glitters."

"Magical," she said. "But magic aside, I've dealt with more power outages than a person should have to in their lifetime. And now this blizzard! I guess I'm not seeing the appeal to dressing in layers and learning that sweat freezes on one's eyelashes and upper lip."

Jason laughed. "So does snot. But that's something you learn when you're a kid."

"That's information I will, unfortunately, never lose."

"You remember everything?"

"Most stuff. Not conversations, like this. Mostly data and lists. It's like when you're doing a mindless task and your brain is focused on that one thing? My brain goes into photographic memory mode. I can't turn it off. But if I'm writing a grocery list while I'm running about the house or singing or even chatting with a friend, then no."

"That's cool. What about books and movies? Do you remember them word for word?"

"Sometimes. Again, it depends on my focus and if I'm distracted by friends sitting beside me in the theater. I can absolutely quote every line from the *Italian Job* remake."

"The one with Mark Wahlberg? Wasn't that one the best?" Jason asked. Then he took on a feminine tone, "'My name's Becky, but it's written on my shirt.'"

"'Listen, Becky, I'm gonna need your shirt and your truck.'" She quoted the next line from the popular movie.

The man's laughter was the sexiest thing she'd heard in a long time. Amelie stepped forward, not really thinking, and touched his shirt, dead center over his chest. "Thank you," she said.

"Sure." He clasped his hand over hers. "Just doing my job."

"You're doing more than that. You've given me back the confidence I thought I'd lost since leaving France. You didn't coddle or chastise me after that attack. You said 'good for you.' I need that respect."

"Well earned."

And then she reacted, because it felt right.

The man's mouth was warm, firm and fit against hers as easily as her decision to kiss him had been. She stayed there, inhaling his skin, his breath, his power. One of his hands hooked at her hip and nudged her forward. She pressed her breasts against his chest and then…realized what she was doing.

Amelie pulled away and touched her mouth. "Sorry. I—"

"Please, do not apologize for a kiss," he said. "It'll give me a complex."

"Oh, your kiss was great. Your mouth is so delicious—I mean, kissing you probably wasn't the right thing—"

He stopped her protest with another connection of mouth to mouth. A hot, demanding union that drew up a sigh from the giddy swirl in her core. She settled against him, and when they parted this time, their eyes met. The crackle of the nearby fire mimicked the spark that had ignited in her belly. Everything about her felt melty and relaxed, attuned to his breath, his glance, his subtle nudge of palm against her hip.

Those freckles were like catnip to her purring desires.

Another loud crackle and pop alerted Jason. He looked aside, then pushed her away. "Oh no!" He raced toward the fireplace.

A fire had started on the rug before the hearth. Nothing a glass of water couldn't douse but—her notebook was in flames.

"The sparks must have started it." Amelie grabbed a bowl from the sink and filled it with water.

By the time she made it to Jason's side, he'd stomped out the flames. The rug bore a small black burn in the tight nylon coils. But her notebook was a tattered, ashy mess.

"The list," she said. "It's all gone."

He shot her a direct look. "Forever?"

Chapter Fourteen

The list was a complete loss. Jason had tried to salvage it, but no going. He'd stomped out the fire the spark had started, making sure no hazard remained. Yvette had scrubbed the rug with a towel and tossed the burned notebook. Those old rag rugs made from tightly coiled fabrics always stood up well to stray sparks. They were a northern Minnesota cabin standard.

"The information hasn't been lost forever," Yvette said as she sat on the couch. "But I'll have to start over now."

That was one thing to be thankful for—that she didn't lose the information after downloading it from her brain onto the page.

"I'd appreciate you giving it another go," he said. "It could prove helpful to figure out what the hell is going on."

"Do I have to do it tonight?"

"No." Jason blew out a breath, surprising himself when he felt his muscles stretch wearily across his shoulders. He checked his watch. "It's been a long day. And it's late. It won't matter if you start now or tomorrow."

He sat on the couch beside Yvette. Amelie. He'd better

stick with Yvette for the sake of her cover. She'd brought out an extra quilt, and he couldn't avoid the return yawn when he saw hers. Putting up his feet on the coffee table, he settled into the comfortable couch and closed his eyes, pulling the blanket up to his neck.

"I'll sleep here," he said. "I know this cabin has only the one room with two beds."

"You're welcome to one of the beds."

"Thanks, but I like falling asleep before a fire," he said quietly.

"Yes, it is cozy. Do you mind if I sit here awhile longer and take in the ambience?"

"Go ahead."

She sat next to him, and he smiled inwardly. Nice to have the company. And she smelled great. Among so many other things that turned his senses up to ultra-alert. The softness of her skin teased, so close but just out of reach. The accidental nudge of her knee against his. The sweep of her hair across her shoulder.

Outside, the wind had settled some, but Jason expected the drifts to be tall and deep by morning. He didn't mind a good snowing in. Especially when it put him in proximity with a pretty woman. And she had kissed him right before the rug had taken flame. Funny to think, but they had created their own sparks.

He wasn't against making sparks with a beautiful woman. He'd gotten to know her better. She was alone and uncertain. He had known that feeling when first moving to Frost Falls to take on the superfluous job of police chief. But he had made the job his own and was very protective of this town now. Sometimes a guy needed a push in a new direction to restore his energy and positive outlook.

But now that he'd been pushed, he faced the full shove right out of the position he'd grown to love. Damn it, he didn't want to lose this job, as insignificant and quirky as it happened to be.

But he'd be lying if he said he was satisfied living in this small town. Female companionship was hard to come by. He generally dated women from other towns. Not even dates, more just hookups. How to intertwine his job with a happy social life? Marriage was something he looked forward to, but that would never happen if he didn't start playing the field and getting serious.

"About that kiss earlier," he said, eyes closed, content to relax in the warmth.

"I never flirt." She snuggled close against his side. Mm…that contact did not preach relaxation. "I always mean what I say and do."

"Unless you're spying for Interpol."

Her sigh hurt him more than he expected. "I'm not lying to you, Jason. I trust you. *You.* The guy who confessed to being a spy himself."

"Sorry. You're right. I appreciate that you say it like it is. No playing around."

"There's nothing wrong with a little play."

"Gotta agree with that."

When she twisted and leaned in, Jason tilted his head. The kiss was a surprise, but one he surrendered to like a refreshing free-fall dive into a summer spring. With the fire crackling across the room and casting an amber glow through the evening dark, the mood took on a sultry tone. Yvette's mouth was sweet and seeking.

Her breasts hugged his arm. He shifted on the couch to hook his hand at her hip.

This was too good to be real. He didn't want to get his hopes up, but it was difficult not to. Yvette was the sort of woman he would like to date, to have in his life long-term while he learned about her hopes, her dreams, her desires. And could he ever share the same with a woman?

The clutch of her hand at his flannel shirt tugged, insistent and wanting. He glided his hand up over her shoulder and tangled his fingers in her hair. As soft as he'd thought it could be.

The kiss almost went deep and delving, but all of a sudden, Yvette pulled back and smiled at him.

"Good night, Cash." She kissed his cheek, then laid her head on his shoulder.

Mercy. Now he would never fall asleep.

BUT HE DID.

Jason awoke from a snore. The room was dark. The fire glimmered with low red embers. His face felt... cold. As did his feet and legs. Sitting up, he noted Yvette had curled up beside him, her head on the arm of the couch and her stockinged feet against his thigh. There along his leg he felt the most indulgent warmth. But she'd stolen the blanket, and—damn, it was cold in the cabin.

And he could make one guess why.

Getting up carefully, so as not to disturb her, he wandered into the kitchen and opened the fridge. The inner light did not blink on. No electricity. The storm must have taken out the power. Not unexpected. But why hadn't the generator kicked in?

He checked his watch. It was 5:00 a.m. Hell of a time to wake. If he went back to sleep, he would fall into a comfortable snooze but be groggy around six when he normally woke, yet if he stayed up he'd be tired later in the day.

A shiver that traced him from neck to toes decided for him. It was too cold to sleep. But did he really have to bundle up and go out to check the generator?

He glanced toward the couch. A warm body lay there, beckoning his return. Only a few steps away. No need to face the brutal weather.

Jason shook his head. He wasn't one to push the easy button. And if he didn't check the generator now, the cabin would only grow colder, and the risk of the water pipes freezing was a real possibility.

Putting on his coat, boots, gloves and scarf, he worked quietly. Yvette didn't stir on the couch. Yvette, of the luscious mouth. The woman did not tease about flirting. Their make-out session, though too short for him, had stoked a fire within him. He could go there with her. Beyond the kiss and into bared skin and moans. But only as a fling. Because she lived in France and had no intention of staying in Minnesota. And if he started something with her...he didn't want to get his heart broken. It was tough enough being a bachelor in a small town.

Opening the front door and bracing for the cold, he swore silently as his skin tightened. The air hurt his face. Closing the door quietly behind him, he assessed the situation. The snow was not so deep in front of the cabin. Thanks to wind drift, he could still see most of the driveway and up to the gravel road. Here and there, sharp-edged drifts cut across that road. The plow only drove through on Mondays. Which had been yesterday. Though Rusty Nelson, of the gas station, did take his blade through town because The Moose always gave him a free meal in payment. As for the outer, less traveled roads, everybody would have to sit tight. The snowmobile would glide across this fresh powder like a dream.

Walking around the side of the cabin, Jason navigated the dark dawn with ease. He loved the way the darkness could be bright in the wintertime, illuminated by the white landscape. The world was quiet, blanketed to solace with the glittering snow. The stillness amplified his steps, his rubber-soled boots crunching the snowpack.

He bent and scooped up some snow and tried to form a snowball. It held, but not well. Which meant the snow was not too wet. A good thing if he wished to hop on the cat and ride into town.

Keeping his head down and his eyes peeled, he looked for anything out of the ordinary. Tracks, evidence of anything or anyone who may have attempted to broach the cabin during the night. Cut the electrical power. But the snow cover was pristine.

The back of the cabin was hugged by a snowdrift that reached half a foot up and over the window glass. The two walls that shielded the generator had been worthless. The cover was drifted up high; snow completely covered the generator. Jason swore. Somewhere under all that snow sat the key to getting the electricity back on.

He weighed the options. He could get a shovel out of the garage and dig down and try to figure out what was wrong with the generator. The cabin would not be livable if it had no heat. But he didn't have the time to play handyman. The electrician from Ely, a town about thirty minutes east, would be able to get out here, but he couldn't know if it would be today or in a few days.

The other option was to bring Yvette into town with him. There he could do his job and keep her close until they could find the perp.

Nodding, Jason eyed the garage. No drifts before the double door. Thankful he wouldn't have to shovel his way out, he wandered back around to the front of the house.

THE INVITE TO stay at the police chief's house was unexpected, but welcome. Having woken up shivering, Amelie now kept the blanket tight about her shoulders and wandered down the short hallway into the log-walled bedroom. The idea of stripping away her clothing to shower did not seem particularly wise. Instead, she added another sweater over her shirt and then, with the blanket again draped across her shoulders, pulled on another pair of socks and rolled them to cover the hems of her leggings.

"I really hate Minnesota," she muttered.

Though she was never one to hate anything. It wasn't the state—it was this cold. For certain, France did have its chilly moments in the wintertime. However, she'd become accustomed to working in an office building, insulated from the elements. Maybe the summers here were warm and sunny. In this part of the state, surely the nature must be amazing. She'd only read about the Boundary Waters and the forest that hugged the upper part of the state, but for an outdoorsman, it must be a dream.

She did want to venture out with her camera again. And if that meant braving the frigid weather, then so be it. Because it was high time she started facing the facts. That pros and cons list? She'd lied to Jason. It had fallen heavily in favor of the cons. And if she was honest with herself, the idea of returning to her current job did not appeal.

Could she make a living as a photographer? It had started as a cover job for her assignments. A good agent tried to choose a cover she was familiar with, so she could easily blend, and Amelie had always loved photography. Thanks to her father's life insurance policy, she had a healthy savings account that would allow her to quit her paycheck job while seeking something that could satisfy her need for fulfilling work. It was something she needed to seriously consider. And soon.

She wandered back out to the living room. Even if she didn't appreciate the current climes, the male species was something to admire. Case in point? Jason stood before the hearth, ensuring all sparks were completely dampened. Bent over in those blue jeans, he provided a great view of his nice, tight—

"You pack?" he called over a shoulder.

"Uh…" Pack? Oh, right. "A few things." She set down her grocery-run backpack that she'd filled with clothing. "How long do you think it will take to get the electricity working?"

"I'll give Karl a call when we get to town," he said. "Storm dropped a good twenty inches last night. We'll have to take the snowcats into town."

"I'm good with that. For as much as I hate the cold, I actually enjoy dashing through the snow in a horse-less open sleigh."

He chuckled. "Good one. You'll learn to like our weather. It's good for the blood."

"It is?"

"Yeah." He slapped his chest, and Yvette could only imagine doing the same, yet gentler, and…under his shirt. "Keeps the blood pumping." His cell phone rang, and he answered as he wandered to the foyer and started pulling on his outerwear. Amelie now realized the Wi-Fi had been available when she'd checked for texts upon rising.

"Yeah?" Jason said to the caller. "You're kidding me? Where?"

Amelie pulled on the snow pants that had been pro-vided by the cabin. They were thermal and designed like overalls, so they provided a layer of added warmth and protection from the elements.

"I'll be there in…" Jason eyed her, then gave her a forced smile before answering the person on the phone. "Give me half an hour." He hung up and then tossed her the knit cap that was sitting on top of his gloves. "Alex found a body in a running vehicle near the edge of town."

"A body?"

"Yeah. Uh…" He winced as he appeared to consider his words. "It's the perp."

"What?"

"Alex ID'd him as the mafia hit man, Herve Charley."

"How did he die?"

"Carbon-monoxide inhalation? Won't know until I can take a look. The medical examiner is already on her way. The main road has been plowed. I'll have to drop you at my house and run. Hell, maybe I should take you to the station. Be safer there."

Amelie pulled on a pout. "I was looking forward to a hot shower. Is your place really a target for crime? And you did say the suspect is dead."

"I thought we'd determined we don't really know what the hell is going on."

Amelie swallowed. He was right. She really needed to get smart about this operation. Because it was a mission she needed to participate in.

"Aw, don't give me the pouty face. Fine. You get a shower. And then you're heading to the station where I, or someone, can keep an eye on you."

Amelie bounced on her toes. It was a small victory, but it lifted her spirits. And she needed that.

Chapter Fifteen

The forest green SUV had been pushed into the ditch.
Purposely. It hadn't slid off the icy gravel road while
traveling. Though, certainly, the roads were treacherous this bright, sunny morning. Ice glinted like a be-
jeweled crust under the cruel sunshine. Last night's
blizzard conditions had kept every smart person inside
and safe in their homes. Save this one. But the vehicle
couldn't have been in the ditch for long. The tire tracks
leading into the ditch were crisp, only lightly covered
with a dusting of snow blown by the wind.

Jason stretched his gaze along the road and spied another set of tracks. Faint, but again, snow had drifted
slightly to emboss the tire treads. And they were different than those of the ditched vehicle.

"You see that?" he said to Alex, who stood waiting
for Jason outside the patrol car.

"Yep. Another vehicle either forced this one in the
ditch, or someone stopped to help but left."

"I'm ruling out help," Jason decided. If it had been
anyone from the town, they would have called dispatch
to alert him to the situation. "You run a plate check?"

"Yes. Vehicle belongs to Carol Bradley. She reported

it missing from her garage—door open, keys hanging on the key holder inside the garage—forty-five minutes ago."

"Oh, Carol," Jason muttered. "You were just asking for that one. So the perp stole a vehicle that was virtually handed to him in the first place."

Stepping carefully on the icy tarmac, Jason inspected the exterior of the vehicle. Grayish-white dust from the salted roads shaded the green paint. Because of the angle the truck sat at, the passenger's side hugging the ditch was buried up to the bottom of the side windows. The engine had been running when Alex had arrived on the scene, and he'd shut it off. And…the back right wheel of the car had sunk into the ditch, allowing snow to cover the exhaust pipe.

"Not good," he muttered. The exhaust had nowhere to go but inside the vehicle.

"Carbon monoxide?" Alex asked from where he was walking to determine that the only footprints were boot marks from him and Jason.

"Looks like it," Jason called.

"Someone could have run him off the road. Guy got knocked out. The other car backed up and drove off. This guy never woke up," Alex conjectured.

"We'll see."

With a lunge, Jason stepped up onto the running board edging the driver's side of the truck. He peered inside and found exactly as expected. The driver, Herve Charley, was immobile, buckled in, his jaw slack. Alex reported that he'd initially opened the door and shaken the man but had quickly realized he was dead, so then he'd stepped back so as not to contaminate the scene.

Jason stepped down and opened the door, having to push it with some strength to fight against the angle at which the vehicle was tilted. Sliding between the door and the car frame, he leaned in and inspected the guy's face. He didn't notice any bruising on the forehead or temple areas where a sudden slam of the brakes might have sent him flying forward into the windshield. And to know if his chest had hit the steering wheel hard would require the medical examiner.

Charley's eyes were closed. His skin was still pink, but his lips were bluing. Carbon-monoxide poisoning did not tend to blue the skin, and, if Jason recalled a few previous experiences with the like, the lips turned bright red. Certainly, the cold could be a factor in the odd skin color. A heater didn't do a person much good when the wind whipped the icy air through and about the steel vehicle.

He wouldn't touch the body without gloves. The medical examiner would chastise him for that. No visible weapons. No pistol, no knife. He couldn't have purposely parked at such a strange angle, and halfway in the ditch. Maybe he had slid a ways and Jason had read the tracks incorrectly. Because why would someone run him into the ditch? Who knew this man was in Frost Falls? Had he started a fight with someone?

Didn't make sense. He'd escaped from jail. Charley should have been lying low or long gone from the town by now.

He scanned the truck's interior. On the passenger seat sat a plastic grocery bag. When Jason lifted the edge, he spied inside a half-full plastic bottle of a bright blue energy drink and an opened pack of salted beef sticks.

Turning the key in the ignition to get power but not spin the engine, Jason listened to the radio station. It was the Duluth top hits channel that played current songs all the way back to the '60s and the '70s. He checked the gas gauge. Half-full. No other warning lights.

Had Charley been staking out Yvette? He was parked a mile out on the east road, which led to the Birch Bower cabin. Nothing else out this way, save the rental cabin. But what had stopped him from proceeding to the cabin? The road, while slick, was not drifted over. Easily drivable at a slow speed. Had he seen Jason head out this way on the snowmobile earlier in the day? Waiting for him to leave? Possible.

But the additional set of tire tracks bothered Jason. They had stopped right behind the SUV. No boot tracks, though. Whoever had driven the other car had not gotten out. Alex's guess about another vehicle pushing this one into the ditch, then taking off, could be right on.

Switching off the ignition, Jason stepped out of the truck as Elaine pulled up in the medical examiner's van. Must be her turn to drive the vehicle. The county shared one van between the four offices in the Boundary Waters area.

"The victim did not get out of the vehicle," Alex reported. With a gesture toward the SUV, he added, "He's wearing those cowboy boots. I checked. No tracks outside to match. Just our boots. Although, with the ice and drifting, even if he had gotten out, those tracks would have been dusted away."

"Thanks, Alex." Jason tugged at his skullcap to cover the tops of his ears. He wandered to the rear of the vehicle and inspected the chrome bumper. Sure enough, a sharp dent crimped the end. "Someone pushed him into the ditch. But I feel like he might have been parked here."

"We got a vigilante going after the bad guy?" Alex asked.

"No one knows about our resident bad guy," Jason said.

Except Yvette. But he'd been with her all night. And while Bay and Marjorie knew to keep a tight lid on police business, he could assume the three women he'd questioned about Yvette Pearson's death had already released that information into the gossip grapevine.

He waved as the medical examiner approached. "Elaine! You made it."

Already snapping on black latex gloves, Elaine executed careful steps over the icy road. "I'm a hardy sort, you know that, Cash. Icy roads don't intimidate me." With a nod to Alex, she stomped across the snowpack to peek inside the cab. "Sitting here overnight?"

"Alex found him on morning rounds. He always checks on the Enerson couple down the road."

"That couple must be pushing a hundred, the both of them," Elaine said.

"Einer turned a hundred and one last week," Alex called as he wandered back to the patrol car, most likely to retrieve a thermos of coffee.

Jason wished he'd consumed some coffee before coming here. He'd even suffer the bitter, dark stuff Alex tilted down like an addict. He'd pulled up to his house on the snowmobile, Yvette behind him. Handing Yvette the key to the front door, he'd told her to make herself at home. The last time he'd given a woman free rein in his home, she'd put pink pillows on his couch and had suggested he get a juicer. All he could do was shiver at that memory.

Elaine put up a boot on the SUV's side runner, and Jason grabbed her elbow to steady her while also holding the car door open with his shoulder.

"Thanks, Cash. You think it was carbon monoxide?"

"I do. But there's damage to the back bumper and additional tire treads. Someone nudged the vehicle into the ditch."

"Interesting," she muttered out from inside the cab.

While waiting for Elaine's initial inspection of the deceased, Jason watched Alex tilt back the thermos. The one thing Jason never missed was his morning coffee. But this morning had been unusual in that he'd woken snuggled beside a beautiful woman. Both of them fully clothed.

Something wrong with that picture.

On the other hand, he never expected anything from a woman unless they had communicated clear signals to those expectations. It had been sweet to find Yvette's warm body curled up against him this morning. Shared body heat on a stormy winter night. Nothing at all wrong with that.

But what did it mean for their future? Why was he even thinking future about the woman? Was it because she was the first woman he'd met in a long time who hit all his *this feels right* buttons? Or was he desperate and lucky to find a beautiful woman, about his age, in the same vicinity as he was?

No, it wasn't that. She was smart, courageous and

in need of his protection. And the courageous part appealed to him. A woman who wasn't afraid to defend herself and could take his garbage? Could he get more, please?

A future would be great. Even if that only entailed the two of them getting to know one another better and doing more than sharing a snuggle. An official date would be a great start.

Elaine jumped down and tugged off her gloves then stuffed them in her left pocket. From her right pocket, she pulled out thermal gloves and slid them on. "No telltale cyanosis. Which means it wasn't carbon monoxide. Though it may have lulled the deceased a bit."

"What's cyanosis?"

"Skin turning blue."

"Right. I noticed that, but, well…" Jason peered inside the cab. The body sure looked as if it had suffered from inhalation of a poisonous substance. He adjusted his stance, pressing back the door with his shoulder, but also fighting the whipping wind that suddenly decided to sweep the snow up and into their faces. "What did you see, Elaine?"

"Did you notice the fine crystal on his collar? And the smell of his breath?"

"I didn't get that cozy with the guy."

She smirked. "That's why I get paid the medium bucks. Cyanide poisoning is my initial assessment. I can only confirm with lab tests. But I don't think he took his own life. Which may coincide with the dented bumper and extra vehicle tracks. Someone might have wanted to ensure he was dead."

"I'll call Ryan Bay and have him come out to help us

process the scene," Jason said. "Things will go much faster. Then we can all get back to a warm office."

"Bay didn't stay in Frost Falls? Didn't you offer him a cell to camp out in?"

"I'm not exactly sure where he stayed last night. He's been cozying up to Marjorie's husband for dumplings a few nights now. Might have earned himself a bed there." Jason tugged out his cell phone.

"Oh, those dumplings." Elaine nodded her head appreciatively.

Jason stepped aside and let the door close with a good push from the wind. He scanned the ground again. His own boot tracks were barely visible for the icy surface, and he followed Elaine's smaller tracks to the back of the vehicle where she stood. The drifting snow covered them quickly.

The BCA agent's phone carried over to messages, so Jason told him where to meet him, then tucked away the phone in a pocket.

He stepped up beside Elaine, who had turned her back to the wind. She looked out over the snow-packed field, which gleamed with sunshine. "So now we've got a hit man's killer running around town?"

"This case is starting to get very interesting," Elaine said. "Mystery. Thrills. Murder. I gotta say it does add some excitement to the usual natural-causes pickups. These parts, the elderly tend to drop like flies. But you see one death because of age or cancer…" She shrugged. "You've seen them all."

"Not sure I should be glad to oblige your need for excitement, Elaine."

She smirked at him. "You love it, too, Cash. I can see that glint in your eye."

He crooked a brow and looked down at her. "My eyes don't glint."

"Yeah? Tell that to your Frenchwoman."

"My French—what?"

She chuckled softly. "Marjorie told me."

Jason shook his head. "The gossip in this town."

"The whole county, Cash. The whole county. When's Bay going to arrive?"

"His phone went to message."

"Could be a while. I'll get the gurney. You guys help me bag and load up the body."

"Will do." Jason headed toward the back of Elaine's vehicle to get out the equipment they'd need.

If the man in the green SUV had been sent to kill Yvette, then why would someone take him out? Had a cleanup been dispatched to take out the inept hit man? Possible. And probable. Anything goes when the mafia was involved. And, very possibly, Interpol.

Uff da. This was getting deeper than the snow.

Chapter Sixteen

Amelie lingered under the hot water. She hadn't had decent water pressure in the weeks she'd been in the country. Washing her hair under the lackluster stream back at the cabin had been a challenge. Now the water blasted her skin and massaged it and—oh. Just. Ohh…

Another bonus? The house had central heating with electricity that worked. Heaven.

After what she determined was half an hour, she decided a good guest would not use all the hot water, so she reluctantly stepped out onto the plush bath mat and wrapped a thick towel about her wet hair and another around her body. Tucking her feet into the slipper-like socks she'd hastily packed, she then wandered down the hallway to the extra bedroom Jason had said she could use.

The room was…some grandmother's creation. It had made her laugh when she'd first walked in to leave her bag. Crocheted pillowcases and bedspread, and the lace curtains were the same off-white as the bed dressings. The furniture was straight out of the '50s with a plain pressboard headboard, and the dresser looked like one of those old-fashioned televisions that, indeed—upon closer inspection—had a record player on one side and the other side fitted with drawers for clothing. So lost-in-the-past yet teasing Twilight Zone. Jason must have inherited the place from a relative. Or so she could hope his idea of decorating style did not include such strange furnishings.

But she wouldn't look a gift horse in the mouth. It was either this or shivering back at the cabin. She did not care to be alone and too far away from the handsome police chief who could provide her protection when she most needed it.

Amelie hated to admit it to herself, but she did like the presence of a strong, confident man. Sure, she'd trained in self-defense. But with the state of her mind and emotions lately, she'd gladly step back and allow him to stand before her if that's what he could do.

Dropping the towels aside and combing out her hair before the full-length mirror on the back of the door, she relished the warmth that did not necessitate she immediately get dressed.

Her cell phone rang, and she picked it up from the bed. No ID, but she recognized the number.

"Settling in?" Jason asked.

"You don't know how much I missed water pressure."

"Did you save some hot water for me?"

"Are you coming home to shower?" Amelie bit her lower lip. That question could be construed as suggestive. But…depending on how he replied, she'd get a bead on his feelings toward her.

"Was that an invitation?"

Score! She turned before the mirror, studying her naked profile. If he came home right now...

"Sorry, I shouldn't be so forward," Jason said. "I, uh, have a lot to do here at the station with this new twist to the investigation. I can't say much more. This is an active investigation. And you're..."

"No longer in danger?"

"Can you come over to the station and we'll talk?" he asked. "I need to wrap my head around as much info as you can provide."

"Can we meet at The Moose? I'm starving."

"I don't know..."

"Sorry. I didn't mean that to sound like a date."

"It's not that, Yvette. I'm just not sure it's safe for you to be wandering around town, putting yourself out there."

"The guy is dead, Jason. What aren't you telling me?"

He sighed. "He is."

"What if I walk over to the station right now and pick up something for us to eat along the way? It's a straight shot. You can stand outside and watch me walk there."

"I've got a better idea. I'll meet you there, and we'll walk back to the station together."

"Great. I could go for a big serving of meat and potatoes."

"You've settled into the Scandinavian aesthetic."

"I know. And I fear for my waistline because of it. Give me ten minutes to get dressed and I'll meet you there?"

"You're, uh...not dressed?"

"Just stepped out of the shower."

A heavy exhale sounded on the line, and Amelie smiled. She'd given him something to think about. And she certainly hoped that thought lingered with him for a long time.

"See you soon," he said quickly, then hung up.

JASON PUSHED ASIDE the evidence bag he'd gathered from the ditched SUV and tapped the plastic. Inside he'd collected Herve Charley's cell phone, truck keys, twenty dollars and a fidget spinner, of all things. Not a single weapon. No gun. No garrote or knife. This hit man liked to get up close and personal with his marks.

Ryan Bay had called. He'd made contact with the FBI. Charley was on their list. An agent was headed to Duluth to stand in on the autopsy right now. And likely they'd send an agent to Frost Falls.

All this evidence would be sent to Duluth for forensics to put it through their tests, and it would be shared with the FBI. Verification that Charley had contact with Yvette Pearson was important to tie the two cases together. Because if not, there could be another killer on the loose. As well, Jason wanted to see what connections, if any, he could find between Herve Charley and Jacques Patron.

It was a hunch. He had no real evidence to link them. But if Patron was the only one who knew Yvette was staying in Minnesota, in a small town with no more than a grocery store and a diner/gas station/strip joint, then that led to one conclusion: Patron had sent the hit after her.

As Jason scanned what little public information he could access on the Interpol assistant director, he remembered Yvette telling him how she'd proven herself to Jacques by reading lists and then later writing them out. A handy skill to have, especially in the spy business. And if the expense for training her for fieldwork had been put out, only to find she wasn't cut out for such harrowing work, then surely the director would want to utilize her unique skill in some form. And he shouldn't be willing to dispose of that same skill for some little infraction.

Whatever she'd read on that list had been confidential and likely hadn't been something Interpol had expected to receive. Someone must have wanted *her* to see it. Could that someone have known of her memory skills? Or was it that they knew she had a connection to Patron? Were they outside Interpol? Or had it come from inside? That made more sense, considering the difficulty of learning about Yvette's skills and then targeting her email specifically. And was the email sender someone dangerous enough to put a hit out on a fellow employee?

This smacked of duplicity. And that grabbed Jason in the gut and twisted. Hard. He knew what it was like to deal with double-crossing spies. And not only his job but his personal reputation had suffered because of it.

Two years ago, in Verona, Italy, he'd trusted the Italian agent who had been assigned as his liaison while he'd been in the city on a critical operation. Despite Jason's trust of his employer at the time, the Central Intelligence Agency, he had never walked into a situation blind. When he'd learned who was to liaise with him, he'd checked her out. Charleze Portello had been with Interpol as a field operative for six years. She spoke five languages, was skilled in various forms of martial arts and had helped take down a billion-dollar counterfeit-antiques operation in Morocco. Impeccable credentials.

He'd never dreamed she'd turn out to be a Russian honeypot sent to learn what he knew and follow him right to the target.

That had not gone down well with the CIA. Which was why Jason currently wore a cloth badge on his coat and sat in a cold office before a computer that should have been bricked a decade earlier.

Leaning back and blowing out a breath, he shook his head. Feeling sorry for himself? That wasn't a Cash condition. His father had taught him better than that. All three Cash brothers were confident and able, and the vein of cockiness infused by their former marine dad ran hot and heavy in them all. Jason had loved working for the CIA. And he would be a liar to say he didn't miss the adventure, action and intensity of the job. But life had decided he was needed in this town at this moment in time. And…he'd accepted that.

But soon enough, that was going to be ripped from his grasp. Was he not meant to settle and be happy? Why did he keep stepping into jobs that weren't meant to last? Was it something he did? He didn't so much love this town as he did the people in it. And while he understood that Frost Falls was small and a police station was no longer a necessity, he'd hate to see it go. It was a town landmark. And who would be there to direct Ole Svendson to put his clothes back on and get off the main drag?

Things had to start looking up. And they were. With forensics reports due from Duluth, Jason might be able to close one case if Charley's DNA could be matched to Yvette Pearson's evidence.

Unless a new hit man had arrived in town.

Chapter Seventeen

To say that every diner in The Moose was watching Amelie standing next to Jason as they waited for their to-go meals was putting it accurately. All eyes were on them, accompanied by smirks, nods and raised eyebrows. Of course, whenever Amelie cast a glance toward the curious onlookers, they all resumed what they had been doing. Even if it meant completely missing the edge of the coffee cup and spilling down the front of that snowflake-patterned red thermal sweater.

Out of the corner of her mouth, she asked Jason, "Are we a local event?"

"Apparently, we are." His freckles were even more pronounced thanks to the bright white sunshine that beamed through the diner windows. Amelie admired those same freckles in his liquid green eyes. A sight she could take in forever. "What are you looking at?"

She leaned in close and whispered, "Your freckles."

"Stupid things."

"Why do you say that?"

"Never liked them. My brother Justin once tried to scrub them off me. With a Brillo pad."

"What's a Brillo pad?"

"It's made from stainless steel and is used for scouring food off dishes."

"That's terrible!"

"Par for the course when you grow up with two brothers. I served him his just desserts. More than a few times. Hey, Hank!" He waved to a gentleman leaving the diner, who returned a wink as he opened the front door.

"Marjorie's husband," he said to Amelie. "My dispatcher."

She loved his self-satisfied smile. It popped in the dimple on his cheek. It was all Amelie could do not to lean forward and touch that indent. But the townsfolk had been served more than enough entertainment for one afternoon. And, weirdly, the place had gotten packed since they'd arrived five minutes earlier. Had all those texts and whispered phone calls brought in the entire town—some having to forge unplowed roads—to watch their very single police chief flirt with a woman? Or even more exciting, to possibly overhear some news about the murder investigation?

Amelie chuckled and turned a blatant smile to the peanut gang along the counter, who all quickly snapped their heads around to pay attention to their cooling meals.

"Here you go, Chief Cash." The waitress set a bag on the counter and took Jason's credit card and slashed it through the charge machine. "Will that be all?"

"You betcha. Thank you very much, Charlotte." Jason tucked away his wallet and grabbed the bag. When they walked to the door, he waved to the audience who followed their exit. "Nothing to see here, folks! Just having a little lunch."

Once outside, Amelie shivered against the brisk cold, but she laughed as their footsteps made them dodge a heap of unplowed snow in their path and they bumped shoulders.

"Am I ruining your reputation?" she asked as they crossed the street and headed toward the station.

"If there was anything left to be ruined, I might be worried. But you gotta give them something to whisper about every now and then, eh?"

"If you say so. But speaking of reputations... I shouldn't ask, but I have to. Tell me why you left the CIA."

"Do I have to?"

"I did tell you my sad tale."

He chuckled. "Fine. I didn't leave, I was fired. But my boss wanted me to suffer even more, so he 'placed' me—" he made air quotes "—in a suitable job that required filling."

"This job you have now? It's such a small town. I'm surprised there is even a police station in it."

A passing station wagon honked, and Jason nodded and gave the driver a wave. "Frost Falls used to be four times the population it is now. Wasn't even three years ago it was booming. Workers from the iron range lived here. Then the Red Band iron mine went bust, and everyone packed up and left. It was a lot of migrant workers, but many locals as well. Since there was already a police station, the chief of police stayed on as he watched the town's numbers dwindle. He died of natural causes two years ago. And when they should have closed the station and left the law enforcement to the county, some smart aleck in the CIA decided he'd send one of his agents here as a means of punishment to watch over the peanut gang."

"Did you have to take the job?"

"No. But it was a job, and it's located within an hour's driving distance of both my brothers and my parents, so… Hell." He stopped at the corner of the red-brick station house and looked straight at her. It was his hefty sigh that told her his truths were valuable. And she would handle them with the care they deserved. "At the time, I wasn't in a mental place where I was willing to stand up and fight the system. I was real down on myself and decided to take my punishment as due."

"Punishment for what?"

"I botched a mission."

"Is that all? But…agents do that all the time. Well, not all the time. But it happens. Backup measures are usually in place—"

"I let a known terrorist walk out of my crosshairs," Jason said firmly. He closed his eyes and swallowed. "Because she got to him first."

"She?" Amelie noticed the muscle in his jaw tighten. "An Interpol agent?"

"How'd you guess?"

"You were not pleased to hear I worked for Interpol. I had no idea at the time, but that explains your reaction."

"She was using me the whole time. I thought she was a liaison provided by the Italian headquarters. Turns out Interpol wanted their hands on the target for their own reasons. And it wasn't to take him out. I want to believe it was some kind of trade to the Russians. Far as I know, the target is walking free. It's not right."

"A lot of what goes on in international and national security agencies isn't always deemed right. But who is the judge of what is right and wrong? There are many situations that can be viewed both ways."

"I know that. One man's freedom fight is another man's misdirected protest. The target had taken out women and children, Yvette. Dozens of them. His weapon of choice was pipe bombs placed at coffee shops in the Washington, DC, area. It was a malicious and vulgar crime. I hate myself for letting him walk."

Amelie knew now wasn't the time for argument or reasoning. It was a challenge dealing with the power an agent wielded. Certainly, she had been faced with many such challenges. And ultimately? She'd not been able to pass the cruelest test. To shoot or not to shoot? She'd not realized which side she fell on until it was almost too late. Fortunately, she'd been able to step away and still retain her job at Interpol.

Jason had been punished for something that hadn't been his fault. One of her own had tricked him? Likely a honeypot sent in to cozy up to him, earn his trust, learn what he knew, then report back to headquarters. It happened all the time.

"I won't betray you," she said. "Promise."

He nodded but didn't say anything. He didn't need to. Thanks to his training, and his experience in Italy, he couldn't trust her. Not completely. But she was prepared to earn that trust.

"Thanks, Jason. You didn't have to tell me that. I appreciate that you did. It's freezing out here." She managed a face-crunching smile, then ran ahead and grabbed the station door and held it for Jason.

"Jason." A woman with frosted brown hair cut close to her scalp stood from behind a desk. Must be the dispatcher he'd mentioned. "This must be your French— er, uh, Yvette, wasn't it?"

Amelie tugged off a mitten and offered her hand. "Nice to meet you. You must be Marjorie."

"You betcha. You two dining in Jason's office?"

"You know we are," Jason said with a tone that indicated he wasn't about to take any of the woman's sly teasing. "I'm waiting on a call from the FBI," he called as he entered his office and held the door for Amelie. "Patch it through when it comes, Marjorie."

"Will do, boss."

He closed the door, and Amelie took the food bag to set their meals out on his desk. "Do I get the grand tour?" she asked.

"Uh, sure, but this old station house is the least interesting place in the whole town."

"Oh, I don't know. Marjorie's Christmas decorations certainly do brighten up the outer office."

"They stay up until Valentine's Day, and then we have hearts until St. Patrick's and—it's never boring out in reception. Okay, then! Here's the tour. This is my desk. This is my computer. This is me. That's my deer rack collection." He pointed to the two racks, each more than sixteen points, hanging on the far wall. And next to it hung… "And that is the calendar the print shop in the next town makes of local heroes—they donate profits to the Camp Ripley charity."

"Is that man standing beside a real wolf?" Amelie

bent to study closely the calendar hung from a bent two-inch roofing nail. It featured a sexy, bare-chested man with dark hair and a six pack that competed with his incredible dimples.

"Yep, that's my brother Joseph. They call him the Wolf Whisperer. I told you he works for the DNR and has an intimate connection to nature, wolves especially."

"I love wolves. They have such a history. Have you heard of the Beast of Gévaudan in France?"

"Can't say that I have."

"It's an eighteenth-century werewolf legend."

Jason chuckled. "Sorry to disappoint, but there are no werewolves here in Minnesota. You like that kind of stuff?"

"What kind of stuff?"

"Werewolves and vampires and all that weird nonsense?"

She cast him a flutter of lash. "I wouldn't chase a sexy vampire out of my bed."

"Yikes. You women and your…weird fascination for all things…weird. I don't understand why having some fang-toothed monster gnawing on your neck is supposed to be romantic."

"Well, I'm not much for being gnawed myself. Are you on a month?" She flipped up a couple pages of the calendar.

"I was in last year's edition."

"Doesn't surprise me."

This time she took him in from head to just there below his belt. Heh. Was the man blushing?

"I'll have to see about finding a copy," she said. "Especially since beefcake is another of my interests."

"I think my mom has ten. Or a hundred. So that's it. My office," he said. "Pretty exciting, eh?"

"I like it all. Quaint, but underneath it all I'm sure there's a vibrant and busy law enforcement team ready and willing to protect its citizens."

"Always." Jason thrust back his shoulders. "Now let's eat and then get to work."

"Is the food that terrible?"

Jason's voice summoned Amelie from thoughts that were far too deep for what should be a pleasant lunch. Forcing on a smile, she shook her head. "It's too good. I could get used to this home-style cooking. And that's the problem."

"I've never had a problem with a turkey and gravy sandwich."

"I can see why. It's…mmm…so good."

Jason leaned forward and caught his cheek in a palm. "Could a turkey sandwich entice you to stay in Frost Falls longer than you'd planned?"

"My gut answer? Yes." Amelie squeezed her eyes shut. Had she just said that? And the reason it had come out so easily was because there was an excellent incentive for sticking around: freckles and a sexy smile. But. "But I didn't have a planned end date for this stay. And I'm not sure I can survive this place much longer."

"You've been cooped up in that cabin for weeks. Anyone would go loony bin. You should give some consideration to sticking around awhile. Let me show you how to enjoy a Minnesota winter."

She ran her tongue along her upper lip. Not an offer any sane woman would refuse. "Don't you have a girl-friend, Jason?"

He winked at her. "Does it look like it?"

"No. But that makes me wonder why."

He crimped a brow.

"What's wrong with you?" she said on a teasing tone.

"Not a lot of young, single women here in Frost Falls. Or haven't you noticed?"

"Isn't the Saturday-night stripper single?"

He shook his head and chuckled softly. "What about you? Is there a boyfriend back home in France?"

"There isn't."

"Yeah? So what's wrong with you?"

"I work too much and have no social life. But no cats yet."

"That's a good thing."

"So now—" she leaned in closer over her takeout container "—the burning question."

"Shoot."

"Are you interested in me, Jason?"

"Hell, yes."

"I like a man who knows what he wants." She sat back, pleased with that quick and confident answer.

The intercom buzzed, and Marjorie said, "Ryan Bay is on his way."

"Thanks, Marjorie. Bay is with the Bureau of Criminal Apprehension. He'll want to talk to you," he said to Amelie.

"Sure. Standard procedure."

"Nothing to worry about."

"I'm not worried. I've done nothing wrong."

"Nothing except attract a hit man to Frost Falls."

"Is that an accusation? I'm not sure I care for that."

"Sorry. It's not your fault." He set down his sandwich and leaned forward. "Why would someone take out a hit man?"

"Mafia, right?"

"He was a hired gun. Connected to local mafia. And now he's dead," Jason said.

"You said the vehicle was stuck in the ditch. Was it forced off the road?"

"Yes. There was a dent on the bumper and tire tracks indicating that. But the driver wasn't dead when he hit the ditch. Maybe? I initially assumed carbon-monoxide inhalation. Happens in these parts during the winter months. Car slides off an icy road, gets half-buried in the snow. The driver takes the safe route of not venturing out in a blizzard and doesn't know the safety precautions for staying in a vehicle when trapped in the cold. Gotta remember to check the exhaust pipe if you're letting the engine run to stay warm. Doesn't take long for carbon monoxide to enter the brain and lull the person to sleep. For good."

He pulled off the plastic cover from the coffee cup and sipped. "But the medical examiner spotted signs of poison."

"Poison? Why would someone take out the person who was supposed to kill me?"

"I don't know. That's what I'm asking you."

She detected an accusing tone and didn't like it one bit. Sitting up straight, Amelie took another bite of her sandwich.

"You don't trust me?" she asked.

"I really want to." He challenged her with a steady gaze. Damn, those freckles would be her undoing. "But I know very little."

"I know even less. I'm as confused about all this as you are."

"Every thought I have about this case leads me back to Jacques Patron."

"But he's…" She paused. No confirmation of his death had been given. As far as she knew, he could be AWOL. Could he be a double agent?

"Did you have a chance to write out the list while at my place this morning?" he asked.

"No, I'm sorry, the hot shower seduced me."

She caught his appreciative nod with a subtle lift of brow.

"I intend to get to that as soon as we're done here," she said. "Promise. I want to help you. And if there is someone wandering Frost Falls who is so dangerous as to defeat a hit man, then…" She set down the last corner of the sandwich and tucked her shaking hands between her legs. "I'm a little scared."

"Don't be. I will protect you, Yvette. Amelie."

"I know you will." She stood and gathered her container and plastic utensils and put them in the bag they'd come in.

She turned and wandered toward the window overlooking Main Street, trailing her fingers along the scuffed sill. "I suppose a town this size doesn't see hit men all that often."

"You better believe we don't." He tossed his things in the bag and joined her.

His presence softened her fears. Standing so close to him, she felt lighter, safer.

"Thank you for what you've done for me, Jason." Her gaze met his, and her lips parted softly. "I mean, Chief Cash."

Heartbeats thundered as memories of their kisses resurfaced. She moved closer so their legs touched. "You kissed me yesterday at the cabin. A girl might expect another…"

"Nothing wrong with a kiss. And if I recall correctly, you were the one to initiate the kiss on the—"

She kissed him quickly, pleased at his surprised response as his open arms slowly and assuredly wrapped around her back. He felt right pressed against her.

His fiery kiss quickly melted the ice that had taken up under her skin like permafrost since moving to Frost Falls.

She giggled.

Jason pressed a finger to her mouth. "Quiet. These walls are as thin as paper. Marjorie will hear."

"That's all right!" Marjorie called out from the other room. "I'm happy you finally have someone to kiss, Chief Cash!"

Amelie gaped, then muffled another giggle.

Jason raised a brow as if to silently say, "See?"

Amelie's cell phone rang, then immediately buzzed, indicating the caller sent a text message instead of waiting for her to answer. She stared at the screen ID and blinked. Her heartbeat thundered. She opened her mouth but no sound came out.

"What is it?" Jason asked.

"It's a message."

"Yeah?"

She turned the phone toward Jason. "It's from Jacques Patron."

Chapter Eighteen

"I thought he was dead." Jason took Yvette's phone from her and read the message to himself: You there?

"I should text him back." She reached for the phone, but Jason clasped his fingers about it. "Jason?"

"I'm not sure about this. I know what I heard on that message. It was a gunshot."

"That doesn't mean anyone was harmed or even died."

"True. But the guy hasn't contacted you since you arrived—what—two weeks ago? And now he does only *after* the hit man has failed? This doesn't feel right."

"You think that's a text from someone else? Using Jacques's phone?"

"Not sure. I want to do a trace on this text."

"I thought your dispatch came up with nothing on the first trace to your phone?"

"She did, but it's worth another try. Can I take this with me?"

She was beautiful when she was thinking. Bright blue eyes unfocused and head tilted slightly down.

She nodded. "Okay. I don't have any important information on it. Just a few calls to the grocery store and, of course, to Interpol in Lyon. I'll write down my password." She grabbed a napkin, and Jason pulled a pen out from his inside coat pocket so she could write it down.

He took the napkin and wrapped it once about the phone then slipped that and the pen into his pocket. "Just to be safe. If he's alive, that's good, right?"

"But if he is, don't you think I should return his call soon?"

"Let me answer with a different question. If you don't return his call, will the man think you're dead? And more important—will believing you are dead please him?"

She worried at her lower lip with her teeth. Thinking again. Which was exactly what he needed her to do. Everything about this situation seemed to point the compass toward France, and Yvette's boss.

"I'm not stupid," she said. "It could very well be as you suspect. I'll wait until you can track the origin of the text. If it came from Jacques's phone…"

"Interpol wouldn't confirm Patron's death. If they don't know what Patron is up to, they could have begun an investigation of their own. Which means it's possible they don't know where you are. Patron hasn't told anyone. That doesn't sound like standard procedure when an agent goes dark. At the very least, it's noted and the director would know, yes?"

Yvette nodded. "You're right, I don't know Jacques as well as I think I do. And I have a list I need to get out of my head. Once again."

"It could be key to solving this case," Jason said.

AMELIE SETTLED ONTO the chair behind the police chief's desk with a blank sheet of paper before her.

Jason breezed back in from reception, tucking away his cell phone in a coat pocket. "You going to be okay for half an hour by yourself?" he asked, zipping up his coat. "Alex and I are meeting Bay to go over the medical examination on Charley's body."

He wandered over and stood beside the chair. He smelled like fresh, clean air. His overwhelming presence lulled her into a swoony smile.

"I will be with Marjorie standing guard out in reception," she teased. "This shouldn't take too long. What will I do when I've finished?"

"If I'm not back, you can…" He looked around the office, then opened the bottom desk drawer to reveal the contents. "I've got provisions. Snacks and Sudoku. Marjorie will talk your head off it you let her, and she's got a lot of work to do this afternoon. Think she's going to head downstairs and do a little cleaning in the cells, too."

"I won't bother her. Sudoku, eh?"

"For stakeouts."

She lifted a brow in wonder.

"Eh." He shrugged. "I might get to use that book someday. There's always hope."

He leaned over, and when Amelie sensed he was going to kiss her on the top of the head, she quickly tilted her head to catch that morsel against her mouth. He didn't hesitate, finding their connection like a pro. The man pushed his fingers up through the back of her hair, holding her gently. He tasted like all the things she needed right now. Safety, connection, intimacy.

Releasing a tiny moan as his kiss deepened in exploration, Amelie twisted and moved up onto her knees. She spread her hands up the front of his coat, wishing it were anything but the thick black waterproof fabric. Like bare, hot skin. Could a girl get a little taste of that?

Sliding down her hands, she felt the hard shape of his gun hugging his ribs, and then, at the bottom of his coat, she pushed her fingers up underneath it. The Kevlar vest he wore was solid, but thin. His flannel shirt hugged the top of his jeans and…oh yes, there.

He smiled against her mouth, then with a glance toward the closed door, turned and whispered, "You doing some investigation work of your own?"

"I am. And I found what I was looking for." Hot, bare skin. Tight, hard abs. A dangerous tease. "I wish you didn't have to leave."

"You make me wish the same thing." He nuzzled his forehead against hers. "I'd take you along with me, but this is police business and…"

"I get it. I'm not an investigating officer." Amelie took in his scent, his skin, his breath. The moment was so intimate, yet in the background lurked calamity.

With a quick kiss to her mouth, he said, "I'll be back."

"I'll be waiting for you."

"Does that mean what I think it means?" he asked.

"I never flirt."

"You always mean business. I got that about you." He kissed her again, taking the time to make it linger as he swept his tongue against hers and tasted her deeply. Then he swore softly against her mouth, nodded and stood up. "If I don't leave now…"

"I get it. I feel the same. Things are going to happen between us."

"Yes, they are."

"Go," she said. "I'll write out the list. Then we'll… see what happens next."

He strode to the door, pulling a knit cap over his head. "See you soon!"

She waited and waved as he passed before the front window and strode down Main Street. The man couldn't return to her fast enough. Because he had started a fire inside her, and she wouldn't be able to stop thinking about him until all his clothes were stripped away and that investigation practice turned into real-time experience.

Until then, she did have a more pressing task at hand.

Leaning forward on the not-too-comfy chair, Amelie wrote out the numbers and letters that formed a list she'd viewed weeks earlier in the strange email that she now felt sure had been sent to her with an ulterior purpose. It couldn't have been an accident. Someone had wanted her to take that information to her boss.

And her boss had known exactly what sort of damage that information could do. To him?

More and more, she believed Jacques was involved in something underhanded.

It was slow going this time around because it was difficult to avoid thoughts of Jacques Patron's true intentions. What information was she streaming out onto the paper? It was something worth killing for.

After half an hour, she wrote out the last line. Times, dates, locations and…that mysterious fourth column.

Each entry was a jumble of letters and numbers. It had to be code or...maybe a password?

Stretching her arms over her head, she turned and stood, peering out the window. Jason was still gone, and she hadn't heard a peep from Marjorie after she'd called out that she was going downstairs to straighten the cells.

She wasn't about to go out wandering on her own. But she was antsy now, and the office had chilled noticeably. Pulling on her coat, she dallied with the idea of running down the street to Olson's Oasis for something to munch on. No. Jason had snacks in the drawer. And he'd never forgive her for leaving the station.

Picking up her camera, she wandered out into reception. Amelie trailed a finger along Marjorie's pin-neat desk, taking in the photos of Marjorie and a man with blond hair who must be her husband. A bobblehead of a black cat with green rhinestones for eyes sat next to a desk phone. And a cookbook titled *Hot Dishes* that was flagged with colorful Post-its was splayed open, cover facing up.

She stood back and snapped a few shots of the reception area, being sure to get Jason's office in the background. She'd never been much for interior shots. Nature was most interesting to capture on film. Backing up against the door, she decided a step outside would be worthwhile, because there was a large oak tree that loomed in the back parking lot. And she'd stay close to the station.

Jason's truck was still parked in the back lot, as was a green Honda. Must be Marjorie's. The oak tree's canopy was vast, leafless, and stretched overhead as if an open umbrella.

Tilting back her head, Amelie snapped some shots. Inhaling the crisp winter air, she smiled. Yes, this could become a career that would make her happy.

Chapter Nineteen

"The cyanide killed him," Elaine said over the phone line as Jason scrolled through Herve Charley's cell phone looking for clues. He and Alex stood in the gas station parking lot, where the green SUV had been towed to wait for the Duluth tow to come and take it away. Ryan Bay stood over by his car, on the phone. "I found traces of it in the beef jerky. Clever."

Jason eyed a couple bundled against the day's ten degrees as they passed by, probably on the way to The Moose for some pie. "Whoever followed him must have planted the beef jerky. Probably drove up behind him. Nudged the car into the ditch and waited to see if the driver would react. No reaction. Assumed he was dead, and drove off."

"A fair assessment. The body was clean of any DNA not unique to the deceased."

Jason swore under his breath. They were dealing with professionals. Two of them. One dead. And the other?

"Thanks, Elaine. This may have become an international case. Bay is on the phone with Interpol again, trying to get some real answers about the one suspect that sticks out like a sore thumb."

"Who do you think the perp is this time around?" Elaine conjectured, "A vigilante going after someone who tried to harm another?"

"Why would someone take out a hit man, Elaine?"

"I don't know—"

"Well, I do. It's because the first one has been replaced after a shoddy effort at eliminating the target. Which means Frost Falls has another hit man running loose. The FBI has verified links to the Minnesota mafia right now."

"Which means someone is after your woman."

"She's not my—"

"Where is she?"

"At the station." Jason checked his watch. It had been half an hour since he'd left Yvette. He should check in with her. "I gotta go, Elaine. Thanks for the info."

Dialing Yvette's number, he suddenly jumped when his pocket rang. Alex cast him a wondering look.

"Shoot. Forgot I'd taken her phone as evidence." He patted the pocket and hung up. "I'm heading back to the station. Make sure everyone is all right. Have Bay give me a call as soon as he's off the phone with Interpol."

Jason started walking down the street. For some reason, he quickened his footsteps.

THE SKY WAS white and the sun high. Amelie could even find some good in the cold, because it tingled across her face, making her feel alive. The idea of spending more time in Frost Falls to photograph the scenery, to perhaps even venture into the Boundary Waters Canoe

Area Wilderness, was appealing. It would be a great addition to her meager portfolio.

Everything felt normal. Yet a weird feeling of dread prompted her to suddenly twist at the waist and scan the parking lot behind the station. She hadn't heard anything beyond the hum of the heater that puffed out condensation from the rooftop of the station. Narrowing her gaze, she took in the surroundings.

JASON RAN DOWN the street toward the station. His rubber-soled boots took the snow compacted on the tarmac with ease. Four blocks and no one was going to break a sweat in this frigid weather. By the time he reached the parking lot, he cursed when he saw Yvette's figure standing against the hood of his truck.

What was she doing outside?

"Yvette!"

She turned and waved.

Jason spied the flash of red as it glinted across the hood of his truck. "Get down!"

Racing toward the truck, he lunged forward, gripped her by the shoulders and knocked her down to land on the snow-packed tarmac. Their bodies rolled, and he barreled over the top of her. The camera she'd been holding clattered across the snow. Protecting her body with his, Jason looked up and around the front of the vehicle.

"Someone just shot at you," he said. "I was right." He pulled out his gun and switched off the safety. "There's another hit man in town."

Chapter Twenty

"Stay down," Jason demanded to the woman beneath him on the snow.

Yvette nodded. Her eyes were wide, but he detected more common sense than fear in them. She'd been trained for hostile situations.

He scrambled around to the end of the truck bed and crouched low, pulling out his gun. He swept a look around the rear taillight. No movement in the parking lot. Aiming out into the parking lot, he didn't spy the shooter.

Jason's exhale fogged before his face.

The growl of a snowmobile engine firing up alerted him. He sighted a flash of silver that would place the machine in the alleyway behind the antique shop two buildings down.

"I'm going after him!" he called to Yvette. "Get inside the station!" His protective instincts forced him back to the front of the truck where she now crouched. "You got this, yes?"

She nodded. "Go!"

"Tell Marjorie to call Alex here."

His snowmobile was parked ten feet from the back

door. Firing it up, he navigated forward out of the parking lot and to the alleyway. He waited until he heard the other snowmobile reach the intersection of Main Street and the corner of the block. The driver was dressed all in black. No cap or earmuffs, and he didn't wear gloves.

"Not a resident," Jason confirmed.

Confident that whoever drove the snowmobile was the one who had shot at Yvette, he gunned the throttle and his sled soared forward just as the other snowmobile took off through the intersection.

Gun tucked in the holster at his hip, he would not fire on the shooter until he could confirm he was indeed the suspect. Worst-case scenario would see him chasing a kid out for a joyride. But his gut told him this was his man.

Picking up speed as he passed through the intersection, Jason saw the suspect turn and spy him. Jason performed a circling motion with his hand, signaling the man to pull over. A press of a button on the handlebar turned on the police flasher lights.

That resulted in the suspect kicking it into overdrive.

Jason had expected as much. He was a hundred yards behind but intended to close the distance before they got too far out of the city. On the other hand, he was an experienced snowmobiler, and even if the suspect had some skill handling a sled, he wasn't dressed for a ten-degree day or a race through the frigid air and newly drifted snowpack.

The road heading north out of town had been plowed by Rusty Nelson early this morning. Jason's machine soared along the hard-packed snow that had formed on the tarmac. Perfect track for racing snowmobiles.

In these conditions, he could handle this six-hundred-pound machine like a dream.

He thought momentarily of how close Yvette had come to taking a bullet. Why had she been standing outside? He'd seen her camera on the ground. Taking photos? He should have been more clear about her staying inside.

Was the shooter a replacement for the previous hit man? Dirty business, that. But all was fair in spies and deception. If that was what was going on.

Jason had been capable of such dirty dealings. Once, he'd been sent in to replace an inept field asset, but termination had not been a requirement. And yet the same could have happened to him after he'd missed the kill shot. He'd been taken in so easily by the female agent. Had truly believed she was on his side. Damn it!

He gripped the handlebars and ripped the throttle, cutting the distance between himself and the shooter.

Had Interpol issued an official agent termination order for Yvette? Because she had read sensitive data? It was possible yet highly unlikely. But if so, her boss was either trying to save her neck or cut her throat.

The suspect veered from the main road and took off across the ditch. Snow sprayed in the sky, glittering against the too-bright sun that proved deceptive in that it wasn't able to warm this frozen tundra.

They headed northeast. That direction would not allow an easy escape.

The falls, the town's namesake, sat half a mile ahead. Frozen this time of year. Always fun to take the cat out on the slick riverbed, but if a person didn't know the area, the falls could prove dangerous. He and Alex put up orange warning flags and stretched a bright orange safety fence before the falls, but it seemed every few years some unfortunate soul crashed his snowmobile or took a flight over the falls, which dropped twenty feet to boulders below.

AFTER JASON LEFT, Amelie squatted near the tire for a while. Back flat against the front quarter panel and palms against her forehead. That had been a close call.

She should have never been out here to give the shooter such opportunity. Taking pictures, of all things.

The glint of something silver caught her eye. She crawled toward the pushed-up snow that demarcated the edge of the parking lot in front of the truck. Something was wedged into the snow.

She started to touch it, then got smart. Pulling her sweater sleeve down over her fingers, she used that as protection to grip the object and pulled it out.

This was what had been fired at her. A dart with a red tip.

"Not cool," she muttered, because the implications were creepier than if it had been a bullet.

Springing up, yet staying bent and low, she crept over to the building, plucking up her camera along the way, and then around to the front door. She quickly went inside and rushed to Jason's office to close the door. Marjorie must still be downstairs tidying up the cells.

She pulled open Jason's desk drawers and in the second one spied some plastic evidence bags. Dropping the dart into the bag, she then sealed it.

Patting her hip for her phone, she cursed the fact she'd given it to Jason. She looked around the desk for a weapon, but there was only a locked gun case with one rifle in it.

There was another hit man?

Of course, they wouldn't let this rest without eliminating the target. Whatever this was. And whoever they were.

As she settled into Jason's chair, fingers gripping the arms tightly, Amelie asked herself plainly if Jacques Patron were friend or foe.

Her father had valued his friendship with Patron. And her mother—well, she didn't remember her talking about the man. Perhaps she'd even avoided him. Amelie recalled a few times when her mother had bowed out of joining her father over drinks with Patron at a local taproom.

Had Patron gotten into dirty dealings? Was he protecting himself?

And was he dead or alive?

Chapter Twenty-One

The falls loomed ahead. In the summer, it was possible to walk from the creek above, using a jagged rocky trail, to the gorge below where the water fell softly and landed on mossy boulders. There were no nearby trees to block the wind or even provide handholds. It was a tricky descent without snow and ice.

In the wintertime? Only an idiot would try to land at the bottom starting from the top. And more than a few did in search of Instagram-worthy shots of the spectacular frozen falls. The smart ones wore crampons and used rock-climbing gear. The stupid ones? Jason had rescued a handful of injured climbers over the past two years. Couple of broken arms and a head injury from falling ice chunks. The fine was two thousand dollars if he caught the culprits.

But right now he was more concerned about the one idiot who had no idea what waited for him. Snow blanketed the land as far as the eye could see, and the whiteness played tricks with the eye, disguising ridges, valleys and even edges where the land stopped. The suspect would drive his snowmobile right over the falls' edge if Jason didn't intervene. The last thing he needed was another dead hit man on his hands.

Gunning the engine, he pushed the cat to full speed and gained on the suspect. Veering right, he cursed that he only wore a ski cap and no helmet as the snow spraying up from that move spat at his bare cheeks like pins. He paralleled the suspect, who pulled out his gun and fired at him.

The bullet went wide. Jason wasn't worried about being a target—not at this speed. He jerked his machine to the left, forcing the other to veer left. Gauging he had less than fifty feet before the snowy land gave way to a twenty-foot fall, he stood and tilted his body to pull a tight curl. The nose of his sled butted the other snowmobile's nose, and the impact caused the driver to fall off in a soft landing.

Jason gunned the cat and managed to slip ahead of the other snowmobile and clear it before that machine, unmanned, soared over the falls. His own machine skidded up a cloud of snow behind him as he wrestled it to a stop but two feet from the falls' edge.

Muttering an oath worthy of this annoyance, Jason shut off the snowcat and pulled out his gun. He headed toward the man, who struggled in the knee-deep snow. Difficult to find purchase in the fresh-fallen powder. Jason stomped through the crusted surface, wishing for snowshoes.

"Hands up!" he called.

The suspect pulled up an ungloved hand. Sunlight glinted on the gun he held. Jason pressed the trigger but didn't squeeze hard enough to release. He held steady.

The shooter's hands were too cold. Trembles gave

way to jerky shudders. The gun dropped out of his frozen fingers. It sank deep into the snow. The suspect's knees bent, his body falling forward. His face landed in the snow as he struggled against the freezing elements and the inability to keep his body warm enough to stand upright.

AMELIE ANSWERED THE landline on the desk the moment Marjorie opened the office door and popped her head in.

"Hello?" Amelie said. She waved at Marjorie to indicate she stay put.

"I've apprehended the suspect," Jason said. "Just wanted to make sure you were safe."

"I am. Marjorie just got in from downstairs. I'll tell her to contact Alex now."

Marjorie signaled with an *okay* shape of her fingers and left for her desk. Amelie heard her say Alex's name.

"I'll be there in half an hour," Jason said.

She nodded. "You should know he wasn't shooting bullets."

"What?"

"It was a tranq dart." Amelie eyed the evidence bag; a few drops of water had melted from the snow on the outside. "He wasn't trying to kill me. It would be a strange weapon to use if death was his objective."

"Interesting. Someone wanted you incapacitated—he had to have been following you. Waiting for…"

"For me to make a mistake and walk outside, giving him a clear target. I'm so sorry, Jason."

"We'll talk when I get in."

"I finished the list," she added quickly.

"Excellent. See you soon."

THE SUSPECT WAS not speaking English. And it wasn't a Texan drawl this time. Jason knew very few French words, but he did recognize the language. Interesting. For about five seconds.

Patience did not come easily today. He was frustrated and yet invigorated at the same time. This was a mystery. Something he'd been wanting since taking the desk here in Frost Falls. If he was going to prove his worth, this was the case to do it. The powers that be wouldn't want to close the station after he'd solved such a big case. This would put Frost Falls on the map. He'd prove he was an asset to the town as well as the county.

Beside him stood Ryan Bay.

"You recording this?" Jason asked.

Bay nodded and pointed his cell phone toward the prisoner. "Go ahead."

Jason turned to the prisoner, who sat on the bed in the cell, head bowed. "You used a tranquilizer dart," he said. The prisoner lifted his head. The man understood him. He had to if he had made his way around the United States to Minnesota from wherever the hell he'd come from. "You didn't want the woman dead?"

The suspect tilted his head subtly, then bowed it again.

"Who do you work for? The Minnesota mafia?"

The prisoner smirked but neither shook his head nor nodded in confirmation.

Then Jason tried a hunch. "Interpol?"

The slightest tensing of the man's jaw told Jason so much. He'd hit on something. He exchanged a raised eyebrow with the BCA agent, who nodded.

Was this hit man really on the same team as Yvette? Jason had to search the Interpol database. With the fingerprints he'd taken upon booking him, he could do that search. But if he was from Interpol, and the previous hit man had not been—what was going on?

Alex wandered down the stairs, and Jason asked, "Did Marjorie run the fingerprints?"

"She's still trying to upload the scan. Sorry, Cash. Won't be much longer."

The station still used the old card-and-ink method of fingerprinting. Which meant they had to upload a scanned image of the fingerprints to run them through the database. What he wouldn't give for the fancy digital scanners all the well-budgeted stations used nowadays.

"I'll check with Interpol," Bay said. "It may cut our time and we won't have to deal with this insolent."

"Good plan," Jason said.

"I get my phone call," the man said from behind the cell bars.

Jason turned at the perfect use of English. The bastard.

"That you do." He took the receiver off the landline attached to the cinder-block wall and handed it through the bars, letting the cord dangle from a horizontal bar. "Alex will assist you with dialing. Good luck getting through though."

He hesitated before walking up the stairs behind Bay. The last time he'd left Alex alone with the prisoner, the man had escaped. Only to be found dead hours later. Jason considered it for a moment. This time the suspect could have his food stuffed through the bars, if it came to that.

He also knew that phone hadn't received any reception since he'd been working here. Maybe a broken wire. Maybe even a frayed cable on the outside phone lines. Too bad it wasn't in the city budget for repairs.

He took the stairs two at a time, following Bay, and stepped out into the frigid air with a brute shout as the brisk chill instantly permeated his flannel shirt. He'd left his coat in the office.

"I'll be right in," Bay said, walking toward his car. "I need to make a few calls."

"You can use my office phone," Jason called, but the man was already rushing toward his vehicle.

Running around to the back door, Jason entered the building, stomping his boots free of snow on the mat.

Marjorie greeted him with a smile.

"You get the fingerprints scanned?"

"Running them right now. The Wi-Fi has been wonky since the storm. But I crossed my fingers and promised my firstborn if it would hold out. The connection is running slower than the old dial-up, but we should have results soon."

Jason swung around Marjorie's desk and eyed the spinning colored ball on the computer screen that indicated it was doing its work. Slowly.

"Miss LaSalle is in your office. I fixed her up with coffee and last year's local calendar. I keep a few copies in my lower drawer. For emergencies."

She ended with a "toodle-loo!" leaving Jason shaking his head. How had Marjorie known Yvette was interested in the calendar?

He knocked his fist against the thin wall as he opened the door to his office. They really needed to insulate these inner walls.

Chapter Twenty-Two

Well, hell. Not like he wasn't proud of the July center-fold that featured him washing the station patrol car shirtless. Heh.

Yvette was seated behind his desk, sipping coffee and grinning widely. Wow. Her eyes actually glinted. Just like Elaine had said his eyes had a glint. Huh. Guess it was possible. And never before had he seen such a bright yet devious smile.

"Hey, I gotta give back to the community somehow, right?" Jason hooked a thigh up on the corner of the desk and leaned over to spy the source of her amusement.

"Marjorie said this was the office copy." She tapped the July spread. "But she already texted me the link to the online version. You definitely go above and beyond with community service."

"I do like to serve the greater good."

"Greater good, indeed." She winked and then covered an even wider smile behind another sip of coffee. "You interrogate the guy who shot at me?"

"He's not overly talkative. Cross your fingers the Wi-Fi stays connected so we get a fingerprint match soon."

Yvette crossed her fingers, then pointed to the plastic evidence bag at the corner of the desk. "It's the dart that I plucked out of a snowbank. No fingerprint contamination. Promise."

Jason took the item and studied it. "I've seen these in syringe form," he commented. "Used when security professionals are holding down an aggravated target. Firing one out of a gun at a human seems so…"

"Sporting? Like a hunter after his prey?"

"I was going to go with creepy."

He turned the bag to study the dart tip. The only way the shooter could have guaranteed a good placement was to get close to Yvette. Ten to twenty feet maximum. He'd seen the target acquisition red light on Yvette, and yet, he hadn't seen anyone in the area so close. He'd had to have been at least half a block away. Likely, he'd intended to tranq Yvette, toss her over a shoulder—and then what? Take her to crime scene two to finish the job?

"I'll send this to Duluth for forensics to test it. See what this dart contains."

"Jason, I'm so sorry," she rushed out. An exhale preceded a watery look up at him. "I was bored. I'd finished the list. I figured if I stayed right by the station, it would be fine to snap a few shots. I've been so foolish since arriving here. You can see why I would have never made a good field agent."

"Don't give yourself such a hard time. Nobody's hurt. That's what matters."

He noticed Yvette's subtle shiver. Her discomfort gave him the shivers, too.

"They didn't want me dead. At least, not right away,"

she said. Her voice trembled. "They want what's in my brain first."

He set the dart on the desk and stood, hooking his thumbs at his belt loops as he scanned out the window behind her. He didn't want her to see his concern, but they both knew how desperate this situation had become.

"The perp is behind bars," he offered.

Yvette sighed. "That's what you said the last time."

That statement cut at his pride. He'd screwed up with Herve Charley. No matter that it hadn't been him watching the prisoner at the time of his escape. Jason took responsibility around here. He had to.

Marjorie beeped the intercom.

"Cash, we got a hit on the fingerprints. And the CIA is on the line for you and Bay."

Really? What the hell was the CIA doing nosing in on the scene? Bay had contacted the FBI. They should have matters pertaining to Charley in hand.

"Thanks." He glanced to the desk phone. He'd prefer to take the call in private and not with an Interpol agent in the room. "Be right there."

Yvette stood, but he shook his head, gesturing she sit back down. "You stay in here."

The last thing he needed right now was the CIA sticking their noses in his business. They'd controlled him up until they'd dumped him here in Frost Falls. What next?

"Fine." She sat. "But you know how thin these walls are."

He winced as he opened the door and stepped out

into reception. Wasn't much he was going to keep private, and especially not with a conference call.

"The CIA?" He looked to Bay, who was nursing a cup of coffee in a paper cup advertising The Moose logo. "Thought you were connecting us with Interpol?"

"I was, but I got a ping from the CIA looking to conference with us. And…here they are." He nodded to Marjorie, who pushed a button on her phone.

"Jason Cash," the man on the line said. "Marcus Fronde, counterintelligence director for the CIA."

Jason knew the man. Not personally, but more than a few times his name had appeared on a dossier for an overseas job. Counterintelligence? They got involved when a foreign entity was in the mix. They must have gotten wind of Bay's call to Interpol. But from the FBI?

There were too many fingers in the soup for Jason's comfort. And the last agency he wanted to deal with was the CIA.

"You've been busy up there in your frozen little town," Fronde said.

"Yes, sir. That's what they sent me here to do. Keep the peace and enforce the law." He glanced to Bay. Surely he'd been briefed regarding Jason's history. He didn't react, merely crossed his arms high over his chest.

"Not working so well, eh?" Fronde said. "You've got a homicide and a dead shooter with known connections to mafia activity in your area."

Jason swallowed and turned his back to Marjorie, who respectfully penciled something on the calendar splayed open on the desk before her. "Keeping an eye on me?" he asked.

"Always. You've got Agent Bay there?"

"Yes, sir," Bay replied. "We're coordinating with Interpol. Or attempting to. The target in this case is one of their agents."

"You realize when an investigation goes international, the CIA wants in?"

Yes, he did. And no, he did not want a CIA agent charging in and taking over his investigation. He didn't mind sharing with the BCA. Bay was nothing but a handy reference should he need his assistance.

But to step aside and allow a CIA agent to do the job he was supposed to do?

On the other hand, they could probably twist the information he needed out of Interpol merely by cachet alone.

"I've got things under control. And with my experience," Jason said, "I know what to do. Though if you can hook me up with a liaison to Interpol, I'd be appreciative."

"Forget the liaison. I'll be sending out an agent. Should arrive this evening. Tomorrow morning at the latest. They'll relieve you of the case."

Jason opened his mouth to protest, but the call clicked off.

He thrust a fist before him in frustration. The urge to swear, and loudly, was only tamped down by pressing his lips together and compressing his jaw.

"I get your anger," Bay said. "I've read your bio."

Great. Just freakin' great.

"I can handle this," Jason said.

"Another set of eyes and ears isn't going to obstruct the investigation," Bay said calmly. "As you said, they will have more leverage with Interpol. Can't understand why they're giving us the cold shoulder, especially when one of their agents is involved."

"Yeah? Maybe two of their agents are in the thick of this."

"What are you thinking, Cash?"

"Her boss, Jacques Patron. He could be pulling strings on his end, covering things up."

"So he's moved to the top of your suspects list? We don't have confirmation that he's dead or alive."

"Right. And that feels twenty kinds of wrong to me. Admit it, that's suspicious."

"It is. So why not welcome the CIA to assist? Come on, Cash, it's all water under the bridge now. Doesn't matter who works the case so long as we get a good outcome."

Jason nodded. "Just hate to see Frost Falls lose this station. You know they're going to shut us down come March, forward all calls to the county?"

"What?"

Jason tightened his jaw at Marjorie's outburst. Shoot. He'd meant to tell her that at a better time.

"Sorry, Marjorie. I've known about it a few weeks. Was intending to tell you. I thought this case might give us some leeway. Maybe even impress all the right people."

"Uff da." The dispatcher sat back in her chair, shaking her head.

"It's not so much the station you want to save," Bay said, "as your reputation. Admit it, Cash. You were a damn good CIA agent. Your sniping skills were highly commended."

"Can we have this conversation some other time?"

Jason said with a glance toward Marjorie, who now looked at him like a deer in headlights. "The case is all we need to discuss."

"Sure. But don't get your hopes up about the station staying open." Bay tossed his empty coffee cup in the garbage can beside the desk. "I'm going back down to see if the prisoner may have changed his mind about talking.

"I'll be close." Jason stepped away and into his office, closing the door behind him. Anything to get away from Marjorie's sad stare. But the escape wasn't exactly what he'd hoped for, because Yvette looked up from her place behind his desk.

"What did the CIA have to say?" she asked quietly.

"Uh, just keeping an eye on me."

"They're stepping in, aren't they?"

She'd heard it all. Damn it.

Jason could but nod. He shouldn't take this so hard, but—damn it, this had been his one chance to prove himself!

"Then we'd better hurry," she said. "And figure this out before that happens." She pulled a piece of paper out of her pocket and handed it to him. "The list."

Chapter Twenty-Three

Jason unfolded the notebook page, which still dangled ragged bits from where Yvette had torn it from the spiral binder. The writing was neat but tiny. She'd said she thought it was an invoice. Dates and locations didn't necessarily imply invoice but could rather denote meetings or pickups or even exchange of goods. Something had occurred at the listed location on the corresponding date. Something associated with a dollar amount. The amounts were even, ranging from two thousand to eighteen thousand euros. Some amounts were listed with a dollar sign, which might indicate a difference in who was giving and who was receiving.

"Could be gunrunning," he mused out loud. The Duluth harbor on Lake Superior was one of the largest US outlets for importers of illegal firearms.

"You think?" Yvette exhaled an exasperated sigh. "I hate firearms dealers. They are the nastiest of the nasty."

"Indeed, they are. But it's a guess. Someone was receiving money for…something. At these dates and locations. And some amounts are listed with a dollar sign so I have to figure it wasn't just euros involved. Interesting."

"Then why would *I* have received that email?"

Jason shrugged. "Someone letting the cat out of the bag? Trying to call attention to it without being the one to do so. Could be anything. Corporate shills. Assassins. A list of eliminated targets and payouts."

"You really think it came from within?"

He wasn't one hundred percent sure about that. Or anything, at this point. But his Spidey senses were tingling.

"Your boss," Jason said. "Remind me how he acted when you'd told him you had this info stored in your head."

She leaned her elbows onto the edge of the desk. "Jacques has always been a calm, cool man. Hard to get a read on him. His eyes are gray."

"That have significance? Eye color?"

"Soulless," she said. "And his hair is graying, so he was always sort of…not there. Easy to blend in. Which made him a great agent, I'm sure. But as a fellow worker, I could never get a read on him."

"And yet, I initially sensed you had a good rapport with him? That you liked him? You call him by his first name. That indicates something more than a mere business relationship."

"I did. I do. Like I told you, I remember him from when I was a teenager. I've grown up trusting him. So, yes, our relationship is personal, but on a friendly level." Yvette wrinkled up her face. "But after receiving that message, I'm not so sure what that relationship has become. Is he dead or alive? What's going on, Jason?"

Jason took a moment to put himself in the head of a French Interpol director who knew a woman who carried a list in her head—a list he apparently had read quickly, then burned it. Those were not the actions of a man who had nothing to hide.

Had Patron removed Yvette from Lyon to then make her death look like an accident? Why send her all the way to Frost Falls? What was the mafia connection? Was there a connection? Could Herve Charley have been a random hire? No, he'd read about the French connection in the stats.

"No one knows where you are? No family? A girl-friend?"

She shook her head.

He snapped the paper with a forefinger. Had to be sensitive information. Was Jacques Patron protecting someone? Himself?

"Tell me more about Jacques Patron," he said to Yvette.

A knock on the door preceded "Cash?"

It was Ryan Bay.

"Come in."

Jason slid a thigh onto the desk corner and crossed his arms over his chest.

"Talked to Interpol again and sent them the prisoner's fingerprints. They are cooperating with this information. Still couldn't get any info on Patron. Said they're looking into it." Bay handed him a single printed paper. "You won't believe who we've got below."

Jason's eyes dropped to the prisoner's name: Rutger Lund. Thirty-seven years old. A field operative. For Interpol.

He glanced to Yvette. They'd sent one of her own to take her out? Yikes. How was he going to tell her that? Did he need to tell her that? Yes, he did.

"What's up?" she asked.

"Got the prisoner's name," Bay said to her. "Rutger Lund. You know him?"

She shook her head. "Should I?"

"He's an Interpol agent," Jason said.

Yvette's jaw dropped open. And Bay pulled up a chair to sit down.

"YOU GOING TO do this, or am I?" Bay asked Jason.

Jason pulled his desk chair back and gestured for Yvette to sit down. "I'll do it."

"You guys suspect me now, don't you?" Yvette sat, and when neither of them answered her, she beamed her big blue gaze up at Jason. "You do."

"Didn't say that," he said.

"Well, I'll say it," Bay tossed out. "We've got an Interpol agent hiding out in Frost Falls under an assumed name…" He handed Jason another sheet of paper from the file folder. "Her real name is Amelie Desauliniers. Has worked at Interpol for two years. Six months in the field and another eighteen—"

"For their tech department. I know," Jason said. "She's told me as much."

Bay stood and leaned his palms onto the desk. This was the first time Jason had seen the fire in him show in his curled fingers and tense jaw.

Jason took an instinctual step toward Yvette. He stood beside her but a step away from touching her. "She was sent here because she had sensitive information in her head that her boss feared could get her killed," Jason said.

"What sort of information?"

Yvette turned the list Jason had set on his desk toward the agent, and he took it and read it. Bay shrugged his shoulders. "What does this mean?"

"Not sure," Jason offered.

"Well, ask her!"

"I don't know what it means," Yvette replied. "It was a strange email that turned up in my inbox. It didn't have an origin, and it self-destructed after a few minutes. But it was enough to put my boss on the alert and want to send me away for a while."

Bay winced. "I'm not following."

"She's got a photographic memory," Jason explained. "She remembers things she reads, like books and lists, but doesn't necessarily know what it is she has seen."

"And you believe her?"

"I'm the one who's been the target," Yvette said firmly. "I'm not on a case, or running a ploy or—I haven't been a field agent for a long time. I'm just trying to stay alive while we figure this out."

Agent Bay scanned down the list. He tapped his fingers on it. "Three columns of data. Looks like a date column, possibly location and…"

"Time," Jason offered.

"But this fourth column is a mix of numbers and letters. A password? For what?" He shot a steely gaze at Yvette.

But she had no answer. If her boss had wanted this out of everyone's eyesight, including his own…

Over her shoulder, Jason asked, "How do you code operations?"

"That's probably need to know."

He gave her an exasperated look. "I'm not asking for state secrets. I'm trying to keep you alive."

"Right. Uh, usually a three- or four-letter sequence. First few letters of the operation code name. If something were called Blacktail, for instance, the code would be B, L, A, C."

"Gotta be a lot of operations that begin with *black*, don't you think?"

"That's true. Maybe I don't know for sure. You think there are operation code names on that list?"

"I don't know. Let me see that list, Bay."

The agent handed it over, and Jason took a few moments to read it.

"This last column for each entry is eight to twelve characters long. It's gotta be passwords. What makes you so sure your boss, who sent you off to a foreign country and then basically left you here without contact, isn't working for someone else?"

"If he was protecting himself, then why not take me out right away?" she asked. "Fire me or have me eliminated that night I went home. Instead he sends me to Minnesota? For what reason?"

"To get you far away until he figured out what to do with you," Bay offered. "And it would it be cleaner to take you out on foreign soil."

"How so? Taking out a target on home territory would be neater, more contained and something a person could control."

"True, but the evidence would no longer be in Interpol's backyard."

"And if my guess about the mafia connection to France is correct," Jason said, "then perhaps he wanted her in his hire's range. Maybe Jacques is a double agent. Or he's protecting a double who has been taking payouts."

"But agencies employ double agents all the time," Yvette said.

"Don't I know it." Jason shook his head and growled at the same time.

"Oh right," Yvette said. "Her."

Bay and Jason exchanged a look.

Jason scrubbed his brow with the heel of his hand. "That's not what we're discussing. Maybe Jacques wanted this information hidden," he tossed out. "Forever."

"Are you implying he had no intention of ever bringing me back in?"

"I don't know. He is the one man who knew what was on this list. And is he still alive?" He looked to Bay.

"I asked and was told that was need-to-know information," Bay said.

"Don't you think that's a little strange?" Jason asked.

Bay shrugged. "Yes, but they have their secrets just like we have ours. They work much more closely with the CIA. Do you think the prisoner in your jail cell knows what the list is for?" Bay said. "He has to."

"Why does he have to? He's only been sent to take out the target."

"He didn't want me dead," Yvette said. "He wanted me incapacitated."

"Right." Jason had forgotten that detail. "So he could then extract what you know. Maybe he does know. And if he's Interpol…something doesn't add up here. Someone knows something. And I need to find out who and what that is. We need to talk to him again, Bay."

"I agree."

"Come on." Jason headed out of the office but called over his shoulder, "Yvette, or Amelie, look over that final column again. See if it makes any sense to you now."

Chapter Twenty-Four

Jason paced before the cell bars. It was cold down here,
but the prisoner had not taken the blanket to wrap about
himself. A sturdy man, he was about Jason's height and
build and had slick black hair and dark eyes. He sat on
the bed, back to the cinder-block wall, knees bent. He
faced the bars. Marjorie reported he'd eaten every bit
of his food. (And Jason would, too; those meals came
directly from The Moose.) He was also fastidious about
his personal grooming and had requested a book, any
book, to read. One of Marjorie's romance novels sat
splayed open on the bed beside him. Jason wouldn't
even smirk at that. He'd sneaked a peek at a few pages
when Marjorie wasn't looking. Those books were interesting.

And written in English.

The BCA agent stepped up beside Jason and gave
him a look. Yes, he was ready.

"Interpol, eh?" Jason said to the prisoner.

The man maintained his gaze but said, "I wasn't able
to place a call."

And now he spoke English perfectly well. "I know.
Repairman has been called for the faulty wiring." Yes,

like a year and a half ago. "By law, I'm supposed to report your whereabouts to Interpol."

"That is not correct."

"How do you know? Are you familiar with Interpol
procedure?"

The man looked aside, bowing his head.

"Did Jacques Patron send you here to pick up Amelie Desauliniers?"

The man crossed his arms over his chest and tilted
his head back against the wall. No comment.

"You weren't sent to kill her," Jason said. "So I have
to figure that means you either came to take Desauliniers home—though, why you'd do it in such a covert
manner does puzzle me. And if you're not returning
her to Lyon, then the only other option is to extract information."

"Phone. Call."

"Like I said, a repairman has been called. Another
storm is headed toward us, though. Makes travel difficult. You'd better hunker down for the wait."

"You have a cell phone in your pocket. Desk phones
elsewhere," the prisoner insisted.

"I do, but you are not in a position to access them,
are you?"

The man crossed his arms tightly and looked aside.

Jason toed the base of a cell bar. "This is what we've
learned from a database search. You are Rutger Lund.
An Interpol agent. Home base, Marseille. Seven years
in the field. Expertise, black ops. Apparently, covert
sniping and operating a snowmobile were not in your
training."

"You have no idea what you are sticking your nose into."

Jason propped his forearm against a couple of the cell bars and peered between two of them. "Why don't you enlighten me?"

He didn't mind getting flipped the bird. He hadn't expected the man would engage in a sharing session with him. But he had gotten a roundabout confirmation that he was Interpol. And that only troubled him further.

"I'll let you sit on ice awhile longer." He glanced to the thermostat on the wall, right next to the phone. "These concrete walls are thick, but they don't insulate against the weather well. Talk to you in the morning."

The man swore in French as Jason and Agent Bay headed up the stairs.

UP IN JASON'S OFFICE, Amelie studied the list. With the CIA headed this way, they had their work cut out for them. She knew the CIA would take over the case, and she also knew that Jason would take that as an affront. He hadn't come right out and told her, but he needed to solve this case. A small-town cop planted in the middle of nowhere who had once traveled the world on covert missions? Hell yes, he probably needed this like a person needed oxygen.

And if she could help him, then she would.

She scoured over the paper. Cash payouts? To whom and what for? Interpol was huge and employed thousands across the globe. If this was a confidential list, it could only have been meant for Patron's eyes. The fact she had received it? Someone wanted to out Patron.

Because if it implicated anyone other than her boss, why wouldn't he have acted on that information immediately and—maybe he had.

No. Then there would have been no reason to send her out of the country.

"I'm missing something."

The final column, Amelie had postulated, could be passwords. But for what? Each was associated with a different date, location and dollar amount. Was it a locker that held the payout, accessible only with the correct password? But the dates were all past. Why include the password if the pickup had already occurred?

She closed her eyes and recalled the day she'd opened the suspicious email. Unless she wrote things down, she wouldn't recall it all exactly, but she could remember the layout of the document on her computer. Two single eight-and-a-half by eleven-inch pages. Four columns. The final column...had those characters been underlined?

She opened her eyes. "Like clickable links?"

The email had disappeared after ten minutes. It hadn't gone to the trash file. Not recoverable. Yet nothing was ever completely lost from a computer's hard drive. Security agencies employed talented individuals who could access even the most buried information on a hard drive. It wasn't in her skill set, but the tech manager was certainly qualified.

The first hit man had to have been ordered by someone who didn't want the information falling into other hands.

But as for the suspect sitting in the jail cell below? He'd wanted her alive. And had very likely taken out the first hit man.

Yet her death was for the ultimate reason of...what? If they'd kept her alive, it had to be for a reason. To extract the information she knew? But it seemed as if Jacques might already know that info, so he couldn't be related to the second shooter.

Amelie leaned back in the uncomfortable office chair. She felt at odds and alone, standing in the middle of a flooding room. She had no allies. Even Jason couldn't be considered one. He was only doing his duty. This investigation had begun with the body of a dead woman. An innocent woman caught in a fouled assassination attempt.

She bit her lip. That poor family.

"How's it coming?"

She stood abruptly with the list in hand. "I didn't hear you walk in."

Jason lifted a brow and cast her a discerning look. Even though the look was meant to be questioning, she still swooned at the sight of that freckled gaze. "You figure out the final column?"

"I think these are passwords," she said. "I recall now, on the original document, the fourth column was underlined."

He lifted a brow.

"Like clickable links," she suggested.

"Good going. How do we access the original document?"

"We don't. Not unless we turn this investigation over to Interpol."

"Not a good idea. I have reason to believe someone is involved in a cover-up," he said. "And I'm beginning to think it was cash payouts."

"Payouts to whom?"

Jason shrugged.

Amelie wrapped her arms over her chest and bowed her head. The sensation of tears niggled at her, but she would not cry in front of him. That was not professional. And she had to look at her exile here as a continuation of her job. For her own sake, she had to stay strong and figure this out.

"What is it?" Jason leaned over her and stroked her hair.

His kind touch tugged at her tears, but she sniffled and shook her head. "I'm sorry. It's all so much. I feel abandoned. Out of place. Feeling sorry for myself, I suppose."

"You have every right. You are alone in a strange country. And a damn cold and inhospitable country at that."

"Why couldn't he have sent me to Florida?" she said with a lighter tone.

"Your boss ever mention friends in Minnesota? Allies? Employees?"

"You think he chose this state for a purpose?"

"The Minnesota mafia does have a connection to France."

Amelie met his gaze. Damn, he was so handsome. Why had she met Jason Cash in such a situation? Any other time, she would have reached to touch those cute freckles on his nose.

He gave her shoulders a reassuring squeeze. "What are you thinking about right now?" he asked.

She set free the smile that was always so close when in his presence. "Your freckles."

He wrinkled his nose. "You spend a lot of time thinking about my freckles."

"They're sexy."

Amelie leaned in and kissed him. She twisted on the chair, and he knelt between her legs. Cupping her head with his hands, he deepened the kiss in an urgent and insistent way. He tasted like coffee. His heat fired within her like no hearth fire ever could.

She gripped his shirt and tugged him closer so she could wrap her legs about his thighs. He bowed his head and kissed down her neck and throat. She almost moaned with pleasure. But she was aware that Marjorie could be in the next room. A few minutes of this pleasure was all she asked.

When his hand brushed her breast, her nipples tightened. And she dared the quietest moan. Jason answered with his own restrained sound of want.

He broke the kiss and pressed his forehead to hers, closing his eyes. He breathed a few times, heavy and wanting, then stepped back and pulled her up to embrace.

"I want you," she said quietly.

He nodded against her head.

"I want this to happen."

"It will," he said in a quiet, low tone that stirred at her humming insides. So sexy to have to be quiet when all they wanted to do was rip each other's clothing off. "Not here."

"'Course not," she said on a breath. "You have an investigation going on."

He gave her another quick kiss. "I do, and it's only just gotten started. Oh, you mean that other investigation? The one regarding the hit man and the French spy?" He smiled. "I prefer the first, but duty does call. Let's solve this case. Save the girl. And then…"

"And then?"

"And then we'll see what happens next."

Chapter Twenty-Five

Snow whisked across the tarmac, plastering the main road thick white. Jason stomped the flakes from his boots before entering the station. He'd walked Yvette across the street to Olson's Oasis after Colette had waved her down. Said she'd ordered a helmet for her and it was in. The two women had started chatting, so Jason had pleaded off and told Yvette no more than ten minutes. He'd be watching the store out the station window.

The station smelled like roasted turkey, gravy and lots of buttery mashed potatoes. Marjorie did not have a meal on her desk. She handed him a cup of coffee as he entered.

"You already eat? You should go home, Marjorie. Storm's not taking its time today."

"I intend to. Just grabbing a few necessaries in case you need me to make some calls while the station is closed. I've already talked to county dispatch. They are on call. I fed the prisoner again."

"I guess you did. A Thanksgiving dinner?"

"*Uff da*, it's freezing down there and we are not Guantánamo. I gave him back the pillow you removed, too."

"Marjorie."

She lifted an eyebrow, and Jason conceded with a nod. "Fine. He's going to have to sit through the storm down there. I'll turn the heat up a few degrees."

"Already done." Marjorie pulled on her bright red parka. "I left some snacks, too. Cronuts and popcorn. He'll be fine. Isn't the CIA headed our way?"

"You betcha. Just heard from them. On their way from the Minneapolis airport."

"Through the storm?"

Jason shrugged.

"I know you don't want them stealing your case," Marjorie said. "Maybe they'll allow you to work with them?"

"Doubt it. Me and the CIA—it's bad blood, Marjorie. Agent Bay shouldn't have said what he said earlier. But I'm not going to pull a hissy fit. If they want to take over, it's their case. But until they get here—and I'm predicting the storm will hang them up somewhere around Hinckley…"

"Good eats in that town," Marjorie said.

"They'll have to hunker down at Tobie's. Best cinnamon rolls this side of the Twin Cities."

"So speaking of all the things Agent Bay has let slip." Marjorie walked up to him and wrapped a scarf about her neck. "You going to tell me more about the station closing?"

"I don't know much, Marjorie. City budget cuts. They plan to close us in March. I thought I could do something, maybe this case would bring attention to us and they'd reconsider, but…" Jason sighed. "I'm sorry."

"It's not your fault, Cash. This station has been on

its last legs since the iron mine closed. Maybe it's time I retired, eh?"

"Uff da," he said.

"Exactly. Bay is down with the prisoner. Not sure what he's up to, but that's where he is. Where's your woman?"

"She's not my woman, Marjorie."

"You want her to be your woman."

"Would you quit calling her my woman? She's... I like her. Okay?"

"There's nothing wrong with kissing a woman you want to protect. And now that the prisoner is behind bars, what will she do with herself? Oh, there's a handsome policeman willing to keep her warm on a stormy night."

"Marjorie!"

She chuckled and headed toward the door. "It's not very often I get to tease you, Cash. Let me have this one." She waved and left the station.

And Jason smiled to himself. He'd let her have that one. Because he had gotten the pretty one.

"Five minutes," the waitress told Amelie, who sat at the counter nursing a cup of coffee. "I need to let the pie thaw a few minutes before I cut it."

Amelie had ordered a couple of slices of pie for herself and Jason. A surprise. The Moose was close enough to the station, and she'd scanned the area. Hadn't felt a sense of unease. She'd be safe by herself for the time it took to finish this cup.

"Pass the sugar."

Amelie startled when the woman next to her at the

counter asked for the condiment. She noticed her sitting at the counter when she'd walked in. Her coffee cup was half-full. She was beautiful. Dark black hair was cut choppy just below her ears, and lots of smoky eye shadow drew attention to her gray eyes.

A perfectly groomed eyebrow lifted in question as she silently stared at Amelie.

"Oh, yes, sorry." Amelie slid the sugar shaker toward her. "My mind was elsewhere."

"Probably on the crazy weather, eh?"

She had a definite French accent, Amelie thought. Not unusual in this town, for she'd learned that many passing through came from Canada. French Canadians traveled down to Minnesota to shop because the exchange rate was so good. Add to that, the Boundary Waters Canoe Area Wilderness was a gorgeous vacation site.

"I'm getting accustomed to the weather," Amelie provided. "What about you? New in town?"

"Just passing through. The hubby and I are headed for Canada. Relatives. You know."

"That's the accent I recognize."

"Yours sounds French, as well. But not Canadian. What part of France you from?"

Amelie felt a sudden and distinct twinge in her gut. That instinct alarm that she had been trained never to ignore. Of course, the woman was simply making conversation. While talking to another woman her age, not from the area, sounded like heaven, it was weird that someone would be passing through during a storm. On the other hand, these Minnesotans were a hardy breed, and a few flakes never kept them in one place for long.

"Refill?" The waitress filled the woman's coffee cup and then looked to Amelie.

She shook her head. "I'll be back. I'm headed to the, uh…" She pointed toward the corner that turned into a long hallway leading to the restrooms.

"I'll go check on the pie right now." The waitress walked off.

After a sip of her coffee, the woman with the dark hair beamed a smile at her. Amelie felt that grin on her back all the way down the end of the counter. Even after she rounded the turn, it burned up her neck.

Why was she getting this feeling? Simply because the woman wasn't from around here? Amelie wasn't, either. Still, most travelers would plan ahead in such weather.

With the bag containing the helmet in one hand, she pushed open the bathroom door and paced before the stalls. The strong lavender air freshener gave her a sudden headache.

The same kind of headache she got whenever she thought about Jacques Patron.

Turning to push open the door, Amelie caught it roughly against her palm. She stepped back to allow the new person to enter. With an "excuse me" on her tongue, Amelie stopped speaking at sight of who it was.

"Hey, sweetie." The beautiful woman with the smoky eye shadow grinned at her. Except this time, Amelie didn't need instinct to know that grin was malevolent.

JASON PICKED UP the list that lay on the desk before him and wandered to the window to peer out. Main Street was clear. Back to the list. Jacques Patron was protecting someone who had been taking bribes or kickbacks. That was his conclusion. It made sense. A date, a location for pickup and a dollar amount.

Of course, the list could not be something Patron had made himself. The only reason a person would make such a list—and put it in the hands of an Interpol employee—had to be for blackmail or push. But why involve Yvette?

Jason honestly did not believe she had a clue what she was involved in. She wasn't lying to him. She couldn't be. So that meant someone knew she had a relationship to Patron and that upon seeing the list, she'd go to her boss. And he'd known what it meant as soon as she'd shown him.

He felt sorry for Yvette. All her life she'd known the man only as a kind friend of the family. And now he had betrayed her.

Did it matter who Patron was protecting? He could be protecting himself, for all Jason knew. What did matter was that an innocent woman had gotten trapped in the middle, carrying information she hadn't asked to know in the first place. And now someone wanted her dead.

He tapped the last column on the list. Clickable links? To what? Videos? Of? The person accepting payoffs?

"Makes sense."

The only people who had any clue what was on the list were Yvette and Jacques Patron.

Jason had heard a gunshot at the end of the message Patron had left him. Yet…he hadn't heard a human grunt of pain following. Most people vocalized when shot, even if it was just a moan. Which meant...

"He's still alive." Had to be.

Interpol was generally open with information when asked through the correct channels. And yet, if an investigation into one of their own was underway, they would likely keep that close to the vest. As Jason had done. But if the CIA had already stuck their noses into this, there could be information that Jason wasn't allowed to know.

Time to go with his gut.

"Patron is protecting himself," Jason decided. And he knew it was true.

He checked his watch and frowned. It had been twenty minutes since he'd left Yvette at Olson's Oasis. He glanced down Main Street again. Where was she?

Jason grabbed his coat and soared out of the office. Only to come face-to-face with a smirking man in a black suit, wearing no outerwear. His shoulders crouched forward against the wind.

The CIA had arrived.

Chapter Twenty-Six

Amelie came to with a snap of her head upward. Ouch. She sat upright and blinked. Where was she? She had been in the ladies' restroom at The Moose and—the woman with the gray eyes had walked in and smiled at her so wickedly.

A shiver crept along her arms. She wore no coat, just a sweater, jeans and boots. Taking in her surroundings, she didn't hear anything, but—what was that? Wind whipped wildly against the windows that filtered in hazy light. The storm sounded angry. The concrete floor was littered with dust and debris. She sat on a wood chair with flat side arms, and one of her wrists was bound to that arm. Her other wrist was free, but her arm sat heavily on the chair. She didn't feel tied up, not at the ankles or around her waist or chest. And to test, she slid forward on the chair.

"Not so fast, sweetie. I need you to relax."

Her instincts had been right. The woman had kidnapped her and taken her…somewhere. How much time had passed? How had she gotten her out of The Moose? She must have had help.

Scanning before her, Amelie took in a vast, empty

building. Looked like an old garage, the kind used for fixing cars. There were two big doors through which cars could drive in and out, and a small walled-off office toward the front. One window with yellowed glass was frosted over. But no tools or furniture, save the chair she sat on and a wood table beside her. Actually, the table was a plank of plywood sitting atop two wood sawhorses. A makeshift operation.

"Where am I?"

"I honestly don't know," the woman replied. "Some abandoned garage. This town is overrun with empty houses and buildings."

Her accent no longer carried the Canadian cadence.

"Who do you work for?" Amelie had the clarity to ask. She still hadn't seen the woman. She stood behind the chair.

"None of your business, sweetie."

"I am not your sweetie. Do you work for Jacques Patron?"

The woman laughed and walked around to the side by the table. She set a pistol on the plank and lifted what Amelie now noticed was a syringe. A spill of black hair fell across her left eye and cheek as she studied the clear plastic tube on the device.

"You haven't figured it out yet?" the woman asked.

"If I had, I wouldn't be sitting here right now."

"You do have the list in your head. That's what I've been told."

"I…" She wasn't going to provide information when it wasn't clear what the woman knew. "What's your name?"

"Hey, if you don't want to be friendly, sweetie, then

names are off the table. Let's quit with the girlfriend chat. It's cold in here, and I'm sure you'll want to get some warmer clothes on when we're done."

"Does that mean you're not going to kill me?"

"If I kill you, I'll never have access to what you know."

"You don't have access to it now. What's going to change that?"

"This." The woman held the syringe closer to Amelie. "Sodium pentothal. It'll make you tell the truth."

A drug used to obtain information from unwilling subjects. "It might relax me and make me tell you who my secret lover is, but how will it extract information you don't even know about?"

"You tell me."

"About my lover?"

"I'd slap you, but I'm not as cruel as you think. It was a necessary evil bringing you here on the sly. And as for secrets? The whole town knows you're sleeping with the police chief. *Dieu*, he's a handsome one. Now let's get serious. You're going to tell me what was on that list. Line by line."

A snap of a fingernail against the plastic syringe brought Amelie's attention up and to the left. She met the woman's gray irises. She didn't know what the drug would do to her. It was supposed to relax a person's inhibitions and even make them suggestible. But would that also unlock the things she stored in her brain? Things she was normally only able to release by writing them down? A physical action that worked as a sort of dictation machine from brain to hand to page.

"I don't think it'll work," Amelie said as firmly as she could.

By all means, she'd like to stay alive. And if retaining the list in her brain could do that for her, then she would talk her way around it until they were both shivering from the cold.

Where was Jason? Could she hope he'd sense something was wrong and find her? The town was small, but as the woman had said, there were many abandoned buildings and houses. Too many for Jason to go through one by one, and in the storm.

How long had she been out? He must have missed her by now.

"I have to actually write out the information," she tried. "Which means I'll need paper, a pen and probably a whole pot of black coffee."

"That's not the way this is going down." The woman's grip on her arm felt like an ice princess personified.

Amelie struggled. She was basically free, save for her left arm being tied down to the chair arm.

"Sit still or this needle will end up in your eye!"

A male voice alerted them both. "Leslie Cassel."

Both women stopped struggling. Amelie squinted to eye the man who stood near an open door, which let in bright light and snow flurries. He was not Jason. Yet she recognized him immediately.

"She's going to bring you down, Patron," the woman—Leslie—said. "We've been on to you for weeks." She stabbed the needle into Amelie's arm.

"Can't risk Interpol learning about my indiscretions," Jacques said.

A gunshot sounded. Leslie screamed. And Amelie grabbed for the syringe, still in her arm.

Chapter Twenty-Seven

Blood spattered Amelie's cheek. Leslie had been hit, and she'd dropped to the floor behind her. Had it been a kill shot? She did not groan, nor did Amelie hear her moving. But she wasn't in position to turn and assess with Jacques Patron standing thirty feet away with a pistol aimed at her.

She glanced at the syringe she'd dropped on the floor. The plunger had not been depressed. *Merci Dieu.*

"What the hell is going on?" she asked, more out of anger than fear, or even a desperation to make conversation and delay the man's likely goal of shooting her. Out the corner of her eye, she spied Leslie's pistol that lay two feet away on the wood plank.

"Doesn't matter, does it?" Jacques had a calm manner to his speech when he spoke French. An affectation that had once reassured her. Now it made the hairs on the back of her neck stand upright. "I hired an idiot to do a job I should have taken care of in Lyon."

Jason had been right. Jacques had been protecting himself all along. Amelie's stomach performed a squeeze, and her heart dropped. Why Jacques was hesitating was beyond her. He was a skilled operative who had never paused to pull the trigger when called for.

"You don't want to kill me," she said calmly. "If you did, you would have done so, as you've said, right away in Lyon. Is it because you don't have the list?"

"Oh, I know what's on that list. I thought I could make it go away by sending you away. After all, you are Vincent's daughter. We were friends. But then I got smart."

"I still don't know what's going on, Jacques. And if you think about it, that means you are the only one with all the facts. You can trust me. Let me walk away from this."

"You may not know." He redirected his aim toward the floor near her feet. "But they do." He fired again.

Behind her on the floor, Leslie yelped and cursed.

In the commotion, Amelie grabbed the gun from the table. She stood. Her left wrist was still bound to the chair, but she could take aim and defend herself.

She heard Leslie's body shift on the concrete floor, as if she were dragging herself.

Jacques laughed and splayed his hands up near his shoulders, the gun barrel pointing toward the ceiling. "Go ahead, Desauliniers! Take your best shot!"

Never had mockery cut her so deeply. Because he knew…

"Tell me why you did this," she insisted. Her aim targeted the man's heart. "What do I know?"

"He's been taking hush money from the mafia…" Leslie said from the floor. "They're running guns through the Superior Lakes. Patron is their French connection. You're our only proof… Amelie…" Leslie gasped. Coughed. "What's…in your…head. A list with links to security videos showing Jacques accepting payoffs."

How did she know so much? And she knew her real name. And Jacques. Apparently, she was investigating him. And had tracked his connection to Yvette here to Minnesota…

"She's with…" Amelie quickly did the math. Jason had mentioned the man they had behind bars was an Interpol agent. He must have had a partner. "Interpol. Because you know her," she said to Jacques. "You called her by name. And she didn't kill me because they need me to—" Jacques took aim at the floor again. "No!"

Another bullet fired. With a hard bite on her lower lip, Amelie realized she hadn't fired the gun she still held in defense. Not even to protect Leslie.

No sounds from behind her this time. Had he killed her?

Amelie stretched out her arm, willing herself to pull the trigger. Yet a tear threatened at the corner of her eye. He'd killed Leslie. The man had lied to her. Had used her. And had sent a hit man after her. The same killer who had murdered an innocent woman. And now Jacques was here to finish the botched job.

Her fingers clutched the weapon surely. Why couldn't she pull the trigger?

Images of her mother flashed before her. She hadn't told Jason the entire truth. Scared and wanting to know if her mother was all right, Amelie had sneaked out and into the living room, crawling behind the sofa. The man who had entered hadn't noticed her. And she'd seen her mother. Kneeling on the floor, head up and pleading with the stranger who Amelie could never see or reconstruct in her memories.

Amelie's life had never been the same because someone had pulled the trigger and ended her mother's life.

She never wanted another daughter or son to know the loss of a parent. No matter their crimes.

Jacques's chuckle was unnerving. The man was unhinged. If he had been taking bribes and had sent a hit man after her, then he deserved to die. And yet, Amelie wanted him to pay for his crimes. Most importantly, for the innocent woman who had died by mistake, and for killing the woman lying on the floor behind her.

"I'm waiting," Jacques cajoled with a tormenting tease to his tone. "You can't do it. You father would be very disappointed in you, Amelie. You couldn't cut it as a field agent because you couldn't pull the trigger. What makes you think you can do it now?"

She didn't want him to be right. But—what was wrong with her? All she had to do was pull the trigger. She had been an ace aim in training. She didn't have to kill him. She could aim for his shoulder so he'd drop his weapon, and then send another bullet into his thigh to incapacitate him.

Yes, she could do that. Maybe?

Jacques shook his head and tutted as if she was a child. "Just like your mother. On her knees and unable to defend herself when the stakes were at their highest."

"My mother was assassinated," Amelie yelled in English. She didn't want to play nice with the man anymore. "Wait. How could you know she was on her knees?"

Jacques's smirk curdled Amelie's blood.

"No," she said with a gasp. "You?"

He shrugged and nodded, before saying in English, "She was a liability to your father's work."

"You bastard!" The gun suddenly felt three times heavier. It slipped in her grasp.

And Jacques chuckled. "You can't pull the trigger!"

"She doesn't need to," called out another male voice. "Because I can."

Chapter Twenty-Eight

The target turned toward Jason.

Jason had heard him talking to Yvette. It was Jacques Patron. Very much alive. And that man intended to kill his own agent. He wasn't sure if the woman on the floor was dead. Or what had gone down in the conversation that had all been in French, save the last few lines. But it all stopped now.

He'd panicked when Yvette had not returned to the station. He'd raced to Olson's Oasis, and Colette had said she'd seen her stop in at The Moose. There, the waitress had told him about the unfamiliar woman with the great hairstyle and how she'd followed Yvette into the bathroom. It had been easy enough to follow the trail of a woman's boot prints—deeper in the fresh-fallen snow because she'd been carrying a load—and to the tracks that had led toward the south end of Frost Falls, where a string of abandoned shops and businesses had sat empty for years.

As Patron raised his arm to fire off a shot, Jason squeezed the trigger. No waiting. No pausing to allow the villain his "this is why I did it" speech. Just take him out, efficiently and quickly. No foreign double agents to redirect his focus. But Patron was damn well going to live to answer for the crimes he had committed against his agency and Yvette.

Jacques yelped and clutched his thigh with his gun hand. Not a direct hit on the femoral artery. Jason didn't want him to bleed out. But a painful strike that should lodge in bone.

Another shot landed in Patron's shoulder. The bullet entering muscle and bone brought him to his knees. Still, he held the gun. And managed to fire. The shot went high, pinging a steel ceiling rafter.

This time, Jason aimed, breathed in—and on his out breath he squeezed the trigger. The bullet pinged Patron's gun, sending it flying from his grasp to land spinning on the floor six feet away.

With the hostile disarmed, Jason ran forward and kicked the gun he'd wielded toward the wall. Out of his peripheral vision, he saw Yvette struggle with the leather strap binding her wrist.

He rushed to help her. "Are you okay?"

She nodded. "Check Leslie. The woman on the floor. You didn't kill him."

"Didn't need to. Don't want to." Jason tugged out his cell phone and hit a speed-dial number. "Alex."

"Yes, Cash?"

"You locate Bay?"

"You betcha. We're waiting for orders. The CIA agent is wondering where you've gotten to."

Jason had told the agent he had to run out to his truck for something and to make himself at home in his office. He could have used him for backup, but—hell, he'd needed to move, and fast.

"I found the perp, Alex. Come to the old Reynolds Repair garage south of town."

"Will do, Cash."

Seeing the strap about Yvette's wrist was actually a thin leather belt, Jason helped her get out of the clasp. She gripped his forearms as if to steady herself.

"You sit," he said. "Take the gun." He nodded toward the pistol on the plank. "Keep an eye on Patron. Can you do that?"

She nodded. She was flustered, but he had confidence she could hold a gun on her boss. Another bullet wasn't required to subdue him. Yvette could maintain her innate need to not harm another human being. No matter what the man had done to her.

Jason bent to inspect the woman on the floor. A bullet had nicked the side of her neck, and she was bleeding profusely. Her eyelids fluttered.

"She's alive." He tugged out his phone again and dialed. "Alex, get an ambulance on the road as well. Call Ely. Bob Hagar drives the ambulance. He can navigate this storm like Rudolph through a whiteout."

"On it, Cash."

The woman had taken a bullet to her shin as well as the thigh. With some field triage, Jason could keep her stable. Shedding his coat, he unbuttoned his flannel shirt and pulled it off. He needed to put pressure on her neck so she didn't bleed out.

The woman's eyes fluttered. Briefly focusing on his bare skin, she said, "Nice."

With a smirk and a shiver now that his bared chest had taken on the chill, Jason pressed the shirt against her neck.

Over his shoulder, he saw Patron topple in a faint.

Yvette took that cue to join Jason's side. "Is she going to be okay? Her name is Leslie Cassel."

"Should be. Did she kidnap you?"

"Yes, but she's on my side. Interpol has been following Jacques for weeks. They needed the information in my brain to implicate him for taking bribes from a gunrunning operation moving through Lake Superior."

"Figured it was something like payouts," he said to Yvette. "Might have been his reason for sending you here. He had contacts in the area. Minnesota mafia."

"It makes too much sense now. And Interpol didn't call me in because they must have had no idea where to find me until recently. Jacques kept my location a secret."

She blew out a breath, and her body tilted against his. She was exhausted and probably didn't realize she'd leaned on him. Jason hugged her about the waist and bowed his head to hers. The moment was bittersweet, but he intended to remember only the sweetness of her body against his. "I couldn't pull the trigger, Jason."

"Because you're a good person, Amelie. Don't feel bad for that."

"But it's my job."

"It was your job. Now your job is to make sure Jacques Patron pays for his crimes."

"I can do that. I will do that. Now tell me how to help. Unless it involves getting half-naked?"

He chuckled and pulled on his coat and zipped it up. "That was a good shirt," he said. He switched positions with her, leaving her to triage. "Watch her. I'm going to take care of Patron."

He cuffed the man, who struggled, despite what had to be painful injuries.

"Got 'em," Jason said, feeling satisfaction for a job well done. "And without the CIA's interference."

They would assume control of the case from here. And take credit for it all.

Didn't matter. Jason had gotten to Amelie before Patron could harm her. He wished he could have found her sooner, so he could have protected Leslie. This case had gotten him scrambling, and all had ended well.

With the suspect in hand.

"You saved me," she said from across the room. "I knew you would."

Jason caught her smile. It made the stormy day feel like springtime.

Epilogue

Days later...

Jason and Amelie stood beside the hospital bed where Leslie Cassel lay, recovering from the gunshot wounds. The damage had landed within centimeters of her artery, but fortune had not wanted her to die. She was eager to return to France and her job as soon as she could.

"I apologize for jumping the gun," she said to Amelie.

"I don't understand." Amelie moved closer while Jason clasped her hand. He'd taken to holding her hand lately. A lot. And she loved every single clasp.

"I won't apologize for kidnapping you. That was part of the job." Leslie smirked. "You know how we need to be covert for the integrity of an operation. But I should have waited. Lund was in jail…" She gave Jason a sharp glance.

Jason put up his hands. "I had no idea the guy was Interpol until a few hours before you took off with Yvette. Amelie." He gave her a wink. "I suspected he was another inept hit man. And really, for a trained agent, he should have known how to handle a snowmobile much better. I saved him from a plunge over a frozen falls."

"He told me that." Leslie smiled. Rutger Lund had been released immediately after Interpol had verified their agents had been sent to Frost Falls to extract the information from Amelie so they could make the case on Patron. He'd stopped in to visit Leslie before flying out of the country. "But I panicked. It was supposed to be a two-man operation. Pick up Amelie Desauliniers. Extract the information from her head. Send her to a safe house. We couldn't let you know we were from Interpol, Amelie, because we weren't sure if you were colluding with Patron."

"How did you finally decide I was not?"

"I didn't know for sure until the moment he faced you down in the repair shop."

"Nothing like coming down to the wire," Jason said. "Patron has been arrested."

"Yes, that's good," Leslie said. "But we never did get the information. And I'm sorry, Amelie, that things could have gone so wrong in that garage when Patron showed up. I thought I could handle it myself, but I needed backup."

"Apology accepted," Amelie said. "I know what it's like in the field and second-guessing your own judgment." She dug into her pocket and pulled out a piece of notebook paper to hand to Leslie. "Here's the list you wanted. But don't worry. I've already sent copies to the director at Interpol. Enough damning evidence to prove Jacques Patron was taking bribes from a gun-runner connected to the Minnesota mafia. And we've recovered the links from the original email, which lead to CCTV videos showing the handoffs in various major European cities."

Leslie folded the paper and closed her eyes. Pale winter sunlight beamed across her face. "Thank you. Are you going to be all right?"

Amelie nodded noncommittally. "I've already spoken to the director about the incident and have been debriefed. It's been suggested I remain in data tech, but I'm not so sure anymore."

"Don't let this scare you away," Leslie said. "You joined this organization for a purpose, yes?"

"I did. But that purpose may have been misdirected. It might have been more of a fearful reaction to a past event that made me follow in my father's footsteps. I'm going to give returning to Interpol some thought." Amelie looked to Jason, who squeezed her hand.

And Leslie also looked to Jason before smiling at Amelie. "I get it. This weather sucks. But the scenery…" She shook her head appreciatively. "I hear there's a calendar a girl should look at?"

"I think I know where to find you a copy," Amelie said. "We'll leave you to rest."

The twosome left as health services wheeled in a savory-smelling lunch. As they entered the chill outside air and walked toward Jason's truck, Amelie felt that what she'd told Leslie was the truth. She did need time to think about the job she'd always thought was the right fit for her. But it wasn't anymore. She had a misbalanced pros and cons list to prove that.

She'd been granted another week's leave before she was expected to report for duty. And she'd take it.

Jason opened the passenger door for her and helped

her up inside his truck. Once seated, she reached for the door, but instead, Jason stepped up onto the side runner and leaned inside the cab to kiss her.

Even with the wind brisking her cheeks and bare hands with an icy chill, the heat they generated when their lips touched warmed her whole body. Amelie pulled him closer, and he leaned inside, reaching to embrace her about the waist as he deepened the kiss.

Leaving this man would be a challenge. But who said it had to happen right away? Or even... Dare she consider it?

When he broke the kiss, Jason bowed his forehead to hers, and for a while they simply shared the intense silence. Finally, he said, "Amelie. I love that name. I'll never forget that name."

Her heart did a flip-flop.

"I know you don't belong here," he said. "But maybe you could stay awhile longer?"

He wanted her to stay? Yes! "I do have a week leave. What if I extended my vacation here?"

"You'd do that?"

"I've been changed by my service with Interpol, Jason. I need to think of what it is I really want. Am I doing it because my parents were in it? Was it a fearful reaction to watching my mother get killed?"

He kissed her forehead. "Questions that only you can answer."

"What about you? Is the station still closing?"

"Probably. The CIA tossed me a freebie, though, and didn't step in on the case as I suspected they would. I got the credit for this one. And the sheriff's department called me this morning to offer me a position in Ely. I'm considering it."

"Is Ely another small town like this one?"

"A bit bigger." Seeing her frown, he added encouragingly, "They've got tourist attractions. And the wolf center."

"Wow. Exciting times abound here. But still cold, right?"

"Still cold." He leaned in, nuzzling a kiss at the base of her ear, then whispered, "If you stay awhile longer, I'll keep you warm."

"That's an offer I won't refuse."

* * * * *

LET'S TALK
Romance

For exclusive extracts, competitions
and special offers, find us online:

- 📘 facebook.com/millsandboon
- 🐦 @MillsandBoon
- 📷 @MillsandBoonUK

Get in touch on 01413 063232

For all the latest titles coming soon, visit
millsandboon.co.uk/nextmonth

MILLS & BOON

THE HEART OF ROMANCE

A ROMANCE FOR EVERY READER

MODERN

Prepare to be swept off your feet by sophisticated, sexy and seductive heroes, in some of the world's most glamourous and romantic locations, where power and passion collide.

HISTORICAL

Escape with historical heroes from time gone by. Whether your passion is for wicked Regency Rakes, muscled Vikings or rugged Highlanders, awaken the romance of the past.

MEDICAL

Set your pulse racing with dedicated, delectable doctors in the high-pressure world of medicine, where emotions run high and passion, comfort and love are the best medicine.

True Love

Celebrate true love with tender stories of heartfelt romance, from the rush of falling in love to the joy a new baby can bring, and a focus on the emotional heart of a relationship.

Desire

Indulge in secrets and scandal, intense drama and plenty of sizzling hot action with powerful and passionate heroes who have it all: wealth, status, good looks…everything but the right woman.

HEROES

Experience all the excitement of a gripping thriller, with an intense romance at its heart. Resourceful, true-to-life women and strong, fearless men face danger and desire - a killer combination!

To see which titles are coming soon, please visit

millsandboon.co.uk/nextmonth

JOIN US ON SOCIAL MEDIA!

Stay up to date with our latest releases, author
news and gossip, special offers and discounts, and
all the behind-the-scenes action
from Mills & Boon...

 millsandboon

 millsandboonuk

 millsandboon

It might just be true love...